A SHIELD OF SNOW

A NOTE TO THE READER.

THIS BOOK DEALS WITH SUBJECT MATTER THAT MAY BE HARMFUL TO YOUR MENTAL HEALTH INCLUDING CONVERSATION AND ON PAGE DEPICTIONS OF: ENSLAVEMENT (IT IS NEVER GLORIFIED IN THIS BOOK, NOR WILL CHARACTERS MIRACULOUSLY FALL IN LOVE WITH THOSE WHO PRACTICE ENSLAVEMENT, BECAUSE, BARF). CHILD LOSS AND ATTEMPTED SUICIDE.

FOR A FULL LIST OF CONTENT WARNINGS, PLEASE TURN TO THE BACK PAGE.

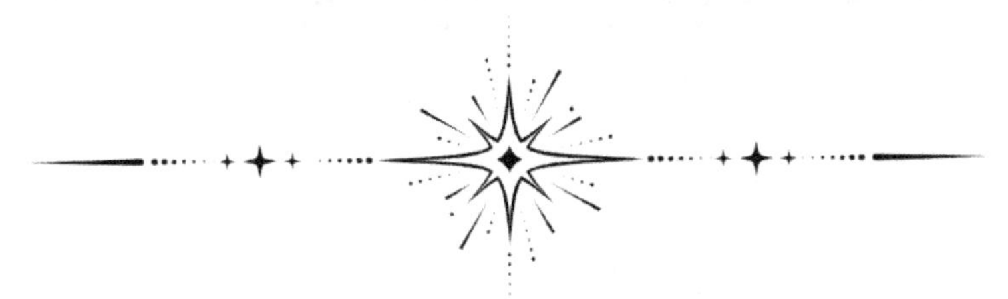

TO THOSE WHO HAVE FOUND
THE COURAGE
TO SAY...
"NO MORE. THIS STOPS WITH ME."

MONWYN
BASILIA
PENUM
Eira's Rift
COLPASS
CORDILLARIA
STORMRIDG
Moonledge
Sinnonbreak
RUINS
OF HAIN
LÆNNAN
LYK
BALDORVA

N
W E
S
SILVERSTEP
SNÆRSHADE
SEA
NORTIA
RUINS OF INGLIS
THE RIFT
VERUS
MYNDER GAEA
RUINS OF TALEER
SOLNNA
ÆRTA

VERUS TEMPLE HIERARCHY AND ÆRTAN PANTHEON

THE MANTLE
Religious Head of Ærta

DEVOTEES
Mantle's council and kingdom advocates

OBLIGATES
Chosen children committed to Ærta's betterment

PRIESTESSES/ PRIESTS
Religious practitioners

ACOLYTES
Priestess or priests in training

MAJOR GODS

THE GODDESS ←——————→ GAMMOND
Creator · God of Wisdom

MOSSIUS · MERRIAS ←——————→ MAGIS
God of Healing/Medicine · Goddess of Judgement · Human Conjurer

THE CHILD
Protector of Innocents

MINOR GODS

DERROS: God of the Seas
LYKKSUN: Goddess of Sun
JOSA: God of Music
MARESSA: Goddess of the Forests
VIKTOS: God of Thunder
THORAMIKA: Bear Goddess

CONTENTS

Prologue: Sweetlips, AKA, The Minnow   1

1. The Hunt   7

2. The Past Stays in the Past... Kinda   17

3. Fish Do Not Have Ears   27

4. Bushes and Brambles!   31

5. My Angry Bits   37

6. With Them Goes My Heart   45

7. Dicks, Pricks, and Licks   55

8. Through the Eyes of a Child   65

9. That's What She Said   71

10. Hambrose   83

11. Messy Hessie   91

12. Engagement is Another Word for Altercation   99

13. You Big, Dumb, Stupid Dumb Face!   109

14. How Do You Initiate Marital Legal Injunctions Against Your Fate-Bond?   117

15. It's About Damn Time!   125

16. The Cure-All is a Warm Cup O' Love   131

17. Come With Me   137

18. My Favorite Song   141

19. That's Actually the Dumbest Thing I've Ever Heard   149

20. Stick to the Plan. There is Only One Plan. One I Say!   155

21. A Cedar Coffin? Smells Like Claustrophobia to Me   163

22. The Primus-King Has a Type: Pretty and Ignorant   171

23. Like, Your Time Will Come, Bro.   179

24. Early to Rise   187

25. How I Measure Up   195

26. The Power of a Name   205

27. Pa.   217

28. Mouth Stuff   223

29. Pain   231

30. How the Fighty Doth Fall   241

31. Cato's Ick Word   255

32. Sugary Shake Down   261

33. The Confessional   273

34. No Touchy   281

35. What Lurks in the Dark   293

36. I'm So Fucking Romantic   301

37. What is Love? Baby Don't Burn Me   313

38. The Tangled Triad... Well, More Tangle, Less Triad   323

39. As Pa Always Says, the Time to Repair the Coop Isn't When the Fox is Ahuntin'	327
40. Girlfriends	335
41. Searching the Stacks	339
42. Hi Ho, Hi Ho. It's Off to Work I Ho.	345
43. Because I'm Hungry	361
44. How Easily Love is Shared	367
45. The Goddess's Will, My Fat Ass.	373
46. Our Mother Who Art in Cradle, Pillow Talk Be My Game.	379
47. Truths Are Sharper Than Lies	385
48. Blind Devotion is the True Cause of Early Onset Hair Loss	389
49. I've Changed My Mind. Maybe Lies Are Sharper.	401
50. Two Paths	407
51. Sometimes Choice is All You Have Left	411
52. I Fucked Up	417
53. Tck, tck, tck	421
54. Visitation Hours	423
55. Safe House Envy	429
56. Until the Soldier Softens	437
57. I Am One of Them	441
58. It. Is. Me.	447
59. What Kind of Fuckery is This?	453

60. There Are Things Not Meant For A Grown Husband's Eyes   459

61. Because a Person You Don't Know is Still an Important One   469

62. Literally Not as Bad as a Shovel to the Tootsie   475

63. Serpentine Bladehoof   481

64. Encroachment   489

65. Full Circle   495

66. What Love Demands   501

67. The Portrait of Love   505

68. A Bonded Bundle Bedding   511

Epilogue: The Nether   521

From E.A. with love   522

Content Warnings   523

PROLOGUE: SWEETLIPS, AKA, THE MINNOW

EIRA

HOW DARE YOU!

My head snapped backward as Ambrose's voice thundered through the connection. I sandwiched my head between my hands and held on.

DISCLOSE TO ME YOUR LOCATION AT ONCE!

A warm palm settled in the middle of my back as the aroma of beans and ham wafted up from the bowl that slid under my nose.

"Have we been found again, minnow?"

"Yes, Pa. We sure have." I leaned back and stared into the crinkly eyes I loved so much. Skin red and windburnt, a nose that some would say was too big for his face—those wrinkles that webbed nearly to his temples were the only indicator that he was smiling beneath his "winter beard," which was looking much whiter than the spicy rust-red it had been when I last saw him.

I KNOW YOU CAN HEAR ME, NETHER HARPY! ANSWER ME!

I flinched at the mental intrusion.

"Take your ease, Ulltan. You've been moving snow all day. It's time to rest." My mother sank down into the chair opposite me and placed a crusty loaf of piping hot bread in the table's center. "Eira, tell that husband of yours to stop his screeching. Creator's tits, child, you've told him of our plans. Why does he continue his ranting?"

"Love, Momma, because of love." I laughed, and she returned my smile. I couldn't help it. I knew my men were beside themselves, but I'd formed a plan and *planned* to stick to it... no matter the pain it caused my heart. "And because in Monwyn, the boys think they know best."

Momma chuckled, her sparse brows arching in mock surprise.

"Be that as it may, Eira, he should trust that you are making a decision that is best for—"

My head snapped back.

PIRATE LARM FOLLOWS CATO AROUND MOPING LIKE A LOST PUPPY AND CATO PUNCHES EVERY MAN THAT CROSSES HIS PATH! HE FELLED ABERUS FOR SAYING, "I HOPE YOU FIND HER, BROTHER," AND JANCE FOR SMILING IN A MANNER CATO DEEMED PITEOUS.

My mother ripped a hunk of bread from the loaf and placed it in my bowl.

"Are you alright, daughter?"

I nodded.

"Yes, I'm fine. You'll understand when you meet Ambro—"

EIRA VERRAS CHULAINN!

WHAT?! I snapped through the connection, unable to ignore Ambrose any longer.

Oh. There you are, wifey. I miss you very much, and—shut up, Catommandus, no, I will not relay your commands through the brain Bond. This is "my" Bond, not yours. Back up, tiny prince. Stop! Get—oof—back, she ca-can't hear you even... if... you yell. Evandr, Papa Cato is threatening Daddy Septimus again. He said he would hammer a pickaxe through his nose until his brains ran liquid.

Ambrose giggled through the connection, and my stomach sank. Gods, how I missed them.

"Is he still speakin', minnow?" my father asked.

"Yes, and he may not stop for some time. Ambrose is *verbose*." I spooned a heap of savory beans into my mouth and listened to the one-sided play-by-play happening inside my mind.

"Let's see. From what I'm able to gather, Evandr is chasing Cato through the snow with a crude shiv of some sort. And Larm, the one who took on Cato's characteristics after they thawed, is crying, or perhaps clawing at... well, I'm not sure. The link is choppy."

My pa patted my hand.

"And this is commonplace for the men in yer life?" My father's bushy brows knit tightly as he dunked a fistful of bread into his bowl.

I shrugged and nodded, a half-smile tugging at the corner of my mouth.

Are you there, Eira?

Yes. I'm here, husband. I continued on with my dinner, knowing well that the conversation might be lengthy. It usually was.

Tell me where you are, wife.

No, I said simply, just as I had every time they'd caught up with us over the last three months.

Wife... His voice trailed off. *I find myself in a predicament. I am absolutely miffed that you walked out on us—flew, rather—but my constant fears calm instantly when I hear your voice.*

Mine, too. The admission felt hollow, like my soul had without the nourishment of their presence. *Ambrose, soothing spouse that I love more than seven slices of decadent lemon cake... tell me of home.*

Momma and Pa shared a knowing glance and stood, taking their meals to the far side of the small room.

Oh, gracious, where to begin? Baby Verra is turning soft pink! Her little eyes are more violet now and, Eira, if you hold her tiny hands, she hops up and down on her bitty hooves and—

That's wonderful, but...but will you start with Allaine, please?

Of course.

Even through our connection, I could feel more than hear his voice deflate.

Greggen has mended enough to roam free without the healer's care, though Catommandus keeps constant tabs on him. My guess is that he plans to use the Scion against the Baldorvans, and Allaine is the proverbial dangling carrot that keeps Greggen in line. Allaine... she is cautiously happy. She truly loves him, wiflet, no matter that he is now a revolting cyclops of a man. Oh! Gods, and Cinden, she has gone as fat as a pig primed for slaughter! She is waddling around, ordering Ethens about. I suspect, by her wheezy-breathed proclamations and fiery levels of indigestion, that she may give birth early.

I worked backward, counting the months on my fingers. By my calculations, she was nearing her eighth month, but not knowing the exact moment that she and Ozius conceived, she could be well into the later stages.

Fear gripped me in its tight embrace.

Ambrose, please send for a non-Monwyn healer. A Solnnan could potentially make the trek and see to her.

I could, perhaps, but I do not understand why—

Because the Monwyn way of locking a woman into a stifling, stinking room until she gives birth with only the company of an idiot healer and his idiot sidekick is—

Eira.

Don't "Eira" me! Your customs treat mothers-to-be like—

Wife!

What?!

The connection went momentarily silent.

I know that our Joining was overshadowed by the insanity that happened shortly after, but how do you not recall Papa Burchard's gift to you? He changed the practices, remember? He announced it at our breakfast. The midwifery school? Shameful spouse, you do not recall it on account of your loudly weeping vagina. Cato's royal title was restored, and I was forgotten in an instant. Nothing more than a contract husband.

Tears stung my eyes as Petulant Ambrose reared his head.

The truth was, I *had* forgotten.

The announcement *had* been overshadowed by the days that followed: Lemder's blackmail, Cato leaving, and the brutal murders of the women I held dear.

The birthing wing now stands on the eastern side of the palace. Aberus had a heraldic device made up for the first initiates of midwives and signed off on their husbands' letters of approval. He appreciates that having our own people in charge will save the royal coffers a coin or two.

It was probably better that Ambrose couldn't see the sneer on my face. I anger-chewed a morsel of bacon.

Gods alive, Aberus makes it hard to like him.

Ohhh, myyy... and speaking of Aberus. Ambrose's devious laughter floated through the connection. *I do believe he has quite the crush on our sweet little dollop, Richelle, but it seems that her own twinkling eyes have shone upon... another...*

What? I sat up, chomping at the bit for a snippet of court gossip.

You will never guess, wifey...

Zotikos! Jance! Imella's man, Hughes! Ummm. The head gardener, Maihon? They would be adorable together, and little Mae would have a mother!

No, nope, nu-uh, no, but that would be picturesque.

I tapped my toes on the floor and drummed my fingers on the table.

Tell me, tell me!

You tell me one thing first.

Okay, what?

Do you still love me, Eira? I treated you poorly the last I saw you and I need to make amends, to do it right, to tell you that I love you, that I am "in" love with you. Yes, asshole, I will tell her you love her as well. No, I will not recite the fucking poem—Cato wrote you a poem. It's horrific; his meter is inconsistent, and his metaphors have the same depth of meaning as a random pebble in a still-life painting.

A glowing warmth surrounded me, easing the emptiness in my chest.

Ambrose, I love you. With all that I am, I love you. Please tell Cato he is forever where he belongs, tucked safely in my heart.

She says she misses dick, mostly mine, but yours on occasion.

Ambrose! I covered my face with both hands, shaking my head.

Oh, it's Bem.

What's Bem?

The knave who has Richelle's puss a-purring.

My mouth dropped open.

Silence.

Wife, are you there? Where have you gone?

My loud laughter filled the cavern that was my temporary home.

I'm sorry, Black Bear, I'm here. It's just... Bem? Bem, Bem? Poor postured, greasy-haired Bem? No wonder he started dressing nicer and bathing. I assumed that the change was due to him assuming the role of Protector.

No, no, not at all. Apparently, he is quite the romantic—who would have known?

Silence fell once more.

Are you there, Black Bear?

Eira... Cato leaves soon. He and the Mantle... my-my sibling, Rayæl, are already plotting. Gotwig speeds toward Baldorva to gather information. And though I personally cannot fathom his returning to those who had enslaved him, he knows the land, and perhaps it will do him good to undermine such a revolting system.

My heart hammered against my chest, panic swelling at the prospect of not seeing Cato until after the dust of our inevitable war settled.

*Gotwig is the best for the job, Ambrose, just like—*I held my breath, letting it out slowly—*just like there is no other but Cato who could lead Ærta to victory.*

I'd rehearsed that speech every day since my father had snatched my shade-form from the sky.

Eira, please don't leave me alone forever.

I twisted the gold and silver band around my finger—the physical representation of the love in our unique family.

One... two... three... breathe, Eira.

Sweetlips, are you exercising? Well done! I commend your efforts, but make sure you inhale as you lower, exhale before flexion. Try with me; I'll count this time. Ready... okay, and one... breathe... and... two.

Ambrose, I can't wait to be with you again. It shouldn't be long now. Goodbye, Black Bear.

Eira, wai—

I severed the connection and brushed away the tears that always marked the end of our conversations.

A hanky flashed in front of my eyes, startling me.

"Thank you, Gotwig." I dabbed at my nose and then slid the linen back to him. "Like we planned, they assume you are bound for Baldorva."

My instructor-turned-mentor wrinkled his nose and his hand cringed back, while he puffed on his pipe.

"Please keep your secretions to yourself, Troth Eira."

CHAPTER ONE

THE HUNT

CATO

Verus, two days north. Border of Gaea... fourteen hours by horse. On foot—with the idiots at my back—a lifetime. Misbehaving demon-puff... a matter of minutes? Half of an hour? Who the nether knows? Weapons: nine on my person. An extra dozen strapped to Megrimir's tack. The plan: triangulate her known whereab—

"Have you pinpointed her location?"

I snatched the parchment from my bag, ignoring the man calling out to me, unrolled it, and flattened the crude map against the smooth skin of a tall birch. Did she think I could not track her? Did she assume herself safe because her "pa" could, what... shovel snow... make a lake ripple? I may not be blessed with the divine powers to conjure, but I had outsmarted my own æther-filled father countless times. Not her parents, not her ass of a contract husband, or the Goddess herself would keep me from my mate. She was mine just as much as I was her—

"Papa Catommandus, I—"

"For the last time, Larm. Stop. Calling. Me. Papa." I pressed my forehead to the tree trunk and breathed the chilly air deeply into my lungs, rethinking my life's dream of raising a passel of children.

"Apologies, Cap'n. However—"

"Larm. It is Cato. Call me Cato. We are grown men, the both of us; furthermore, we are not on a ship and—"

"But Commander Ambrose requires me to use his—"

"Commander Ambrose is a jackass."

Pen in hand, I marked the location where Ambrose's Bond with Eira had begun and then noted where it had faded away.

"Godsdammit!"

My fist met bark.

I punched the spot where the three interlocking rings met until the parchment shone red. She should be here. She should have been *right* where I stood. But looking around, I could find not a single clue as to her whereabouts. The snow-covered ground was a soft, flawless blanket. There were no signs of human life: no snapped twigs, no disturbed low-hanging branches.

"Pa—Cato, sir."

I stiffened when Larm's abnormally cool hand settled on my shoulder. Where he touched, a frigid line snaked its way toward the sliver of exposed skin at my throat.

My stomach churned with anxiety.

Even with the unpleasant side effects, Larm's gesture brought a modicum of comfort.

"What, Larm?"

He inhaled deeply, something he did before nearly every sentence.

He patted me like a fucking dog.

"When I lost my missus, I thought life was done. I wanted it to be done. Take solace in knowing that your lady walks the soils."

His grip tightened briefly, then disappeared, and then I heard the crunch of his footsteps as he walked away. I took my own deep breath and tried to expel the frustration, refocusing, again, on the mission at hand.

Above all, I missed my wife and would welcome her back into my arms like I would welcome my own mother if she miraculously rose from her grave, but I was also dealing with a profound sense of anger. She'd left me. And the hole she left burned deep in my chest.

I stared at the intersecting rings on the map before re-rolling the parchment and sliding it into its leather case. Something didn't add up. And that something had everything to do with conjuration.

Larm waved me over, not looking up as he rummaged through the small, scuffed-up healer's chest he'd procured from his saddlebag. For the past three months—the most agonizing period of my life—the ritual had occurred so frequently that I no longer needed prompting to hold out whatever extremity was bleeding.

He shook a tin of clotting powder onto my knuckles while my ever-growing resentment grappled with my ability to give a damn. I gave no fucks for his dead wife or his family. I sure as shit did not need his advice, but the last time I had upset the pirate-turned-Frostchild, the consequence had been mutual regret. How was I to know that re-tying the knots tied by a seasoned pirate was an insult akin to slapping his grandmother? His hurt feelings leaked through our fucked-up parental tether, and my resulting shame found its way back to him... casting him headlong into a depressive spiral... which led to me weeping into Ambrose's shoulder. It had lasted days.

"I am sorry for the loss of your wife, Larm." I forced out the words.

He grunted something unintelligible, tilting his dark head in acknowledgement, but kept his focus on my hand as he wrapped it in a narrow length of linen.

He sighed.

"After the babes went, my lady lost her will to eat, lost her will to fight. I don't blame her, never will. But they don't go hungry where they are now."

My chest constricted.

"Where are you from, Larm? Surely not Ærta?" I softened my tone as I questioned him.

I had tried to place his heritage before, but Larm always deflected. His accent was common enough for the continent, but his cadence had a foreign quality that bore no similarity to the surrounding kingdoms.

"Tale for another day, Cap'n."

I nodded, letting the honorific slide, and glanced off into the distance where Evandr and Septimus sat on a felled log, their pale heads close together. My uncle was teaching the Scion to tie a hangman's knot, just as he had me when I was a boy. Evandr manipulated the rope skillfully and, when finished, looked up into Septimus's glowing face.

I spat in the snow.

Evandr had awoken from his freeze with a profound and disconcerting love for my uncle, who reciprocated in kind. *My* best friend and the man who'd abused me—beat me into a bloody mess as a child—were inseparable and so *disgustingly* joyful. Every time I laid eyes on the cheerful duo, my ire flared a degree hotter.

Septimus's eyes sparkled, a mirror of Evandr's, just as Larm's eyes were now identical to mine. Evandr—already as pale as Septimus, on account of my father pulling his æther for so many years—looked like he *actually* sprang from the loins of the filth that was my relation.

A fucking curse from above.

Through his brief coupling with the woman I loved, Septimus got what he'd always longed for—a son of his own.

"Fath—Sir." Larm offered me his waterskin, and I took a quick swig of the slush.

He bobbed his head toward the happy family.

"Don't let that break your focus."

I tore my eyes away, but my gaze landed on another source of frustration and concern.

Ambrose.

He sat off in the distance, perched upon a rock, staring out into nothing. The confounded snow, which should have fully melted by now, swirled around his head, and the inky tendrils of his unbound hair blew in disarray.

"He'll come around, sir. He gets like this each time he speaks with her. I reckon a day or two and he'll get back to normal."

I motioned for Larm to hold back while I stalked across the clearing, digging into my satchel as I went.

"Ambrose, put this on." I grit my teeth at the wetness that finally breached the thick leather of my boots.

Solemn eyes barely registered the nalbound cap in my hand before glancing away.

"I am fine."

"You are not. And I will not suffer the punishment of our irrationally angry spouse if you perish before she sees you again."

I raked my fingers through the tangles in his hair, wound the mass into a knot, and then shoved the cap firmly over his head until it covered the bright-red tips of his ears.

"She will find my newly mangled visage repugnant."

Gods, grant me mercy.

"Move over."

Ambrose sat motionless. I saddled up next to him and shoved his bulk aside.

His head dropped to my shoulder, and I fisted my hands, suppressing the urge to strike out—I would endure his touch. For the love of my brother, I would endure this. His hand rested on mine, and I squeezed my eyes shut until the churning in my stomach calmed enough to resume breathing.

"Eira likes scars, Ambrose. It is a woman thing, I think—proves our masculinity and protective capacity." *Gods, I sound like an idiot.* "She loves mine. She traces them with her fingertips, kisses them, and lick—"

"Catommandus, do not delude yourself. She slobbers all over your off-putting complexion due to the Dick Bond and nothing more. Meanwhile, *I* must put in an effort."

Kill him. End his malaise.

I pinched the bridge of my nose.

Gods fucking dammit.

"Ambrose, there is no other as... as alluring as yourself. The droop in your lip does not diminish your charm or negate your attractiveness, and the scar adds character to your ruggedly handsome countenance."

His body softened against mine.

"Then why haven't you sought me out for your own comfort? Why have you kept me at arm's length?"

My back went ramrod straight.

For fuck's sake.

"Calm your cock, Cato. I do not mean sexual comfort." Ambrose sniffled and wiped at his nose. "Without she, there is no we. It is the joy that Eira and I experience together that makes playing with you tolerable." Ambrose folded his hands. "My wife and I come together over coming. No Bond required."

I scoffed.

Am I offended? I think I'm offended.

His shoulders shook.

Godsfuckingdammit. I had no clue how to restore him to his former self.

What would Eira... Ugh. I knew precisely what she would do. I wrapped my arm around his shoulder and pulled him close, warming his back with my cloak. *She would cuddle him like the disgruntled child he is.*

I rocked him slowly, clenching my jaw so hard it sent a sharp pain down my neck.

His trembling intensified.

Not working. Josa's godsdamned taint.

"I want a kiss," he stated. "It will help."

My stomach sank as the Bond actively rejected another human in my arms. But his tears destroyed my heart.

He turned his face to mine and puckered his lips—*oh gods*—he closed the distance—*Cradle save me*—and his tongue snaked out.

"You dishonorable piece of shit! You tongue-fucked my nose!"

His loud laughter echoed around the cluster of trees, and I shoved him away, only to be wrapped in his bear's embrace. Chapped lips peppered dry kisses over my cheeks and chin as I struggled in vain.

"We are a sad pair, are we not, Cat? And all because of a lovely little cunt... the most divine of Goddess-made vaginas." Ambrose crushed me to his chest, squeezing the air from my lungs. "You know what I miss most, other than the aforementioned cunt?"

"Release me, adopted tyrant!"

My hand flashed toward his head, but he anticipated the move, twisted his torso, and flung me to the ground. Wet snow worked under my collar, permeating the wool I wore.

I fucking loathed wet wool.

Ambrose kicked a lump of snow—forlorn and despondent again.

"Her soft-bodied hugs, the conversation, her adorably crooked labia. Who even am I? Is this what love does to a man, Catommandus? And my hair." He compressed his lips and closed his eyes. "Without her nimble fingers massaging my scalp, as it has become accustomed to, my crowning glory lacks life; its once brilliant luster gone dim."

"Have you tried, oh, I don't know, combing it instead of whining about it?" I rolled up to my feet, concealing a tightly packed ball of snow in my hand. *I'd give him something to cry over.*

Ambrose narrowed his eyes, the mossy green darkening as the sunset haloed his body in rays of gold.

"What are you about, Catommandus?" His voice dropped low.

I cocked my head to the side. "Whatever do you mean, *Highness Ambrose?*"

A rare rush of adrenaline enlivened me. A worthy adversary. I would scrub his only slightly marred face into the ground until he begged for mercy.

Ambrose's shoulders tightened. He shifted his leg back, snugging his booted toe against the log.

It had been three days since my last altercation—the inept highwaymen had lasted only minutes—and my body screamed to let loose once again.

His core tightened, preparing to attack.

My plan: hip throw his giant's body and crush his windpipe beneath my knee.

"Do not delude yourself into thinking you are the only man who can anticipate one's movements, Cat—"

"Is this how brothers initiate a fuck?"

My hackles rose, bristling at the intrusion. Were it not for his skills as a tracker, Septimus would be face down in the dirt, rotting until the wildlife consumed him.

"Disgusting. My Enchantress should never again have to endure your debauched ways."

I snapped and sent the snowball flying, aiming directly for Septimus's perfectly straight nose, wishing the ball of ice were my dagger.

Evandr's chest eclipsed my view with inhuman speed, intercepting the true-flying projectile. It thudded against his neck and dropped into his cowl.

"Cat, don't, man." Evandr cocked his hip and crossed his arms. "I've told you plenty to leave him be."

Septimus's smug face peered around Evan's broad shoulder. His icy-blue eyes met mine, his repulsion almost palpable, his lips hitched into a victorious smile.

I narrowed my eyes, grimacing at my once frost-covered friend.

"Had I known, Evandr, that fucking Ambrose would have infuriated Septimus to the level of stroke, I would have done it years ago."

Ambrose twisted to look upon the pair standing behind him.

"Septimus, if you think Eira was not the catalyst behind this development"—he gestured between us with an indifferent flick of the wrist—"then you are as bullheaded as she believes. My wife's interest in the lustful arts is unparalleled. Oh! And if your *new son* has failed to mention it, Evandr and I took turns... um ... entering each other's exit for the better part of a year."

"Yeah, we did. And Nortia, she's a nasty girl." Evandr smiled, the white crescent stretching from ear to ear. "Back at Verus, she twirled tongue loops around my—"

Ambrose rolled his shoulders back, fists clenched. He stepped toward Evandr, who scoffed, not at all concerned about the incensed man towering over him.

"Have you lain with *my* wife, Scion?" For perhaps the first time since Eira flew away, Ambrose displayed an emotion other than sorrow—the angry bite in his voice gave me hope.

"Who hasn't lain with your wife?" Septimus removed his gloves, one finger at a time. His cold eyes bore into Ambrose's, and for an indulgent second, I imagined squeezing the sky-colored orbs until they burst and squelched between my fingers.

Ambrose lunged, but I placed myself in front of him. While on the surface he appeared hale, he was still recovering from the violence he'd endured at the hands of the Primus-King's underlings. He'd lost significant weight, much of it muscle, and a fight with Evandr or Septimus could be his last.

Digging my heels into the snow, I shoved back against Ambrose. Septimus curled his lip derisively. The scene played out in my head—I had experienced it countless times. Septimus would goad Ambrose into lashing out, giving the asshole just cause to pummel him in "self-defense."

Unfortunately for him, he raised me too well.

"Are you remembering that night, Uncle?" I said. "How often do you revisit pushing yourself between her thighs?" The corners of his nose flared indignantly. "The way she watched *me*, her eyes never leaving mine as she clenched around your cock? Are you aware Ambrose had used her only hours before? Gods, how slick she was."

I smiled at the memory. My woman had the strength of ten men and the courage of a goddess. Without pause she'd accepted Septimus into her body to give Evandr another chance at life.

The corner of Septimus's eye twitched. *You are slipping, old man.*

"Knowing that you covet my wife pleases me to no end."

Septimus arched an unbothered brow, but the evidence of her effect on him was there, thickening in his pants.

"If she requires my body upon her return, *boy*, then I shall provide it."

"Not if you are dickless, Uncle." Ambrose growled behind me. He shoved against me with such force that I had to brace myself on the log to keep him subdued. "I will unleash such rage upon you that Eira's shadow tantrums will seem like a tepid spring rain. Your name will be synonymous with ruin. I will corral Monwyn's geriatric manwhores and through them, craft your new legacy as the client who is more genital wart than cock. I will dismember you with my toenail clippers and feed your offensive appendage to Cat's dog."

"My what?" I stood straight, and Ambrose stumbled.

"Oh, dash it, Catommandus!" Ambrose steadied himself on my shoulders, as true fear sparked in his eyes. "Do. Not. And I repeat. Do not let on that I slipped! Cat, I will end your life without an ounce of remorse before I spoil her surprise."

"But Ambrose, she—"

He fisted my collar, twisting the fabric until breathing became difficult.

"Listen, she found a mutt at her last location and had it sent to Monwyn. I demanded it be called Pup Ambrose, but she yelled and fussed until I promised to allow you to name the mongrel. It is hideous from her description. Stiff fur and scrawny; an uneven set of whiskers and misshapen head." My heels rose off the ground. Ambrose's nose touched mine. "You will act so fucking surprised, Cat. You will clap your hands and smile and dance like a happy toddler, or I will gut you and then feed you to the creature. Do you understand? Cease your ridiculous smile. You *will* take this seriously."

A dog.

She got me a dog.

Fuck me, but I didn't know love could intensify at the utterance of a few words. In my mind's eye, a war hound appeared next to Eira and our passel of brats—another protector for my progeny.

The slap of Ambrose's palm against my cheek echoed around the clearing.

"What the actual fu—"

"Catommandus, swear it. Swear it now. If you upset her—"

Bristling, I shook off his hands and straightened my cloak.

"I will not lie to my wife, Ambrose; it sets a poor precedent and—"

"Enough!" Septimus yelled, drawing our collective attention. "Be a pair of obedient wives and shut up. If only your husband were here to beat you into silence."

Evandr chuckled at the jab, to which Septimus flashed a winning smile. "He's calling Eira the man in the relationship. Get it? Ha!"

Kill Septimus. Murder Evan somehow. Live happily ever after. A fairy-tale ending.

Chapter Two

THE PAST STAYS IN THE PAST... KINDA

Eira

"They've left. Let us resume our journey."

I peered around our temporary home and back up through the small tunnel that Gotwig had crawled out of an hour ago. Hughes, Imella's former manservant, poked his head through the hole, the dusky-pink sky a halo around his head. He plucked his spectacles from his nose and rubbed the lenses on his coat's lapel.

"Consort, shall I assist you?" The red-bearded man inquired in his ever-formal manner.

"No, Hughes. I'll try one more time but thank you."

I sensed my father at my back.

"Ready, minnow? Ye shouldn't even need me to assist ye this time. Ye've picked up so much."

I nodded and smiled up at the weathered and whiskered face of my Pa. Cold air filled my lungs while I sent a trail of effervescent energy through my chest and down my arms.

I called to the æther.

Part for me, please, and allow me to guide you.

Instantaneously, my view changed. Like a silent glacier slipping from a mountain, the river of white flowed into the empty cavern that had been our temporary home as I guided it carefully—it had to be perfect, refilled without flaw, or Septimus would suss us out.

My father guided my mother up a hill of snow until they stood next to Gotwig and Hughes.

Now the hard part.

I crouched and trudged up the hill as I replaced the snow behind me... without looking. From my mother's nod of encouragement, I knew *this* time I had it right. Gotwig held out his hands and aided me over a small lip of ice.

"Nicely done, daughter mine." My momma plucked a wayward hair sticking to my oil-smeared lips. "Now, let your pa cover the evidence and you make your way north. We'll meet you at the sled."

I shielded my eyes and took in the scenery.

We'd spent three days underground waiting for my men to move on, and in that time the snowfall all but ceased. I swear, the moment they left, the snow tumbled from the sky like teardrops from the Goddess's eyes.

"See you there."

The blustery winds sent my blunt-cut hair over my shoulders and into my eyes. I had debated cutting it off again, but after a memory of Cato twirling the length around his finger and Ambrose brushing it smooth after a bath, I asked my mother to even out the inconsistent lengths instead of letting temporary aggravation win out.

"Their party heads southwest." Gotwig took my elbow, as was our routine when setting off into the wilds these days. The odds of separation in a sudden squall were too great.

Hughes stepped next to me.

"The Frostborn travel with them, Eira."

I tempered my sudden excitement, drawing comfort from Hughes's calm presence.

Pure luck allowed Gotwig to acquire his contract after Ambrose denied him employment. Hughes was invaluable on various fronts. His detailed reports allowed me to keep my wits when my tenacious spouses closed in. He allowed me to feel connected to them, dampening my urge to run into their arms.

They had all been invaluable.

Once, when I caught sight of Cato, my skin had burned my mother so badly she still bore the scars on her hands. She saw me through the devastation, cooling me with handfuls of snow, while Gotwig endured the siphoning of my æther. Pa held me in his gloved hands, his body wrapped in a thick, protective blanket as he rocked me through the episode.

"How are they? How do they look?" I asked.

"All healthy, Consort. Your husband remains leaner than before, but his color looks less pallid."

I breathed a sigh of relief. I had *thought* I knew anxiety, but it was not until I left my heart in Monwyn that I tasted genuine fear, true loneliness.

"And Cato?"

"Scowly," Hughes replied.

Thank the gods.

We took turns assisting each other up and over a steep, icy grade. Perhaps a snow-covered fence or short hill lay beneath.

"Eira, are you prepared?" Gotwig asked, while producing a third scarf from his bag and twisting it around his ears. "Have we left any stones unturned?"

I walked past him, my legs sinking to the calves.

"You would have found them if we had. You would have flipped them over and tossed them into a lake."

Gotwig huffed, the white fog of his breath blending in with the moderate fall of snow.

"I do not possess nearly the omniscience you believe me to have." He sneered at me, pressing his lips in disapproval.

I hid a smile. We'd spent so much time in close proximity that I could now pick up on the minute change in the cadence of his voice when he received a compliment.

"I'm simply observant. Any peon could achieve the same if they applied themselves."

Hughes flicked his eyes to mine, sharing in a moment of conspiratorial understanding.

We continued on, picking our way over the terrain.

"Jilly sent your mother word. She awaits your arrival." Gotwig checked his timepiece and then snapped it closed. "We expect to make Timber by nightfall, barring any surprises."

"Can we *not* have any surprises, Eira?" Hughes muttered.

I giggled. I couldn't help it. The last *surprise* involved an ambush of biting pixies, who happened to be attracted to Hughes's red hair.

My Pa, bless him, had been trying to teach me how to fish using the æther. Instead of gently tossing the trout onto the bank, I sent it shooting through the trunk of a tree. And who knew pixie colonies inhabited trees? *Or* that the æther acted like an aphrodisiac when it hit them? Poor Hughes wore an impressive amount of fairy frosting—which happened to glow a greenish-gold, just like a lightning bug.

"Right. And Momma trusts Jilly with her life and, therefore, mine."

"Correct." Gotwig inclined his chin. "Did your mother ever tell you that Jilly stashed her in a keg of pickle brine? She stayed in the barrel for two days until the guards stopped sniffing around."

"No, but I imagine that explains why the smell of fermenting radishes turns her green." I paused. "Maybe that's also the reason I can consume a gallon of them. How pregnant was she when you all escaped?"

"Quite." Gotwig held his hand out in front of his stomach.

Our steps slowed as we came upon a muddy path that extended from east to west. Gotwig and Hughes inspected the road before flagging me forward. Hughes bent low, ear to the ground, listening for the rumble of hooves, and Gotwig examined the fresh tracks left by a heavy, wheeled cart.

"Hughes, travel back to Monwyn. Our Baldorvan contact should have replied in this timeframe. Send the information to Solnna, refresh your reserves, and then meet us at the new checkpoint. Troth Eira will have infiltrated the Primus-King's circle by the time you return. Make haste."

Hughes clipped a bow and left as noiselessly as he always arrived. I watched him walk as far as a copse of trees, and then he disappeared behind a leafless oak, seamlessly blending into the scenery.

With a gentle nudge to my elbow, Gotwig and I set off again. Another mile stretched between us and our rest.

My heart ached. My chest felt heavy with the weight of despair. And every time Hughes, Pa, or even Gotwig left to hunt or scout, it amplified my stress. At least they returned. To imagine how Ambrose must feel made the æther seize in my chest—thank the Goddess he had Cato.

"Lord Gotwig?" I asked, distracting myself from the sad void of my thoughts.

"Hmm?" He pushed a limb from our path, and the snow fell like glitter as it caught the light.

"You... you loved my mother?"

A long stretch of silence followed, and I thought that perhaps I'd dug a little too deep. I heard his slow intake of air.

"Change the past tense to present, and you will have your answer."

Oh.

Now *I* hesitated to speak, but curiosity wouldn't allow me to close the door.

"Does it bother you to be here with her and Pa? So close and yet—"

"No, Troth Solnna, it does not."

"Not even knowing that they—"

"It is enough for me to see she is happy and well taken care of." We skirted around to a narrow point in a frozen stream instead of walking across its ice-covered surface. "And as far as Ulltan is concerned," Gotwig pointed toward a mound of white that blended in with the other hills surrounding it. "He is the partner she needed in life, and I am thankful they found each other."

He turned to me and raised a questioning brow, no doubt intrigued by my overdramatic frown.

"That's just real goddessdamned selfless of you. I'd shit my britches if Cato or Ambrose found somebody else. Probably twice if the other was a human as kind as Pa."

Gotwig rolled his eyes so hard his irises disappeared.

"I am overly aware of how hot your jealousy burns. Your eyes go dull when listening to reports of the kingdom's functioning, but the moment Hughes says Verus sent a priestess to guide Ambrose through his recent trauma, you heat our shelter to melting... even when you discover she is eighty and four." Gotwig's smile dripped with sarcasm as he dropped my elbow and took three ogre-sized steps backward. "Now, can you perform this feat without trying to end me for the second time?"

"Really?" I pursed my lips and eyeballed the retreating man. "First off, Ambrose is a man of varied and unique tastes, and he becomes agitated during dry spells." I let the æther flow, threading the energy through my arm as carefully as silk floss through the eye of a needle. I focused on the mound ahead and clenched the muscles of my stomach, causing the æther to flow faster. "Second, yes, I can do this... but take another step back."

Gotwig took *two* giant-sized steps to the right.

Dick.

Like a massive, fluffy pancake tossed above a griddle, a disk of ice rose into the air. I held it suspended while encouraging the frozen water to stay unified.

"And, as I have told you, Lord I-hate-the-cold-because-the-awakening-stole-my-body-heat-and-now-I'm-a-perpetually-grumpy-icicle. That was an accident. When I saw the pup, I just—"

"Decided my final resting place was to be beneath a mountain of slush." Gotwig pulled a pipe from his belongings and struck a match.

The mischievous giggle that escaped me floated on the wind between us, playing in and out of the frozen precipitation.

Gotwig came to stand near me again. The last time I attempted to clear the ice, it took the little pupper and me nearly a quarter of an hour to dig him free of his accidental entombment.

I nodded, satisfied, as I scanned the low-profile sled that was now revealed before us, checking for damage or wear.

Gotwig waved my parents over—I hadn't even noticed their approach.

"All well?" Momma asked, surveying the sled's polished wooden runners... and then Gotwig.

"He's *fine*, Momma." I pinched his gaunt cheek. "Can you even kill a man who has already died?"

My pa's chuckle made me grin. "They never forget the oopsies, now do they?"

My mother continued her inspection.

"Sid, do you need to ride with Eira?" She pressed her wrist to Gotwig's forehead, checking for fever or chill.

Sid.

Sidnatious Gotwig.

I clamped a hand over my mouth to avoid another reprimand, which drew Momma's attention anyway.

"Silly girl, do you think I shouted his *last* name between the sheets? How awkward would that have been?"

"Ahhhhhhhhhh! Not as awkward as this conversation!" I sang out while shielding my ears with mittened hands.

Pa's chuckles turned to guffaws of merriment. He nudged my mother with his elbow, proud of her quick wit. "Spouse of mine, should I regale her of my first experience with lovin'? Why, the first time I undressed a..."

Oh, my gods.

"Stop! Both of you. I may be approaching year thirty, but this is not and never will be an appropriate topic!"

My parents chuckled, and even Gotwig's face cracked into a semblance of a grin. He patted my mother's hand where it rested on his wrist, checking the pulse I was pretty sure he didn't actually have.

"I'm hale and hearty, Vonnie," Gotwig assured.

My mother pinned him with a skeptical look.

"Let's be off, then. For the first leg of the journey, I'll sit with Eira. I've quite the chill, and she runs as warm as a snow bunny's bum."

My father helped her into the sled and then held her gloved hands to his mouth, puffing warm air through the knit. Her smile deepened, and my heart swelled in my chest. I hopped into the seat beside her, and together we snuggled close while Pa tossed a thick wool blanket over our legs.

In an instant my mind returned to the past, flooding with the memories of a safe and cozy childhood—my fur-lined leather coat smelling of wood and tallow, gliding over an ocean of snow and ice. I sank into the nostalgia.

"Let's revisit the plan, Eiry."

Calm gone.

"Momma, we've been—"

"Hold tight!" Pa shouted from his perch behind Gotwig.

The sled lurched and bumped, and we gripped the rope that lay across our legs as we shot off. Gotwig shifted on the rear curve of the footboards, tucking his frigid hands behind my back as he gripped the seat.

"I'm jealous that Pa doesn't have to wave his hands or pause to channel the æther. He just thinks it, and *woosh*, we're off like a schooner riding a storm."

Momma blinked at me, her expression dry. "Well, practice more."

I curled my lip in indignation, and we fell into easy laughter.

"Now, repeat the plan, please, and loud enough that your father and Sid can hear."

Gotwig tapped my shoulder in agreement.

I inhaled deeply and launched into the plan that I'd recited a dozen times before.

"I am to meet your old friend Jilly at the Timber Tavern. I will assume the identity of her niece, who hails from the mountain town of Stacks. I join the influx of immigrants who have left their kingdoms for fear of Solnna releasing their wicked magic beyond their borders and sinking Ærta into the sea. I will work in the tavern until I am given kingdom employment. The Gaean Obligates, Yemailrys and Kymor—who I can't wait to see again—will secure that employment, and the Mantle has ordered them to ensure that it places me in the path of the Primus-King. When I see him, I will wreck his body, destroy his world, and take his life by the most violent means possible."

"Eira Verras Chulainn," Momma mom-voiced me sternly.

I hunkered under the blanket, refusing to respond to her castigation.

"You will wait *patiently* for your father and Gotwig to join you, and they will decide the course of action after assessing the situation. I am against you going in at all, but who am I to naysay the Mantle?"

"Momma." I eyed her blandly. "I explode at will. I've sunk ships single-handedly. I—"

"Do not need to further traumatize yourself for something that began before I bore you into the world. *You* are backup in this plan. You are the scout this time—get them in and provide the details they need to get the job done. If something goes horribly wrong, you may then, and only then, unleash the... What does your husband call it? Your demon fluff?"

"Puff. But Momma..." A sick feeling flooded my body, like it did every time I thought of what my mother endured. The Primus-King—my sire—I fought back the tears. He had forced a child upon her.

I was that child. And I felt as if—

"Eira," I didn't meet her eyes, just stared off watching the forest as we slid by. "It is not your place to avenge me. You are *my* child. *Mine.* But I will not discuss my past with you, as it is mine to keep or share as I see fit."

"You should have aborted me."

"I tried."

I flinched and twisted, peering into olive-green eyes. A single brow arched as she gazed back at me with zero remorse.

"So why am I here? No, wait. Don't answer that. The Goddess willed it, right? It was the game of the divine."

"More like an insufficient supply of herbs."

"Damn, Momma!" I couldn't help but chuckle, the tension breaking, even with the morbidity of the conversation.

I felt her chest rise and then fall.

"Daughter, I *will* tell you this. I worked for many years to undo the damage done to my body and mind. I am at peace with my past and the path that I now choose to walk. I do not see him in your face, child. I see you, the girl I am so proud of."

A lump I could not swallow formed in my throat.

"And as it turns out, Eira, love and free will are amazing medications. Both of which I made efforts to administer liberally in your upbringing—curse the Mantle and Their meddling."

I inclined my head and looked up to the sky, where the first stars emerged from a swirling swath of navy and azure.

Her words settled warmly in my chest.

A sparkling trail flared in the night. I made a wish.

Take a goodnight kiss to Ambrose, little light. Whisper in Cato's ear... Tell him that love transcends all distances.

I glanced back at my mother.

"You all made me who I am today."

"A brat?"

"Momma!"

"Well, you are a brat, dear, but I think it's a side effect of your tough-as-nails nature. That and having a Pa who coddled you."

A wool-covered hand patted my head, and my mother barked out a humorless laugh.

"My minnow is a self-determined girl."

"Because you are a sensitive snowpuff. You let her get away with actual crimes, Ulltan."

"Be that as it may," my father said, his deep voice muffled by the passing wind, "the conversation has gone well off course. Lord Gotwig and I will strike when the time is right. Ye, tiny fish, will be... What's the fancy-man word you used?"

Gotwig cupped his hand around his mouth, the wind now blowing hard enough to make conversation difficult.

"Reconnaissance."

"That's the one. *Reconnaissance.* Ye gather the information and then lay low. Don't ye go swimming up no stream ye ain't got no business being in."

But it is my business, Pa.

I bristled at the insinuation that it wasn't.

Had they seen Nan hanging there... what that despicable man had done to her body? Had they been there to hear the thud of Imella slumping to the ground? Watch my husband's tears as he shoveled dirt into her grave?

"Gracious, girl." My mother fanned the heavy blanket, and steam rose around us. "Sid, do you remember how warm she was as a babe?" She turned to me.

"He loved holding your toasty little self, and I appreciated every second you were free of my teat. Between my bouts of tears and cluster feeding your tubby little self, I hot-flashed as bright as the burning Solnnan sun."

A million questions assaulted me at once.

"And your mother was my Gram, Gotwig?" I twisted around, grabbing the back of the sled, remembering the information Papa Burchard had revealed to me. *Goddess rest him.*

Gotwig's face remained neutral as he sought permission from my mother.

Momma dipped her head.

"She was my mother, yes. She took you and Vonnie into her home when you needed refuge. She was thrilled beyond measure to have a makeshift family after many years alone."

My æther swelled so tightly in my chest that for a moment I felt faint. I loved my cotton-haired gram more than I loved cake. When she'd stood upon Merrias's blade, it was a tipping point for both of us—the cradle for her, and for me, in many ways, the final paring away of my childish understandings of mortality.

"Did she know that I wasn't..." I let the sentence fade away, worried about the potential discomfort of the topic.

"She knew that you were not of my body but also knew that you *were* from the woman who had my heart. Did you know it was she who introduced Ulltan to your mother?"

"Wait, what?" I jerked my head around. My mother, whose finely lined cheeks shone rosy in the last remnants of the twilight, smiled demurely. "She sold out her own son and introduced you to Pa? Ma! You told me you met him at the butcher shop, slobbering over a rasher of bacon, you lying hen!"

All three of them burst into laughter.

Gotwig cleared his throat. "After you were safe in the North, I made the trek back to Verus to begin my work and ensure the plan we devised came to fruition. Your Gram began matchmaking the moment the door shut, and rightfully so. My return was never promised."

"So how *did* the two liars meet?"

Momma rolled her eyes.

"Was it romantic? What did Gram do?"

"No." Momma fanned the blanket again. "Not at all. I didn't really like him. You see, your father was far too conceited, and I, mature beyond my years."

I gave my pa an over-the-shoulder once-over and snapped my mouth shut.

His unruly bush of a beard covered half of his face, and above it he was as bald as the eagle tattooed across his freckled back. His paunch fell over his belt, and his toenails—I shivered in revulsion, recalling the last time I saw them—were a horrendous and gnarly mess.

Welp, no accounting for taste, I suppose.

My parents' secretive smiles were the last thing to fade before darkness consumed all but what the moonlight touched.

CHAPTER THREE

FISH DO NOT HAVE EARS

EIRA

Two miles from Mynder, Gaea's renowned, malachite-drenched capital, we stood behind a tightly bunched line of hedges. From the scattering of litter, broken glass, and parchment, we were not the only ones who'd made a privacy panel of the thick evergreens.

"Eiry, take this." My mother untied the apron she wore and tied it around my waist. She was never without it on account of her messy duties as a midwife. I ran my hand across the honeycombed smocking that made up the top quarter of its linen length. "Now you look less like a sack of grain and more like a matronly barmaid."

"Matronly is exactly what I aspire to be. Ugh."

I peered down and took in my garments, which were a far cry from the luxurious gowns of the Monwyn nobles and very much the opposite of the diaphanous silken confections of the Solnnan court.

Scratchy beige wool encased me from tits to toes; the fabric was so coarse, heavy, and entirely devoid of decoration that I did in fact resemble a bag of bulgur wheat. The sleeves fit tight, the neck was high and clinging, and frankly, had my mother not pulled in its shapeless volume with her apron's ties, I could have hid a small army beneath the canopy that flared out from just above the bust. Ambrose would be appalled—he loved seeing my curves. I could just hear the strangled sound of disgust he'd make.

Cato would simply cut the offending garment from my form and toss it on the hearth.

Ah, well. I wasn't here to impress.

Gotwig circled me, assessing what he could in the low light.

"Gaeans prize that which is natural above all. If the Goddess created it, then it should be enjoyed in its purest form. You wish to join this city because you wish to live as she intended, yes?"

"Correct."

He propped a leather bag on his knee, checking the supplies within for the sixth time since we'd hidden the sled a mile south.

"I'm here to learn the ways of a simplistic life and dedicate myself to the cause of Mossius and Merrias."

"Which is?" Gotwig paced to one side and then the other, the bag gripped tightly in his hands.

"To embrace Gaea's deep-held values and moral code."

"Yes, and?" His head bobbed up and down as he, uncharacteristically, continued to pace.

"And murdering the king of the realm by the most violent means possible."

His eyes snapped to mine. Even in the moonlit dark I could see their chastising shine.

"Troth Solnna."

"Lord Gotwig."

He closed the distance, moving silently toward me, without even crunching the snow beneath his feet.

"And?" There was no humor in his flat tone.

I blew my hair out of my face, and the wind immediately sent it flying back between my parted lips.

"And to ensure the health and prosperity of a traditional lifestyle that eschews the use of conjuration in all forms... even though I have used it in many forms."

"Because?" he prompted.

"Because the Goddess bestowed upon humanity all they required for them to thrive. The use of conjuration goes against Her plan."

My mother combed my strands back and wrapped a long length of gray wool around my head, securing it with a wooden clasp.

"Daughter, your bag contains gold. Not enough to draw suspicion, but enough to buy a shift to wear under this mess of a dress."

"Momma, if I add another layer, I'll perish from the heat before I can get to the murder." Perspiration beaded on the inside of the fibrous wool, a distinctly unpleasant sensation.

She tsked and tossed a cloak over my shoulders.

"You certainly won't seal the deal if you're scratching at that sensitive skin of yours. Eira, purchase an undergarment so that there is a barrier between you and the fabric. I can just see your murderous plan of attack foiled by a yeasty rash."

"Now, Vonnie—"

Big, burly arms enveloped my head, cutting off my ability to hear.

Pa. He'd employed the same tactic since I was a child. It didn't matter if we were in company, at the millinery shop, or at the Glass Palace for that matter. This was his way of saying, "This is adult speak, minnow. Not for the ears of a lil' fish."

Muffled voices rose around me—one more feminine, the other soft and low—until finally, I was released.

"Ulltan, she's closer to thirty than thirteen." Momma patted Pa's arm.

"A father's heart don't care about age, Vonnie. We ain't encouraging her to act on her whims." My father spun me around and brought his face close, his eyebrows drawn. He tapped me on the nose. "Those whims of yers have gotten ye into a whole heap of predicaments since ye was but toddling."

My mouth dropped open as I propped my fists on my hips.

"Pa! Just what are you imply—"

He wrapped his arms around my head again, pulling me close to his chest; the faint smell of smoked herring and old leather reminded me of home.

Voices rose again, but this time I called to the æther and poked a tiny tongue of black flame into my father's potbelly until he begrudgingly let me go.

"I understand, Ulltan, but the difference is that we will be close to her. Jilly can send word to the checkpoint in just over an hour if anything should go awry."

Pa crossed his arms over his chest.

"I know it. But I still don't like it."

Gotwig snapped his timepiece closed, the metallic click all too familiar. "I am loath to interrupt the squabbling of spouses, but it is time."

"Of course." My mother's expression was stern and serious.

My father's eyes glistened in the snow-lit shadows.

I inhaled a deep, frosty breath, letting the cool air soothe my nerves and cycle through my wool-fevered body.

"I love you all. I'll be okay."

My mother straightened the cloak's ties once more.

"You have the strength of Nortia, Eiry. And don't you forget it."

CHAPTER FOUR

BUSHES AND BRAMBLES!

EIRA

"**A**nd stay out, you dank turd dangling from a dog's bottom!"

I jumped backward as a man's body sailed through the open door, spilling onto the porch.

Huh.

I leaned back and read the sign again.

Timber Tavern.

"Insult me again and I'll take more than your money, foul-mouthed glob of a diseased dick's splatter!"

A tiny woman waved her long, curved smoking pipe into the air and kicked the felled man square in his ass. He sprawled down the short flight of steps and into the road.

"Ya heard me wrong—*hiccup*—your ears done deceived you!" The obviously soused patron crawled a few feet away, reaching for the stiff felt hat that had rolled off his head.

The woman took a slow drag from her pipe.

"Did I? Did I then, Cam? Go on and tell me how's was I supposed to interpret, 'Your cunt is looser than your lips, woman!'"

Oh, fuck. I'm affronted for her.

Drunk Cam sputtered out something unintelligible and shoved his hat over his thick mop of black hair. He lifted a shaky hand in the air and pointed it directly at her thin chest.

"Now, Jilly..."

Ah, that's Jilly.

"Had I said, 'were your bubbies as big as that mouth of yours—'"

Cam never got a chance to finish.

As if summoned by conjuration, a broom appeared in Jilly's hands, her pipe clenched between bared teeth.

"Were your pickle as proud as the words you hurl, your pants would be in perpetual protest!" The woman shot off the porch amid a swirl of heavy skirts, the broom hoisted over her head like an axe ready to cleave his head in two.

Cam, who'd just found his feet, dodged and rolled as the broom smacked the ground where he'd lain only seconds before.

Fury incarnate, Jilly pivoted on her toes and sent her bristle-headed javelin sailing in an impressive arc.

"Woman! Control thyself! Get—*hiccough*—back to the kitchens and—Mossius's fine kneecaps!"

The tightly packed head of husks punched forward, catching the man in the back of his thigh as he fled.

"And stay out! No good, pox-marked prick!"

The diminutive woman retrieved the broom and slung it over her shoulder, standing ramrod straight like the most decorated of Ærtan soldiers.

"JILLY!"

I jumped, tossing my hand to my heart as a young man hollered beside me. Light from the open tavern door seeped out from behind him. "Jilly! Hester's in the hall, and she's gettin' naked!"

"Brambles and bushes," Jilly lamented, chucking the broom onto a bench and running through the entrance.

"Alright. At least I know it's the right place." I muttered under my breath. Jilly's head darted back out, inches from my face. "Fuck!"

She pinned me with a look of concern.

"Hessie's britches disappear the second her tankard touches tongue. Come on, give me a hand."

Welp.

I tossed my bag over my shoulder. "Corralling naked drunks is in my wheelhouse of skills."

"Hester gets right handsy." Jilly gave me a curt nod and smoothed a ringlet back into her puffy lace cap.

"Excellent... like any normal day in Monwyn."

I followed her over the threshold and into a haze that smelled of warm yeast and tobacco. A massive hearth put off a bright light that nearly blinded me after I'd stood so long in the dark. The fireplace took up the entire back wall, and a large copper hood perched proudly over the stone structure, channeling its thick plume of smoke up the chimney. A lone minstrel plucked the strings of a lute—rather poorly—as he sat perched on a barrel atop a small stage in front of the roaring flames.

To the left, a crowd of men stood around staring at... something. I had no idea what they were all looking at, gathered as tightly as they were, but whatever it was, it was serious business. Shoulder-to-shoulder, they vied for a better view.

"Kiss me in the nethers! They've gone bone-dry with age!" a slurring voice crowed.

Gracious.

"This once spunky beav is an ashtray of soot compared to the pond she once was."

My eyes caught sight of the woman that I assumed, on account of her bare and drooping buttocks, was Hester.

"Lutr, love!" the old woman croaked out, "Let Hessie take her teeth out and show you what a good gumming is—"

"Back, you! Back, I say!" Jilly flapped her arms in front of Hester's red-cheeked face while maintaining an impressive tooth-hold on her pipe. The lace around her cap popped up and down with her angry little hops. "Lile Benot, grab her skivvies, dear, hoist them up."

"B-but Jilly!" The youth that had earlier alerted Jilly to Hester's antics swallowed hard, the pronounced Adam's apple in his throat bobbing.

"Don't touch me, boy. Lutr's makin' love eyes at me!"

Hester tossed her stringy, thin hair back... and spat out her teeth.

Oh. Well. Still, not the wildest thing I've seen.

Her top set of wooden teeth flew, landing on the crossed arms of the tallest and most disgruntled-looking man I'd seen outside of Monwyn.

"Leth Hethster tend to that thurkey neck, Luthr." The *very* inebriated woman gyrated her hips to a rhythm all her own, shimmying her butt so it rippled like silk. She was surprisingly spry.

Jilly caught the woman in a bear hug, pinning her arms to her sides.

"Lile Benot! The undies, boy!"

Hester bucked and jumped with the vigor of a much younger woman trying to throw off her captor.

Lutr stood as stone, his wide-set eyes giving no clue as to his emotions.

Lile Benot cringed—poor child—but dutifully dropped low, reaching for the linen garment around a set of dancing feet. Hester reared anew and shoved the loose skin of her rear against the cheek of the horror-stricken youth.

"Mossius, healer lord!" the boy wailed. He closed his eyes and pawed at the floor, searching for her underclothes in vain.

"Dear gods," I whispered, "the boy will be traumatized."

I tossed my bag onto the bar at my right, knocking over a tankard of ale, much to the chagrin of the barmaid cleaning a mountain of dirty cups.

"So sorry," I apologized quickly and then charged in. "Hester!"

The pickled exhibitionist fought harder.

"Cease your squirms!" I barked the order with so much authority that Cato would have snapped to attention. "You're stripping the innocence from that boy one gyration at a time!" I snatched the sloppy set of teeth from Lutr's chest and plugged her mouth. "And put your teeth in for the Goddess's sake."

The wriggling stopped, and three heads swiveled in my direction.

Hester stared at me for a moment... and then something changed in her gray-blue eyes.

I recognized the mischievous glint. The same little spark would often alight in Ambrose's eyes before he turned peevish.

Her mouth dropped open, and she slung her head back—she was primed for a ruckus.

"No, you don't!" I reared my arm back.

"Ack! Jilly! She means to assault—"

Smack!

I brought my palm down on her flabby ass with the same force that it took to subdue a frisky Ambrose. Hester's mouth dropped open, her shock evident.

"Now, into your underthings this instant, madam, or I'll..."

Fuck. What will I do?

I looked around the room... where every single patron looked back at me.

Hester screwed up her face, gumming her mouthpiece into place, sputtering out a few unintelligible words before turning her attention back to me. "Go on then! What will a chubby-arsed peasant do to the likes of—"

"HESSSTTTEERRR!" I screamed at the top of my lungs.

Jilly, Lile Benot, and Hester hopped back, putting distance between us.

"What in the gods'—" Hester spat, turning to flee.

Remembering one of my momma's well-employed behavior-correcting tactics, I attempted out-freaking the freak.

I lifted my knees as high as they would go and stomp-walked toward the bare-assed old woman.

"YOUR BUNS ASSAULT MY EYES! THIS ISN'T THE BAWDY HOUSE, HESTER! IT'S A BAR!"

Once, as a child, I'd made a scene, screaming and kicking when I didn't get the sweet that I wanted from the market. My mother had dropped to the ground, wailing and kicking her feet, crying to the cradle above about her "poor hungry tummy." Gammond's giant gonads, I'd been horrified... And Momma, true to her nature, gave not a single shit about my embarrassment. For the next twenty-some-odd years, I lived in fear that she'd pull the same stunt in front of my friends. Nether, until I was ten years and seven, I took the long path to town, avoiding the market at all costs. Until I met the shop owner's daughter and began trying to flirt my way into her pants. And then did the same to his son a week later. That had been a series of ill-fated decisions that kept me from cake for yet another year.

"NO BUNS IN BARS!" I shrieked while dancing about and flailing my arms.

Hester sneered, grabbed her drawers, and yanked them high above her navel. She glared. "Jilly, what kind of riffraff are you letting into this establishment?" She glanced between Jilly and Lutr while shuffling backward until her back pressed against a stair banister. "Clear out your company, or I'll..."

I stalked closer, giving no quarter.

"Jilly? Jilly, stop this tyrant from—back, you!" She poked her finger out like a sword, stabbing at my chest.

I pressed on, and Hester fled again, crawling up the stairs. The uneven clip-clop of her inebriated movements died out as she disappeared into the tavern's second story.

I rubbed a hand across my neck and cleared my gritty throat.

"I need some water."

A clap sounded behind my back. It began slowly but transformed into a full round of applause, complete with whistles and whoops.

Oh, gods.

"She bested old Hessie!"

"Finally, someone who can keep her clothed! Those side-swinging tits gave me nightmares last month."

"Don't disparage her body," I snapped back at the stunned man. "Hester looks amazing for her age. You saw what I saw. And, by Derros, she has *maintained* her energy. Shame on you, sir."

The man's head lowered, his eyes cast down. Several Gaeans smacked their hands on the tables, amused by their friend's chastisement.

"Who's the new face, Jilly?"

"Tongue like a striking serpent on that one!"

Great job lying low, Eira.

I waved a shy fan of fingers, chuckling awkwardly.

"Hi. I'm Birdie." I lifted the sides of my skirts, holding them wide, and bobbed a poor curtsy. I'd practiced the little stumble over and over while Gotwig chastised the "proper" movements out of me. "Jilly's niece. From the mount—"

"Birdie, dear! Why, I hardly recognized you, as big as you've grown!"

Jilly flew at me, arms wide. She caught me around the hips in a warm embrace and spun me around before pulling the collar of my cloak more snugly around my face. "You'll catch a chill if you aren't bundled snug as a bug."

I glanced down at her, returning her hug and smiling with feigned familiarity.

She released me but clung to an elbow.

"Lutr, you remember Milly, my sister? This is her little Birdie."

Lutr nodded, just a single dip of his shining bald head. "Yes. I remember. I saw you when you were four. You were cute. We played hide-and-seek. You look like your dad."

Oh boy, Lutr would never make it as an Obligate—awful liar.

Jilly fluttered around.

"Gracious me, niece, you must be exhausted after your trip. Head up the stairs. Your room is the sixth door on the left. Lile Benot will bring up a hot meal and your bag. Shoo now, don't make me take up the broom again."

Jilly swatted at my rump, and I climbed the stairs, relieved to get away from the crowd's attention.

I heard Jilly chatting with her clientele behind me as I continued my ascent. "Milly's husband, Arnault, is a moose of a man. Birdie gets her height from him but her coloring from our side."

I pushed open a heavy wooden door at the top of the steps. Its hand-painted sign read, Paying Guests Only.

"Shit!" My hand flew to my chest.

A serious and entirely clear-eyed Hester beckoned me to the hallway's end.

"Come on, girl, we've no time to waste."

CHAPTER FIVE

MY ANGRY BITS

EIRA

"So, downstairs?" I followed Hester into a decent-sized room with a single window and a wealth of massive furniture.

The door closed behind us with a soft click.

Hester turned and furrowed her sparse brows as she sized me up, scrutinizing me from head wrap to boots.

"When you dabble in the game of espionage, young one, distractions become a permanent part of one's nature." She moved quickly to shutter her window, cutting off the little light the moon afforded us. "Not a single soul attempts to mess with a crazy old crone, and that's the way I prefer it."

She rolled up the waist of her forest-green-and-gray paneled skirt until her long but scrawny calves came into view.

I nodded my understanding. "I usually toss a tit out."

The corner of her mouth tugged down in a cynical smile.

"Had I your ample bosoms, I would no doubt deploy them under duress. Now, strip."

I undid my cloak and tossed it onto the nearby bed.

"Full nude or underwear nude?"

She cocked a brow.

"I'm impressed. You're either a well-trained Troth or a slut."

I twisted the length of cloth from around my head and shrugged out of my scratchy dress.

"Why not both?"

"Full. Anything the concoction touches will feel its power."

Hester sped around the room, opening drawers from her literal wall of chests, collecting handfuls of roots and foliage. The massive cherry wood chest of drawers with heavy bronze pulls reached to the low-hung ceiling.

My stomach sank as a familiar astringent smell assaulted my nose. "Are you a healer, conjurer, or a priestess?"

Hester stopped short in her collection mission. Arms full, she moved toward me, each step measured and slow.

"Nay, girl. Neither." Her droopy lids opened wide, revealing eyes filmy with the haze of age.

It took all of me not to retreat as she pressed in on me. She came so close that I could smell the woodsy, honeyed scent of the bag of saffron she held clutched to her chest.

"I'm a hedge witch," she whispered, one eye squinting in time with her words. "Now lie on the bed, upside down. Hang your head over the side."

"Hedge witch?"

"Your ears do work, then?" She pointed her elbows at the quilt-covered bed and then set her burden on a three-legged bedside table. "Go on, hurry."

I took a wide path around Hester and tossed my legs over to assume the position requested.

Momma knows these people, Eira. She would never put you in harm's path.

I dropped my head back and watched the scene unfold, upside down.

"Explain *hedge witch*, please. I'm not familiar with the term. In Nortia, witches are conjurers and therefore outlaws. So...?"

Hester skittered like a crab, swiping ingredients and taking whiffs of the items she procured. From her wardrobe—which contained not a single item of clothing—she retrieved a set of nested earthenware bowls.

"I know the plants. Make the potions. Eat this leaf and fart, toss this salt and keep the haints at bay. You know the sort."

Do I?

"Are you Cult Mossius?"

Her flickering fingers stilled for a split second before resuming their ministrations.

"No," Hester said the word with a certain sort of venom.

"Ah, a Cult Mossius reject?" I pried, immediately clueing in on the slight stiffening of her hunched shoulders. The wrinkly skin around her mouth tightened—I'd hit a nerve.

The witch remained silent as she retrieved what looked like a handful of eggs from a drawer more suited for sweaters. In a quick succession of one-handed smacks, she cracked one, two, and three greenish eggs into a powdery mixture.

"Jilly warned me you may be impertinent. Your mother, kind as she was, couldn't leave well enough alone, just like you."

"You know my mother?"

Hester sat on the floor, close to my head, and extracted a whisk from under her bedframe.

"Of course." Hester sniffed the concoction and tested the viscosity of the paste as she held her utensil aloft. "All of us wanted her smart self for our research partner... before we became 'Cult Mossius rejects.'"

She stabbed her finger into the bowl and painted the pasty mixture across my brows.

"What is it?" The stinky slop felt heavy on my forehead.

"In two days' time, you will check in with the city's magistrate. Newly arriving immigrants must present themselves for assessment to gain employment. If you are found lacking, the Cult will determine your suitability for improvement."

"And what if the Cult determines I can't be *improved*—am I sent back home? Turned out on the streets? That'd be gross, by the way. Who would turn away someone seeking refuge if they were unable to—"

"No."

A tepid glob of paste hit the top of my head.

"Whoa, Hester! Is bald a Gaean cultural custom? What are you—"

"Hush. We begin your transformation. And this is no depilatory cream." She scrubbed her fingers into my scalp after coating the ends of my hair.

"Gods, Hester!" The smell—like rotten eggs and sulfur—burned the breath from my lungs. "What foulness are you coating me in?"

She slopped another handful on my head, massaging it in.

"You know, you bear a remarkable resemblance to the Primus-King's eldest daughter. Perhaps a little fatter than "curvy" implies, but chestnut hair, teal eyes, a straight nose with a slight tilt at its end."

I pressed my lips together.

"She was kidnapped. Mmhmm, that's right. Over two and a half decades ago. Can you imagine having your child taken from your home?" Her voice went low, as if she were sharing gossip with a close friend. "Now, old Hessie isn't one to chatter, but it seems that the evil conjuring queen of Solnna kept the child under lock and key. After the failed civil war, the daughter escaped under the cloak of an eerie fog. The Primus-King has search parties all over the continent. Awful business, that."

I nodded my understanding. This was the story the Primus-King was selling.

"So, if I'm not going bald, I'm going—"

"Blonde. Unless I've added in too much lye or alum, then you *will* go bald and, most likely, skinless."

For fuck's sake.

Hester smiled widely, the pearl inlay of her wooden teeth gleaming in a most becoming way.

"I pray, then, that you are an accomplished... What did you call it? Hedge witch?"

"Yes, that's right. Is your asshole hairy?"

Hester whisked a little more powder into her bowl.

I blinked repeatedly.

"I honestly don't know. Probably?"

"No matter. We'll pluck those out. That skin is too sensitive for the likes of this brew."

I quieted while she carried on, spreading a thin layer over my arms and legs and a smear over my pubic hair.

"Normally, we'd sit you out in the sun for a few hours to marinate, but time is of the essence. I'd say twelve hours as you are, and then we shall apply the saffron and lemon juice. That one is applied hot."

"Twelve hours!"

She replied by swiping her thickly coated hand across my mouth.

"You've a little mustache, Birdie. You'll need to seal those lips to prevent potential poisoning."

Touché, Hester, touché.

Effectively silenced, I took the time to study the old woman as she carried on, humming a tuneless song under her breath. Her fingers were bent with age, and as she slathered me with the rank paste, I noticed her knuckles were markedly swollen. She had well-maintained nails, despite the unkempt hair hanging in dull-gray strands around her shoulders. And though her clothing was much too large and in ill repair, she had no odor that indicated a lack of resources or hygiene.

"Legs up."

I complied, and she slid two rolled-up blankets under my ankles so she could reach the undersides of my legs.

After what felt like two hours, Hester dropped heavily onto the bed with a sigh. She leaned over and assessed my hair by rubbing off a small amount of goo.

"It's striped like an orange tabby cat right now. Pray to the Goddess you won't require a second bake." She scooted back and leaned against a parchment-covered wall. Childish renderings of plants, pups, and happy snakes hung haphazardly. With their asymmetrical hearts and the backwards letters formed by tiny hands, they had clearly been created with love.

I cracked my lips apart and blew away the dried crumbles of her potion.

"Hester?"

She laid her head against the wall and closed her eyes.

"Hester?" I said more firmly.

Her nostrils flared, and she sighed deeply.

"I am *beyond* interrogation, Birdie."

"But I am *remarkably* curious, Hester."

She huffed and shot off the bed, heading toward a blue-and-white water basin sandwiched between two hanging swags of evergreen.

"Go on then, ask your questions, girl."

After smoothing her stringy strands behind her ears, she committed to vigorously scrubbing the bowl and utensils with powdered soap.

I shifted my hips, trying to get more comfortable.

"Why are you helping me?"

She chewed on the inside of her cheek while drying her tools on a linen and then, with a loud bang, closed a drawer, stowing her wares. Deep worry lines creased her forehead.

Hester came my way and dropped down to sit cross-legged on the floor.

My heart beat momentarily out of rhythm as her demeanor changed. She sagged in on herself like the weight of the continent settled upon her diminutive shoulders. Her age showed then.

"Hester, are you okay?"

She peered into my upside-down eyes, blinking a single time.

"I arranged your mother's Joining to the Primus-King."

"You..."

My mind tried to process her words, the syllables rearranging and twisting before colliding into each other in a clash of realization.

I flinched, wrapping protective arms around myself. Bits of dried paste and thicker goo ran down my biceps, but nothing could distract me from the jumble of my racing thoughts.

My skin heated, and sweat beaded on my forehead.

And the æther.

It hummed and buzzed within my chest, like it'd been waiting to unfurl its shadowy plumes.

One... two... Momma must have known I'd meet her.... Calm, Eira, stay calm. Three... four... breathe. Goddess, oh my Goddess. Surely Momma would have known; surely, she would have—

I leapt off the bed. I couldn't keep the æther grounded lying prone like I was. I clenched my muscles, holding back the emotion that thundered inside me, demanding release.

"Do not disturb the mixture!" Hester waved her hands frantically, indicating the bed. "Resume your position before—"

"Fuck the mixture!"

I frantically searched for my discarded clothing but froze when I caught the pale, lumpy reflection of a mashed-potato creature. I shuffled to the mirror mounted above the washbasin.

"Holy shit from the divine bum above." I raised my hand to my face, refusing to believe what my eyes most assuredly saw.

I was not myself. I was without hue.

This makeover went beyond the Verus Grooming room, which included extra hair fibers and skillfully applied makeup. This transformation had turned my brows the color of corn cakes, my lashes a light gold, and my darkest, walnut-colored hair yellow. Gaudy, flaming Solnnan butterfly-wing yellow.

I was unrecognizable; the hairs on my arms and legs were nearly invisible. My eyes, which Cato described as "angry-ocean-water-teal," now appeared much greener than blue, staring out from the new me. My lips appeared more prominent and rosier, and the pink undertones of my complexion stood out brightly.

"You're burning!" Hester came up behind me and held her palms in front of my shoulders. "The mixture does naturally warm, but it is emanating. You are having an allergic episode! Come, we—"

I snapped around.

"My mother endured rape and abuse when she was barely on the cusp of womanhood." I walked Hester backward, the anger and æther combining, and steam leaked from my fingertips. "Can you rationalize why you chose that for her, Hester?"

The paste began to scorch my scalp and face.

I glared, gritting my teeth together as I channeled the pain deeply into my being, a conduit that allowed me to keep from lashing out. Gotwig would have applauded my self-control.

"Explain it to me, Hester, and do it quickly. I can only *rationalize* not snapping that thin neck of yours because my mother trusts Jilly—and by extension, you as well."

She nodded, not quite meeting my gaze.

"Yes, of course. I will explain all, but the paste must be removed. The mixture has become volatile." Hester raced to the bed, her skirts unfurling from the roll at her hips as she reached under the frame and yanked. "Help me, child."

Still brimming with resentment but fueled by both magical and chemical heat streaking across my sensitive skin, I gave aid, tugging on the rope handle of a shallow barrel.

"Josa's taint!" I furiously fanned the skin of my upper thighs. "Hester, I'm lava levels of boiling."

"Get in. Hurry, girl, or the magistrate will accuse you of bearing plague at the checkpoint."

I performed a one-legged hop into the center of the standing bath and began scrubbing at my stomach.

"Don't rub! Don't risk breaking the skin!"

"Get it off of me then!" I was starting to panic.

Hester broke into a run. She tossed up a wall panel near the washbasin and withdrew a cleverly concealed canvas rope.

"Catch it!"

I snatched the bronze-capped length from the air as a hysterical Hester pumped the handle it had been coiled around. The old woman jumped and pushed with all her might and then tugged with just as much fervor as soon as the lever depressed.

"Hester, what the nether are—"

Water.

A blessed, freezing, powerful stream of water shot into my temple. Surprised, my heels hit the barrel's edge, but I maintained my balance.

"Don't get it in your eyes. Hold it, girl, hold it high."

Where the water hit my burning skin, it felt like taking a naked plunge into the Penumbrean Sea in the winter months.

"Derro's watery waves!" I scrunched my face and tried pretending that I was back in Solnna, luxuriating in their rain bath after taking too much sun. Those were Ambrose's hands running through my hair, and the panted breaths were Cato taking in the scene... not a wheezing elder sloughing off what I prayed was only paste and not bits of my skin.

"There we go. Dry off. I'll fetch the aloe—it'll soothe the angry bits."

Chapter Six

WITH THEM GOES MY HEART

AMBROSE. THE WILDS OF GAEA. THREE MONTHS AFTER EIRA'S DEPARTURE.

"You are positive that you know the way?" I pushed my spectacles up the bridge of my nose and peered into the distance over Cato's shoulder.

"Ambrose. Do you even know me?"

Insolent little bitch.

I continued staring, unwilling to meet his eyes. The priestess I'd been speaking with said this was all a part of my issues with loss, and I knew she was right. Even so, I opted to ignore his face and scoff at the state of his shit-covered, in-need-of-a-polish boot in the stirrup.

He was leaving.

It was time.

And I was bereft.

"But Catommandus, the snow—surely it changes the topography of the environment, rendering your map useless. You will get lost and—"

"Ambro—"

With a smart slap to Horse Ambrose's flank, I cut short the farewell. The destrier sidestepped. Cato jerked around, daggers shooting from his eyes—the sweet eyes of my sort-of-lover.

"Do not *Ambrose* me again, Cat. Our wife is missing—no, no, she is willfully avoiding us, and now you ride off into the cold to hash out the stratagems of an international conflict!"

"There is no war yet. Cease your dramatics. The Mantle and my generals must make haste to form a plan for the eventuality. Surely you understand this is bigger than your daddy issues."

Cato sighed, and his eyes softened. I wanted to punch the short princeling in his throat and pop that look of pity right off his big-pored complexion.

"What I *understand* is that you have a Larm, fucking Septimus has Evandr, and I have nothing, no one. I just had to go and fall in love." I hugged my arms close to my body. "And what did it get me? She left me, despite our vows... Just like Mama and Father, just like my goatling, just like the parents who gave me up. Do not deepen your scowl! Unfurrow your brow at once."

"For fuck's sake, Ambrose."

"Oof!" Horse Ambrose's rump collided with my shoulder as Cato guided him around.

I stumbled backward, wrenching an ankle in the process of catching my fall.

Evandr and Septimus chuckled behind me. Gods alive, how I hated them. I hated what they represented and hated their newfound happiness. Hated how close they were and how they could talk and laugh well into the night.

Tears, hot and stinging, pricked the backs of my eyes.

It's how Eira had been with me—not only my lover, but my best friend. She, above all, cared for me and my well-being... knew how to touch me, which situations mandated which type of cuddles. My chest felt as if an ogre had taken a tree-sized mallet to my heart. My soul ached even more profoundly.

A firm hand righted me, then slipped from my shoulder, moving up to cup my jaw.

Cato lifted my gaze to his, where he sat astride his mount. The thin, golden aura danced in his dark eyes, and I choked back a sob, knowing the realities we both faced.

He whisked a tear from my cheek with his gloved thumb.

"I love you, Ambrose."

I nodded, unable to form words without an avalanche of tears spewing forth.

"I l-love y-you, too."

To the nether with it.

I let my tears flow, the warmth running down my cheeks and cooling in the frigid air.

Cato stroked the raised scar that cut through my beard.

"I will give Their Holiness, your sibling, the letter you penned. Expect a weekly correspondence from me when you arrive back in Monwyn. I am not leaving you or Eira, and I *will* see you both again."

"Catommandus, I feel as if I should continue to search. She is so—"

"It is too dangerous, Ambrose. Already, we ride too close to Gaea. We cannot risk your recognition. Promise me you will do no such thing."

"I will not tie myself to such a promise," I scoffed. "I am my own man."

"You are *my* man, if Eira is to be believed."

Cato quirked a brow, and I felt the telltale heat of a blush move across my cheeks.

"Well, I, uh..." I bit the corner of my lip, and then my Scion's mind snapped firmly into place. "You absolute cow's ass! You seek to manipulate me with your flirtations!"

Cato shrugged one of his wide shoulders and winked.

"Ambrose, my first order will be to send the units gathering at Verus to the Primus-King's doorstep. He will step down and submit himself to the Mantle, or I will render him lifeless. She will be safe and back in my arms within the month."

I covered his hand with my own, bracing it against my cheek.

"*Our* arms."

He rolled his eyes and nodded halfheartedly.

"And then we will chain her to the palace and—"

"Spank her plump ass and fuck her senseless, and cuddle and—"

Cato looked at me askance.

"I was going to say plan out our beautiful future, but your proposal holds as much merit... perhaps more." He pulled his hand from my grasp and sat up straight. "Now, listen. When you arrive in Cordillaria, keep a watchful eye on Greggen. Though I reshaped him into a tool, if the Baldorvan informants have breached the city—which I am positive they have—he is not to be trusted."

I bobbed my head. Personally, I wanted Greggen dead for the pain he'd caused my soft-hearted harpy, and for his role in my mother's death, but I understood the logic in keeping him at our mercy. He was so disgustingly in love with Allaine that it had been fairly simple to keep him in check. I could just glance in her direction, and he snapped to my bidding. Well, less of a snap and more of a careful saunter—he was still learning to navigate life as a single-eyed man.

"Catommandus, does Bem still have Greggen's eyeball? What does he do with the body parts? I am not at all sure that it is healthy for—"

The crunch of snow announced the rest of our unmerry little band.

A wad of spit landed near my foot.

"Please, Goddess, end this disgustingly sentimental moment," Septimus's smooth voice mocked. "Catommandus, did you not suck his dick well enough last night? Did you leave him unsatisfied? No surprise. It is your calling card, prodigal prince."

Cato glowered from his steed, his mouth setting into a thin line.

I patted Cato's thigh.

"Oh, no, you have it all wrong. Cato is not a giver, honestly. He is more like the shared plaything of my wife and I. Eira and I enjoy nothing better than team sports."

"Uncle, you live only because I leave for Verus and the kingdom needs your know-how," Cat growled out in a menacing tone. "But when this matter is settled, the world, and I, will no longer have need of you. Ambrose, love..."

I raised my brows, caught off guard by his endearment. He stared into Septimus's eyes.

"... the memory of coming between your soft, warm lips will stay with me for the duration."

Cato gripped my head and yanked my face to his, our mouths crashing together. His tongue parted my lips and entered, tangling with my own.

Septimus gagged. And to be honest, I also felt the lurching of Cato's throat. He'd not been able to stomach the touch of another, I think, on account of the Dick Bond he shared with our wife.

"Fucking filthy, appalling men. Your father would disown you, the both of you!"

I leaned into the faux kiss, running my hands up Cato's chest and moaning like the Goddess was fellating me, and then quickly unlocked our lips, lest he regurgitate his meager breakfast upon me.

"Good boy, Ambrose. Good boy."

We shared in a conspiratorial smile as we pulled away.

"Thank you, my thick-dicked daddy. I am such a slut for your praise."

I trailed my finger up the length of Cato's thigh as he sat back on his mount, looking a little green around the gills.

"Leave Catommandus before you compel me to slit my wrists. Evandr, avert your eyes," Septimus gritted out.

"No use. Dick's already hard." Evandr's hearty laughter cast a rock into the ice-covered lake of tension.

I continued my exploration, palming a single globe of Cato's rear. I watched his throat working to hold back the bubbling sick. Catommandus would agree that the lilting song of Septimus's furious huffs would *absolutely* be worth a bout of vomits.

Septimus stepped toward me.

"The feeling of your wife's walls clenching around my shaft sets a standard that other broodmares cannot meet. That you seek lesser pleasures speaks to your inability to satisfy her."

My muscles coiled.

"Steady, Ambrose," Cato murmured.

I breathed deeply, trying to dispel my anger, but rage twisted through my body like poison through the bloodstream.

He'd had my wife.

My uncle, my supposed relation—blood shared or not—wedged his pierced dick into the body of my bride and released himself into her perfect cavern.

I wanted him dead for his transgression.

"Our pillow talk is workshopping the most *satisfying* ways to murder you." I said in my most sycophantic voice. "It gets him off quick."

Septimus sneered and kicked a chunk of mud-covered ice at Horse Ambrose.

Cato ignored him and inclined his chin.

"The lot of you are charged with maintaining the safety of Monwyn. Return home and fortify the kingdom for the impending war."

Without an ounce of pomp or fanfare, Larm readied the last of their provisions, and together, without a glance back... they left me.

"Ambrose! You are giving him reasons to taunt you."

I snapped my head around and stared at the man I'd once considered Joining with. Thank Viktos, I'd dodged that short, bulky, infuriating bolt of lightning. *Ugh.*

I dabbed my dick with a bit of linen and tucked myself back into my pants before discarding the square. Evandr, mannerless oaf that he was, shook his cock, sprinkling a bit of urine onto his boots before shoving it back behind his laces. *Disgusting.*

"I am permitted to feel *and* express my emotions. My mother did not raise me to hide my feelings behind a mountain of bullshit like the other boys."

Evan popped his lips.

"Yeah, right. Imella would have told you to stop your sniveling."

I shrugged.

"Yes, but she would have done it while rocking me in the comfort of her bosom."

Evandr pinched the bridge of his nose with his dirty piss fingers.

"Ambrose, you've sniffled and sighed your way from one side of the continent to the other." Evandr walked ahead, scouting the area while I cleaned my hands in the snow. "It's gotten old, my friend."

I gazed at my nicked-up hands, turning the palms up and then down, inspecting their cleanliness. *My* scars did not lend me a ruggedness as they did for Catommandus, nor did they imbue me with the rakish handsomeness as they did for pirate Larm. No, what I saw in the mirror was a man who had entered the arena and lost.

I tugged my chartreuse scarf more closely around my face, doing what I could to protect my sensitive skin from the elements.

At least I am here, though.

I hadn't admitted it to a soul, but after my wife returned me from the brink of death, I pondered taking my life out of fear she'd no longer love what I'd become. I wasn't sure *I* could love what I'd become.

But I'd made it through.

And more than anything in my life, I wanted her back, nestled into our bed, braiding my hair, allowing me to bathe her voluptuous form so I could prove to her that I still had worth.

"How profoundly love has changed me, Evan."

"*How profoundly love has—*"

"Hold your mocking tongue, Uncle. You will atone for—"

"—fucking your wife... with her full and, shall I say, most enthusiastic consent?"

I stood to my full height and loomed over the washed-out, pale piece of excrement. With an undertone of vulgarity, Septimus's tongue swiped over the corner of his mouth, and clawing fingers of hatred drew the heat from my bones. Were I honest with myself, it wasn't just hate; it was embarrassment. And I loathed it. Why should his dubious actions make me feel like a scolded child?

Priestess Eglantine counseled that I should allow myself to feel my feelings as they came but to recognize that perhaps, given my propensity to catastrophize, I should remember that what I see may be an overinflation of what is actually occurring.

"Is that what you weep over, false prince? Knowing that my velvet-covered steel took her to the brink of ecstasy while you writhed helpless in your sickbed? Goddess alive, her tight cunt milking my shaft for every last drop of seed was—"

I snapped.

She was mine. And I protected what was mine.

The nails of my left hand dug into the flesh of his neck as my mace appeared in my right as if by conjuration.

I'd dye the blanket of snow with his brain matter.

"Ambrose, stop!" In my periphery, I saw the outline of the screaming Evandr barreling toward us with his unnatural Frostborn speed.

Fuck it, I'd take my chances against him.

"Give my gratitude to the Nether Lord, Uncle."

Septimus flailed, clawing at my face as I sent my weapon on a trajectory toward his temple.

"Ambrose! NO!" Evandr bellowed.

A movement in the distance caught my attention.

"Spy," I hissed, pulling my killing blow. "Get down."

I flung Septimus, and we dropped to the ground. Seconds later, Evandr dropped into a crouch beside us.

"Where?"

"There in the distance."

Septimus's eyes followed my finger, which pointed to a shadow moving between the trees some quarter of a mile away.

Evandr crawled in next to me. Where his body touched mine, it felt like the cold seeped into my bones.

"Look, Ambrose, I can deal with Cato trying to kill him, but you—"

"Shut up!" I palmed the Scion's head and twisted it in the direction of the interloper.

"It moves toward Monwyn," Septimus barked in my ear.

"Do you think it spotted us?" I asked, noting the shadowy figure picking up speed.

Septimus inclined his chin.

"We have no time for loose ends." I got to my knees, ready to pursue.

"Evandr, give chase. Bring the demon back, and I shall find out what it knows."

"Yes, Father."

Before I could shift my weight to run, Evan took off, startling a fox from the brush and then outstripping it across the clearing.

Septimus's stupidly blue eyes glittered like a starry sky. "Is my progeny not magnificent?"

"I am appalled, simply aghast, that you allow such familiarity. It is actually creepy."

Gods he is magnificent, though!

Fueled by whatever the fuck the Nether Lord had done to him, Evandr raced across the expanse, growing in both width and height. By the time the forest swallowed him, he rivaled the smaller trees for height.

"Honestly, I feel as though Larm could take him quite handily." I dug around in my pocket, searching for the hideous cap Catommandus made for me before we set out. I'd "lost" the three or four others he'd knitted me on account of the way they deflated the volume from my mane, but in this cold, I tugged the thick cap over my ears. "Evandr shows, but it is Larm who *truly* grows. No mystery there, though; Cato's splatter-batter was bound to result in a spawn more virulent than your own."

Evandr emerged from the forest, not lumbering as you would expect an ice giant to do, but sprinting from the wood with the confident grace of a wolf bounding across a ridge.

He'd caught the deviant, and the ensnared form struggled in his grasp, kicking and bowing its back, doing everything in its power to escape.

Futile.

Frost-Evandr paid it no mind, not even blinking when the silver spurs of the swinging, booted feet pierced holes in the gray-blue skin of his stomach. Blood rained from the punctures down to his groin—the azure streaks were luminous and reminded me of the strange glowing squid that swam in Monwyn's western seas.

Ah, shoes—a man, then, and not another nether creature, thank the Goddess.

Since Eira's departure, we'd fought off enough trolls and blade-footed pixies to last a lifetime.

Evander continued forward, squeezing the man in his arms, until he ceased his flailing.

"Hopefully, he's grown accustomed to his newfound strength. I tried for days to remove the goblin stains from my tan leathers to no avail. If he pops this one like he did that grizzly little urchin, I'll have no garments left—my gods, he is hung like the most colossal of mules."

Septimus muttered out some curse, but I still could not avert my eyes. Evandr's dingles dangled nearly to the middle of his tree-trunk-sized thighs.

"And you, Septimus, how do you figure you'll keep him in clothes? Hmm? Stripped of your lands and titles as you are, the task will be a daunting one."

I could feel my uncle's icy stare, just as frigid as the wind that blew around us.

Evandr came to a stop, and his bare skin, before my still disbelieving eyes, faded into its normal, pasty hue. He tossed a slender man at our feet as his skin momentarily sagged before tightening around his shrinking frame.

The sight of his transformation raised the hair on my arms... which was a much calmer reaction than when he and Larm the pirate had initially converted into ice ogres. I chuckled softly. There had been so much screaming. I was yelling. Bem was bleating. Aberus had picked up that plump little dollop, Richelle, tossed her over his shoulder, and run. Catommandus pissed himself, though he blamed the wet pants on their thawing.

"What is your name? Who do you work for?" Septimus apprehended the cloaked figure, while I tossed Evandr the spare clothing from his pack.

Silence.

Septimus yanked the man to his knees and bound his wrists behind his back.

"I will peel the skin from your tongue, worm."

I shoved my way next to my odious uncle, attempting to get a better look at our captive.

"Septimus, must you always start with violence? Offer him a warm meal, for goodness's sake. In this weather, it would be much more enticing than"—Septimus tossed back the man's hood—"Oho! I know this fellow. Hughes, is it? Let him up. This is Mama's former guard."

"I do not care if he is—"

"Untie him!"

Septimus eyed me but did as asked, releasing the red-headed man, who stood quickly and brushed the snow from his clothes.

"What brings you out in this weather, Hughes? The last time we spoke, you were bound for the Isles of Inglis."

I dug around in my pack and withdrew a bit of jerky, offering it up and pressing it into his gloved hand.

"A new contract was secured." Hughes's eyes flicked toward Evandr, who was pulling on a pair of mismatched socks.

"Do not concern yourself with him. He'll not harm you. He is my wife's creepy love child." I waved a dismissive hand. "As you are aware, she possesses unique abilities, and subsequently, she has passed those on to her offspring." I chuckled, thinking about how lovely Eira was in her demon puff form—all billowy and iridescent. "Ah, and speaking of my lady wife, I pray there are no hard feelings between you and I, Hughes. Though Mama had the best of intentions in transferring your services to my love bunny upon her death, I feel, as her husband, that I am the only protection she needs."

Hughes clipped a bow and then straightened his spectacles. "I harbor no bitterness, Highness."

"Good man, Hughes, good man." I nodded and turned to repack my bag. "You be off then."

"Indeed. At once, I'll be on my way, Prince Ambrose."

Hughes spun on his heels and headed back toward the forest.

Septimus and Evandr closed the ranks behind me.

"I should have asked him how he kept his frames clear of the fog. Mine glazed over the moment I perched them upon my fine—"

At once, everything clicked.

"A new contract. That motherfucker."

Hughes shot off, tearing across the snowfield.

I pursued him, moving faster than I have ever moved before. I heard Septimus's footfalls behind me.

Hughes swerved left, gaining distance, but at the mere thought of him slipping from my grasp, I was imbued with a spark of energy. I launched myself, tackling him to the ground.

"Where is my wife?" I gritted out between clenched teeth.

My fingers dug into his shoulders, pinning him to the earth.

His eyes remained passive. His lips sealed.

Septimus cracked his knuckles as he came to our side. "This is no coincidence. I will break him."

I shook my head.

"No, Uncle. He is mine."

CHAPTER SEVEN

DICKS, PRICKS, AND LICKS

EIRA

"Holy fuck, Jilly. How do you keep up with all of this? With all of them?" I stabbed my finger toward the band of merrymakers, many of whom were pounding their fists against the table, demanding their fourth and fifth rounds of beer. "Is it like this every night?"

There must have been sixty bodies packed into the Timber Tavern, and more kept coming. Every other minute that fucking door would swing open and another man would walk in. Like yesterday, throngs of patrons stood shoulder to shoulder; tonight they gathered around the tables, their attention riveted on whatever drinking game they played.

"It is." Jilly dunked two handfuls of copper tankards into a sink filled with sudsy water and then repeated the action twice more. "We lie outside of the city gates, so are not beholden to the laws of the capital." She nodded toward the most boisterous of the groups. "Gambling is forbidden in Mynder."

"Gambling?" I stood on my toes and peeked over the bar, trying to glimpse what the men slid across the tabletops. "Coins? Malachite?"

Jilly shook her head while I wiped the sweat from mine. "Sugar."

"Sugar?"

"Sugar." Jilly drew fresh beer into the mugs and slid them in my direction. "Now go on, take these to the magistrate's table. Catch his eye, Birdie, and then play nice. You'll make your case to him tomorrow."

"Right." I gathered up the foaming tankards, three in each hand, and made my way through the ever-increasing crowd. My swollen feet ached, and my knees felt like I'd climbed a hundred flights of stairs.

I'd been working the tavern floor since my eyes opened, and with every hour that ticked by with no end in sight, I gained a new appreciation for the maids and menfolk who did this day in and day out.

"Play nice, Birdie," I murmured under my breath.

So far, my attempts at catching anything more than a cursory nod of the magistrate's head had failed. I'd cleared my throat, bumped the table, and sighed in distress; all had gone ignored.

The magistrate glanced up as I neared, and I unleashed my most winning smile in his direction, plopping his drink down before serving the others.

This smile had dazzled Cato and subdued Ambrose in more than one fit of petulance!

His disinterested eyes went right back to the pouch in his hand, weighing it and turning it over in his palm.

Well!

I sidestepped and dodged my way back to the bar, feeling all kinds of disgruntled.

Jilly glanced at me expectantly while blowing warm air into her wash-water-chilled hands.

"Nothing. He was entirely focused on his sugar bag."

I shoved my sleeves above my elbows, grabbed two tankards, and shot them into the sink.

Hidden behind the tall bar, I released my æther and my frustrations, heating the water until bubbles began to surface.

"New plan." I pressed the two warmed vessels in her red-splotched hands. "If you need it heated again, let me know."

I unwound my head wrap, unleashing hair so golden that I could have been mistaken for a bushel of wheat.

"What are you—"

"I'm bringing out *my* game pieces. Pass me that knife."

With a look of confusion, Jilly handed over a blade, which I promptly took and thrust into the heavy wool of my neckline. A puff of heat struck me in the face when I slit the gown from the middle of my breasts to the top. The two halves fell open, revealing a more than ample view of skin.

"Prostitution? No, ma'am. You'll see me shut down, Birdie." Jilly flapped her hands in front of my cleavage. "Cover up, girl, *you* are a modest maiden, or have you forgotten?"

"Modest maidens have tits, Jilly. And they can still be modest-minded *and* show them off. Plus, I'm so fucking hot I'm likely to drip sweat into their drinks. That's what will get you shut down."

I checked my reflection in the bottom of a shiny pot. No need for face powders. My cheeks shone cherry-red, and my dark lashes contrasted with my blonde brows. I ran my fingers through my hair and then lifted each breast, going for an optimal display.

Jilly paced back and forth, wringing her apron in her tiny hands.

"I'm a trained Troth." I picked up a plate of cheese and popped a cube in my mouth. "These girls have landed me many a potential partner." I chewed and swallowed what was most assuredly not cheese. "What is this?"

"Bean curd. Cheese and wine are not permitted in the city. They have been deemed unhealthy by the Primus-King."

My face fell.

The Primus-King was an *actual* tyrant.

"And the sugar?" I nodded toward the gambling patrons. "Is that why they're using it for—"

"Correct. Not allowed."

Shit, this place is worse than Monwyn.

She shrugged.

"According to the law keepers, it's done with the intention of expanding our longevity and keeping our waistlines slimmer."

"And the citizens are okay with their monarch making that decision for them?"

"Well, yes. For the greater good of our people."

My eyes landed on a table of hollering men, my lips pressed into a sarcastic line.

"And that's why there are a hundred men ready to come to blows over..." I stood on my toes, "... two tablespoons of sugar?"

A silent 'oh' shaped Jilly's lips, her small, guileless eyes stretching wide.

"Why, Jilly, you nefarious little profiteer." I twirled around and glanced back at her over my shoulder. "And you worry about *me* taking the lawman to my bed... when he's clearly already in yours."

Her gritty little chortle followed me across the floor.

I sized up my prey as I offered bean cubes to the patrons on my left and right.

Alright, Eira, you may be a bovine by Gaean standards, but a cow with big teats gives more milk than a cow with... no teats? A bull? Whatever.

The magistrate was a fine-looking fellow in his middle years. His light brown hair complemented his rich black skin. A few silver coils hid in his beard, and I could make out prominent laugh lines on either side of his full lips. Yet, his complexion was free of wrinkles or blemishes.

Chatting with anyone and everyone who would engage with me, I circled the tables, all the while keeping a close eye on my target.

Tactic number one... a bee to honey.

"Here, love, don't put your cards down. Open your mouth." I pressed a curd cube past the lips of a profusely sweating patron. This game must be for a whole pastry's worth of the sweet stuff.

"Now *this* is service." He laughed uncomfortably while tapping his cheek. "A kiss for luck?"

I bent and pecked the top of his bald pate.

With a deep inhale, he fanned his cards across the tabletop, closing his eyes as if saying a prayer.

"Wilmer! By Merrias! You did it, man. You've taken the lot!"

Shining brown eyes peered into mine, tears of happiness pooling in their corners.

"She's my good luck charm, she is! Lend me another kiss, lovely lady... you got a name?"

"That's Jilly's niece, from the mountains. Wish she'd a come here sooner, eh, Wilmer?" The customer to his right said while smacking him on the shoulder.

I blushed and backed up a step before bending into a shoddy curtsy, intentionally butt-bumping the patron playing his hand against the magistrate.

Tactic two... damsel in distress.

"I'm so sorry, sir!" I set my platter down and, in doing so, knocked over a half-filled tankard, its contents spilling and running across the table. "Oh, sticks and stacks! I'm such a pain, always running these hips into something or someone. I am so *very* sorry!" I effused.

I ran my hands over my mark, checking for the injuries I knew weren't there.

"Not at all, I'm fine, quite alright," he said while blindly reaching out, too entranced by his cards instead of me. He batted away my searching hands, and as I leaned forward, he smacked the mound of my left breast once and then again.

Tactic number three... Why, it's just little old me!

"Oh!" I gasped and covered the top three inches of my seven-inch cleavage. "Oh, I... I..."

The men at the table looked up just as the last smack had landed. The magistrate's eyes darkened. I looked from side to side, as if trapped.

"Zandus! Apologize at once, or I shall have you cuffed for assault," hissed the magistrate. He slammed his card hand on the table—and with a little help from my toe under the table leg—caused the spilled beer to splatter and then run.

"Magistrate!" I nabbed the cloth from my apron and flew around the table. "Gracious Gammond." I hid a forced yawn behind the hand I smacked over my surprised mouth. It would aid in wetting my eyes, giving the appearance of nascent tears. "Oh, your fine coat! I have never beheld a garment so grand, and now I am the cause of its ruin!"

With panicked energy, I dropped to my knees and began blotting the magistrate's crotch.

"Please forgive me, sir. I've had little training—it's my first day!" I turned my blot into a stroke, running the cloth over his lap with both hands... perhaps groping more than wiping. My very nice swell of boobs—if I do say so myself—heaved and jostled under his nose.

"All is well, my lady... I... I, ahem."

"Sir, you cannot possibly forgive me so easily. I'll work extra shifts and pay you whatever the cost may be..."

I glanced up and let my words trail off, innocently parting my lips while I held his gaze.

You could have scooped up the silence with a spoon.

Surprisingly, the magistrate maintained his strict eye contact, never once straying to my heaving bosom. *Dammit!*

"This is an old frock. You've caused no trouble, um..."

"Birdie." I breathed, slowing my ministrations, my hands coming to rest in his lap as if guided by fate. "W-well, my given name is Peregrine, after the—"

"Falcon." The magistrate murmured softly. "The fastest bird to fly the Gaean skies."

Um... sure. Quick bird. Real speedy.

I nodded shyly before pulling at the heavy fabric of the gown caught under my knees. I didn't have to *fake* needing his aid. "Mama said my hair was the same color as one of their—"

"—feet."

I was thinking beak. Bird beaks are yellow, right?

"Mhmm. Yes. Just like their majestic... feet."

The magistrate proffered his hand and helped me rise while I stepped all over the hem of my sack dress.

"Thank you, sir." I stood and smoothed out my skirts and then my hair. "You are ever the gentleman."

His wide, beaming smile revealed gold and malachite decorations adhered to his eyeteeth.

Over the next three hours, I served drinks by the hundred, washed what had to have been eight sinks of dishes, popped fourteen million bean cubes into the mouths of sugar gamblers, and shot dozens of shy glances at the man who would determine if I was *acceptable* enough to remain in the kingdom.

"Birdie dear, go wake the minstrel, good-for-nothing lout." Jilly waved at the entertainer who'd fallen asleep on the chin rest of his fiddle. A crowd of empty ale tankards sat at his feet.

"Jimothy, wake up." I shook the shoulder of the stupidly handsome man. "Jim, she'll fire you this time, and then where will you be?"

His uncannily beautiful blue eyes met mine, and he blinked his perversely long lashes.

"B, she's canned me four times in the last month." He dropped his instrument to his lap and began plucking a tune.

Jim winked in Jilly's direction, and the more mature woman's cheeks turned red before she twisted away to her duties. "Now, be a good little server girl and go fetch me an ale."

"Now, do what? Pardon, but I can be hard of hearing sometimes."

The sharp smack of palm on ass caused me to stiffen.

My æther surged, dancing in my chest like the bubbles that danced atop the ale.

Neutral. Neutral, Eira. This little handsome fucker—

"What the fuck, man!" Jim yelled as his arm snapped back, and he tumbled from his stool.

"Minstrel Jimothy, a hand laid upon another person with intent to harm, coerce, or cause strife is an arrestable offense in this kingdom. Apologize to Miss Birdie at once."

"Fine! I'm sorry, Birdie, maybe keep your fat ass contained to the kitchens and—okay, okay, gods! Let go of me! Stop! B, I'm sorry, real sorry!"

"Go upstairs and sober up, Jim." The magistrate shoved the minstrel toward the stairs. "Miss Birdie? I do hope you are uninjured. I'm sorry it took me so long to come to your rescue."

Rescue? Be glad I didn't eviscerate the little weasel.

I hugged my arms around my waist.

"Other than my innocence, I am fully intact and sound of body." The fast-acting æther settled its churn, but my irritation at having been slapped continued heating me to a boil. "Thank you, magistrate..."

"Badyr. Please, call me Badyr."

"Oh, sir, I couldn't possibly. You are a man of the law and therefore deserve the respect due to your station."

The magistrate stood a little taller and pulled at the hem of his fine frock.

"Such a sweet little bird." His lopsided grin came off as quite fatherly.

Barf.

Were Cato here, he would have outright laughed. *Sweet* was not a word he'd ever use to describe me.

Sweat trickled down my back.

Every random thought of my Fate Bond threw me into an anxiety-fueled fever.

"I must get back to work. Thank you, magistrate... er, Badyr, sir." I bobbed another poor curtsy.

"Jilly, I'll fetch the extra barrel of pickles from the cold shed." I waved and rushed to the back room.

The magistrate's voice followed me. "Jilly, may I have a word?"

I hit the back door with both hands and then shoved my sleeves up while quickly heading to the tree line. I picked my way to my favorite snowdrift, situated between two evergreens. I fell backward into the mound, making it my throne.

"Ahhhh." I kicked off my shoes, rolled off my stockings, and poked my feet into the hill, feeling the snow liquefy around my toes. I closed my eyes and took a few minutes to simply exist, breathing in the cool air and refocusing my mind.

"Goddess's divine blessings," I groaned, as the cold infiltrated my gown.

The snow melted around my wrists and forearms, the cool trails of water slithering from my hands to elbows. My head cleared as my temperature normalized.

The magistrate seemed okay—for a Gaean—and I had no doubt that he would find me fit and grant me leave for employment now. The pulsing throb in my feet was evidence of my willingness to work.

I wiggled deeper into my ice throne.

After official admittance to the kingdom, that's when the hard work would truly begin. I'd be a liar if I said there wasn't a part of me, just a little dreamy part of me, that hoped that I'd be placed in a sweet little study where I'd be in charge of some shipping industry while I kept watch on the comings and goings of the Primus-King. But I already knew where I was headed... palace scullery maid. I was going to live the glamorous life of scrubbing latrines and polishing shoes while making note of the Primus-King's schedule.

I heard the creak of wood on hinges.

"Birdie?" Jilly called from the tavern's back door.

I didn't respond immediately, too lost in the icy relief flowing up my ankles.

The barkeep's footfalls crunched as she approached.

"Birdie, you certainly did your job with the magistr— Oh! Tree trunks and thorn thickets! Don't move!"

My eyes snapped open to a frantic Jilly brandishing her pipe.

"Jilly, what's—"

"Vipers!"

She took off running, dropped to her knees and dug through the snow.

"Oh." I raised my arms to my eyes. "Why hello, little worms."

Three pointed heads raised from cool little coils wrapped around my wrists.

I chuckled.

"Jilly, I thought they were water. Are these snakes? How delightful, I've never seen a snake—"

"Don't move, girl!" Jilly shouted, coming up to her feet with a long branch grasped in her hands. A puff of smoke enveloped her head as she clenched down on her pipe.

She ran toward me, stick waving.

"Jilly! Wait!"

I sat up quickly, stunned by the sight of a dozen more snakes coiling around my legs.

"Birdie, lie back! Don't move! They're venomous! A single bite and—"

I held my hands up again and peered into six vertical pupils set into bright-green irises.

"Birdie!"

I gave my arms a shake, and three long bodies fell from my wrists and into the snow.

"Why, they're as pliant as pudding. Don't hurt them."

Jilly stopped short. "What in all the unnatural...?"

The serpents slithered around but stayed close.

"Just because you have sharp teeth doesn't mean you'll always bite, Jilly."

The snakes flowed over the snow, tucking themselves close to my sides. The thin ropes slid and slipped over each other, forming tight piles of variegated green and gold nestled tight to my hips.

"Well, I'll be damned." Jilly let her stick drop and tugged her lace cap over her ears. "Birdie, they're using you like a warm stone in a sunbeam. And do you know what this means, girl?"

Jilly smiled wide, her yellowed teeth showing signs of decay.

"That I'm extraordinarily hot?" I replied, smiling at the tongue-in-cheek comment.

Jilly didn't take the bait.

"No. No, no, no." She came forward, using the smoking end of her pipe to shoo a wayward viper toward the woods edge. "It means that this confoundedly long winter is coming to an end. The thaw is finally coming. The serpents only end their winter brumation when it's time for spring."

Sharp-footed pixies tiptoed up my spine.

Spring meant Cato would soon head to Verus, and if the Primus-King wasn't brought low... Baldorva.

"Birdie, are you okay? Did one bite ya?"

"No... I just... I'm just missing home. And hoping to return sooner rather than later."

Jilly braced her fists on her hips and tapped an impatient toe.

"Well, you've got yourself a good head start, girl."

"The magistrate?" I nodded resolutely. "Yes, admittance to the kingdom is a good first step."

"Admittance?" Jilly chortled. "You'll wish it was just admittance."

"Why's that?" I flounced my gown, hiding a lingering snake in its folds, lest Jilly see it and choke on her pipe.

"He wishes to court ya."

"Do what now?" My brows shot clear to my lemon-yellow hairline.

"He's requested you meet his Lead Mate to reckon out if you're a fit for his family."

"Oh, fuck." I fell back into the snowbank and covered my eyes with my arms.

"Not to worry, dear. You'll be placed and given employment before that can happen. Palace maids can't take husbands."

"Good," I mumbled. "Because I already have two."

CHAPTER EIGHT

THROUGH THE EYES OF A CHILD

AMBROSE

"This is disgusting, even for my standards."

"I'm inclined to agree, Father Septimus."

"Oh, pish-posh, Evandr, you would let your creepy frost-daddy take a shit on your forehead if he asked you to. And besides, I am doing a favor for a friend!"

Flog in hand, I lashed out, striking Hughes across the shoulders. His flesh split and ribboned down his torso.

"Argh!" my wife's informant cried out. Sweat dripped down his brow, joining the sheen of ruby red that coated his skin.

"Ah ha-ha, blurghbbler bleg," the baby in my arms bubbled. *Gods's mercy she is lovable.*

"Awwww. You think that's funny, wittle bitty goatling? Want Unkie Amby to do it again?"

Crack!

"Ahah ha ha ha ha!" Verra's little fists waved in pure happiness, and I let the whip fly again.

"Argh!" Hughes slumped, his shoulders in danger of dislocating, strung up as they were.

"Ha-ha-ahhhhhh, blurbblerg ba."

I shielded my little satyress from the spray of blood that shot in our direction and then tucked her further into the wrap that held her secure to my chest.

"Ahh, is there anything sweeter than the sound of a little one's laughter?"

Septimus and Evandr stared in combined shock—Septimus grimacing so hard his nose wrinkled.

"Both of you should be ashamed." I pressed the whip's handle into the tot's hand, and she brought it to her mouth to soothe her sore little gums. "How do you imagine Cinden is supposed to perform the duties required of a mother when she, just last night, birthed Ethens's big-headed spawn from betwixt her thighs? This is what being a good *friend* and good *uncle* looks like."

Evandr hopped up on the limb-stretcher-table-thing and swung his legs. "Ambrose, I think, given your new-to-torturing status, Septimus should take over."

"SHE IS *MY* WIFE!" I shouted, laying my hand over the baby's ears. "I am her husband, and I will go to any and all lengths to see her brought home. Even if that means"—I snatched up a spiky set of knuckle-cover-whatevers and plunged them deeply into Hughes's thigh—"that I must learn the finer points of torment. You know, Septimus, you had every opportunity to teach me, as did Catommandus; you both squandered your time being all broody. I forgive you, though, *mostly*. My priestess-guide tells me forgiveness is an important part of overcoming my issues with abandonment."

Hughes vomited a stream of yellow bile onto the floor as I tried unsuccessfully to wrench the spikes from his leg.

"Answer me, man. Where is she? Where is my harpy?"

His only answer was the defiant flick of his bloodshot eyes.

The door swung open.

"Bark! Yap! Yap! Bark!"

Why me?

"Who let the dog in? Evandr, catch it!" Cato's godsdamned mutt shot through the chamber, anger frothing from its miniature body. Evandr gave chase, but the one-eyed mongrel contorted its scrawny ribs and wove in between Septimus's legs.

"For fuck's sake, Evandr! You are a frost giant, a fast-as-the-nether super being. How can a rat in a fur coat best you?"

The pale idiot dove, and the dog dodged, baring its remaining teeth in the most unintimidating of snarls. It convulsed and shivered in the same disgusting manner as when it defended its bowl of mashed meat.

"Yap, yap! Grrrrrrr!"

Evandr went to his knees, crawling, and the pup leaned all of its five pounds against Septimus's calf. The fucking animal protected the vilest thing to walk the halls of Cordillaria!

I tossed my arms above my head. Working in these conditions was simply unthinkable.

"What kind of operation are we running in this palace? Evandr, you are kneeling in bodily refuse! Septimus, avert your judgment-laden eyes! I am appalled—embarrassed—that Hughes must bear witness to our deficiencies."

Propping my boot on the aforementioned's thigh, I heaved. The squelch and suck of separating the metal barbs from his flesh sent the baby into another round of giggles.

At least my Verra appreciates me. "Mwah." I kissed one of her itty-bitty budding horns.

"Highness!" Bem hollered as he sauntered through the door, head held high, boots polished to a gleam. His cleanliness and fresh scent were still disconcerting enough to keep me suspicious.

"His Majesty requests the presence of the—"

"Yap! Yap-yap." Cato-dog-us tore across the room, catapulting himself at Bem. It latched onto the man's calf and shook its head as if it tore into the neck of its prey.

"Raaaaawwwwrrrr!" Bem scream-growled at the mutt, who yelped and scurried across the room, tail tucked between his legs.

Verra wailed, startled by the heinous sounds of incompetence.

"Protector Bem!" I lamented. "Look at what you have done! The nasty fellow has tracked Hughes's excrement through the entire chamber. There, there, tiny kid, Unkie is not upset at you." Verra screamed her sorrows, and I rocked her while patting her sweet little bum. My head snapped back to Bem. "*What* is so important that Aberus would interrupt my husbandly duty?"

Bem, the mannerless cad, scratched his ass before crossing one ankle over the other and leaning against the threshold. He glanced around the room with the most peculiar look of longing, as if the torture chamber was the place that held his fondest memories.

"The King wants tah discuss the matter of succession with y'all." He lifted his arm and trailed a finger down a chain that was anchored to the ceiling, gazing at the damn thing like it was a lost lover. "Now that His Highness Cato is at Verus, and war's on the horizon, he..."

Hughes rattled his chains, diverting my attention.

I pinched the bridge of my nose. I couldn't take much more of this.

"Prisoner, stop squirming. With the babe up in arms and your creaky squeaks, I cannot focus!" I admonished, picking up the pace of my pats and adding a bounce into my step. "Bem. Again." I flicked my wrist in the Protector's direction.

"What I had said was—"

Garbled words hit my ears.

"Hughes! Insolent man! What? What do you want? Your confounded mumbling has me—"

"Kaz a non on, on e rud."

"What did he say?" snapped Septimus. He sped toward my detainee and hauled him up by the underarms. "Speak, or I will gouge out your stuttering tongue!"

"Well, but then he'd not be able to talk—Hughes, do be a gentleman. Quit the slurring."

Bloodshot eyes focused briefly on mine before rolling back and then refocusing.

"Kaz ta non... non ea sea ruds...." Once again, Hughes's eyes hid under his lids. His head flopped to his chest in an entirely undignified way.

"Well, that's just great. Well done, Septimus."

"Write that down, false prince," Septimus ordered.

I glanced once to the left and once to the right.

"Why certainly, Uncle, it's not like my hands are full. Let me find my parchment while these two perfectly literate humans stand there doing nothing."

"Kaz ta on... or anon... ease... rud." Septimus prodded Hughes's head, but the man didn't come to. "He speaks in riddles. We must decipher his puzzle. Anon. Anonymous, perhaps? Kaz ta. Kas tan? What did you hear, Evandr?" Septimus let Hughes's body slump and then snapped his fingers. Dog-a-mmandus leapt into his arms like a trained performer's pet. *Filthy, disease-ridden mutt.*

"Dunno." Evandr shrugged a shoulder.

"Never again should you, *nephew*, be allowed to practice the fine art of persuasion. You are an embarrassment."

I actually couldn't take much more of this. I turned my attention to the Protector.

"Bem, after you have scrubbed the floor to a shine, see to it that Hughes is washed and fed. Sew his ear back on as well. Never could I have imagined that the thing would have come clear off." Verra squawked. "No, ma'am, that is our secret. Your mother would have my balls if she knew it fell into your swaddle."

I pointed to the flesh lump, which I'd placed into a metal bowl the moment I'd realized the baby had it in her inquisitive little fist.

Bowing and shuffling toward the discarded skin, Bem paused and looked at me in confusion. "Ya wish me tah mend the man? You intend tah set him free then?"

I shook my head.

"No, not at all. But he has taken exceptional care to ensure my wife's secrets. I could not have asked for a better henchman to look after her needs. It's quite commendable, really. And a bath always makes me feel my best. I will continue his torment after I speak with my brother." I hopped backward as Bem advanced on me quickly. "Yeesh! Bem. Apologies. I-I am not used to seeing you wear such an expression."

Protector Bem, ear in hand, beamed, his gap-toothed smile revealed a mouth of cracked teeth on his left side. For a moment, I thought that literal stars shone in his eyes, but I realized it was simply the reflection of the spiked wall behind me.

"Ya plan tah build him back up so you can shatter him again?"

"Ummm... sure..." I took a measured step toward the door, snuggling Verra closer to my chest.

"Masterful," Bem whispered, tears welling in his eyes.

"Riiiight. Well, Septimus, bring the ankle-biter; we must keep the stinking terror alive until Eira returns. Septimus!"

My uncle, yanked from his pondering, sneered.

"K-kast an on ease-rud. Hmmm. Cast on and eat, rud, rude rod? Hmmm. Cast on and eat rod," Septimus wondered aloud.

"Uncle," I laughed. "I do believe that spicy little Hughes just told you to eat a dick. What an amazingly courageous spy. I am beyond thankful he is on Eira's side."

Chapter Nine

THAT'S WHAT SHE SAID

Eira

A dmittance day.

"Hester, you could at least wear your stockings on the *inside* of your shoes. There is not a head that hasn't turned our way. I'm trying to lie low."

Hester stomped through a watery mud puddle, splashing all the children within a five-foot radius. They squealed in happiness.

"Hester!"

"What, you boring old goat?" She kicked out, and one of her loose yellow stockings pooled around her ankle. I motioned her to my side, and reluctantly, she stomped in my direction. "If their eyes are on me, they aren't on you." She rolled up the waistband of her skirt until her knobby knees were visible and yanked up her soaking-wet stocking. "Besides, I have an image to maintain."

"Town madwoman?"

A knowing smile tugged at the corners of her mouth. "You just be glad I wore my teeth. See the line?" She pointed over my shoulder.

"Lykksun's lap!" I took in the growing throng of refugees. "Jilly should have sent me alone. I wouldn't have missed *that*." I gestured to the orderly line of people to whom a group of priestesses was ladling out water. "There must be three hundred or more."

People in various states of dress, from a wide range of social statuses, stood or sat on a paver-dotted sidewalk. Some of the women wore silk-lined fur, others threadbare tunics, but despite the disparity in dress, they all seemed to wear the same expression: exhaustion.

"Be that as it may, it's easy to get turned around in Mynder—it's huge!—and Jilly thought I could point out the important buildings while in the city center."

I nodded. That would help me get to know my new surroundings.

We took our place in the line, and I spun, getting my first good look at Gaea.

In my head, given the fact that my evil father oversaw the kingdom, I had imagined streets teeming with trash and horse shit and buildings that leaned from deferred maintenance.

Mynder was actually lovely, all polished wood and lush evergreens interspersed between budding oaks and birch trees. Even on the heels of a harsh winter, it seemed... alive.

"Keep that up; you look like all the other newcomers twirling about," Hester whispered. "Now, look to your left, the big building in the distance with the domed roof." She pointed. "That is Twins Temple. The entire town goes there to pray twice weekly. Make sure never to be late. The service is mandated by law."

I dipped my chin in acknowledgment and focused my eyes on the massive structure. I could only see its top half, on account of the many buildings in my way, but the part I did see rose at least four stories tall. The dark-gray building boasted swirling motifs of inlaid malachite in several hues of green. The twisting shades put me in mind of Ambrose's eyes.

"And beyond that?" I gestured past the temple to an architectural wonder partially obscured by the domed roof.

"That, my dear, is Cult Mossius." Hester paused. "And the shorter wooden structures in between, houses for the citizens."

I couldn't look anywhere but the dome.

Cult Mossius. Where Mama received her education. Now, *it* was just as ominous as I'd built it up to be.

Constructed from Cato-sized blocks of forest green stone and that glittering black rock that made up Verus Temple, the monolith stood in stark contrast to the homes of lumber and log. The morning fog had yet to fully dissipate, and the double flame sculpture that shot up from its roof seemed to disappear into the hazy sky above.

"Form a second line! You," a priestess shouted as she smiled and waved, "lead the back half up to the registration table. And welcome to Gaea, pilgrim; safety and prosperity lie within our gates."

Hester bent low, plucking little tufts of green sprigs from beneath a melting lump of snow. I took her by the elbow, and together we walked, nearing what appeared to be a horse barn, with a tent erected in front.

I looked over my shoulder, suddenly feeling incredibly small in the big city. All these people flooded into Gaea's capital because they feared people like me...

"Hehehehe, looks like old Hessie taught you a thing or two about wranglin' a man."

"What?"

Hester twisted me sideways as her maniacal little chuckles tittered in my ear.

The magistrate—a very well-dressed man of the law—presided over his operation with his hands in the pockets of his perfectly tailored long coat. The intensity with which he inspected a refugee's knapsack spoke to his dedication.

Troth face, activate.

I lowered my lashes and imagined the first time I set eyes on Cato. The blush spread over my cheeks, and I felt it all the way to my toes. Slowly, I glanced up, not beaming or giggling like an immature miss, but simply acknowledging his presence with a small, secretive lift of my lips.

The magistrate tilted his chin, near imperceptibly, and then moved to—*Oh! It's Troth Yemailrys! I'd know those boulder-sized breasts anywhere!*

My throat constricted with emotion. Though it had been almost a year, the friendships—or maybe more accurately, trauma bonds—we forged in the Verus Maneuverings had tied us tightly. The Troth sat at a trestle table, surrounded by ledgers and inkwells.

I approached the covered stall that shielded her from the elements.

"Name?" Yemailrys asked, her tone all business.

"Peregrine Springwoods."

"Kingdom of birth?"

"Gaea, mountain region."

"Is your entry sponsored?"

"Yep!" Hester danced around, swinging her arms and rolling her hands. "By Jilly of Timber Tavern. Jilly the Short! The Broomweilder! Pipe Puffin' Jilly!" she sang out.

Yemailrys raised her brows as she eyeballed Hester's wild shuffles.

"It's been a while, Hester. Did Jilly send you in her stead?" Yemailrys asked with a concerned affect to her voice rather than her usual sarcastic tone.

Hester leaped from foot to foot.

"She did, Troth, and this is Birdie! She's got them big biddies, like you. Jilly can't leave the bar! Too busy."

Yemailrys's lips thinned. She nodded like it wasn't the millionth time someone had commented on her proportions. I felt a moment of shame knowing that it was the first thought to come to my mind as well.

"Are you currently ill, or have you been ill in the last three weeks?" Yemailrys asked me, her face as impassive as stone.

"No."

"Are you currently pregnant, or have you been in the last year?"

"No."

"Do you have any living children?"

"No."

"Have you borne witness to a conjuration?"

"No. But I did hear Solnna was full of conjurers," I replied. "And that the Primus-King would keep us safe from the like."

A murmur of agreement swelled from behind me.

"What skill sets do you possess?"

Hester's stringy mop of gray hair popped up in front of my face. "She can carry five mugs in one hand! Seen her do it!"

Yemailrys waved Hester away. "Thank you, Hessie. Peregrine?"

"I'm a quick learner. I've always worked around the house for my mother: dishes, cleaning—oh, and I aided the laundress back home. These hands can sure scrub one out!"

"Thank you," Yemailrys said while scribbling notes into her book. She eyed me. "Because you carry more weight than what the Primus-King deems optimal for longevity, a lengthier examination of your person is required."

"Are you fuc—" My face went flat as I cut short the obscenity.

"It's 'cause you're fat, Birdie dear. My sire was a fat man who lived to ninety and two. Don't worry!" Hester bellowed, loud enough to prompt a chorus of giggles from those nearest.

It took every ounce of my restraint not to toss off my gown and climb upon the table to bare the body that had attracted not one but two fine men to its bounty. Instead, I lowered my head.

"Will I have to remove my... my stockings?"

Yemailrys peered at me with a kind expression, but I could see the humor lighting up her eyes. "I'm afraid you are required to fully undress, but please, don't feel any shame. In Gaea, we hold the body to be sacred, a meeting of both soul *and* skin."

"Except not fat ones," Hester said. "Or old ones like me! Here, I'll take my clothes off, too!"

The magistrate came jogging to our side of the table.

"That's not necessary, Hester." He gently took her hands and moved them away from the buttons on her shirt. "We know you were raised well. Why, look at you, you must be well over eighty."

"Eighty and four!" Hester's head bobbed up and down. She clapped her hands on her stomach like a seal begging for a tasty smelt treat.

"What? And still so spry?" The magistrate fastened the button at her neck and then took a step closer.

"Miss Birdie, P-Peregrine, if I may refer to you as such?"

I nodded.

"I assure you that Healer Amias will in no way insult you or make overtures about you-your body."

Amias! Oh, fuck! How the nether had I forgotten the Scions of Gaea! Lok and Amias would be lurking around.

"And if it makes you feel safer, I will stand guard along with Hester here."

"Y-yes! I need you there!" I stammered out.

Because if I recall, Amias is the Primus-King's favored Obligate! I tamped down the hot feeling of impending doom. I didn't want to have to go all demon puff yet. I didn't want to scorch the fucking refugees or terrify them out of their wits.

The magistrate hesitated before plucking up the courage to place his fingers on the underside of my elbow and steered me—by the grace of the Goddess—in the direction of a makeshift healer's theater.

"Not only was Healer Amias trained in Cult Mossius by the Primus-King himself, but if any hair remained upon his head, it would be a brilliant shade of red. You see, he was born Obligate. Do you know much about the Obligation?"

I shook my head and hugged my arms around my waist, feigning shyness.

"I'm afraid my education only extended to cleaning and mending."

And transforming into a vindictive and cold-hearted cloud.

I glanced around, making note of the children playing in the street. Of the smiling citizens of Gaea who didn't deserve to be eviscerated by a shade-haint.

"Both noble professions," the magistrate said in a tone that left no doubt as to his earnestness. "Now, come along."

I flicked my eyes to Yemailrys and her face of pure indifference. *Magnificent Troth.*

"Lead the way, magistrate, sir."

"Badyr," he reminded me.

I nodded but fixed my eyes ahead as the curtain swept to the side. I saw him before he saw me.

Amias.

Obligate Amias.

The man who traveled to Verus with Scion Castor, who was killed by Cato's hand, and Scion Ozius, whose rotting head was presented to me as a Joining gift.

He hadn't changed—not really.

Though dressed in opulent robes of gold, with a healer's pouch tied to his waist, he was still the pleasant-faced man with a beard as bushy as a snow fox's tail.

Currently, he administered drops into the eye of a young man with a rash covering the right side of his face. Behind him, other pilgrims and refugees stood in various states of dress: no shirts on some, no shoes on others, and one with a pant leg rolled to her knee.

"Scion-Healer Amias, may the Goddess smile upon you this day. I have a young woman who is feeling timid about the inspection. I have assured her that—"

Amias turned.

Soft-brown eyes locked with mine. Where did his allegiance lie?

I calmed the æther that fluttered in my stomach and stood like stone, weighing the choice to flee or fight.

"Welcome, daughter of the Goddess."

Oh, gods! He knows about the goddess blood!

"You have nothing to fear from me," he said as he spread his arms wide, his baggy sleeves hanging. "The Mantle smiles upon Their children, and we are, in Their eyes, beauty made flesh."

Or a deceitful fiend made flesh!

Amias waved me over, but I clutched tight to the magistrate's arm. If I had to use him as a bargaining chip or shield... so be it.

"Here we are, Peregrine. You stand over there and disrobe, right next to that wall. Hester, I have a jar of salted meat in the aid center; fetch it, please."

Hester shot off.

With that, the magistrate walked over to the half-wall.

Of course. I nearly rolled my eyes. *The lawman gets to view the show.*

The infirmary was just a hastily converted barn with a canvas roof. Every sixteen feet or so, another low wall jutted out, and I could see the heads and the occasional torso of the other weary travelers.

To my utter surprise, the magistrate turned, giving us his back.

"Allow me to help you with your dress."

Amias took a step forward, and I, a step back.

He pressed his lips into a thin line, and the slight change in his expression sent the æther swirling—it was an untrusting force, to be sure.

Amias pressed closer. I could feel the air from his exhalation just as my back hit the wall.

"Their Holiness sends greetings," he whispered as he bent to lift the hem of my gown. "My offices in the palace are located on the third level, western wing. There is a vial in the red-lacquered apothecary cabinet, third row, labeled 'blisters.' Choose the lightest blue liquid. Death occurs within minutes of ingestion. Carry out the deed in Verus's name."

Orders given. Orders heard. My stomach sank. Every hair on my body stood at attention. My mother and father would be furious, but if my dealing the death blow kept my father and Gotwig out of harm's way, so be it. Just as the Mantle had embodied righteous justice when faced with a traitor, I would be the agent of consequence. I was Merrias's granddaughter—judgment was in my blood.

My dress passed over my head, and Amias laid it carefully on the back of a chair. I stood, shoulders hunched, arms crossed over my bare chest.

"The Primus-King is paranoid and hypervigilant. Ingratiate yourself with one of his children or wives to gain access to his person." He withdrew a glass disk from the pouch he wore and then held it up, catching the natural light and casting its beam on my face.

Blinded, I flinched. Amias captured my jaw and tugged.

"Open your mouth—ah, a fine set of teeth. Did you know the state of one's gums can tell us much about a person's overall health?" He said it loud enough that those in the next stall over would hear.

"No, sir. But I scrub mine with a cloth in the morning and at night."

"A good practice. Might I also suggest scraping your tongue with the handle of a metal spoon? It tames the odor of one's breath."

Dick.

Amias glanced at me, a good-natured smile firmly in place. He palpated my neck and then laid his hands over my heart. His expression turned to one of concern.

"You are feverish."

"I ran here."

"*You* ran?"

"Sure did," I whispered back.

Brows knit and worry lines defined, Amias ran his palms over my stomach and then hips. He glanced up, tilting his head to one side—curiosity brimmed in his expression.

Calm. Peace and calm, you little bubbling nuisance! I repeated the litany in my mind, trying to silence the æther, asking it to slow its churn.

I stared at Amias in challenge. Did he possess the same odd ability as Ozius? Did his hands tell him more than just the texture of one's skin? *Cult Mossius weirdos!* How did this kingdom take a vehement stance against conjurers when they raised creepy-fingered occultists?

"It would seem that many things have changed since Verus." He kept his voice low and swept both hands down my legs. "How did you come to lose this toenail?"

Troll.

"I took it off in a shoveling incident while helping my ma bury her dear old cat... sweet kitty Ambrose. He was impulsive and neurotic, but awfully cuddly."

Amias bit his lips, this time stifling a bark of laughter.

His wandering hands settled again, one in between my breasts and the other right below. *He could feel it.* The webbing at the corners of his eyes intensified.

"Miss Birdie, you don't have long to act."

I nodded while keeping direct eye contact with him.

He dropped his voice low. "*Others* have come to the kingdom recently. Outsiders who share an interest in our politics and borders."

The Baldorvans.

The æther somersaulted as my temperature rose. Fuck me—I thought I had conquered it.

Amias laid the knuckles of his right hand on my forehead.

"Do not fear me, Eira," he murmured. "I am Obligate first and a healer second."

A beat of silence passed between us.

"Anyone who stands as a blockade in my path should fear *me*, Scion Amias."

His brow hitched in surprise, but his chin dropped in acknowledgment.

Over his shoulder, Troth Yemailrys appeared with her book in hand. Her mouth was drawn.

"Healer Amias, the lead healer has surprised us with a visit."

Amias's head snapped up. He snatched my dress from the chair and thrust it into my arms.

"Miss Birdie is hale and hearty, Troth Yemailrys; with the magistrate's signature, she is fit to be placed in the palace as a scullery maid. Magistrate?"

The magistrate spun on his heels, and his eyes popped wide.

"Creator's kneecaps. I-I... Miss Peregrine, forgive me." With unrivaled speed, he pivoted back around. "I assumed you fully attired! And, scullery maid?" The magistrate grabbed Amias's shoulder as the healer tried to move past him. "Madam Troth, Healer Amais, I feel that Miss Birdie would flourish i-in a more familial environment, and... well, what I'm trying to say is..."

He glanced back over his shoulder.

"Magistrate, I'm... Oh! Still not dressed, sir!"

Wide-eyed, he stared, a man caught in the glowing beacon of breasts.

I yanked the gown over my head to save the poor soul from his embarrassment but became entangled in its volume. I fought the fabric, tits bouncing. "Magistrate, Jilly told me of your wish, but—dammit, these sleeves are inside out!" I hopped and wiggled, trying to shimmy into the garment. "I just don't think we're—"

"Dear gods," Yemailrys cursed. "Birdie, dear, you are... Please allow me to assist you." I felt Yemailrys's hands tugging at the sweat-dampened wool. "Do stop hopping; you are drawing attention to your predicament. We need to move things along. Here, let us head to the—Lead Healer! Welcome."

My head and hands emerged from their confinement.

Troth mode.

Eyes to the floor, I placed my palms on my cheeks, feigning embarrassment. I couldn't give two shits about them seeing my boobs—all of Verus and half of Monwyn had been afforded an ample view.

I bobbed an improper curtsy and moved past the—

"Malvin! Malvin, get your toad's face away from Jilly-girl's niece!"

In a flurry of skirts and flailing limbs, a shouting Hester twisted away from a red-faced Amias, who was doing his best to drag her backward.

I looked up.

The man she'd called a frog—the Lead Healer—stood as regal as a king presiding over his court. In a set of muted-gold robes, with a standing fur collar, he cut quite the figure. He gracefully sidestepped Hester and glanced down at his purple-velvet shoes, turning his foot this way and that, inspecting them for dust.

"Hessie, it's been some time. I see you are still... alive... and as effervescent as always. Do stand aside; I am on business for the archhealer."

Hester launched her arms in the air, waving her hands right in the man's face.

"That's what I'm afraid of, you, you amphibious lump!"

His lips spread into a wide grimace, and his enormous amber eyes bulged in aggravation.

Oh. There's the toad.

"Now, Hessie—"

"Don't you 'now Hessie' me! I know what goes on—"

Smack!

Hester dropped into a heap of long limbs, her hip taking the impact of her fall.

"Hester!" I ran to her side, dropping to my knees. Amias joined me and immediately began assessing her. The æther knotted into a ball, ready to flow from my hands and into the Lead Healer's head.

"Don't move, Hester. Your leg's bent all funny."

Hester raised her head, blue eyes blazing. She leveled a finger at the Lead Healer's chest. "Shame on you, Malvin. You had a chance to—"

"Sir." I inserted myself the moment I saw his fist clench. "Sir, allow me to walk Hester home. Auntie Jilly will see her to bed."

The Lead Healer rolled his bulbous eyes and huffed. "Why she is still allowed to reside within the realm remains a mystery. Brotherly love be damned."

"Why you continue to believe his lies is—"

"Hester. Hester, let's go, okay?"

I helped her to her feet, noting the pain that marred her face as she put weight on her leg.

"Yes, Hessie, be gone from here, lest I demand the rest of your teeth pulled from your skull."

"What the fu—" I remembered my role and smacked a hand over my mouth. "What foolishness did you take part in to deserve that, Hessie? Did you take off your clothes in front of the wrong crowd? Come on now, let's get you home."

Hester leaned on me heavily, and I bore the brunt of her weight.

"No, Birdie." She squeezed me close. "It's the malachite. It makes them all go mad!" She spat at the Lead Healer's feet, and his lips curled in unfiltered disgust. She jabbed her finger at Amias. "You ignored me! They ignored me! All because of tradition. Shit on tradition!"

"What a nasty liar you've turned out to be, Hessie... such wasted potential." The Lead Healer turned and flicked his wrist at two servants. "Let us be gone from here and—wait."

Blinking his amphibious eyes, he tapped the tip of his finger to his chin.

"As luck would have it, we are seeking domestic servants at Cult Mossius. Purification division." He pouted theatrically. "They tend to come and go so quickly."

The Lead Healer stepped toward me, and ice poured through my normally hot veins. He circled me, peering close. His flat little nose stopped right below my ear, and the puff of his breath against my flesh made my stomach clench.

"Ah, yes, the scent of peasant stock." He stood to his full height and glared down his nose. "Hester, by the looks of her, I feel that your *Miss Birdie* would do well as a maid at Cult Mossius. Healer Amias, cleanse her and then have her sent to—"

"No!" Hester shouted.

"But Lead Healer, sir." The magistrate found his voice. "I've made my intentions clear with her aunt and my Lifemate and I would like to declare for her... provided the women mesh well when they are introduced, of course."

The men stood facing each other, postures tight, shoulders pulled back.

"Have the bannans been spoken before a priest? Hmm? No? Well, unless it happens by this eve, *my* word is law. See to it, Scion-Healer."

Amias bowed his head. "It would be a most prestigious honor for her to toil alongside our storied healers. Though I daresay the cleaning load at the Cult doubles that of the palace. The woman is not strong of arm."

The lead healer pinched my wrist and eyed my fingers. "Worker's hands. Poorly kept nails and mottled flesh that has seen the effects of both lye and ammonia. She'll do just fine."

Yemailrys waved her quill in the air. "Begging your pardon, but I have already secured her position as a palace scullery. She possesses the skills of a competent cleaner, which are sorely needed, what with the Primus-King's new babes being born."

Geezer of a babymaker.

"Yes, sir, Lead Healer, sir, I'm good for a spit shine!" I nodded enthusiastically. I needed to get into that palace.

Gods, Hester, what have you done?

"Malvin, you odious old bag. You can't take your anger at me out on another," Hester piped up.

"Oh, but I can. And I will suspend her visitation hours if you cannot keep your behavior in check. If you are good, Hessie dear, and keep those awful lies from spilling from those wrinkled lips, I will allow her to seek placement elsewhere."

The toad-faced man gave me a less-than-reassuring grin. He reached out, and I forced myself to stay still while he pinched a bit of my blonde hair between his fingertips. "Yes, you'll do fine."

The Lead Healer swept his robes with a flourish as he turned.

"I am late for my meeting with the archhealer. Scion Healer Amias, have the slender, hazel-eyed male specimen sent to Cult Mossius—along with this female. I expect them both the moment evening prayer ends." The Lead Healer clapped his hands together, and as fast as he had entered, he left, leaving a stunned and silent group behind.

The magistrate trailed after him, continuing to make his case.

"Gods' mercy, Birdie, I'm sorry. I'm so sorry." Hester grimaced and prodded her hip gingerly. "I'd not seen him in years."

Amias and Yemailrys gathered closely around us, offering aid to Hester.

"Lay it out, Amias," I said, looking pointedly at the Scion. "What in the gods' name just happened?"

"You'll be fine, Birdie, but your plans will have to change—"

"Those Healer fools," Hester butted in. "You haven't the faintest notion what *he* does there, Amias."

"Hester, I grew up there. Cult Mossius is—"

"—a filthy pit of sin!" she hissed. "That's what it is."

Amias looked ready to argue but held his peace, the struggle evident in his gaze.

I wrapped my arm around Hester's waist and, as carefully as I could, began our hobble home. It was slow going.

"Hester, what the nether am I supposed to do now?"

She winced in pain with every step she took.

"Birdie, we need to Join you with a magistrate before you find yourself stuck."

Chapter Ten

HAMBROSE

Ambrose

"Cas anon ease rud." Septimus said for the thousandth time. If he didn't seal his lips soon, I would bruise them to immobility.

"Yeesh!" The crowded room took me by surprise. "Brother Aberus, are you held against your will? Blink if I should save you from this terrifying feminine coven. Cough if I should simply render you unconscious."

I strolled into my father's—*brother's*—chamber.

Goddess alive. Aberus, the big-headed buffalo, was surrounded by every woman in the kingdom... with the exception, of course, of *the* woman, *my* woman... who happened to hold the highest precedence among all the busybodying vaginas currently overtaking the royal suite. The tiny teacup he held looked ridiculous in his massive paw, but not nearly as ridiculous as the two fat braids that Richelle and Steffanie were weaving onto the sides of his head.

I frowned at the domesticity of it all. He was king! My wife was missing! Where were the maps? Where were the tiny soldiers that we could strategize with and then make kiss?

"Ambrose, brother mine, come join me."

"And let me hold the baby!" Allaine cried out, her grabby hand all aflutter. "You hog her all day and allow none of us to—"

I glared at the tree-tall menace, untrusting of the woman who stood nearly at my eye level.

"Lady Allaine." I narrowed my gaze. "I realize that you are attention starved, what with your Scion-turned-deviant-turned-husband-turned-servant toiling such long hours, but I am sure one-eyed Greggen will—"

"Ambrose, let her tend to the child," Aberus sighed, holding his palms up in exasperation. "We have business to discuss."

"What? My goatling needs—"

"King's order!" he bellowed.

"Conniving heifers... the lot of you," I muttered beneath my breath, pointedly looking between each woman that made up the clucking gaggle.

"*King's* Order."

Allaine stepped into my field of vision, cutting off my view of her sanctimonious sisterhood. "Is it because of my arm? Is that why you have a problem with me holding her?"

"Derros grant me peace. No, Allaine, you have proven time and again you are physically capable."

"So, what is it, *Highn-ass?*" Accusatory blue eyes pinned me in place like a bolt to a target.

With the most uncaring degree of nonchalance I could muster, I plucked my gassy goatling from her sling and propped her on my shoulder. Though noxious, the tiny toots she produced were as adorable as she.

"Aberus, are the lesser nobles permitted to speak with such outrageous disrespect now that you have perched your massive bottom upon the high throne? Hmm? Oh, and Allaine, so you are aware, it is your lack of judgment that gives me pause as to your parental fitness. Why, just look at the man with whom you chose to Join."

"Ambrose!" Aberus shouted. He pounded the table so hard the tea service quivered.

"What?" I challenged, sneering at his lack of decorum. "Allaine is a poor judge of character. My wittle bitty goat shall be surrounded by—"

Allaine's small-breasted chest smacked into my sternum with a solid thump.

"Verra's mother is a mouthy gold-digger, and her father a saliva-fetishizing social climber!" Allaine spat while quirking that perfectly pointed brow of hers. "If *character* is your metric, they were an *excellent* choice."

Aberus chuckled and then slurped down his tea.

"Well, I, uh... eh, point taken." I patted Verra's back, in case she needed to burp. "But she's sleeping and—"

"And I will rock her at the exact speed and tempo you taught us yesterday... That's an hour I will never get back," she muttered.

"Fine." I reluctantly lowered my godschild from her perch and laid her into the cradle of Allaine's arm. "But I am watching you."

Aberus rubbed the tightening braids at his temples.

"Join me, Ambrose; we have much to discuss. Uncle, would you care for tea?"

"Cats among us run," Septimus whispered while shuffling around in a circle.

"Pardon?" Aberus asked. "Uncle, sit."

Septimus lowered himself into a chair and stared into an empty cup.

"Ignore him, Aberus. Verra's garbled words make more sense than his, and he's been doing this since we left my good man Hughes in the torture—"

Aberus choked on his drink.

"Not in polite company, brother," he chided.

"These hens? Polite? You *have* taken leave of your sanity." I scoffed and flicked my eyes at Richelle, who shot her middle finger into the air behind Aberus's unknowing head.

"Fuck off, short haglet," I mouthed.

"Ambrose, since Mama and Aunt Lilium departed, the ladies of Cordillaria have breathed new life into this lonely palace. Steffanie here is leading a music class for the nobles' wives, and Troth Richelle is instructing dance, all the while establishing the widows' and children's home that will be built in the summer. And what have you been doing during that time? Leisure hunting, it would seem."

"If you call searching for my wife leisure hunting, then yes."

The door opened, and Aberus gestured for Greggen and Bem to join us at the table.

Greggen went immediately to Allaine, sank to his knees, and placed a kiss on the elbow of her seized arm. If he so much as breathed on Verra, I'd take his other eye and feed it to Canine Cato.

His husbandly duty done, Greggen rose and sat across from Septimus. I kicked the Scion's chair, sliding him a few more inches away.

Richelle *and* Steffanie cast judgmental glances upon me.

Witches, both of them.

Septimus continued mumbling into his empty cup.

"Anyhow. With Cato at Verus and not likely to take a wife—and with tensions rising with Baldorva—we must discuss succession."

I dismissed him with a flick of my wrist.

"If you die, I take the crown. I lead Monwyn into a Golden Age with Eira by my side, and our brood of children continues a fine new lineage. What more needs to be discussed?"

Septimus growled a low and stupid sound, just like he did each time my wife's name was mentioned. Well, he could grumble all he wanted; plans for his demise were in place. It was just a matter of time before I saw the last of him. I'd lined Bem's pockets with a heap of gold and promised him that he could Join with Richelle once the deed was done. But first, Septimus had to sniff out Eira's location. Only then, Bem could off the man, thus eradicating the Dick Bond that tied him to my wife.

Everything was on course. Well... it was if Bem could avoid arrest for creepery. Instead of sitting as bade, he stood a foot away from Richelle, just staring at her with his lips parted. Even the bald spots that shone through his wispy, pulled-back hair blushed red.

"Protector Bem, how are you?" Richelle said, ever bubbly, even when obviously uncomfortable.

"Gud," Bem said.

Oh, gods. I'd been tutoring the slouchy fool on the fine arts of seduction, but we'd not been able to advance past the concept of a basic follow-up question.

I eased my glasses down and pinched the bridge of my nose. I was under so much strain that my shoulders nearly rose to my ears. *Josa's majestic taint.* Eira was the only cure for the boulders of stress heaped on my divinely formed shoulders.

Aberus stood, walked to Richelle, and took her hand in his. Her eyes softened the moment she looked up at his fat head. Aberus was disgustingly smitten with her as well, but just like in his youth, he'd decided to learn every minute fact about her—her favorite scent, the shape of her toenails, her mother's second cousin's recipe for rump roast—before daring to flip her skirts. It was appalling that such a cinnamon bun was my relation, especially given that Richelle would be more than willing to sample his sausage.

The king guided Richelle next to Steffanie, who now sat near the crackling fireplace. On his return to the table, he tapped Bem on the shoulder, snapping the Protector out of his stupor.

Aberus sat.

"With war on the horizon and with neither you nor I having an heir, we must select a successor. Cato is pledged to Verus for the duration, I lead Monwyn's armies, and you defend our seas. Our lives are at risk and our closest relative—"

"No!" My seat toppled backward as I bolted to my feet. "Do not dare suggest that Septimus wear the crown. Do not!"

Aberus's brow dropped so low that a shadow fell over his eyes.

"Who then, Ambrose? One of our female relations? Would you appoint one of our sisters? Can you imagine Borka on the throne? She would drive the treasury into the ground purchasing horseflesh and fine cheese. Or better yet, cousin Kairus. Do you think the populace will follow a woman who is Assigned to the country that threatens Ærta? Perhaps she would bring along her new Baldorvan friends. Think, Ambrose, more than a hundred years of Monwyn men on the throne, and you would appoint—"

Aberus stopped midsentence, and I could see the cowardice spread across his cow-like countenance.

I propped my chin on my fists and batted my lashes.

"Do go on, brother. It seems the ladies of Cordillaria share a keen interest in what you have to say."

All of them—Steffanie, Richelle, Allaine, and little Verra—shot daggers at Aberus, daring him to finish his sentence. You could have cut the tension with a cleaver.

"They'd do gud, ya know," Bem said out of nowhere. All eyes snapped in his direction. "No war. Food in mouths. Talkin' out the problems. I'm fur it." He nodded.

Richelle smiled and shimmied her shoulders.

Steffanie nodded.

Aberus grumbled.

Septimus stared at his fucking cup.

"Ladies, I-I do believe refreshments are being served in the Ladies' Solarium," Aberus said, waving to the door.

Richelle's mouth opened with a huff, and Aberus had the good graces to look sheepish.

"Hand her over." I signaled to Allaine as the miffed trio made to exit. She placed the child in my arms. "Oh!" A hot stream of spit-up cascaded down my shoulder. "Did the lady giant shake up your tum-tum? How dare she?"

I kissed my satyress on one chubby cheek and then the other, using the tablecloth to wipe her chin.

"Gwooo, blurrrrrblub."

"I know, sweetling, I know." I snuggled her back into her sling and popped a tea-wetted linen napkin between her little gums—her tiny little toofs were causing her pain. "Let us change the subject for a moment. Scion Greggen, update us while my brother tries to save face."

Greggen, stoic and lacking the air of smugness ever since Cato beat it out of him, nodded.

"My people have—"

"No. I'm sorry, but who?" I quizzed. I'd give him no ground.

He lowered his head and set his eyes on the sugar bowl at the table's center.

"The *Baldorvans* I've been tracking are in Gaea. The Primus-King has welcomed at least a dozen into his palace on the pretense of protecting the kingdom from conjurers while he heads to Verus for the war summit."

"Protection? Horse shit. They wish to snatch up my wife and cart her off to breed with that despicable warlord who rules at the whims of slave mongers." I squeezed my eyes tight and then sprang them wide, making my best surprised face for Verra. She loved it, of course, and giggled happily while reaching for my braid. She caught the rope of hair in her fist and chomped. "What does that make, *three* who wish to sire a spawn on my woman? Oh no, technically four, let's see—the Baldorvan warlord, Septimus, Catommandus, and me. Of course I want her to bear my babes as well; I'll not go uncounted."

Greggen and Aberus shared a look.

"And is that truly enough for them to start a war of the hemispheres?" Aberus asked, his tone serious.

"Were you not yourself just fuming over the lack of an heir, big brother? Want my advice? Don't shake that massive head of yours; I'm telling you anyway."

Aberus pretended not to listen as he hailed a servant carrying a stack of parchment on a silver platter.

"Pick a wife and 'git tah fuckin,' as Bem would say. Solve your own problem, brother dear... as my wife would say."

Aberus sifted through his missives, and I used the time to clean under Verra's grubby little nails.

"Let's see." He cracked open a cerulean wax seal. "Catommandus sends his greetings. He requests that we prepare seven units of cavalry to make the trek to the temple before summer." He slid his finger under another seal, one I knew to be my sibling's personal scarlet wax. "The Mantle requires that the four Ærtan monarchs and their second-born heirs meet Them in a month's time, and," Aberus sighed, "in lieu of a child from my body, they want you to attend me."

That got my attention.

"But Aberus, who will preside over Monwyn if all three of us are called to action?"

"You see our predicament, brother. The moment you left and the minute Catommandus took the western road to Verus, our lack of family members became an issue."

"Kazt anon ease rud."

"No, Septimus, you dolt." I scolded my idiot uncle, who now had a vice grip on his empty teacup. "You were there; he traveled west of our location.

W-e-s-t. You are slipping, old man. This jumbling of letters you've fixated on grows tiresome. No wonder you cannot locate my—"

"KAZ ANON EASE RUD!" Septimus slammed his palms onto the table and leapt to his feet. Shards of pottery flew across the tabletop. He reached across the table and snatched me by the shoulders, causing Verra to let out a shrill squawk. "Cat's on the east road! Catommandus is on the east road! Do you not understand? The east road leads to Gaea! He sent *us* away. He seeks my enchantress! He has fooled us all."

"No," I hissed, batting at his hands. "Cato would never turn his back on Ærta. And have you not understood *me?* We are a Bonded bundle, a-a tangled triad of lovers, a committed union. He would never turn his back on *us.*"

"I would have fucked your ass raw if it meant she'd be mine." Spittle flew from Septimus's mouth. His hands shook, and his shoulders quaked. "I would have played along, and then I would have stolen her at the first opportunity."

No. No, he would never—

A sharp little hoofer struck me in the chin. Verra's lovely lavender eyes stared into my soul as if she knew something I did not.

"No..." I told her in a stern tone. "Unlike these lot, I trust my adopted brother-lover."

Septimus appeared at my side; his demonic head nearly perched upon my shoulder.

I reared back when his hand settled on my arm. He held fast.

"He played the long game, Ambrose, just as I taught him." Septimus's voice shook with a deep-seated anger. "It has all been a lie."

I turned my shoulder, shielding Verra from his intensity.

"We have *loved*, Septimus. I know you do not comprehend such an emotion, but together we share the most sublime of spouses and through her, we share each other."

"He duped you." Septimus patted my arm, the comforting action as confusing as it was terror-invoking. "Were it not my enchantress, I would applaud his grand design."

My eyes leapt from object to object, seeing nothing as my mind struggled to fit the pieces of this predicament together.

Surely not. He would never. Would he? Was this his plan all along? Could Cat have...

Hot tears stung the backs of my eyes.

He was entirely capable. He had plotted and schemed his whole life.

I removed Verra from her sling, placed a kiss on her forehead, and then passed her into Greggen's arms.

"Return her to Cinden on the morrow. If any harm befalls her, you best run back to your homeland of filth—though even there I will hunt you, just as I hunt Catommandus."

Aberus came to his feet.

"Brother Ambrose. Think rationally; Cato is ensconced at Verus Temple. Are you truly contemplating fratricide on the mumblings of a half-dead spy? The taking of your brother's life?"

"Why not?" I replied calmly. "It's a family tradition."

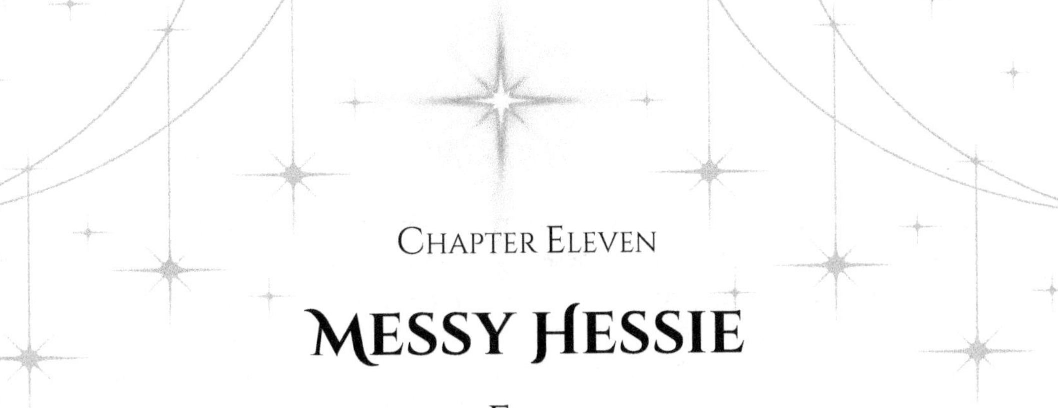

Chapter Eleven

MESSY HESSIE

Eira

After bathing and dressing her in a clean nightshift, Jilly and I propped Hester up in her bed.

Give her your blood, Eira. I pushed the thought away.

Jilly sat alongside the ailing woman and combed her hair down her back. "Hester, you need to see a healer."

"I won't go, Jilly." Hester winced as she turned to meet Jilly's eyes dead-on. "You know I won't."

"That's fear logic, Hester. You've got a significant injury. There has to be some healer in this city that you trust."

I dragged a chair over and sat near the foot of the bed. I tucked the quilt around Hester's feet.

"Nope. Not a one." She wagged a finger at my face.

"That's fine, because neither of you are going anywhere until you drop an iceberg's worth of truth."

They shared a look, but neither made to talk.

Mmhmm. Well, I had a few tricks to make their lips start wagging. I leaned forward, elbows on my knees.

"You know the funny thing about an iceberg?" I sighed deeply and rested my head between my hands. Hester faked a yawn, and Jilly inspected Hester's ear like it was the most interesting ear she'd ever encountered. "You only see what floats above the surface, but hidden below, that's where its real weight lies."

I nodded, more to myself than to them. Icebergs, though pretty to look at, struck terror into the hearts of fishermen. A partial understanding of the truth is just as treacherous, as it's the unseen depths that cause the most damage.

Silence.

Gods, they were like two girls in their fourteenth year. How people that age could be caught at the very height of their dramatic dealings and still cling to their innocence was beyond me. How many times had I put my mother through the same? She deserved a place in the Cradle above.

"Ladies, something you both need to understand about my life is this: I make plans. I make lists that need their own lists. I plot things out. I lay the groundwork with the best of intentions. But then fate tosses those plans on their planny asses." I scratched my belly and yawned. "Should I be more concerned that my well-laid plans have been tossed out the window on account of some age-old medical drama?" I kicked my shoes off and let them tumble to the floor. "Should I be frightened by the prospect of adding a third husband to my ever-growing man-menagerie?" I flexed my grubby toes. "Did Mama tell you that I have two already? Or did she keep you in the dark as you are now keeping me?"

Silent fucking defiance. Jilly continued combing the three godsdamned hairs on Hester's head, and Hester perused the childish artwork that decorated her wall.

"Do you all feel like the Lead Healer is a man I should fear?"

Though hesitant at first, both women nodded in unison.

"Well, you're both wrong." I shoved my sleeves up over my elbows. "Do you know why?"

Both shook their silent heads.

Crack! An electric shock split the air.

Dance your syncopated rhythms upon my fingers.

"Because I can fucking adapt."

Black flames surged from my hand and transformed the silence, not with a roar, but with an unbearable heat that pressed against every corner of the room. The licking tendrils of shadow rose higher. Shocks of lightning jumped from fingertip to fingertip, arcing as I poured my æther into the dark plumes.

Jilly's eyes widened in desperate fear, and Hester's, though unnervingly dry, held a stark, dawning horror.

Ash fell like a sudden squall of snow, the ceiling turned gray with char, and the paint bubbled on the walls.

"Gods' mercy!" Jilly wrapped her arms around Hester, who shielded her face with both hands. Too overwhelmed to scream, their mouths froze open as if my shade stole their cries.

And still I let the æther flow.

Beads of sweat dripped into their eyes, and Hester's wet hair put off steam.

Thank you, friendly fire. You are a thing of true beauty.

I called the scorching shade back to me and let its flame burn low while I twisted my hand back and forth, watching its unruly yet hypnotic sway.

"You are an Other... a... conjurer." Jilly's voice quivered, just the same as her hands.

My answering smile held no warmth.

"Lucky for the Gaeans, I care about preserving the lives of the innocent. But make no mistake. If small men, or great men, leave me no option, I will scorch this land until all that remains is a dry, dead husk."

Hester struggled against Jilly's hold, but the small woman held her tight. "Your hip, Hester, settle down."

I whipped my gaze to the window, and the iron latch holding it shut shattered, hitting the wall and then clattering to the floor. *Thank you for opening, little latch. I'll see you fixed.*

Cool winds blew into the room, dispelling the overwhelming heat from the air, chilling my fevered skin.

"Mama didn't fill you in on this part, did she?"

More head shaking.

"Welp, I'm a bona fide conjurer, ladies. Not a great one, mind you, but those ships in the Solnnan skirmish certainly didn't sink in a storm. Would you rub my feet, Jilly? I am embarrassed to say that I am not at all used to the workload, and these swollen seal pups are barking."

Jilly rearranged her cap and then quickly scooted down the bed toward me. With surprising strength, she took my heel into her hands and started kneading. She looked at Hester, and I caught a subtle pursing of the hedge witch's lips.

"Hester, Jilly wants to say something. Why are you discouraging her?" I asked. "Stifling someone's voice is sooooooo Monwyn."

Hester's sparse brows knit close.

"I'm a Troth, Hester. Again, not a great one, but decent enough at reading people. What is it you want to discuss, Jilly?"

Jilly worried her lip between her tobacco-stained teeth.

"I... well—"

"Jilly," Hester cautioned. The older woman reached out and laid her hand on the diminutive woman's forearm... which made Jilly pause her foot rub... which made me want to cry a little.

"It's time." Jilly patted Hester's hand. "I'm tired of hiding and am more afraid now than I was then."

Oh, goodness. I sat up, dropped my feet to the floor, and caught one of Jilly's hands, taking it between mine. I recognized the desperation in her tone and saw the shift in her posture, the droop in her shoulders.

Silent tears traced the deep wrinkles in Hester's cheeks.

"Alright, Jilly girl, alright." Hester pushed the blankets off her chest and shifted, grimacing as she dragged herself nearer to Jilly.

"Birdie," Jilly reached for the ribbons that held her lacy cap secure. "Your mother came to the attention of the Primus-King when she and Hester aided me in escaping Cult Mossius. Hester was an instructor, and your mother a healer-in-training." She worked the cap from her head, and an abundance of curly, white-as-a-snowflake hair dropped around her face and shoulders. When it fully uncoiled, I quickly spotted the unnaturally bright-maroon roots at her crown. She pulled the mass over her shoulder and tilted her head. She ran a finger along her ear. "Your mother removed the pointed tips, and Hester filed my teeth straight to help me blend in. We lighten the hair on my head every three days."

What in the...

I stood and studied the top of her exposed ear; sure enough, the faint line of a fine scar ran the length of the inner cartilage.

"They used to be as pointy as a slice of pie." She let her hair drop, covering her rounded ears.

Pointy ears, filed teeth?

"What... what are you, Jilly?" I caught myself and shook my head in apology. "No, wait, that sounded awful."

She smiled gently, understanding my impulsive reaction.

"I'm a gnome."

My jaw dropped; I couldn't help it.

"A gnome? Like, from the stories of the Isles of Inglis? I thought... I thought you'd be—"

"—shorter?"

"Well... made up, a work of fiction... but also yes, shorter. Let's see, *Magika and Menagerie* described gnomes as short of stature but solid of body, like a heavily clayed soil." I tapped my finger against my chin. "Broad of nose and slick-haired like a river otter."

Jilly's lips curved into an endearing smile. "That does describe my mother quite accurately, though you would have received a sound wallop had you compared her to an otter."

I managed a laugh.

"The book said the gnomes went extinct after the Great War. Something about them siding with the humans and angering the Nether Lord."

"Falsehoods. Rumors we spread for our protection. We've been here amongst you the entire time: the satyrs, centaurs, and gnomes. And that whole Nether Lord thing was cooked up like a loaf of bread."

Well, he sure isn't. I'll never forget the sight of him rising from the fissure I created.

I scrubbed my face with both hands. The puzzle pieces I juggled in my mind weren't creating a complete picture yet.

"Back up for me, please. Momma and Hester were at Cult Mossius, and you were..."

Hester pulled herself up to a more secure sitting position. "Cult Mossius is devoted to healing, to studying everything the earth provides us and how it can impact our bodies and lives."

Jilly parted her mass of tresses and pointed at her head. Not only were her roots maroon, but her scalp had an orange tinge as well, right where the hair met skin.

"I was studied for years; portions of my scalp removed, the fluid from my liver siphoned—it's what gives the Obligates their various shades of red hair color, you know. The quantity given, along with their natural pigmentation, accounts for the differences when ingested."

A punch to the face would have been a softer blow.

"What? Are you fucking serious?" My head snapped up. I was horrified, shocked to my core. "Ingested? The fluids taken from your body?"

"Yes, people love their ceremonies, and that particular ritual sets the Obligates apart from the rest of society. It gives them an air of mystery."

"And you escaped?"

Hester took Jilly's hand in a gesture so familiar it made my heart squeeze. Jilly turned her head and kissed Hester softly. They shared in a sweet moment.

"Barely," Jilly chuckled. "Hester and your mother sprung me from the Cult. I'll never forget that night."

"Wait, why the fuck did you stay so close? How—why would you—"

"Mynder is my home, Birdie. And sometimes you choose to stay and fight for your home and for those you love and won't leave behind."

I dragged my fingers down my cheeks.

Hester gave a curt nod and then smiled the cheekiest of smiles.

"We can laugh about it now, but Merrias above, we were so scared that night. After disguising her as a Solnnan healer on pilgrimage, we snuck Jilly through the halls. Within minutes, we ran into my brother, your... well, your father."

"Y-your brother?" My voice was a broken whisper, thick with accusation. "You... you are his sister?" I stumbled trying to get to my feet, my hand flying to my mouth. The floor felt unsteady, and for a terrifying second, nothing felt safe. Nothing felt real.

My thoughts spun. Was this some elaborate trick? Had I been a complete fool? Was Hester another part of the Primus-King's cruel design—his uncanny ability to stay ahead of my actions? Bile rose in my throat, hot and bitter. I stared at her, my aunt, my vision blurring, desperate to find some telltale sign of dishonesty in her eyes, any hint of the evil I knew ran in his blood.

Hester's eyes shimmered. Jilly held her, supporting her with unspoken tenderness.

"I was knowingly going against him; I'd never done that before." Her voice hitched. "He taught the healers then, just as he does now—such a brilliant mind."

Hester stared straight ahead, looking into her past. I gulped the air, reminding myself that my momma would never place me in harm's way. Never. I still couldn't force myself to sit near the woman. I hugged my middle and paced the floor.

"Your mother taught me to see that the Cult's studies, though they advanced our understanding of medicine, weren't worth the harm they caused. We snuck Jilly through the halls, and having altered his schedule, my brother intercepted us. Your mother, quicker of wit than us all, faked a fall, tumbling right into the king himself."

Jilly laughed quietly at the reminiscences.

"Can you just imagine the king of the country, arms and legs flailing? It was quite the scene. Anyhow, she busted her brow wide open on my brother's nose, and they both lay there bleeding in a heap, too stunned to move. Jilly walked right past him and out the door to her freedom."

"And my momma into her prison."

Hester nodded.

"We think their blood mingled then. For weeks after the incident, he pursued her, showering her with gifts, elevating her in the ranks. Placed her on the most interesting studies. She enjoyed the attention, and... and I convinced my brother that perhaps they should Join. I thought she could influence him as she had me and end the studies on the Others."

I practically fell into the chair, too stunned to maintain my balance. Hester pushed a hank of hair from her eyes and then folded her hands in her lap.

"My brother is the product of a long line of kings who determined that any study is acceptable—that the greater good of the knowledge gained can offset the harm. Your mother, however, was convinced that the sentiment was wrong and that not even a single creature should be kept for study if they didn't, or couldn't, give express permission. Goddess, Birdie, there was no evidence of my brother ever being brutal. Never. And Vonnie was so willing to Join with him if it meant she could bring about change."

Jilly nodded and interjected, "She agreed immediately."

"It was only after the Joining took place that h-he—" Hester stuttered and went silent.

"I know what he did to her," I said bleakly, "and I am aware that I am the result."

Jilly scooted toward me and let her legs dangle over the side of the bed.

"He was," Hester continued, "he was exceedingly fearful she would leave him. He ignored his other wives. There was only Vonnie. It was like some powerful force altered the mind of the man I knew. Anyhow, she escaped, and my brother cast me out."

"For aiding her?"

"Officially, it was for presenting the idea that the malachite affects our minds... but yes, he suspected me. Even after my expulsion, he's stayed in contact; to this day he sends a monthly sum and writes me weekly, always sending his love."

Jilly used her apron to mop up Hester's non-stop flow of tears.

I studied my relative, comparing her to how I remembered the Primus-King—lively blue eyes, graying hair, with a softer white around his temples.

"And now you help me to atone for your guilty conscience?"

She breathed in deeply and exhaled slowly.

"No, my sins are my own. But I would see him ended in the gentlest way possible. When your mother contacted me and made me aware of the Monwyn murders, it was clear to me that he is still willing and capable of great harm. I love him despite his flaws. That's a hard thing to hear, I suppose."

A knock sounded on the door. Lile Benot poked his head in.

"Jilly, the magistrate is downstairs waiting; he brought these papers."

"Thank you, hun, I'll be right down."

Jilly read the missive as Lile shut the door.

"Birdie girl, now, I'm not telling you how to carry out your plans. But I suggest you Join yourself to the magistrate this very evening and rework your strategy. If you enter the Cult and you are discovered, you may never again see the sun. Troth Yemailrys has sent word that she will appoint you to the gong farmery if we can secure a proposal this eve."

"The what?"

Jilly screwed up her face in distaste.

"Well, it's nighttime employment—quite respectable. You would scrape the palace cesspit. That's a—"

"I know what a cesspit is. It's a tank of shit!"

"It's a noble profession, pays well, and—"

"—is sure to result in divorce. Is divorce legal in Gaea? Huh? Because after standing in a shithole all night long, my *third* husband is sure to demand one!"

CHAPTER TWELVE

ENGAGEMENT IS ANOTHER WORD FOR ALTERCATION

EIRA

I took the stairs one by one, dressed in a loose and frumpy gown of lightweight wool, its only decoration four laughably large wooden buttons that ran from my neck to navel. Its lines were not sewn to flatter, but it was a deep, almost black gray—the nearly Nortian color bolstered my confidence. Hester said it washed me out like a plucked peahen. Underneath the scratchy bag, an old, much-too-tight chemise gave my irritated skin some relief and my breasts a bit of lift, even if it bit into my chest, forming a quartet instead of a pair.

Jilly tucked her arm securely into my elbow.

"Smile now, girl. Show him those teeth," she whispered. "Snare 'em with sugar."

At the bottom of the staircase, I glanced up slowly—for spectacle's sake—knowing that my soot-darkened lashes framed my eyes and made them stand out brilliantly next to my lightened hair. A single short braid intertwined with a thin green ribbon that stopped at my nape. It was the first time in months that it had been styled and pulled back out of my face.

I caught the magistrate's eye and let a smile, which I hoped rivaled the sunrise, spread across my face.

He took to his feet, and his ecstatic grin rivaled my own. *Lord Gammond, he's a smitten kitten.* The magistrate dipped his chin to a tall and willowy woman standing to his side. He whispered something into her ear, and she beamed, waving a long-fingered hand in my direction.

My gods. She's adorable. Tall and thin with a bright and rosy complexion that contrasted so beautifully with the magistrate's skin of raven-wing black. Her ice-blue eyes sparkled and matched her modest yet silky knee-length tunic. Oh, and how jealous I was of the long leather skirt she layered beneath her top. The hide looked remarkably soft and supple. She reminded me of Allaine. Ugh, the reminiscence nearly made my smile falter. I hoped my friend was well. When last I'd seen her, she'd been in a deep depression.

We crossed the tavern floor, and to my surprise, a hush fell over the room.

The gamblers put down their cards, and the drinkers their mugs—I nearly expected a round of applause.

"Ahem," the magistrate cleared his throat as we approached. His lady rapidly tapped his wrist. "Right, yes." He scurried around the table to pull out two chairs before tucking Jilly and me in tightly. "Miss Birdie, it is lovely to see you again." His mask of calm authority slipped back into place as he resumed his seat. "Please allow me to introduce my wife and Lifemate, Sparrow."

My eyes nearly bugged from their sockets. Surely, he was jesting.

Sparrow?

The lovely woman let go of a tinkling laugh that revealed a smile of gold-and-green studded teeth, the entire top row glittering.

"When Badyr spoke your name, I just knew the gods conspired to bring the flock together!"

They sure are conspiring...

She hugged her husband's arm and dropped her head to his shoulder. "I've tried for years to procure an additional mate for us."

Badyr tilted his head to rest atop hers.

"How lovely." I adopted an expression I hoped read as harmonious. Simply hearing the words "additional mate" made the æther in my chest sink to my stomach. But I couldn't think of my loves—it would only lead to tears.

"Since the moment we started courting, Badyr and I knew we wanted a large family."

My waning attention snapped back to the couple seated across from me. Sparrow gazed up at her husband, who looked down at her adoringly. They were so darn cute.

"Do you see yourself Joining with a large family, Peregrine?" The magistrate asked in a voice laced with hope. "I know this is happening fast, but in light of the unfortunate timeline..."

"Yep. Sure do. Love kids." *If they are silent or playing far away.* A barmaid plunked down four ales and a plate of crackers. I grabbed a mug and gulped the frosty contents. Over the rim, Sparrow's eyes shone like the sky. *I bet they need a second pair of hands. Mamas don't get paid to watch their own kids—which is criminal.* "And I love the idea of playing games in the evening and sewing tiny clothes." I hoped those were things wives did. My mother was always out delivering babies or checking up on patients, and as a new wife myself, so far my duties included... well, welcoming my husbands into my mouth or between my legs. Sometimes both at once, depending on the circumstance.

"Badyr!" Sparrow squeezed his bicep again and emitted a high-pitched squeal. "I think I love her."

"Uh-ugh," I sputtered on the ale's frothy foam.

Troth mask, Eira!

"I'm kidding, I'm kidding." Sparrow held her hands up in apology. "I tend to get a little ahead of myself."

I inclined my head and laughed along.

"How many children do you have?" I asked.

"Oh, none," Sparrow stated matter-of-factly. "Badyr and I don't share in a physical relationship."

Well, fuck me running. I could have sworn I heard Goddess Merrias's deep chuckle in my mind. My plan had been to plead a nightly headache until the Primus-King was dead.

"You've not—you don't... butter the bread?"

The mates simultaneously shook their heads.

"And have you, Badyr, ever..." I circled the fingers of one hand and plunged my pointer finger through the loop in a childish gesture.

The quiet crowd pressed in around us, anticipating his answer. I could feel the collective breaths of the nosy gamblers on my neck.

"Music, by gods!" Jilly flapped a hand behind my head, frantically motioning for Jimothy to strike up a tune. I should have realized one's "purity" would be a sensitive subject in the morally conscious kingdom.

Creator's tits. I could explain away the extra marriage on account of my king-killing mission, but my Black Bear would never forgive bodily infidelity. *Never.* Already I prepared to throw myself at Ambrose's feet the moment we reunited. Taking Septimus into my body saved Evandr, yes, but I didn't know if it had cost me my partner.

The chords of a lute struck up, breaking the escalating tension. *Thank you, Jimothy!*

"I have never shared in amorous congress with another, no." Badyr patted Sparrow's hand. "Sparrow is not inclined to the physical, but we share a deep and profound love. And you, Peregrine, a-are you pure?"

I groaned inwardly. *Fucking Gaeans.*

"I searched for peace in sunshine...
On mountaintops and in dreams."
My vision blurred, breath no longer filling my lungs.
I knew the rich baritone—smooth like silk, as warm as my lover's embrace.
Goosebumps dotted my arms.
"Birdie, are you alright?" Sparrow asked. "Badyr, she's faint!"
"Peregrine?"
"Fetch water!" Jilly snapped. "Chip some ice off for her, too."
"It found me instead in your arms," I uttered under my breath, speaking the words that completed the inscription on the inside of my twisted-metal ring. The æther spiraled, heating the dual metal. After Gotwig's spies retrieved it from Cordillaria, I'd never once removed it; it was the only physical link I allowed to my other life.
My heart thundered, thumping wildly against my ribs.
"Here, lady, drink this." The barmaid pressed a cold glass into my palm. I chugged its contents before the water could boil from the æther circulating between my hands and chewed the ice to buy me precious seconds.
"Birdie's got the nervous jitters, is all; it's a family thing, it is. We go all feverish at the first bit of excitement!" Jilly whacked me on the back so hard that ice flew from my mouth, slid across the table, and landed in Badyr's lap. Before I could apologize, the song ended.
With an appreciative energy, the crowd exploded into applause, whistling and whooping while I sucked the air into my lungs and called upon the goddess. A shadow loomed over me, casting its profile onto the table. My æther swam, collecting along my spine as if it could reach the man at my back.
Jilly swung around, still patting me.
"You've got the job if you want it, minstrel. And the quiet fellow, Larm, was it? He can stay if he'll agree to share the room. I ain't got a bed long enough for his feet, though."
"Larm?" I whispered. "LARM!" His name left my mouth in a sob.
I jumped up so fast my chair tipped and clattered to the floor.
My Frostborn.
He was here.
Tears blotted out all but the faintest outline of the slender form that stood on the stage.
I wasn't sure how Badyr and Sparrow would interpret my ugly cry, but I didn't care. Our divine child—Cato and mine—ran toward me, arms thrown wide.

"I don't... my goodness... how I've missed you."

At Larm's touch, my topsy-turvy world righted.

This feeling was different from anything I'd experienced before. Panic, worry, relief, pride. Like a snowball to the face, the amassed emotions nearly felled me.

"I missed you." Larm's long sigh melted into a soft laugh.

Where my chest pressed against his stomach, the constant heat that plagued me cooled.

"Larm, oh, my Goddess, Larm. I have no words!"

He dropped to his knees, tilting his face to mine. Even with weather-roughened skin and deep wrinkles from the sun, he was perfect.

I ran my thumbs over his thick brows and then turned his head from left to right. Brown skin with carnelian undertones gave him a warm glow. A delightful spray of freckles ran across the bridge of his nose and under his eyes—

My husband's eyes.

I choked back a sob. A perfect replica of Cato's gaze stared at me. Deep brown like the richest soil, a blade-thin edge of gold surrounding their pupils.

"You are so handsome, my Larm. Breathtakingly so."

The surprise of seeing him unfrozen and alive—my gods—was there any greater feeling?

"Who ya reckon that is?" A patron two tables over asked loudly, crunching a cracker between words.

Oh, shit. Shit, shit, shit!

The room was silent... body-in-a-crypt silent.

The gamblers didn't gamble. The barmaids had ceased barring.

"Dunno." A man across the room shouted. "What'll happen next, ya s'pose? Badyr gonna off him?"

"Wanna place a bet on it? Eh?"

"Naw, not the lawman. Not in cold blood. Ya think that young'un will sing us another song? Do ya know the one about the sailor kissin' the mermaid?"

Oh, fuckity fuck.

With effort, I twisted in Larm's tight embrace to behold my—

"Merciful gods!" I screamed.

"Come now, that's no way to greet the man you love!" *Cato...* Motherfucking Catommandus Borko Odell, whatever-the-nether-his-other-names-were, flung his hand out, pointing to Larm.

He sauntered forward. I lost my ability to breathe again. I was stricken... with horror.

"Oh. My. Dearest. Gods."

With the charm of a trickster demon, Cato flashed his perfect smile while rubbing his baby-bald chin with thumb and forefinger. No beard. Not even a speck of stubble. And what in Goddess Maressa's name had he done to his brows? They were plucked line-thin and curved like a crossbow's prod.

"Not the first time I've been compared to the divine," Cato crooned.

His tucked but fully unbuttoned shirt of Solnnan pink fluttered as he sailed over to Jilly, who sat smiling up at him like a cat who'd been tossed a tuna steak. His chest hair, that magnificent pelt of sexy fur, was gone. He was smooth as a water-slick whale. And... oh, divine Creator. A tattoo. A massive blue rendering of... of...

"A harpy!" I yelled. "With her tits out?" *Merrias, kill me. I can't take any more today.* The creature, its body that of a bird and its head a woman's, stretched from his shoulder to his sternum.

"Ah, fair-haired lady, you know your lore. The tits were modeled off my favorite gal." He gripped his fist and flexed his pec, making the harpy dance.

I looked closer.

Oh.

My.

Gods.

The likeness was not perfect, of course, but the full lips, almond-shaped eyes, and the left nipple slightly higher than the other. *My* face looked out from a monstrous feathered body. And in its clawed talons, the me-beast clutched a bleeding heart. And not the cute kind that we used to draw in the snow back home, but the inside-of-a-man's-chest kind, resplendent with severed arteries and dripping blood.

"That is..." I stammered incoherently. "So stupid. I-I..."

Cato tossed his head and shook the nebulous mass of loose curls that fell around his shoulders. One side was braided back and pinned to keep it from falling into his eyes.

He let his gaze roam over me, making a show of looking me up and then down.

"You dare insult my ink, she who soaked her head in a pail of piss?" *Ouch!*

Cato flung his voluminous coils again and pursed his oil-slicked lips.

The legs of a chair scraped across the floor.

"Sir! Do not think to impugn the unique beauty of Miss Peregrine." The magistrate's hand dropped to the small blade sheathed at his hip.

Fuck, fuck, fuck!

Cato's mouth twitched.

"Ah, yes, *Miss* Peregrine. Hair like dried stalks of dead wheat in the fall." Cato flourished his hand and then dipped into a low bow. "I am called Tom, good sir, and I see from your stance that you are a man who wields an abundance of authority. I am but a lowly poet; please forgive my perceived slight to your—"

"Wife-to-be," Badyr growled with an edge I'd not heard before. His eyes glittered dangerously, and for the first time, I saw him as a man and not a means.

Sparrow stood next to her husband and, with a surprising amount of her own strength, said, "*Our* wife-to-be, sir! And she'll not be insulted in or out of our presence."

"I said I was sorry, yeesh." Cato twisted an empty chair and tossed his leg over the seat. He sat with a thud, propping his boots in front of Jilly's face.

"Do all musicians lack manners?" She batted his feet to the floor.

"Only when pursuing delicious little snacks like yourself." Cato winked at Jilly and nabbed a cracker from her plate.

The apples of Jilly's cheeks glowed rusty red.

"Well, now." She pinched Cato's chin in her fingers. "You provide a jaunty tune at their Joining, and your transgressions will be forgiven."

A lick of scorching jealousy dragged its fiery finger across my chest. I'd hate to throat punch Jilly; I really would.

"Ah," Cato glanced from Badyr to me. "Congratulations to the three of you. When will the nuptials take place?"

"This very eve."

The subtle tick in Cato's jaw belied his rage.

Oh, no, no, no.

"Is. That. So," he clipped, leaning back and taking in the room, no doubt weighing the odds on his ability to slit the throats of all present. My money was on him.

"The weddin' and the beddin! Bets on Badyr knockin' her up? Books are open, gents. I've got two spoons of the sweet stuff on a babe in 'er belly come winter," a patron hollered, brandishing a small book.

"Me first! My coin's on a girl child," squealed Sparrow.

The inner corner of Cato's eye tightened.

Merrias, grandmother, stop him from spilling blood.

To any other, my husband's overly broad smile would appear genuine, but I knew better. The brittle lines bracketing his mouth spelled danger. The sharp glint in his eye was the same as when his dagger slid through Scion Castor's neck the night we fled Verus Temple. My man—though understanding the power that came from peace—reveled in the application of violence.

Cato gripped his bicep, fingers sinking into its muscle. His eyes slid to Larm.

"But Peregrine, the love of your life has left his home and followed you to this Goddess-blessed kingdom. Why, his dear father passed to the cradle not a day after you left, and Larm's inherited the entirety of the swinery."

For fuck's sake, Cato. Swinery? My city boy was clueless.

Sparrow squared her shoulders. Badyr tapped his dagger's shiny pommel.

Not good. Not good at all.

In an act of desperation, I clutched Larm's hands to my chest.

"Larm, is this true? Did your wicked father greet Merrias? Does he stand upon her blade of judgment?"

"Yep. Dead," Larm said, nodding a couple seconds too late. His eyes shifted between Cato and me. "The whole of the swinery belongs to me now. I must have eighty and seven hogs."

Oh.

My poor Frostborn was not a creature born of duplicity. His face was all wrong for the tone in which he delivered his lie, and his narrow shoulders bunched up around his ears. My chest tightened at his discomfort, and I wanted nothing more than to deliver a sound smack to Cato's rear for putting him in this position.

"Yes, Peregrine, your man can finally keep you in comfort without his father causing strife. You'll no doubt wish to pack quickly. The sunshine is melting the snow so fast we'll be knee-deep in mud in a day or two." Cato's grin was sickly sweet.

Larm cleared his throat as new wagers began to fly all around us.

"Yes. Keep you. No dad. Many pigs." Chuckles sounded around the room. Larm clasped his hands together and wrung them like a wet rag. "Much mud. Very muddy. Pigs like mud, but we don't. Let's pack."

The magistrate rounded the table, clutching Sparrow's hand tightly. She looked at me with an open expression of sadness, her hope waning.

"Is this true, Peregrine? We would never stand in the way of love." Sparrow squeezed my shoulder in a supportive gesture. "Badyr can fetch the priest if so, and we can see the two of you Joined this very eve." She tilted her head to the magistrate, who returned her intense expression. "True love—a mate of your heart—is not a gift to give up."

Under my hands, Larm's body, once merely cool, chilled to the frigid temps of a Nortian night. He stopped breathing; his breath caught in his chest.

"Larm?"

"I-my... my wife... is." His eyes glistened with unshed tears.

"Oh, Larm," I cooed while stroking the back of his neck. I dropped my chin to the top of his head and held him, forgetting the others who surrounded us. He knew loss—profound loss—and I'd not cause him more for the sake of a charade.

I broke away and bade Larm to stand.

"No, magistrate, *Tom* here is the town rascal and knows nothing of what he speaks." I met Cato's gaze. With no beard to hide it, his jaw tensed and slackened like the head of a drum. "Larm is the brother I never had but always wanted. We are not lovers."

I felt my Frostborn's relief as if it were my own.

"Then shall *we* move forward, dear Peregrine?" Sparrow asked with an infinite measure of longing.

The wagers increased twofold.

"We will have a good life." Badyr stroked his knuckles down the length of my forearm.

"Do not!" Cato launched from his seat. "DO. NOT!"

All heads in the room snapped in his direction. Jilly backed away.

"Do not do this," he slurred. Cato gripped the table's edge, the self-control he held so dear slipping away.

"Pa—Cat," Larm said in a measured voice. "Let's head outside and take a breather, yes?" My Frostborn went to Cato, unfazed by his outburst, and ever so gently pried his fingers from the tabletop. "He's got soldiers' nerves, ma'am, that's all."

Cato's breathing turned labored.

The Primus-King could wait. The magistrate could wait.

"Badyr, Sparrow, I'm so sorry, but I must decline your offer to Join. I've family to care for."

Their crestfallen expressions saddened me more than they should have—the human cost of intrigue.

"Birdie!" squeaked Jilly, pulling my attention in yet another direction. "Wh-what about..."

"In the mountains, your friends are kin. I'll be back soon." I looked between Cato and Larm and beckoned them toward the tavern's back door.

CHAPTER THIRTEEN

YOU BIG, DUMB, STUPID DUMB FACE!

CATO

*S*hed—*fifteen feet to the right. Tree line surrounding snowbanks. Conditions: muddy enough for a sloppy fight. Weapons. Two on my person, seven on my steed, two miles due south. Greatest threat in the area: my battered fucking heart.*

The feeling of my soul rekindling its lost spark brought me to my knees. Colors were once more vibrant and not the washed-out palette of muted hues that had dulled my vision in her absence.

The tavern's door shut, and I buried my face in her skirts... and wept—tears providing a rare catharsis.

"My heart. My temple. My goddess." I tilted my head back and stared into the face that had been too long a memory. "My wife."

I could feel my control fading further. All the time training to maintain my composure in her presence was for naught. The Bond between us felt like a physical presence, an unseen but ironclad link.

My family surrounded me. The Goddess had finally found me fit. She had smiled upon me and—

"What the actual fuck, Cato?" Eira shouted, stamping her angry foot on the ground. Eyes flashing, hands fisted... she was furious. And I fucking wanted her like I'd never tasted those lips, never smelled her scent, or licked the salt from her skin.

Viktos strike me dead, but my lifeless cock stirred to throbbing. I had all but forgotten I was a man with a man's base urges.

I grasped her thighs, kneading the flesh below her ass.

"Do you know what you've done?" She grabbed hold of her skirts, yanked them from my hands, and then stomped over to a small hill of snow. Larm jogged behind her, following like a well-trained pup.

Eira twisted and fell back into a shallow depression before crossing her arms over her chest and tamping down the uneven snow near her feet.

Water soaked into the knees of my pants. I peered down at my empty hands. *The fuck was this?* Kneeling before her, pouring out my feelings, fucking sobbing like that weakling Ambrose and... and she dared to walk away?

My unhinged joy subsided, eclipsed by my far more rational pent-up aggression.

It was time for *her* reckoning.

"What *I* have done?" I surged to my feet and stalked to my sour-faced mate, clenching my teeth to keep from yelling. "Enlighten me, *wife*; fill me in on exactly what *I* have done."

Eyes the color of a storm-tossed ocean snapped to mine, glaring with equal parts conviction and accusation.

"Godsdamn you, and godsdamn this divine Bond!" She kicked out, aiming for my shin. I darted out of her foot's reach and batted her leg away. Her heel lodged into the snow. "Oooooh, I swear to—"

"You swear? What is your swearing worth? You *swore* yourself to me. To remain by my side. Did your divine mistress bestow upon you the power to roll back time and try again? Try to... I don't know, greet me with a fucking smile? A hug?" Her mouth fell open. *Good.* "When I dared to dream of our reunion, it played out in a tumble of limbs, professions of undying love, and my cock in your—"

A palmful of wet-packed snow met my face, knocking my head to the side. "The fuck, Eira!" I brushed the frozen remnants from my jaw.

Larm chuckled.

I saw red.

"Cato, you have singlehandedly ruined the plans I have *painstakingly* laid in place! You have ruined it all! Ruined it!"

With the edge of my hand above my brow, I swung around, blinking wildly.

"Single-handedly? No others involved? Do you not see the other man standing just there?" I shot my arm out, pointing to Larm, and with a reflexive backhand, smacked another cold projectile from its trajectory toward my face.

"Eat shit." Eira pouted those full, angry lips, and I awkwardly shuffled to keep the bulge in my pants hidden from Larm's view. *Fucking Dick Bond.* "It doesn't matter the variety—horse, bull... dog."

My shoulders were tight, a knot of pure tension. Every muscle screamed for release, either in a fight or... something else. But all I could do was stand there, caught between fury and my body's betrayal.

"And your plan? Pardon me, madam, but was it to mount the lawman until you swelled with his lawful little spawn?" The image sickened me, and a guttural snarl tore its way out of my throat. "What then? Setting up playdates with the Primus-King's ninety-seven toddlers until you, what, convince them that their daddy is the bad man? Three months, Eira, three! No explanations, no communication. Nothing!"

I was spiraling. I was yelling. I was slipping.

My every word was a lash, every breath a gasp of pain. My vision narrowed, and her face, defiant and exasperating, swam in and out of focus.

Unable to contain the eruption, I spun and stalked to the nearby shed, letting go of my frustrations, punching the fucking door until its hinges groaned and splintering pops greeted my ears.

"Fucking Bond. Fucking emotions. Fucking—"

"Snakes!"

I smashed the door again and again, leaving spots of blood—a fitting memento of our tumultuous reunion.

"Snakes! They won't leave her be, Pa-Cat. Vipers everywhere!"

"Larm, it's fine, sweetheart, really. They don't do anything but lie here."

The sudden placating softness in her tone struck me as odd, demanding my attention.

"What the nether are you saying, Larm?" I turned, took in the scene, and ran, exploding with speed to reach her side. "Stay calm. No sudden movements." Like catching frogs in a stream, I struck, snatching a serpent behind its head, holding it in my fists while it bared its fangs. I caught another and slung both into the woods.

"Cato, don't! They've no wings!"

What does my bumpkin wife think these are?

I dropped, pulled my dagger, and cleaved the heads of three serpents in a single, frenzied swipe. All three plopped into the puddle at my feet. But there were more. Movement flickered at the edge of my vision—a cluster of the vile things slithered near my wife. No hesitation. My dagger was a blur of silver, a flashing extension of my arm. I launched into a rapid assault, stabbing down again and again. I slashed across their bodies, the cold steel splitting icy scales.

"Cato! No! Please stop! No, no, no!" Her pleas stilled me a moment.

"What in the Goddess's—Eira, what the fuck?"

A dozen twisting bodies encircled her wrists like bracelets. The vipers slithered along her dissolving throne of snow and tucked themselves close to her hips.

"Do you feel better now?" she spat. "Murderer!"

I bared my teeth, seized a serpent coiling at my feet, and let it soar, a rope awkwardly tumbling across the clearing.

Her eyes glinted dangerously, sharper than my knife.

"I do not. No." I pressed my fingers to my forehead.

"Violent outbursts do nothing to solve problems. You know this. And now," she collected an armful of serpents and held them to her chest, "and now you have dashed the lives of their relatives." Tears cascaded over her cheeks. A yellow viper raised its head and hissed.

"Violence would do a great deal to solve my *current* problem." I growled at my *clearly* addle-brained mate. She tapped the snake's head, thumping it repeatedly until it settled down.

Our eyes locked in a silent standoff.

In my periphery, Larm fidgeted in discomfort.

"They like the heat," she sobbed. I watched in disbelief as a wayward serpent made to burrow into her shoe. "Bu-but now you've killed them."

I assessed the carnage. The splattered snow, the headless serpents. My wife, their pale-haired queen. *Fuck me.* There was the remorse. I never knew remorse until Eira. A side effect of our love that I was not too keen on.

Her eyes traveled up my legs.

"You have an erection," she stated it like I was unaware of the bulge in my pants... or the fact that Larm stood an arm's length away.

"Ridiculous," I murmured, while untucking the tails of my shirt and arranging them over my crotch.

And then she laughed.

Her ill-timed giggle echoed off the trees and bounced off the tavern's wall, rich and unbridled. The song that taunted me in my dreams made real.

I dropped my head between my shoulders, fell to my knees, and crawled the distance that separated us.

"We are a mess, love. I have been in absolute disarray without you." I reached for her but jerked my hand back as a hidden serpent emerged from under her gown. "Call off your guard. I have need of my woman."

"They don't listen to me." She laughed again and stood, shaking off another two or three small snakes. Not a one of the slithering shits hissed or reared their heads.

They raced back to the woods. *Cowards.*

"Willful, are they?" I gathered her hands in mine and brought her fingers to my lips. "Like someone else I know." Breathing her in, I slid her hands between mine, re-memorizing the smooth feel of her nails and every wrinkle of her knuckles. My palms tingled, coming alive. "My world." Emotion welled in me. "My home."

Tears cascaded over her raw cheeks. The flesh there was so pink it looked as if she'd suffered the burns of harsh lye.

"It seems we had similar ideas," I said, combing my fingers through her hair, skimming them around the edges of the inflamed flesh near her ear. "My disguise may have been less painful to don, however."

She shook her head.

"It's nothing. Compared to the loneliness..." She hesitated, swallowing her sorrow. She shook her head again, unable to go on.

My anger diminished. In an instant it became compassion. I was a fool to think she hadn't suffered. To have put my agony above her own had been an act of misguided self-preservation. Wrapping her in my arms, I buried my nose in her hair and held her until I felt her soft palms push against my chest. I relinquished my hold, just a little, so that she could trace the blue outlines of the severed heart inked into my skin.

"It is Ambrose's design," I whispered, admittedly concerned over her feelings toward the piece. She skimmed a nail along the raised line of the scar now hidden by the rendering. "After you left, he defaced a majority of the palace heirlooms with its likeness. Every portrait of a past Monwyn monarch now bears wings and a fine set of breasts. Aberus was beside himself, as you could imagine. Banished Ambrose for the duration of three weeks."

"He did what? But Ambrose, Goddess love him, is still recovering! How dare Aberus do such a thing?"

"He languished the time away in Colpass, having your new matching wardrobes created. I'd have preferred another three weeks of silence, but I was not consulted on the matter." I cupped Eira's chin in my hands, abhorring the look of guilt marring her features. She sucked in a nervous breath, and I watched as she fought to find her resolve.

"Talk to me, strong-willed wife—perfect mate."

Her lashes flickered as she waged an internal battle. She tilted her stubborn chin and flattened those stunning lips. She pinched the edge of my shirt and slid the buttery fabric between her fingers.

"Cato, there isn't a distance I wouldn't travel to ensure our future—not an ogre or troll I'd not face, not a human I'd not take to task—but you, my reason for our separation, will need to, right now, turn your ass back down the path you came from and return to Monwyn."

Ah, yes, there she is.

"Absolutely not," I said. There was no reason to mince my words. I'd come for her, and with her I would leave.

A cloud rolled in, blocking the sun, cutting off the rays of light filtering through the tree branches above.

"I present you two choices, Eira. Pick either; it does not matter to me which. However, time is of the essence, so decide quickly."

She bristled, shaking those square shoulders as she stood up to her diminutive height—and her tits swayed. Fucking nether, if she chose to wield her body against me, I was already defeated. I stared above her head, counting the buds on a long limb.

"Is that right? Two choices, and I am to pick one? How magnanimous of you. How thoughtful of a husband you are."

"Quite." I nodded. "And just think—unlike you—at least I am *giving* you a choice." It was a low blow, but, gods, how she had damaged me every time she did not come home. Every time I knew I'd found her, I could feel the tingle in my hands... and still she hid. "Your choices are as follows, and both are straightforward courses of action. First, if you wish it, *I* will dispose of the Primus-King as the Mantle's representative. You will stay with Larm while the deed is carried out, and then we will make our way to the coast. Or option two: we run and leave this all behind. *Choose.*" I withdrew my timepiece from my pocket and checked its hands. "You are afforded half of a minute to mull them over."

Eira's white-blonde brow arched high enough for me to see it even as I counted my hundredth bud. She slapped the shit out of my hand, knocking the timepiece from my fingers.

"No, sir." She took a step backward. "Allow me to counter your two choices with two of my own, husband. And keep in mind, I love you more than a multi-tiered cake."

She looked down and shuffled her feet, putting distance between us under the guise of checking for a lost viper. She'd not fool me.

"Snakes," she lied, gaining a few inches to the left.

I almost laughed but spared her the embarrassment.

"Just making sure none are underfoot." She bent, swatted away the dirt on her shoe, and angled herself toward the clearing between the tavern and trees.

My eyes narrowed to slits, and my cock bucked in my pants as her perfect round ass spread with her bend. The most pleasant sensation settled in the base of my spine as she retreated another three steps, still working the serpent angle.

Goddess Thoramika, be on my side.

My wife was my favorite prey to hunt, and she fucking knew what she was about—even her slow show of departure had me digging my toe into the ground, seeking traction for the moment I would spring. I stretched my neck from one side to the other and made a show of searching the ground.

"I only detect a *single* forked-tongued creature among us."

Her indignant mouth dropped open as she whipped straight up.

"Will you apprise me of my options, unless, of course, you would rather I fill that mouth with something more satisfying than words?"

Ah, yes. My defeat might come from the sway of her hips... But how sweetly she fell in line at just the imagery of our passion.

She chewed at her bottom lip, and I could see her pulse quicken at the base of her neck. Her shoulders shifted ever so slightly to the open space between Larm and me.

Yes. Fuck. I am begging you. Run, wife... run and see what monster finds you in these woods.

"Fine."

"Fine?" Not the answer I had expected.

She changed course, and I tracked her measured and unhurried movements. She was sizing up another potential path of escape, turning with the precise, deliberate air of a general surveying a battlefield. Her hands were clasped behind her back; her nose tipped imperiously into the air.

"One: you and Larm will head to our rendezvous location and stay with my parents until our plan is carried out. We've worked on this for months, and you needn't insert yourselves." She transferred her weight to her right foot, lowering a half inch as she bent a knee. Did she think to outrun me? *Goddess, let her try. I pray to you, beseech you, Infinite Mother.*

Eira pondered, chewing on that fucking lip, flicking her tongue out to—I snapped back to awareness. *She is good.* My wife knew how to distract me; she knew exactly how to throw off my focus, and I was willfully falling for her seductress's ploy.

Fucking cock—the downfall of humanity.

She tapped the tip of her nose thoughtfully.

"Honestly, Cato, backup would be welcome, just as a precaution, mind you. And I'd love another set of eyes watching over my parents."

The slick but soft sound of her toe twisting into the partially frozen ground raised my hackles. My vision constricted, tunneling until only she existed.

I held my ground.

"And what, my love, is the second option you wish to present?"

Her eyes flicked to a spot behind my head.

Not falling for it, crafty conjurer.

She fanned her arm out to the side, trying to divert my attention, but I refused to look away from her eyes. Her eyes told me what I needed to know.

"I leave again, and this starts anew. I'll not have you in harm's way, no matter how long it takes. The clock resets."

Like the silvery cloud cover drifting over a bright moon, her pupils shimmered. Any other would mistake it for a shift in the light, but I would never again be fooled by its subtle gleam. It was that same shifting haze that I saw before she ripped my soul from my flesh and dissipated, leaving my arms and home empty.

"Does it then, lady wife?"

My hands drifted to my chest. I exposed a single side of my naked torso.

"You underestimate my willpower, Cato. Sex appeal may work on a younger woman, but I've lived a little too much in the last year to be drawn in by brawn."

"Mmhmm, undoubtedly." I slowly and methodically shrugged from the silk, revealing my other shoulder, a move I'd used to get my way with her in the past. My woman appreciated a solid pectoral.

I let the shirt fall to my hand.

Eye glimmer... slow inhale... eye glimmer... quick intake.

"Now, Larm!" I shouted.

Springing, I lassoed the tightly woven silk over her half-shadowed form, mentally thanking Primus Zuddaz for the idea of the extra-tight weave containing her. They used the same technique to trap steam in their dye baths in Solnna. Larm scooped up the shirt's other side and tied it as I retrieved a triple-layered, silk-lined bag hidden in the wide cuff of my boot.

"Catoooo! You deceitful, big-headed lump of a—Ahhhhh!"

We stuffed her, head first, into the bag.

"Well done, Larm! Now go. Head southeast."

Chapter Fourteen

How Do You Initiate Marital Legal Injunctions Against Your Fate-Bond?

Eira

"Get me out of this bag, Catommandus! If you don't let me out right now—did you just smack me? You dare assault me?" I kicked, striking... well, I didn't fucking know, but I nailed it again for good measure. How dare he smack my bottom while I'm bound and defenseless?

"A love tap is all," came his muffled reply. "Hush and behave."

Behave? Did he just—

I flailed in earnest and attempted to demon puff my way out, but to no avail. My battling just made my prison swing harder. I seethed. I could run through walls and squeeze my way through fractured glass, but somehow, this bag cut me off from my abilities! I was livid!

"Wallop me again, Cato; do it and see if I don't invoke my godsdamned grandmother Merrias and end this confounded Bond! Ahhh!" My stomach sank and then flipped, my body suddenly weightless. "Cato, you dick-brained son of a—oof."

My stomach hit something solid, knocking the air from my chest. *Horse Ambrose, fuck! We'll be halfway to the Isles before morning.*

I fought my bag prison, punching and thrashing. When I got out of here, I'd demand a divorce—no, wait—I'll kill him and save us the legal strife. Oh wait, we weren't *really* Joined. Good. I'd just walk out of these woods with my Frostchild.

"I'm hungry!" I yelled. And was ignored.

"I have to pass water!" I tried again.

Nothing. I might as well have been talking to the wind. Swaying back and forth, I contemplated my next move: punching Cato in the throat so hard that he dropped from baritone to bass. I stewed in the dark, not even a pinprick of light to illuminate my confines.

"I'm in need of a fast fuck!" There was a pause in the movements I could hear around me, but a beat later they picked up again.

"Pa-Cat," mumbled Larm from somewhere above me. "I'm thinking things over, and I'm not sure my life-giver is pleased with the direction we're headed."

The crunch of footsteps alerted me to a presence on my right. I lashed out but struck air.

"Am I not also your life-giver, Larm?"

"You are."

"I find I am *most* pleased with the turn of events," Cato replied.

"Yaa!" I kicked with the strength of my ancestors. "Gammond's gonads!" My toes smarted like I had punted a marble statue.

"I don't know, Cato, sir."

Larm... Larm was the weak link.

"Larm, sweetheart, listen to me. Kidnapping is not a plan; it's a crime. I give you permission to shun your idiot life-giver and assist your more grounded and thoughtful one. Okay?"

Several minutes passed by.

"Larm, dammit, release me! I'm sick and tired of—oof." My butt thudded against a hard surface, and the constant swaying finally ceased. An eye-searing flash of sunlight blinded me, but I came up swinging anyway. "Cato, you frozen turd from an elk's—ahhhhhhhhhhhh! Run!"

I hauled ass, not caring which direction I headed.

"Fucking run!" I screamed over my shoulder. "Giiaannt!" Legs churning, I barreled through two tall pines, dodged a birch, and then set myself toward a dense copse of evergreens. "Merrrrrriiaaasss! Merrrias!" My heart raced as I pumped the legs that hadn't attempted even a quick dash in the past months. "The fuck, the fuck!" I tore over a snow-topped mound and—wait.

My husband.

My Frostborn!

I slowed to a stop and spun.

"You're a conjurer, Eira!" I reminded myself out loud.

I focused, sucked the cool air into my lungs, and called to the æther, gathering it to my core. *I can do this; I can.* Calves burning, I retraced my path, stumbling over the roots of a massive oak. You'd think Goddess blood would provide a modicum of grace to its bearer—or perhaps the æther would keep a conjurer afloat. I was living proof that neither of those assumptions was accurate.

"I'm coming, Cato! Get thee back to the nether, demon scourge!"

I leapt through the twin trunks and caught sight of the behemoth looming in the distance. Holy mother above, it was huge. "Turn your eyes upon *me*, beast!" I hollered, heading straight for the monster. Frantically, I searched for Cato, desperate to see that he remained alive.

The murky water of a nearby puddle caught my attention, and I called the liquid to me. It reacted instantly and flowed around my fingers. Though abysmal at water conjuration, my Pa had taught me how to spear a fish with only a cup's worth—a compact stream shot through the eye resulted in a quick end and little mess.

"Dieeeee—Oof!"

Hit by a sudden force, I toppled. I squeezed my eyes closed and clawed at my assailant as we rolled over prickly pinecones and old acorn shells. With a thud, we came to an abrupt stop.

"Cato?"

A strong hand cradled my head. I stared up, stupefied.

"Are you hurt, love?" He bent low and ran the tip of his nose along the bridge of mine. "That was quite the tumble."

Given his state of calm, it dawned on me that I was the only one trying to fight for our lives, which meant...

"Cat. Wh-what *is* that?" I flicked my eyes toward the mass of cobalt blue in my periphery.

"That's our kid." He gestured over his shoulder and grinned. "I rather think he inherited his peaceful temperament from me."

"Our kid? Our..."

"Close your mouth, wife. Larm is self-conscious of this form. It is still new to him."

"It's still—our kid..." I trailed off, wondering if I'd struck my head after all. I felt my scalp for bumps or cuts.

"Let us go closer, love," Cato dropped his voice low. "His bite is, in fact, worse than his bark, but we are safe, idiom aside." Cato helped me stand and went about knocking pine needles from my hair. He kept looking over to where my eyes had still yet to stray, and his smile deepened each time—I could sense within him a deep sense of pride.

"Oh, okay. I—worse than o-our kid... bite... big..."

"Sure. Something like that." Cato looped my hand through his elbow and brought my dirty knuckles to his lips.

"My reaction was similar the first time. You should have seen Aberus, though. You are handling the transformation much better than he. I am not exaggerating when I tell you that his curls stood on end."

Cato swept a hand toward the giant.

"Meet our Frostborn."

I couldn't muster the voice to joke that he should be called our "First-born" instead.

"Larm," I breathed out, my voice having gone airy.

You could not have prepared me.

The massive being in front of me was like no creature of lore I'd ever read about—was like nothing my grandmother described in her stories... stranger than anything I'd seen flying in the Solnnan skies.

A marbled complexion of deepest sealskin gray and cobalt blue, hands triple the size of Aberus's massive paws, and a solid body lacking in the heavy paunch that I'd seen on many a troll... He was beautiful, and he was mine.

Larm. My Frostborn.

He bent at the knees and took a seat on the trunk of a felled tree. The wood creaked and groaned under his weight. He crossed his colossal feet at the ankles; his toes had talons, slate-colored and hooked.

Cato leaned into my side.

"He thought he might scare you, so we didn't pursue. He held me down until I could shake off the need to give chase."

I nodded my acknowledgment, still at a loss for coherent words.

"Come meet our boy," Cato said. He pulled me by the hands, and in a stupor, I followed.

"Our boy?"

Cato chuckled.

"I know I always said I wanted girls, but I quickly came to the realization that as long as they were healthy—and could twist an ogre's head from their shoulders—I could love a stinky little fella."

"Frost giant." I felt ridiculous repeating it, but my legs were shaky, and my mind still reeled from the shock of it all.

"He's got my eyes, love. And your... well... he's all mine, I'm afraid," Cato said, his laugh soft and light.

Together we slowly approached Larm. I admired the matte perfection of his stone-like back and wanted to feel the texture of his lovely skin. The closer we came, the more my æther seemed to calm, swirling in a gentle scroll instead of bubbling like the burps of a fermented food.

We circled the log upon which he sat, and I came face-to-face with the product of the extraordinary Bond between me and the husband of my heart. *My* Larm. The bounty of the Goddess's blessings—or rather, the Nether Lord's.

"Larm? Can you hear me?" I whispered, reaching a tentative hand toward him.

He nodded his gigantic head, his ebony curls now a rich midnight blue.

"Oh, I'm sorry, I shouldn't—" I dropped my arm, remembering my manners, but in an impressively fast motion he caught my fingers and pressed my palm to his cheek, sighing as he leaned into the touch.

His breath was so powerful it ruffled my hair. His skin was blessedly cool.

"Warm," Larm said, in a voice so deep it evoked the sound of rumbling thundersnow.

"You can speak like this..."

"You should see him fight." Cato squeezed my other hand. "Less than a week ago, he removed the limbs from a marauder with just his fingernails. Snipped them off cleanly. Change back, Larm, we remain too close to the city for my comfort. Let us press on."

I closed my eyes and prayed for clarity.

"About that, Cato—"

Nope, can't talk. Only stare.

Awestruck—it was the only word to describe the transition taking place before me.

Larm's skin deepened in hue, especially around his joints, as did his hair. His skin sagged momentarily, but like a hide on a drying rack, his flesh tightened around his shrinking form. My gaze locked on him, devouring every detail of his alteration. Was he alright? Did it hurt? A thousand questions tumbled through me, but my tongue felt too thick to ask them.

"How positively beautiful you are, my Larm." I stroked the stubble on his human chin, needing to confirm he was still solid, still real.

"It's taken me a while to come to terms with the changes, but it's getting easier."

A dull ache spread from my stomach outward.

"And I wasn't there." My knees buckled, and Cato guided me to the log. I sat next to Larm and pressed my head into my hands. "I created you, and then I left."

A palm settled on my neck, and Cato sank down beside me, resting his chin on my shoulder.

"I was there, Eira. I took care of him."

"But I... I didn't consider. I just left."

Cato drew small circles beneath my ear, his calloused thumb another reminder that while I hid out in a bunker of snow, he toiled—aided Larm in his conversion and Ambrose in his recovery.

"At any point did you give up on me? On us?"

"Gods, no." I shook my head. "Never." I leaned into my husband, pulling on his strength. "I left *for* us, Cato. So that we could live without the constant threat that seeks us and ours."

I sought Larm's hand and folded my fingers around his. Cato nuzzled my neck with his smooth, beardless cheek.

"And here I thought you left because Septimus pissed you off."

"Pffbt," I blew out my lips and stiffened, remembering the last night I shared with his deviant uncle. How he'd thought to abuse my body while finally slaking his lust, how badly I'd wanted him to, and how I had used him in return, finally claiming the mutilated body of my Mated Bond.

My stomach tightened in anguish, and my thighs in arousal. It was a sick and confusing feeling to endure.

Sin. Selfishness. Revulsion. Repentance.

Cato's warm breath tickled my chin; his curls blocked my sight.

"Eira, do not allow guilt to fester within you. It is a useless emotion that keeps you stuck in a chamber with no exit."

Larm scooted closer, sandwiching me in safety. "I don't judge you for it."

Tears. More of them. Was my "Chosen One" purpose to prevent a catastrophic future drought? Because I actually felt qualified for that.

I mustered my courage.

"I believed in what I was doing, in the choices I'd made. Until the moment I saw you. Then I second-guessed it all." I choked on my sob.

Two arms wrapped around my back, one warm, one cool.

"You no longer need to," Cato said. I felt Larm nod.

"I do."

"You do not. Eira. We are here. We leave now, and we start our life as a family."

Family.

My heart nearly burst.

I lost myself at the sight of Cato's joy. He pressed his forehead to mine. The deep cinnamon-brown reflection of his irises stole my breath.

"The Primus-King and the Mantle can wage their own battles, my love. Let the gods tear themselves apart. Aberus and the high lords can drown in their dealings, because in two days' time the three of us set sail from Inglis, bound for the lands beyond Baldorva, our new home."

My heart sang as loudly as it wept. We could do this. We could build something new. I didn't care if we were poor or homeless. I just wanted—

"Will Ambrose meet us at the ship?"

The golden rings around Cato's pupils constricted.

"I certainly hope not."

As I scrambled to my feet, my dress caught, and the earth rushed to meet my face... just as time slowed.

CHAPTER FIFTEEN

IT'S ABOUT DAMN TIME!

EIRA

"**G**randdaughter, you called?"

A mouthful of mud muffled my reply.

"Did I?" I spat, rolled over, and found my feet before scooping the wet earth from the shell of my ear. I flung the mud from my hands and did my best to clean them on the stomach of my gown.

"Loudly," Merrias replied.

Sweat-soaked and smeared in streaks of red, the goddess strode toward me, the Arbiter Blade in her grasp. She was entirely unclothed other than the solid black boots that cut off at her knees.

"The war has begun?" I asked, yanking the hem of my gown from Cato's frozen grip. *Had he tried to grab me? Probably.*

I inspected my little family. Both sat as still as statues. One of Cato and both of Larm's eyes were closed, and their mouths looked to have been frozen mid-word. The effect was too awkward to be comical.

"Not officially. The fighting has yet to begin."

I turned to my grandmother, giving her my full attention.

"Are you naked and covered in blood for fun, then?" I arched a brow in question. My eyes roamed over her mature yet strong body. Gods above, I hoped to age so well.

On wide hips and thighs, her sturdy and robust body moved toward me with the powerful grace of a warrior. As she approached, it became clear that some of the ribbons of blood were, in actuality, pink veins crisscrossing just beneath her flesh, glowing softly. The subtle rosy light was more pronounced around her neck and groin and nearly invisible in her arms and thighs.

"No. Your skull-rattling screams interrupted my bathing preparations." She grimaced. "And knife play holds no appeal for me in the bedroom. On the field of combat, however..." She paused. "After a bit of sport, the pantheon of lesser gods is one fewer this evening. Who cares about the god of sunfish, anyway?" She pointed her blade at Cato's chest. "This is your Fate Bond?" I nodded. "He is... smoother than I recall."

"He's in disguise."

She canted her head to the side and tossed her weapon over her shoulder; it disappeared as it hit its arcing zenith. Merrias then studied Larm as she walked toward him, squinting as if pondering a riddle.

"The Frostborn." Merrias propped a fist on her hip and looked down her nose at him. "You, granddaughter, will do well to remember that the Nether Lord does not bestow favor without the expectation of repayment." She shrugged, unbothered by her nudity. "Perhaps he'll make an exception for his granddaughter."

Merrias turned sharply, waved a beckoning hand, and made her way to a boulder a few yards away. She sat on the protruding stone, legs spread wide, the pose of so many overconfident men.

Okay, well then. We were without a doubt built in the image of the gods right down to the... celestial folds.

"It still vexes me that his essence pollutes you. Fucking Primus-King."

"Well, Grandmother, take solace in the fact that you are the only one to come when I call. The Nether Lord only emerges when we're already buried under the avalanche."

Merrias waved a dismissive hand.

"Eira Chulainn, descendant of *my* blood, your moment of weakness in Solnna did not surprise me—though it left me questioning your loyalty to the Goddess."

"What? That's horseshit."

"I do not judge your human's heart for aligning with the Depraved One—I, too, have made brash choices in the name of love. But every choice bears a consequence."

I held my ground in front of Merrias.

"I didn't align with anyone, Grandmother. The only choice I made was not to let him die. I've stayed true to the Goddess and to you."

She laughed, a humorless sound, the harsh noise scattering a handful of birds.

I dropped down to my backside, not caring that the mud seeped into my dress.

"When you cemented the Bond with Scion Ambrose, it was the Nether Lord's essence that sustained his life. Having his constant jabber in your head was not the only price. Like Lykksun to Catommandus and Viktos to Septimus, your spouse is linked to He Who Rules the Nether. And for the cradle's sake, you couldn't have picked a more powerful host. Ambrose is born of two Obligates during Verus's Rite... under the sign of my Goddess mother, no less. Only his petulance is more powerful than his potential."

I scoffed. She may be a Goddess, and he may be a handful, but he was still *my* husband.

"Ambrose is high-spirited, but he cares deeply for—"

Merrias raised a silencing hand, and my mouth snapped shut.

"Yes, child, and that is where the problem lies. The two Bonds chosen for you were selected precisely because of their abilities to set *aside* their feelings for humanity."

Merrias closed her eyes and inhaled. As she pulled the air into her lungs, the smears of blood that coated her skin seeped into her flesh. The pinkish veins at her wrists and neck drew it in, glowing a rich ruby red. By her exhale, her flesh gleamed clean and bright, like a Troth on Grooming Day.

She held her hands out to me, and I settled my palms atop hers.

"This is why your blood heals, Eira. Through me, you contain fragments of all that lives. You can energize others, lengthen their lives, heal their wounds, and stave off death for a time. I caution, though: it does not make one immortal."

"Is that a threat?" I asked. "Threats seem beneath someone who can erase an entire village with the flick of a finger."

Merrias traced the lines etched in my palms. The trail of her thumb stung like little pricks of a needle.

"I approve of your feistiness, granddaughter, but no. Venture another guess."

The merest hint of scarlet glowed under the thinner skin of my wrist, directly under the pads of her thumbs.

"The Primus-King? Does he assume my blood will grant him immortality? Does he fear death so much?"

Merrias dipped her chin.

"He bargained away his people for Leyometh's essence, thinking it would grant him eternity. Now, as he ages still, he grows desperate."

"Why does he seek to push off the inevitable if he believes his destination to be the cradle? Why would he not wish to take his place with our Divine Mother?"

Merrias dragged her finger up my forearm, watching the glow spread with an expression akin to pride.

"You will not like the answer."

I swirled an uncaring hand in the air, breaking off her contact and signaling for her to continue.

"These days I don't like any of the truths I am learning, but hearing them is better than not."

"Such a brat. Who raised you to be such?" The corner of her lip twitched. "Eira, the Primus-King acts as he does and makes the choices he does because he loves his people."

I fought to keep my eyes from rolling.

"Ugh, yep, fuck that answer. Wad it up and stuff it right back into your mouth." I rested my hands on the ground behind me and dropped my head back.

Happy, fat clouds mocked me, frozen in a beautiful blue sky.

"Bullshit." I muttered. "A heaping pile of steaming shit."

"Evil is rarely begotten by evil intent, granddaughter. His intentions are pure; his actions are otherwise."

Merrias stretched her arms above her head.

A sheath of shimmery gossamer enveloped her. Like cobwebs of charmeuse, the fabric was a simple ivory hue, and yet it reflected a rainbow's worth of colors where light struck just right.

"But he *is* evil. Merrias, he forced himself on my mother and then harvested her blood for his own benefit."

The Goddess crossed her legs and bounced her foot.

"The most wretched among your kind dote on their spouses, laugh with best friends, and kiss and cuddle their pets. Even the Magis loved our daughter, despite his enslaving and abusing an entire population... until I separated his head from his body, that is." Merrias chuckled flippantly, and my skin heated. Steam rose from the ground where my feet met the moist soil.

"Why are you telling me this, Merrias?" The mud surrounding me bubbled like thick batter on a hot skillet. "You wish me to forgive my mother's rapist? The man who took my Nan from me? You want me to forget all he has done because his kingdom abounds with a fit, healthy, and happy population? Does that absolve him of his transgressions?"

Merrias pressed her lips tight, and for just an instant, I saw my own mother in her face.

"My goal is to ensure the Goddess stays firmly at the top of our divine hierarchy. What is your goal, Eira?"

Merrias patted the spot next to her.

I stood and stomped over but didn't sit. Instead, I planted my hands on my hips and scowled.

"*My* goal, Grandmother, is a lifetime of sharing snacks, cuddles, and dicks."

Merrias pointed to her side again, and as if compelled, my body rushed forward, my butt meeting boulder.

"And the Goddess through whom all life comes? Is she piled somewhere on your snack plate?"

I huffed loudly and then paused, catching sight of Cato and Larm. I could all but see the connection that existed between them. Perched upon the log, my husband's right hand was still clawed where he'd snatched my dress, but his left was placed on Larm's shoulder.

"Speak plainly, Grandmother."

"All will have to choose a side—the Goddess or the Nether Lord."

She took my hand in hers again and continued.

"The Primus-King, Bonded to Leyometh, offers that his people will bear arms in the Nether Lord's name—you've seen firsthand how refugees flock in droves to become Gaean citizens, yes?"

I nodded.

"He builds an army, one that, if coupled with the might of the Baldor-vans, will be larger than that which worships the Divine Mother. They will strip her name and memory from the world." Merrias patted the top of my hand, just like my grandmother used to do when we sat near the brazier, sharing herring and hot chocolate.

"Why haven't you struck the Primus-King from existence, ending both your troubles and mine?"

"Because my blade will eradicate the essence that flows between the Primus-King and the lesser god, Leyometh, not simply cut the ties. Were Leyometh a major god, he might withstand the loss, but he is not. When my Bonds are severed, the pain is immense. The same would render Leyometh comatose or worse, and if he cannot guard the Nether or keep alive the flames of hearth and home, there will be catastrophic consequences. And that is not accounting for the revenge of an aggrieved father. The Nether Lord would be indiscriminate in his slaughter: humans, magical creatures, gods. What purpose would the pantheon have without a people to oversee?"

"So, like the Mantle, you feel the task of offing the Primus-King naturally falls to me?" I peered at the goddess through the sides of my eyes. "Won't the Nether Lord come after me as well, if I kill the Primus-King and fuck up Leyometh's essence?"

"Is your life more valuable than all the humans that walk the soils?"

I blanched, and she patted my knee once again.

"Eira, no." Her tone softened. "Powerful amongst the humans you and your birth father may be—which is why your hand is required to deal the blow—but neither of you can destroy a god's essence. If you bring him down, his body will die, but Leyometh's essence remains."

"Of course it does." I sighed in resignation. "Well, lucky for you, I have a plan in place to do the job already; that is, if it is not derailed by the fools that love me."

Merrias caught my chin in her fingers and forced my gaze to hers.

"Murder, cheat, or steal if you must, but do not let this end with our Mother's name lost to time, and for the Goddess's sake, stop denying the power that you carry. It may be your greatest bargaining chip."

Sharp-footed pixies tiptoed down my spine.

The goddess smiled flatly and then stood, striding toward my frozen family. She leaned low and skimmed a cracked fingernail down Cato's nose.

"What are you doing? Don't touch him!"

Again, my mouth snapped shut, not of its own accord.

The crooked cartilage popped, the sound akin to teeth ripping through the gristle on a fat-marbled steak. The two halves separated, causing tears to leak from his eyes and stream over his cheeks. Blood issued from both nostrils. Merrias pushed the tip of his nose with a single finger and then pinched the bridge together, like she was forming the spout of a new clay pot. Where her fingers caressed, his nose obliged, becoming as straight as an arrow's shaft.

"Though Lykksun chose well in the male, Catommandus, he is as head-strong as they come."

"Fuck!" Cato blinked and jerked forward, grasping his face with both hands. Larm fell backward, head over feet, off the back of the log.

Merrias turned to me.

"Your Frostborn is strong enough to control your Fate Bond if the need arises. Goodbye, granddaughter."

CHAPTER SIXTEEN

THE CURE-ALL IS A WARM CUP O' LOVE

CATO

Weapons. Commandeered by the crafty fucking conjurer I wedded. Location. Thirty fucking minutes from the Gaean border. Most dangerous thing in these woods? My impulsive godsdamned wife and traitor of a frost child.

"Larm! Unhand me! Put me down this instant!"

Like a herd of cattle driven through the forest, giant Larm and his thick-skulled mother stomped over the underbrush, chuckling and chatting like long-lost friends—ignoring my shouts, oblivious to my spur-shod boots puncturing his marble-hard forearm. And he carried me across his chest like a babe suckling its mother's teat! To say I was chagrined would be the understatement of a century.

If I could but reach my blade, I would render him fingerless—not that it would make it through his thick digits—and then turn her over my knee. Except it would be useless, because they would continue to scheme up seventy-four more ways to pry the lid from my jam-fucking-packed jar of stress!

"Fucking nether! I did not think to pack a bone saw when setting out to rescue—"

"Cato, hush. You will wake the whole of Gaea," Eira hissed, pointing her finger at me as she chided me soundly.

I will throttle her. Throttle her and then fuck her and then throttle her again. She'll probably enjoy it, though.

I thrashed to no avail, and Larm, in his abundant need to coddle me, patted me on the chest with a massive, taloned paw. Blood coursed hot through my veins. This was decidedly *not* how the plan was to take shape.

We had plotted out fifteen differing scenarios and gone through a dozen dry runs for each!

"*Me?*" I hurled back at her. "*I* will alert them? Not the hulking blue beast-man cracking off branches and stomping through the fucking forest like a buffalo through a beer hall? Not the scream-laughs of my mate gone mad? And, Eira, his story was not in the least bit funny and—"

"Turn him upside down, Larm. Maybe he'll cease his screeching." The giggle that normally fell so sweetly from her tongue set my teeth on edge.

"Eira. I. Swear. To—"

My woman stopped abruptly and looked up at me with dangerously narrowed eyes.

"Look, Cato, until you stop trying to physically abscond with me, Larm's in charge. Get on board, *Your Highness*, or you get a babysitter."

I snapped an arm from my confines, aiming to wrap my fingers around that tempting neck of hers. Larm, swift as a fucking fox, jerked his shoulder back, and my fingers closed around air.

"Now, E, Pa-Cat, I think it's time you both settle yourselves."

My wife tilted her head, nearly bending her neck in half to glare at us. She arched a wildly blonde brow.

"Larm, why in all of Ærta do you call him pocket?"

She set her fists on her hips, and Larm—gods, for a fleeting moment I thought he meant to make a meal of me—smiled. It was entirely unsettling. Until now, I had not witnessed the gruesome grin dividing his face in two. Eira's eyes sparkled, glinting and reflecting the same odd affection that stirred within my own chest. The moment was beautiful. *She* was breathtaking.

"Not pocket... *Pa*-Cat. It's, well, brother Evandr calls Septimus something more familial but the Bond that Cato"—Larm hefted me in emphasis—"and I share is more complex than what they seem to have. I keep forgetting he prefers Cato."

Like a demon spawn, her eyes shifted from Larm to me, her expression transforming from one of adoration to one I knew meant imminent violence.

"Larm, my beautiful Frostborn." Eira patted Larm's tree trunk of a leg, ignoring the thigh-sized appendage mere inches from her nose. "I think the name is darling. And your Pocket doesn't mind it in the slightest. He suffers from chronic grumpies."

"Thanks, E. I understand; my dad was much the same. He has slept the long sleep for nigh on fifteen years, and I miss him fiercely, which makes these new ties more complicated."

Eira leaned her head against Larm's kneecap and nodded while she embraced his leg.

"Though I've experienced what many would call instant affection for your Pocket, the emotions don't override the confusion the mind experiences. When you're ready, I'd love to hear more about your father and family."

Larm smiled wider, revealing a shorter, gold-capped lower tooth.

A deep pang of guilt centered itself in my chest. I did feel irrevocably bound to the giant, but fighting against the Fate Bond was a continual test of my control.

Eira snuggled her face into Larm's leg, and he sighed. I bristled. As he'd mentioned no less than five times, he loved the feeling of her warm skin on his chilled flesh.

"The name is ridiculous, and you will cease using it, Larm."

Eira's impertinent mouth puckered.

"Cato, leave off, or I will instruct him to shove you into his *pocket*." She pushed a wayward hair back. "You'd fit."

The conspiratorial chuckling began anew, and I sent up a prayer, now thankful for my restraints. The Goddess smiled upon her Chosen One by guaranteeing my entrapment. I was nearing a level of fury that would render my dear little family speechless—or unconscious. Was it problematic to hope a band of brigands would set upon us? At this point I would pummel the first man or creature to look at me askance.

"A complaint about my size, wife?" I fumed, but not because of the low-hanging fruit she had snatched and hurled—my stature had been the butt of many a man's ill-thought jest. No. The truth of the matter was that after a handful of hours spent with Eira, Larm had divulged more to her than he had to me in the last three months. And it... well, it hurt. "If you find me so unappealing, Eira, consider my diminutive form off-limits." I laid back into Larm's embrace and ceased my struggling.

"Larm, lower your Pocket."

"Fuck all!" I plunged toward the ground, preparing to tuck and roll, but in a flash, I found myself dangling from Larm's gargantuan paws. His iron-tipped nails dug into my biceps. My feet dangled. "Retract your claws, giant!"

The sharp, needle-like sting pierced my flesh.

"E? Should I?"

Eira shook her head in the negative. "No, he's an asshole who barely registers pain and will dart away the moment there's an opening. But a little lower, please. Your Pocket is a wily imp."

My toes met the ground, but my heels remained elevated.

"Thank you, Larmy." Eira pecked a kiss on one of his indigo and gray knuckles.

I stared at the spot while dragging the cool air into my lungs, trying to no avail to squash the jolt of jealousy that spiked within me. *My mate. Mine.*

"Cato, husband?" Her voice drew me from the darkness, soothed and ensnared me. As always, she made me her contented captive.

Lifting up on her toes, she balanced her chin on Larm's fingers and then gazed into my eyes.

"Were it not for the sake of humanity, Kitty Cat, I would lead our escape to another land." She reached up, and her nimble fingers came around my neck, working the taut muscles near my nape. Her expression softened as she dreamed or thought or reflected. "Ambrose would hate a commoner's life, but he'd come around after a month or two of snuggles and hair-washing sessions."

Bullshit.

I spat on the ground near her foot.

"Cato?" She grimaced in confusion. The stars fell from her eyes, dropping and punching holes through my heart.

"Ambrose should be dashed upon the rocks with the rest of them," I gritted out, not mincing my words or hiding my truth.

"Husband..."

She didn't flinch, nor did she lash out as I'd expected.

"Cato." She twisted a curl around her finger and tucked it back with the aggravating mass that I couldn't wait to clip away. I should have shaved it bald before I'd left, but the style was too reminiscent of my time in Verus and might lead to recognition. "I know you don't mean it. What's our Black Bear done to make you so angry?"

Eira came closer, her lips a hairbreadth from my ear. The warmth from her skin emanated, surrounding me in a cloak of familiar comfort. She dropped her voice.

"You weren't aggrieved when last we shared you." Her cheeks brightened to a most becoming coral. I closed my eyes, drawn in by her closeness, my body's response a wicked betrayal of what I wished it to present. "As I recall, you quite enjoyed the two-on-one treatment."

Larm groaned, a monstrous sound of discomfort.

I clenched my jaw until I could no longer keep silent.

"You should recall that I am a man accustomed to playing the long game."

Eira dropped back to the flats of her feet, her brows knit tight.

"What are you trying to say? Speak plainly."

I would have thought my statement quite clear. *Fuck it.*

In an explosion of force, I tucked my elbow and twisted, taking the Frostborn by surprise and gaining my freedom.

Larm swatted out, but I evaded him handily, dipping and lunging toward Eira. She'd not registered my intent. I seized her shoulders and maneuvered her against the trunk of the nearest tree.

"Cato! What in all—"

Shoving my hips forward, I blocked her attempt to flee, holding her firm.□

"I would have fucked the Nether Lord himself to see the heaviness of passion in your eyes." I crowded her, caging her between my arms, dipping my chin to capture the faint scent of vanilla that somehow always clung to her. "At a single word from your lips, I would endure the punishments or pleasantries of your choosing, the feelings of others never factoring into my actions."

She shoved me in the chest, but I refused to give ground.

"Cato, you're upset. You've let your insecurities get the best of you. When-if things go back to normal, the three of us will sit down and—"

I grabbed her shoulders.

"Look around, Eira, the *three* of us do not exist. Ambrose is not here. He wallows in depression instead of seeking you through trial and blood." I hardly recognized the vehemence in my quavering voice. "Nothing stops my pursuit of you. Do you hear me? Ambrose, the coward, the defeatist, is not worthy to walk the same earth upon which you tread."

Shimmer... deep inhale... glimmer. Not fucking happening.

"Okay, well." Eira wedged her hands into the crooks of my elbows and attempted to set me aside. "Larm? You over there? Your Pocket has gone six snowflakes short of a flurry, and we need to seek a priestess."

"You need to—"

She broke free.

My arm shot out reflexively, my hand collaring her neck. The erratic tempo of her heartbeat played under my palm, fueling my impending lapse into insanity.

Shimmer... deep inhale... glimmer.

"Don't you *dare* leave me again," I growled, wrestling myself for control but wanting so badly to give in—to show her exactly the reach of my emotions. "I will not forgive your next abandonment, Eira. Ambrose may pine for those who desert him; I will not."

My fingers tightened, emphasizing my seriousness.

Her eyes welled, twin pools in a Solnnan oasis.

"You fucking crushed me, Eira. You destroyed the trust between us, the same trust that allowed me to accept another being in our lives."

Her mouth parted, her lush lower lip trembled, destroying me all over again.

"Cato, I'm so sorry. So immeasurably sorry for the pain I've caused you."

Three months. How was "sorry" supposed to restore lost time? The anger I held at bay ripped at me like the jaws of a starved wolf upon a flock of unpenned fowl. The period of separation may be minute in the scale of a lifetime, but even the most mundane seconds spent together felt consequential.

"*Sorry* is meaningless. You left me without a goodbye—without even the courtesy of a kiss to see me through."

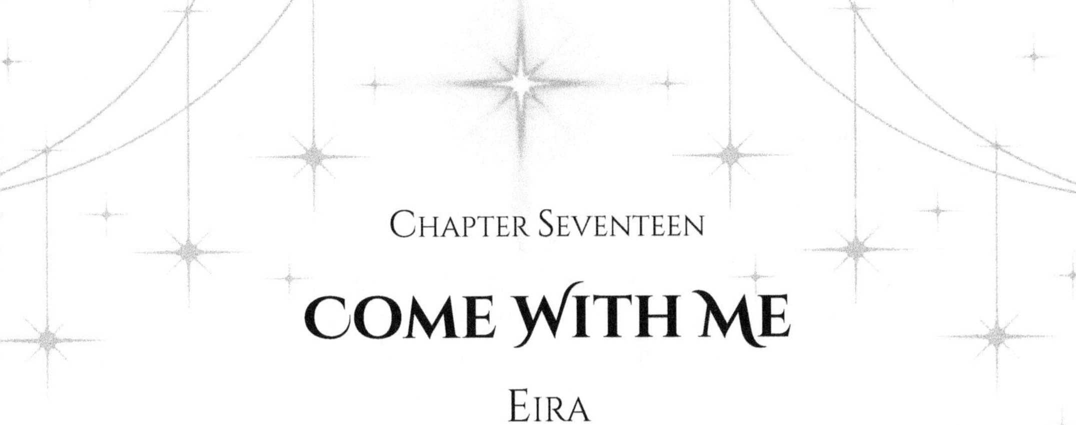

Chapter Seventeen

COME WITH ME

Eira

I silenced him with my lips. Had he ever experienced heartbreak before me? I supposed not, as he'd purposefully sworn off relationships from the time he was a decade and five. He'd had so little experience in matters of the heart.

For the Goddess's sake, I remember wasting away in bed for a week after breaking off a month-long affair with Thealor, a gorgeous member of the whale processors guild. I'd told him if we ended up together, I'd just end up walking all over him and crushing his spirit—he was too nice and incredibly gentle. My Pa had been so devastated, disappointed he wouldn't have a son-in-law in maritime trade, that he shed more than two tears. *Eiry, my minnow, he'd provide for ye and make a nice home, yes?* I'd hugged his big shoulders as I snuck him extra bits of fish jerky that evening. *I know, Pa, but I'm too much of a woman for him, and besides, I head to Verus after the next thaw.* My momma had agreed with me, and about two weeks later, my tongue was cervix-deep in the lovely fair-haired Marilla as I plotted how I might convince my parents to allow her to act as my companion at Verus instead of Nan.

"Eira," he whispered, pulling me from my wandering mind.

I kissed him again, relishing the prickles of goosebumps spreading along my arms, the quickening of my pulse. I poured love into my husband through the kiss, and in doing so began to crawl out of the hole I'd dug for myself these last three months. I'd sobbed, curled up in whatever makeshift bed I lay in each night. My tears, like the most devoted suitor, had visited every day. Ten and eight or nearing thirty, it turns out that the agony of losing someone you love remains the same.

Cato hummed with mingled relief and desire. The rumbling I felt through his chest caused my eyes to roll to the back of my head and my thighs to shake. Were he not pinning me to rough bark, I would have melted to the ground.

I licked the seam of his lips, wanting more. I was beside myself with the need to taste him, for our bodies to be linked.

An intense ray of sunlight broke through the canopy above, surrounding us—Lykksun's chosen in his rightful place once more. The Goddess Maressa sang out her song of approval in the rattle of swaying branches, the drips of thawing snow, the scurry of squirrels as they skittered up the trees.

The Bond strengthened. It tightened and coiled between us, a physical pull that I felt above my navel. The æther sparkled and popped. My scalp tightened, and like I'd inhaled too much smoke from Gotwig's pipe, a light and effervescent sensation elevated my body's awareness.

How had I found the courage to leave this? What measure of strength, or madness, possessed me to separate from this man?

The sudden change in his stance alerted me to his waning restraint. Beneath my fingertips, the thin lines that framed his mouth deepened as he wedged a knee between my thighs.

"I'm here. *We* are here," I breathed before his mouth met mine again. With each desperate touch, I begged his forgiveness, using lips in lieu of words.

He sighed through his nose, and his shoulders lowered a full inch as he relaxed into me.

"Here. With me." He pulled back, drinking in every detail of my body. "My Eira. My wife."

Under his scrutiny, I felt... oh goodness, I felt inadequate.

My hand went to my hair, attempting to smooth the dry frizz that topped my crown. My skin flaked, and my brows had suffered chemically induced balding at their centers. I'd not taken the best care of myself. The days of planning and hyperfocus took their toll, and the depression certainly hadn't helped. Gods, I was sure I looked like I'd washed up on the shore after a storm. I looked anywhere but his eyes.

"Wife." Cato's voice was sharp, snapping me back to the present. "Eyes to me."

I shook my head. Thinking I wouldn't see him or Ambrose in the near future—perhaps ever again—my appearance and my well-being had become an afterthought.

"My world, my heart, you will never be less than perfection in my eyes." He tilted my chin up, shaking me with gentle emphasis. "And that has nothing to do with the Bond... nor your hair." He captured my hand and placed it over his heart. "Your worth is measured by your actions, and only a little by the outstanding curve of your ass."

There he was. My husband. Soft eyes and the lower half of his face coated in blood from his newly shaped nose.

He laughed, caressing the hand he covered.

My throat tightened.

"I-I've gotten larger, and my skin is mottled and—"

"And I desire you." I cast my eyes downward, but Cato nosed my chin up. "Gammond's light, how badly I want you."

His naked admissions still sent heat scalding across my face.

"Eira, change is inevitable in life, and I adore watching your metamorphosis." He scrunched up his now perfectly straight nose. "Also, having spent time with my father, you must know that I am destined for baldness, weak teeth, and skin as dry as an overdone pastry. I must practice wooing you with words so you will overlook my eventual flaws."

I playfully smacked his shoulder.

"Silence those lips, you handsome thing. You are also part your mother."

"Ah, well." Cato shifted to the side and hooked his ankle around mine. "Will you continue loving me when I am fat to the point of waddling and my wrinkled lids bag over my eyes?"

"Yes," I said without hesitation.

"Yes," he replied, his mouth smiling against my neck. He nuzzled my chin with his hairless cheek, the sensation foreign but not unpleasant. "Yes." Cato laced his fingers into my hair, lightly grasping the length at my nape. "Eira?"

"Hmmm?" He traced the edge of my ear and then dipped his finger into the notch between my clavicles.

"Spread your godsdamned legs."

CHAPTER EIGHTEEN

MY FAVORITE SONG

CATO

"**N**ow, Eira." I dropped my hands to the ties of my pants and yanked the cord loose. If I did not bury my cock in her soon, I could not be responsible for my actions against the innocents who might wander along. She was my refuge, the only thing that seemed to keep me tethered to reality. "You have tested my patience, and now I will take what is mine. Honestly, I am aggrieved that the Bond did not press you to attempt a public fucking at the tavern." I turned, my fingers still exploring the soft skin of Eira's neck. "Larm, leave us and go wait."

My woman's gaze widened—godsdamn but I could lose myself in those eyes, even if they were worriedly shifting between me and our clingy giant spawn.

"But, Cato?"

My anger, my relief, my need of her—all of it churned and built, the pressure manifesting in a throb at the base of my spine.

"If you thought a kiss would satisfy me, you clearly misread my intentions."

In the stormy depths of her shocked expression, I caught a brief but hazy glimmer.

She wouldn't dare.

"Did you not hear me, Eira?" My hands shook as I ineffectually ripped at the closures of my pants. I sucked air into my lungs, gulping hard, doing my utmost to remain stable. "Larm. Go. Return to the inn."

Eira made to sidestep, but on instinct, I shifted and blocked her, cutting off her path of escape. Her breasts compressed against my chest, and for the briefest moment my vision swam at the plush feeling of her softness.

"Cato! You and Larm can't stay in Gaea; it's too dangerous."

She fisted the sides of my shirt. Her brows drew together, and tears replaced the glimmer I had feared signaled her departure.

The looming shadow of my Frostborn cut off the sunlight.

"Larm. You *will* obey me in this matter," I slurred out, not sparing a glance over my shoulder. My vision sharpened, and my sense of smell intensified. "To the inn, at once."

"E, what's happening to him? Should I—"

Eira lurched toward him at a run.

She made it two steps before I jerked her back to my chest, cloaking us in her scent: the vanilla that clung to her hair, and under that, clean sweat, and the heady musk of her growing desire.

"Larm. No, he's—this happens when—"

My fingers tightened around the column of her neck, cutting her words short.

"Larm. *Now.*" I tried in vain to lessen the violence in my voice, to tamp down what on the outside must look like an act of brutality—the war-rior-king demanded her flesh, and his patience had long since worn away. My heart hammered against my ribcage.

Take her. Claim her. Yours and yours alone.

"Larm," Eira said, her voice tight. "It's... I'll explain it later. Head to the inn."

Larm reached out. "E, I'm afraid he—"

I went for my knife but found its sheath empty.

"Do not touch her!" I warned. Some part of me rightfully felt shame, but I was beyond the bounds of self-control.

Eira captured my empty hand. She wove her fingers through the digits that begged for a blade. She wrapped my arm around her body and settled my palm over her breast.

"Take what you need, husband."

My eyes rolled to the sky as she backed up, pressing her hips into my cock. The velvet of her voice, thick and smooth, was heady with the sound of her arousal.

"He won't hurt me, Larm, I promise. Go."

"I will never, *never* harm her." He had to know. I would die before I hurt her.

Eira's hands dropped to her skirts, and I tightened the fingers around her neck.

Mine. She is mine. Not Ambrose's. Mine. Not Larm's. Remind her, Cat. Brand her. Make it known.

My exhalations turned harsh as I vied for a modicum of restraint, wanting to spare our Frostborn the sight of me fucking Eira like the monster inside me demanded.

I was losing the battle.

"You belong to me. *Me!*" I growled, droplets of spittle flying from my lips.

"E?" Larm's question hung in the air.

"Fucking leave!" I yelled, my hips thrusting against her ass, pleasure jolting through my dick and settling in my stomach.

Eira whimpered, the feminine sound destroying my remaining composure. She glanced back, and her pupil-blown gaze found mine at the same moment her hand shot out, pointing toward Gaea. "Go, Larm. Quickly."

I twisted her, no longer concerned with who or what bore witness. My hips bucked into the swell of her stomach. I relished her submission.

"Eira." I drove her backward, my hands gripping her hips. Her back met bark—she would require the support. "I issued an order and expect it to be followed."

She nodded and unconsciously bit her bottom lip while rolling the fabric of her skirt above her knees.

"More. Hide nothing from me."

"Nothing," she sighed, bunching the fabric to her thighs, her golden tuft of hair peeking from above the slit that I'd kill to sink myself into... had killed to fuck.

She wore no underthings. The Goddess was pleased with her son.

Own her. Make her claim her place.

My mouth watered, my tongue yearning for her taste.

"You smell of the earth, musky and tart." I dropped my hand and gripped her center, squeezing until her labia parted. "How fucking dare you take this from me? Steal away with the most precious of my possessions. Lower your brow at once."

She cocked it higher, and rage spiked through my skull, half blinding me.

"Impertinent little bitch."

Crack!

My head snapped to the side, and a feeling of utter euphoria enveloped me. No other would have dared. *Hers. By the gods, I am hers.*

"Watch your mouth, sir. I'll only abide so much of your rough treatment." She looked up from under her lashes and moistened the corner of her mouth with the tip of her tongue.

"I fucking love you, Eira Verras Chulainn." The tickling sting of her palm on my cheek made my sac tighten painfully. "And, sweetheart..." I throttled my cock, feeling like a whole man for the first time in too long. I stroked myself slowly, sliding my fingers over my foreskin, knowing she loved watching it glide over my head. My cock ached and thrummed. "You will withstand everything I give you. Correct?"

"Correct."

I shoved her to her knees, her little mewl of need lost in a groan as she came face-to-face with my ardor.

"This, wife, is how the repentant are forgiven their transgressions."

"I beg your forgiveness." Her nimble fingers went to the buttons at her chest. She plucked one, revealing a splinter of flesh. Pine needles poked at her knees and shins, but she didn't care. My pleasure was more important than her comfort. "How should I atone? A prayer?" Her second and third buttons followed suit, and I glimpsed the heavy swell of her breasts. The rosy semi-circles of the tops of her nipples showed over the low neckline of a threadbare chemise. It tied directly under her bust, lifting her chest in a tantalizing display.

"No, my love, for you will find yourself unable to speak."

Her lips parted in question, and I drove my cock into her wet mouth.

"Fucking yes." I withdrew and plunged again.

"More." My woman went feral, lips sucking, tongue licking my underside, and tracing the ridge of my crown. "Deeper," she demanded.

I gasped and made to withdraw, knowing I would spill too soon, but Eira clawed at my hips and sank her fingernails into my ass, jerking me forward. The sting of sharp nails sent me into a spiraling haze. I clutched the tree trunk behind her head to prevent my knees from buckling.

She pleaded for more, her choked hums communicating what her mouth could not.

Her head butted against the trunk—I continued pumping my hips and fucking her sweet mouth while she stroked my length.

Fucking nether, how she took me—tongue lapping, cheeks sunken.

"I have *never* seen a sight as beautiful." I cupped her chin and slowed her ministrations, watching my insertion as I leisurely ground into her, fighting against the demand of her eager mouth. "But I'll not—"

She smacked my hand away and bent forward, licking along the thick vein of my underside. Precum spilled from my tip, and she lapped at it like a greedy miser snatching at gold.

"You vicious little brat." I would have laughed if I were not so close to losing myself.

"Eira," her eyes flicked up to mine, glazed over with desire. "Hear me well." I paused to catch my breath. "I'll spill myself between your thighs and nowhere else."

"Shut up." Her fingers sought out her clit. Her groans vibrated along my length as she took me harder, bobbing her head until she reached my base.

"Godsdamn, woman!" I stumbled back, forcing her to release me.

For a single beat Eira paused, eyes unfocused, and then she twisted over and positioned herself on all fours.

I was no longer the one in control.

She yanked her gown up, baring herself to me: slick, ruby flesh, darker around her glistening entrance.

"I will die having known true joy."

"Do you like it when I grovel for you?" she asked, looking over her shoulder. She dipped, and her round ass thrust into the air.

"Lower, darling."

She smirked and then wiggled her rump like a cat before pouncing on its prey, her breasts flattened on the ground.

"Like this?" She rested her chin on the cold, damp earth and stretched her arms forward, clasping her hands together.

"Full contrition?"

"Completely at your mercy."

Gods above.

Dropping to my knees, I palmed her cheeks and spread her wide, kneading the supple flesh—surveying my domain.

Mine.

I ducked down, laving the flat of my tongue from her clitoris to entrance, and then snaked it into her divinity.

"Cato!" She reared back.

"Remain still."

My hands slid under her bunched skirts, roaming over her back and around her waist—

"Cato," she cried out again, pressing harder into my face. "Now. I want you now."

"I see you did not acquire patience in your time away."

I straightened and throttled my cock, drawing circles in her wetness, coating my erection in her dew.

"Please, husband. I've dreamt of you every night. My flesh turned to fire with no recourse to extinguish the flames."

I lined myself up with her entrance and pushed, feeding her but a single inch.

"Whose fault is that, Eira?"

She squeezed her muscles, gripping my arousal... clenching my head so hard I fought to keep upright.

"The P-primus-King's."

Oppositional little shit.

"Mmm, I think not." I pulled out, admiring the now shining tip of my cock. "Try again. As I recall, the Primus-King took no vows to remain by my side."

"Cato, fuck me! Where is my warrior-king? Where is—"

"Give me the credit I deserve, love." I repositioned and sank my tip into her again, relishing the pop of my crown as it pressed past her entrance. She cried out the most pitiful of sounds. "Both Ambrose and Septimus would be sleeping in their graves had I not mastered that creature."

I clasped her hips, keeping them under my control as I edged her, dipping in, fucking just a little, and then retreating.

"Yes, oh, gods, yes!" Eira wailed. "Cato, no!"

My eyes fixed to the spot where we joined, and above it, the puckered flesh I adored. The little freckle next to it. The hills and slick valleys of her labia. *Flawless.*

She attempted to set a pace, but I gave no ground, rocking back when she sought more.

"I pictured their deaths, plotted the removal of their appendages; I took solace in imagining the crescendo of their combined screams. Only one sound could be sweeter... you know the song of which I speak."

I thrust hard, yanking her onto me by the creases of her hips, sheathing myself to the hilt.

"Cato!" She screamed my name, the cry an homage to our coupling. I closed my eyes to the beauty of it all.

"Yes, that very tune."

"Fuck, fuck, gods, don't stop, please." Eira rocked forward and then pushed off her knees, thick ass clapping against my pelvis.

"Take it, love; take everything."

I was done. I'd lost. She was my undoing, and I regretted nothing.

The pressure in my cock built, but I held myself steady while she fucked back onto me. I tried to imagine the most gruesome scenes, the most boring of conversations as she chased her completion, but then she shifted and reached back between her legs, her fingers splitting around my erection. She felt me slip in and out of her while grinding her clit on the heel of her palm.

Like the simpering female in one of Ambrose's absurd romance stories, my godsdamned toes curled.

"Uh-uh-ohhhhh, yes. Harder!"

Planting a foot on the ground beside her calf, I rose up and hammered down, drilling into her heat, hypnotized by the glimpse of her tit squeezing from her open neckline.

"So good, Eira, you feel so fucking incredible."

Her staccato cries rang out, her words punctuated by the beat of my thighs against her ass. "M-missed you so mu-much." Her lips parted, and the side of her face smeared through the mud and wet grass. "I'm com-coming."

She spasmed around my cock, panting, thighs rigid.

The base of my erection tingled and tightened as my load surged in thick streams. I watched her through a fog of ecstasy and drove into her once and then again. My vision distorted, and I clamped my teeth tightly—if Eira's screams didn't alert the Gaean guards, my shouts would.

Though my heart still hammered in my chest, I came back from the Goddess's plane.

"Lykksun's kneecaps," she breathed as she collapsed and rolled to her side. A magnificent smile gleamed through the dirt caked on the side of her face. "That did wonders for my mood."

My deeper laughter joined hers, and I followed her lead, going to the ground and pulling her to my side.

"Sheathe your sword before I decide to wield it again." She giggled.

"Gracious, wife, can I not cool my steaming loins before our next encounter?" I squirmed and managed, with her help, to tuck my good man back into my pants.

"You know my appetite," she murmured into my ear while turning my face to hers.

Gentle lips met mine.

"Hello, Cato." She bent her head and kissed me again. "I missed you."

A rush of warmth spread from my chest outward, and I felt the tiniest tug around my navel.

"Are you feeding off me, wife?"

She turned sheepish eyes on me.

"Just a little. I like the feeling of your energy best. It makes the æther snappy."

"Take all you need then, sweetheart." I laced my fingers through hers and brought her knuckles to my lips. "But while you sap me of my soul, explain to me how it took you all of an afternoon to turn our ice child into an unrepentant mama's boy."

That's Actually the Dumbest Thing I've Ever Heard

Ambrose

"Wake the Mantle! Alert Them, tell Them I have arrived!" My voice carried around the vestibule, startling the dawdling pilgrims from their pious gawking.

The wrinkly hag sitting behind the desk grinned widely and scurried around, all floating silks and fine robes. The tall, scaled collar she wore jangled as she ran toward me.

"Scion Monwyn! To what do we owe this honor?"

"Madam, I demand to see Their Most High—unhand me!" I shook the priestess's aged mitts from my elbow and stepped from her reach, trying to catch my breath after enduring such a scandalous affront. "I am a man Joined!" How dare she touch what belonged to another? Were these commonplace actions? "Do you not see the ring that graces my ear? The diamond and jet whale that signifies that this commodity is no longer traded upon the open market?"

"Oh, I-I, yes, Scion, of course."

She scuttled backward, duly chastised. *Serves her right.*

"Hey, Vi!" Evandr clapped the back of the priestess's shoulder like they were the best of pals. *Unmarried men are such cads.* "How's the temple been?"

The priestess broke into a surprised smile.

"Scion Evandr!" They hugged and swayed back and forth before she laced her arm through his elbow. *Shameless!* "How is Solnna? What brings you back so soon from your Assignment? We were so pleased to hear that no ill befell you during the attacks. The temple, as a whole, was beside itself with worry."

"Me? Hurt? Never." Evandr lifted a meaty arm and flexed his sizable bicep.

Ugh, how did I permit such a blatant narcissist to plunder my perfect pucker? And why the fuck am I, the prince of a noble kingdom, not being attended?

"Did I misspeak?" I slapped the top of the desk and then kicked its side for good measure. "Did I?"

All eyes drew to me. *Thank fuck.*

I whipped my head around, surveying the slack-mouthed crowd, looking for my sibling, when a hand raised.

"Ye said tah wake the Mantle." The pilgrim bowed respectfully.

I rummaged around in the pocket of my leathers.

"Dear pilgrim, reap the reward of your keen ears." I tossed the scrawny man a fat ruby and watched his eyes widen as he snatched it from the air. "Priestess! WHAT IS IT THAT I SAID?" I bellowed.

The pilgrim ran off, and the priestess sought refuge behind two acolytes. She eyeballed me over her human shield's shoulder.

"Y-you said to wake the M-mantle, Lord Scion."

"I said, wake the Mantle," I repeated with a calculated calm, no doubt filling their souls with a certain dread. I struck a power pose, feet splayed, one hand on my hip, the other over my heart.

A quick movement startled me. "Gads!"

I hopped aside to avoid a potential attack.

"Wake the fucking Mantle!" Septimus roared. The fiend yanked the dagger from his belt and sent it smashing through the decorative lamp perched on the side of the registrant's desk.

"Gammond's giant gonads." I pinched the bridge of my nose, knocking my frames askew.

My uncle was *actually* too much.

"If the Mantle does not appear within the next four minutes, I will set fire to every man, woman, and child in this temple!"

As if the desk itself responded to his intensity, flames caught and spread, eating stacks of parchments in their wake. Oil leaked and spread down the furniture's sides; blue lines of fire licked the marble floor.

My breath hitched.

The expanding pool of flame was a haunting reminder of my wife and her stunning black fire—everything pointed back to her.

"He's nether-touched!" A woman screamed.

"Demon spawn!" another yelled as they ran from the chamber.

"Fire! Alert the Mantle, call the guards!" The priestess flapped her arms above her head as pandemonium ensued. "Fire!"

Pilgrims dashed toward the entrance, and acolytes dove, attempting to save handfuls of charred documents.

"One minute remains before I melt the toddler clinging to your skirts!" Septimus stomped into a puddle of flaming oil and pointed his blade toward a terrified mother.

I waved a flippant hand in Evandr's direction. "Ugh, can you stop him? Rarely will he heed anything I say."

Evandr hopped from one foot to the other, unsure of where his allegiance lay—with Verus or his frost father.

"Oh, go on, Evan. This drama grows tiresome."

Evandr nodded and lunged for the large bowl of ink-drying sand. He tossed its contents onto the burning mess and beat down the remaining blaze with his leather-gloved hands.

"Guards! Guards!" The priestess cried as she ran, searching for solid cover.

"Had you just called them in the first place..." I blinked and inspected the ring I wore on my finger. Silver, smelted from the same chunk of ore as the one that graced my wife's hand.

The telltale sound of boots pounding out a rhythmic cadence alerted me to a new presence. The doors at the back of the chamber flung wide.

"Thank the Goddess," I prayed aloud. "But I require the *full* army. Rustle the rest from the barracks."

A bevy of red-clad soldiers tore across the marble floor, spears and blades at the ready.

"Arrest that man!" The priestess squawked from her new hiding spot behind Evandr's square bulk. She pointed a shaking finger at Septimus, who bared his teeth in her direction.

"Uncle, that is overly theatrical; do stop."

"Set your blades upon my flesh!" Septimus yelled, pounding a fist against his chest. "To my side, Evandr!"

Evandr—submissive frost boy that he was—hustled to my uncle's side, leaving the priestess unguarded. Her fearful eyes rolled wildly, like a horse spooked by a bear in the forest.

"No, no! It is I who requires—to me, I say! Commander, to me!"

A squadron of Verus guards ran at us in tight formation, their singular focus Septimus.

"Enchantress!" His battle cry reverberated off the walls of the antechamber, and his silver hair glowed gold in the light of the wall lamps, adding to his diabolical performance.

"You know what? Frankly, I am sick of him too. Put him behind bars. That's fine." The guards charged, and I stepped aside. "I swear to the Goddess, if he or Cat are in the vicinity, I am *always* the afterthought."

The struggle ensued. I could do nothing more than cross my arms and wait it out.

Oil splattered my spectacles.

"Fuck it all!" I removed them and worked to clean their soiled lenses.

"You gonna stop that?" Evandr asked, his tone tinged with alarm. He stood near me, shaking the soot from his gloves, no thought given to his peppering of my fine, fawn-colored ankle boots.

"No. Not until he ceases using that wholly unimaginative pet name for *my* wife. If they kill him—though our party will lack a decent tracker—I will never have to hear that particular phraseology again."

A guard toppled past us, falling on his ass. Another joined him, careening headfirst into the desk and crumpling to the floor.

"He trains against groups of four. Commander, send at least five in one go, and we can be done this millennium. You are wasting time that I do not have."

In my periphery, a floating cloud of crimson and ivory drew my attention.

"There you are!" I sprinted through the line of guards poised in front of my sibling, shoving them aside. "They Who are Most Exalted And Who Is The Picture of Heredity Perfection, call forth Your General, Catommandus of Basilia."

"Scion! Do not dare to lay a hand on—" Palming the face of the priestess who threw herself in my path, I tossed her aside. How *dare* she insert herself into a familial matter?

I wrapped my sibling in my arms and kissed one of Their veil-shrouded cheeks and then the other, ignoring the incensed yelps and the hiss of drawn swords.

Rayæl's soft laughter reached my ears, followed by Their long sigh.

Diminutive fists pounded on my back.

"The Mantle cannot be touched by unblessed hands!"

"Release Them at once!" Another short woman tugged on my arm.

"That is ridiculous." I bumped the aggravating gnat with my hip and sent her stumbling back. "I am a literal Scion. Whose hands are more blessed than mine? Can you point to one more blessed? Hmm?"

My slim-shouldered sibling assured Their handlers of Their safety.

"My child, release me, and tell me the reason for your sudden..." —They peered around me and then stood straight again—"... and most astonishing appearance."

They lifted a delicate, ring-covered hand, the gold and multi-hued bracelets jangling to Their elbow—the room silenced

"If only I could subdue my wife so casually," I muttered.

Turning, I made note of the technique used to *subdue* Septimus. A length of leather stretched through his teeth, pulling his head back at an unnatural angle, and both his arms were wrenched awkwardly to his sides, his elbows locked in place.

"Ensconce him in a chamber with no furniture, food, um, windows." I tapped my chin thoughtfully. "No decor... He turns everything into a projectile. Oh, and, Commander, don't hit him; he likes it. Awful business that."

The guards dragged him away, the soles of Septimus's shoes shrieking on the gleaming tiles. Already, a crew of servants hurried to clean the mess with mops and buckets.

"Scion Ambrose, Chosen One, what brings you to Verus Temple so early? Kingdom representatives are not required to present themselves for another fortnight or more. Escorts do not leave until the morrow."

The Mantle waved forward the priestesses who saw to Their comfort. I bent and rearranged the disobedient curl of the taller one and then adjusted the shoulder seams of the other's robe. *A bit of excitement is no excuse for dishevelment.*

"No. I'll be back for that later. Did you receive my request for a solo bathing chamber?"

"I did, yes."

"Good, good. Now, I must speak to my brother-lover. Order him into Your presence, please."

A priestess gasped, and I shot her a look. The Mantle's perfectly arched brows rose under Their sheer cover.

"Scion Ambrose, perhaps, another term to describe your relationship with—"

"Oh pish, silly prude. He and I share no blood, my wife *always* takes part, and the three of us are entirely monogamous—barring one or two incidents beyond my woman's control. You remember her, yes? Thick of thigh, fine of face, the most perfect, pink puss—"

"Ambrose! Let us retire to a private chamber and discuss the matter."

"Yes! A slumber party. What does Your bedchamber look like? Let us go there and make like siblings do. I'd like to—Oh dear." A priestess crumbled to the floor, and her counterpart dropped to her knees, fanning her face. "Hmmm. You Who Are All Mighty And Whatnot, I take issue with the fortitude of your employees. Why has this one wilted yet again?"

The fanner's head snapped up, an unnerving amount of malice in her sneer.

"You cannot step a single one of your ogre-sized feet into the space where the Goddess communes with—" Evandr stepped in front of her, blocking her from my sight.

Good.

"I commune while I shit, personally. Sibling, do you commune while you defecate? And though I prefer to read ledgers while breaking my fast, the evening snack is reserved for tales of romance."

"Scion, please." My sibling fluttered a graceful hand toward the grand staircase. "Let us adjourn to Devotee Mariad's office. You will find it most welcoming."

"Fine, but call forth Catommandus to attend us. Where is he? Out training soldiers?"

The Mantle's bejeweled hand settled on my wrist.

"Ambrose, General Catommandus has yet to report to his post. The temple received a missive days ago stating that a rebellion had occurred in Monwyn, causing his delay."

"A what now?"

My vision faltered as my assuredness—my unwavering trust—shattered. Doubt rose within me like the hulking head of a leviathan cresting the surf.

"Ambrose, hey man, stay calm."

I snatched Evandr by the collar and drew him to my face, my fists shaking with rage. Frost formed at the tips of my fingernails, but I ignored its becoming glitter. Evandr's eyes widened.

"Fetch my blades. Catommandus is dead to me."

CHAPTER TWENTY

STICK TO THE PLAN. THERE IS ONLY ONE PLAN. ONE I SAY!

EIRA

"You are telling me, *Birdie*, that you cannot comprehend the one thousand and four reasons that your so-called 'plan' will end in a disastrous cataclysm of doom?"

"No, Cato, I *cannot*," I mocked his overly formal tone. "And for the third time, button your shirt. Those are my goods, and I'll not have another fresh-faced Gaean stop to ask you for directions. These people have no boundaries and apparently haven't traveled further than their own doorsteps. How 'which way is the hatmaker's shop, handsome?' translates into an 'accidental' caress of your chest is beyond me. She should consider herself lucky that she now knows where to get a new, stylishly unmangled hat."

"You suffer from a wicked case of jealousy, you know."

"No, I don't." I stuck my nose in the air. "I was just hastening her visit to the hatmaker, is all. And how in the nether did you know where the shop was?"

Cato flourished his hand and bowed.

"I do my homework *and* turn it in on time."

"I'd wager that you were an insufferable child."

I did an about-face and trudged forward, running to keep pace with Larm and Amias's long-legged steps.

Cato snatched my hand and pulled me backward.

"Jealousy is my favorite shade on you, Eira. So pretty with that color high on your cheeks."

Whirling around in a twirl of baggy skirts, I pointed at Cato's bare and hairless chest. "Look here, I am not jel—"

"Here?" He cocked a brow and stepped forward, the soft skin of his sternum pressing into the pad of my finger. "Right here?" He glanced down at our point of contact.

Whew, did someone light a beacon? Maybe an evening bonfire? I glanced around, suddenly parched.

Traitorous vagina... stupid Dick Bond.

"Momma always said separation makes the heart grow fonder; she failed to mention its effect on one's genitals."

He continued to advance until my palm splayed in the warm valley of his pectorals.

"Tell me you love me," Cato whispered.

Gods alive. He devoured me with his eyes, acting as if he didn't hear the old man berating a youth about his late delivery... as if the pack of dogs barking at a flock of chicken escapees was a band of Ærta's most talented musicians.

My body sang right along with the raucous clucks.

"I... Cato." I couldn't force my hands to my sides where they belonged. Instead, deep in my enemy's territory, I scraped my nail down his chest, tracing the harpy's thick, feathered thigh to the heart clasped in her talons. "I love you like—like how the moon loves the sun when he emerges at dawn, painting her in shades of red and gold."

A warm breeze blew, sending the discarded wrapper of some vendor's fare dancing around our feet.

"Like the sun mourns the moon the minute she must go..." he replied.

"Ahem." Amias shoved himself between us, tipped Cato's head back, and peered up his nostrils. "All seems in order, but if it happens again, contact a healer," he said loudly and then lowered his voice. "If the two of you carry on as you are, you will garner suspicion."

Cato openly scoffed, and Amias pinned him with a look that said, "Shut the fuck up."

"I will reiterate this to you both. Larm does not meet the description of the original man requested by the Lead Healer—close, but not exact. If we are to pass him through the gates, we must give them no reason to inspect us closely. Currently, you," he pointed a finger in my face, "are arousing more than just suspicions."

I glanced at the front of Cato's pants. *Ope.* I nodded contritely and stepped away. Hand to my shoulder, Amias ushered me forward, and we continued our walk.

"Cato, you and Larm arrived together. You passed the inspection and were thus granted permission to serve as the tavern's new minstrel. I allowed you to tag along to acclimate yourself to the city. Do you both understand your backstories?"

"Of course I understand, Amias," Cato spat. "I may not be an Obligate, but I have more training in intrigue than the two of you combined."

I kept my face pointed forward but worked to soothe my man.

"Cato, you're worried, but we will meet every other day. I'll feed you information, and you will relay it to Momma, Pa, and Gotwig. Amias reports to the Mantle, and Yemailrys and Kymor both know I'm here. Larm will be with me; he will come to my aid if the need should arise."

I heard Cato's intake of air and the slow release of his breath. "Which is the only reason I can abide any of this horseshit plan."

Silent now, we meandered through a street lined with small shops, keeping our eyes on the massive structure ahead of us.

"The gates are just there." Amias pointed to a space between two larger buildings, one an inn and the other a restaurant that smelled of fresh yeast.

Cult Mossius took up nearly the whole sky.

The remaining rays of sunlight gleamed on the sparkling charcoal-and-jade building, which stood proud behind a stone fence that topped out right above Larm's head. A steel gate, wide open in welcome, was flanked on either side by a smiling set of guards and a red-clad—Oh! It was Troth Kymor!

I wanted badly to run ahead and greet her with a hug but stopped myself, remembering my place. I'd not seen her since Verus, and though little shadows had formed beneath her eyes, she looked hearty and hale.

"Welcome to Cult Mossius." She bowed, and her dark-blonde braids, which ended in a lovely puff at the top of her scalp, bobbed. Her warm, brown complexion was as radiant as the expression she wore.

"Our newest family members have arrived!" A shorter fellow, dressed in the robes of a priest, tapped Kymor on the back and then clicked his stylus against the parchment clipped to a board in his other hand. "Come forward then; we are pleased to have you in Gaea. Scion-Healer Amias, you are looking fit as a fiddle-leaf fig!"

Amias and the priest shared in a brotherly hug.

"Well met, Father Tor-Vale. How goes the Goddess's work this glorious eve?"

"I daresay, it goes well. We have cured the soy farmer of his rash, and Lady Beachwood's hemorrhoids no longer pain her after the birth of her well-proofed little bread bun. Ah! The jowls on that chunky little cabbage. You have never seen the likes." Tor-Vale puffed out his cheeks, and they both fell into a bout of boisterous laughter. "Now, is this charming woman the Lady Peregrine called Birdie?"

Tor-Vale bid me forward, and I performed my poor curtsy.

"Peasant hips." He squinted over his parchment, scrutinizing me closely. "Check. Let's see, um, hair the color of dried straw, eyes teal, height... not so much." He cackled. "Rather like me in that aspect. Ha, ha! Welcome, miss!"

"I'm pleased to make your acquaintance, noble sir." I performed another shitty curtsy, and the man clacked his stylus while he preened at receiving the accolade.

"Well, isn't she a delight? And let us see, the man who will join us is—"

"I am he, kind sir."

Fuck a butt in the frozen tundra!

I stared straight ahead, unable to draw breath.

Cato sauntered forward, sliding in front of Larm, chest puffed and teeth flashing in the cockiest of smiles.

"Ah! Yes." Tor-Vale said, flipping through his notes. "Dæne, formerly of Solnna. The Lead-Healer was impressed with your physique. Hmmm, hmm, mmmm," Tor-vale hummed a jaunty tune.

"As well he should be. I am a man in my prime."

If "prime" means mate-less, then yes.

I glared sidelong at Cato and caught the dismissive flick of his fingers.

"Well-muscled? Mmhmm, mmhmm, check. Spry?"

Cato fell to his back, rolled up on his shoulders, and then sprang to his feet without using his hands. He bowed to a gathering crowd and then bent over, balanced on his hands, and began performing one-armed feats of strength.

"Oh, my. *Check*!" Tor-Vale clapped to the beat of his own chuckle. "Hazel eyes..."

Cato jumped upright, sauntered over to Tor-Vale, and batted his flirty lashes.

"Hmm, well, I would call those basic brown, but the lovely golden sunburst gives them a hue some might call hazel. Check!"

Cato winked, and Tor-Vale lapsed into giggles.

Watching over her colleague's shoulder, Troth Kymor caught my eyes, serving up an expression that anyone else would read as "neutral." Knowing her, I certainly did not. In terms of personality, Kymor would be considered dry to downright standoffish, so the slight flare of her right nostril, to me, screamed, "WHAT THE FUCK IS HE DOING?" I squinted ever so slightly, wondering the same.

"Lastly, tall and slender," Tor-Vale frowned, flipping a parchment back and forth. "Scion-Healer Amias?" He clicked his tongue. "Do you think…" he trailed off, tapping that stylus and leafing through pages. "Hmmm, though I trust you implicitly, the Lead Healer will have a fit if I place the wrong male in our program. Allow me to fetch him and—"

"Father Tor-Vale!" Amid the thickening crowd, a voice called from behind us.

Nooooo, oh my Goddess.

"Magistrate Badyr! Hello, fine sir. Ah, and I see the lovely Lady Sparrow lights the eve with her smile."

The æther leapt to my throat.

Oh, fuck, fuck, fuck. This is all I need. Two spurned lovers and—fuck me—three spurned lovers—wait, do I count Larm? And a lie hanging over all of our heads.

"Indeed, she does; my Sparrow led the devotionals at prayer, and I have never been prouder to call her mine."

I felt rather than saw the couple draw closer, positioning themselves at the front of the crowd.

Think, think, think!

Cato would be sure to resort to violence if challenged. Larm would go all giant if someone threatened his Pocket… and if the guards harmed a single one of Larm's toenails, I would level this city in a matter of—

"I couldn't help but overhear your conversation. Having been at my post when these refugees were processed, I will tell you with the full authority of my station that the man you see there," Badyr pointed to Cato, and I called to the æther, channeling it to my fingertips, "is Dæne, formerly of Solnna."

My knees buckled, but I remained upright and quickly faked a sneeze to hide the lurch in my posture.

Good humans exist. They truly do.

"He lacks the accent of the southern kingdom," Tor-Vale said while walking a circle around Cato, investigating him closely. He stopped and nudged Cato's unbuttoned shirt to one side, frowning at the tattoo.

"My mother's people were Taleery, and she preferred us to speak the common language at home," Cato interjected.

Never lie when you don't have to.

My pleading eyes flicked to Badyr and then to Sparrow, who acknowledged me with the softest smile. She bowed her head.

"The Taleery warriors saw Ærta through the Great War," she said, placing a hand over her heart. "May their memories ever reside in our minds."

"That they did. That they did," agreed Father Tor-Vale. "Well, he's a fine specimen for sure, magistrate, and the new miss here certainly doesn't have the look of the Lead Healer's typical recruit either. Perhaps the Lead is branching out? Alright. Check! Thank you, magistrate; your word is as pure as the gold that caps my teeth!"

"And a fine set you have," Sparrow said, her voice full of cheer.

Badyr dipped his chin, his eyes closing briefly. "I wish the new recruit much success and an abundance of happiness."

I could have wept—I made a mental note to scour the continent for a bird-named-baby-making third for them. No wait, fuck that. My ice-for-brains husband could take up that banner; as he loved to remind us, he was overqualified in intrigue.

"Good eve, and may Mossius keep you both healthy," I replied to Badyr and Sparrow, throwing all my sincerity into my voice.

Arm in arm, they walked away, Sparrow's head resting on her Lifemate's shoulder. *Mother, keep them. Goddess, protect them.*

My rampant heartbeat slowed, just as my aggravation mounted.

What was the point in making a plan if your spouse tossed it out the window at a moment's notice? Would he continue tossing away my ideas when we were old and gray?

I chanced a look at Cato.

"For fuck's—" I snapped my mouth closed.

Shirt hanging from his shoulders, chest on display, my husband flexed his pec, sending his harpy into a dance to the beat of Tor-Vales's claps... and Larm's jigging feet.

This was my life. Those were my boys. There was no denying it.

"Ahem." Kymor cleared her throat, drawing the entertainers away from the attention of the enraptured audience.

Tor-Vale twisted around, all manner of flustered. He was a bureaucrat caught shirking his duties for fun. He settled and gave us all a sheepish grin. "Troth Kymor will show you to your lodgings."

He passed us on to the Troth.

"Welcome to Gaea," Kymor said in her flat, low-toned voice. She very deliberately opened her arms, though she stood rooted in place. I went into her embrace, and she enveloped me tightly. Her lips came to my ear. "Has Emissary Monwyn suffered an illness? Seizure, perhaps?"

I squeezed her tighter, not yet wanting the hug to end. She was my chosen sister, and together we'd shared in more traumatic experiences than pleasant ones.

"Yes. Yes, he has. An injury to the head."

She pulled from me, took a methodical step back, and exchanged places with Tor-Vale, who was rocking Cato in a snug embrace that I knew would set his teeth on edge.

You asked for this, asshole.

"Family members and friends may visit every other day following the noon bell." Kymor relayed the message to Larm and then embraced Amias with a quick squeeze.

Larm nodded and then shared in a hug with his Pocket, no doubt exchanging words I couldn't hear.

"Follow me, recruits," Kymor said.

Cato charged through the gates and walked beside the Troth, wiggling his fingers at the armed guards that lined a cobbled path. At least a dozen stood on each side, lining the way to Cult Mossius.

Between the tightly packed soldiers, I made out priests and healers turning the recently thawed soil of raised garden beds. That was dedication; the sky was nearly dark.

"The Primus-King welcomes you to Cult Mossius. He places your health and prosperity, and that of all Ærtan citizens, above all other concerns," Kymor began an obviously rehearsed speech. "As employees and recruits selected to become a part of its functioning, you are entitled to the food, medicines, and daily regimens that will ensure your time with us is productive. The couriers run from sunrise to sunrise, and if you receive a missive, respond immediately. Time is of the essence when lives are at stake."

"I'm here to clean, right?" I asked. "Who is going to send me a missive?"

Kymor stopped abruptly and turned on her heels.

"Cleanliness is important for the healers and patients alike. It prevents disease. It safeguards the frail. How would the Cult function if it were not for our devoted staff of purifiers?"

Eek. Kymor was *not* making light.

"No, yes. I understand."

She pivoted sharply, and we resumed our walk.

"Private lodgings are provided; overeating, alcohol consumption, and sexual relations are forbidden while employed. Exercise and daily outdoor activities are mandatory."

"This is my actual nightmare," I mumbled only loud enough that Cato, who'd fallen back by my side, could hear.

We reached the end of the paved path, and my anxiety spiked without warning. Yes, I'd planned for months. Yes, it had all already gone awry. But now a new course was set and the sails were unfurled.

The æther responded like a rock sinking to the pit of my stomach.

"Well met, Troth Kymor! Mossius's flame illuminates your fine countenance today. Welcome, recruits!" a door guard effused while tugging the handle of a carved wood door, inlaid with a branching tree of beaten copper and variegated green stones.

"Good evening, Callox. Tell your little ones I look forward to seeing them at the Naming celebration next week."

"I will. All four have made their guesses as to the Primus-King's daughter's name."

Kymor smiled, a practiced tilt of her lips, and walked through the door without further response, her heavy red-and-sage robes trailing behind.

I stepped over the threshold.

Welp.

Chapter Twenty-One

A Cedar Coffin? Smells Like Claustrophobia to Me

Eira

We joined Kymor, walking on the same shimmering black stone that made up Verus Temple. Unshaded lamps dotted the corridor at even intervals, casting bright wheels of light on the walls. My imagination may have gotten the better of me when picturing Cult Mossius. This was just a boring, regular, long-ass hallway.

We strolled for what felt like several minutes.

"The Cult's heart lies ahead," Kymor stated, just as a glaringly white aura appeared at the tunnel's end.

We emerged into a large atrium, at whose center an elevated brazier burned, crackling three stories above our heads. Its rectangular, white-and-gold-veined marble base was as wide as a seven-horse caravan, and it was polished to a high shine. Even more impressive was the cobweb of copper piping that snaked across the room—a dozen or more of the tubes connecting to the furnace-hot heart. Vines and greenery coiled around the metal. Some produced flowers, others hairy tendrils that draped across multiple pipes on multiple floors.

The pungent smell of mint and lavender wafted in the chamber's warm air.

"This is not at all what I expected," I whispered to Cato, who craned his neck, taking in the sight.

"Nor I," he agreed. "I pictured dark and dank cells where wizened healers worked by candlelight, poking their prey with long needles."

Kymor led our party forward.

"Cult Mossius takes the shape of a wagon wheel. The atrium in which we stand is at its center, the hub if you will, and the eight corridors that surround us are its spokes," she explained, pointing around the open chamber. "The seventh floor houses the green rooms, where medicinal plants grow year-round. The fifth and sixth are dedicated to research and experimentation. The recruits' living spaces are on the fourth floor. Patients with rare ailments have their quarters on the second and third, and the healers, priests, and practitioners reside on the first.

A sharp blast trumpeted from above, and I jumped into Cato's arms.

"Gods' balls!" I hollered loud enough to turn the heads of several people walking by.

I looked up to see steam pouring from a section of copper pipe, before a metal flap smacked back over the opening, cutting off the hot flow and horrid sound.

Kymor snorted and hid her smile behind her hand.

"Saplings!" A group chorused from the floors above. Cackles followed, and then a dozen or so arms waved at us from various balconies.

I waved back, smiling shyly at the grinning faces that leaned over the half-walls of each level.

"That happens every ten minutes or so. Come with me."

Kymor led us around the brazier's base, and my breath caught. I did not expect the back wall to be transparent. Small glass panes were a luxury, and wall-sized pieces unheard of. The closest glazier masters I knew of resided north of Solnna near the desert. Getting this massive panel here must have cost more than Ambrose's princely holdings. It boasted of immense wealth.

I pressed a hand to the glass, focusing on the room beyond.

Butterflies took flight in my stomach as my eyes beheld a twisted-wood throne sitting at the head of a table whose top was painted with a likeness of Mossius. The god's eyes were a welcoming shade of blue, and his grey hair hung to his shoulders. His face was wrinkled and wise, and his mouth was set in a serene smile.

I leaned a shoulder into Cato. "I'm guessing he and Merrias are not the kind of twins who look alike. If so, they got it all wrong."

Kymor clapped her hands, drawing our attention.

"Our illustrious leader sits in state within the room twice per week, hearing the findings and progress of his Lead and Archhealers."

A door opened behind us, and a gaggle of healers poured out, continuing a heated debate.

"When does the Primus-King take audience? How often?" I asked, probably a little too enthusiastically.

"Is there but a single entrance?" Cato's question followed close on the heels of mine.

The healers, ever curious, surrounded us, one looking at Cato through a quizzling glass.

"I am telling you, Hammont: the application of yellow wood root slowed the progression by at least two weeks."

The man twisted Cato's head and peered into his ear.

"Bah, that remains to be seen, Moll. Two subjects responding positively is a coincidence. Seventeen, and I'll pen the primer myself."

A red-faced fellow and a statuesque woman halted in their tracks and pulled out their own glasses, giving Cato a once-over.

The woman, satisfied by whatever Cato's cuticles could reveal, turned her glass on me—her lovely cobalt eye magnified to the size of a lime.

"Welcome to Cult Mossius, recruits. And if I heard your queries correctly, yes, my fair-haired friend, our gracious sovereign also makes time to listen to the complaints and compliments of servants like yourself as well as the nobles of his court. His concern is for all citizens," the woman said, proffering a hand that smelled of ammonia. I laid my fingers in her dry, cracked palm, and she inspected my nail beds. "May the Goddess guide you."

"This way to your rooms," Kymor said as the others went on their way.

We took a sharp left into the westernmost spoke and proceeded to the end of another long hallway. Kymor stepped into a small wood-paneled alcove, and Cato and I took our places behind her. It seemed a little late for prayers, but the Gaeans were a devout bunch.

"Going up." Kymor pulled a door from a hidden pocket in the wall, sealing us into a cedarwood tomb.

Immediately, I went on alert.

"What is this—Oh, Goddess!" My back hit the wall. The room jerked and moved in a syncopated pattern, starting and stopping every few seconds.

"This is not... I don't want... Open the door and let me out."

I tossed my arms out against the wall but could feel even more of the creaky movement through my palms.

"Breathe, Birdie. With me, in... and out. Good, again." Cato slipped his arm around my shoulder, and I tucked myself into his chest, closing my eyes.

"I want out. Get me out," I pleaded. Sweat beaded on my forehead, and my vision tunneled. I was locked in a moving coffin.

"It's perfectly safe, Birdie. Calm yourself. If the steam fails, we are still suspended by sturdy ropes," Kymor offered, doing her best to mitigate my panic.

My face flushed hotter, and my bowels churned. *Suspended? Over what?*

"My chest is too tight. I c-can't—"

The lift halted, shuddered, and began to move again.

"Look at me, love," Cato whispered softly. "Let me see those gorgeous eyes." His hand cupped my jaw. "Shall I give you something to occupy your mind?"

My breath came in tight, frantic pants. I tried to turn away, my body wanting to flee, but he held me firm and leaned into me, bending his head.

"My most recent fantasy involved dipping your tits in a bowl of beef gravy and licking them clean."

"Cato that's—"

"—titillating? Thrilling? Deeply arousing?"

I choked a laugh.

"Concerning."

He applied pressure to my shoulders, helping to ground me.

"To be fair, I went days without nourishment and months without you—she who sustains my spirit."

I bit down on my lip and focused on the pulsing of my æther. It recognized its person, sought to gather directly below his touch.

Kymor cleared her throat and extended a finger toward Cato.

"Dæne, I would ask that you mind your erection as we exit the lift. It has formed a noticeable tent at crotch level." Kymor steepled her fingers and held them up, not an ounce of judgment in her voice.

Lift *almost* forgotten, I sputtered a laugh.

Cato rolled his eyes and moved back, adjusting himself as he went.

"Better?" he asked.

"No," Kymor stated flatly. "It now lies crooked, drawing one's eyes to the asymmetry of your sunrise."

The lift halted with a jolt. The door opened, and a fine specimen greeted us.

"Level four."

"Thank you," Kymor nodded, and we stepped out into yet another long hallway.

The older man with ham-sized biceps pulled a long brass lever, and the lift dropped from view in a billow of steam.

"Ohhh," I inhaled deeply and was hit with a pang of nostalgia.

Cato arched a brow.

"You *would* pine for the scent of rendered whale fat."

I shrugged at his *correct* assumption. The lamps running along the walls must have recently been filled.

"Not so much pine for as occasionally long for." I hugged my arms around my waist.

"That, Birdie dear, would be the definition of pining." He chuckled and shifted closer to my side while keeping his eyes straight ahead. "One day, I will take you to your home. I want to see the ice hut where little Eira grew up and witness the light in your eyes when you show me the places you have painted in my mind."

"Trying to get on my good side?"

"Is it working?" His cheek dimpled.

"Stupid Dick Bond," I mumbled. "No. You deserve an earful, and I intend to deliver."

As we reached the corridor's middle, Troth Kymor gestured to the left and then right.

"All recruits, no matter their occupation, are housed in this hall or the one directly across the way. Prayers occur at Twin's Temple in the evenings, and dinner follows. Currently, the other recruits are dining."

We passed a dozen or so open doorways; the dark and unoccupied chambers revealed nothing of what lay within.

Kymor halted abruptly.

"Dæne, your room is to the right, and Birdie's is to the left." She reached through the leftmost doorway, twisted a lamp's knob, and illuminated a tiny but serviceable room. "Follow me."

"Where are the doors?" I asked, running my fingers along a seam where I thought, like the lift, one was hidden.

"There are no doors." Kymor turned in her stiff-necked manner. "There is nothing that occurs here that should be kept secret."

"No?" I dropped my voice, "Because he snores and grinds his teeth loud enough to raise the deceased." I hitched a thumb at Cato. He lifted a shoulder, unable to deny the accusation.

Troth Kymor shooed us into the room's furthest corner and then poked her head out over the threshold. Once satisfied no one was around to overhear, she turned back to us.

"Yemailrys filled me in on the occupation change, though hurriedly. But why are you both here in the first place? Do you seek asylum from attacking conjurers? Is Monwyn under siege?" Never one to beat around the bush, Kymor stood at attention, her hands firmly pressed to her sides.

"We don't have the hours it would take to explain it all. But please trust me when I say it's important."

"Of course it is. The Mantle's word is above all others. I will move messages between you and Scion Lok if need be. He is not appointed to the palace or temple and has the freedom to come and go more readily. He will see intel to Verus."

I inclined my chin and didn't bother telling her that I had a Gotwig and a frost giant at my disposal. Given the tension in her voice when saying *conjurer*, I didn't think it would go over well.

"So, no doors?" I pressed, both incredulous and anxious at the thought of swapping secrets in the open.

"Birdie, focus on the larger issue," Kymor said, popping her head back into the hall and then returning.

"Right, of course." I scrubbed my hands over my face. "Wait, where are Lok's duties if not the palace or Cult Mossius?"

"The Primus-King found him too surly for a front-facing placement. He oversees waste management."

"Shitty attitude, shitty job?" I quipped, remembering our rather terse interactions at Verus.

Cato's mouth twitched; Kymor's did not.

"The city of Mynder has never been more orderly or cleaner. He has taken to the post enthusiastically. Shame on your judgment. Again, focus."

I stood straighter but couldn't help shuffling my feet, thoroughly chastised. She was right, of course.

"We, the collective Obligates, will work to provide a simple means to an end."

Uh, oh. I nodded, noting the deeper message of her words. Cato, cleverer than most, understood as well. I didn't need to look at him to know the exact level of scowl he'd wear.

"I assumed that the *end* would be carried out by others."

Kymor scoffed.

"That was an ignorant assumption, Emissary. She is the Mantle's servant first and foremost."

I reached out to steady Cato.

"She is my—"

Kymor, unknowing of or uncaring of the escalating situation, raised the flat of her palm directly in front of Cato's face.

"Sir. You are not permitted to infringe upon the directives given by They Who Serve the Mother Goddess."

I moved toward the bed as Cato's accusatory gaze seared into the side of my face. Would it be problematic to use my womanly wiles to distract him? Yes, but if I had to open-door fuck him to calm him, well, it was my lot in this life as his Fated Bond.

"If you are looking for simple, Miss *Birdie* may not be your best choice—she and the word *subtle* should never be uttered in the same breath."

It took every speck of my willpower not to point out that he had indeed just uttered both.

"Miss Birdie?" Cato hissed, his voice barely above a whisper. "When did you plan to share *that* particular tidbit?"

The tension in the room bore down on me like a polar bear pursuing its prey.

"I was not planning to share it." I met Kymor's eyes, not daring to look at my irate spouse.

"That is sensible, Birdie." Kymor nodded. "Dæne, you are not supposed to be here; thus, operational security precludes her sharing it. A man of your educational caliber should recognize that."

I reached out to Cato and grabbed his forearm with both hands. I felt the flex and release of his tensing fists. Kymor stood as coolly as ever, oblivious to the fact that Cato had no qualms about dispatching members of any persuasion, he, she, or they.

"Your ignorance matters little. Your presence here is of no assistance, even if we had been forewarned. Dæne, formerly of Solnna, signed on as a research specimen, and Birdie as a purity recruit. Your paths may cross, but I do not suspect it will be often."

Cato gestured to the lack of a door, and a few moments later, I picked up on the chatter of an incoming crowd.

"Ah, they have returned." Kymor stepped into the hall and flagged the group down. "We will speak again. Your respective ministers will dole out your duties." Kymor bowed low. "Raina, Alder, your new recruits have arrived."

CHAPTER TWENTY-TWO

THE PRIMUS-KING HAS A TYPE: PRETTY AND IGNORANT

CATO

One primary target. Man: slim, tall, unbalanced gait, no visible armor or obvious training. Items to render a man lifeless, twenty-seven within arm's reach. Stabbing implements: Three glass cosmetics bottles. Two metal combs, one wide-toothed and the other slim. Five sharpened styluses and a single metal nail file. Tools of strangulation: Two leather belts. Two sets of braided laces. Four hair ribbons, silk. Pocket watch with a sturdy chain on the desk. Bludgeons: forearm-sized candle holder. Copper drinking vessel. Marble figurine of Merrias and Mossius above the bed. Weapons on my person? My godsdamned hands if that fucker doesn't cease salivating over my wife.

"Dæne and Birdie, this way—make the acquaintance of ministers Alder and Raina."

"Oh my, we don't often see the thick of hip in the Cult." The thin, willowy, and passably attractive minister squeezed Eira's biceps and then held both of her cheeks in her palms. I dug my nails into the skin of my hands. "I'm Raina, and I oversee the upkeep of our patient chambers. Alder, feel her; the softness is delightful, in truth."

She dropped a hand to Eira's hip, running it over the swell of her backside.

This is how we would be discovered. My envy, the downfall of Verus Temple.

"Healthy tone despite the extra mass." Sandy blond, handsome, and full of youthful vigor, the male minister swept his cursed paws along Eira's waist, nodding in agreement. "And teeth?"

My wife bared her teeth in an exaggerated smile, and then the man hooked his finger over her lip and tugged.

I blacked out temporarily. *Play your role, Cato. Fucking play it!*

I took a single step backward, ensuring I could not snatch either minister by their graceful, swanlike necks.

"A strong set and no evidence of thinning gums."

"Strong indeed." Eira nodded animatedly despite the fucking finger in her mouth. "Raised on pork and leafy greens." She patted her belly and then struck her backside.

Leafy greens, my ass. Her ass, rather. Fucking nether. Now I'm sporting a hard-on.

Minister Alder dropped to a knee and grasped Eira's ankle, squeezing it while working his way up. "Bend at the joint, please."

He hinged her leg, raising and lowering it, and then had the mannish audacity to hike her skirts. *My limbs. My legs. My ass. My wife.*

"An overeater, to be sure, sedentary perhaps, but quite healthy." Raina palpated the dense thigh muscle of the "country girl." "No evidence of muscular atrophy."

Raina squatted low and shook the silk of Eira's inner thigh, watching her lushness move and bounce.

My nails breached the skin of my palms.

"Yes, sir, mountains of laundry and farm stuff, day in and day out."

"Pffftt." The only "farm stuff" Eira partook in was riding my cock.

My flippant exclamation drew the attention of the group, but Eira lifted her skirts higher, retaking command of their observations. They continued groping her, and she just danced her scrumptious self around like a—

"I am Dæne, formerly of Solnna. I put myself forward for your examination!" I haughtily proclaimed, stepping between my woman and the seeking hands of the offensive ministers. "Which of you oversees the research specimens, of which I am one?"

I shrugged off my shirt and tossed it to the floor, catching the eyes of a few others milling about and doing their best to hide their eavesdropping.

"Dæne is a man born to lift and toil." I could have vomited, referring to myself in the third person. Instead, I fisted my hands behind my back and flexed like that narcissist Ambrose any time he caught his reflection in a glass pane, mirror, or highly polished brass. Glancing down at the two squatting molesters, I flashed my most winning smile—these foolish dimples alone could send Eira into orgasm.

And apparently many others. *Ugh.*

"That would be me. I am Minister Alder, and indeed, the Lead Healer has sent us another quality sample."

Raina elbowed Minister Alder, and they both rose, their heads reaching well above mine.

"Alder, he is shorter than the last four, but let me guess..." The woman eyed me with a look of derision. "You can run a mile. You can jump high. You can lift heavy things and move them from point A to point B, but you've never once successfully lifted a book to your face?"

I own more books than you have hairs, woman of darkness.

"Now, Raina!" Minister Alder admonished while chuckling through a simpering grin. "The Primus-King has a type. The subject can't help it if he—"

"Have *you* read a book, Birdie?" Raina made a show of looking around her counterpart and brushing a steel-gray tendril of hair over her ear.

"Two!" Eira effused. "The letter-teaching book and *The Children's Guide to Growing Up Gaean.*"

Raina applauded as one might for a child who had babbled their way into forming some garbled semblance of an actual word.

I hated them. All of them.

"Oh my, you are well learned then; it will take you far, Birdie. With intelligence and that unique shade of hair, you must have been the catch of the countryside."

"I received an offer of Joining just yesterday!" Eira threaded her fingers together and rose on her toes. She was so fucking adorable that I wanted to whisk her away to a remote mountaintop where only we resided.

"And you refused the suitor?" Minister Raina looked authentically curious.

"Mmhmm, I want to be a lady's maid for a fancy Gaean and live in a fancy Gaean house. My Auntie Jilly says this is how to make my dream come true. Not to Join with the first handsome man to tie me down."

Handsome? I added the magistrate to my mental dossier. I'd present her with his fucking face if she found it so attractive.

Raina reached beyond me and stroked her elegant fingers down the side of Eira's cheek.

"Auntie Jilly is right. We will teach you the way of discipline and structure. Do as you are bidden, Birdie, and we will see you rise to the ranks of Lead Purifier... or even Chatelaine, the keeper of the house keys."

"No, I can't even imagine!"

My clever wife had them eating from her palm; her innocent act was as charming as a puppy tumbling over its own paws.

"Give yourself over to my instruction, and we will see it so." Minister Raina winked, and Eira giggled... giggles that should be mine. "This is not an easy life, Birdie, but one with a higher purpose."

"Fellas, I see you lurking." Minister Alder clapped twice, and those who'd been ducking in and out of the chambers behind him jumped to attention and lined the walls, standing like the poorest excuse for soldiers. The minister threaded his arm through my elbow, and my stomach soured at the contact.

Loathing the Gaean penchant for overfamiliarity, I forced myself to relax, to slacken my muscles, but kept my mind sharp.

"Recruits, allow me to introduce Birdie and Dæne. Our new lad Dæne has renounced the Solnnan kingdom and shunned his father, who was found to have harbored a conjurer," Minister Alder spoke the last word in a low and haunting tone.

"Oh, my gods!"

"That's fucked up, bro!"

Alder gestured for quiet before continuing.

"Dæne was forced to deal the final blow that ended the conjuring scourge, and our Primus-King granted him asylum and pardoned the crime—no, not crime, the justice he brought about. He will join the Brotherhood Research Experimentation."

"Aww yeah, Brotherhood!"

Three men pumped their fists into the air and hollered like a bunch of fools betting on a race.

"Brohos, unite!"

My list of loathing was running out of room.

"Take him into the fold, fellas, and show him the ropes, eh?" The minister chuckled and stood to the side, extending his twig-like arm toward my new *brothers*. "Enjoy your time, Dæne; you've earned your spot in the Cult."

I'd enjoy wrenching your shoulder from its socket.

I spared a glance at Eira and swallowed back the lump gathering in my throat. Would walking away from her always feel like reopening a nearly mended wound?

"It was nice meeting you, Dæne. I'm sure we'll talk again." She offered me her hand.

My every impulse was to slit throats, sneak out, and never return—but Eira. She bared her soul to me through that glance, and as I took her smaller hand into my own, it was as if I could hear her thoughts. *Trust me, husband. Have faith in me, Cato.* No Brain Bond was required for me to understand that my belief in her was necessary to repair our damaged trust. She graced me with a soft smile, and I shuttered my eyes, wanting it to be the last thing I saw before being taken from her.

I steeled myself, nodded, and forced my legs to step into the fold of a back-slapping mob of men who smelled like they'd bathed in concentrated sandalwood oil.

"Alright, man! Let's find your uniform. I'm Rollo."

Rollo, a pale man-child with a mop of red curls, smacked my back and then took my hand, forcing it into some elaborate, bespoke handshake.

Instant hatred.

I forced my lips to curl into a smile, fervently hoping that it would come across as wholesome and not demented. Granted, if the man kept stealing glances behind my head, it may not matter.

"New bro!" The next two men I encountered jumped into the air, smacking their chests together.

I contemplated murder-suicide.

"Come on, man, let's go!"

They hooked their arms over my shoulders and steered me away from she who mattered most in my world, ushering me into what I was sure would be my personal nether.

As we navigated the hall, I flicked my eyes to the right and left, memorizing the chambers and faces we passed, cataloging and storing any oddities that struck me.

"We all wash together and catch up on the day, ya know? Make a plan for tomorrow, think about how we can improve, and give a hundred and fourteen percent to the cause."

"A hundred and fourteen, you say? Out of...?" I let the question linger amid blinking eyes and blank expressions.

One man, who had not deigned to give me his name, came to stand in front of me and placed both of his disgustingly soft-skinned palms on my naked shoulders. *I might actually upheave.*

"Yeah, man, we gotta be better than the best, ya know. Above even the *most* beyond, bro. It's why we're here." The young man, whose hair sat in an artless mass, knotted atop his head, peered into my eyes as if he held the knowledge of all Ærtan philosophers combined.

I stared back, visualizing choking him out with his own topknot.

"You got real pretty eyes, Dæne."

"And you have very handsome... fingers."

He punched my shoulder, and we resumed our walk.

At the end of the recruits' hall, we took a sharp left and then proceeded through a set of mahogany double doors.

My vision clouded.

The space we entered reminded me of the hot springs in my holdings of Basilia. Heavy with steam and smelling of herbs and astringent, we stepped into the cloud, which dissipated some as we neared a large pool. I let my eyes roam. The copper piping stretched the length of the ceiling, and three smaller pools were situated toward the back of the room, sunk into a floor of sage-green and sky-blue glass tile.

Snap!

I cocked my head to the side, sure that I had imagined the crack of a towel against my ass.

"Get naked, bro!"

"Last one in takes Wren to the Naming ceremony!"

Three presumably grown men raced to strip out of their ankle-length tunics of wheat-colored wool, revealing perfect replicas of the barely-there undergarments Eira preferred—two triangles tied at each point. With not an ounce of shame, they pulled said ties and tossed the garments upon the wet floor. I was appalled—wholly disturbed.

"Come on, Dæne. It's alright, man. The Goddess made you, brother, four inches or twelve. If it gets the job done, there's no shame. Amiright?"

This man, I would murder swiftly if only to silence his mouth sooner. With deep-brown skin, matching eyes, and hair in a series of tight braids, his slim form put me in mind of some Monwyn men before their tenure in the mines. With a smack to Rollo's toned ass, he launched himself into the air, pulled himself into a tight ball, and plunged into the pool.

Droplets of displaced water rained down my cheeks.

Vulgar children.

"Junnie is right. You were chosen, man. Be proud," stated a honey-blond with a similarly lean musculature, all long limbs and sinewy arms. "Chosen, bro... chosen." He bowed his head in solemnity.

Rollo and whoever the fuck the last one was ran across the floor and dove headfirst into the central pool. They emerged, flinging their heads back, showering a cascade of water onto the floor.

The nether. This actually is the nether.

"Dæne, Dæne, Dæne!" they chanted.

I disrobed, folded my clothing into perfect squares, and set them far from the trajectory of their idle hair flings.

"My man! You got a hog. Girth over span." Rollo jumped up, attempting to dunk Junnie under the water. The red hair that peppered his chest was a startling contrast against the ivory of his heavily freckled skin. "Many a lady likes it that way."

"How would you know? Huh?" Junnie laughed, attempting a shoddy shoulder takedown.

I placed my hands on my hips and sneered down at the three hardly-men staring at my dick. The fuck was wrong with today's youth?

"Nice tatts. The ladybird's got good tits," said the unidentified third, walking closer, squinting his eyes, and reaching out like he was fixing to touch my person. "Boobs built to nurture, bro."

They shared a laugh.

Perhaps my wife had been correct in her assumption of my inability to carry out a mission where she was concerned. Never did I think to encounter *three* Ambrose-level simpletons.

"Naw, Junnie, his thigh snake's where it's at. Snakes, man, they, like, keep down the vermin population, ya know? They do the Goddess's work so bros don't gotta."

"Yeah, man, you're right, brother. Snakes are good for the earth and stuff."

One... two... breath... three... this works for Eira... four and five...

A stream of cold water struck the middle of my chest and puddled at my feet.

The triad laughed, splashing each other for sport.

My eye twitched. I would throttle the miscreants and leave their bodies floating until they bloated with—

"You wrestle, bro?"

Another splash hit me squarely on the crotch. Cocking my head to the side, I studied the presumptuous young man.

"Yes, Rollo, yes, I do."

I dove, aiming for his neck.

Chapter Twenty-Three

Like, Your Time Will Come, Bro.

Eira

"The uniform of the domestic. Keep it clean, keep it starched; you are in the service of the Primus-King, and he is first and foremost a man who prizes organization."

Minister Raina handed over a folded uniform of lime-green linen on which sat a pair of half-boots and an apron that looked as if it could stand on its own.

I took the bundle and ran a finger over the stiff fabric.

"Beeswax keeps the fabric watertight and easier to clean." Minister Raina sat on the small bed that ran the length of my chamber's far wall. It would accommodate a man taller than Cato, but Ambrose or Allaine would be hard-pressed for comfort. A thick woolen blanket was turned down to reveal sheets with the sheen of a recent press.

"Wow! The city-dwelling Gaeans are so smart," I gushed, knowing full well that we used the same waxed sheets to seal jars and keep foodstuffs fresh back in Nortia.

Raina folded back the voluminous sleeves of her dark-emerald robe, revealing a tight gray undertunic and a wealth of silver and malachite bracelets on both wrists. She winced as she shifted.

"You've much to learn, Birdie. You are an empty bowl, ready for me to fill with know-how. Go on then, don your nightslip; you'll find it in the chest. As you change, I'll tell you of your placement."

She pointed across the room to three drawers, nestled beneath the wardrobe.

"You are assigned to the fifth floor, Oak Hall. In the morning, you will report for duty and check in with each healer in your assigned area to inquire about their needs. There might be vials to clean, floors to scrub, or sheets to change. It is of the utmost importance that you are diligent in your duties and pay careful attention to every detail. If you make a mistake, immediately send me a missive by courier. Delayed communication costs lives."

I nodded in response while opening the first drawer. It was full of lotions and stockings, a wicker basket of tinctures, and thick woolen pads.

"For your menses, cramping, headaches, and stomach ailments. You will also find a daily regimen to keep you in tip-top form. Those nine vials—take a capful before each meal."

Nine?

I tugged on the second drawer and found it stocked with undergarments. I turned. "Do city Gaeans wear chest supports?"

She scoffed.

"No, not at all. The droop of one's bosom is a testament to a life lived."

"And the chafe of one's nipples?" I countered.

Raina pulled a face and then a glowing smile lit her from within. I wondered at her age. Her skin said late thirties; her hair, the color of a freshly forged blade, late forties.

"They will acclimate in due time. However," she pointed to the third drawer, "wear the tightest of your provided slips. The blend of silk and linen will keep you comfortable. Go on now." Minister Raina leaned back, closing her eyes as if to catch a few moments of rest.

She rubbed her temples.

"How old are you, Birdie?"

"Twenty and seven, minister."

"Nearing the end of your prime." She blinked open sapphire-blue eyes. "Are you sure this is the life you wish to pursue?"

With the most innocent look I could muster, I bent, grabbing the hem of my gown, and twisted as I tugged it over my head, covering myself with my elbows. I could give a shit about who saw my breasts, but it would sell my chosen role of simple country girl—which I found both funny and absurd. Why did people think that growing up secluded made you prudish or less intelligent? Working on farms and growing one's food took smarts and physical endurance... And you saw all kinds of animals locked in their mating dances.

"Minister Raina, will we truly see the Primus-King?" I wrestled on a sleeveless mauve slip and turned back around. "I won't know how to act."

"We will. Do you know the protocol when he walks by?"

I procured the chair from the writing desk, propped up the minister's legs—much to her surprise—and sat next to her on the bed. I'd glimpsed her swollen ankles as she'd stretched her feet.

"I don't; please tell me. I don't want to mess this up."

Raina stifled a yawn.

"As he makes his inspection, he will acknowledge each of those in his employ. Your palms should rest lightly on his elbows, and his divine hand will be laid upon your heart. Your bodies should *never* touch, as such closeness is reserved only for his wives and children."

"I fear I'll pass out and fall straight to the floor if he so much as nears me." I fluttered a frantic hand in front of my face. "Oh, gracious. When is the next inspection?"

I needed all the information I could get, but being close enough to embrace the man would be far too risky—blonde hair and brows wouldn't be enough to avoid recognition.

"Hmmm, between his youngest daughter's Naming celebration and entertaining foreign guests, he is sure to be busy. Normally, it would be every four days."

"When was he here last?" I grabbed her hand and squeezed it as if overcome by anxiety instead of revulsion. I looked up, making my eyes large, and allowed my lip to quiver.

Minister Raina's brows furrowed.

"The day before yesterday. Birdie, you are a woman grown. The Primus-King is but a man. A powerful and wealthy man, but one who acknowledges the importance of even the smallest country mouse."

"Minister, I just don't know if I'm cut out for—"

"Birdie." She laughed, and her rosy cheeks dimpled. "Gaea's earthly father knows nothing but love." She filled her chest and slowly exhaled. "It's that nasty Lead Healer to worry over. He's as crotchety as they come but leaves us be if all runs smoothly. He lives to impress the Primus." She rolled her eyes.

"And he looks like a frog," I whispered.

Raina's cackle bounced off the walls. I tossed my hands over my mouth in mock embarrassment.

"Birdie!" a masculine voice yelled from the hall. "Hey, Birdie?"

The minister tossed her feet from the chair and shot up straight, squaring her shoulders as three young men, one smug-looking Cato, and two young ladies squished into the room, forming a practiced ring of bodies. All eyes were on me, and feeling smothered, I tried unsuccessfully to inch my way to the door.

"Lookin' good, Raina," one of the young men said, winking at the minister in clear suggestion. Raina was not impressed.

"*Minister* Raina, to you, Brooks."

"Ouch," replied the man, who then stabbed a make-believe knife into his chest before falling to his knees and letting his tongue loll out. His baggy, oatmeal-colored tunic pooled around his legs.

The other men wore the same, and the ladies, nightshifts like my own.

"Raina, you didn't tell us Dæne was, like, a three-time Solnnan wrestling champion." This particular man, with damp hair flowing to the middle of his back, tossed himself on my bed and stretched out, propping his feet on the wall.

"He twisted Rollo into a knot. Flipping hilarious. His ankles were over his head!"

Raina, stance rigid and gaze haughty, thinned her lips. "Birdie, I leave you in the incapable hands of the *Brotherhood*." She grimaced. "I will check on your progress tomorrow."

With that, she fled the room, and my eyes immediately found Cato, who was fighting to soften a sneer.

"Yeah, Birdie, bro, I, like, showed Rollo what was up in the domain of wrestling artistry... and, um, stuff." With his most serious expression, my husband clasped his hands and made his pecs hop up and down.

I lost my composure—all of it—and descended into a cackling fit.

Cato tilted his head to the side, his mouth falling open in disbelief.

"Why are you, like, laughing, Birdie, bro?" He seized me around the waist and pulled me to his side. "You wanna have a go with the champion?" He dipped like he was preparing to hoist me over his head.

"No!" I shouted, my giggles filling the room. "Who are your new friends, Dæne? Introduce me, you mannerless ogre." I wiped the tears from my eyes and squeezed my legs tight, fearing a laughter leak.

Cato swung around and pointed first to the man lounging on my bed.

"Like, this is Junnie; he's Nortian, says it's real cold and stuff up there, like, northward." He pointed to another with a set of intricate braids. "My man Brooks is Gaean; he started here a few months ago, and this..."—Cato paused and then began a poorly executed series of hand clasps and elbow bumps with the most appetizing redhead I'd ever seen—"... is Rollo, my, uh, new bro."

"You'll get the shake soon, man," Rollo assured Cato, his pale-blue eyes alight with hope and encouragement.

Oh, my Goddess, they are so adorable. The way he encouraged Cato immediately endeared him to my heart.

"Hey, this is my girl, River." Brooks dropped to the ground, pulling the petite brunette down with him, settling her into his lap. "We're a perfect match." His arms came around her, and in his loving countenance, you could see how much he cared for the woman.

"Hi, Birdie. You'll love it here." River snuggled him back and placed a peck on Brooks's chin. "Wait, are you research or purification?"

"Purification," I replied, taking note of the green line of ear studs that began at the top of her ear and ended at her lobe.

"Well then, you may love it a little less." She looked me up and down, not in a mean way, just curious, and then laid her head back on Brook's shoulder, gliding her lips across his skin. River was a woman besotted. I recognized myself in her. "Robyn is domestic, too." She nodded to the tall and extremely muscular woman who had since joined Junnie on the bed. She finger-combed the long strands of his hair over her lap while she cradled his head.

"Bird name!" I shouted, bouncing in Cato's arms. I pointed to Robyn and then to myself.

The room erupted into easy laughter.

I smiled along, all the while adding her to my "potential Badyr and Sparrow spouse" list.

Cato joined Junnie and sat on the floor, propping his back against the set of drawers. He crooked his finger and winked.

Heat flared between my legs, and the walls of my passage thickened and throbbed. *How does the blink of an eye send my æther spiraling?* I sat next to him, demurely tucking my legs under my rear. *Oh, boy.* One time, after three months, had not been enough to quell my desires.

"So, like, brothers, debrief me of the daily operations and functioning of Cult Mossius... and stuff, like, brother."

I slipped the most Trothy of Troth masks over my face. Cato's misuse of the young folk's slang, coupled with his highly formal, princely speech patterns, would end this charade before it truly began—my laughter would be the giveaway.

Junnie reached across Robyn, plucked a corked bottle of ink from my desk, and tossed it into the air, catching it as it descended. He repeated the action once and then again. "Yeah, okay, so like, the biggest thing is we honor the Goddess, ya know?"

"Yeah, man, I know, the Goddess." Cato struck his chest twice and then kissed his fingers before saluting the sky.

I bit my cheek until I tasted iron, physically having to stop the donkey bray of a guffaw building in my throat.

The brothers followed suit, serious and entirely sober. Chest tap. Kiss. Salute.

"The Goddess." I shoved a knuckle into my mouth and bit down hard while nodding and pointing to the sky with my other hand.

"We wake in the morning and hone our bodies with powerful and explosive training." Rollo raised his tunic, showing off a delicious set of abs. "Then we, like, nourish ourselves with the finest of foods, because that's the same as, like, a prayer to the Divine Twins when we, like, take in the food of the earth and stuff."

"Indeed—and stuff," Cato replied.

"Divine Twins. Yep." I raised a finger and pointed to the ceiling once again while biting down even harder. Cradle above, please let them think my tears are an emotional display of piety!

Cato placed an arm over my shoulder and twirled a strand of my hair around his finger, tugging a little too tightly. It helped to center me and, at the same time, allowed me to lean toward him without appearing overfamiliar.

"Yeah, man. And then we head to research. Sixth level, Amethyst Hall. Some days are tough, man, but like, you're strong, Dæne."

"So strong, bro. Look at my veins." Cato pumped his forearm.

"Like, oh my gods, so strong," I said while squeezing my elbows together and pushing up my chest. Whether they thought I was mocking him or overcome by his physical charms, they'd be right. Arm veins. So gross, so alluring.

"Then we go to dinner and prayers, 'cause true health starts here, bro." Junnie chimed in while he patted his heart. Robyn rescued my bottle of ink and then went to work gathering Junnie's hair into a tail. "Then it's back here to our girls." He kissed the inside of Robyn's wrist. "Best part of my day."

"So, about that," Cato said, tugging my arm across his stomach and hugging it close. "How strict is the 'no fornication' policy?"

River sat up, eyes earnest. Her black coils sprang softly around her cheeks. "Extremely. We guard our purity until we are Joined. I heard two recruits were caught last year and got kicked out of the kingdom with nothing but their names. Stripped them down, took them to the border, and set them on the highway to fend for themselves." She shuddered, her thin shoulders collapsing inward.

"Mouth stuff is fine though," Rollo, the freckled beauty, said, his pouty lips pulled down forlornly. "If you've got a girl."

Oh dear.

I crawled away from Cato and held my arms wide, just as Ambrose would have done for me. The hurt in Rollo's kind eyes gutted me.

My nightshift snapped tight, and I was pulled backward just as Rollo neared.

Cato shook his head at the man but said nothing.

"Man, your day will come, Rollo. You gotta be, like, open to the cosmos and stuff," Brooks said.

Rollo inhaled deeply and looked off into the distance, his glacier-blue eyes gone dim.

"To bed!" A voice hollered from the hall. "All recruits to bed!"

Like a Cato-trained battalion, the recruits hopped to business.

Before he stepped across the hall, Cato turned to look back. He formed a little heart with his hands just as the lamps dimmed.

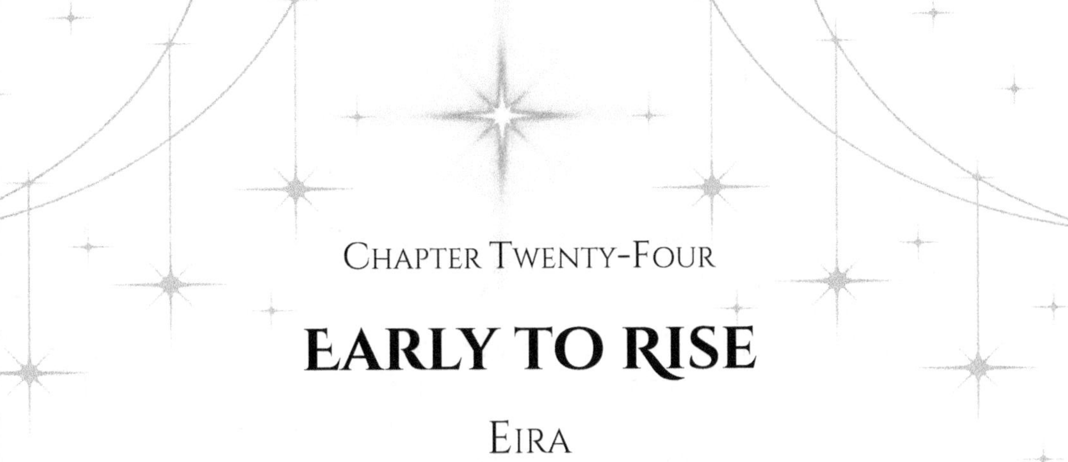

CHAPTER TWENTY-FOUR

EARLY TO RISE

EIRA

"**R**ecruits to the floor!"

My eyes snapped open.

"Where am I? Right. Gaea. Fuck it's early. No problem. I can do this." I talked to myself, hoping it would keep my drooping lids from closing once again. "Get up, lazy girl." I tore off the sheet. "You're a strong gal, energetic, and—eeek!"

Cato jolted awake when I stepped on his face.

"Morning." He caught my foot, kissed its arch, and then crawled on all fours, speeding toward his room like a baby making a break for a plate of forbidden sweets.

A quick "I love you; be safe" floated back to me.

The corridor lamps illuminated shortly after.

"Uniforms on, hair bound!" Another shout issued from the opposite end of the hall.

A recruit bearing a tray stacked with paper-covered parcels and a basket of bottles stepped into my room. "Break your fast, know the Goddess's love."

"Thank you." I took the packaged fare and a drink and turned quickly to dress.

The glaringly lime-green tunic that was to be my uniform covered me from chin to right above my ankle. I was used to hems that hit the floor, so seeing my boots felt strangely out of place. The garment fit closely to my chest and flared from the underbust before dropping gently over my hips. Though the fabric was airy and light, the tunic buttoned tightly at the wrists and neck. I might not boil, but I *would* asphyxiate. I grabbed a belt and cinched it at the smallest part of my waist, and then wrapped a ribbon around my head, fashioning it into a bow that sat directly atop my crown.

"This is your quarter of an hour warning, recruits!" The mystery herald bellowed, sending me into a panic.

Food. Eat. Go.

Biting into a buttery biscuit into which two fried eggs, a wealth of salty greens, and a slice of sharp-tasting cheese had been sandwiched, I applauded the cook, wherever they may be. I chased the fare with... I didn't know what the nether it was. The drink was fizzy and tangy but not at all like the Solnnan or Gaean wines I'd tasted.

"To your posts!" The herald shouted again, followed by a multitude of fast-moving footsteps.

I popped my head out the door, and Robyn signaled to me as she headed toward the lift.

I followed, scurrying to catch up, dodging the other bodies amassed in the hall.

"Come on, Birdie, I'm on the same floor, Birch Hall."

We crowded into the lift, and just as the last man stepped on and squished against me, the damn thing noticeably sank.

Breathe... breathe, breathe... You are a demon puff. You fly. This is fine!

Fingers threaded through mine and squeezed.

"You'll get used to it. I promise," Robyn whispered.

I nodded but covered my eyes with both our hands.

The door parted amid a flurry of activity. Healers ducked in and out of rooms, some showing the telltale signs of having been awake throughout the night, others as chipper as a coffee-fueled Troth Richelle.

"Oak is that way; see the leaf?"

I looked in the direction she pointed. "Sure do. Thank you, Robyn."

She hurried to the right, waving at another group of recruits. I walked toward an arched threshold adorned with an oblong *thing* with drooping lobes, praying that the beaten copper showed the correct form of vegetation. In the center of the atrium, I did a quick spin and made note of the other leaves above each doorway. The only one I could identify with certainty was the needles of a pine... which I didn't think should count as a leaf at all.

I found my hallway and stood, slightly stupefied as others moved decisively toward their destinations.

"Shit!" I started as a burst of screeching steam released somewhere above me.

"Sapling!" shouted another recruit, who smiled and saluted as they jogged by.

"You've arrived. Do not dawdle."

I bobbed a curtsy to the white-haired person in an apron similar to mine. Beneath his, though, he wore a basic shirt of natural linen.

"Pardon me, healer, it is my first day on the—"

"We've no time for formalities. Lady Haycroft is in the throes again. Clean the vessels quickly and dip each in witch hazel. Return them to her side. Go."

I was halfway through another curtsy when the healer pointed impatiently at one of the many unmarked doors. His stern expression sent me darting through.

The smell hit me like an avalanche.

I doubled over and vomited, the mess splattering over the pristine marble floor.

"I'm s-so sorry, my dear," came the pained voice of the sunken-faced Lady Haycroft. I took in her glassy eyes and the sickly pallor of her skin.

I heaved again.

"Now, here, Lady, there is nothing to apologize for." The healer entered the room, rushing to his patient's side. "Your body and its functions are nothing to be ashamed of."

Choking back embarrassment and burning bile, I glanced around the chamber until my eyes landed on the same style of spigot and hose that Hester had used in her room. A large marble basin stood positioned below it, and a neat row of bottles stood above. All were labeled clearly: ammonia, soap, vinegar, and witch hazel. Linen towels, a mop, a broom, and a bristled brush hung from a series of wooden pegs to the right of the wash station.

I dashed to the sink, wetted some towels and—

"Careful, girl! It comes out boiling!"

The flow washed over my hands, and I faked a flinch, waving my arms in the air as if to cool them. Heat didn't affect me like it did others, and my lack of reaction would be enough to garner doubt, especially to the observant. I slung the towels into a bucket, grabbed the mop, and made haste in cleaning up my mess before collecting a stack of shallow bowls and soiled vessels.

"Y-you shouldn't have to do this, Healer Richmonde. I am ashamed for you to see me." Lady Haycroft sniffled, and the healer dabbed at her tears.

"Not at all. Your focus should be comfort, nothing more. Don't your boys visit today?"

I listened while scrubbing, stopping every other dish to press my face into my shoulder as another bout of dry heaves wracked my body.

"Never do they show, healer, but that is the way of things when we age, is it not? It's for the best—better to spend my last days here and leave them only the good memories of their mother."

My throat constricted, but no longer from the nausea. I kept washing.

A short while later, vessels cleaned, I headed toward the bed with a stack of fresh basins. The healer massaged Lady Haycroft's hand, her thickened veins standing out prominently from her thin flesh.

"The sons Haycroft are no doubt working hard to spread the glorious wares of the Primus-King's vineyards, or they would be here by your side. You raised fine boys, strong and intelligent. Here now, let me fetch your extract." The healer rose and produced a small tincture from a slender apothecary's cabinet located near the bed. "Drink this down." He tipped the silvery liquid to her lips.

"Being their mother is my greatest joy." She fell into a fit of coughing, and Healer Richmonde waved for a bowl, holding it under her chin as blood and mucus flecked its interior. Though he hid it well, concern deepened the lines bracketing his mouth. "I wish Lord Haycroft had... had been alive to see them elevated to the Assembly. My sister told me that both received invitations to the Naming ceremony ball. I am beyond proud."

"How splendid. The Primus-King must hold them in high regard."

Lady Haycroft relaxed and lay back against the stack of pillows, closing her eyes.

The healer took a moment to examine the contents of the sullied bowl. His lips thinned.

"Why do you linger, recruit?"

My mouth dropped open, but no words came forth.

"To the next room with you."

Startled into action, I set out.

I pushed the next door wide and entered a chamber of calm.

"Healer Kristen, how should we administer the salve?" Four healers stood in a semicircle, watching another prepare. The taller woman shrugged out of her green robes, revealing a sleeveless tunic and a magnificent, colorful octopus inked into her arm. Perhaps she was Solnnan? She was clearly a lover of the sea. She combed an escaped strand of wheaten-colored hair, smoothing it to rejoin the tail at her nape.

"Paint the bandages with a thick layer of the mixture and ensure nothing on your person can drag or rub against young Gavin's skin." Healer Kristen plunged her arms into a sink filled with water and then dried them on a linen. "Gavin, my brave boy, are you ready to begin? Yesterday was much better than the day you came to us. Another month and you'll be back home terrorizing your sister."

The healers similarly disrobed and hung their outer garments on a row of pegs by the door.

Oh, my stars.

The cracked and blistered lips of the patient parted, but only slightly—the boy lay so still I would have thought him Cradle-bound.

Gavin lay on his stomach, covered in dozens of linen strips, his thin body blending in with the tan sheets beneath.

"Two on one side, two on the other." Healer Kristen stood at her patient's side. "Recruit, cut new strips, and see that they touch nothing but each other as you stack them." The healer jerked her head in the direction of a fabric bolt hanging from the ceiling. Those I assumed to be healers-in-training took up their places. "The bandaging should never dry out; it would cause undue pain and could harm newly formed skin when lifted."

I rushed to the rolled linen and located a pair of shears on the table below. Reaching above my head, I unraveled a length and dutifully began cutting strips, estimating how many were needed to cover a small human.

"With your partner, you will slowly remove the soiled bandage, watching beneath for any disturbance to the flesh. Do not make fast movements. Though, as children, we are told to 'rip off the bandage,' the adage applies to papercuts and knee scrapes, not burns to the degree our Gavin has acquired. Let us begin."

I continued my task, focused on making straighter cuts without slowing my progress, but the low whimpers of the child's muffled cries paused my hand in mid-motion.

"Such a brave young man. Gavin, hold tight."

I chanced a look over my shoulder, and my eyes welled. Tears fell over my cheeks, but with them came the determination to work faster.

Gavin's shoulders were an ocean of shining red, striped with waves of pink and white. His lower back resembled a taut leather hide, and though his left side appeared healthy and unscathed, his right bore countless lines of stitching.

The youth's legs spasmed as the final bandage was removed.

"Another day of good healing, young man. Every day we see progress. Recruit, the bandages. Hold them across your forearms thusly." Healer Kristen lifted both arms, elbows bent.

"Of course," I nodded, following the directive.

As Gavin's skin, slick with fluid and striped with deep fissures, was revealed, the smell of blood and decomposition intensified. In some places, the cracks were so severe that they exposed the raw, red muscle beneath—Divine Mother.

My head spun.

I leaned a hip against the wall for support and held my arms aloft.

The faces of men, both innocent and guilty, flashed before my eyes—I'd delivered this same pain while wrecking the grounds of Cordillaria.

The guilt I'd avoided came crashing back upon me like a hammer to an anvil.

More than a dozen had perished, burned in the inferno of my grief over Nan's death—not a one of those soldiers had strung the noose. Not a single one.

You could take away his pain, Eira.

"Steady, recruit; if Gavin can endure it, so can you," Healer Kristen said, no accusation in her speech. She plucked the tip of one bandage, offering its opposite end to a trainee. "Paint both sides, move quickly." Together, they layered a thick, jelly-like substance onto the linen. With precision and speed, the men and women covered the boy, and with each application, his cries eased.

"Well done. On to the next room, recruit. Recruit? You did well."

"Yes, thank you." I snapped back into the now.

The hours bore on.

I found myself speeding from one chamber to the next, lost in the blur of a quickly disappearing day. I fanned an old man taking his last breaths while priestesses prayed, and his Lead Mate and two lesser wives moistened his lips with salve. I held the bowl as a healer lanced another's wound. The woman sat through the procedure, squeezing her brother's fingers for support. I scrubbed and cleaned room after room, as well as the chamber pots of young and old alike.

By the time Robyn fetched me for dinner, I lacked both the energy and stomach for food.

She hugged me, and I rested my head on her shoulder, too fatigued to shed tears.

"Let's head to the baths, Birdie."

We passed the dining hall but kept walking. Before reaching the bathing chamber, Robyn hailed a courier and sent a missive to the ministers notifying them of our whereabouts.

I waded into the water, heedless of my surroundings, and for once not jumping out of my skin when the steam blasted from above. I sank to my neck.

"What's happening?" I held my palm in front of my face and turned it, intrigued and a little alarmed. My feet and hands tingled, and the superficial scrapes I'd received restocking a cartload of pumice into a storage closet stung.

Robyn trailed behind me, wading in by means of four short steps.

"The pool is infused with witch hazel and a melaleuca extraction. Just go under and scrub and you'll come up as clean as can be. You don't need sudsing soaps."

"Truly?" I plunged under and vigorously scrubbed my scalp before rubbing down my body.

I emerged, my hair heavy and dripping. The medicinal pool had stripped away the day's grime—a small relief. The oppressive scent of illness no longer clung to me, replaced instead by the faint smell of camphor and herbs. Yet, as my body felt renewed, a deeper stain seemed to remain, a cold and quiet despair that no amount of washing could cleanse.

I could save them all. It would take so little.

"I promise you'll get used to it, Birdie," Robyn said.

"Why would I want to get used to it?" I asked while resubmerging myself to the shoulders. "All the suffering and pain—it's awful."

We waded out and sat on a bench, toweling off our hair.

"Because they need us."

Chapter Twenty-Five

How I Measure Up

Cato

"**B**ro, over here!" Rollo hollered, lacking the basic decorum of social graces. How did he think yelling would benefit those in their convalescence? Or the healers speaking to each other about their plans for administering care?

Arrogant youth.

Rollo saluted, like some shit-for-brains cadet... and then forced me into the movements of the absurd handshake he performed in place of a proper greeting.

Clap the forearm, Cato. Grip and slide. Hook the fingers. Snap—no, fuck—point then snap. Clap the palms twice in quick succession. End by punching his fist with the strength of a frail infant.

I'd split his knuckles wide if he inquired of the greeting customs of *my* people.

"S'ok man, lemme check you out. Tunic, check. Sandals, check."

"Ass, check!" A masculine howl came from behind.

Palms drummed on the cheeks of my buttocks, and I went rigid, a red haze across my vision.

"Hahahaha! We got him, brother. You gotta get quick Dæne!"

"Yes," I seethed. "I *gotta* get quick... bro."

"Ro-ro," Junnie whispered to Rollo. "Stand up, man, chest out—here she comes."

The Brotherhood collective adopted the cocky, puffed-up stance that accompanied too many a man in their second decade.

I positioned myself at the back of the group so that I could watch for Eira as she headed off to work. She'd slept fitfully last night, and my eyes hadn't closed until I'd snuck into her room and counted her even breaths.

I scanned the atrium and the visible halls.

Eira wanted my trust, and she had it, but there was no way to shut off the barrage of calculations and determinations that swam through my mind—ways in which this could fail, and how to circumvent those eventualities.

"Hey girly!" Brooks sauntered toward another group of barely-adults. The young ladies tossed their hair and pranced about like skittish ponies. "So, you pretty things thinking about the ball?"

I thought I spied my wife's blonde head rush past the balustrade above us, but the figure moved too rapidly for surety.

"Yeah, maybe... Who's your new friend?"

"Dæne." Rollo interrupted my watch by draping his arm around my shoulder as was his habit. I glowered and stood rigid. "So, about the ball, would you, like, wanna...?"

A sprite-like girl with blue eyes too big for her head and a cutesy little nose took a step toward me.

I took a step back and sneered, lest she misread my action.

"Does Dæne like to dance?" She hopped at me, and her skeletal fingers walked up my arm.

"Dæne does not," I retorted, peering down my nose at her—never had this scowl failed me.

Her shiny smile widened, and her bulbous catfish eyes reflected untoward intent.

Dear gods.

I drew back, shaking her corpselike phalanges from my elbow.

"I bet you just haven't found the right partner."

Were she feline, her salmon-flesh-hued lips would have curled to her whiskers.

Catching Rollo by the elbow, I placed him front and center, cutting off her disconcerting gaze.

"Girly, my bro, Ro-ro, wishes to extend to you an invitation to the upcoming, like, soiree." I dug my thumbs into Rollo's spine, forcing him to stand taller.

"Yeah, um... I..." He wavered. Instead of exuding pride in himself, he bashfully rubbed the back of his freckled neck. "Yeah, Wren, you gotta know I think you're pretty and I like, like you."

The flippant little mite stretched out her neck to peer around Rollo.

"What does Dæne like?"

I handled Rollo like a shield, positioning him to block her as she attempted to appropriate my space.

"Age," I spat. "*Dæne* likes maturity." Brooks and Junnie grimaced, eye-balling me like I'd lost my good senses. "And giant tits. Big, like, mature..." I racked my brain rolling through the index of Ambrose's childish vocabulary, finally settling on "milk monsters."

Goddess, forgive me.

Wren's bud of a mouth popped open, making an unseemly smacking noise.

"Um, yeah. Sooo..." Rollo ran his fingers through his hair and palmed his neck again, seeming to deflate before my eyes. "Well, uh, we gotta go."

I nodded sharply, and the Brotherhood closed ranks.

We walked a long corridor. Ever vigilant, I continually glanced over my shoulder, scouting for signs of the addle-brained Wren or others of her ilk.

"Fuck it all," I grumbled, as I tripped over my preposterously long tunic whose hem dragged the ground.

"Rollo, like, I told you, you've got to assert yourself. Make her fall for you, man," Brooks said, walloping his forlorn friend on the shoulder. "Show her the person you are. Keep showing up, bro."

I fought my gown, kicking out my toes to avoid trampling it again.

"That's how love works, brother, it grows. You keep feeding the plant to make it bloom and stuff," Junnie effused with a hand over his heart.

Was this... was this the common ideology in modern-day courtship?

"Feed her bro, and watch her petals, like, unfurl," Brooks added, splaying his fingers to imitate a flower as it greets the sun.

"Absolutely not," I interjected. The bros stopped and stared in confusion. "If the *girl* is not interested, move on. Do not sully your good name by acting the cad. And do not waste your time on a human who does not deign to reciprocate your feelings." The three men shifted uncomfortably. "Bro," I added, going in for another ludicrous handshake.

"Fuck, Dæne, that was like, all kinds of deep," Junnie said, hands on his lean hips. "That mean you're not gonna go for Wren? Rollo's still gotta chance?"

My eyebrows shot to my forehead, but I hastily dragged them down.

"Did you not hear a fucking word I said? Wren is not interested in Ro—"

"Oh, right. Not enough tits. Rollo's still in, boys!" Brooks let a punch fly, his fist landing on my shoulder with a pathetic thud. I balked at his poor form, making a note to address it with him later.

They took off again, their hoots and hollers stoking the flames of my already heightened annoyance.

"Brotherhood!"

"Broho's!"

We sped toward an arched doorway surrounded by an outstanding array of purple and lilac stones. The stunning mosaic of pink, lavender, and violet amethysts put me in mind of my most favored quarry back home. I allowed myself a moment to trail my fingers over the smooth gems.

"Alder! Alder! Alder!"

A door swung open, and the minister welcomed the rowdy crew while they loudly chanted his name.

"Come, gentlemen, measurements first!" The minister clapped.

I entered a single step behind the others.

Healer's tables: Four. Calipers, tongs, measuring sticks. Tonics and tinctures in abundance. Escape routes: the way we entered, unless an exit exists behind the curtain. Three healers present, one presumably Nortian judging by the heavy beard and lightweight robes. The second, Scion, hair a distressing shade of cherry. The third... round of hip, soft of arms, pale of hair, and—ah yes—low or no vision.

The healer's iris jerked rhythmically to the left. She sat in a chair near a grouping of tables, a healer-in-training at her side, stylus and parchment in their hand.

"Dæne," Rollo whispered from the side of his mouth. "Disrobe."

With not a bit of ceremony, he tossed his tunic over his head and crumpled it into a ball, which he launched at Minister Alder.

The minister caught it mid-air and laid it across the top of an apothecary cabinet on the closest wall.

The other bros followed suit.

I removed my tunic, folded it, and placed it at the head of a table. The tiny thong, our mandated underwear, crept up my crevice.

"To the floor, gents. We have new prospects and wish to update your charts, excluding Brooks, of course."

Rollo winked at Brooks, who smacked his hand against the sparse fur of his chest and then saluted the ceiling.

"Form a line, fellas. Healer Baaba, are you ready to begin?"

I positioned myself as requested, standing beside Junnie.

"We are," said the seated healer, whose assistant bent to whisper something into her ear.

"Let us proceed, then, shall we? Scion-Healer M'Xoshan, your instruments." Minister Alder procured a tray from the shelving that ran the length of the back wall and walked it to the healer's side.

"Rollo, have you continued the regimen of tonics and not strayed from your diet?"

"Yes, Scion-Healer."

The healer's red braids swung over his shoulder as he bent and wrapped a ribbon length around Rollo's ankle, calf, and then knee.

"Now squat and hold, great. Very nice, Rollo, you have increased your muscle mass."

"Fuck yeah!" Brooks and Rollo slapped their hands together in an arch. "Alright, man!"

The healer continued measuring, speaking numbers out loud for the healer-in-training to scratch onto their parchment.

"Now breathe. Mouth open." Rollo dropped his jaw, and the Scion-Healer stuck his nose into his gaping maw and inhaled. "Mmhmm, mmhmm. Teeth healthy. Tongue?" Rollo stuck his out. "Pink, clean."

The healer took Rollo's jaws into his hands and turned his face to and fro.

"Good. Now the new man."

Scion-Healer M'Xoshan flicked his onyx eyes to mine. He balked, his eyes growing wide.

"Finally, we stray from the standard. I told the Lead Healer it was time, and *finally* the arse listened." He whipped out a measuring device and slapped it against his palm.

"We are ready for the full description when you are," Healer Baaba said, steepling her fingers under her double chin.

"Ahem, yes." The Scion-Healer clasped his hands behind his back and walked a circle around my person. "Male specimen. Broad of shoulder, dense of muscle. Tapered waist with perhaps a small excess of adipose tissue above each hip, probably due to a meat-rich diet. We can slim him down if you think it's pertinent to do so. Skin is a medium bronze, likely due to his mother's desert heritage. The lighter-golden tresses around his forehead are unusual, however, his time in the sun would explain their differing color. Registration said you hailed from Solnna, yes?"

"North of Solnna, correct," I answered.

"Stand on one leg. Excellent. Now the other, yes, yes. Impeccable balance. Oh, gracious Gammond! A missing toe. How did that make it past inspection? Such a flaw could spell—"

"Was it a defect of birth, Dæne?" Healer Baaba cut off the spiraling Scion.

"No, as I told Scion-Healer Amias, it is the result of a spade accident while working the dyebaths back home."

M'Xoshan dropped to his knees and swiped his finger across the tip of my missing digit. After years, feeling had not returned.

"Ah, a scar and shoddy stitch line prove the tale correct."

"Then it poses no issue going forward. What you describe is a laborer's body. This could prove an interesting variable in our research. Measurements?" replied Healer Baaba.

The measuring length came out, and I stood as a stone while every inch of me was assessed.

"Ah, well then. Big head, height typical, what of his testes?"

The Scion-Healer pulled my ties, and in an instant, he was on me, squeezing and prodding each of my testicles.

"Two. Even in droop. Comparable to the diameter of a small walnut."

Small what?

"Naw Dæne, don't look, like, sour, man. Walnuts are strong, bro, super hard."

"I am not sour," I shot back. "Walnuts are a noble cuisine." I bristled, loathing the idiocy of youth. "Noble."

"No irregularities, no lumps or bumps. Firm but with adequate give. Phallus length undetermined on account of shrinkage."

The bros chuckled under their collective breaths, and I grew tired of the implications of the assessment.

"Sphincter and internals?"

"Both function without issue," I answered. "My internals are spectacular."

"Good, good. Place your hands on the end of the bed and bend."

The chortling on either side of me grated on my nerves, but I followed the directive without fuss. I was not embarrassed in the least.

"Bear down on my finger; it will ease insertion. A little pressure now. Alright, well done, and squeeze. Mmhmm, nice tone." The finger swirled uncomfortably in my rectum. "Do your bowels empty regularly?"

More laughs.

"Indeed," I mumbled. "Nearly at the same hour of every day."

"Impressive. And the consistency?"

The laughs turned to mocking cackles.

I'll rip the larynxes from their giggling throats and feed them to my war hound.

"Dæne, is it watery? Pudding-like? S-shaped?"

Junnie snorted, and in my periphery, Rollo doubled over, holding his middle.

"I-it's straight, I think? Like moist clay? Fuck off, Rollo." I saluted him with Eira's favorite middle-fingered gesture.

"That's fine. Fine."

"More than fine. The picture of health, I'd say… like, bro." I straightened and made to retie my scant undergarments.

"Just a moment, we require samples." The Scion-Healer waved behind his head, and Minister Alder came forward with an armful of flasks.

Junnie whipped forth his donkey-long length—Ambrose would be green with envy—and urinated, his stream inspected by the watchful eyes of M'Xoshan.

"Junnie, increase your water intake; you should be producing more fluids."

"Yes, Scion-Healer." He nodded.

Next came Brooks.

"Perfect color, excellent volume, scent normal. Well done, keep it up."

Rollo stepped forward and accepted his container.

"On the dark side of normal, but much clearer than last time. Rollo… I think you're ready."

"Rollo!" Minister Alder clasped the young man's hands and shook them excitedly. The bro beamed as a deep blush stained his cheeks. Junnie clapped him on the back in a hearty congratulations. "Impressive volume."

Impressive volume? Clear urine a celebration? Ridiculous.

"My dinner portion, if you can beat me, Dæne." Rollo cocked a fiery brow, flinging the challenge in my direction.

"Dæne. Proceed. Ignore that silly ham."

"Accepted," I silently mouthed the word over the healer's shoulder.

Pissing for distance in a line of soldiers or drawing a dick in the snow with your stream, all were a part of the penis-having-experience. That was child's play—I would instruct them in how a *man* answers nature's call.

I snatched the vessel, gripped my appendage, and let my powerful stream flow.

Junnie and Brooks watched intently while Rollo sweated. I would enjoy gorging myself his dinner directly in front of his smug face.

"Nearly clear, impressive issue *and* quantity. Dæne, I applaud your commitment to hydration."

I may have preened a little at the compliment, casting a glance of superiority at both Brooks and Rollo, the latter of whom rolled his sad little loser's eyes.

"Minister, the stools, please."

"Fecal matter?" I asked, rather put off by the idea of taking a shit and subsequently watching the idiots compete over the speed, quality, and quantity of their aforementioned stools. "On command?"

"Ha! You are witty, Dæne, another admirable quality." Alder shook a finger at me. "But no, not those kinds of stools."

The minister ducked behind a curtain and returned with a stack of wooden seats. He deposited one in front of each of us.

On my left, Rollo leaped over his and sat. To my right, Junnie propped a foot on the rung of his, and Brooks leaned both elbows on his stool's padded leather seat.

"Semen samples." Scion-Healer M'Xosha said while handing me a shallow pan. He worked his way down the line. "From all of you."

What?

"I got a teaspoon of sugar for the first that blows," Rollo said under his breath.

Come again?

"I'll see that bet. And throw in a wedge of cheese," Junnie replied.

"You will not, Rollo. No sugar," the minister chided as Rollo took his cock in hand, shaking it and running his fingers along its length.

No fucking way.

"Ahem." I cleared my throat, looking away from Rollo, only for my eyes to settle upon Junnie, lip tucked under his teeth. He spat on the dick in his palm and went to work jerking his thick-headed member.

I stared down at my limp man. This scene was entirely unarousing.

The healer-in-training tapped their stylus against their parchment, eyes dull with boredom. Healer Baaba stifled a yawn with the back of her hand.

Rollo grunted beside me, now fully engorged, using a two-finger and thumb method to make circles around his swollen tip.

Goddess fucking damn it all.

Little Cato, retracted, seeking refuge somewhere in my pelvis.

Now that Eira was in my life, I was not a man built for the idle jack-off. She was voracious for my cock. Why the fuck would I ever use my hand?

"Take your time, Dæne; perhaps close your eyes," the godsdamned healer said in a soothing voice.

Come on, Cat, you have endured torture. I pinched my eyes and pictured my favorite sight in the world. Eira on her knees... Eira locking eyes with me, over her shoulder, while presenting me with her wet and willing—

"There we go, Dæne, the turtle's head peeks from its shell."

For. Fuck's. Sake.

"Uh, yeah, uh-huh, yeah," Junnie groaned out, while the soft squelches of his masturbation disturbed my concentration.

I squeezed my eyes tighter and fisted my cock.

"Fuck, yesssss!" Rollo came, moaning beside me.

I gritted my teeth.

Eira. Gods, that smile, the teasing little hitch of her lips when she played the brat, not wanting to outright ask me to fuck her... ahhh, and her demanding voice when she finally did. Mmmm. There we g—

"Dæne, Dæne, Dæne!"

I blanched, both eyes snapping open.

They surrounded me. All of them—even Baaba with her hands folded as if willing my dick to life.

"Dysfunction of the erection can happen to anyone," she said gently.

"My erections function just fine," I spat. "If I were afforded privacy like a normal fucking human, I could—"

"Dæne, bro, you gotta relax, man. Loosen your throttle," Junnie said in encouragement. I stiffened as his hands landed on my shoulders, kneading the bunched muscles. "Don't choke the Goddess's gift; caress it, my man. Treat it like you will your Lifemate the night you lose your purity together."

Homicide might improve the ambiance.

"Get a girl, man. It helped Brooks," Rollo said, reaching toward my cock. I smacked his hand away, appalled. "Just trying to help, bro. A firm and long-lasting hard-on is a sign of optimal health."

Minister Alder darted off behind the curtain, where there was the sound of a door opening and the minister calling out indistinctly.

An additional entry point.

The curtain ruffled.

"Miss me, boys?"

Divine Creator Above, hear the plea of your mortal son: strike me dead. Render me unconscious so that I may know peace. Shine your light upon Eira. Bless her with a long and prosperous life.

"Wren, would you aid Dæne?" asked Minister Alder, as he escorted her into the room. "He is suffering from a dysfunction of the genitals that—"

"I suffer not from a lack of vigor but lack of priv—"

She whipped out her tits.

I shuddered, horrified by Wren's taut-tipped bosoms wobbling as she danced and swayed with her hands above her head.

My dick shriveled.

"Cover your youthful chest, madam!"

"Youthful? I am a woman grown, you stupid piece of shit!"

"Then I shall have no compunction rending the life from your—"

"Oh, fuck, right, man. Minister Adler, Dæne's into old tits. He likes big, ole um... milk monsters." Rollo shaped his palms around a set of imaginary breasts. "But I think yours are great, Wren." He smiled, going red in the face, dipping his head in her direction.

The waif of a woman curled her lip, her blue eyes bulging in anger.

"Milk? Mon—wait!" The minister bounded off again.

As if reading my intent, Wren blocked my path.

"Back. The fuck. Up," I growled. "My body belongs to one woman, and *you* are not she."

The room went silent. Junnie, Healer Baaba, and the healer-in-training shrank back.

"That is so fucking sexy," Wren, the woman-child, purred out in her best attempt at a sultry voice. "Saving it all for your Lifemate." She licked her lips and stepped toward me.

"I've found one!" Minister Alder yelled, reentering the room. "Phyllis, Dæne requires stimulation. Your breasts, good lady, bear them in the name of the god Mossius, our Healer Lord."

My face fell.

Phyllis—though a handsome woman—undoubtedly had great-grand-children at home

"If Mossius wills it," the grandmotherly woman said, bowing her head, hands going to her robes.

I ran. I snatched up my minuscule underthings, and I fucking ran.

THE POWER OF A NAME

EIRA

The term respect didn't encompass the awe I felt for the healers... for the recruits.

Time was meaningless on the fifth floor. I was dead on my feet, but the healers never left their bedside vigils, and there was never time for a few quiet moments to collect oneself. Shit, it was only after Robyn found me, scouring what must have been my seventy-fifth bedpan, that I finally stopped moving.

Upon reflection, I wasn't sure I'd ever endured hardship.

Yes, I'd had my fair share of injuries, but I healed instantaneously the moment I became shade. I'd brought Ambrose, Cato, and even Evandr back from the hands of death, but adrenaline had made those instances nearly painless—just a cut and some blood, and I saw them live again.

People like Allaine, with her seized arm—gods, how did she quietly manage the discomfort every hour of the day? The suffering I witnessed today didn't end, or if it did, not quickly. And in too many of the cases, the pain was permanent.

And how selfish was I to do nothing more than watch?

I could heal them.

After our bath, Robyn and I returned to our tiny chambers.

"Here, Birdie," Robyn pulled a soft garment from my wardrobe and guided it over my head. "Listen up. You *have* to end your day when your shift is over so that you can do it again tomorrow. The last four recruits didn't make it past day three, and I knew they'd head back to city life within the first couple of hours. You're stronger than they were."

I remained silent, not knowing how to respond.

"You need to eat at some point. If you neglect yourself, your body will give out long before your mind does."

I nodded, but it was like the smell of infection and festering skin sat on my top lip, making it impossible to feel anything but nauseous.

"Courier incoming!" heralded a voice from the hall.

I bent over my desk and scribbled upon a parchment, handing it to the courier as she made her rounds. Robyn dug in her waist pouch and gave the woman a handful of missives.

"I write to my family daily, Birdie. It helps." Robyn smiled, and I returned the gesture weakly. "So does time with the Goddess. Let's head to the temple. Sometimes prayers are the best medicine."

We walked the corridors and headed to the exit, our destination the famed Twins Temple.

I hoped Cato's day had not been filled with similar horrors. If they thought to test their concoctions on his body or hurt him for the sake of trying to heal him... I would force him to leave, even if it meant I had to abandon my mission.

Outside, citizens clamored all around us, and the smell of fresh-baked foodstuffs floated on a cool and gentle breeze. All the ice had melted, and only a single mound of snow remained that I could see.

"Robyn is that—" I squinted in the eve's waning light.

"Yes, the temple lies in the middle of a manmade forest. Pretty neat, right?"

In the heart of Mynder, next to towering apartments and a handful of shops, lay the most perfect woodland, its trees all laid out in perfect rows. We followed close behind a family of five and headed toward an arched tunnel created by the knotted and twisted trunks of malleable saplings. It was an astounding amalgamation of nature and art.

We stepped onto a cobblestone path that led through the bent trees. Thin copper pipes outlined the walkway, fueling moon-and-star-shaped lanterns that stood as tall as my hip. Woodless fires danced within, casting golden light onto the ground. It was the stuff of my childhood dreams made reality.

Above our heads, last year's dead moss draped from tree to tree, and fathers lifted their children to hang small handmade ornaments from the natural swag. I spied a tiny wooden chicken, a painted flower, and several entirely unidentifiable objects made by creative little hands.

"They're tokens of thanks. The priests collect them once a month and take them to the Primus-King. He blesses them and then gifts them to the infirm when he visits the Cult. Some are placed in the Prayer Fires on high holy days as well."

"He visits the sick?" I asked.

"And sits with them for hours when he can. I don't know how he manages it *and* keeps the kingdom going. The Primus-King has the energy of a man half his age. He might be in attendance tonight, though it's unlikely, what with preparations for his daughter's ceremony well underway."

Though I hid my emotions behind a placid mask, my mind went on alert, filtering through a host of what-ifs. *If he recognizes me, how should I respond? If I become overwhelmed, can I keep grounded?*

Priests and priestesses milled about, offering blessings and chastising the teens who were loitering around the statues that flanked the path. We passed vast numbers of the devout—a sea awash in the gold and green of Gaea and the reds of Verus—and beheld the temple proper.

Huh.

It was plain.

I mean, the dome that sat atop it was... nice, but I had expected more. A gemstone or twenty thousand wouldn't have been out of place with what my mind had conjured up. I'd seen a sketch of it once when I was a girl, but maybe Rizellen, the Gaean merchant, had been trying to win over an impressionable Troth, because this was about as inspiring as a soup bowl upended atop a bag of flour.

"Hmmm." I stood, hands on hips, neck craned.

No painted glass windows, no architectural flourishes. No fancy lights. It was, at its core, basic.

Robyn caught my frown and the crook of my elbow. "Just wait."

Two priests greeted us and beckoned us through the boring wooden doors.

"May the Goddess shine Her light upon you both."

"Know Her love, children of Gaea."

Arm in arm, we walked into...

"The truest beauty is found within," Robyn whispered, her smile beaming with pride. "Well, that's what they told us when we were kids. I'm inclined to believe it, though."

"Ho-ly shit. How in all of Ærta did they get them to do that?" I asked, pointing to the ring of trees that lined the perimeter of the main room. I stood transfixed, astonished by the trunks that rose tall and the branches that shot off and then joined, twisting into complicated knotted patterns. At the centermost point, up in the fucking air, hundreds, maybe thousands of branches of differing thickness, converged into the shape of an oval, in whose center stood a carved likeness of She Who Gave All: rounded stomach, hair a wreath of coils, arms held out as if embracing her creation.

On either side of her thickset thighs stood her twins, each with a palm laid on her waist.

"I dunno," Robyn chuckled, leading me through the chamber.

At the far end of the temple, the people gathered. Lush, floral-patterned carpets covered the floor in an array of greens, golds, and reds. A semi-circular dais was set against the back wall—the steps on both sides formed by the same intricately knotted branches. Copper pipes arched above the ceremonial stage and skirted around a large six-pointed star carved from smooth, snow-white marble. Twin flames tangled above the star at the mouth of each pipe.

My heart began to palpitate and flutter, and the æther buzzed in the tips of my fingers.

"Hey Robyn, we saved a spot." Brooks hailed us with a wave of his hand. "Birdie, you good? Domestic is tough."

I nodded and smiled as we wound through a short row of the parishioners, many already kneeling at prayer.

"Exhausted, but yes. Thanks for asking."

Brooks crooked his finger, and I bent low.

"So, Dæne had, like, a tough day, alright? I don't know how to help really, but like, tell him his pecs look good maybe?"

"What happened?" I asked calmly, my voice hiding the rising panic suddenly welling within me. "Where is he? Is he hurt?"

Brooks tilted his head and, not so subtly, pointed to a spot behind him with his elbow.

"Just his pride, bro, just his pride."

I saw him then, my husband, my love... my *visibly* agitated chosen mate.

Cato was kneeling, arms crossed, back spear straight. He pouted so severely that two lines, not one, formed between his brows.

Next to him knelt a striking woman with raven-wing hair. She stared up at him with big, besotted eyes of Monwyn blue. She poked his stomach with a pointed finger, and he smacked her hand away as if she were a mosquito buzzing around his head. She jerked her hand back, hugging it to her chest, but continued blinking her long, flirtatious lashes.

Cato's eyes met mine, and the side of his mouth hitched, dimpling his cheek. My insides melted. Even with his line-thin brows and baby-smooth jaw, he righted my toppled world. His smile intensified as I drew nearer, both dimples making a rare appearance.

"Birdie," his voice soothed the fraying edges of my spirit. In this temple, he was *my* blessing.

"Move over, youngin'," I instructed the woman at his side. I didn't care who the fuck she was. She was in my spot.

"Do what?" Her mauve lips puckered in a pout. The glare she sent me was sharp enough to shave with.

"Or don't. That's fine." I dropped and squished myself between her and my man. The angry imp had two choices: retreat or hold me on her lap.

"Ugh! Who even are you? Like, get off me!"

"Oh, pardon me, it's these ample hips of mine." I shoved her pert buns with my fat ass. She tumbled to her side.

"Mmm, yes, they are ample, aren't they," Cato crooned in a playful tone.

I swatted his thigh in a gesture coyer than scolding and leaned in close—the lady beside us already an afterthought.

"Brooks said you had a rough day?"

"Not as tough as yours, it would seem." Cato dipped his chin while assessing me. "Dark circles, teeth worrying that succulent bottom lip, nails bitten so short that—"

"He couldn't get his dick hard," said the still-too-close girl over my shoulder.

Cato leveled a look at the raven-haired beauty. Dark, calculating eyes and pearlescent teeth flashed in a predatory gleam, one that the unwise would mistake for a smile—the last sight his adversaries saw before he snuffed out their life.

I did a double-take, unsure of whether I should laugh at or eviscerate the woman shoving at my flank.

"Wren, that's a low blow." Rollo knelt on her other side.

"Oh! Bird name!" I clapped, much to the confusion of those surrounding me.

Wren frowned at Rollo and then leered at me while doing her damndest to recapture Cato's attention. She ran the point of her pink tongue along her lip and pushed out her chest.

Rollo tapped her on the shoulder.

She snorted like he was the *actual* biggest inconvenience of her short life.

"No, for real, though. A man's load is, like, his sacred covenant with the Goddess, alright, and the healers use it to determine the magnitude of his health. You have no idea how hard it is to—"

"I know how *hard* it isn't." Junnie came to his knees and kneeled on Cato's right, pulling River down with him and tucking her close. She nuzzled into his side. "Look, you're just gonna have to relax, Dæne. We're all there supporting you and—"

Cato ran his hands over the shadow forming on his jaw.

I was confused.

"Your being there *is* the problem. When did masturbation become a team activity?"

I was *so* fucking confused.

Cato's cheeks warmed, and I placed a hand on his thigh.

"So... so, Dæne, the healers required a-ah—" I sputtered over my words, attempting to put together the pieces of the disjointed story.

"—a sample, yes," Cato grumbled. He laid his palm over mine, the hard calluses of his sword hand rough on my over-washed skin.

"And no privacy was afforded for you to um—"

"—produce said sample," he bit out.

Oh, for the Cradle's sake. Embarrassment was an emotion I'd never seen him wear, and I wanted to whisk him away from the eyes falling upon him, now *and* retroactively.

"And these guys made fun of you?" I gestured to the Brotherhood.

Junnie clapped Cato on the chest and then draped himself over his shoulder, speaking directly to me.

"Made fun of? No, never. We cheered him on, bro. Patted him on the back. Wren shook her tits around, but he still couldn't—"

"Oh, did she?" I angled my head back and studied my husband.

He scoffed loud enough to draw attention.

"As if her plum-sized breasts could arouse a man of my tastes."

Wren shrieked.

"I think they're real nice, Wren." Rollo nudged her with his shoulder. "I think they probably, like, overstimulated him. Ya know?"

She bounced her head in the affirmative.

"Naw, Ro-ro, that's not it. He likes big ole breasticles. We've all got our thing, and Wren's don't work for him. I like tall girls; Junnie likes... well, he likes River." Brooks smiled at the couple, who were so sweetly in love. "The Goddess made us unique, bro. Nothing to be ashamed of. And he can try again tomorrow, but like, Dæne, my man, you gotta rub one out, or like, it's back to the city. Research brothers have to be, like, the *most* prime of specimens."

Ah, yes, there's the panic. It never drifted too far from my side.

My mind raced. If he couldn't produce, it would be a way to force him to safety. And though he'd fight it, I wanted Cato as far away from Gaea as possible, even if, selfishly, I basked in the security of his presence.

I touched his forearm, making the gesture appear as unfamiliar as I could. The wife in me burned to tear open his silken tunic and remind him *just* how virile he was.

Cato tensed, his tendons cording under my touch. "What I would like, *bros* and ladies, is to not be talked about as if I am—"

I gasped, and Cato went rigid.

"It's him." The æther drummed against my chest wall, the beats just this side of painful.

Cato's eyes tracked mine, landing on the man who emerged from a from a doorway hidden under the limbs on the back wall.

I suppressed a shudder, not for the coward who locked my mother away, but for the open hatred that shone from the face of my mate.

Nan, Imella, Lilium, little satyr, Momma.

I leaned in close and dropped my voice. "Play your role, Dæne."

At once, Cato adopted a serene smile, which I mimicked.

Robyn, who'd found a space between Rollo and Wren, shifted forward and caught my eye; her smile, one of genuine delight, reached from one ear to the other.

"That's him," she mouthed, while twirling a strand of her dark hair around her finger.

Junnie leaned forward.

"And those studs are his boys. Royal bros one, four, and eight: Zephyr, Merritt, and Flynn. I hear they all possess *the touch*. They like, head the Cult Mossius council with the Archhealer and stuff."

Robyn nodded. "It's hearsay, of course, but like the Obligates, they are blessed." She raised her arms and studied her palms. "With a touch, they feel and understand the plight of a person's body." Fingertips to her forehead, Robyn curled to the floor in deep prayer.

"Like Amias... and Ozius," I murmured to Cato as I covered my brow. Together we bowed our heads. "Do you remember after the Rite, when Ozius touched me and said I didn't carry Ambrose's child?"

"Yes." Cato's voice was cold, but as we lifted upright, his gaze was soft and congenial.

"Most beloved citizens of Gaea!" The Primus-King raised his arms and voice.

"Praise to our Primus-King!"

"Long life to our savior!"

"Keep us safe, majesty! The conjurers will take our children!"

The conjurers are your children. I wanted to yell it, scream it to the audience... but how long ago was it that I had felt the same? I had been convinced that *conjurer* was a word synonymous with *evil*.

As the assembled citizens mirrored their leader's outstretched arms, held their littles aloft, and chanted for his continued health, I stared into the eyes of my father—no, never that name for him.

We could end this now.

My temperature rose, the æther prickling under my skin.

"Steady," Cato said, as he turned to embrace me, as if caught up in the moment, like so many of the others surrounding us.

Safe in his arms, I studied the Primus-King. He was handsome enough, I suppose.

On account of draining and using my mother's blood, he appeared to be a man in his early sixth decade. He should have been a wrinkly old bag like Hester—he deserved to be a dry and dusty pile of bone.

"I'll pray for your bush snake to spit venom, bro." Brooks tossed his arms around Cato and me and smacked a wet kiss on his cheek.

"Brooks, if you do not unhand me this instant, like, bro, I will—"

"Wren!" I squealed as the beauty attempted to slither past me and fold her arms around Cato. "Can you believe it? The Primus-King!" I butt-blocked her and then caught her up in my arms, mashing her lithe body into a Nan-like bear hug.

"Birdie, let me go," she hissed into my neck. "I can't breathe for all your tits in my face!"

The crowd quieted, and I released her; she dusted her dress off like I was something filthy.

The Primus-King stepped behind a simple wooden table and held a candle to a large silver bowl. As the slips of parchment within ignited, and the smoke carried the prayers to the Cradle, he tapped his brow and whispered a prayer.

My eyes were shaped like his. My bottom lip similarly thicker in the middle.

"We welcome into our kingdom the refugees of Ærta." He strode to the front of the table and stood with his hands clasped. "Be at peace, brothers and sisters, for there is safety within these walls. Merrias vows her protection, and her twin Mossius guides us to live this life of abundance. I invite the tiny tots forward."

Gray of hair but barely a wrinkle to speak of, the Primus-King bent low and hoisted two of the dozens of children who ran to surround him and his sons... my brothers.

I didn't let myself dwell on that.

"There is nothing more beautiful than our little ones, and there are no lengths a parent would not go to protect our treasures."

The crowd murmured their agreement.

"They Who Commune with the Goddess, The Most Exalted High Mantle, calls for me and mine to make the journey to Verus Temple as tensions rise across the continent and known world. We convene for the cause of peace." He kissed the blonde curls of the little girl perched on his hip and then set both children on the floor amid the still-growing ring of others.

You could feel the tension swell amongst the gathering. Eyes flickered between mothers and fathers. Among the younger generation, those old enough to have heard the stories of war hugged their arms around their middles.

"You cannot leave us, sire!"

"Who will see to the Cult?"

"To us? Who will ensure the kingdom's safety?"

The Primus-King lifted his arms, and silence descended once more.

"Zephyr and I journey to Verus after my youngest's Naming celebration, but do not fear, for I would never leave you unattended. Merritt and Flynn, in council with the Assembly, will rule in my stead, and though they are not men of the military, as our Zephyr is, I have made provisions. Emberkin Arro, third in command of the lands of Baldorva, has made his way across the sea to—"

The rest of the Primus-King's sentence drowned in a violent wave of objections.

Men surged to their feet, hoisting angry fists into the air. Mothers took their daughters' hands and pulled their sons close.

The Primus-King simply nodded and listened to the cries of his people as fear swept through the crowd like a sudden squall.

"Slavers! You would bring us slavers?"

"Baldorvans in Ærta!"

"Shackling humans: how can you condone such a thing?"

The concerns of the throng swelled. People looked from left to right. Some were wide-eyed in shock, others on their feet and headed to the door. One bold man retrieved his child from the Primus-King's feet.

"Hear me, Gaea, hear me." The Primus-King intoned in a gentle but firm voice. "The Mantle Themself opened the borders in the last Obligate session. Troth Kairus of Monwyn and our late and adored son, Scion Ozius, were Assigned to the country."

"Adored son? It was he who sent us Ozius's head to Monwyn as a Joining gift!" I hissed.

Cato took my hand, and I sealed my lips, just as a man appeared in the back doorway.

The Baldorvan stepped forward. A fucking Baldorvan.

Like he'd brought with him the eye of a Solnnan storm, a terrifying and sudden stillness fell around us.

"My Goddess, he is exactly what my child's mind imagined a Baldorvan to be."

Cato remained silent, his head forward, his mind working.

Emberkin Arro strode onto the dais, flanked by two more of his kind.

On his exposed arms, boldly inked lines formed thin bands around his elbows and biceps, matching those that slashed across his cheeks. I counted three black lines spanning the bridge of his nose and four on each arm. Two rings of silver pierced his left nostril, and his ear was notched in three places, splitting the lobe. The iron grey at his temples melted into a head of dark, reddish-brown, shoulder-length hair. Pleated skirts concealed his legs, and as he moved, muffled thuds spoke of the armor that lay beneath. Two guards in hooded robes of deep ochre—their faces obscured by thin veils of black—stood at his sides.

"We welcome you and your companions to Gaea. With danger encroaching on our doorstep, you answered our plea for assistance. We are in your debt." The Primus-King drew his arm back, signaling the chairs located along the back wall.

The Baldorvans took their seats.

"Good citizens, Gaea works to broker peace in the face of catastrophe."

Emberkin Arro sat spread-legged and at ease. His companions—who were creepy as all fuck—perched on the ends of their chairs, backs straight, hands tucked into the sleeves of their robes, entirely unmoving.

"The enemy is not Baldorva, my children. Their customs may be different from ours, but the true treachery lies in the hands of the trickster Queen of Solnna, who named Baldorva in the fake attack on her lands. She and her mother and her mother's mother kept the conjurers hidden, raising them and grooming them all the while. She forms an army unmatched and plans to take the continent. We cannot work alone if we are to circumvent her efforts."

The murmurs of the crowd rose again.

"Emberkin Arro has pledged to keep you safe and, Goddess willing, Zephyr and I can convince our Most Esteemed Mantle that war is avoidable with Baldorvan aid. Let us pray as the Goddess has taught us."

The congregation bowed their heads and placed their fingers to their brows—all but one man a few rows away from me. As he followed suit a half-beat later, my pa winked just before he covered his eyes. Dressed in the guise of a Gaean peasant, he blended in well, his woolen cloak hiding his rounded belly.

"Let fear not collapse our strong foundations. Through the Goddess, we know love. Through the Goddess we know harmony, and through her," The crowd sat upright as the Primus-King indicated Emberkin Arro with an open-handed sweep, "a means of hope is granted."

A priest and four priestesses entered the room. Behind them, a swath of servants carrying bread-and-vegetable-laden baskets doled out their bounty. Members of the populace thanked the servants as they passed, pressing the gifts into the hands of their neighbors.

"Long live the Primus-King!"

A chorus of accolades rose around us as the littles at the front clamored to their feet to receive rounds of bread from the Primus-King's own hands before rejoining their families.

The priest stood upon the dais now, waiting for the last of the servants to join him. They linked hands.

"As we close our prayers, as we have done for the past three months, we implore the Goddess for the deliverance and safekeeping of Emryss, the Primus-King's eldest daughter, betrothed to the warlord, snatched from her crib by the matriarchs of Solnna. Her father and future husband would see her home. Never forgotten, no longer lost."

The prayers came to a close, and the congregation stood, but I found myself unable to rise.

He'd named me...

Cato cupped my elbow and forced me to stand.

"I'll walk this one home, bro," Cato said, winking at Junnie.

It took all of my energy, but I smiled and waved as the others shared a conspiratorial chuckle and left.

"Let's, like, find privacy, Birdie."

"Yes, but first," I glanced over my husband's shoulder, tears gathering in my eyes, "Cato... meet my pa."

Chapter Twenty-Seven

PA.

Cato

"**I**'m Ulltan. Follow me, son."

I pivoted and came face-to-face with the smiling eyes of Eira's Pa. Love was *truly* blinding.

Either my wife was entirely unobservant, which I knew to be untrue, or affection had rendered her incapable of seeing the obvious. How she never questioned her paternity living with the mass of a man before me was inconceivable.

Rough and red weathered skin stretched over a wide face that bore not even a hint of resemblance to hers. His nose was long and wide, and though his smile was easy like hers, he lacked teeth from his canines back.

Eira leaned into her father's side as we made our way to the temple doors. The crowd much lighter now, we stepped into the night.

"I've a son! How lucky am I to no longer bear the brunt of coddling her alone?"

"Pa!"

Ulltan hefted a meaty hand in my direction and shook mine with enthusiasm.

"Eiry, is this yer Bond husband or the contract one?" He asked while shaking me so vigorously that my teeth rattled in my skull.

"Bond, Pa, this is Cato," she whispered. "But here, he is called Dæne. Pa, you heard... Am I—was I betrothed to a Baldorvan Warlord?"

Faster than I anticipated from a man so many years my senior, Ulltan pinched my chin with his dry-skinned fingers. I held myself steady but went immediately on guard. This might be her father, but I had learned long ago that familial ties did not guarantee safety. And, barring Eira, it still jarred me to receive unauthorized touches.

"Yes, darlin'. But yer Momma never agreed to the union."

Ulltan turned my face from side to side, inspecting me in the low light of the pathway's lamps. His eyes narrowed to shards.

"So yer the man who lied to my minnow about who ye were, plotted to snatch her from Verus, and then saw her Joined with yer brother so ye could continue havin' yer way with her?" His brows lowered over his eyes, the thick and unruly hairs casting thin shadows on his cheeks.

"I—yes," I stammered. "I did."

And I refused to repent for my actions—not to him, not to the Goddess.

He tossed his head back and howled.

"That's near enough to how I reeled her momma in, too!" Mirthful tears gathered in the corners of his eyes, and he dabbed at them with a handful of his cloak.

"Pa, that is *not* how you and Momma came to be."

"Well, that may be a bit of a fish tale." Ulltan held his hands close together, then spread them wide and farther apart with each word, as if the fish were growing right before our eyes. "If I'm to be honest, this little one—all chubby thighs and rosy cheeks—certainly played her part in our comin' together. My minnow, gracious Goddess, how she cried and cried unless I carted her about for her overtaxed Ma. Lucky for me, I'd lugged whales on these shoulders all my life."

"Pa!" Eira stomped her foot, grimacing.

"What?" Ulltan flinched in surprise as he looked at his vexed daughter sideways. "How else would I've acquired these muscles? Whale meat weighs a heap, it does, daughter mine; you well know it."

Her father remained clueless as to his accidental implication.

Eira broke into a fit of laughter, the sound so pure it lifted me from my now pervasive sense of dread. Could a heart burst from joy, or was it only grief that could shatter it? She had every reason to be jaded and bitter; she had taken emotional body blows that would have left me hollow. She was much tougher than I—her laughter free and unforced. I allowed myself to soak in her radiance before clapping closed the metaphorical visor of my emotional helm.

"Ulltan, why have you come?" My delivery was harsher than intended, and both the Chulainns looked me up and then down.

"'Cause I'm her Pa, young man. Do I need a reason?" Under his cloak, he pushed his sleeves up to his elbows. "'Cause I'll give you a reason if need be."

"I—no, for fuck's sake, it came out wrong. Is something amiss?"

His affable grin returned.

"No, not at all. Your boy, Larm, found us per yer instruction, though."

My chest puffed up in pride—our Frostborn successfully carried out his first official order.

"Yes, sir, he found us, explained the change in Eira's destination, and I wished to look in on my daughter's wellbein'. Fish bubbles and whale farts, but Vonnie scolded me somethin' fierce. Said coming here would be like as not to complicate matters, but a pa's heart ain't at rest when his little'uns cavortin' with trouble."

That I understood.

I had always been a strategist, but the moment Eira sauntered in and knocked on Ambrose's back, my mind took on a new and more vital objective. My every plan—once the defense of my own kingdom's interests—were now solely to ensure she flourished.

We retraced the illuminated path that would see us back to Cult Mossius, passing those at prayer and those at play. Lifemates embraced in the shadows, and children skipped around, weaving through the legs of their elders.

"Son-in-law, share with me yer thoughts, my boy. You heard the Primus-King, how do ye interpret his intent?"

Ulltan's immediate acceptance and familiarity took me aback, just like the heavy hand that lingered on my shoulder. A pang of grief for my deceased father took me by surprise. I shoved it away and focused my thoughts on tactics and motivation.

"The Primus-King is setting himself up to act as the great arbitrator—Ærta's savior. Co-opting the Mantle's overtures to Baldorva, though shocking, was a well-reasoned play," I supplied. "For the most part, the people accepted his interpretation of events and intent."

We slowed our pace and let a line of priestesses cut in front of us.

"Can you imagine the prestige he would garner if he arrived at Verus claiming to have single-handedly stopped a war before the first sword fell?" Eira asked. She reached up and sent a small painted ornament spinning. "All would praise him."

Without warning, Ulltan stopped and bent over until his eyes were on the much lower level of Eira's.

"Daughter, ye look tired. With yer man here, trained in the arts martial as he is, would ye not consider allowing him to step into yer wee boots and let him gather up the bits and bobs of information that we seek?"

"No, Pa. I'm not coming back to sit with you and Momma while somebody else tries to fix my mess."

"*His* mess, minnow. The Primus-King's. Place the blame at the feet of its rightful owner, little one. Go on, now, hug yer old Pa; with the Gaeans as touchy as they are, it won't rouse no suspicions."

A wobbly-lipped Eira went into her pa's arms, and it confirmed to me that more than anything, I wished to be the boulder she clung to in life's storm. I wanted to be what my father was not for his wife and children.

"I knew you wouldn't budge, daughter mine, but I promised yer momma I would try to persuade ye. She's beside herself knowin' yer at the Cult instead of the palace. She told me to tell ye not to let yer soft heart get the best of ye."

Eira bristled but held her tongue.

"And Gotwig? What does he say, Pa?"

"Well..." Ulltan went crimson above his beard, rocking Eira from side to side. "He, uh, well, Sidnatious said, 'wonderful, shall we place bets on whether her veins run dry from healing feeble old men, or from trying to spike the city's drinking water with her blood?' Yes, I believe that's what he said, word for word."

"He said wha—"

Ulltan squished Eira's head into his chest, cutting off her words. I would remember the tactic.

My wife flailed; her father offered me a wink.

"Gotwig's headed to Verus to convince the Mantle not to level charges against ye, son. When it came to light that ye took it upon yerself to—how'd ye find us anyway?" Ulltan swung around and asked in the middle of his own sentence, very much like his daughter would have done.

"Pa!" Eira walloped her father's ample stomach, fighting for release.

He leveled me with a look of curiosity.

"The smoke of Gotwig's pipe. The distinctive smell of clove and citrus carried on the wind." I shifted my weight to better gauge Ulltan's reaction. "Though I have little understanding of how you remained hidden... I tracked you by the occasional whiff of tobacco. Only when I rid myself of the dead weight in my party was I able to pursue you with the full arsenal of my abilities. How *did* you manage to evade me?"

Eira cleared her throat, stepped back from her father's embrace, and instinctively moved in my direction.

"We were underground, in caverns of snow and ice." She wrung her hands together and inched nearer. "You slept upon our roof one night." Tears shimmered in her eyes. "I think your proximity was the only reason I lasted as long as I did. The Bond's relentless pull is stronger the further apart we are."

"Rocked her while she sobbed, I did. Turned her nose up at her momma's soup, and I forced her to a healer."

Eira's shoulders slumped, and Ulltan reached for her at the same moment I took her by the elbow. I slid my thumb across her lashes, dashing away the wetness before it fell.

"Do not cry, love; you made the right choice for you, and I will never begrudge you for it."

She popped an impertinent brow, even as she wept.

"You won't? I'm fairly certain that the words you spat were—"

"I may continue to sulk." I winked—a gesture I knew caused that little heart of hers to flutter. "But I will always forgive you."

"Listen, children," Ulltan said while reworking the brooch that fastened his cloak. "The plan remains the same, but the focus is now played out on two fronts. If the Primus-King leaves the palace, Larm and I will intercept him and put the matter to rest." Eira took over the task of pinning her father's garment, as his arthritic fingers fumbled with the pin. "We'll make quick work of it. Y'all produced a *big* boy—takes after his Gramps."

"Pa, don't put yourself in harm's way. I can do this. You've seen what I am capable of."

Ulltan took Eira's smaller hands into his enormous set.

"If given the choice between yer life or mine, tiny fish, I will always choose yers. Don't ye naysay me. Ain't enough hours in the day for me to explain how a pa feels about their baby. Not another word."

"Pa, you don't know me at all if you think—"

"—that the last word will ever be mine?" Ulltan turned to me, his gaze steady. He clasped my hand and placed Eira's palm in its center. "I also know the lengths a husband will go to protect his wife."

There was no need to nod, no need to reply—an unspoken pact between two protectors.

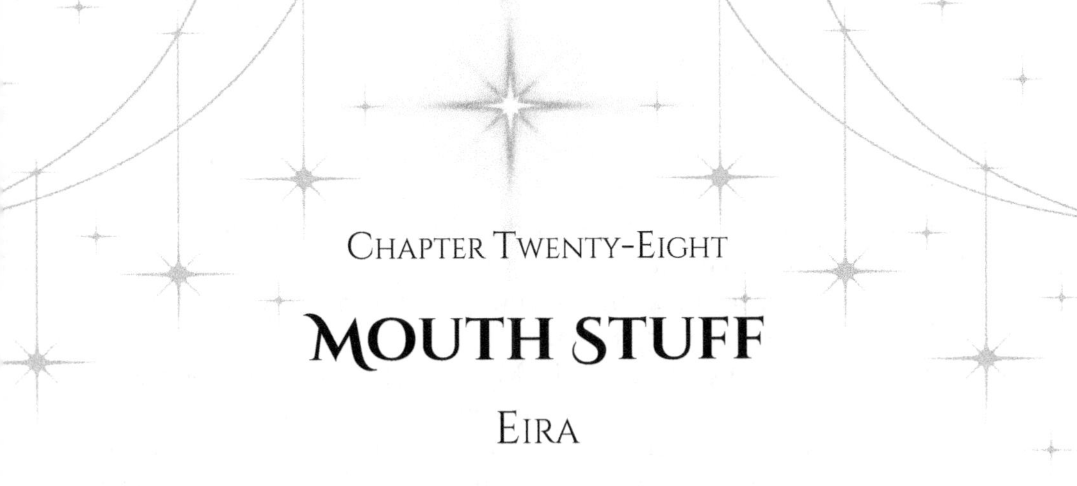

CHAPTER TWENTY-EIGHT

MOUTH STUFF

EIRA

The lamps dimmed, and the hall went pitch black.

Never had a bed been more comfortable. I scooted down as far as I could and propped my heels on the wall, groaning as the pressure in my feet dissipated. The ache in my back slowly relaxed.

Shuffling sounds and murmurs could be heard from both sides of the corridor; no doubt, Robyn sought out Brooks, and Junnie found his way to River. Sweet Rollo probably dreamed of his Lifemate. I pressed my lips into a smile when I picked up on the telltale scuttles of Cato crawling into my chamber.

I pushed off the wall, moving back, when the bottom of the coverlet lifted, and he ducked under, pressing kisses on my bare legs. He silently massaged my ankles and then calves as he climbed his way up my body.

His head emerged next to mine.

"One day I will simply open a door and join you in our bed." He ran his newly straightened nose along the bridge of mine. "Has it yet been a year of sneaking around and covert assignations?"

"Nearly," I whispered while making room for him to rotate and lie on his side. He pulled my thigh over his hips, sliding a knee between my legs. "And Merrias should have left your nose alone. I loved your bump."

I felt him shrug.

"Do not fret. I've not gone a consecutive five years without a break; your ruggedly handsome husband will return. Though I will lament the loss of my newfound ability to breathe from my left side—a most pleasant side effect of Merrias's tampering."

"Oh, goodness, well, perhaps give up your fighting ways in exchange for fresh air?"

"The last time it was little Mae who dealt the blow, not some deadly assassin. She kneed me in the face as I swung her to my shoulders."

I could just imagine it. Mae squealing in delight, Cato ignoring the blood coursing down his chin.

"How was day one of playing the purification recruit, my love?"

I buried my face into Cato's chest.

"It was... exhausting, eye-opening. My mother is correct in counseling me to mind my heart. Were I Assigned to this kingdom, Cato, I would give myself over entirely. You should see the child on my floor, with his awful burns, and the mother dying so painfully slow. I keep thinking, what would it cost me but a few drops of blood?"

Though I couldn't make out anything but the line of his profile, I felt him tense.

"Your life, Eira. That would be the cost." Cato's arm tightened, the drum of his heart amplifying to match the rising intensity of his voice. "Listen to me. Do not attempt it. Do not *think* it. A single miraculous healing, and the Primus-King will know. Any hope of escape will be gone."

"Cato?" I traced the scar that I could no longer see beneath his ink but could still feel.

"Yes."

"When I made the decision to come here, I made it with the full knowledge that *here* is where I might meet my end."

Cato suppressed a reflexive gag. His respirations sputtered as he fought to bring his body under control.

I smoothed the loose curls over his ear and pressed my forehead to his.

"Eira, your care for the lives within these walls is endearing. I would usher even the frailest to their grave to keep you whole."

I used the coverlet to dab away the sweat forming on his brow.

"Tell me of your day, husband, and we will rework our plans," I said, hoping to help him from the bog he waded through. From the moment I woke to the seconds before sleep claimed, a plethora of poor outcomes cycled through my mind. They no doubt consumed his.

Cato grumbled but acquiesced.

"Today was horrendous. I despise every human I have encountered in the Cult. All of them. The only silver lining was the realization that I skipped over the "bro" phase of my journey to manhood... like, oh my gods."

Our mingled laughter soothed my spirit like a strong drink never could.

"Mutual masturbation and celebratory slaps aren't your thing?" I jested, knowing that Cato's tolerance for antics had ended well before he could grow a beard.

"No, for fuck's sake. I firmly believe that some pursuits are to be carried out behind closed doors... despite what *you* have encouraged me to partake in." Cato nipped at my earlobe. "For you, I step out of my element on the regular. Watch the woman of my dreams fuck a Scion? Why not? It makes her smile. Fuck the Scion while he fucks my wife? Sure, it makes her come twice as hard... and me come twice."

I slapped a hand over my mouth to keep from squealing out loud. My cheeks heated as the æther took a merry jog to my vagina.

"Eira, my gods, you should have seen Rollo and the bros. Jerk, jerk, spurt, just as comfortable as if they were sitting down to a picturesque dinner with their mothers."

I faked a gag.

"And what will you do tomorrow?"

His chest expanded so wide that my back pressed snug against the wall.

"I honestly do not know, love, but I will not leave you here to fend for yourself." Cato sighed. "Never could I have imagined *this* to be the test I would fail. Mayhap I can conceal a sticky substance in my hands or... or Goddess forbid borrow some from a servant—Ugh. Brought low by my dick's demand for emotional connection."

"Is-is your manhood okay?"

"My *manhood*?" Cato questioned.

I shoved him playfully.

"Your pride, asshole, you know, *manhood*. Men get really attached to their... functioning."

I felt the vibrations of his quiet laughter against my breasts.

"No, love," Cato snugged his hips closer to mine. "I am surprised you have yet to note how very *okay* my manhood is in your presence."

"Mmmm," I hummed as he pressed his heavy arousal against my pubic bone. "Do you think the Bond has rendered you numb to the allure of all others?"

Cato smacked his lips.

"Asks the woman who eagerly satisfies two virile men, while experiencing that same Bond. I would counter your question with the same."

A gritty, greedy chuckle issued from my throat. *Yes, I have no issues in seeing the allure of others... and he knows it.*

"I suppose it is difficult for a woman of such ravenous appetites to understand that a man might require some level of trust and affection to function at his best."

"It does go against popular opinion."

Cato slid his palm up my sternum and chest, his fingers wrapping around the column of my throat.

"Lucky for us, I care nothing for the sentiments of others."

"Even Ambrose?"

A burst of air hit me in the face as Cato flopped onto his back, his erection deflating in record time.

"We have to talk about it, husband number one." I wiggled free of my tight spot and straddled his hips, jailing him until we'd hashed this out. I pushed my fingers into the muscle below his clavicle and rubbed at the gathering tension. "I'm legally Joined to him, Cato, and I love him, just as you love him. Just as he loves you and me. I do *not* believe you played along with our lovemaking just for my sake. At least... I don't want to believe you did."

He shifted beneath me, and I followed the path of his biceps as he folded his arms under his head.

"It is rather complex."

"Do your best to explain it... and regrow your chest hair as soon as we are free of this place. May the Goddess, in her infinite mercy, not let my last grope of a man's body be a bald one. She knows my penchant for a pelt."

"You are a woman of base tastes."

"I can't argue with that... though I think I prefer my ladies' lips to be bald."

Cato cleared his throat, and as I'd hoped, I felt him stir to life beneath me.

We passed the next few minutes in silence, kissing.

"When we are, all of us together, it feels good—physically, of course, because why wouldn't it? A hole in a warmed-over wedge of cheese entices some men."

"Who?" I asked, emitting a wry chuckle. "You?"

"I have yet to develop a sufficient rapport with brie," Cato said in mock seriousness. "I admit that at first, I entered the physical relationship because it meant I could keep you closer. It was in Solnna, however, that I came face-to-face with the ferocity of his devotion to you. It was that which allowed me to consider him as a part of *us*. I understand his devotion on a profound level. I respect it, and that respect conferred a level of attraction." Cato took my hand and settled it over his chest. The steady beat beneath sent the æther tumbling. "But, my love, when it is *just* you and I... it feels transcendent."

It was as if a cool breeze lifted the hair from my nape and skimmed over my shoulders as he spoke. I inhaled, welcoming the divine sensation.

"Eira, if given the choice between a comfortable existence with the two of you, or an extraordinary one where you and I soar through this life as one... I choose you. I choose *only* you."

I lowered myself to my elbows and lay my cheek against a day's growth of stubble.

"I can't abandon him, Cato, nor can you. He's endured a lifetime of abandonment at the hands of many—you and I included—and yet, he unshuttered his closed-off heart. We can do the same for him. It may sound disingenuous to downplay my privileged situation, but I'm content with a happy life that is occasionally transcendental. Can you be as well?"

Cato lifted my rear with his knees, angling my face to his, claiming my lips once and then again.

"I do love him, Eira, but in *my* way. Ambrose was never my brother—he wasn't allowed to be. Not in the way Aberus was. Father saw to that by separating us while we were young. Despite the distance, along the way to Verus, I think—though it pains me to say it aloud—the imbecile squirmed his way past my barriers and assumed the position of my best friend."

"Aww, Cato." I kissed his closed eyelids, feeling like I'd burst from the sweetness. "Best friends who—"

"—share."

"Fuck," I said simultaneously. "Granted, you have never once been the fuckee. Would you like to be?"

I scooped my hips forward and backward, grinding myself along his cock.

"Hmm. The idea of him..."

"Go on..." I encouraged, positioning myself more securely atop my most favorite armament. Cato shifted invitingly, and I purred in delight.

"It makes me shy."

"*Oh.*" I'd expected some form of sexy banter or an explicit comment meant to send me over the cliff while I dry-fucked him—I wasn't prepared for his vulnerability.

"I like to have control, and I am uncomfortable relinquishing it."

"And that's perfectly acceptable," I squeezed my thighs and tilted my hips, imagining Ambrose at Cato's back or me perched on Cato's face while I kissed Ambrose and he thrust himself into Cato's tightness. "But if you would like to practice... I know someone who would be more than willing to wield the sword."

"I will say it again, and listen to me well, woman. I have no interest in Wren."

Did he just?!

"Sir!" I screeched, sending my fist flying toward his pretty new nose.

Wrist caught and arm twisted, I found myself flipped, face pressed into the mattress.

"*This* is my position, wife. Allow me to remind you of where *you* belong."

The slip of Cato's tunic along my legs as he hastily bunched the material was an unanticipated aphrodisiac.

I slickened at his absurdly misogynistic proclamation.

"Recruits!"

The room brightened, and the wall lamp fired to a blaze.

Cato shot backward, and I fell to my side, ready to feign sleep.

"Bro!"

Junnie's amused face popped through the threshold, followed by a grinning Rollo and Robyn... and Wren.

"Go. The. Fuck. Away," a quickly escalating Cato growled. "Before I—"

"Look at you, bro!" Rollo pointed to the wedge tent at Cato's crotch. "You did it, my man!"

"Dæne." Brooks elbowed his way to the threshold, hands held up in apology. "We're just looking out for your purity, bro. Things can get heated, being all like, in close proximity and what have you. Pent-up desires and stuff can lead you down, like, the path of immorality."

"Gross." Wren's shard-like eyes pierced mine. "What's a cleaning girl like you even thinking, throwing yourself at a research boy?"

"Who, me?" I rose on my knees, turned, and shoved Cato backward. His head met my mattress as I descended. "It's just mouth stuff. I promise I'll leave his purity *intact*."

I allowed them just a glimpse of the tenting caused by his erection before I blocked the view with my bent elbow. He watched me like a man drugged, eyes hazed over and mouth slack, as I trailed my fingers along the pulsing vein of his underside and dipped my head low.

"Dæne! My man!"

"Shut up, Junnie!"

"Turn off the lights. Come on."

"She's what gets him hard? Ugh, slut!"

The light went out, and I pushed Cato's tunic above his hips.

His hand found the back of my head; he gripped my hair tightly, forcing me to look up. His pupils were dilated, focus riveted to my lips.

"Indeed... Birdie is most adept at *mouth stuff*." He thrust up while guiding my head down.

I swirled my tongue around his leaking tip and took him to the base, relaxing my throat as his hips jerked in response.

Question my man's virility? Like, fuck you will... bro.

CHAPTER TWENTY-NINE

PAIN

EIRA

"Healer Richmonde, we are men of import! The tone of this missive was one of pure disrespect. The brothers Haycroft take orders from the Primus-King and no other."

I kept my head downcast and tried to slip past the two men blocking the chamber door. They were making me late to my room, which would then cause a chain reaction of delays. My arms shook under the weight of a heavy stack of bowls, and yet, they paid me no attention, even as I wavered. A person from my homeland would have opened the door; the men of Monwyn would have taken the load from my arms.

One of the brothers, in a long coat of fine burgundy linen and tight brown leathers, flung out his arm, shaking a parchment. He hit my stack, shifting its weight, which sent me into the wall.

Three bowls clattered to the floor, but thankfully didn't break. I'd just spent the last hour washing them.

"Clumsy." He turned, sniffed, and went back to his rant.

Okay, well, I fucking hate him. Great way to start my day.

"The matters of state cannot be interrupted in these trying times. You of all people should know that, healer. The threat Solnna poses impacts us all."

The two red-faced Gaeans clasped their hands behind their backs. The twins had jet-hued hair cut to their scalps and close-cropped beards covered their jaws.

"Receiving this scathing note from the courier was downright unseemly." The slightly taller of the identical men shoved the parchment under the healer's nose and flattened it with a snap. "Imagine, if you will, my servant reading the words, 'A pox upon your houses, brothers Haycroft. May your children abandon you in your hour of need and may your chickens succumb to a shit plague,' in front of both Zephyr and Merritt, the heirs to the Gaean throne! Who writes such a thing? Who would dare?"

I bit my cheeks to keep the corners of my lips locked firmly in place.

I do, motherfucker. I dare.

The courier service worked faster than I expected.

"We do not raise chickens; we are not peasants." The other brother, Haycroft, piped up.

Huh. Apparently, neither of them had ever been on the receiving end of the common Nortian curse.

"Had the Primus-King been in attendance as per usual, I would have demanded the writer flogged! I would wield the whip myself!" Spit flew from his lips as he spoke. "Mother may be ill but—"

"She's not *ill*. She's dying." I shrank back, mentally chiding myself for the sudden outburst. Even if my delivery had been soft, I knew better than to assert myself with the upper crust of society. That kind of slip-up would see me in chains. *Get your head in the game, Eira.*

A hand lashed out.

"Ouch!" I fell to the floor, bowls breaking and shards of glazed pottery flying. I pressed my hand to the stinging spot under my eye, and my fingers came back tinted red.

He hit me. He... he hit me.

Æther spiked through my palms, begging to be released into his skull, even as my mind tried coming to terms with having received the blow.

Calm, Eira, meek. You are a servant.

"Purification recruit fancies herself a healer?" the taller twin said as he righted a ring, adorned with a chunk of malachite the size of his ego, back on his finger.

One... two... three... breathe... four...

"What? Has the loudmouthed lowling gone silent after realizing to whom she spoke? Will you beg me not to report you? Look at me when I address you."

The man cocked his dark slash of a brow.

I stared past him, eyes dry, teeth clenched.

He struck, and I braced myself for impact.

"Do we employ cows now?" Fingers dug into my chin and cheeks, sharp nails sinking into my soft skin. He tightened his grip, but I refused to acknowledge him.

"Julian, stop. Just look into those vacant eyes. Not a thought behind them. What she claims about mother is no doubt—"

"True," Healer Richmonde interrupted the standoff. "My Lords, we have no way to identify who wrote the missive, as it is unsigned and so many pass through the Cult, but the recruit is correct in her assessment of your mother's condition."

Lord Julian spun on the healer. "Why were we not informed?"

Healer Richmonde inclined their head in thought.

"As with many patients, they do not wish to burden their loved ones and—"

"How long does she have?" Shorter twin Haycroft asked, concern marring his unlined brow.

The healer gestured noncommittally.

"Only Mother Merrias knows for sure, but if she is not with us when the door is opened, I would not be surprised."

Lord Asscroft gripped his brother's elbow, visibly shaken. "Open the door," he commanded.

Healer Richmonde led the way.

I steeled my nerves and prepared myself for the smell. There was nothing I could compare it to, and despite the efforts of the recruits who worked through the night, the scent took me aback once again, though I managed not to become ill.

The brothers rushed to their mother's side. Richmonde examined my face.

"Life is truly cyclical, recruit. In old age, we are once more reduced to the state of a babe, and it is our children that guide us into the next world." The healer checked their timepiece. "You don't need stitching. It isn't deep."

"B-boys. My beautiful b—"

Lady Haycroft was still with us, though barely. Her voice broke off. Her eyes glistened.

"Mama," Lord Julian took her hand into his, as careful as if she were made of blown glass. "Mama, why did you not send word?"

After meticulously cleaning the small cut on my face and ensuring that not a speck of blood remained, I left them to their tragic reunion to sweep the bits of glass from the hallway.

And then I was on to the next room.

Swift steps made for fast work as I gathered sheets for washing and replaced the lost stack of bowls. Young Gavin was as I'd seen him yesterday, and though I could see no difference in his flesh, Healer Kristen pointed out several areas of new pink skin, and under her tutelage, her trainees did the same.

I wondered what would happen if a flake of the scab forming on my face found its way into his poultice... but quickly shoved the thought away.

In the fourth room of the day, the healer prepared to lance a wound that wouldn't cease bleeding. They'd tried everything from herbs to pressure to bandages and then attempted to place a set of pinchers on whatever was causing the issue. Nothing would stem its flow.

Sweat poured from my brow, and for once, it wasn't from the confounded heat that constantly afflicted me. I worked a bellows, blowing air into an inlet hole that stoked the flames of a brazier. Above me, a metal pin was heated to glowing.

I remembered the day of the Rite, when I'd received my brand. The pain was so intense that I'd passed out—and that was a fast poke.

"When the lance is introduced, the trainees will hold you. The natural reflex is to flee from pain or jerk away, but it is integral for your safety that you are immobilized."

My eyes were the size of saucers. I was not cut out for this life; healers and purification recruits earned their place in the Cradle.

Be brave, Eira, be resolute.

"Greyla, you may scream or lose consciousness. Both are fine. Do you have any quest—" A frantic knock sounded.

"Recruit, the door."

I dropped the bellows handle, thankful for a reprieve.

It was Robyn.

"Minister Raina calls for Birdie." She held a missive between two fingers and handed it over to the healer, who quickly scanned it. "I'll take over her duties."

Shit. I was in trouble.

I moved toward the door, only for Robyn to block my way.

"Birdie, it's Dæne. He's—oh, Birdie, he's—"

"Where is he?" I shook her hand off, preparing to run.

"Downstairs, Amethyst Hall. Be careful; don't make a scene. The Baldorvans are touring, and you and I will lose our jobs if the ministers catch wind of our swap."

I nodded. "Thank you, Robyn."

Speed-walking across the atrium, the lift came into view. Sure enough, the fucking Baldorvans and a crowd of priests blocked the damn thing. It would be a half hour before the lift freed up.

"Fuck!" I jumped, startled by the release of the copper pipes. Steam spurted forth and... and gave me an idea.

I ducked into a vacant room and steadied myself before becoming shade. Evanescing through walls might have been faster, but I didn't know the layout of the Cult well enough, and if anyone saw me passing through a random wall, all nether would break loose. Cult Mossius at its calmest still resembled an anthill: swarms of people constantly running about.

Floating along the ceiling, I hovered in the dark apex of a corner until the copper piping burst open again.

The steam didn't burn me, but it did propel me at an alarming speed. The dark was disorienting, and in mere seconds, the pressure forced me down and burped me out into a bright room. The gust that issued behind me forced me to the room's floor, where I quickly sought refuge in the shadow of a chair's seat. The room was so well lit that a random shadow would be wholly out of place.

Open, open! I kept my gaze on the copper flap. Cato needed me. I should've waited for the lift instead of rushing in like—

"The Baldorvans agreed to a truce if she is delivered into their hands."

My shade expanded. Winding tendrils licked the chair legs. I floated to the table's underside as I continued to swell.

It was he... the Primus-King. I recognized the timbre of his calm and steady voice.

His time had come.

Three sets of legs. All of their owners would need to perish; none could live to tell the tale of how the fire started.

I sent out a wisp of shadows, coiling them around the table's leg. The chair at the head of the table scraped the floor as its owner stood.

As my view cleared, recognition dawned. We were in the glass-walled chamber below the massive brazier. Witnesses would be inevitable, but I could call upon the æther to keep the door's metal lock shut after setting the blaze.

Come to me, flames. Dance upon my father's wicked form and—

A baby cooed, the sweet and unmistakable sound dousing my fury like so much water.

The infant squealed again, and I turned toward the noise. Two tiny feet poked out over a much older pair of knees. A chubby fist, with little stars for knuckles, gripped the Primus-King's fingers, his gold signet ring visible on his thumb.

"Father, Emryss is our sister; she is family. We cannot hand her over to them. Take the towel, Father; the baby just ate and—well, too late."

Chair legs scraped the floor, and I watched an ankle cross over a knee as the other pair of legs shifted. Fur-lined silk dragged across the white marble floor.

"It is nothing, son of mine. I've been covered in spit-up most of my life; the flood is well worth the visit with my grandchild."

"Both of you, focus," an aggravated voice chastised. "You both fail to see the bigger issue. We do not have her, Zephyr. If she cannot be found, it is Father they will take in her stead. The Baldorvan Seer proclaimed that the god Leyometh demands the return of his essence, and until that time, they will continue enslaving any of those who revere the Goddess. It is our sister—bless her name—or he. If Father is taken, the kingdom will fall apart in a matter of weeks. Father, you *are* Gaea, the very reason for its glory. Our people thrive because of you."

The Primus-King folded a hand around his grandchild's rounded stomach.

I studied that hand. Calluses textured the side of his thumb and index finger; ink stained his nails. Scholar's hands.

"My sons, my heirs, you have been raised to take the reins. I will go to them. I am not likely to survive the next two years, as I ingested the last remnants of my Lifemate's blood prior to visiting Monwyn. My wife, Vonnie, didn't attend the Joining. As for Emryss, that loathsome Scion-Prince and his ill-mannered brother caged her, held her captive, never once leaving her side. I managed a single dance with her; I knew her to be kind... just deprived of a father's love. I could have convinced her to join us if only I'd had the chance."

A chance? Why had he not come as himself if he only wished to converse? Why had he hidden his identity?

I knew the answer.

If he'd come as the sitting monarch of Gaea, he'd not have had the opportunity to take me by force if I spurned him.

"What of the Others? Father, there must be more than just her. We will continue our search."

"Merritt, you know the answer. We've combined my emissions with that of centaurs and wraiths, witches and human women. Though the touch has been, by the Goddess's grace, granted to many of my sons, naturally conceived or inseminated, none of my offspring bear the blood gift. Vonnie and then Emryss were made unique."

His issue was combined with? Was he...

The pipe spat steam, and I flew into its opening.

Cato first. He came before all others, even if it was to our detriment.

Two wrong turns and one crowded room foiled me before I burst into a closet filled with supplies, some of which, thankfully, were uniforms. In my fluster, I'd forgotten I'd reemerge in the nude. Again, the kind of action that would get me caught.

Should I have killed them all?

I dressed quickly, the tunic too long but sufficient for my needs. I sped through the archway surrounded by glinting purple stones.

There was no need to search for which room contained him.

The war had begun; I'd recognize the bark of that order anywhere.

I was swept up into chaos before I even opened the door.

"Cover your breasts, harlot!"

Cato brandished a tongue depressor at a topless Wren and the other, more mature woman who had cornered him.

"Dæne, like, you almost had it, man! Give one a squeeze or—"

Cato launched a bedpan at Junnie's chest, hitting him square on. The young man doubled over. Rollo went to the bro's aid, ducking as another vessel flew.

"I almost had it *before* you ignorant cretins introduced the demon and her grandmother!"

"Your eyes were closed, bro; we'd just thought if some tits were there when you opened them, you'd pop off."

Minister Alder flailed his arms, calling for order. "I think, Dæne, that it is time to reconsider your life as a research specimen. Your lack of virility notwithstanding, the violence you are capable of is highly concerning!"

"Dæne," I whispered the name, and Cato turned to me. His head fell back against the wall, his shoulders fell, and he no longer resembled a wild animal running from a band of hunters. He swallowed, straightened his posture, and nodded at the minister.

"With recruit Birdie's assistance, I believe I stand a chance at producing a sample... like, bro."

Minister Alder hesitated.

"Mossius as my witness, Alder. Bro stood like a stele last night." Rollo, face full of concern, shot a stiff arm into the air. "Rock solid, my man."

My eyes bounced between the multitude of people in the room. Three naked men, two healers, two topless—apparently untempting—temptresses, a woman scribbling notes, and the minister all looked back at me with pleading eyes.

"It would keep us from chancing the Lead Healer's wrath." Minister Alder dipped his head as he worried the skin around his fingers with his nails. "Birdie, might you..."

We couldn't risk expulsion. Not now. There were layers to the Primus-King's treachery. We needed proof and word sent to Verus. It would be more than I could handle on my own.

"I would be honored to... assist." I curtsied, holding the panels of my tunic wide. The proper decorum for medically induced ejaculation was glossed over in Troth training, so I erred on the side of politeness.

"Oh, praise her name! Let us not suffer the Lead Healer's wicked mouth this day."

I held Cato's eyes but couldn't help tossing a sidelong glance at Wren before the minister shooed her away through an adjoining door. She was miffed, and I, all of a sudden, was as smug as a sneaky snowfox finding a hole in a henhouse.

I observed the others observing Cato, who stood proud in his tiny underclothes. He was damnably beautiful, all inked muscles and hard planes. The sneer on his face may have kept his audience at a distance, but it drew me in, the Bond alive and intense.

"Healer, is it necessary for so many to watch?" I asked, without looking at her or her assistant, my eyes adhered to Cato's crotch. I was thirsty, and he provided my favorite refreshment. My passage grew heavy—she bloomed under my mate's gaze, no matter the surroundings.

"It is, recruit. The issue must be witnessed. Research demands it to maintain fidelity."

I nodded.

"Fidelity, of course. To ensure the sample is..."

"Untainted," the other healer supplied. "From the selected source."

"Right. Well then, Dæne. In the name of science, do you mind if I..." I pointed to where the wool of his tunic was pilled and stretched. Let me find out that Wren had pawed him. Young she may be, but consent was a lesson to be learned at the earliest age.

"Yes, Miss Birdie. I'd be most obliged if you would... assist me... bro."

The atmosphere shifted, the high energy settling as I neared my husband.

Keep your eyes on me. No others exist.

"The Goddess favors you, Dæne, formerly of Solnna; you possess the body of a warrior and the face of a king."

My warrior-king.

Cato cleared his throat, nostrils flaring, his penis stirring to life. He positioned his back against the side of a healer's table and held on to its leather top with both hands.

"Well done, recruit!" Minister Alder clapped behind my head, and then his chin perched upon my shoulder. "Now, to keep him erect—"

"I've got this, Minister. Respectfully."

The door opened behind us, and I quickly closed the distance, covering Cato's eyes with one palm and stroking his length with my other.

"Don't succumb to the distractions; close your eyes, Dæne. Let me help you." I slicked my tongue over Cato's nipple, and his fingers dug deeper into the table. "That's it, handsome, pretend it's my thick, beautiful ass in your hands."

Cato groaned, the gravelly sound seducing me. I squeezed my thighs, delighting in the divine throb he elicited.

I reached beneath his clothing, keeping as much of him covered as possible, and skimmed my fingers over the droplet at his tip. His response pleased me so thoroughly that it was difficult not to fall on my knees and worship him properly.

"Welcome to research, Emberkin Arro. You've caught us at an excellent time."

Cato's tension returned in full force. His arms stiffened, his jaw clenched, and his body coiled into an unforgiving mass of aggression.

"Minister? Is mouth stuff permitted?" I asked.

"I—well, healer, would it taint the sample?"

"Alder, she's good at mouth stuff, I promise," Junnie piped up from "like" a foot away. *No boundaries. Not a single one.*

I could feel their collective eyes on my back, and not in disgust or upset. They wanted Cato to succeed—I could practically hear their prayers—no wait, Rollo was verbally evoking Mossius's aid.

"If the mouth is removed prior to ejaculation, the sample may be studied and—"

"The woman is to fellate this man? As research?" A rough voice gritted out, followed by a malicious laugh. "I suffer a fever. Will she see to me after this patient? How does a Baldorvan become a specimen, eh?"

A chorus of male laughter broke out.

"As a cadaver," Cato hissed into my ear.

"Eyes closed," I demanded. "Now."

Cato squeezed them shut, his jaw flickering as he clamped his teeth tighter.

I gathered the hem of his tunic and scrunched it up, catching his flagging member in my hand. Spitting into my palm, I glided the tips of my fingers along his underside until I could feel the bulge of the vein I loved to trace with my tongue. With my other hand, I cupped his sac, appreciating its weight.

"The woman knows her way around a weapon. I will avail myself of her next," the Baldorvan interrupted again. The unmistakable sound of a belt loosening hit my ears... and Cato's.

His nose flared at the corners, the beast within him awakening. He would blow our cover.

"Eyes closed, handsome. I love the way you feel." I dropped to my knees and took his cock to its base, sucking him in until he bottomed out at the back of my throat.

What the?

My eyes widened. An inked serpent coiled around his leg where the conjurer's protective ward used to be. The lengths Cato had gone to ensure he'd not be recognized while he sought me out turned me molten. Gods, how I craved this madman. Arousal spiked within me, my core tightening. Let the Baldorvan watch; let him witness what he would never have—love. Pure and magical love.

"That's the little bitch from upstairs, Julian. Consider my poor opinion of her changed."

The twins. Great fucking day.

I tightened my lips and sucked until I heard Cato's moan. I increased my speed, hoping to bring him about faster.

"Fuck," Cato groaned above me. "Fucking outstanding."

I added a hand, pumping him into my mouth while sucking him so hard my cheeks tunneled.

The goddamned door opened and closed again.

Was the Goddess herself against us? I doubled down, palpating the skin between Cato's sac and backside. His erection softened as he fought to maintain concentration.

"Ah, yes, Father, thank you for joining us. I hope your travels were easy," Minister Alder said.

"Oho! The Mantle was remiss in detailing the nature of our welcome to Gaea."

I froze.

Ambrose!

Yes, wifey?

CHAPTER THIRTY

HOW THE FIGHTY DOTH FALL

AMBROSE

"What do we have here, Minister?"

I tossed my ruby-and-gold-striped silks in a practiced swirl about my ankles and flounced across the floor before leaning a hip on a tall stool.

I kept my face serene as I watched her work—so talented, so giving.

Though her hair was now the hue of freshly barfed bile, the stirrings of attraction inundated my very soul. Is that what love does to a man? When she swelled with my son, would her puffy cankles please my eye? Oh, probably; she'd be sexy waddling around like one of those chubby, black-and-white ice birds that she chattered about so often.

My wife.

She kept her neck arched and lips tight like the good girl she was, and I drank her in. Her form was impeccable, thighs splayed wide as she kneeled, hands working in tandem to draw forth pleasure... awe-inspiring.

My heart was not my own. Not anymore. No, she held it firmly in the care of those cracked and peeling nails.

My brow furrowed as I continued my perusal.

Had I been remiss in not demanding she return to me? I'd assumed her to be hale and hearty and wished to allow her freedom to pursue her goals. Seeing her now, though, I wondered if I'd failed at my husbandly duties.

The heavy hand of shame settled upon my shoulder.

Cato and I had fought fiercely over my choice, coming to blows more than once, and now there was the evidence that he may have been in the right all along. Her brows cried out for a pluck... her skin needed a treatment of butters—shea, coconut, *and* cocoa. She required several days of pampering to restore her radiant glow.

I assessed the graceful hollow of her cheeks and the flash of her pretty pink tongue.

Eira was love in its most human form, and I would see things righted. I would dress her down—literally, not figuratively—and we'd spend the day in the bath working to rebuild our physical connection through massage and mud treatments and fucking and fine foods.

There was no holding back my appreciative sigh.

I moved to the other side of the table to better view her at work. She hadn't seen me yet, but there was no need for eyes when you were connected by a Bond as tightly as she and I.

Enjoy that thick dick, my nasty harpy. Cato will find himself split from navel to sternum before nightfall, if the weather holds. I have made arrangements to stomp on his deceitful entrails under the beauteous copper lanterns, but the rain and wind simply cannot make up their minds.

My glorious wife, a masterwork of soft curves and handholds, attempted to keep the steady rhythm of her mouth around Cato's erection, but my magnanimous presence slackened him, the blood draining from his dick as fast as the light from his dull brown eyes. Stupid poo eyes. I hated them.

"Welcome to Cult Mossius, Father; the Primus-King informed us of your arrival!" The minister clapped his hands and performed a series of quick bows. "Here we have the examination of our newest research specimen, hand-chosen by our illustrious Lead Healer for his looks, abilities, and intelligence."

I allowed my eyes to rove over Cato, the betrayer—he could certainly see all seven feet of me. I'd made sure of it, placing myself just so.

"Hmmm. Minister, was it the missing toe that placed him above the other potential candidates? Or his pint-sized stature?"

Ambrose, don't goad him. If he fails to reach completion, he loses his position, and our chances to observe the Primus-King dwindle even further.

Sounds like a him problem, lovely one.

I moseyed across the floor, no longer satisfied with seeing just the back of her head and a few glimpses of her profile.

"Ah, the woman. Minister, by the gods... I see why *she* passed muster. I should like to inspect her myself."

Lykksun's divine kneecaps, cut it out, Ambrose.

My fingers sought her chin and lifted before the minister could reject my request.

"What the—" Eira cried out, dropping the dangling dick in her hand. "What have you... "

Eira's eyes, those beautiful swamp lichen orbs, filled with tears... but not the fun kind she'd once shed from a dick stab to the uvula.

Wifey had missed her husband.

"Is she as soft as she looks, Father?" Emberkin Arro, the scrumptious bit of a Baldorvan, asked while adjusting himself. "She has the kind of flesh a man could grab onto."

Eira scrambled around, grasping for the cock she'd lost, all the while fighting her natural inclination to gaze upon her husband. Me. Her *actual* husband. Not some spiritual forest fuck bullshit.

Ambrose, Black Bear, the illness—I was told you'd fully recovered. I see that is not the case. Forgive me, my love. Forgive me for not being there to do more.

A veritable picture book of emotions flashed over her fair visage. My awful little Troth, she was incapable of true neutrality.

What? No! I am a man whole, but you will spend years atoning for your absence. And though appalled by your clandestine behavior with Uncle Septimus, after weeks of grappling with my emotions, I've decided to love you still.

She blinked the tears away, the faintest smile appearing on her blowjob-swollen lips.

I will, Ambrose, I will. A-and you are still the most handsome man I know, despite y-your...

"Recruit! What is amiss?" Minister Alder rushed to my side. "She is not used to being in the city. I am sure that is why she is staring at you so awkwardly. Please accept my apologies, Father."

Eira pointed a wavering finger.

"I-I, uh, yes. I've never seen something so fine. They glitter like the stars above." She pointed to the jeweled bracelets I'd borrowed from my sibling. All the other priests who had traveled with me had been envious of the finery as well. *Covetous bitches.*

The Baldorvan, flanked by one of his veiled guards, pushed their way forward.

"Allow me to show you mine. Yes?" The Baldorvan produced his tattoo-covered hands. On them, bands of silver, red diamonds, and black opal drew my attention. I found myself impressed and perhaps a tad envious of the number of rare gems gracing his person.

Eira spun on her knees, poking a finger into the slaver's thigh. "Save your breath. I'm not impressed by wealth... noble and gracious protector of Gaea." She bowed her head demurely and patted the spot where she'd just jabbed him.

The ambassador rubbed his beard, licking his foul lips—*foul* could only be a metaphorical description—the man not only had impeccable hygiene but also an enticing combination of features. Piercing eyes of the lightest slate were fringed by impossibly black lashes, made doubly thick by the line of kohl swiped under his eye. His nose, long of bridge but wide at its base, was reminiscent of an arrow's head, and his lips... Well, they were okay. His canines were capped in a silver that matched his eyes. And his skin... mmm... tan like the people who hailed from the desert, with reddish undertones that I'd like to—

"Minister, can you couple with your slaves in Gaea? In Baldorva we'd not debase ourselves, but here I could make an exception for the gentle-tongued whore."

Did he just call her a—

"She is no slave," I seethed, clamping my teeth behind my smile. "There is no place in Ærta where such heinousness is permitted. Whore though? Eh, perhaps."

"Sex worker, Father, don't disparage," Eira murmured, covering Cato's deflated failure with her hand.

"Ah, a coin for the whore, then? I have many coins. I will give one to her benefactor now and another when the deed is done. Is the limp dick your handler, sex worker? Have her sent to me tomorrow." The foreigner dug around in his pocket and then flipped a coin at Cato's chest. It rolled down his body and clanged to the floor.

Minister Alder stuttered something unintelligible. Cato's thighs tightened, ready to pounce. I imagined embedding that coin into the thin slit of his eye.

Ambrose, please! Change the subject before Cato explodes!

Why? I do not see why they shouldn't fight. Tiring him out will make Cato easier to murder. And by the looks of him, Cato is not in any danger of an explosion.

I stepped between my woman and the Baldorvan at her back.

"I do apologize, Emberkin; however, the exchange of coin for sexual gratification is not permitted in Gaea." I shrugged off my overrobe and pushed my slipping spectacles up my nose. "I bet she'd do it for a sugary snack, though."

What the fuck, Ambrose?!

Eira, do not scream; it gives me the most grievous of headaches. I need all my faculties to change the subject, as demanded.

Emberkin Arro leaned to his leftmost guard, whispering something not meant for the ears of the others in the room. His eyes flicked to my wife, and I plotted his death.

"All in jest, Minister. Gaean snacks are entirely lacking in flavor." Fisting my hands at my back, I rounded and bent over a seated healer, glancing at her scribe's notes. "If you will, bring the focus back to the tour. All of us—minus these tempting twins—came to witness the Primus-King's special project. The Lead Healer is quite proud of his research outcomes, and Verus wishes a full report upon my return."

"Yes, at once!" Minister Alder flapped his arms and gathered the audience closer. "Here in research, we test the strength and abilities of young men who meet a particular standard set by our Primus-King."

"Bros! That's us," a sinewy blond hollered while initiating a bizarre handshaking ritual with another.

They barked like dogs and thumped their chests.

Yeesh. Wife, are these truly the best specimens Gaea offers? Well, that redhead is fuckable, but the others...

Ambrose, stay focused, please, I'm begging you.

My love-weakened heart could not stand the sadness flowing through our connection.

I am a benevolent spouse and will always seek to solve your problems. Do you hear me? Punch his left testicle if you hear me.

Ambrose!

I drew the air into my lungs and channeled my inner thespian.

"Noble healers, good Minister, what seems to be the problem with this specimen, then? And what in the gods' names are you testing for?" I looked high and then low before snatching up a metal implement from a table and holding it aloft.

The minister fluttered nervous hands in the direction of my evil former lover.

"Dæne is a unique candidate. He surpasses our physical criteria as far as exertion and endurance are concerned, and he is as quick-witted as they come. We have run into a small issue, though, and cannot continue on with him, unfortunately. I am afraid that even an interesting prospect can't forgo any steps in our process; Dæne will leave us tonight."

"Alder, bro, give him another shot, man," the red-headed sculpture interjected.

"Dæne is, like, a super good wrestler and stuff," a lovely brunette offered.

The minister shook his head, his mouth drooping at the corners.

Ambrose, we have a plan. Larm is here, and Pa and Momma. And now, I need Cato here because—

And, oddly, I was not invited.

I inspected the implement, holding it close and turning it about.

Please, Black Bear. I can't, I just can't—

—be separated from him again?

My barbed words cut straight through her; I saw it in the roll of her soft shoulders. She wrung her hands together and—my breath hitched.

She wore it still.

And I had been so quick to place my ire at her feet.

The gold-and-silver ring caught the harsh light of the room. It was the outward sign of our love.

Minister Alder patted Manbun's back in a fatherly gesture. "I am sorry, young sirs, but we must move on and—"

"Minister, I say, have you employed the queenmaker's touch?" I splayed my fingers, fanning them out, inspecting their precision file. "Emission guaranteed, no erection required."

"Pardon?" The minister replied, intrigue replacing his disappointment.

I cracked my knuckles.

"Gods above, an entire kingdom of body-loving naturalists, and not a single one of you understands a man's functioning at all. Fetch me a lubricant, and I shall demonstrate."

I snapped, but not a soul stirred to carry out my bidding.

That normally works at home.

We aren't at home.

"I'll allow it," said the seated healer, who had the most divine alabaster complexion my eyes had ever beheld.

The minister hesitated and then nodded to a woman scribbling notes. She hurried to the cabinets along the back wall and pulled forth a jar filled with a thick white substance. Emulsified oil, most likely. Not my favorite, but Catommandus was undeserving of a silken slip, so no matter.

With a confidence befitting my fake station of emissary and priest, I shooed Eira away and came to stand before Cato, leering at him through my frames.

What an ugly nose he has. How have I never noticed it?

Eira sobbed through the connection.

It's not a reflection on you, sweet harpy. You had no choice in the Dick Bond.

Cato's eyes bore into mine. He lacked the proper expression for a man staring into the eyes of his savior—I'd change that momentarily.

I pinched Cato's wrist with two fingers and held his arm aloft, sniffing.

"Minister, you are positive this is your chosen specimen and not some odd variable tossed in to measure the validity of your hypothesisious?"

The healers in the room outright laughed. I looked between them. My question was of a serious nature. Why in the nether would they have chosen this flea of a man?

It's hypothesis, Ambrose!

Hush, wife, I was close enough.

I tapped a finger into the divot of my clean-shaven chin and then tweaked the stiff side curl of my mustache.

"Dæne, is it? Come. Bend over the end of the table and spread those mediocre thighs of yours."

Cato glared, and I batted my lashes while pointing to the table.

Color bloomed at the base of his neck. I grinned.

Going to fight me, big boy? Attack a man of the Goddess in a crowd of witnesses?

The pressure building between us could blow the roof clear off Cult Mossius.

I arched a brow.

Cato narrowed his eyes... the challenge accepted.

The man who once completed the puzzle of my incomplete heart marched forward like a soldier to battle, his eyes flashing a warning as he passed.

Cato smacked the leather table as he bent at the hips.

Let his reckoning begin.

Stop that!

I held the lubrication jar aloft.

Get thee from my head!

"Please come closer, everyone, gather round so you can learn the finer points of a *very* clinical practice."

Oh, my Goddess. Ambrose, who are you even supposed to be?

Like a scene in my books of love, the others in the room faded away.

Cannot you tell by my new coiffure, wife? Or are your eyes only for another?

I twisted the jar's lid and sniffed its contents.

I am the balding man who insists on preserving the remnants of his former glory by combing the meager wisps of his dwindling youth diligently to one side. I am the man recapturing his vigor through the gloriousness of his facial hair, when that of my head has failed.

I dumped the jar upside down, studying its viscosity, nodding as I found the substance acceptable.

Hear me, wife! I am Father Regulus, right hand of the Mantle, Their Most Revered and Holy Servant, Sovereign of Verus, Shepherd of the Ærtan Flock, but mayhap more importantly... I am the aggrieved husband and shunned lover who has come to mete out justice!

Eira's face collapsed. She bent double, burying her head in her hands. Contrite... just as she should be.

I turned on my heel and walked the ring of humans, stopping before each to show the contents of the jar—I memorized their features and took their measure as I passed by, ever the observant Scion.

"Listen well, students. Deep in the dark cavern, there is a secret gem nestled amid the brown stones. Only a practiced miner can reveal its profound mystery."

Be serious, Ambrose.

I am deadly serious, wifling.

I pointed to the ceiling, and the bell-shaped sleeve of my robe fell to my elbow, revealing the magnificent sage embroidery worked into my cuff.

"The introduction of a single digit is best practice, but looking at the size of this asshole, we will begin with two."

Ambrose, you will hurt him. Calm yourself before you make matters worse.

Hush, negligent spouse. This is a matter between men.

I dunked my middle and index fingers into the unscented concoction and then inspected them for adequate coverage.

"You, haystack hair, Cult Mossius fluffer, lift the specimen's man-dress and part his flat cheeks. Make sure all have ample view as I impart this wisdom in the name of research."

Ambrose Berra Odell... whatever your other names are, the moment I get you alone—

Eira hurried to Cato, who gave her a terse nod. Their eyes locked; trust poured between them. Revolting.

Eira bent, and my eyes lingered on her broad ass. She gently tugged at Cato's garment.

Did the room get hot? Stiflingly so?

Hurry, wife. I grow tired and have a massage and fine meal waiting in my chambers. My apartments are divine, the servants gorgeous, the—

How gorgeous?

I heard the gravel in her voice clearly through the connection. Ahh, even with the grotesque state of my once glorious mane, she desired me—this love of ours was true.

Jealous wifey, do not fret. Though my eyes may linger along the lines of a lean Gaean limb, the curve of a perfect handful, my body has not known another. I made my vows to you before She Who Gave All. And Cato doesn't count. I hate him.

"Temple slut, expose the starfish."

Eira went left, hesitated, and then turned right.

"Just mount the table." I indicated the space behind Cato.

The Baldorvan chuckled, but I silenced him with a sharp snap of my fingers.

"Fine." Eira complied without berating me.

She reached over Cato's shoulders, skimming her fingers over his lightly haired buttocks before splitting and revealing his puckered flesh.

I fought back a sudden wave of melancholy, felt the burn of some healer's astringent stinging my eyes.

"Address me as my station requires," I barked at Eira.

"Fine, *Father*." She popped a provocative yet bushy brow.

Be careful, buxom brat, or fake-husband will receive your punishment.

I held her angry gaze and, without preamble, I struck, burying my slick digits to the second knuckle.

"Fuck!" Cato shouted, tensing around my two thick fingers.

"No, no." I flicked his ass cheek. "Do not squeeze; push."

Like the hardhead he was, he grunted, not heeding a single word of my advice.

I shoved forward and twisted my wrist.

"Gods-godsdamn." Cato clawed the leather cushion.

Eira, fickle mistress that she was, hugged Cato's head to her chest while he drew ragged breaths.

"Relax, Dæne. The priest is correct. The sphincter tissues are quite sensitive," the healer stated.

"Yes, relax, tightass," I concurred.

Eira whispered into Cato's ear and stroked his hair. Under her comforting guidance, he started to loosen.

Minister Alder ducked so close he nearly blocked my view. "A-and this will result in a sample?"

"It seems rather unpleasant." A taller healer, a man I'd not been introduced to, followed close on his heels, leaning in for observation.

"This, no, but this"—I changed tactics, locating the Goddess-given diamond that nestled so perfectly in the cave of secrets. I palpated the spot, dancing my fingertips over its slope—"in addition to the superb set of mammorials smashed against the specimen's face will hasten the process."

Mammaries, you giant goose!

Cato groaned and pressed back. His respiration increased.

"There you are, Dæne, well done," Eira whispered, rubbing his stupid bald face all over her tits. "Such a good specimen."

Cato's dick swelled in earnest, and I could practically see the æther bubbling within Eira.

This was how it should be—all of us together.

I missed her cunt fairies more than I missed my own mother, Goddess rest her bones. But I ached knowing we would no longer share in the enchantment of pleasing our lover in tandem. Cato would learn: if he could not love me at my worst, then he did not deserve to love me at my best.

"Father, might I have a go?"

"What!" I bellowed at the white-haired healer whose chin practically lay upon my shoulder. Jealousy reared within me like an angry green goblin. *How dare someone touch what belongs to—*

"Pardon me, Father, I suffer from low vision and see the majority with my hands."

The woman, clear-lashed and so uniquely attractive, leaned in with curiosity.

"Oh. Well, of course, yes." I nodded, slipping my fingers free. My erratic heart rate slowed.

Cato gave a low rumble as his head rested on the finest cleavage in all the lands.

"Will you allow the healer to enter you, Dæne?" Eira asked, running a hand down Cato's ridiculous crown of looping curls.

"Yes," he hissed through a clenched jaw.

With my hand on her elbow, I positioned the healer and slicked her fingers. She patted around and located the bull's brown eye.

"Though *my* gem is the very manly size of a walnut, you will find his to resemble its diminutive cousin, the simple acorn. Mmhmm, yes, now slide forward, twist and—"

Cato hummed, stifling the full-blown moan that I knew him capable of.

"Stay focused, Dæne," Eira murmured. "I am interested in the, um, potency of your sample."

"Well done, healer. Now, set a rhythm, slow and gentle but steady."

Cato's thighs tensed. He panted the sounds of a man nearing the heights... and I thanked Verus for the heavy traveling leathers beneath my robes. Never would he witness my response again.

"Clockwise, pat, pat, counterclockwise the same," I sang out the rhythm and inspected the healer's handiwork, adjusting her wrist ever so slightly. "Speed up. Mmhmm, pat, pat. Pat, pat."

Cato's knees buckled.

"You have inspired an impressive erection in the otherwise dysfunctional male," Minister Alder supplied.

"The vessel," the healer said with excitement. "His testicles tighten."

Minister Alder scurried over and held a shallow bowl under Cato's cock—his admittedly beautiful appendage.

"Come on, Dæne, bro!"

"You, like, got this, my man!"

"Silence!" I commanded, throwing a cautionary hand into the face of the yummy redhead. "Or we stand to lose what was so hard-fought."

Cato growled low in his throat while grabbing handfuls of Eira's bounty.

Ambrose, he's, he's losing it.

No tears, honey cunt. I'll not be the man who lets you down.

"Now that you have, er, invoked the stimulation, you may perform a very scientific jerkoff. Allow me to demonstrate."

I wrung my fingers around that middling erection, clenched my jaw, and tugged.

Eira whispered something in his ear.

"Oh, gods." Cato's head flew up, his lips parted.

I watched my wife, wondering at her reaction to it all.

My nasty little love demon was beside herself with lust, pupils enlarged, sitting back on a heel that wouldn't provide her nearly enough stimulation. I'd slake her later; she'd been without me for too long.

I pumped Cato fast, slipping my hand over his head, running my fingers over the ridge I knew was so sensitive. He stiffened.

"Fuck. Gods—Eir—gods."

Cato released a wealth, his essence collecting in the vessel below... like the pulp of my stomped-upon heart.

Thank you, Black Bear. You were amazing! Look at them all.

I turned, and my waning confidence buoyed.

The men, exuberant in their youth, raised their fists in the air, and the Baldorvan nodded, his mouth drawn in appreciation. One twin frowned while the other adjusted his pants.

"Fantastic!" Minister Alder cheered, passing the sample to the tall healer. The man walked into an adjoining chamber. "The sample looked promising, though the determination is not mine to make."

With bated breath, we waited.

Seconds ticked by, and then minutes.

The healer poked his head back through the threshold, grinning from ear to ear.

"The sample is perfection."

Cheers came from all around, garnering congratulatory slaps on the back. Perhaps I'd missed my true calling. What would life have been like had Monwyn not forcibly smashed the princely coronet upon my brow?

Minister Alder clapped his hands, sleeves swinging.

"Wren is fertile! Let us not wait to administer the sample. The criteria shows they are an excellent match."

WHAT?!

"Praise Her!" I fell to one knee, Eira's mental scream folding me in two. My spectacles clattered to the floor.

"Congratulations, Dæne, let me hug you!" Eira wrapped her arms around our false husband as he made to bolt and held him in an iron-tight embrace. "Father, will you offer congratulations with more hugs, tighter hugs?"

FIX THIS, MOTHERFUCKER! FIX THIS OR I WILL BURN YOU AND THIS GODSFORSAKEN CULT TO SOOT! I CAN'T HOLD HIM BACK MUCH LONGER!

I shot to my feet and headed toward the adjoining chamber.

"Healer, sir? Oh, healer! What part of the research is this?"

Minister Alder grabbed my elbow, but I shrugged him off.

"This is the pinnacle, Father Regulus. Here we achieve true perfection. But—but you are not allowed to—"

"Oh!" I barked out. "What fine examples of woman parts."

Two vaginas blinked at me as I walked through the door, one beautifully brown and ruby, and the other, the finest cherry-rose. With widespread legs and their hips up on inclines, one leafed through the pages of a book while the other chattered softly.

"Yes. Our female specimens endured the same rigorous testing as our males."

"Do they now?"

The healer hesitated briefly but then waved me over.

"Come closer."

I feigned interest in the vulvicular details of the vaginas, all the while inching toward the cabinet where glass tubes of baby batter were sorted into a neat row.

"And what lies beyond the flaps and folds? Forgive an old priest his ignorance."

The healer swabbed the genitals of each woman with not an ounce of the respect that the sensitive lips of divinity deserved.

"Ah, a network not unlike the..."

I spotted the splooge.

"How interesting, the felappionia tubes you say?"

"Fallopian."

I silently slid in the direction of the samples and squinted, bringing into focus the tube that sat upon the parchment marked *Dæne*.

"And which of these divine creatures is Wren?"

"Me!" The blue-eyed beauty waved a hand and then went back to her conversation.

Ambrose, what's happening? The boys took Cato to bathe. I have to go back to work!

"Ah, well, healer, I should like to perform the *spermination*, as I farmed the seed myself, yes?"

Black Bear, please! I cannot take this! I cannot! The thought of—

Hush, Eira, I cannot think!

"That is quite unorthodox, Father, so I think not—"

Eira hollered from the other room. We all glanced toward the other chamber.

"Oh! Haha. Emberkin, your strong and manly hands seem to have taken on a mind of their own. But, uh, back the fuck off, great protector, sir. I am a lady with morals."

Do not agitate the Baldorvan.

He squeezed my ass! Double palmed me!

"Gracious, just a moment." The healer walked toward the door.

I acted swiftly, popping the top of Cato's spillage and swapping it with a tube sitting on the parchment marked *June Bug*. The semen flowed free.

"Gad!" Palm to mouth, I nearly retched. What disgusting game did they play? Breeding humans and insects?

The door shut, sealing out Eira's voice.

"Oh, curses! I didn't seal it properly." The healer shoved me aside and procured Cato's swapped tube. He held it aloft, looking at it through the light. Hardly a drop remained.

He placed it back on the cabinet and clicked his tongue. "River, nothing for you today. I'm so sorry. We'll require Junnie to produce another sample."

I'm gonna stab him, Ambrose. He's got me all caged up against the wall.

"Wren, are you ready?" With a precision only healers seemed to possess, he procured the bug semen, inserted the glass length into the woman and— "Clench and hold, Wren."

I gagged. Vomit nearing the precipice.

It is fixed, Eira. Do not go puff demon.

"Thank you for the demonstration, healer; I must be off!"

The man nodded absentmindedly as I rushed toward the door.

"River, on second thought—damn these clumsy hands—let us not waste what Junnie has so thoughtfully provided."

I swung around.

Too late.

Chapter Thirty-One

CATO'S ICK WORD

Eira

The early morning hours were upon us.

One would have thought neither of us capable of sleeping, but after finishing out my shift, finding Cato and having an absolute meltdown over the conversations I'd overheard between the Primus-King and my brothers. I sobbed over the fact I hadn't splattered their brains over the pretty glass walls... weeping for never having had siblings... or nieces and nephews. Then Cato hashed out the political and dynastic implications of the Primus-King's personal breeding experiment—for two revolutions of the timepiece's hands—so the moment Cato crawled into the tiny chamber and nudged me toward the wall, slumber claimed me. He no longer snored with his new nose, and though I should be thanking Merrias, I was shaken by the change.

"Your knees are bruised."

"They're fine, but please continue." I wiggled my toes, and Cato took the hint and continued the foot rub he'd initiated to wake me. "I can't care about my knees," I yawned, open-mouthed and unashamed, "when my stomach is rumbling."

In the flickering light of a single taper, Cato crawled next to me, careful to move without making a sound. I felt the soft brush of his nightclothes against my back, the steady rise and fall of his chest, and the reassuring weight of his arm draped over my waist. He snugged his hips to mine. We were a perfect fit.

"Reiterate to me what Minister Raina said when she addressed you after dinner. Spare no detail."

I mulled over the conversation again.

"She said I was to dine with Father Regulus as a thank you for assisting him in your *extraction*."

Cato cringed.

"Thank you for ensuring we could remain together, Cato. I know it was—"

"Humiliating, uncomfortable... absolutely worth it."

I pressed my lips into a tight line, but he smoothed a thumb across them, lingering in the soft slope beneath my lip.

"It was a more pleasant form of torture than my previous experiences, though mark my words, I am leaving this place before Wren's womb has a chance to ripen." Cato made a gagging sound.

With fingers walking over my hip, he encouraged me to turn and face him.

I cracked a smile, though I knew it didn't reach my eyes.

"I would have eviscerated her *and* your ill-gotten love child."

"As well you should." Cato bent low and placed a kiss on the sensitive hollow beneath my ear.

"Will you extend my thanks to Ambrose after you debrief him at dinner? And shall we go over the line of questioning again?"

It was my turn to cringe.

"Yes, I will, but please, by the Goddess, spare me another talk of strategery, General Catommandus. No more lessons in interrogation. I'm intrigued the fuck out."

"I have methods aplenty to make you talk, my love. Perhaps a hands-on lesson?"

He lifted the blanket and disappeared, nipping my waist with sharp teeth. I shrieked, and his hand clapped over my mouth.

"Shhhh." He smiled against my stomach.

Cato pressed my thighs open and settled between them. His lips coasted lightly over the tops of my breasts, and I squirmed at the ticklish sensation.

"Settle," he murmured while gripping my hips. "And though a trying experience for myself, do not think I was unaware of the tune your body sang while witnessing my—"

"—milking?"

Cato popped up to his knees, tossing back the blanket.

"That is disgusting, Eira. You have managed to turn my stomach. Me, a man who has, with regularity, reached into the gaping cavity of the disemboweled." He clutched handfuls of my belly and shook it until I couldn't contain my laughter.

"But how was the orgasm?" I fanned my fingers out and slid my palms over his pectorals. "Sounded top tier from my position."

He blinked rapidly, his expression gone blank. I lifted and threaded my fingers into his mop of curls, tugging. He bent and dipped his tongue into my navel.

"Not nearly as cataclysmic as being fairy cunted."

Giggles burst from my mouth. Cato pressed a pillow to my face as he dropped and curled around me like a... well... very much like a cat.

"Shut up, Birdie," a sleepy groan came from down the hall.

"Arrrr ooo twyin to keel me?" I asked in a muffled voice.

Cato pulled the cover up and over our heads as I turned to face him. I quieted and counted the steady beats of his heart.

"Eira, when you are summoned to dinner... the Baldorvan."

"I know, I know." I skimmed my lips over the scar beneath his ink. "Stay away, don't go near him; you will burn the world if he touches me."

I'd heard it all before.

Silence.

"You must seduce the Baldorvan."

"What?" I smacked the side of my head like my ears were filled with seawater. "Say that again?"

"After dining with Ambrose, seek the foreigner. Feign illness or a need to relieve yourself and locate him. Ingratiate yourself and gather intel that we can use to stymie future attempts on your person. Eira, with what you overheard, it is clear that the Baldorvans will not rest until Leyometh's essence is returned. Convince him that this Emryss is a farce, and plant the idea that the Primus-King is a viable substitute."

"You've lost your fucking mind. I'll not willfully seduce such a vile human. Cato, you can't be serious."

I ripped the cover away, but Cato pulled it back into place.

"Keep your enemies close. The adage is old, but it is one that holds true. Earn his trust, plant false information about the lost daughter—it will reach the ears of his countrymen. Trust me. Change *his* mind, and the Baldorvans will turn on the Primus-King."

I fought Cato's embrace, but he caught my arms.

"Eira, it also provides another safeguard for you... for Ærta."

"Safe? How? You're asking me to... to fuck *another* man whom I loathe. First Septimus and now him? And for what?"

"I know, my love, I am well aware. But men guard their prizes like they do their treasure. Become his prize, and he will rain nether upon those who would seek to claim you. You are resilient and resourceful, and you alone have the unique means to remove yourself from potential escalation. If it comes to it, raze this city and leave, never look back."

I struggled, but Cato did not relinquish his hold.

"No."

"Yes. You had the chance to live with me as husband and wife—you chose vengeance. Were the goal simply the death of the Primus-King, I would guard you like the treasure you are. The Baldorvans will never stop. The forces they mobilize could engulf the continent, an army whose single focus is taking you from me. So we will do what it takes. Everything it takes. This is an 'at all costs' mission—this is the price we pay."

"You should have stayed away. You never should have sought me."

I wrestled free of his grasp and rose. He followed closely behind.

"Listen, Eira. Listen to me." Cato took my wrist in emphasis. "See me now as the tactician, not the husband. We lay the foundations for a multi-pronged strategy, which gives us a greater chance of success. Make the Baldorvan want you, crave you... trust you. Then feed him the story you wish him to believe. And if what you say is true, and the Primus-King has been impregnating other species and trapping them here, the Mantle will want proof of the allegations. I will find it. Larm will act as a go-between for Verus and me."

"I don't want Larm in danger, Cato. And certainly not you."

Strong arms encircled my waist.

"Larm is a giant, Eira. A fucking being made of ice and muscle. He felled an ogre with a single shot to the chest, ripped the wings from a harpy, and burst the skull of a highwaywoman like he was crushing a grape in his fist."

"But he's still—"

"—ours," Cato breathed.

I nodded, my heart full of trepidation.

"Luckily for us, we produced a boy-creature given to thoughtfulness and foresight. Now, give these orders to Ambrose: he is to seek out the betrothal contract binding you to Baldorva. Is that clear?"

"Yes."

Cato paused, and his body softened.

"While here, until I make my way to the palace to be with you, I will search for the others. Nothing has hinted at one with the æther among us, but... Are you okay, my love?"

It turns out I *could* shed more tears.

"Cato, what you are asking... can *you* handle it? Is it absolutely necessary?"

"I can endure anything that perpetuates your freedom."

My sniffles were the only discernible sound in the quiet. I knew I could do it. Verus taught us to entice a target, whether physical attraction existed or not, but I didn't want another conquest. I just wanted to go home with my husbands.

"Cato, Ambrose must agree. Already I've broken my vow to him by allowing Septimus into my body."

"To give Evandr life!" he barked.

My hands burned like boiling pitch, but Cato didn't flinch from the contact.

"Eira, if I can withstand the agony of having witnessed the act, then Ambrose can man up and—"

"He's *not* you, Cato."

Chapter Thirty-Two

SUGARY SHAKE DOWN

Ambrose

"No, do not set the red dish next to the orange; it clashes with the centerpiece. Who taught you the art of tablescape?"

"Apologies, Father, I shall move it at once."

"See that you do."

Tossing the third set of robes on the feather-stuffed mattress, I paused, caught by the reflection staring back at me.

The gilded mirror told the truth of the last three months.

I closed my eyes and remembered the teachings of my new mentor. "I am always worthy of love."

"Pardon me, Father?"

I ignored the servant and traced my collarbones.

This body of mine, once ivory-skinned perfection, had changed. My jaw bore the jagged scar of our flight from Solnna, and my stomach no longer reminded me of the carved terraces of a hillside farm. My crowning glory, my flowing tail of jet, had suffered the abusive shearing of my blades.

A forceful knock sounded, and my stomach jumped to my throat.

"The door, man. Get the door!" The incompetent servant, bedecked in livery of dreary Gaean green, hopped to it as I jogged to the moon-lit window and strategically positioned myself in its glowing light.

I am worthy of love.

"Father Regulus."

I opened my eyes and beheld not my heart's desire, but an austere woman of middle years.

"As asked, recruit Birdie has permission to dine under your care. I will return in an hour and—"

"Greetings, Minister Raina." I bowed, low and sweeping. She set me with a stern look that put me in mind of my own mother when she'd caught me rifling through her best lip stains. "You need not return. The Lead Healer has granted the Cult's most prestigious cumslut to serve as my personal laundress. Both noble professions, both used to removing stubborn stains. Be off now. Get, get."

The minister puffed up her thin-boned chest.

"Sir! Do not impugn the recruit's good name. Birdie is a hard worker, decent, and tough."

"Here." I tossed a bag of gold, thinking she'd snatch it from the air like all the other grubbing servants. It hit the woman squarely in the windpipe and thunked to the floor.

"Why you—!" She pinned me with a most disturbing glare.

"Do not judge a man of the cloth! I'll not sully her purity or whatever. I require a delicate hand to maintain my garments. As you can see, they are without parallel." I gestured to the pile of discarded clothes. My sibling had outfitted me in Their castoffs. Secondhand silks—who could have ever imagined I'd see the day? "The Lead Healer assured me that the straw-headed bumpkin was a famed laundress from the foothills and that her aunties, Hester and Jilly, were his bosom friends and could vouch for her skills." His actual words had been something closer to "yes, that'll rile the wrinkly hags," but I didn't know them, so I couldn't care less. "The missive arrived by courier just minutes ago. Take it."

I dug around in the folds of my peach-and-pearl garment. The color washed me out entirely, though it complemented my eyes. I dropped the letter into her hand and watched her scan the parchment.

She tsked.

"Birdie." The minister spoke over her shoulder. "It seems you've acquired new lodgings. I can never keep the hard workers. It was my pleasure serving our divine Lord Mossius with you. I will take my leave and see to it that your belongings—"

"Dæne!" Eira choked out from somewhere beyond the threshold. "Minister Raina, tell Dæne of my good fortune, and River and Robyn, please, promise me you will. Let them know I will serve Father Regulus. Make sure Dæne knows."

The woman nodded her head, her tall body blocking the view of my wife.

"Of course, Birdie. I will."

The minister tipped her chin and lingered in the doorway.

"You. Out!" I snapped at the servant, who quickly kowtowed and fled. The minister backed out, unable to sidestep the terrified man and, with an informal bow of her own, left.

"Father?"

Clunky boots slid into my sight as the door clicked closed behind her. I was afraid to lift my eyes any further, but *she* was finally here... my wife.

I fell to my knees. Tears cascaded from my eyes, dashing my ability to see her when, finally, I mustered the bravery to look up.

"I never knew how desperately I needed you until you became nothing more than a memory, husband."

I twisted my hands into her skirts, lest she disappear again.

"Forgive me, Eira, and please, by the gods, do not force me into exile again."

"What the f-fuck are you, you apologizing for you overgrown b-brute," Eira stuttered between wracking sobs. She dug into a pouch at her side, withdrew my lost spectacles, and perched them on my nose.

I saw her then, as clear to my eyes as she was in my heart.

"Black Bear." She joined me on her knees and pressed her face into my chest. "My husband."

I stared at her unsightly piss-yellow stalks and felt the heat of her nasal secretions as they bled through the fine weave of my attire. I tucked her safely under my arm.

"Ambrose, I was selfish, I know, but I never wanted you to set foot in this kingdom of evil."

"Evil? Now, Eira, I applaud the histrionics for our overdue reunion, but I have found Gaea to be most accommodating, and the Cult was, well, inspirational in its devotion to care."

She shook her frizzled mop.

"There's more to it, Ambrose. I've much to tell you about this place."

I rested my chin on her head and rocked her gently.

"Eira, the Cult is not the problem we are here to solve. You must remember that. I have been in counsel with the Mantle." I pressed her shoulders back and grimaced at her snot-slicked upper lip. She clung to me as I wiped her face with my sleeve—my sibling could afford new silks. "We agreed to the following. I, with my religious brothers, will escort the Primus-King to Verus. While there, if he publicly denounces the Queen of Solnna, there are grounds for a trial. Calling for insurrection—civil war—goes against the legal tenets of Ærtan law. He's legally unseated and jailed, Verus appoints a Primus, the Baldorvan leaves, and we begin anew." I dusted my hands and flung off the proverbial dirt.

"No," Eira stated flatly, angling her head to wipe her eyes on my sleeve.

"No?"

She shook her beauteous head against my chest.

"The Baldorvans want the Primus-King or me... well, Emryss, that's what the Primus-King named me before birth. They won't *just* leave. And Grandmother Merrias wants the Primus-King eliminated, not jailed. Also, there's another small problem."

I reached above our heads and procured a linen from the dining table.

"Blow." Eira scrunched her nose like a bunny rabbit but did as asked.

"Smaller than two warring gods and a deranged monarch? Non-issue. Do not worry."

She wrung her hands in worry.

"I am legally betrothed to the Baldorvan warlord. Pa confirmed it."

I froze, my mind charting a path into an unknown future.

"Ambrose? Black Bear? Come back to me."

Delightfully hot fingers caressed the edge of my jaw, but my mounting anxiety disallowed me from enjoying her touch.

"You are mine before man and Goddess. Your signature resides next to *mine*. That cannot be undone by the laws of Monwyn, nor those of Verus."

"But what of the laws of Gaea? Or the laws of a nation that gives no thought to the freedoms of its people?"

I shivered in Eira's arms, wavering like a banner in high winds. Her hand settled against my cheek, and I leaned into its unnatural warmth, closing my eyes.

"You feel perfect in my arms, wifling." I soaked her in until I felt her shift. I would have stayed on the floor for an eternity had she wished for it, but I understood at once. "This cannot be comfortable on those precious knees. Come." I rose, holding her small hands in mine, remembering the loving touches they had lavished upon my person. "You will note that I have drummed up a meager repast for us—just something small. I fretted that they may be furnishing you with more greenery than substance."

She nodded, wiping the wetness from her face. Helping her rise, I made to settle her in a velvet-topped seat, but her look of alarm gave me pause.

I pulled the chair further back, but her lip began to wobble.

"Can I sit in your lap instead?"

"Of course."

I slid into the seat, my hand never leaving the small of her back. She curled her legs up and settled in, her weight an immediate comfort to my battered spirit.

"Oh, Ambrose"—her voice caught—"fish jerky?" I'd placed that dish closest to the table's edge. She procured a sliver and nipped off a bit. She offered me the remainder, and I happily took it from her fingers, chewing thoughtfully on the briny fare.

We ate in quiet contemplation, her feeding me little nibbles from the array of breads, vegetable medleys supplemented with grain, and platters of small game as we shared a tankard of the fermented tea that the Gaeans consumed at every meal.

"Ambrose, how are you? Really?"

My chest rose steadily. I wished to tell her that I was a man without parallel—the envy of all who beheld me—shaped to perfection by the Goddess's hand. But that would make me a liar.

"Damaged."

The dark crescent of her lashes fluttered against her cheek, and I kissed away the tears at their corners.

"But every day I am working to repair."

She rested her head on my shoulder. The warmth of her breath along my neck was more restorative than all the meditation and positive visualizations combined.

"I think Cato is feeling similar."

I didn't hide the curl of my lip. *He* was the catalyst of this destruction in the first place. The reason I'd risked riding here at a breakneck pace... the cause of my disfiguration.

"Good, he is deserving of such."

"Ambrose," she chided.

"I will not hear it, Eira. That nail fastened the coffin's lid when he kissed me goodbye, knowing well, he'd never see me again. Look me in the eye and tell me he did not plan to abscond with you."

She covered her face with her hands and cried out in muffled sobs. I murmured words of comfort in her ear. She was not at fault, and I loathed him even more for the pain she took on, trying to excuse his indefensible actions.

"It is more complex than that, Ambrose. Please trust me when I tell you he loves you and that... that I couldn't, wouldn't, leave without you. The Bond makes Cato—"

"Your favorite." I fiddled with a bit of green garnish hanging from a soup of potato and carrot.

Eira's head shot up, her eyes blazing. She swatted my nose, and I captured her offensive hand.

"No, sir! I have told you once before, but apparently the Nether Lord froze your brain as well as your body." She yanked her hand free and wound her arms about my neck, her fingers stroked the remnants of my thin hair.

"I love you and I love Cato, both of you, not one above the other, not one this month and the other the next. Do I love you differently? Of course. I loved Nan in a different way from my mother, and Kairus differently from Cinden. Ambrose, you are not Cato, and I don't *want* you to be Cato. He has never, not once, helped me pick a gown or fashion my hair. He'd vomit if I asked him to plan a ball, and... he doesn't hold me like you—doesn't pamper me or make bawdy jokes."

I had to look away, feeling unworthy of the praise. I was no longer that man—the one so self-assured, the god carved from a flawless rock of quartzite.

"Black Bear, can you imagine the unsightly mess he'd make of a soiree? He'd drape the hall in pale-orange cloth and serve that flavorless concoction that he eats on campaign. We'd drill with swords instead of dance."

I grimaced.

"He would have weapons imported instead of wine. Would undoubtedly malign the guests for their poor posture," I added.

"And he would send them off to bed while the sun remained in the sky."

This is what I missed most—not the cunt fairies, or the way she combed my hair more gently than anyone else. We tittered like the coconspirators we were, and I fed her bits of bread dipped in butter, as we planned a Cato-style gathering, from rough, bleached-out linens to the inevitable hour of knitting he would foist upon the unsuspecting guests. Together, we eased back into the comfort of our partnership.

"Oh, before it slips my mind. Cato asks that you locate the betrothal contract that binds me to Gaea. He worries that because the agreement precedes our vows, it may render our union invalid. He wishes to study its original text but must remain in the Cult for a few days yet, at my request." Eira shivered, and I released her, thinking my cool skin caused her a chill. Searching hands sought me out, and she tucked herself back into my chest. "The breeding *thing* and the possibility that somewhere Others are imprisoned is entirely warped. Ambrose, the very idea of picking and choosing which people get to live or reproduce is awful."

I procured a slice of roast fowl as I pondered. I wasn't at all sure I agreed.

"Wiflet, the Gaeans adhere to revolting cultural practices, but, in the name of argument, would healthier children not be a boon to society at large? Gracious, if they could restore me to my former self, I'd gladly lie upon the healer's table."

Eira frowned and took a deep swallow of tea, her vexed eyes peering at me over the tankard's rim.

"Is Allaine not deserving of her existence, even with her seized arm? And little Mae, Maihon's daughter? She looks different and communicates uniquely, but is her smile not the picture of perfection? Would Scion Zotikos be considered flawed because of his marbled skin tones? Or would Richelle be considered unworthy because she's prone to heaviness?"

"Well, no, but..." I thought about each of them, how all of them gave something to the world, and how my former flawlessness had done little to shield me from life's travails. "No, wise harpy, they are all blessedly made. I see your point."

Eira's nimble fingers, smelling strongly of cleaning soap, plucked at the fastening of my ostentatious tunic as we held each other. Her cheek was stamped with the pattern of pearls and goldwork embroidery that graced its neckline.

"How boring would it be if we were all the same? Well, maybe not if we all looked like you. That might be okay," she said, brightening the room with a radiant smile.

I placed my hand over hers and allowed time to pass. I would never take another minute with her for granted, even if her hair remained the texture of a porcupine's bristly coat.

"Ambrose, thank you for preventing Cato from fathering a Cult child, at the risk of being found out—Josa's divine taint, the thought of another carrying his—oh gods, I can't even voice it. I would die. Just die." Eira sliced a finger across her throat, and I felt the blade across mine. "Anyway, before we continue down the path of plots and plans... husband, I'd like to show you how much I missed you."

She worked fast. One... two... three fasteners undone, and my chest was laid bare. I caught the garment's edges and concealed my manly fur. She was feral for my downy softness, but I could not rightfully take her body while concealing the damnable truth.

She pawed at my pecs and groaned like the seductress she was. Her eyes gleamed with mischief... and promise.

"No, no, I'm quite sated... from the chicken." I batted at her nimble fingers. "Let us continue our dialogue... in the barracks, perhaps—have you toured them? Fortified for attack, teaming with able-bodied soldiers."

A slow and predatory smile curved her lips.

"You've been such a big"—she grasped my dick—"brave"—she licked those lush fucking lips—"Black Bear. And Cato has only satisfied me once since his return." I was done for. Only my dick was larger than those innocent pleading eyes.

Oh, dear... dear... dear... dear. Blurt out the truth and never orgasm again? Or fuck it out and pray for the best?

The foundations of my marriage rocked as hard as my wife grinding against my legs.

Think Ambrose!

"Assume the position, husband, wife needs to rut."

Oh, well, she made that easy.

"Eira, you are entirely unromantic."

A derisive snort escaped her as she shot straight up.

"Am not! I am mushy and lovey-dovey and, dare I say, whimsically affectionate. But if you'd rather *not* have your garden watered after such a dry spell..."

Blood filled my cock as she worked me with her hand. Why was the stroke of my wife so much more enticing than all the fleeting moments of fornication before her? Godsdamn, but my teeth were already on edge.

It's because I'll let you fuck my mouth orrr pussy.

Gods save me! I snapped the brain Bond closed.

Pussy. She loathed the word but knew well the spell of vulnerability it cast upon me. A single vulgarity and I donned the shackles of submissiveness.

"No. You are completely lacking in romantic finesse."

I watched her mouth fall open, her plump bottom lip putting me in mind of her other juicy portions.

"Would you rather I take *your* ass, my big, strong, Black Bear?"

"Eira, yes, of course I want you, it is just that... after our separation... I need to be wooed, my flame slowly rekindled into a raging fire. What kind of person just flounces through the door and says, 'you wanna put your stuff in my muffin?' Hmm? Did foreplay go out of fashion during my period of convalescence?"

Eira's gaze darkened and then shimmered an incandescent gray.

Cato had warned me of the glimmer.

I ignored her and consulted the fine craftsmanship of a silver spoon, inlaid with a channel of purple wood.

"Ambrose? What. Have. You. *Done?*" Eira cupped my chin and forced my eyes to hers. "Never have you denied me your body. What are you *not* saying?"

My dick throbbed. Gods, but it fucking ached at her demanding touch. My resolve began to slip.

"P-pardon? Oh! Look there!" I gathered my robe and stood, dumping her from my lap, avoiding her conjurer's face. There was no telling the spells or charms she had learned in her absence.

"OUCH godsdammit!" She scrambled to her knees, and I fled, seeking the only weapon substantial enough to deliver me from her wrath.

My cock nearly speared a rack of lamb as I rounded the table. My birth father spoke of capturing her in a bag of tightly woven silk. Larm postulated that a bucket of water might contain her, but he'd not witnessed her dive into the depths of Solnna's harbor—the water parted for *she*, not the other way around.

"Ambrose, if you don't get back here and start your lips to flapping, I will fly down your throat and stop up your stupidly regular guts..."

I bolted, seeking refuge behind a chair.

She gave chase, her voice increasing in volume as she neared.

"I'll swear off sex for seven years! I will—oh!"

I thrust my hand forward and sprung my trap with a flourish, pulling away the concealing cloth with a snap.

"Oh! Oh! Oh!"

Eira performed the clap-and-squeal.

I live another day.

The thick slice of strawberry cake held her enraptured. The heat of its recent bake ensured its sweet scent carried far. I held the confection aloft, her eager sniffs disturbing the heavy dusting of sugar coating its top.

"How'd you get this?" She asked, her little fingernails dancing along the edge of the plate. Her eyes were as wide as Cato's nasty little mutt when Septimus fed him scraps from the dinner table.

"It's illegal here, Ambrose. Sugar is more precious than coin."

The hostile energy swirling about the chamber settled. Ohhh, how I knew my woman. I tempered the smug smile that fought to bloom on my face as I led her, cake first, to sit upon the edge of the feather-stuffed bed.

Luckily, such a mattress would collapse into a formless cave under the weight of two tangling bodies. Its lack of adequate support may be just enough to subdue my ardor, thank fuck. She wore no chest support, my pleasure pillows roamed free from their normal trappings and sang to me their siren's song.

I flashed my lengthy digits in her face.

"When your ring bears the Mantle's seal, doors you didn't know existed readily open."

I ripped off a chunk of pink moistness and shoveled it into her open maw.

"Mmmmm. Oh, my gods, Ambrose. Right now, you are most certainly husband number one."

"Oh, my succulent sea lion… I was always number one. First to kiss you, first to fuck. First to pierce my ear and bind us for eternity."

Pupils blown, knees parted, she slurped my finger and sucked. Her head lulled back, eyes closed, neck bared to me. I was lost. *I* knew it had more to do with shoving illicit sweets deeper into her cherry-red mouth than it did simulating oral sex; my dick didn't care.

My vision swam with the memories of her skillful tongue wrapped around me. My perfect lover: suspension of sexual guilt coupled with a willingness to delve deep into the world of pleasure. She was everything, and she deserved everything.

"Eira?"

"Mwaht?" she spoke with a mouth half-full. I did not chastise her lack of decorum, not now.

"Here, my benevolent harpy, have another. I *live* to see your smile."

And smile she did, shuffling her happy little feet on the polished wood floor.

A few more bites and I placed the cake platter on the bedside table. Though she pouted, she acquiesced to its removal, opting instead to lay her head on my shoulder.

"Ahem." I cleared my throat. "Eira, who holds my heart in her palms. Future mother of my babes."

"Kisses? I've missed your kisses, husband," she interrupted.

She puckered, and I gave in.

One last caress.

I settled my lips on hers and growled my need against their warmth. Nothing so chaste should fan the flames of want like this simple meeting of mouths, but her heat… it flowed over me, melting the glacier that had taken up residence within me.

We parted, lips a hair's breadth away. Her eyes crinkled at the corners, and I memorized her smile. In that moment, I decided. I wouldn't keep anything from my spouse; only heartache lay along the path of deceit. I stared at the papered walls, focusing on the bay laurels, whose stamped leaves twisted below the crown molding.

I placed my hand upon her thigh. She reached across my lap and procured her sweet treat.

"Eira. Catommandus's emission was given *very* clinically to one by the name of Brooks."

I shrank back and turned my cheek, preparing to feel the sear of her shadowy shade.

Unfazed, she bit into her cake, brittle hair swinging.

"Really? What are they playing at with that?" She shook her head in confusion. "Maybe it's good for the skin or something."

Goodness, she took the news well. I tapped my naked chin.

"I do not think it so, or I would have lived a life blemish-free."

She chewed thoughtfully, the wheels turning in her mind. Her brow furrowed.

"What do you suppose Cato's semen would do for a man like—"

"Oh! My slipup, yes, incorrect body of water. *River* was the name of the semen recipient. Lovely vagina, ruby nestled in a shell of deep bronze."

Oh fuck...

The hem of my tunic smoldered, and I stomped my feet on the fast-moving smolder.

The plate in Eira's hand began to shake.

"Let me just take that, before—"

It shattered, casting violent projectiles into the walls and the knot-carved headboard. A shard struck her shoulder, the blood welling in a ring.

"Sweetling, hang on now. I made every attempt to stop the sperminizing, but it happened so quickly."

Eira's body vibrated as her eyes glazed over in a glimmer of gray.

"Ambrose." She stared ahead, eyes seeing nothing and everything at once. "Husband."

"Yes, my world?" I reached for her but drew back with a yelp.

She was an inferno—my living, breathing funeral pyre.

"I'm going to fuck the Baldorvan emissary."

Chapter Thirty-Three

THE CONFESSIONAL

Eira

"Cat's plan is preposterous. He encourages infidelity as he knows it goes against my morals and that it will require me to initiate divorce. It drives you into his arms."

"No, it drives me into the Baldorvan's arms. Do you think Cato wants me with another? He hardly tolerates you."

"Then you agree! He despises me and conspires against us!" Ambrose stopped abruptly, but I continued stomping through the corridor.

The Gaean palace was a puzzle, not a home—more hedge maze than domicile. I marched, passing yet another copper tree whose beaten metal branches reached the ceiling before spidering out and concealing the pipes that fueled the lanterns dangling from above. Gleaming sheets of bronze and gold decorated the opulent corridors, giving off a tangy metallic scent that hung in the air. The walls gleamed, reflecting back on themselves, and they had me completely turned around.

Ambrose, come on!

I wheeled around and tapped my foot on the black-veined marble floor, the impatient smack of my leather boots echoing.

Get your raggedy servants's ass back here this instant! My husband stabbed his finger at the floor, his face pinched in consternation.

Ooooo! I narrowed my eyes and stomped to his side, taking my spot, one step behind him.

"You know what? You and Cato need to sit down for a lover-to-lover meeting. You are both in the wrong, and you are both brainless. Now tell me where Emberkin Arro resides."

Ambrose shook his head in defiance.

I'll find him myself, asshole. I dashed down a hallway to the right and came upon a dead end, a wall resplendent with a metal rendering of guess what? A godsdamned tree. I retraced my steps.

"Nature is dumb. I hate trees. I want to be back home where everything is just ice; snow is just... watered-down ice. Nothing changes; bugs don't bite you, because they all freeze in the ice. *Nothing* changes."

Oh! Is Emberkin Arro's room down this hall?

I bolted, but my head snapped back as my body continued forward. "Ack!"

Tugging me by the forehead, Ambrose hauled me against his chest.

"Bless you, my child," he intoned for the benefit of those near enough to hear. He brought his mouth to my ear. "Calm your delightful tits, woman, and hear reason—good day, sir, madam." Ambrose smacked his giant palm to the nobleman's forehead and then his wife's. "Blessings in the name of She Who Is Most Divine."

The couple, momentarily stupefied, bowed and murmured their thanks.

I plastered a reverent smile on my face and averted my eyes from the high-ranking nobles—there was more malachite in their teeth than in the Twins Temple.

Tell me where the slaver sleeps, Ambrose.

"Praise Her!" He walloped me on the godsdamned forehead again, and I clenched my fists to keep from frying him with black fire. A door opened to our left, and a classroom's worth of children spilled into the hall.

"Repent your sins, lowly child of Gaea, so that you may serve Her better. Good day, madam, what a large flock you have."

Ambrose blessed each child in turn until, finally, the hall emptied once more.

Guide me to the fucking foreigner, Ambrose. I'm going to serve him up some cunt fairies and convince him that Emryss is two continents to the east, or that she's a bit of Gaean propaganda.

My back slammed against the cold surface of the metal-covered wall, hard enough that the lanterns above swung from their boughs.

If you bestow my fairies upon any other, I will kill him and you. Do you comprehend me beneath your helm of urine-tinged atrocity?

The fingers clasped around my neck sent chills down my arms, literal whisps of creeping frost. His mossy green eyes were uncharacteristically hollow—the agony buried within them was not a cost I was willing to pay.

I-I won't do it. I promise I won't.

Ambrose's shoulders slumped.

Take me back to the room Black Bear. Nothing insurmountable hinges on my seducing the man. I can infiltrate the palace staff and plant false information nearly as well in the guise of your laundress. Servants talk; it will reach the Baldorvan's ears.

Ambrose leaned an elbow against the wall, his face contorted. His suffering staggered me, but our surroundings robbed me of the ability to offer solace. I reached out, but he halted me, bowing his head and covering his eyes as if sharing in a prayer. Helpless, I mimicked the gesture, despising every second that ticked by.

Take me back to the rooms. I want a bath and to finish my cake.

With a shuddering breath, Ambrose straightened and nudged me on the shoulder, forcing me to walk at his front.

Hush, wife, your Bond voice is grating.

Ambrose, please—

He closed off his mind.

We continued down the length of a hall, passing a group who hit their knees the moment they recognized the vestments of the Verus Order. My priest-husband raised his hands and thumped them, two by two, leaving angry prints on their faces and an old man's shining pate.

"May your crops be bountiful and your children more attractive than their parents."

A few heads turned at the benediction, but most bowed at the waist and pressed alms into his fingers. He pocketed the coins and took off down the hall before the last of the devout rose from the floor.

Slow down. I can't keep up. Why are you soldier-walking?

Taking two steps for each of his, I huffed and puffed, trailing behind him until I spotted a servant turning a key in the lock of a room a few feet ahead. The woman jiggled the handle to ensure its security, and the instant she turned her back, I channeled the æther and asked the lock's pins to spring free.

Look at those tits!

What? Where?

In the most athletic action of my life, I hip-checked the door and then lunged, snatching two handfuls of Ambrose's jewel-encrusted robe. Golden spangles and shimmering silver threads ripped free in my grasp as Ambrose tripped over my deliberately placed foot. He toppled, and together we vanished into what proved, thankfully, to be a storage closet and not the Primus-King's private chambers.

With the softest click a conjurer could magically muster, I locked us into the pitch-dark room.

Black flame sparked from my fingers. Not enough to fully illuminate the space, but enough to see Ambrose, all six-something feet of his crossed arms and stern face, and about a dozen rolled up carpets.

I raised my hand, casting light behind his head.

"Gods, Ambrose, just look at it. This is deliberate erasure—remove all the Solnnan items from the people's eyes and remove the reminders of their humanity. Fine silks and fruit will be next, mark my words."

Like a torch illuminating the dark walls of a cave, I moved my flaming fingers closer, inspecting roll after roll of the textiles that lined the walls. Their dense piles depicted suns radiating glorious gold and ruby rays, and their unmatched geometric schemes, in rich purple, rose, and lavender, spoke of the land of their creation.

"An effective play on the Primus-King's part to be sure." Ambrose touched his fingertips to the wool loops of a brilliant topaz star. "Many a monarch has done the same to eradicate a guild or company not following his orders."

The æther sank like an anchor in my stomach.

"Ambrose. I've gone about this all wrong," I said, bringing us back to the now.

He peered at me from the side of his eyes and then dropped to sit on a heap of prayer rugs, straight-backed and justifiably ornery.

"Yes, you have."

"I deserve that." I stepped toward him and placed the flame above his shoulder, where it hovered, suspended in the air. My Pa had shown me how to do it—he could hang water droplets like prisms from a window, and often filled our cavern with rainbows to pass the days.

I climbed up behind Ambrose, the carpet cushioning my knees, and combed the mussed wisps of his remaining hair to the side. He didn't communicate as well when disheveled.

He sighed heavily and settled back against my chest, and I pressed my cheek to his faux bald spot while I held him. His skin was surprisingly cool and comforting against my unnatural warmth, like walking into a crisp, cool morning after the kitchen fire had been stoked too high. I soaked it up.

"Ambrose. Every night before I begged sleep to claim me, I shared our goodnight kiss with my pillow." I wrapped my arms around his waist. "I was so distraught that when I began consuming my feelings in servings of soup, I held fake conversations between us. Pillow Ambrose aided me in sticking to a healthier regimen. It was our day-to-day life that I ached for the most. I never seem to tire of you."

Ambrose swiped under his spectacles but remained quiet. His sleeve came away wet.

"My sweet Black Bear, I want to continue the life we built, and I would want to even if you were poor or only five feet tall, or if you weren't born Scion." I eased him forward and worked the knots from his shoulders before continuing down his back. Both of my men held their stress in their bodies, Cato in his forehead and shoulders, Ambrose in his back and neck. "If I could go back, I'd choose you—despite the fits I threw, how I stamped and cursed your name, the night I nearly broke after finding Nan and your mother. Seeing my name next to yours on our Joining contract... I'd fight for that again." If the contract were here, I'd not be able to read it through the blur of my tears.

Ambrose slumped and wrapped his arms around his knees.

"The seduction of the Baldorvan," he said.

"It's not happening."

He turned, only to lurch back as his face nearly collided with my flame. I shoved it higher, mentally chastising myself for its placement. Ambrose took it in stride, panic-checking his ridiculous mustache and huffing *only* twice.

"Eira, do you know the feeling when you fuck someone the same night you meet them, an-and you intend to feel nothing other than the insides of their various holes, but then, that physical connection alters your perception of them and makes you feel like you *should* perhaps have feelings for them? So you end up thinking that you might want to, I don't know, dine with them or take a little moonlit walk... only to a few days later, have the blinders ripped from your eyes as you witness their dubious hygienic practices, or realize they are so dim they couldn't find their way out of a room with a single door?"

I tightened my embrace and pressed my face into his shoulder, hiding my smile. His strange, yet heartfelt admission was delivered so tenderly, I'd not risk the upset.

"I'm... I'm afraid not, no. But I think I understand what you're getting at. Like when someone starts to grow on you despite the intent of your dalliance to be a, ummm... a sploot and scoot."

Ambrose cradled my arms and began to sway from side to side.

I felt his nod.

"You see, I was the other person—the easy conquest that many fancied themselves in love with until they realized that I wasn't worth their emotional output. I think that is the reason I never fell in love, because I knew they would at some point see the real me and leave."

"Ambrose, I refuse to believe—"

He squeezed my hand, a gentle warning to hush.

"But you, Eira, unlike myself, you *would* make them want more. Those clandestine physical connections would become feelings the moment they heard you laugh or the instant you tell them some endearingly mundane anecdote about your frozen childhood. And *that* is what I fear most. It is not the physical aspects of adultery—no one could best my abilities in the lover's dance. Another will take you from me when *you* realize that you could have so much more."

If I weren't already weeping...

I twisted around him, letting go of his back to bring my tear-streaked face level with his. Pulling his hands to my chest, I intertwined our fingers in an unspoken vow.

"If they couldn't see what I so clearly see in you, they weren't worthy of your trust, much less your heart." The reddening whites of his eyes made their mossy irises stand out. "No one's capacity for care, not even the Mantle's, rivals yours. Who, other than you, would have looked at little Verra the goatling and immediately given her a home instead of running in fear? And after adopting her into your care, you put her safety above your feelings and left her in the arms of another. Ambrose, my kind and worthy husband, I'd not have escaped Verus or Solnna were it not for your sacrifices."

My fingers instinctively rose to the scar that marked his jaw, a testament to a moment etched forever in my mind—blood pouring through his fingers as he held his face together and carved my path to freedom.

"An-and you think Emberkin Arro does not possess good qualities? He seems a charismatic sort, witty and thoughtful, and I know he is a warrior in his own right. He is basically a-a Catombrose, an Ambrandus. An amalgamation of your husbands in a perfect silver-templed blend. Do you not see it?"

Cool hands settled beneath my elbows.

"Um. No. Not at all." I shook my head, wondering how he'd come to that particular conclusion. I saw nothing of either of them in the man. But anxieties were often irrational, and fears rarely scale to reality. "Ambrose, were he the handsomest man to walk the soil or the most charitable human in Baldorva, he would still be half the man you are, and no kindness or enchanting quirk exists that would allow me to see past his participation in the act of enslavement, not a single one."

Ambrose chewed the inside of his cheek and sighed deeply. He held my hands, turning them about, inspecting them like they were newly acquired gemstones. He touched his silver ring to my two-toned one.

"Eira, Cato's plan... You will carry it out."

"No. I am relieved *not* to put my skills to the test. Remember, I didn't *actually* finish Troth school." I attempted to lighten the somber mood to no avail.

Ambrose steepled his hands over mine and leaned in.

"The Primus-King avoids the Baldorvan. The foreigner makes him wary. Emberkin Arro said as much during our nude prayer session."

"Your nude... You know what, never mind." I stood and wrung my hands. Neither Ambrose nor Cato seemed to grasp how profoundly their presence complicated things. If I were alone, my job would be simple: protect one human—myself—eliminate one human—*hopefully not myself.* "The point of being here, Black Bear, is to *get* close to the Primus-King. So you see, ensnaring the Baldorvan in my penis-fly-trap is unnecessary."

Something changed in the small closet.

My eyes darted around, searching for the cause of the atmosphere's shift.

My black flame, usually steadfast, wavered and sputtered, flickering erratically.

"Ambrose? When did—are you doing this?" He came to his feet and smoothed his knuckles over my lips. The cold seeped into my flesh, and tiny bumps rose in the wake of his touch.

Ever so slowly, he tilted his chin.

"Ever since the Nether Lord restored me, I cannot seem to get warm. That is, until the moment I saw you on your knees. It was then that my shivering ceased."

Terror trailed the chilly tendrils that burrowed into my chest. The æther stilled.

Had the Nether Lord picked his champion in the race to see me bred? Was this the reason for his hostility toward Cato?

Without a word, I threw myself against him, and locked my arms around his waist, desperate for the solid comfort of his presence.

"We'd best go, wife, before it gets to be too late."

I didn't move, worried that maybe it already was... for all of us.

NO TOUCHY

EIRA

"Emberkin Arro is housed in a suite of apartments on the second level. His appointments are marvelous. All golds, both muted and glowing, with accents of ivory. Stout furniture carved from single logs of ebony, if I am not mistaken. Oho, and his little servants, now there are some strange fellows. They say nothing, never. I crushed one's toe beneath my heel, grated the other's knuckle during our manicures, and slid the file point under his cuticle. Not a grunt or sound of pain."

I stopped and watched my husband forge ahead, all the while chattering about the violence he'd rained upon the guardians. He spun around, glancing one way and then the other.

Problem? Eira, have you grown tired from the exertion? The palace does sprawl, to be sure.

A frustrated grunt escaped me as I held my arms stiffly at my sides.

"Should I be worried that *you* favor the Baldorvan?"

The sauciest little smirk played on Ambrose's lips as he snapped his fingers and indicated the spot next to him.

Meow, wifey.

If it weren't for the group of well-dressed men walking our way, I would have refused to budge. Instead, I padded toward him, eyes downcast, until his feet came into view.

"We only dined together once... and shared in a rather intimate rub down—"

"Performed by whom?" I hissed. Gods, I was such a fucking hypocrite.

"Oddly enough, for someone as enlightened as I, and not prone to jealousy, I must confess that I quite enjoy the sharp sting of my demon puff's claws."

"That. Wasn't. An. Answer," I growled low in my throat.

He stepped closer, his opulent robes caressing the toes of my sturdy boots. I could feel the coolness pouring off him, and I wanted so badly to press my sun-hot flesh against his.

Mmm, lower the temperature, wicked one, before we create a cloud of steam.

Husband, your robe is... um... showing your enthusiasm.

He shuffled and tugged my body in front of him, just as a door to the left opened and the faceless Baldorvan creepers stepped out, flanking its threshold.

"March back to him, heir apparent of Gaea, and notify the Primus-King that he has a single month. One. And while you are in his presence, pray tell him to stop sending his fucking child to deliver *his* messages."

Emberkin Arro emerged from his room, shirtless, covered in swaths of black ink and glittering metal. A bar ran through one of his nipples, and from the other dangled what Cato had once told me was a fire opal. Two rings went through his navel, with a suspended gray rock of some sort hanging into the divot. Were Cato here, he would have regaled me with its properties and uses... and I would have stared at his thick fingers and forearms as he gesticulated throughout the twenty-minute lecture.

Oh, hush, you were with Cato just yesterday. And if I know my wife's appetites, you've gobbled him down twice daily. And that's a sapphire whose hue I would call, hmmm, smoky dockside.

Out of my head, right now!

Ambrose bowed as one of my half-siblings passed by, I think Zephyr. I peeked up as he stopped to pay his respects to the Verus priest, wanting to study him closer. He was pretty. Not handsome, not alluring, or mysterious. He was lovely like Kairus, with long blond hair styled in two braids that reached his hips and bright, clear green eyes. They reminded me of the glowing lights that sometimes appeared in the Nortian night skies. His smile was warm and genuine, and sleeping on his shoulder was—if I remembered those chubby little toes correctly—the baby boy from the glass-walled chamber.

"Father Regulus, I cannot wait to meet again to continue our discussion on the Goddess's divine words. Your take on bodily love was refreshing, and though my father holds to the old ways, I see your point regarding the... flexibility of purity." The prince adjusted the baby as he spoke to Ambrose.

How long have you been in Gaea, husband?

Long enough to be poignant, it seems.

Ambrose fussed over the heavily embellished collar of his robe, smoothing a pleat and then dangling a golden tassel at Zephyr as he edged closer.

"Certainly, Highness Zephyr, as you command." Ambrose broomed the heir's cuff and then let the tassel fall. "But leave tiny Oaklen with his mama's this time? His screech is otherworldly."

My Verra is blessed with poise and calm. This babe fought to pry the four remaining hairs from my scalp while doing his damnedest to call the banshees from their hiding places.

My eyes flicked to Ambrose.

He's also our nephew, husband. You're his uncle. Have you thought about that?

"It is as you say." Zephyr, about as tall as Cato, patted the little one's bottom as he bounced in place. "But you must take it up with my wives, Father; they command the household, and this tiny boy and his daddy are cast out until this tooth breaks through."

Oaklen's eyes opened and settled on me.

Eira, he has green eyes like mine, has he not? How unfortunate, though, that his hair is the same color as a boiled yam.

The heir clipped a short bow.

He's adorable, you mean old ogre.

The faceless guards advanced as the prince made his farewells and left.

Much to my confusion, Ambrose splayed himself out, adopting the pose of a starfish. Their gloved hands moved swiftly and impersonally over his chest, through his legs, and down each arm.

"I told you my thighs were ticklish!" Ambrose giggled while shoving the leftmost guard in the arm. The guard rocked to the side but said nothing.

They turned to me.

"Nope. Don't touch me. We've never been introduced, and if you don't ask first, you don't get to grab the goods."

They advanced, and I swatted the hands that came toward me once and then again.

Eira! You are here to seduce, not cause a scene.

Emberkin Arro, who had until then lingered, leaning on the door frame, came forward, barefoot. His flowing, wide-legged pants concealed his movements beneath their graceful sway.

I know, but him, not them!

Ambrose nodded to the Baldorvan as he approached.

"Emberkin Arro, I've brought a gift."

Ambrose pushed me forward, and I smacked *his* hand for good measure.

Arms crossed over his chest, the slaver, puffed up with self-importance, circled like a vulture, his expression unreadable as he assessed me.

Lykksun's kneecaps, Eira, push your chest out. Nibble that bottom lip. You resemble a ghoul with poor posture.

"Father Regulus, all will adhere to the protocol. Any who enter will submit themselves to search. There are no exceptions."

The cloaked creeper grabbed my hip.

"Look, foreigner, if you want a chance at entering this," I spiked a finger toward my woolybush, "I suggest *you* do the searching—oh, pardon me, as a slaver, you probably refuse to carry out such trivial tasks with your own noble paws."

Emberkin's brows shot to his hairline.

Ambrose grimaced and whacked me on the forehead.

The fuck!

"Gracious gods, you impertinent child of Ærta! You will say fifteen prayers to Viktos asking him to forgive the thunderously vile utterance from your mouth. Forgive the country mouse. She has no understanding of your significance on the world stage."

Emberkin stopped in front of me, tilting his head to the side.

"So, the woman is a whore after all. One whose services you have also enjoyed, Father?"

"Now, Emberkin, I would never skirt the law. I am a man who—"

"—is now beholden to me." The Baldorvan stretched his arms above his head and yawned. "Yesterday, this woman addressed you by your name, despite the fact you had not once spoken it out loud. The encounter was *not* your first meeting, was it?"

Eira, is he correct? Were we so careless?

Ambrose folded his hands together and bowed his head.

I don't... don't remember. He's sharp. We must be sharper.

"Celibacy is not a requirement for those on the path of the divine, Emberkin Arro."

"So, you say, but is a priest who lies a man to be trusted?" He focused on me as he addressed Ambrose.

I jabbed the closest guardian in his chest.

"Fine. Here." I bent over, pulled my skirts up, and revealed my legs. "Take a good look." I stood and pulled at the neckline of my gown, giving the faceless fuck and the foreigner a view of my cleavage. "Now listen up. I'm pure. Get it? No one has plowed this puss, not even the long-dicked deacon." I yanked my thumb toward Ambrose. "To work at the Cult it has to be so."

Emberkin weighed my words, his face expressionless.

"As you can tell by my squishier attributes, I am not a woman meant for the struggles of recruit life. It's exhausting. I can barely keep my eyes open after my shifts, and the pain it leaves in both my spirit and these feet," I shook my head, "shew, I don't know how they do it."

The slaver narrowed his eyes, no doubt wondering if he should accept my story.

"I need to pave my way in this city. I don't have a Lifemate, and I have no skills but the ability to remove a stain and press a wrinkle. But if it means my hands won't burn from the constant contact with ammonia, I've decided to try lying on my back."

And now for the show.

I pretended to shrink, to vanish into the floor, to pull a curtain of shyness around me. Many a Troth had employed the determined "innocent" act, and I wagered that Emberkin Arro could be similarly swayed. I focused on keeping my shoulders rolled inward and chin slightly lowered, all the while letting him glimpse only the most minute signs of my supposed internal battle.

And then for the killing blow.

I, the lowly farmer's daughter, somehow found courage... somehow overcame her virginal fears and found the will to submit herself at the slaver's feet.

Drape your hand over your forehead, wife.

No, too theatrical. Watch this, though.

I dropped my gaze and then peered up for just a fleeting second, only to pretend to be enraptured by the steel of his glinting silver eyes. My lips parted around a breath.

Oh, yes! The frightened little swallow was brilliant. I'd fuck you.

The slaver waved away his guardian and closed the distance between us. He regarded me with a closed-off expression but pinched a bit of my hair between his fingers.

"Let us dine together. See what it is you might offer me."

Under the weight of his stare, I acted as if I were utterly transfixed, even beginning to speak before thinking better of it and holding my tongue.

"Go on..." he encouraged.

"Father Regulus... he has informed me that you may have... *unique* tastes."

"Has he?" Emberkin Arro leaned closer, placing his ear next to my lips. "Tell me."

Tilt your head and let your breath tickle his neck, wife.

I followed Ambrose's directive.

"Bondage, humiliation, foot stuff." I ticked off a list with my fingers. He nodded with each word I rambled.

Ambrose, give me some weird shit.

"Nasolingus, sploshing, coprophilia—" I repeated each word he fed me. *Eeeeek! Less weird!*

"Breath play, spanking, somnophilia, voyeurism."

Better, thank you, Black Bear.

Mwah. Kiss, kiss.

Emberkin Arro's tattooed hand came to rest on mine. With his thumb, he traced the irritation left behind by my "days-long" battle with ammonia water. Because I'd taken to shade recently and my cuts and bruises had all but disappeared, I'd soaked my hands in the concoction before preparing to leave the cult.

"If I wanted what I could have in Baldorva, I would have brought a woman with me." Long muscles danced in his sinewy arms as he straightened his back and laced his fingers together. "What I desire is different."

Oh gods, he's a formicophilist! Eira, retreat!

A what?

Insects! In-sex!

"What?" I squeaked out loud, "What is it you desire?"

Declare menstruation, sweetling! Tell him a sudden ague of the head has taken you by surprise.

"What I desire is softness."

"Huh?" I answered stupidly, finding his statement a juxtaposition to what stood in front of me. You'd have to like pain to some degree to have needles purposefully jammed into your skin. Right?

He skimmed the back of his knuckles along my jaw.

"Soft," he repeated. "Soft curves, soft skin, soft touches. Soft words."

Oh dear. We are doomed. Eira, I will take over the fucking. Move aside.

"Huh..." was the only thing I could think to utter again. Ambrose's hand settled on my shoulder.

"Will that be a problem, whore Birdie?" Emberkin Arro asked.

The entire mission has gone to flame! You possess the body of a squishy goddess, but the charm of—

"In my country, the women are as the men. Skin inked and pierced, muscles lean, frames tall. They are raised as warriors. I wish to experience something different before a wife chooses me. Flesh unmarked, plush form, gentle caresses."

My mouth fell open, but I rectified the misplayed action by chewing on a chipped fingernail.

I'd rather shit on him, Ambrose. Wasn't that one of the options?

"Well, Emberkin Arro," I lowered my voice. "The priest preferred things rough, so I may require guidance. And before we make an accord, I do have one request."

"What is it?" Emberkin Arro pressed his fingers into my cheek, turning my face from one side to the other.

"The herbs to prevent conception. They are not permitted here. When you return to your country, I can't be left with a babe in my belly. Not if I am to eventually find a Lifemate in this kingdom."

Ambrose, take us to Amais. His offices are in the palace, third floor, western wing. Trust me.

"Understood." The slaver nodded sharply. "Birdie, do you know how I might acquire—"

"Emberkin, if you would follow me. The Scions of Verus are loyal to our Mantle and Their representatives. I know just the man to provide the required concoction. Along the way, we can discuss the future... yes?"

Emberkin Arro said nothing but dipped his head.

"Fetch my shoes and robe." He snapped his fingers, and left creeper dashed away and reappeared holding a long gray robe, which he placed over his master's shoulders. The sleeveless silk fit snug to his tapered waist and then flared out, flowing like dye through water as he moved.

Ambrose led the way, Emberkin Arro at his side, me two steps behind... flanked by the twin guards. I could hear neither their footfalls nor breath, veiled as they were.

Ambrose, figure out where the Primus-King's rooms are. This place is more confusing than the ice maze during the whaling festival back home. It took Momma two hours to find me then; it will take her two years if I get lost here.

We made a right down a hallway and traversed two flights of steps. The third level was much less populated than the first and second floors, but the decor remained the same.

Ambrose sidled closer to the Baldorvan, head lowered, shoulder dropped.

"The High Mantle, They Who Commune with She Above, has granted me allowance to entreat in Their absence."

Emberkin snapped twice, and the guards closed in on me and slowed, keeping me back from the two men of import.

Ambrose left the connection open, and a one-sided conversation ensued.

I made no mention because, like you, I am here to watch, learn, and listen.

Silence.

There are rumors that your country allies with the Primus-King in an effort to seize control of the continent's eastern side. Verus seeks to hinder such an alliance.

Silence.

Of course, the woman, Birdie, is here to sweeten the deal. Verus will see to her payments.

Silence.

What do we bring to the table? What is it you seek the most, Emberkin Arro? Or should I say, who?

All the ice in Nortia slid down my spine.

Ambrose?

He snapped the connection shut and rapped upon a door that I couldn't see.

"Scion Amias, it has been too long! Verus misses its son. I come seeking your assistance in a sensitive matter," Ambrose said effervescently.

"Father! It is good to see such a revered man of the Goddess in these halls!"

Amias ushered us into a large space more apt to be called a healer's theatre instead of an office—the space was certainly not a local medicinal. Rows of spotless jars, each labeled with etched copper nameplates, brewing pots, and tools I couldn't name were neatly organized on tall shelves. The entire right wall was dedicated to books and journals.

The room was rectangular with several windows and mirrors on long moveable arms. Those seemed to have been mounted with the intention of directing shafts of light toward specific locations, some for plants, and others, parchment. Foliage cascaded over the railings of a second-floor balcony where I could just make out a red quilt nestled below a round window.

I counted seven timepieces on the left wall. All their hands pointed in different directions, and I suspected they ticked away the cooking time for whatever Amias was brewing on the three hearths beneath them. One roared, having been stoked high, the other merely glowed. The third boasted a multilayered system of metal doors, each with a unique handle on its front.

"Father, how can I be of service? Is the Mantle well?"

"Hale, and in fine temper. Have you had the pleasure of receiving a formal introduction to Emberkin Arro? When the Primus-King and Highness Zephyr travel to Verus, it is he who will step into the role of physical protector of the realm."

"I have not. Well met, Emberkin Arro." Amias nodded and clipped a shallow bow.

"The Mantle applauds Gaea's effort in continuing to secure the relations that Troth Kairus began with the people of Baldorva earlier this year. These are trying times, and we must all rally together."

"They are, Father, they are." Amias peered around Ambrose, his eyes falling on me. "And is that Recruit Birdie from Cult Mossius? I dropped you off myself, but a few days—oh goodness, these fine fellows are handsy."

Amias moved a single foot in Emberkin's direction and by doing so, unknowingly initiated a pat down. Both of the faceless creepers pawed him, going as far as to lift his arms and shake the material of his sleeves, before plucking a metal spoon from a deep pocket.

I fluttered my fingers in a wave as he was deemed no threat and released.

Emberkin Arro wasted no time positioning himself in front of Amias. He simply stood, his authoritative presence demanding attention.

"Did you wish to say something, Emberkin Arro? Are you in need of a poultice, or have you come for a tour of my research? Currently, I seek a way to remove the pus from a boil without incising. I have failed sixty and four times so far."

"I am taking this woman to my bed." The slaver leaned back, looked me in the eyes, and then stabbed a finger at the spot beside him.

Ambrose giggled loudly through the mind meld.

Don't think I'll forgive you... or him.

"The whore requires that I render her infertile. I am surprised she'd not wish to breed with a heartier stock than what has been presented in this kingdom, but I will respect the customs of your bizarre order of Lifemates." The Baldorvan winked an almond-shaped eye in my direction, and I didn't have to fake the blush that spread across my nose. It felt odd receiving a flirtatious gesture from someone other than my husbands... and frankly, I'd prefer him to have no personality at all. There would be no befriending this fuck.

"Absolutely not." Amias raised his palms in a gesture of staunch refusal. "The law forbids it."

"Whose man are you when Verus calls? Hmm, Scion?" Ambrose, who'd been leafing through a stack of parchments, paused. He tossed the notes onto a desk and then picked up a liquid-filled jar, inspecting the floating spheres within.

Amias's gaze flickered from Ambrose to Arro, a note of caution in his eyes.

"What you are asking goes against Gaean law. How will you explain your actions to the Primus-King?" Amias inquired.

Emberkin Arro cocked a haughty brow. "I owe him no explanation, and I am not beholden to your laws. I am, however, a man grown bored, *Chosen One.* I desire quieter entertainment in lieu of participating in my usual favored pastimes. I am sure you are aware of how the Baldorvans like their entertainment. Violent. Bloody."

"No." Amias shook his head again. "The Primus-King—"

"Keeps how many wives? You think he'd begrudge me a fuck with a single woman?" The Baldorvan sneered. "Many gods, many wives." He spat at Amias's feet. "In my country, the women would never stand for such an insult."

"Okay, well in your country—"

Soft, Eira!

"—on-only a single divine being is worshipped, so it stands to reason that a woman would only wish to have a single partner."

Good save, mouthy spouse. Now, tilt your head as if curious and soften your viperous eyes. Later on, show interest in the concept of monotheism. They live for conversion, from what I've read.

"It is so. As is right and proper." Pacing the room, Emberkin Arro set his eyes upon every drawer and leaf, mixture and tool. His guards came to stand by my side.

"Scion Amias, I send my first report on the morrow. How should I inform the Mantle of your behavior?" Ambrose asked.

Amias rocked on his heels.

Good Scion. So very convincing, Ambrose praised.

Isn't he, though? It is surprising that, according to Kol, he couldn't please a woman worth a damn. Some things just cannot be faked.

Amias and Kol? When? After Kairus dropped him?

Mmhmm. Kol said he just kept on trying… so she just kept on going back. Better her than me.

While pressing his thumbs to his temples, Amias let the air pass from his lungs in a defeated gust.

"Fine. But *you* will see to her welfare, Father. The last thing we need is a scandal with our names attached. Verus would be implicated and taken to task without hesitation. Birdie, come so that I might teach you the way." Amias turned and headed toward a wall of built-in shelves. They reached from floor to ceiling.

I watched a smug smile cross Ambrose's face. Emberkin Arro joined him, and together they spoke in hushed whispers.

The creepers tracked me with their eyes as I walked to Amias's side.

"Birdie, the herbs are considered safe, but care must be taken to ingest the proper amount at the same time each week. Watch as I combine the powders."

Amias pulled open a drawer, and I looked on with a keen interest.

"Bag number one is added to bag number two. Do you understand?"

"Yes, Scion-Healer."

He opened another drawer, and without pausing his hands or mouth, tapped the lid of a vial containing a sky-blue liquid—precisely the poison I had come for.

"Bags three, four, and five," his fingers crawled through a column of indexed pouches in the second drawer. "Are added to the mixture and combined into a liquid of your choice. You are to take half this evening and half the following week. Just a moment."

Amias strode past the guards and procured a small canvas bag from a dozen or so hanging near the door. One of them followed while the other stayed facing me.

"Father, Emberkin," Amias called loudly.

"Yes, Scion-Healer?"

I made my move the moment the second creeper looked toward Ambrose, plucking the vial from its home and pinching it between the meat of my thumb and palm, thus allowing my fingers to remain slack. *Nothing to see here.*

"The woman understands how to ingest the suppressant; I refuse to mix it with my own hands so that I will remain in accordance with the laws, even if by technicality." Amias bagged the ingredients and then rushed over to the wall of timepieces to remove the lid from a cauldron using a massive pair of tongs. "I am a busy man. Please be on your way."

"Certainly, healer. I will see that the Mantle receives your well wishes."

In an instant, a bevy of men surrounded me.

We retraced our steps, Ambrose and Emberkin Arro speaking as if I didn't exist, the silent guards ever watchful.

Wife, I believe the connection will reach from the library. I will plant myself there until you seal the deal. Show him how darling you can be. Rain attention upon him and rub his feet until he sighs. Keep your mind open at all times, and most importantly... do not kill the Baldorvan.

The twin guards marched ahead of me and tossed open the slaver's chamber doors.

"Ensure you lube her up. She's bound to be tight." Ambrose punched the foreigner in the arm, and both of them laughed.

I had no voice to scold his vulgarity as panic set in.

I'm having second thoughts, Black Bear. Third thoughts, seventh thoughts.

No, woman I love. There will be none of that. Do as he asks, wifey. Collect your information, make him desire you, and we will rid our world of him and his filthy kind.

I took a fortifying breath as Ambrose squeezed my shoulder, then took my hand and settled it into the palm of Ærta's enemy.

Chapter Thirty-Five

What Lurks in the Dark

Cato

Nine couriers on the night shift. One incapacitated in the scribe's room, the incident made to look like a slip and fall from spilled ink. Parchments in my shoulder bag: six falsified for admittance onto each level. Twelve authentic, to cement my disguise in the minds of others. Weapons on my person: heavy shears, twelve metal-nibbed styluses, and a thin parchment blade.

"Do you have a reply, healer?" I held up a blank missive and a stylus.

"No, courier. Not at this juncture. You are dismissed."

I nodded and headed out the door.

Floor seven had produced no information regarding Others being held in the Cult. Beyond the fact that something they grew stopped up my nose and made my eyes water profusely, all seemed to be above board.

I blew my nose on a linen for the fourth time in two minutes.

Scent was oftentimes the first indicator of a potential hazard, and it was imperative my nasal passages remain clear. Fuck, my sense of smell allowed me to intercept a marauding band of pirates once. The whiff of brine and wave was out of place in the landlocked mountain town, and I was on them before they'd had time to register the point of my blade slipping through their captain's ribs. Of course, trolls, ogres, and wraiths all carried their own perfume.

Level six, I thought, might be the holdings of a nether creature or æther-born, on account of burn marks present on several cabinets, but making my way through thirty and seven rooms revealed no more than researchers' notes and their hearths, many of which connected to the copper piping system. I'd skimmed dozens of journals and found that though many of their findings would eventually be of great consequence to the world of healing, most were just list after list of experimental outcomes.

No floor tiles seemed out of place. I could detect no odd breezes that would indicate false doors. As a matter of fact, I was appalled by the lack of locking mechanisms throughout the cult. I initially suspected that they wished to give the impression of openness but ultimately settled on their foregoing locks so they could move as quickly as humanly possible as they ran from place to place.

The fifth floor, where Eira had spent her time, was enough to bring most men to their knees. I knew my wife, and gods, I wished I could have spared her the trauma of these sights. She was strong—so much so—but her mind held firm the memories and images of suffering. I both loved and loathed it for her. Septimus had tried his damndest to beat the empathy from me, but my mother had fought harder to maintain it. Eira's influence had me grappling to hold on to the few remaining threads connecting me to humankind.

The moment we'd stepped off the lift that first day, I'd begun to scour level four. I'd managed to slip out for a few hours each night and had taken the time to dip in and out of the recruits' rooms. I had found nothing beyond a few pilfered snacks, a few hidden sugar cubes, and a thin parchment-cutting blade beneath Minister Raina's mattress, its weight now familiar in my bag.

After a fruitless search of the third floor, I now jogged down the second-floor corridor called Barley Hall, and stopped in front of a priestess who had raised her arm to hail me.

"Courier, to me."

I jogged to her side.

"Missive to the Lead Healer, first level."

I procured my writing board.

"Begin dictation."

The healer rubbed her tired eyes; the circles below them were purpled with fatigue.

"Subject B succumbed to a paralysis of the lungs. Manual respiration proved inadequate to sustain life. Advise? End dictation."

I passed her my stylus, and she hastily scribbled some illegible name before slumping into a chair and hanging her head. And then I was off, folding the parchment as I made my way to the lift, ducking in and out of a storage closet and two patients' rooms along the way.

"Hold up!"

Instinctually, my fingers sought the blade in my bag as a hand appeared at the lift's door, pulling the barrier wide.

"Sorry. Lady Haycroft is the last of the night." Two men joined me, carrying a shrouded body between them. I recognized one of their faces—another purity recruit—but not the other. "We need to move her fast."

"No problem," I said, moving to the lift's back wall.

I covered my nose and mouth, feigning a polite aversion to the stench—the perfect excuse to conceal my face. *May Merrias guide you, Lady Haycroft. Your timing was impeccable.* Like the recruits, the putrid reek of death no longer fazed me in the slightest, but a common courier would no doubt be affected.

"We double-wrapped her, but the Goddess blessed us with rapid decomposition. A curse folded within a favor."

I hummed some non-answer as the lift jerked into motion.

"First level, off. Mind your step." A servant opened the door, and I darted out in the same fast-footed manner as the rest of the Cult's hurried couriers. His attention turned to the recruits and the body still in the lift. "Lower level? Show me the signature."

My ears perked, and my feet slowed.

A lower level? The dead do not speak—the perfect audience for misdeeds.

"Naw, we're headed straight to the pyres; the wagons are out front. There's nothing left to learn from the lady."

My mind raced as I headed across the atrium. How would I pull the details from the shadows? My muscles felt like coiled springs, alive and ready to pounce. The air smelled sharp, and—

Everything snapped into perfect focus as the metallic whisper of a door's hinge sounded from behind the Cult's heart, the massive burning brazier. I charted a new course and slinked my way around the fire's base. *Be there, you godsdamned tyrant. Let me end this game.* I gave no fuck who might be with him. They could witness the Primus-King's death before they met him on Merrias's blade.

Shit!

My prayer went unanswered; the glass-fronted room *was* occupied, but by three purity recruits, each with a rag and bucket of ammonia water. I retrieved my hanky and cleared my nose once again. I should have smelled their solution well before turning the corner.

A recruit waved, and I returned the gesture with a smile before dashing off.

Were it not for bad luck, I would have no luck at all. Bem would have danced a jig had I gifted him a monarch's ear or toe. I laughed at myself, suddenly wishing for the walls of my home. Before Eira, I actively looked for ways to avoid Cordillaria Palace: dangerous campaigns, forcing outlaws from their dens, touring the coasts and farmlands.

"Ah, well, wishes are for the unmotivated," I spoke Septimus's old adage out loud.

The first floor's eastern side bustled.

Priests and healers chatted while going from room to room. Many were alert and conversing animatedly about their patients' recoveries. A few sported rumpled clothes and the dull, stringy hair of several days of missed baths.

I had a clue where the Lead Healer resided. From the smattering of opinions I'd encountered or overheard—all negative—I ventured that his offices were near the mass of frowning nobility.

I dug around in my satchel and headed in that direction.

"For you, ma'am." I placed a falsified letter into the hands of a woman who wore robes similar to those of Minister Raina, the only difference a second layer of piped gold trim around the ostentatious sleeves.

She opened it, paused, and then stared at the ceiling like she was pondering her life's choices.

"How the fuck do we go through so many towels?" She pressed her ink-stained hands to her eyes. "We can't order fabric from Solnna anymore. Where on the Goddess's great sphere do we purchase cloth from if not from Solnna?"

"Response?" I questioned. A courier was never to offer counsel. They took messages, they delivered messages.

She flung out her arm in an escalating degree of agitation.

"Go ask the Lead Healer! Cause I don't have a fucking clue."

"Is... is that what you wish me to write?" I shifted from foot to foot, feigning discomfort.

The woman remained quiet for a moment, and though she rested her back against the wall and crumpled the missive, she rallied.□□

"No. Begin dictation: use less ammonia to avoid breakdown, but ensure they boil for no less than ten minutes. End dictation."

I collected my signature and then headed in the direction she'd unwittingly pointed me.

After trying one hallway and coming to a dead end, I attempted the next. His office was simple to locate after that—the yelling and vehemently hurled curses gave it away quite readily.

Before I was halfway down the corridor, two couriers burst from the room, followed by two healers hot on their heels.

"He means it; he'll make sure you don't eat for a week or sleep for two," one healer said to the other.

I stopped at the threshold—the double doors stood open, held wide by fancy green ties that looped around two hooks mounted to the walls.

I counted seven healers in the chamber beyond.

"Now you come asking me to clean your mess! I've a better solution." I swapped sides and, from my periphery, watched as a rather odd-looking man pulled three rolled parchments from his desk drawer.

"Lead Healer Malvin, if you would but let me explain—"

"Explain yourself to their families if you must. But spare me your excuses," the Lead Healer hissed. He unrolled the papers and made notes on each in turn. "Now, Leilani, Winkler, and Annia." He pointed to a trio of healers. "You three are exemplars of this Cult; you may return to your offices knowing you have done well by Mossius. You are dismissed."

Three healers walked out the door, throwing each other smiles.

The Lead Healer jabbed his fingers toward the other four.

"The rest of you, return to your homelands and care for those with simpler needs. Surely you are competent enough to tend to a child with a cut or cough. Leave my sight. Pack your things. Courier!"

I scrambled into the Lead's office, missive ready to hand off.

Never once meeting my eye, he snatched the note from my hand and scanned it with his rather remarkable, amber-colored eyes. It was easy to appreciate the uncommon color and toad-like bulge.

"Response?" I asked as he reread. The knot in his throat bobbed as he swallowed. I procured the writing board, anticipating his need.

"Begin dictation." He closed his eyes and rested his forehead on his steepled fingers. "Subject B was the last. No advice. We are at an end."

That's fucking ominous.

"End dictation and get out."

I stood rooted to the spot.

"Lead Hea—"

"Out!"

I dipped my pen into fresh ink.

"Your signature, sir."

He snatched the stylus and scratched his name, and I retreated, pulling a blank sheet from my bag the moment I cleared the door. Pressing the clean sheet against his freshly inked name, I was left with a mirror image copy of his signature.

I nodded to another courier as I jogged the length of the hall and ducked into a communal bathing chamber. As I relieved myself, I traced the backwards signature with fresh ink and then stamped it onto the bottom of my remaining blank parchment. A perfect likeness stared back at me. This was a much better technique than trying to mimic another's penmanship or trace in poor lighting.

I penned "lower-level access" to the top of the missive and then returned everything to my bag, minus the backward copy. I wiped my ass with that and tossed it into the facilities before chasing it down a pipe with the water hose.

"Back already?" The lift operator said, giving me a sleepy half-smile.

"Last one of the night. You?"

"One more hour. Where are you headed, courier?"

I dug into my bag and retrieved the forged permission, holding it up to the light nearest his face.

"Lower level."

He nodded and closed the door.

Excitement and apprehension vied within me as I descended. Kymor had not mentioned a lower level when she'd introduced Eira and I to the Cult. The bitter taste of deception flooded my tongue. I could not imagine her being unaware of its existence, given the open conversation between the body-bearers. Had its omission been intentional on her part?

I placed her name on my mental dossier titled "not to be trusted."

The lift sank so swiftly that I placed a steadying hand on a wall—Eira would have lost her composure at the jarring dip.

The door opened into a small antechamber.

Recruit of indeterminable gender, lift rope in hand. Small chamber, door at the back. Walls lined with shelves. Shelves storing bodies. Shrouded dead: four. Approximate openings: twenty.

I nodded to the worker and headed straight ahead until the corridor branched left and right, revealing two healers' theaters, both brightly illuminated.

"Courier?"

I followed the voice to a recruit crawling around on their hands and knees. They dipped a scouring brush into a steaming bucket of soapy water and scrubbed at the floor.

"You have a missive?"

"I do."

They indicated their wet hands. "Go ahead, please."

I swiped my nose with the linen, retrieved the missive, and cleared my throat.

"Towels are needed on the upper levels. Solnnan imports are no longer allowed. Can you spare any?"

The purity recruit sat back on their heels and tucked their head into the crook of their elbow, smoothing back the hair that escaped its ribbon tie.

"Over there. Take half and no more." They jerked their head to the back wall.

I took the long way around, circling the table, assessing the walls, shelves, and furniture for cracks or fissures that might indicate a hidden room.

There was nothing. Cult Mossius was, as it claimed to be, a place for healing and help.

Tucking the towels under my arms, I met the eyes of the confused recruit.

"I didn't want to dirty where you already cleaned." I took the short route this time, leaping over the wet spots. "That better?"

The recruit chuckled and went back to their chore.

Back on the lift, I leaned into a corner, relieved that I could seek out Eira and ease her fears about the goings-on of the Cult. Tomorrow, though. Right now, the fourth floor was calling me, and my bed was singing its siren's song.

Why the fuck is this taking so long?

I shut my eyes, inwardly chiding my impatience. Exhaustion made me sloppy, and before another day of showing my flaccid cock to a room of onlookers, I needed more than an hour of sleep. At least it was my last day as a specimen. I'd be set out with the trash the moment my dick—

"What the fuck?"

I flattened my hand on the lift's back wall.

The temperature had changed—I'd swear it.

I squatted down, ear to the floor and then the wall as I listened for a difference in sound. Nothing but the creak of ropes and pulleys.

The temperature altered again, slightly warmer where I pressed my cheek. Only seconds ago, it had cooled ever so slightly.

The fine hair on my nape prickled. Had it taken longer to get to the lower level in the first place?

The door opened, and I tipped my stack of towels as if by accident, a cover for my awkward position.

"You alright?"

"Yep. Just dropped the damn things." I restacked the linens and took the hand the recruit offered. He pulled me to my feet.

"Have a good night; shift's almost done."

I smiled and thanked him. "You too."

My night's work was not done, not by the measure of a mountain. There was a level between the mortuary and the first floor.

CHAPTER THIRTY-SIX

I'M SO FUCKING ROMANTIC

EIRA

"Are you afraid?" Emberkin Arro asked me.

I shook my head but didn't meet his eyes.

Afraid? No. I could send you to Merrias in a matter of seconds. Not looking forward to spending my evening with you? Totally.

I stood statue-still in the middle of a gigantic antechamber, watching as he and his creepers removed their shoes and set them along the wall. The Baldorvan snapped his fingers, and his guards leapt to do his unspoken bidding, opening the tall doors that led to his chambers. Each took up their position flanking the entryway.

"The face you wear says otherwise."

And your face says 'dumb,' fucking slaver.

The Baldorvan assessed me as he shrugged off his robe and hung it in a wardrobe meant to store heavy coats and oiled jackets. The coat hangers were gilded, and the furniture handles inlaid with sapphires and fine enamel. The opulence shouldn't have surprised me, given that the ruby-and-gold-striped walls shimmered with flecks of iridescent mica, but just like in Monwyn and Verus, I was floored by the immense wealth of the monarchs.

He procured a soft and loose shirt of combed wool, which he pulled over his head.

As he dressed, I glanced down at my hands, folded demurely over my stomach.

"What would you like my face to say?" I asked.

Slowly, Emberkin Arro peeled himself away from the wall and came toward me in his disconcertingly silent way, stopping only when his toes encountered my boots. He stood towering over me, his voluminous pants swirling around his feet before settling.

"Whatever it is you want."

An inked fist settled under my chin, lifting.

"Incorrect, Emberkin Arro," I said, meeting his soft-gray gaze. "*This* is a transaction, and I am being well compensated to be what *you* desire. I can't afford to be otherwise."

He waved a dismissive hand, and my eyes caught on the tattoo at his wrist—a dozen or so black circles stacked to form a triangle. If it had meaning or was simply decor, I hadn't a clue, but I'd commit as many of his markings to my memory and then do my best to replicate them on parchment when I returned to Ambrose. The renderings could be sent to Verus.

"The priest told me you were without schooling. I do not believe him." He narrowed his eyes. "Are you fooling the fool, Birdie? Hmm?"

I huffed a little laugh, and his gaze sharpened, honing in on my mouth. *Well, this is going to be easy.* He slid the pad of his thumb along the edge of my bottom lip, staring as if transfixed.

I blinked up at him, intrigued by what I saw. *Do nosebergs get caught on those piercings?*

"*This* is how I want you. That sweet smile." The Baldorvan snapped his fingers, turned, and walked between his guards and into his chamber. "Come."

Pffbbt. Like, get fucked, bro. Ope, poor choice of words.

Plopping down on my butt, I struggled out of my boots and then launched them at the wall. One landed upside down and the other on top of Emberkin Arro's soft leather sandals. I smirked, amused by the thought of my blood-and-vomit-coated sole staining his fine footwear.

"Are all Ærtan women given to smiling so often?"

I glanced over my shoulder and found the foreigner hovering near the door again. I rubbed my foot, a little embarrassed by the state of my toes. The dried skin and callus on my heel would have my mother's tongue clicking.

"More so when the threat of war doesn't loom," I answered honestly. "It's difficult to muster the energy during times of political upheaval."

I grabbed my bag of herbs and stood, stretching my back before pausing in front of the left guard.

"Emberkin, do you own this person?"

"Yes," he answered quickly. "Do you take issue with it?"

"Yes." I placed my hands on my hips and leaned from side to side, doing my best to see through the tight-knit fabric that cloaked the person's face. "I do."

"If it frees you from some moral travail, these men were freeborn at birth, and their parents chose to give them over in service to me."

I continued my inspection, noting the hem of the guardian's hood. I suspected horsehair had been sewn into its edge for added weight.

"It does not, in fact, make me feel less offended. I probably dislike you more for it. Do you have a way to bathe in here?"

The warmth of his breath reached me before the gentle press of his chest against my back.

"Of course, why?"

"Because if you want me soft, I've a pound of skin to slough off first."

Emberkin Arro's laughter was unexpectedly delicate.

He hooked a finger, making a gesture that indicated they lay to the left of the bedchamber door.

"Go look. The Gaeans did not spare an expense on the facility."

Curiosity spurred me deeper into the room.

The main chamber was not large, but it was cozy and reminded me of a description I'd once read in a *Magika and Menagerie* chapter entitled "The Fae Lands and Their Domiciles." Thin copper pipes hung from the ceiling at various intervals, and from their tips were tiny flames, housed in clear glass orbs, that illuminated the room. The bed, the focal point, was wrapped in the intricate knotwork wood that adorned the Twins Temple. Three differing colors made up the interlocking basketweave, and from the scent of it, the lightest was most definitely cedar. The smell immediately put me in mind of Cato. The reddish-purple bands, well, I hadn't a clue about their origin, but the dark mahogany was the same as the heavy furniture back in Ambrose's Colpass appointments.

Seal-gray walls surrounded us, and white gossamer curtains framed a window that ran the width of the chamber's left side.

I looked over my shoulder.

"Godsdamn, Emberkin. It's no wonder Father Regulus is envious."

"Fairly spectacular, yes?"

Selling the mountain mouse routine suddenly became easy.

"This is... how do you think they maintain it?"

Emberkin Arro shrugged while drumming his fingers on his elbow.

"I expected the trees, because of course there are trees, but the waterfall feeding into the stone grotto? *That's* a surprise."

The foreigner's apartments expanded backward on both sides of the antechamber, creating a horseshoe shape. You didn't get a feel for its size until completing a full turn and taking it all in.

To the left of where the creepers stood watch was a nook surrounded by bookshelves. A heavy wood table with a slate top was situated between two overstuffed chairs, and atop it, a gilded chess set, its pieces painted to bear likeness to the pantheon, drew the eye. It was a cozy spot to be sure, but it was the right side that currently had me clapping in excitement.

No time like the present, amiright, Eira?

I trailed the Baldorvan and intertwined my fingers with his. He recoiled, eyes wide, lips parted.

Could he sense the æther? Fuck!

He eyed our hands, but I detected no heightened aggression.

"Do your people not touch before they fuck? Pardon me... make love." I winked at him. I couldn't help myself.

"Rarely," he replied, still studying our bound fingers.

"Like many other things you all do, that's stupid."

Whether Emberkin Arro angled his head in amusement or confoundment, I couldn't tell.

"So you say."

I raised our joined hands between us.

"Is this okay?" I paused. "Would you... would you consider this a romantic gesture?"

"It is, and I would."

Ha! Did you hear that, husband? I'm romantic as fuck!

Good gods, woman! You made me spill my herbal tea all over baby Oaklen!

Oops! I backed off the connection.

"Well, Emberkin Arro, gird your loins, because you and I are headed to the waterfall where I will introduce you to pudding-soft caresses and emotion-filled squishes." *Mystical goddess Maressa... maybe I am horrible at romance.*

I tugged on his hand, and with a bit of hesitation, he followed.

"Do your people wash, Emberkin Arro? I'm guessing no."

"What would make you—of course we wash."

No doors blocked the opulent, nature-themed bathing chamber; you just stepped from the wood-paneled floor onto cool tiles of irregularly shaped slate.

"Filthy laws, filthy bodies? I don't know. How about you convince me otherwise?"

The air was thicker here, laden with the scent of blooming things. The soft flow of the manmade waterfall rushed over a metal lip that divided the water into three parts. One thin trickle fed a lush garden of living plants, whose long roots twisted in a see-through basin. The other two fell out over the deep tub, a place to rinse one's hair and body. A wide mirror reflected the scene, sitting above a cabinet. A bounty of baskets overflowed with creams, washes, and tonics, each with delicate calligraphed labels—the luxury almost brought tears to my eyes.

"Disrobe," I ordered.

Emberkin Arro reached for the hem of his shirt and drew it over his head. He twisted and cast the garment to the floor. He was a breathing tapestry of ink. His back, like his front, was a mosaic of black, red, and gray. The only bare patches were the skin above and below the stripes across his nose and a triangle-shaped patch at the center of his chest. Both spots were the rich, earthy color of wet terracotta.

"This might take me a few minutes," I said, settling my bag of herbs on the countertop and arranging them in a row.

His hands went to his waist, and my eyes to the pouches of medicinals.

I mixed the powders and leaves according to Amias's directive, as the man behind me unlaced the closure of his black underpants—like, full-on long pants under the baggy ones he already wore. I nudged the vial of poison into a grouping of tinctures and tonics

"Headaches, stomach pains, gas, constipation... have you tried any of these?" I picked up several and set them back down in a haphazard pattern surrounding the poison.

"I have had no need, and even if I had, I'd not trust anything from a country not my own."

"Does that mean I can have your dinner when we—what is that?" I yelled and pointed.

What the fuck? Ambrose! Black Bear? Are you there?

Yes! Do not shout. I'm running your way. What has transpired? Did he harm you?

No! It's his penis! It's weird!

Silence.

"Birdie? Have you never seen a cock?" the foreigner questioned. "I did not believe the story that you are an untouched woman, but I might have been incorrect."

"I've seen one or two," I lied. *Or seven.*

I rummaged around the baskets until I found a small carved bone cup, which I held under the thin side of the waterfall until it filled halfway. I combined the herbs and water and took a healthy swig, all the while eyeballing his crotch.

What do you mean, weird? Eira, are you there?

I sputtered, trying to come up with an apt description.□□

"Are you disappointed in its size?" Emberkin Arro asked.

"No. Its—its size is functional, but—"

Is it longer than mine?

No.

Thank the Goddess above. I would have fallen apart.

"Then what is amiss?" the Baldorvan pressed. "You are a strange whore, Birdie."

Is he longer than Cato?

Yes.

Oho! The Goddess favors her Chosen Son... but not his middling-dicked former lover. I shall make an offering at the temple. I think a citrus incense, or, well, silver never goes out of fashion. So what's wrong with it?

It's missing its hat.

Come again?

His dick is bald.

Oh, that? I just assumed they formed differently in Baldorva. Hurry, lovey, fuck him fast, I've ordered us a repast of marinated olives, smoked salmon, and fresh bread.

A warm feeling blossomed within my chest.

Grabbing the hem of my gown, I tossed the dress over my head and let it drop. The promise of snuggles and snacks with Ambrose was enough to renew my waning focus. Those were, in all honesty, some of my favorite pastimes.

"Emberkin Arro, sir, your snowman seems to have lost its scarf," I stated with an air of confidence that I certainly did not feel. "And I am a bit shocked."

A knowing look passed over his face as his eyes fell to his penis. A lazy smile formed on his lips.

"In Baldorva, the foreskin is removed when adulthood is achieved."

"Ah, I see. In Monwyn, the women receive a piercing through the nipple and the men through their ears." I wiggled out of my chemise and laid it on the counter. "Do your women have a coming-of-age custom?" Gray eyes settled on my breasts, lingering in obvious appreciation. "Emberkin?" I folded my hands behind my back and swayed, allowing him to see me fully.

He shook out of his trance.

"It depends on their social status. The Emberkin women are inked on the commemoration days of their birth. That stops the year their menses begin. Men do not stop; the final tattoo is placed on the center of the chest after death."

"Neat," I said, only half paying attention.

His penis seemed to work like a normal one, filling and rising. His head was smaller at the top than Cato's, but it had a similar prominent ridge before thickening to its base. Unlike my men, he had no pubic or chest hair to speak of; the effect made the artwork on his body stand out more starkly than it would have otherwise.

There was a subtle shift in his stance, a squaring of his shoulders, a tightening of his abdomen, as he continued gazing at my chest. When he inhaled, a slow, deliberate breath, his nostrils flared just a fraction.

"Do your women have breasts?" I asked, sauntering forward, working my hips from side to side. I skimmed my palms over my nipples and then cupped each of my breasts, hefting them in my hands.

That slow smile returned.

I didn't stop until his erection skidded up my stomach, smearing a bead of pre-cum on my skin before coming to rest in my softness. My nipples grazed his lower chest.

"Yes, though as a people we tend to slimmer and taller builds as compared to those on this continent. Our females, on average, have smaller chests."

"I love a perfect palmful," I whispered, more to myself than him. I loved tits in general, but an apple-sized set sent me over the edge. How I had Joined with not one, but two men was, on many days, beyond my ability to comprehend.

Emberkin Arro cleared his throat.

"You are—you have shared in intimacies with women? That configuration of relationships does not exist in my country."

I barked a laugh that ended in a chuckle.

"I assure you it does."

His arousal stiffened further, pushing into my stomach. I'd give it to the man, he was as granite. I tilted my hips to gauge his reaction. If I could get him off like this, I wouldn't have to find a way to fake lubrication. My vagina was not sold on a slaver, not even a moderately good-looking one.

"Is this soft enough?"

I took his hands and placed them on my chest, encouraging him to squeeze and explore.

He hummed a low but enthusiastic sound and backed away, leading me by the tips of my fingers to the edge of the see-through tub; the basin came up to the level of his hip. He walked to the counter, where he stepped on a pedal that poked out from the adjoining wall. The bath began to fill.

A semicircle of slate steps led up to the lip of the deep basin, and another down into the water. I took each one and, at the top, bent at the hips, hoping that a flash of pink would send him into a frenzy. Apparently, "soft" also meant slow.

"I will join you momentarily, but for now, I am taken in by the view."

I lowered myself, and by the third step, encountered the lap of water, surprised to find it warm.

I glanced over my shoulder, my gaze tracing an unhurried path from his inked toes to the playful smirk on his lips.

"Hurry before I take a chill," I pouted. My foot met the bath's bottom, and— "There are fish!" I tossed my hands in the air and squealed in delight. "I love fish!" I hopped up and down in the belly-high water and then stilled to lessen the effects of the churn I'd caused, hoping to see more clearly through the glass bottom. "This is amazing, but how do they live?"

Inked arms slid around my stomach, the images of an unknown fanged beast on one forearm and a terrifying manticore on his other. The Baldorvan hugged me close.

Put it in already.

"According to the heir called Merritt, there is a large tank between the levels. A turtle occasionally makes its way by."

Smooth lips skimmed my shoulder, and I took a deep, shaky breath, letting my chest expand fully. As I exhaled, I soundlessly blew on my breasts and gave him a view of my hardening nipples. Men always thought *they* made them stand on end, but the truth was that the cold, the water, the air... all of it hardened them the same.

I let out a sigh of pure contentment and let my head sink onto his shoulder, imagining it was Cato at my back.

"Not to be rude, Emberkin, but the priest will collect me sooner rather than later. How do you normally approach your... whores?"

"I do none of the approaching."

I spun in his arms, my breasts flattening against his lean-muscled chest. Pupils dilated, lips parted, and a burnished glow settled over his cheeks.

"You know, as much as I hope your entire kingdom slips into the ocean and never resurfaces, I find myself wholly intrigued by every second or third word that falls from your lips. Here's a solid plan: I suck on that impressively hard erection, and you tell me how the nether it works over there across the ocean."

Eira! Mind your tone. How's the man to maintain an arousal with all the sass you are serving up?

The same way you do. Plus, I'd really like to know more. Did you hear what he said? Oh, wait, of course not.

I refocused. Get the Baldorvan off. Get out. Get snacks.

"That is a plan worth considering, but I'd rather pay *you* for the service." In a flash, he dropped his arms, and I found myself lifted, twisted, and deposited on the stone ledge next to the falls. "Birdie, I've never—"

I slapped a hand over his mouth and the other around the back of his head, butting his forehead to mine.

"If you tell me the Baldorvans don't believe in oral pleasure, I will lead an army to..." He shoved my thighs wide, and my words faded away.□

The intense look on his face, the determination in his eyes, made my mouth, amongst other things, water.

"Pleasure doesn't factor into it. In Baldorva, sex is a contractual exchange. The man keeps a list of his achievements and attributes until the time he reaches adulthood. Using that, the woman selects the man she wishes to breed, choosing him for his physicality or intelligence. When the agreement is reached, our religious order selects an appropriate time for a coupling. She mounts him, his seed disperses, and then she leaves."

I recalled the day Scion Greggen had entered the place of Cordillaria and spied Allaine standing behind me on the dais. The tall Baldorvan had proclaimed to the masses that together they would recreate the lost giants.□I bet his *attribute* list was the same size as his ego.

"So, do you have children?"

"Probably."

"Probably?"

Emberkin Arro licked his lips unconsciously as he stared at my center.

Godsdammit, the Troth in me wants to know more!

"A woman's father has yet to see me as a fit husband, though several have found me suitable for production. This mission may change that."

Fuck my cultural curiosity!

"Is it because you are a gross slaver? Do you get to access your children if you Join?"

"Lineage is traced through the mother, whose parenthood cannot be falsified. I would become the father of any children she may bring to the Hearthing—that is what we call our Joining. My lands and assets are vast, but it is my close association with the warlord that keeps my hearth cold." His hand came to the center of my chest. "Lie back. I've wanted to taste a woman since my first breeding."

"But why would being close to the warlord be considered—"

"I will gag you if you do not comply with my orders."

He shoved me harder as his head dropped between my knees.

"Oh!" Emberkin Arro was not a shy man; he shot straight to the source and sucked my clit between his lips with a verve unmatched. That was never my preferred way to begin the delicate task, but I settled in, faking a little gasp and hip thrust. He growled and moaned and then doubled down, wagging the tip of his tongue over my gem. As Ambrose would say, *yeesh*! I let my knees drop wide and tipped my pelvis up to his mouth, cheering him on with a false cry.

"Yes, oh gods, fuck, yes."

The fast, pointed-tongued method he employed was more distracting than pleasant. More uncomfortable than orgasm-inspiring.

I sealed my lips and mewled and whimpered while I made a mental list of the items I'd need to convince people I was a laundress: a set of irons, more soaps, lye, and various scouring brushes. *Whoa*—Emberkin Arro changed up his technique and slurped my labia like an oyster from its shell.

"More, Emberkin, I'm so, so fucking close." I wove my fingers through his hair and tugged at the silver-streaked strands.

Ambrose?

My queen?

I'm torn between laughing and cringing.

Do not laugh, Eira; he will call for your banishment. Is he too rough? Does his sex face give stroke rather than sublimity?

No. He's trying to catch his meal in the harbor, but his bait's not tempting the cod.

Pardon, do fucking what?

He's down getting his ears sweaty.

I—Eira, we've discussed your use of colloquialisms.

He's eating my pussy, Ambrose! And he's sucking on my clit like it's a sugar-coated Solnnan snack. Like, he's gnawing on gristle instead of—

Shush, wifey, and I shall fix the situation.

"You taste incredible." Emberkin Arro came up for air, lust-drunk, lips shining, and eyes flashing.

I pressed a foot to his chest as I came up to my elbows.

"Let me return the favor," I said in a low, sultry voice. I'd gobble him down twice to avoid a second tongue-lashing. "I want to know your taste, too."

He smiled, a full-on, both sets of teeth gleaming, eyes alight with passion, kind of smile. And shook his head.

Fuck. Damn. Shit.

"I want you to come on my tongue. I want you shaking and squeezing while I lick your lovely slit."

Well, he had the words right.

I channeled Lady Vaughn and her life-altering lesson on pleasuring her *wonderful,* yet old-ass husband. The hands-on curriculum had taught us Troth a valuable lesson. If we appeared too into it, our partner would designate themselves a god of sexual pursuits. Though they would never improve upon their technique, you could trim down the time of their delivery. On the other hand, if you withheld a portion of your enthusiasm and allowed them an occasional glimpse of the heights they *could* take you, they'd insist on trying again and again, working to better their form, but increasing the demand they placed on your body. I was not here to turn apprentice into master.

"I want all of you, Emberkin. Tongue-fuck me until I'm screaming your name."

Eira?

What?

I tossed my head back as I sent a hand to my vulva, spreading my lips with two fingers.

My dick is pulsing in my palm. I am so fucking hard for my wife's body.

I stilled.

"Birdie, I want to drink from your well while you shatter." The Baldorvan dipped his hand below the water and slid it along his inked cock. "I want your slick dripping down my chin."

I haven't made myself come in three months. I promised myself that my next release would be between your legs. Mmm, yes. My semen will spill down your lush thighs, and I'll gather it up and push it back where it belongs.

My lashes fluttered shut.

I will finger you with my natural lubrication, slippery and fast, until you break. Yes, wife... your husband has come home.

My passage slickened. My clit swelled, and the most delightful of pulses took up with me. My fingers danced over my gem, and I groaned a deep and needy sound.

Emberkin Arro sensed the change. He dipped his middle and index fingers into his mouth and then poised them at my entrance.

Eira, I will use your body to slake this torturous yearning the moment I next see you.

I drew my knees up, my thighs spreading. The Baldorvan introduced his fingers, inch by stretching inch. The corners of his arrow-shaped nose flared, reminding me of Cato. Oh, gods... Cato.

My eyes rolled back as I rocked into his digits.

I will edge you until you are sobbing. Oh, my delicious harpy, I cannot wait to—mmmm—slip myself between your dense cheeks and remind that tight little asshole whose cock reaches the farthest.

"Ohhh, please." The throaty moan that cut my words short belonged to one man... *Ambrose.*

The creepers no doubt heard the water sloshing as Emberkin Arro masturbated to the same perfect rhythm he set with his hand.

"Do. Not. Stop," I huffed out.

He bent low and flicked my clitoris with his tongue, the sensation all but sent me to another realm.

Are you close, husband? I want to know when you come; describe it in detail. Your release running over your hand, smearing your stickiness over my lips.

"Fuck, fuck, harder," I pleaded, my head twisting from side to side, my back arching.

Emberkin Arro grunted, and his forearms bulged as he surged from the water. His cock plunged between my legs, his body slamming into mine. The water sluicing down his stomach amplified the smacking sound of his hips against my ass.

I'll clamp chains on those rosy nipples and yank them tight while I fuck your oil-slicked breasts. I'll feed myself into your mouth and put that bratty tongue to use. Let me hear you, wife.

I erupted, screaming into the chamber.

"Amb—" I grabbed the Baldorvan's rear and dug my fingers into his muscular flesh. "Am I what you want?"

"Fuck. Yes." He collided into me hard until his shouts filled the room. He spasmed and ejaculated, his release hitting my walls, his erection throbbing.

I'm at the door, wifey, and ready to rid myself of this forced chastity.

Chapter Thirty-Seven

WHAT IS LOVE? BABY DON'T BURN ME

AMBROSE

"I love you." Eira cried out as she clawed at my chest, attempting to climb me like a cub up a tree.

I had not so much as shut the door before my woman made her needs known to me. We shared no Dick Bond; there was nothing that bound our hearts beyond our own natures, and that was enough.

"I love you, Ambrose. Husband. There is no other like—"

"What of the enormous waxed curls of my pencil-thin mustache?"

"I love them."

"The depressing wisps of my sideswept coiffure?"

"I love each and every—"

I sealed her mouth with my lips and ripped at the ugly, rough fabric that graced her precious skin. Nothing but the finest silks should ever touch her.

Our kiss was a wordless conversation of tasting, of relearning. Our tongues slipped and twined in a heavy-breathed search for the moments we had missed. I backed her into a wall. The hiss of splitting fabric announced her naked flesh, and I found myself unable to open my eyes. She was a goddess and I unworthy of her beauty.

My hands, on their own, gently but firmly peeled hers from my neck.

She grumbled, a low protest, but I had to pull back. We were moving too fast, and I needed her to know she was so much more than a quick fuck.

"No, no," she sobbed, fighting me tooth and nail. "Ambrose, please don't be angry with me. He's not who I want. Never, not at all."

I took a shaking breath, trying to find the words that would reassure her. I forced my eyes open, my gaze falling on her with a kind of desperate need.

I held her arms, not to restrain her, but as if I were holding on to the last shred of my own hope.

Half of her torn dress fell over her shoulder and bared the top swell of one breast. The other half clung to her upper arm, tempting my eyes to what lay beneath. Blood flooded my arousal, nearly to the point of pain.

"Until this moment, I assumed the pinnacle of eroticism to be an impeccably manicured lover outfitted in a garment designed to entice." I took in the tangled mess of Eira's hair, matted as it was to the textured wall. How her eyes glistened and her chest heaved. How her lips swelled, surrounded by the divine mulberry hue where my stubble had abraded her skin. "Oh, how mistaken I was."

I urged her arms above her head, both of her wrists fitting easily in my palm.

"I know now it is the abandonment of those pretensions that sets my soul ablaze."

I scooped my hand into the small of her back and traced the deep curve until I could squeeze the warm flesh of her ass.

Her panting breaths came harder, the rise and fall of her chest causing the wool clinging to her nipple to continue its slow descent. I watched, entirely fascinated, as her dusty-pink flesh revealed itself, followed by the plum of her tightening peak.

"Your coloring is the perfect palette to my artist's eye, and your taste the most sublime flavor upon my connoisseur's palate."

Dragging my tongue from its back to tip, I covered her nipple, relishing its velvety texture before exploring the tiny, raised bumps scattered about her areola. She arched forward, and her flawless tit cushioned my nose and chin. On instinct, my hips jerked forward... a preview of the Cradle.

"Ambrose, I am stupidly aroused. I want you in me, and I am in no mood to wait."

She pressed a knee between my legs as she bowed off the wall. I captured her calf and wrapped her thick thigh around my hip, settling arousal in her cradle of heat.

"The astronomers spoke of the stars aligning in a rare cosmic dance. They speak of it as if it were a miracle, falling to their knees and praising the gods, but compared to this, to the perfection of our fit... the phenomenon is nothing more than a dull celestial happenstance."

I ground my erection between her legs and took pleasure in watching rosy blotches bloom across her chest.

"That, wifling, is how you romance."

I took her lips again, breathed her in, but smelled *him* on her skin.

Hmmm.

The bite of jealousy was oddly arousing. Was it animalistic of me to delight in the thought of eradicating his scent by replacing it with my own? And would he know *my* perfume when I sent her back to him? I tore my mouth from Eira's. She cried out piteously, need naked in her tone. The sound dredged confidence from the deepest well of my masculinity.

"Gods above, I nearly mind-fucked myself into spilling."

"Ambrose." Her hips swiveled on my dick, and I took a moment to savor the sweetness of it all—the exquisite press and release. "Ambrose. Fuck me right now, I will scream, and then the guards will come. I'll be jailed for prostitution, and you will have missed your chance—isn't that romantic?"

I grimaced.

"At least you are trying."

Her bottom lip wobbled, and my heart lurched.

"Now, wife, none of that." I tapped her sweet little mouth. "Okay, go on then, on your back. I want you in basic... plain old... *missionary,*" I ground out the last word, and by the spasm of her midsection and roll of her eyes, I was fairly sure I'd just caused her to ovulate.

Eira ran toward the bed, hopped up to her knees, and then spread those pretty legs while coasting her fingertips down her inner thighs.

Show me my treasure, Lady Monwyn.

Eira worked the skirts of her gown over her knees, breasts swaying with each of her movements.

Slowly and methodically, I unfastened my robe and let it drop. I gripped my erection beneath the leathers, tracing its outline so she could see the torment she put me in.

You are the most beautiful man alive, Ambrose.

Taking my time walking toward her, I unlatched my belt and, with a loud crack, whipped the leather from my waist.

And what else?

She lay back, while keeping her eyes riveted to mine, and hitched her skirts to her stomach.

And you have the longest dick in all the land.

I winked and wiggled my satisfied shoulders while popping the buttons of my leathers.

And what else, my seductive harpy? Hmmm?

My knees hit the edge of the bed just as the last button released.

And you are the worthiest of love.

Erection freed, I fisted my penis and swirled my head into the cleft of her entrance. I tensed my ass and shifted forward, marveling in the contrast of my pale glans gliding into her ruby opening.

"Oh, gods." Her eyes closed, and she contracted around my head. "Gods, gods."

I gripped the rounds of her full rear and lifted as I shoved my hips forward, entering her in a single, swift thrust.

How shall I fuck you? Fast or—

"Yes. Yes!" Her thick thighs hugged my waist, and she drove her heel into my flank, spurring me like an unbroken stud. "Fuuuck, husband. I—" Her voice cracked, cutting off her exaltation.

I lost myself, pressing my thumbs into the deep creases where her thighs met her hips, railing in and out of her until I entered that state driven only by feeling.

"Come with me, wife. Let me feel you." My dick swelled, tightening as my release came upon me. I crawled onto the bed, covering her, fucking up into her until I felt my tip bump her cervix. She screamed, the sound drawing the come from my body. My sac squeezed, and I found my bliss shooting streams into the woman I so dearly loved.

My head dropped back as I rode out the waves. It was a full two minutes before I found the strength to move.

Gently, I initiated disengagement, but her arms snaked around me, disallowing my retreat.

I choked on the emotion of it all, the beauty of the shared moment, the intensity, the—

"Gods, your dick's as cold as a polar bear's toenail." She wiggled her hips. "It feels amazing."

Stunned to silence for only a moment, I tossed my head back and laughed until tears streamed down my cheeks. It was then that I noticed the cloud of steam filling the chamber.

"You are the weirdest human I've ever encountered, sweetling, and I mean that in the most affectionate sense."

She kissed the tip of my nose.

"And I am all yours."

"Wake up, beautiful Black Bear."

Eira spread kisses over my chest, paying close attention to the unsightly scar that cleaved my torso.

No, send Allaine for tea first, I will nap until Bem brings up the reports.

I yawned but didn't open my eyes. I was boneless. The strength of my muscles had fled, leaving nothing behind but a gentle afterglow.

"Ambrose?"

"Hmm?" I turned and pulled the covers over my face, not that I needed them, mind you; my wife's warmth had chased away the damnable cold.

"I need to go see my auntie, Jilly. Can you get me out of here?"

"Of course I can." I wriggled my ass into the curve of her stomach and drifted back to that sweet place between unconscious and awareness. "When did you get an auntie?" I ignored whatever answer she rattled off while imagining her feminine fingers walking down my backside to...

"Will you take me shopping?"

I levitated, throwing the covers from my person.

"Be ready in five, lazybones!"

Tossing open my closets, I perused my borrowed silks, selecting a knee-length tunic of cranberry-and-black shot silk. I would glisten in the rays of the sun, but not so much as to draw undesired attention. If I garnered a few compliments from the local maidens and theys, all the better, but I'd sworn off men. Deceitful bunch of philanderers.

"Eira! Extract yourself from the covers." The lump under the quilt cursed as she pitifully wrestled free of the yardage. "What is taking you so long?"

It took my wife nearly a quarter of a century to dress in her plain wool garment and for us to traverse into the town beyond the palace. Yes, she did have to sew herself into the damaged fabric, and yes, she had to patch up the back with a gusset of wool pillaged from my siblings's stores, but I was not at fault.

"Blame your wiles for the mess you... I... *we* created."

"Ambrose, stop trying to hold my hand! I am your laundress."

I sneered down at her.

"Fine, then you should be holding my packages." I dropped my bounty into her outstretched arms and then patted down the heap of material so that just her eyes peered over the load.

When we get home—

We will cuddle and snuggle and fuck until you ripen.

She stayed silent, but oh, how she glared.

I love you, wifey.

"The Timber Tavern is just ahead," she gritted out, her teeth clenched in a hair-raising smile.

"Wonderful, I am simply famished. Do they serve duck simmered in wine? Maybe a beef medallion in a rich brown gravy? Open the door for me, laundress!"

Ambrose, I am drawing up divorce papers when we get home.

Sorry, not legal for Monwyn ladies, of whom you are one by marriage.

I waited, flicking my eyes between my wife and the door handle.

She grumbled but managed a two-finger hold while shuffling backward and bumping it with her wide bum.

I sashayed into the establishment and flung my arms wide... I loved the drama created by the play of my wide sleeves.

"I am Father Regulus of Verus Temple. I bless you all in the name of She Who Wields The Divine Vagina Which Birthed the World!" Dozens of weary gazes met mine; hands paused in handing off—ah, yes. "One pound of sugar to the man who procures me a room with a view and snacks for my laundress!"

All nether broke loose.

"I got rooms that overlook the shed!"

"Move, Billford! My chamber may be small, but it overlooks the town square, kind of!"

"Two pounds will see me set up for fifteen years! I'll trade ya my house and the missus."

Men scrambled, surrounding me, raising their hands like a cluster of schoolchildren.

"Now, gentlemen, I can only pick—"

"BACK YOU'UNS, BACK I SAY!" The wicked whiskers of a broom slapped down on a man's curly-haired head. Cross-eyed, he disappeared into the mob.

Though I could not see the weapon's wielder, blows rained down, parting the sea of bodies like Eira in a fit of demon-puff rage.

"THIS HERE IS MY ESTABLISHMENT, AND IF ANY ROOMS ARE LET FOR GOLD OR POWDER, IT WILL DAMN WELL BE ME WHO PROFITS!"

"Who speaks?" I tracked the voice until my eyes lit upon the tiniest old lady I'd ever seen. Age had not been kind to her, but despite her maturity, she stood confidently before me, teeth clamped around the long stem of a smoking pipe.

"Auntie Jilly!" Eira offloaded her parcels, foisting them into my arms, and then embraced the old one.

"Hello there, Birdie," said a middle-aged gent, worrying the felt of his hat while gazing upon my wife as if she were a prize ham.

"Sir! How is it that you know my laundress?" I questioned. He ignored me and patted Eira on the head.

"How's recruit life? Have you run into the magistrate? He's been a little low since you called off the Joining."

"Pardon? You, Sir Chubby Cheeks, say that again?" *What Joining?* I eyeballed the adorable chunk of man flesh who dared to touch my woman.

I tended bar for a while and may have met someone. Eira giggled through the connection. *Well, two someones.*

"You'll never believe it, fellas; I moved up in the world in a matter of days. I did my scrubbing job so well, the priest hired me on the spot... and he bought me new clothes." She jerked her thumb over her shoulder, and I held the packages high, smiling my most winning smile.

Woman, you'd better have a more thorough explanation prepared the moment we are alone.

The old one pointed her broom toward the back of the establishment.

"C'mon, niece, let's get ya both upstairs, and you can model 'em for ole Hessie and me. She's still down with that trick hip of hers, and it would brighten her day to see ya."

The one named Jilly guided us up the stairs and knocked once on a door before trudging in. "Hester, I brought you some comp—"

"Ooh, ain't he a right tall glass of fine, pale ale? Come over here and let Hessie take a long drink."

"Oho!" I tossed my packages to the floor and strode in, holding open one side of the coat Eira insisted I wear. In the middle of the room, I executed a spin.

The haggy little bed-bound loaf gnashed her gums at me.

An unholy alliance forms before my eyes. Ambrose, don't charm the locals.

The door clicked closed, and Eira came to my side; she leaned into me, head resting on my arm.

"Hester, this is my husband, Ambrose."

"The second one?" Hester asked, looking me up and then down.

"The *best* one." I bit at the air, snapping my teeth and giving her my best growl.

"By the gods, if I were five years younger."

Jilly dragged over a set of chairs.

"You'd still be a wrinkly old geezer, Hessie."

The woman, Hester, slapped her thighs in dejection and frowned.

"Age is but a number, darling; I've had older," I crooned. "You have stunning azure eyes, by the by."

Hester cackled. Jilly grumbled. Eira attempted to sit in a seat, but I captured her hand and drew her into my lap.

This is where you belong, Eira. Do not forget again.

"Why are you here, Birdie?" Jilly puffed on her pipe in quick, successive sucks.

"Because I need you to get a message to Larm or my father."

"Right then, let's hear it."

Eira steeled herself, eyes closing, chest expanding.

"The Primus-King is breeding people."

Hester and Jilly nodded in unison, their expressions bland and unimpressed.

"Yes, it is well-known that the researchers are experimenting with selective breeding. None who knows of the Cult's workings will be overly surprised. The Mantle is sure to be aware; They select from the Cult's best healers to work at the Temple."

"Yes, no," Eira mumbled, ill at ease.

I smoothed my palm down her back, cooling her rising temperature.

"It's not that part. My other husband has found himself a specimen in that particular program." Hester's eyes popped wide; Jilly's remained impassive. "But you see, I overheard the Primus-King. *He* is breeding with the Others—centaurs and wraiths an-and witches. Though he openly speaks against their kind, he's—"

"—ignoring the sins of his past," Jilly supplied.

Hester hung her head. "My brother still clings to the idea that—"

"Excuse me? Your what?" I nudged my glasses up my nose and narrowed my gaze. Eira turned in my arms.

"Hester is my aunt. My *actual* relation."

I furrowed my brow, taking in the full length of the bed-bound woman.

"You must take entirely after your mother, my cookie lumps. Your curves, for certain, and your snack-sized height."

Hester nodded in agreement and then did her best to prop herself up on the mound of pillows at her back. I tucked my hand between Eira's knees.

"You know, Auntie Hester, just recently, I too discovered a relation I had no prior knowledge of. His name is Zuddaz, and he lives in Solnna. Oh, and I have a sibling! They are probably the fourth most handsome person in existence, though they lack a certain charisma. Lady Hester, I do believe we are kindred spirits."

Her saggy jowls raised as we shared in a smile that was cut short by a wince of pain.

Eira placed a hand on Hester's blanket-covered ankle.

"Hester, if you'd take just a drop of my blood, it might speed your healing. I can tell how badly your hip troubles you."

The elder shook her head so vehemently that her stringy hair twisted about her ears.

"No. It was that blood that started my baby brother's obsession." Her blue eyes filled with tears. "And that same blood will bring his demise. He was such a beautiful child."

Hester peered off into the past.

"Eira," Jilly brought the conversation back, "those are serious allegations, but I believe you. More than anyone, I believe—"

A knock sounded on the door. Eira hopped up from my lap and stood behind me, hands behind her back like a good little maid.

"Enter."

The door creaked open, and Auntie Jilly's pipe drooped to her chin.

"Not you again, scoundrel!" The old goat bolted upright. "Get you from my sight, Minstrel Tom. The last time you showed your face my Birdie lost her suitor. To this day, my customers shit upon the new 'mediocre' entertainment."

CHAPTER THIRTY-EIGHT

THE TANGLED TRIAD... WELL, MORE TANGLE, LESS TRIAD

EIRA

The chair flew and splintered above Cato's shoulder before I had time to react. "Tom" twisted his body, avoiding the impact of the fast-following pitcher. The ceramic shattered against the door, and water spilled and ran under the threshold's crack.

"War's upon us!" Hessie screeched, flailing her thin arms above her head.

Jilly went for her broom, but Ambrose beat her to it. He snapped its handle over his knee and then launched his big body at full force, trapping Cato between the door and wall.

"What the fuck's happenin'?" Jilly squawked.

"My sugar's on the priest!" Hessie squealed in demented delight. I threw out my arms, shielding her from flying debris.

"Ambrose, stop!" I yelled, trying to pull a charging Jilly back to safety.

Ambrose raised his makeshift mace and hammered down in a single vicious blow. The snap of bone and crackle of cartilage giving way forced bile into my throat.

"Fuck! Godsdammit, Ambrose, it is I, Catommandus." Cato raised his hands in supplication as blood streamed from his nose, coating the front of his Solnnan-pink shirt. "It is your brother, for fuck's sake!"

"His what?" Hester screamed.

"I know precisely who you are; no amount of plucking can hide the evil of your deceitful countenance!" Ambrose cast his bludgeon aside and snatched Cato by his mass of curls. He yanked Cato's head sideways and swept his legs, sending him to the floor. Cato executed a blow-softening roll and popped up on both feet, fists at the ready. He stretched his neck from one side to the other and rolled his shoulders.

Oh, fuck. Fuck. Fuck. Fuck!

"Husbands, cease! You will stop at once!"

Neither of them acknowledged my existence as they squared off. Each eyed the other, Ambrose with a look of pained hatred, Cato with a dawning sense of understanding.

"Ya owe me a week's rent for the bind you put me in, rapscallion!" Jilly let loose a jar of herbs, its target Cato's head.

Cato ducked, doubling over. The ceramic missile continued on its path until it shattered on Ambrose's chin, the shards of light green and purple spraying across his face. He yanked the largest bit of shrapnel from his cheek, the edges cutting into his fingers, and with a grunt of rage, hurled it into Cato's chest with an overhand throw. Cato didn't acknowledge the sharp protrusion that stuck out from his chest, even as blood began to trickle from the wound.

"Oh! He maimed my new boy!" Hester reached under her bed and lobbed a large wooden spoon.

Ambrose sprang high.

Cato countered low.

And the resulting clash shook the walls.

"How dare you, Cat? She is ours. Not yours. Ours!"

"Ambrose. Cease!" Cato commanded.

AMBROSE! I cried into the connection.

His head jerked to the side, but my pleas did nothing but cost him his concentration.

Cato's elbow slammed into Ambrose's jaw, and in a shockingly quick burst, he followed through with a punch to the solar plexus. Ambrose sank to his knees, holding his side.

"Brother, listen to me. Ambrose—"

"Brothers!" Hessie wailed, "Which god do I pray to for that package?"

I could stop this. I could—I drew upon the æther but then stopped short.

Three months of tears mingled with the blood on Ambrose's face. I ran to his side, dropping and enfolding him in my arms.

"I am worthy of, of love," he choked out, "even if he does not think me so." His soft sobs were my undoing.

"Ambrose, look. Look at me." Mossy-green eyes squinted open, one ringed in a quickly swelling bruise, the other bright red from a vessel having burst.

"I-I am worth—"

"—more than every sunrise I've known, the stars that make up the constellations. The... the... How can I quantify what is immeasurable?"

Another pair of arms slid around us, bolstering us in their strength. Finally, our tangled triad was together once more.

AS PA ALWAYS SAYS, THE TIME TO REPAIR THE COOP ISN'T WHEN THE FOX IS AHUNTIN'

EIRA

"Hold still, wife." Ambrose tugged my head around by the ridiculously long length of hair held between his fingers. "The multi-tonal array of blondes will mute the garishness of what currently graces your head. Not even you, my pouty princess, can pull off such a color."

"You've been at it for an hour; my scalp has a pulse," I pleaded. As he had between each new section of hair fiber added, he kissed the apple of one cheek and then the other.

"She is fucking glorious, no matter the color of her crown," Cato said, tossing the fourth blood-covered rag into a bucket of water and ammonia. He peered into a tiny wall mirror and pressed a finger to the side of his swollen nose.

The room Jilly afforded us was small, and the still combative attitudes of the feuding mountain men made it feel stiflingly cramped.

Cato paced the length of the room, three steps in one direction and then three steps in the other. I'd taken to covering my eyes and humming Nortian ditties to cover the neurotic cadence of his footfalls.

"The Dick Bond blinds you, Catommandus... your eyes *and* your stone-coated heart. Her brows resemble a troll's pubic pelt."

I scoffed, and my raw-skinned scalp received a sharp yank.

Cato's nostril began to drip again, and he snatched the last linen from the bedside table.

"Please, take my blood. You see that Ambrose is nearly healed. Just a small amount, nothing that will—"

"Get his dick hard in my presence?" Ambrose grasped my head and swiveled me around until we were face-to-face. "Is that how he sustained full mast while sailing the Ambrosian Sea? I suspect so. He relied on your sanguine aphrodisiac to see the task complete."

"No, Ambrose, and if you'd speak directly to him and act like a fucking adult—"

"Lean back. Head in my lap." He tipped me backward and then loudly rummaged through one of his parcels, withdrawing a pair of tweezers. He thinned out both my arches and deforested their center.

"Kiss." I puckered as Ambrose's face descended.

He kissed the tip of my nose and then my lips. "There. You are as stunning as you are spoiled—two exceptional breasts, one perfect husband, and three new dresses."

He released me, and I sat up, snatching Cato's hand as he paced by. Fingers closed around mine, and the tingling energy that passed between us arced as he pulled me off the bed and into his arms.

"I missed you," he whispered. The hair rose on my neck as his stubbly chin skimmed the shell of my ear. "I have become accustomed to your presence in but a few days. This new separation drove me mad."

Without breaking eye contact, black fire flared from my fingertips, charring the wood comb Ambrose had hurled, until nothing remained but a cloud of ash.

"Stop it, asshole!" I twirled in Cato's embrace and faced off with Ærta's most handsome Scion. "No. You know what? Get up, move." I swatted Ambrose's thigh, and he hopped off the bed, incredulous at having been struck.

I pulled my arms from my dirty, torn-up gown and watched two angry faces transform. "Oh. No. This isn't an invitation. This is an intervention." I stayed within the tent of the gown's skirts, purposefully hiding myself from their view.

"As if I have done anything to warrant one," Cato bit out. The rate at which his nose bled increased with each word he spoke.

"You are blameless? Ah yes, the natural-born son can do no wrong," Ambrose countered.

Still ensconced in my ready-made changing room, I dug through two packages, flipping the length of my waist-long hair over my shoulders when it obscured my vision.

Ambrose had allowed me to pick from six gowns, and this sage-hued beauty was my favorite. In a trick that always seemed to impress the men, I shrugged the old dress over my head while dipping into the new, its voluminous but light layers spilling over me without so much as a hint of skin showing. The wide sleeves billowed to my elbows and tapered to my wrists, ending in two soft, pink cuffs of brocade. The same fabric framed the deep-plunging neckline. Tiny hooks with rose quartz stones bridged the two sides. I stepped into a pair of fresh underwear and pulled them up my thighs, using the gown's skirt to hide my legs from view.

"Sit on the bed, please. Both of you." I dragged over the bedside table and sat atop it.

Neither of them moved. That bitch Ambrose peered at his nails, regarding them like a new golden bauble, and Cato stood, arms crossed, pinching his shirt near his elbow.

"That's fine." I smiled sweetly. "Just fine!" Lightning arced between my fingers in a loud stuttering crack. I shot my palm into the air, and a wall of black fire lifted from the floor.

"Back, demon! To the bed, Catommandus!"

Cato jumped to the mattress, the only surface not engulfed in my stinging shade. He held out his hands and heaved a robe-clutching Ambrose up beside him.

"That's better." I dusted my hands, and the flames disappeared.

"You've singed my sibling's garments," Ambrose chastised me as he reached through a smoldering hole in the back of his coat. "How do you expect me to walk back through the town in this rag?"

A half-smile dimpled one of Cato's cheeks.

"You've grown adept, my love. As if I required another reason to find you enthralling."

If he was trying to flirt his way out of this conversation, he was as dense as a...

His other dimple emerged and triggered that steady pulse between my legs. My tongue darted out to moisten my lips. Ambrose struck, smacking the bottom of my chin.

"Don't be a needy slut, wife. You've been fucked aplenty in the last day."

Cato went for his dagger—no, a pair of shears. Faster than I could hurl my æther, he snipped a curled corner of Ambrose's mustache.

"What the fuck, Cat?" Ambrose stomped fitfully while patting his shorn facial hair. "How dare you introduce asymmetry into my aesthetic?"

"You broke my godsdamned nose, Ambrose! Already I cannot breathe through this side. And have you seen my eye?"

If I could control the soil like the Queen of Solnna, I would have buried them *both* to their necks. As it was, Ambrose fingered the remains of his mustache, reminding me of a cat cleaning its paw. Cato had the decency to acknowledge me, leaning in, elbows on his knees.

"Cato, tell Ambrose what you told me. It's important."

Gold-tinged lashes closed and then slowly opened. His cinnamon-brown eyes swirled with an overabundance of emotion. He took my hand.

"I told her that shit was better when it was just her and me."

Cato skirted the fist that flew his way, and I jumped forward, sandwiching myself between the grown-ass children. I elbowed Cato in his ribs.

"And?" I prompted.

"And fucking what?" Cato clapped back.

I threw my hands up in frustration.

"Ah, okay, we've moved from toddlers to teenagers," I said. *One... two... three... breathe...*

Wife, counting will do nothing. He is beyond redemption.

I shook my head. I would make this work—with every tool at my disposal.

"Cato, if you would vocalize the *rest* of the conversation we had, I would appreciate it."

"Are you setting me on fire?" Cato tugged at his soiled shirt in a rhythmic motion, sweat beading at his temples.

"Yes. Yes, I am."

His eyes, already wide, grew larger. His brows shot up, creating two perfect arches above his pupils.

"That is in no way an appropriate means by which to settle—*fuck*, turn it off!" Cato begged as his flesh turned red. "Fine. Yes, Ambrose, it is true. I did enter the physical aspect of the relationship to keep Eira closer. And then I divulged to her some such drivel about coming face-to-face with your ferocity and devotion for her, which allowed me to consider *you* as a part of *us*." Cato waved a flippant hand, as if to minimize the sincerity of his words. "Are you satisfied, Eira?"

An arm settled around my back, and then another.

"Can you forgive him, Ambrose?"

There was a brief moment of silence.

"Do you love me, Cato?" he asked over my head.

Another pause.

"Yes."

Ambrose made some disgruntled sound.

"Do you love me more than Eira? No, wait, do not answer that. I love her more than I love you, so that wouldn't be fair. Um, do you want me to fuck you?"

Whew, I clasped the neckline of *my* gown and fanned my fevered flesh. *Please say yes!*

"Not particularly, no."

I rested my hand on Cato's knee. "And would you like to explore why that is?" I asked, probably a little too hopefully.

"No."

Ambrose visibly shrank.

"But not because you aren't attractive or a solid conversationalist... some of the time," Cato managed without my prodding.

Damn! I cursed.

You are such a slut, wife.

Shut up, so are you.

"Alright." I shrugged, letting that particular fantasy go. "To each their own. Ambrose, Black Bear, can you forgive Cato?"

"For lying and perpetuating betrayal? Yes. Of course I can; from birth my life was built upon deceit. But for taking you from me? Never. I will never forgive him for that."

I didn't point out that Cato and Larm had barely made it past the city limits with me, but opted to clasp my arms around Ambrose's middle instead.

"It will take time to mend that big heart of yours, and I will help soothe you where I can."

He kissed my forehead, and for a moment I lost myself in his mossy-green gaze.

"Is that your attempt at being romantic?"

I jerked back and glared. Ambrose looked over my head at Cato.

"Do you find my wife to be particularly romantic, Catommandus?"

I whipped around when no answer came.

Like a lump on a log, Cato just sat there, chewing on the inside of his jaw.

"Has she written you a poem? A love letter? Planned a romantic evening where your favored foods were served off the platter of her naked bosom?" Ambrose asked.

Cato clicked his tongue and then smacked his lips like a mannerless camel. "Nope, she never has."

"Ummm, when would I have had time to plan such a lavish—"

"Has she ever once initiated a fuck with *seduction*, or does she simply flaunt her tantalizing backside and demand a ride? I'd say that was her signature move."

Ambrose looked down that stately fucking nose of his.

"Cato! Will you not defend me?"

Husband number one shrugged a shoulder to his ear.

"I am afraid not, my heart. Until now, I was unaware that a proclamation of love should involve a meal served upon the plate of my mate's perfect proportions. Now, I am doubting your commitment entirely."

"I hate you both."

I rose to my feet, and two palms struck each side of my ass. The thin silk did little to dampen the sting.

Breathe... one... two... three... four... breathe... five...

Teeth set, I resumed my spot on the side table, just beyond their reach.

"Next issue, husbands," I gritted out. "The Baldorvan."

That got their attention.

With no beard lending it cover, Cato's jaw ticked like a hummingbird's wing. He gripped his knees hard enough to draw Ambrose's attention, and my Black Bear, darling as he could be, covered Cato's hand with his own.

"His dick is longer than yours, Cat."

I stared at the ceiling and counted the remaining numbers to ten.

"Oh, and Eira just told me that she hated you and wished you would have died in Solnna... you know... in her head... where she and I can communicate and act like the total harlots we are." Ambrose slid his tongue over his bottom lip. "Remind me, and I'll regale you of what she sounds like when she's taking it from the new client. Oh! And I am officially her employer now, as well as a *consumer* of her talents. You know, so that I can render honest reviews for—"

"Ambrose, read the room. Don't be a dick."

Cato's hands shook. His eyes fixed to a spot on the floor, and I watched as a chilling emptiness snuffed out the light that had once lit them from within. I reached out, and Cato captured my hand like it was a lifeline tossed amid a storm-tossed sea. Ambrose slung his arm out, wiggling his fingers, silently demanding I do the same.

"I have acquired poison. One that should act quickly and help us avoid causing a scene if I can administer it in secret."

"When did you acquire such a—oh, you sly little Troth—when we met with Scion Amias?" Ambrose asked. "And the terrifying twins did not catch your sleight of hand?"

"Nope." I arched a saucy brow.

"Well done, cunning harpy."

I swelled under his praise.

"As I see it, if I can access the Primus-King's private chambers, I can disperse the poison into a decanter or vessel... or into him directly. But I need your help, both of you. Ambrose, I need a map. While you search for the betrothal contract, find one or sketch one. I don't have time to learn the palace. Cato, I need you to track the Primus-King. If I am to plant information to mislead the Baldorvan, I will not be free to assess the monarch's patterns."

"He is guarded at all times, Eira," Cato stated flatly. "With his level of paranoia, I am sure soldiers watch over him as he sleeps, perhaps even trusted members of his family. Allow *me* to—"

"Scale the palace walls, bust through a window, and stab every human in a forty-foot radius?"

Ambrose bobbed his head in agreement.

"Ooo, Eira, how about you do what Father did and bind the Baldorvan to you and make him your dog? Order him to return to Baldorva and tell the warlord it was all a farce? And make them send us all their black opals." Ambrose offered. "Cato, you should have seen the stones gracing his—"

"I will never." I slashed my arm across my chest in a gesture of finality. "How is that any different from what the Baldorvans do, enslaving the innocent and treating them as animals? I will never become what Ærta stands against. Never bring it up again. And besides, I've already thought it through; I'll enter the copper pipes as shade."

Ambrose shook his head.

"Unless it's the tiniest vial of poison known to man, it won't fit through the system... which I will be installing in Cordillaria the moment we return."

"I know that, Ambrose."

"Do you, though?" Cato asked, his voice concerned, not chiding. He gazed into the middle distance, his mind leafing through the possibilities—analyzing and looking for flaws.

"As shade, I will attempt to absorb the poison, head through the pipes, deposit the poison onto his meal, or into his lungs, and fly back quickly to take my human form. I always come back healed. Always. It will appear as if he died in his sleep."

The color drained from Cato's face.

Ambrose tapped his index finger to his lips.

"The plan has merit, Catommandus. Stop and think outside of your emotions."

Cato snapped back to the present, ripping his hand from mine.

"Did you fail to hear the part where *my* wife ingests a fast-acting poison? Wake the fuck up, brother. Are you so willing to lose her again?" Cato stood, placing his body in front of mine, ever my Protector. "Perhaps Father Regulus could administer the poison? A toast to the man's long life, an homage to the Goddess in an offering of blessed wine. How are these not your first thoughts?"

The room's single window frosted over despite the sunlight beaming through.

"Cato, how is trusting Eira not yours?"

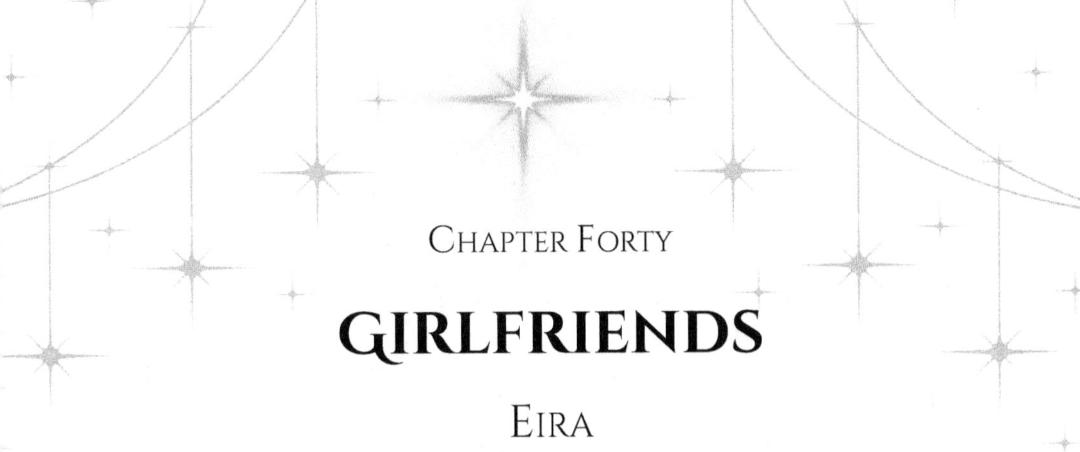

Chapter Forty

GIRLFRIENDS

Eira

I haphazardly waggled my fingers at Robyn and Wren as we passed Cult Mossius, my arms weighed down by Ambrose's "must-have" purchases. The ladies were just behind the fence, waiting for visitation hours to begin.

"Look at that dress!" River shouted, appearing from behind Robyn's back. "Silk?"

"It's the breeder," Father Regulus whispered in my ear. "Can I pay you in lands to be the one to inform Cato that he may father a random woman's spawn? Would you take fine gemstones? A lovely blonde courtesan for you to play with... only if I can watch, of course."

"Absolutely not," I muttered at my husband while beaming at the waving women.

After we said goodbye to Cato, who rode west to inform Larm of our discoveries, we set our plan into motion. The Frostborn would escort Gotwig to Verus with a critical message for Their Holiness: we suspected the Cult was holding Others against their will.

As soon as I could, I would take to shade and attempt to get the proof we desperately needed. Without it, we had nothing, but with it, Ærtan law could force the Primus-King's deposition if our assassination attempt failed.

"Ambrose, with the way you dug at him, I'm honestly surprised you didn't greet him with the news before breaking his nose."

"Yes, well, I don't *actually* want to die. Oh, there's an idea," Ambrose nodded to a line of couriers spilling from the temple. "We should send him a letter: You might be a daddy, daddy. Postscript: You'll never guess who's the mama."

I finger-waved again as Rollo's grinning face rounded the corner.

"We will tell him together. We are all of us a Bonded bundle, yes?" Ambrose grumbled, and I... slipped into a mild depression.

Wifey?

Yes, Black Bear?

If the woman carries his child, what of your heart?

You read me too well.

I hoped that the quickly gathering crowd would misconstrue the sudden, fat tears rolling down my face as the kind that accompanied the joyful reunion of long-lost friends... two days after I'd last seen them.

I think, husband, that babies are born without fault. River isn't at fault. You aren't at fault. Cato is certainly not. But the idea of someone else looking into those big brown eyes or singing the chubby little soul to sleep... oh gods... it fills me with a sickness I cannot begin to describe.

"River! Robyn!" My high-pitched squeal matched those of the two ladies as we shared in a three-way hug. Wren stood back and barred her arm across Rollo's chest when he tried to get near us. "I've missed you all... but not scrubbing shit off the ceiling and floors."

"This is decadent." Robyn slicked her hand over my hip. "And your hair? Birdie, it changes your entire face!"

Ambrose needled his way through our clasped arms and performed a two-handed wallop, smacking each on their foreheads and sending Robyn stumbling back.

"Bless you in Her name! May you not die in the next day or two."

Derros's dong! Bless with less enthusiasm, Ambrose.

Then back your tits off her chest. You cannot control your wandering eye around a fine set.

I disregarded him and steadied the momentarily stunned Robyn. River hid an awkward smile behind her hand, holding back a stream of laughter.

Oh, Ambrose, get this. The Baldorvan nearly came on command when I told him I liked women. He was all, "Impossible! Women do not fuck in Baldorva."

And here I thought him clever.

Robyn's stance changed, and her body went rigid. She pulled back but still held my arms.

"Birdie, Dæne got kicked out." River nodded and drew us all into yet another quick hug.

"No," I breathed, feigning shock. "Where did he go? Was he unable to—"

"—make the whale spout?" Ambrose interjected, wrapping his long arms around us in a cumbersome huddle.

River shook her head, and Ambrose bent to smell her hair.

Cocoa and vanilla. She'll make a fine mother for Cato's big-headed babe.

Ambrose, stop it.

"Minister Alder tried to employ the finger method, and Dæne rendered him unconscious. They escorted him to the front door and deemed him a failed specimen." River scooted closer, avoiding Ambrose's sniffing, as she recounted Cato's last moments. "Wren keeps rubbing her stomach and flashing secretive smiles now. Silly girl. Junnie and I have tried conceiving for the country for two months; there's no way it would happen that fast."

"Conceiving for the country?" I asked, wanting to know more about the *experiment.*

She nodded.

"The children we create are the future of Gaea. They are placed with the best families, will live the best lives, and will go on to produce the next generation of healthier, more productive citizens."

Who will be raised to unequivocally support the Primus-King. Can you even imagine, wifey? What brilliance on his part.

"River, what do *you* get out of it?" I asked. "Losing a baby leaves you with all kinds of tumultuous emotions. Are you prepared for that?"

I remembered going on rounds with my mother back home. For months after a woman miscarried, she insisted on seeing them, even if they'd only been a few weeks along. Almost always, their grief was still present, lying just below the surface of their thankful smiles.

"Of course. I've had sessions with the priests and know what to expect, but ultimately, I am doing the greatest of service and will be compensated for each birth. My older sister bore three before aging out; now she lives in a lovely home and is Lifemate to a healer and his wives."

Sounds pragmatic.

Have you ever watched a woman give birth, Ambrose?

Oh, fuck no, and ruin the beauteous image of my second favorite body part?

"Laundress," Ambrose snapped his fingers, and I barely resisted the urge to snap his bones, "we must be off. Tell your friends goodbye; the linen is in dire need of a pressing." He pointed to the packages squashed between us all.

We made our farewells, taking nearly an hour to arrive back at the palace, blessing each and every person we encountered until reaching Ambrose's apartments.

I tossed the parcels on the table and jumped onto the bed, snuggling a pillow under my head while enjoying the silence. Ambrose removed his layers, hanging each from the arm of a lamp so he could smooth down the puckers and wrinkles. He wore the softest of smiles.

"Do you like having a sibling, a twin even?"

He nodded.

"Yes." He held up a pearled cuff, inspecting the garment for loose threads. "We swapped stories at Verus, and I can fit Their clothes." Ambrose hung the robe in his wardrobe. "It is funny, though... They are the highest-ranking human on this continent, but I think I got the longer end of the stick. They were raised by Devotees and priestesses. I got a mama. They know how to give love, but I am not sure They have ever received it. They do not partake in the pleasures of the flesh. And I wonder if it was because they were never hugged or kissed." Ambrose fluffed his side-combed hair while studying his reflection in a small wall mirror. "But now we have each other, and if They wish it, I will provide an abundance of hugs."

In nothing but his tall underwear, the ones to keep his stomach taut, Ambrose climbed in next to me. He swept my long hair behind my head, ensuring he'd not tug it.

"Wife?"

"Mhmm?"

"When you go to the Baldorvan tonight, I will hunt for the betrothal contracts and map the copper pipes as I go. Do you feel safe enough if I move beyond the connection's range?"

"I do. Though fearsome in reputation, he is demure in the sheets."

Ambrose's expression darkened, all levity fleeing.

"Do not let that fool you, Eira. Ask yourself: Why would a woman not take the third-highest-ranking Baldorvan as a Hearthmate?"

Chapter Forty-One

SEARCHING THE STACKS

Ambrose

"**B**less you, child!" The little boy stumbled back and landed on his bottom. He bolted upright and then scurried away. "Praise Her!"

Is it the lack of sugar that makes the Gaean children puny? That boy would not withstand Verra's gentlest of headbutts.

"Ah, Father Regulus. Your unique blessings will stay with our citizens long after you depart."

"Of course, Highness, that's the point."

The heir, Zephyr, minus his ill-mannered ankle biter, had been leading me into all manner of areas otherwise off-limits to the general public. It had taken me pitching a fit and denying being either "general" or "the public," but that is neither here nor there. I admit, threatening him with excommunication was perhaps a tad dramatic, but the Gaean royal jeweler kept a gem sanctuary, and I was dying to see it.

"So, he, along with a mouth specialist, inset the stones into the teeth of nobles based upon achievement and merit? Like receiving a badge or medal in the other kingdoms?"

"Indeed. It is an outward and permanent show of honor that only my father can bestow."

Zephyr gestured to a room where a passel of children sat at lessons, and I smiled serenely, catching a bit of a lecture on the history of grape production along the rift and northern border.

"And the Primus-King? Where is he this fine day?"

I'd waited for more than an hour to broach the subject of his father.

"Praying with the dying at Cult Mossius. Afterward, he'll stay cooped up in his study until the family takes dinner. Father Regulus, I promise you he does not avoid you on purpose."

"The entire family, you say? Where would you all fit?"

His Highness Zephyr inclined his chin at my incredulous expression, quirking his mouth in amusement.

"Every last one of us who resides in the palace piles into his study. We sit on the floors, couches, or any surface that can bear weight. It is always a happy affair, and if, Cradle forbid, I must take the throne in the near future, I hope to carry on the tradition."

"A noble endeavor." I avoided a gaggle of priestesses as we ventured up a wide staircase leading to the uppermost level. They fancied this father a little too openly.

"The scriptorium lies ahead. You will appreciate the archaic messaging system still in place." Zephyr chuckled. "For all the innovations of Cult Mossius, the palace is behind the times."

Four guards flanked each side of the single door.

All eight of the armored men smiled in greeting. It took all my willpower not to admonish them—Cato would have pulled them from their post for such impertinence. With a disappointing lack of fanfare, not even a formal proclamation, we walked right into the room.

The air, thick with the scent of parchment and ink, was punctuated by the scratching of quills and the rustle of manuscript pages. Rows of scrolls and tomes rested on neatly stacked shelves, some discolored by age, many of them newly bound. Dust motes danced in the shafts of sunlight that illuminated the bent backs of the scribes hunched over their desks. Oh, no, that one was hunched on account of the twin boulders that—"Troth Yemailrys! Why, it has been months."

The auburn-haired, curvy Troth was slow to recognize me in disguise... or perhaps the silly girl still bore me the grudge of our youth.

The Monwyn-raised Troth stood behind the desk, and I rushed to embrace her.

"You look horrific," she whispered. "The rising vomit burns my throat."

"Bless you, Chosen Daughter!" I swatted her forehead so hard she resumed her chair. "Still an ingrate, I see." I whispered back.

Nasty hag. Her father had warned her away from me after my failed attempt at her seduction, and when it was announced we would leave for the temple in the same year, she asked to be held back. Well, I'd gone right behind her back and demanded Father ensure she be present... so that I would have a friend. Impugn my good name because of a "conflict of personality"? I think not. Since when did personality factor into seduction?

"Welcome, and may the Goddess grant you many years. Highness, might I be of service today?" Barely hiding the flush that colored her cheeks,

Yemailrys leapt to her feet again and bobbed a curtsy to Zephyr, who finally made his way to my side.

"No, no, I am giving Father Regulus a tour for his report to Verus. How goes the admittance of refugees? Father, Troth Yemailrys runs the registration when she's not here cataloging. You might make a note to the Mantle that her arrival was a boon to the kingdom."

"No doubt. It was my tutelage that transformed her into the cataloging savant that she is—her ability to alphabetize transcends the norm."

Yemailrys stared at me, face as blank as her brain, before her attention snapped back to Zephyr.

"Eighteen intakes yesterday. Homes found for all but one, who was sent to the infirmary for observation, Your Highness."

"Wonderful, our arms are forever open. Ah, I am being summoned."

I looked in the direction Zephyr waved. None other than that tasty twin, Lord Haycroft, hailed him over. "Troth, please show our esteemed guest the scriptorium. Lord Haycroft's brother experienced a horrific incident just recently. He was at the Cult making arrangements for his mother when he said a faceless aggressor bludgeoned him with a massive set of shears." Zephyr made a cutting motion with his fingers. "But then, I'm told he reeked of forbidden drink when he was found. There's a lesson to be had in his predicament. I'll be just a few minutes."

"I will pray for his recovery." I tapped my fingers to my forehead.

Zephyr walked away, his lovely braids swaying. I counted five seconds before catching Yemailrys by the arm.

"Listen up, Troth—uh, don't roll your eyes at a Mantle-appointed envoy, you nasty little big-boobed tarantula. I need access to Eira's betrothal papers. No, wait, Emryss, that was the birth name. They'll be under that, I suppose."

A single word nearly escaped her lips, but Yemailrys clamped her mouth shut, forcing back the sound. She folded her arm around my proffered elbow and pointed to a line of tall shelves.

"Follow me, Father; you will no doubt be interested in our Guide to Conduct and Valuable Manners holdings, which are in the Children's section."

We disappeared into the stacks, and in a very un-Troth-like action, she fisted two clumps of her waist-length curls.

"She's th-the daughter?" She blinked wildly and shoved a handful of hair in her mouth, chewing on it like some vulgar goat.

"Um, yes, which part had you confused? Stop that." I batted her hand from her face. "Your fine hair makes up, somewhat, for your lack of temperament."

Her glower could flay the hide from a buffalo.

"Ambrose, these people are obsessed with the 'lost daughter of Solnna' insanity. There are hundreds of militias and military groups scouring the continent for her. She's a-a fucking royal. She is loved beyond, without ever having stepped foot in—why would the Mantle want her to kill her own father? What the fuck, Ambrose? What is happening?"

I hastily guided her to the chamber's back corner.

"Chosen daughter, you must repent of your dirty mind," I said loudly. "Bow now, and we shall pray for the return of your wayward labia." I dropped beside her, and together we raised our hands to our brows. "A poor judge of character like yourself may not believe me, but, Yemailrys, the Primus-King is not the man you think."

Even behind her hands, I saw her lips purse in distaste.

"He is—have you met him? He is the kindest man I've ever encountered. And he's Eira's father? Truly?"

Would I ever erase the image of Mama's body as it swung? Limp, waxen. Gone.

"Yemailrys, he slit my mother's throat. He hanged Companion Nan after sewing her lips shut. He took the life of Lord Septimus's wife—"

Her eyes widened in disbelief.

"Lilium? No, she was the gentlest woman. I refuse to believe—"

"He did so with the aid of Scion Greggen, who has admitted his part and has sworn it on parchment. His signature graces the admission, and even now, he only lives by the grace of Prince Catommandus's mercy. If the need for testimony should arise, he will give it."

Her breath hitched.

"Bullshit. The Nether Lord and the Others attacked Cordillaria. The women were simply in the way of—"

"Scion Ozius's head was delivered to my wife as Gaea's Joining gift. Troth Cinden is not aware. Speak of it, and I will see you silenced. The Primus-King forced himself on Eira's mother. She too lives to give witness. Lord Gotwig keeps her safe. Do you need more evidence, Troth? My wife is the greatest good in my life. I will do all in my power to protect her."

A full minute of silence passed.

"No. No, I need no more evidence. What does Eira need?"

"A Baldorvan betrothal contract destroyed"—an idea hit me—"and a distraction to further ensure her safety."

Zephyr spotted us and came our way.

"I know where the contracts are. When does she need the distraction?"

"I will collect you in two hours' time. His Highness Catommandus arrives shortly. Keep your lips sealed."

Chapter Forty-Two

HI HO, HI HO. IT'S OFF TO WORK I HO.

Eira

The creepers were creeping hard this evening.

One patted me down while the other parted my hair with a small blade, searching through the new fibers as if I'd be able to sneak a weapon amid the silky strands. Their eyes—well, their concealed faces—followed me as I passed through the entryway after I'd received my inspection.

Emberkin Arro leaned forward, arms braced on the table, his cool-gray eyes fixed on me.

I waved.

His face softened into a gentle smile as he shook his head in amusement, returning my wave as awkwardly as if it were the first he'd ever given.

Do slavers not wave? Probably not. No manners.

I stepped on the heel of my new ankle boots, freed my foot, and then kicked the leather, narrowly missing the malachite chandelier dangling from the antechamber's high ceiling. The left boot followed, landing nowhere near its mate.

Emberkin Arro's eyes never strayed, even as I stretched my toes and then wiggled the digits—I hated breaking in new shoes, even if they were the softest I'd worn in months.

I walked past the threshold, and the door clicked shut behind me. The guards posted themselves inside today, motionless pillars of yellow gold.

Parchments, melting wax, and a large metal seal ringed the foreigner at the table, looking as happy to have a break from paperwork as he was to see me. Immediately, my mind turned to espionage.

"Good evening, Emberkin." Stiff, shoulders tense, he leaned forward, both hands on the table.

"What?" I turned my head from side to side and then glanced at my chest, hoping that Ambrose's chicken-grease-laden fingers hadn't soiled me when he bent me backward for a "little kiss to remember him by." I'd been breathless for a full five minutes and still smelled faintly of poultry.

I coiled a strand of hair around my finger and let out a strained laugh, as he popped the top button of his gray shirt and lowered himself into the chair at his back.

"It's just that... You may call me Arro, just Arro. Emberkin is an honorific like Lady or Lord—we are given the title of Family of the Flame, or Emberkin, when we reach a certain status or perform certain tasks for the warlord."

"Ah, and if our assignation is to be a *soft* one, the formal address does not fit the narrative. Correct?"

He nodded his head, which opened the column of his neck for my perusal. Inked below his ear was the image of a fire-breathing demon.

"Spoken not at all like a woman from some small mountain town... where no schooling was offered, or so I've been led to believe."

I hummed noncommittally.

"This dress certainly isn't from the hills. And neither is this hair." I executed a twirl, appreciating the dramatic spin of my skirts before I stopped and batted my eyes over my shoulder. "Do you like it?"

He pushed his chair back, legs scraping the floor.

"Very much," he answered.

"Enough to free your people?"

"Enough to order your mouth shut." He patted his thigh, the bulge between his legs growing in prominence. "Here. Now."

"Goodness, Arro, is that for little old me?" I fanned my face as I sauntered forward, my cheeks still burning from Ambrose's parting gift.

Demurely, I perched upon his knee and wrapped my arms around his neck to keep my rear from slipping off his legs... another tactic the noteworthy courtesans were sure to employ... the chubby ones anyway. I averted my eyes and fiddled with the talon-shaped closures on his tight-fitting vest of black brocade.

"Birdie, have you suddenly gone shy?"

Arro traced a finger down my chest, stopping to swirl around a quickly tightening nipple.

"Well." I fidgeted, still refusing eye contact. "Truth be told, I'm not as experienced as you might imagine me to be." I almost laughed at the lie. "And I find that things feel a little different today."

He ran a palm over the outside curve of my breast. I leaned into the touch.

"If you expect me to believe that Verus sent an inexperienced whore to tend me, then I—"

I stilled his hand, and he paused.

"I was literally scrubbing shit from a ceiling the morning before you walked in on me sucking a dick. Ask me how the shit got on the ceiling. Go on." I dropped my hand to his crotch and walked my fingers down his length. "It was shit or dick, and I chose dick. Yesterday, it was Dæne's, and today, Emberk—Arro, it is yours."

His gentle laugh took me by surprise again. I didn't want any reason to see him other than what he was—a slaver.

"Dick over shit?"

"All day, every day. I don't have a strong enough stomach for the latter."

Emberkin Arro tilted his hips and lifted me, settling me more comfortably in his lap.

"I'm afraid I must forgo that most interesting tale, as I am awash in correspondence."

I followed the hand that gestured to the parchment-littered table. Pinching a random missive between my fingers, I held it to my eyes and skimmed its contents.

"The fields are barren... Our God is angry." I released the letter and watched it float back to the table. "Ah, this one is easy, pen the following. Ahem. How do you expect me to fix the fields from here? Tell our God to send rain or lightning... to strike down all the enslavers. Then no one goes hungry. Love, Emberkin Arro. Postscript: tell the warlord to jump face-first into a latrine."

Arro's brows hopped to his hairline. A short, sharp laugh escaped him before he could stifle it.

"You are a bold piece of work, Birdie. I think the warlord would find you... refreshing, yes, I think that's the word I'd use."

"Oh, dear, am I to assume he also lacks a wife?" I poked out my bottom lip and simpered. "Are all the top slavers un-Hearthable?"

He caught my chin between his thumb and forefinger, applying firm pressure, his jaw tight and eyes intense.

"No woman has ever dared speak to me with such disrespect. And certainly not one contracted to me."

Tread lightly, Eira.

"Welp, alright. If banter isn't your thing, a quick fuck and I'll head back to my room for a snack. You know, this might be the cushiest job I'll ever land. Where do you want me? Table? Floor?" I hoped he'd choose the table. I could gather a lot of intel while faking it. "Or you can offer me the same courtesy as you did last evening. I won't say no." I would, however, cringe at his pointy-tongued serpent slithers. *May his future slaver wife suffer a lifetime of poorly executed cunnilingus.*

I kissed the tip of his nose and then picked up another letter—this one a receipt for iron ore and powder.

"The powder is requested to be delivered by the next thaw? Huh. Does Baldorva trade in talc? Do your people use an abundance of cosmetics? I suppose I always thought the slavers to be riddled with acne and—"

The body beneath me went rigid. Breath held, fingers tense around my waist.

"Arro? Are you alright?"

He nodded tersely but stared straight ahead.

"Are you—are you sure? I learned nothing about treating an apoplexy at the cult." *And a stroke would foil our plans!*

I loosened the second button of his shirt and slid one of the talon closures through the loop that held it in place. Snatching up another piece of correspondence, I fanned him with the parchment and read its first line, "I expect your next communication to hold news of her," between waves.

"I am... fine. Fine."

He plucked the letter from my hand and dropped it beside me. It was time to initiate a table fucking. My curiosity was more than piqued by what I'd read.

"Mmhmm, well. Though I may not have had any formal schooling, even someone as lowly as I can see that's a lie."

A muscle jumped in his cheek as he looked ever so briefly away.

"I'm sorry for making light of you. Though I don't know you well, I'd say you'd make a solid, um, Hearthing partner. You're easy to talk to, strong, and passionate about your job. Oh, and you have very pretty eyes." I pulled him close and pressed a kiss to his chin and then cheek.

Below me, his thighs tensed.

Something dawned on me then. *Oh, for fuck's sake.*

I skimmed my palm along his collarbone and brought my lips to his ears before I whispered, "Have you never been kissed?"

He didn't answer.

Of fucking course not. Who in their right mind would allow a warmongering, human-owning disgrace of a person to share in such delight? And why did the chore fall to me? I sighed inwardly. *For Ærta!*

"I find kissing to be the most intimate gesture a person can share." I pulled a Cato and used the tip of my nose to urge his face up. "Would that be something you are interested in experiencing?"

He blinked and looked off to the side.

Was he cute? I tried to look at him through Ambrose's eyes. *He might be sort of handsome.* Striking features different from those of a typical Ærtan certainly gave him a unique appeal. I found myself drawn to the two metal hoops in his nose and to the silver-gray hue of his irises—half-veiled beneath narrow lids framed by thick, black lashes. *Hmm? Maybe?*

"Yes, I am," he said as gravely as a man headed to the gallows.

"Alright. But, but it's generally done with someone you have feelings for, so you may find it less fun than fuck—lovemaking. You ready?" *You ready? How stupidly awkward, Eira!*

He moved his hands about, seeking but not finding the best hold.

"One here," I murmured, while securing his arm more tightly about my waist. "And the other here." I led that one to the curve of my rear. "Close your eyes. Open-eyed kissing should be outlawed."

They blinked shut on command.

"Begin," the slaver commanded, his face impassive.

Begin? Ah, he was as romantic as I. Perhaps more so, if my husbands are to be believed.

I traced an inked line over his nose and fingered the two hoops in his nostril.

"You have lovely lips, Arro. I think they will feel wonderful beneath mine." I followed the winding path of a black swirl near the corner of his mouth and then continued down to an impressive rendering of a dragon piercing its breast, its blood running down its body to fuel the flames in a stone hearth. "You're not at all what I thought a Baldorvan to be. My gram used to tell me you'd come steal me from my bed if I backtalked adults." I turned, bettering my angle for espionage, stretching my neck to glean any words from the parchment nearest me. "Had I known how intriguing you were... how badly I'd want to flick my tongue over that bottom lip... perhaps I wouldn't have stayed my sassy mouth."

I kissed a path up his neck and then peeked to the side, making out the second sentence in the discarded missive. "Our Hearthing is past due. Leyometh demands her return."

I leaned in a little further, and so did he.

Our lips met.

Under my fingertips, his skin went to goosebumps. His hands tightened, and a soft groan vibrated in his throat. I angled my head slightly, letting my hair cascade over one shoulder, and, taking his upper lip between mine, guided his nose from my line of vision. Hoping not to draw suspicion from the creepers, my eyes fastened to the letter. I imagined they watched our every move, but positioned as we were, I relied on the cloak of my tresses to hide my intent.

"I require an heir to maintain my rule, and Princess Emryss was promised to carry my offspring."

I groaned, passing it off as a moan wrought of passion. Fucking men. If they baked the buns, they'd close the baby-making bakery at the first contraction… first menstrual cramp, even.

"Though I have derived much pleasure from your sassy mouth, I would certainly not have stolen you from your bed, Birdie. You would make a terrible dross."

"Dross?"

"It is a word for the impurities that float to the surface when smelting metal, and also the closest translation to what you have named *slave*."

The æther sank to my stomach with the weight of a basalt stone. *Do not bite him. Do. Not. Put. Another. Hole. In. His. Body.*

Arro's hand cupped my cheek, and I sealed my mouth over his, if only to keep my teeth busy.

In my mind, the mouth of a slaver should be cruel and punishing. But wasn't that just the way of the world? They weren't scaly monsters or mythical tyrants; they were men, humans who found some fucking way to rationalize devaluing another life. It was a rare mind that would question the moral foundation of a system that placed them at the pinnacle of the hierarchy.

My temperature began to rise.

Ope, nope. Calm it the fuck down, Eira.

I breathed deeply and imagined Ambrose's cool hands soothing my flesh, sweeping down my back, and settling on my hips. I smiled against the Baldorvan's mouth… something both my men did that drove me to distraction.

"Oh!"

In a single swift motion, I found myself on my back, parchments scattering to the floor. *Godsdammit! Forget the table fuck. Initiate Plan B: floor fuck.*

His mouth crushed to mine.

I tentatively ran my tongue along his parted lips while pushing his shoulders back.

"Floor. Now. Take me from behind," I begged.

"Fuck." He ground his erection against my vulva. "This is... God." Arro thrust against me harder and shoved his tongue past my lips.

"Yes. Fuck. On the floor, Arro. On my knees, take me slowly."

"No." He took my mouth again, tongue sweeping in and tangling with my own.

Wiflet, are you there?

Yes, husband. Wish I wasn't, but yes.

I have information.

A knock sounded, and the twin guards moved swiftly, closing the double doors behind them.

The minutes ticked by while Arro humped and dry-pumped me. I fake-moaned and panted the little breathy whimpers that seemed to drive all the men wild.

The door opened and my husband—Father Regulus—burst into the chamber in a dazzling priest's robe, surprisingly towing a dowdy-looking Yemailrys behind him.

"Emberkin Arro!" Ambrose sang out. "I've procured a treat for us!"

The Troth wore a baggy brown dress, and her normal halo of red-gold hair was braided tight to her scalp. She kept her eyes on the floor.

That doesn't look at all comfortable, wife.

I tilted my head back and blinked at the upside-down image of my beloved.

It's not.

"Why the *fuck* are you interrupting me, priest? Leave before I separate your spine from its flesh." The slaver's voice took on a cold and unsettling edge. On either side of my head, the ropey veins on his forearms stood out. His gray eyes narrowed to shards.

Ambrose sashayed into the room, uncaring, gold robes flying behind him like the wings of a gilded bird. He dragged two of the dining room chairs toward the bed and then flopped down, propping his feet on the edge. He patted the other seat.

"Arro, fierce one. Tonight, I upped the ante in hopes of cementing our deal. I bring you a gift more spectacular than any other you might behold."

What deal?

Hush, Eira, you will distract me.

Emberkin Arro stood, pulling me to my feet and tucking me under his arm. I clung to his side like a woman desperate for an anchor.

"I have my woman. Leave my sight." Emberkin Arro produced a thin blade from his hip. "Man of the Goddess or not, I will shave the skin from—"

"I bring you..." Ambrose intoned before pausing for effect. "Lesbians! The Goddess's most beautiful creation."

Ambrose. Really?

Arro's hand stilled. He flipped his blade back to its sheath.

Eira, understand me, this is important. We need a distraction. A big one. Think about a raucous, wild, chaotic, lesbian fuck session. The sounds that will soon come from the entryway must not reach the foreigners' ears.

Cato?

Cato.

Already, my skin prickled. My body called to its mate.

Yemailrys has given consent?

Oh, my gods, of course, hurry the nether up. Come slap her ass or clap her globes together. That boom will shatter the eardrums of all the palace dwellers—Viktos's true thunder!

Arro's breath quickened. Were lust a portrait, he was its model.

He wasn't smiling, not really, but there was something raw in his expression. His normally pinched face relaxed. Spellbound, he stood motionless, contemplating his decision. I craned my neck, bringing my mouth to his ear.

"It's not illegal here, Arro. You will break no laws by simply watching this manner of coupling. Allow me to leave you with a memory." I bit my bottom lip. The silvery flecks stood out against the darker gray in his irises as I met and held his eyes. "Yes?"

"I..." he whispered. "Yes."

Ambrose, is Cato aware?

Mhmm.

Is he angry?

Very. The connection went momentarily silent. *He has promised to not slay myself or Yemailrys. Well, I told him he could slaughter her after she turned thirty and five. By then, she will be past her prime.*

Ambrose.

Eira, hurry the fuck up. Noise, madam, at once. Squealing, sucking, screaming. It is imperative that it begins soon.

Arro released me and allowed me to lead him across the floor. I pushed him backward and winked as he fell into the chair beside Father Regulus.

"Kiss me," he gritted out.

I bent at the waist, and his hands found my breasts, kneading and squeezing them as our kiss-swollen lips found each other once more.

Arro came up for air.

"Priest. Get out. This is not a public spectacle. If it is my gift, then it is for my eyes alone."

Ambrose pushed his spectacles up his nose.

"Oh, pardon, I was of the understanding that the Baldorvans held public biddings on human flesh. Is that treatment only for the ones you intend to work to death?"

Arro's lip curled. He dropped his hands to the chair arms and shoved to his feet.

I intercepted him and situated my body between the two. Arro seethed. Ambrose sat there bouncing his crossed leg.

Don't agitate the fucker, Ambrose. He pulls out his dagger as fast as his dick.

"The man who wishes to garner my favor keeps his insolent tongue firmly in his mouth." Arro postured, glaring over my shoulder. "Your Mantle sent an imbecile in place of a diplomat."

Ambrose chuckled.

"Just as Baldorva sent a—"

"—warrior," I said, reading the rising tension in the room. Could Ambrose not see the temper he inspired in the Baldorvan? Arro was drawn taut as a bowstring. His fingers curled like claws around the hilt of his blade. "One whose prowess I wish to test in a different sort of combat."

"Proceed," he spat out. "Priest, if you speak again, I will permanently silence you."

Eira, do I need to take over? I am mightily aroused by it all. It is like one of my stories, just imagine it. Yemailrys stands like the innocent you just know she isn't, waiting to be given over to the cruel overlord. Color rises on her cheeks as others barter for her maidenhead, in the hopes of stopping the cattle raids that your village has endured for ten years.

You just want to see her tits.

His infernal giggle transferred through the connection, and jealousy burned bright, a physical reaction in my chest. Me, the woman who'd now spread her legs for three men she wasn't Joined with.

Ambrose shifted in his chair, adjusting himself.

Your envy makes my dick throb, darling. Come now, lovie dove, give your Black Bear a show. I've been such a good boy.

I held back a huff.

"Arro, take your ease." I nodded to the seat he'd left vacant. Thankfully, he sank into it without a fight, though his stance still exuded threat—elbow propped on the armrest, legs spread wide. I stepped to his back, my breath brushing his ear as my hands slipped around his shoulders, fingers tracing the firm lines of his chest. "Isn't she lovely, Arro?"

A faint, ambiguous sound was his only reply.

"The last woman I pleasured had hair the color of sunbeams and the most perfect pair of soft, copper-tipped breasts. I've never had an auburn-haired beauty."

Arro took my hands, kissing the palm of my right and then my left, before I untangled myself from his touch.

Yemailrys stood on the opposite end of the bed that would be our stage. I approached her and reached out.

"Hi, I'm Birdie. What's your name?"

"Catonya," Yemailrys breathed in a higher and airier approximation of her normal voice.

A laugh nearly exploded from my chest.

Ambrose cleared his throat, hacking like a cat bringing up a ball of hair.

I clasped "Catonya's" hand and threaded our fingers together, leading her to the bed's edge. I bade her to sit, facing me and not the salivating men just beyond. Yes, Troth were trained to use sex as a weapon or tool, but I hadn't a clue of Yemailrys's preferences or experience, and one's sexuality was a defining aspect of their life.

"Have you been intimate before, Catonya?" I moved forward, reaching around her neck to untie the leather that bound the tail of her plait. She spread her knees, and I stepped into their cradle, my thighs meeting hers.

"Never with a man. My preference is for women." Her eyes slid toward the Baldorvan. "Though I've been curious as to what it might feel like."

Gods, I will come in my pants.

I ignored Ambrose and placed a knee on the bed to roll around Yemailrys's back. I could shield her from this position. I finger-combed her coils, for a moment envious of their luster and volume.

"May I?" My fingers went to the thread-wrapped buttons at her back.

"Mhmm." I worked each button free, revealing glowing white flesh, spotted with a fine dusting of freckles.

Yemailrys moved then, shifting up to her knees. She turned to face me.

"Should I continue, gentlemen?"

"Yes," Yemailrys answered for them.

A delicious pulsing took up in my passage.

Fuck, yes. And rub your gorgeous breasts against hers. Do it, and I will forgive all your past and future transgressions.

With a single finger, I drew the middle of her neckline down. The fabric caught and then popped over her amber nipples, one pierced in the Monwyn fashion.

Ambrose. Just this once. If she offers herself up to you, you may partake. I have a feeling we will share the tale until we are old and gray.

Ambrose loudly smacked his lips. I wanted to throw him a look as lusty as I felt but didn't dare.

I guided Yemailrys's dress below her knees, catching a glimpse of her copper curls and pink slit as I freed the garment and tossed it to the floor.

"You are stunning, Catonya." *And apparently, I have a thing for red-heads.* "Are you as slick as you have made me?"

I'll have the Monwyn clothier design a wig for our play, Eira. I'll command the irritating shit to shear her head and deliver those very curls if you wish it. She was my subject before she was Assigned here.

So mean, husband. Do you and she share a history?

I took Yemailrys by the hips and guided us into a position that offered the gentlemen a better view of her pretty profile—both on our knees, facing each other.

Ambrose crossed his arms and pressed his lips into a fine line.

Oh, let me guess. You don't have a history, and it upsets you? My husband, Goddess love him. There was sadness in his eyes.

Here, Black Bear, take a look.

I held up Yemailrys's breasts, cradling them in my hands before circling her areolas with my thumbs, never once touching their tightening centers.

"Arro, what do you imagine she will taste like? I think sweeter than salty, more musky than earthy."

A bump sounded from the entryway. Arro's head snapped to the side.

With a strength unknown to myself—and despite her having a solid seven inches of height on me—I twisted Yemailrys by the shoulders and shoved her to the mattress, parting her legs wide. I knee-walked forward and yanked my own dress over my head, casting it aside.

"Wouldn't want that dripping-wet pussy to ruin my best silk."

Ambrose let out a shrill sound of pain.

Are you okay? Was that too vulgar?

No... no... pray continue. Even through the connection, his voice was strained.

Arro's attention was firmly back on the show before him.

"Do you want to see fingers or tongues, Arro?"

"Why not both?" Catonya replied, with a silky laugh.

My entrance swelled, growing heavy and wet.

Sample her tightness, divine harpy, and I will build you a castle with my own hands. Four, if you'd prefer, one in each kingdom.

I cocked a brow, grabbed Yemailrys by the waist, and tucked my pubic bone under her swollen clitoris.

Just one. I lowered my face to Yemailrys's right breast and drew her pierced nipple into my mouth before flicking my tongue over the metal. *A home for the three of us.*

You, me, and Yemailrys? Yes, I can see that working out well.

"Oh, my lady," Yemailrys hummed. Her lips parted, and she pushed her other breast toward my mouth. I licked and sucked, tugging on her nipple until her knees slid back and she opened herself fully, spreading her labia with her fingers. "I cannot wait to see what that mouth can do down below."

Eira, you are a vision, one whose beauty will never adequately be captured on canvas.

Rotating my hips, I gently tilted my pelvic bone until she moaned deep in the back of her throat. I repeated the action, pleasuring her with slow rocking motions until she writhed under me. Her center was warm and wet, and the bounce of her breasts mesmerized me to the point I felt the evidence of my own arousal tickling my vulva, slipping down my lips.

"Arro, let me show you one of my favorite things about loving a woman." I sat back on my knees and pointed to the front of my white linen underwear. My white-blonde curls were visible through the saturated fabric. I pulled the ties at my hips and removed the undergarment.

"Aren't they stunning?" Ambrose whispered with a reverence, his eyes misting over as if he beheld the Goddess herself.

"Unlike anything I've seen."

I tossed the underthings to the Baldorvan and winked when he snatched them from the air and tucked them into his waistband.

A loud bumping sound followed by a thud came from beyond the closed doors.

Shit! That was loud, Ambrose.

"Ah! It must be the drinks I ordered. Finally! The servants in this kingdom should be flogged for untimeliness." Ambrose stood, his erection bouncing under his robes. "Might I suggest snacking on one while she snacks on the other?"

"I agree!" I piped up, maybe a little too chipper.

Ambrose, what's happening?

Don't worry. But for the Goddess's sake, cover his ears and make enough noise to raise our dearly departed from their graves!

Ambrose sprinted to the door. "I am so fucking parched! Praise Her!"

I crawled over a smugly smiling Yemailrys and snatched Arro by his shirt. Dragging him across the bed, I ripped the two sides of his vest and then shirt—buttons flew this way and that.

"It may not be soft, but she's going to ride your mouth, and I'm going to take your cock down my throat, do you understand?"

He nodded once, and I struck, biting his bottom lip and tugging so hard he had no choice but to follow.

"Down." I forced his back to the bed as Yemailrys came up to her knees. "I want to hear her scream while she fucks those pretty lips."

With no ceremony at all, the Troth tossed a thigh over Arro's head and perched upon his face like a queen on her throne. I wasn't entirely sure he could breathe, but if he died, he died. One less slaver in the world.

"Harder," I counseled. Yemailrys squeezed her thighs against his ears, and he took to his job with gusto, a man starved, growling and moaning as he gripped handfuls of her rear and jerked her ass up and down.

"Birdie," Yemailrys whispered. "The Primus-King's office is two floors above this very apartment—Oh yes, oh my Goddess, yes!" Her eyes flicked to the bathing chamber. "The waterfall must start up there—Fuck me, foreigner, fuck me with your tongue! The first day we came here, he gave us his formal address in his study and showed us how the rainwater collected from the palace roof. He said it ran down to the lower level where the mushrooms are grown."

As I listened to her alternating between shouts and whispers, I untied the laces of Arro's pants. His cock sprang free, hot and hard as granite. I lapped the pearl at his divot just before taking him to his base. He shouted obscenities... I think... or may have been begging for air, but I didn't relent, as the noises from the atrium increased in frequency.

"Yes! Yes! Yes!" Yemailrys screamed, while grinding her center on Arro's nose.

From my periphery, I caught a creeper entering the room to stand—

My fingertips tingled. The æther in my chest moved in massive gyres.

Cato—I would recognize him through the realms.

Shame choked me up, followed by a directed sense of anger.

Ambrose, shame on you! He shouldn't be subjected to this.

Figure it out, wife; I am busy! The connection snapped shut.

Fucking Ambrose!

My skin heated, boiling over with a burgeoning sense of desire. The Bond snapped tight. If I didn't find release, I'd end up burning the gods-dammed sheets and melting the people currently rolling in them.

While Yemailrys slit-smothered Emberkin Arro, I changed my position and straddled his legs, mashing my breasts against Yemailrys's.

"Would you mind fucking him?" I asked.

She grimaced.

"Gross. Really? An enslaver? I am not overly disappointed with his tongue methodology, but I've never taken a cock. It seems nasty, all veiny and stiff—"

"Truly? You think he's well-versed in..." My brow furrowed. "Never mind. Use your mouth, then. Please, for me. I've got to save my marriage."

Rightfully, she looked at me in confusion but nodded and waved a flippant hand.

"Whatever. I'll imagine your tits on his chest and get off all the same." Yemailrys rolled her eyes and then shouted again. "Yes! Oh, I'm close!" She dropped her hand to my vulva, collected my moisture, and circled her hand around his erection. "Men are ignorant. They can't tell teeth from talons."

I backed my knees to the edge of the bed and bent low, pressing my chest into Arro's thighs—he'd not be able to rise if he tried.

Fiery prickles danced along my skin. I flushed, uncomfortably hot.

I turned my head toward my man, and desperate for him to understand, I placed my finger to my lips and mouthed *shhh* before crooking it in a come-hither motion.

Cato moved like a man deranged, parting his robe and popping the buttons of his pants as he closed the distance. I arched my back and pushed out my rear, hoping to make his job easier.

My eyes rolled to the ceiling when Cato's hands gripped my ass. There was no other like him. No touch as possessive... no touch as sure.

"I'm...I'm coming!" Yemailrys shrieked, breasts bouncing in the same rhythm as her auburn curls. Either she was having the time of her life, or she was the best fucking Troth among us.

The Baldorvan's hips bucked and thrust as Yemailrys's slickness coated his chin.

My vision softened, my skin sensitized. The haze of arousal took control of my body.

Cato poised his thickness at my entrance, my own shouts building within me. I would reach the Goddess's realm in two strokes.

"Oh, gods, please, please," I begged. My walls parted, much too slowly.

I shoved backward, impaling myself on—

One.

Two.

Three.

Three familiar bumps, cold and metallic, rubbed over the gem deep within me.

"I have searched the world for you, Enchantress."

"What the fuck!" I yelled and began to spasm, orgasming around Septimus's pierced length. He thrust, pounding me like a hammer on an anvil.

"Harder, fucker. Harder," I hissed, keeping my voice low. There was no stopping it. The Mated Bond tugged just as firmly as the Fated one. I spread my legs, threw my head back, and saw the stars.

"I'll kill you," I whispered when my breath returned.

"Do your worst," Septimus said. He thrust once more and poured into me, growling and taking his pleasure.

Yemailrys's head whipped up.

"He's about to blow."

Septimus shot off, the last pulse of his semen splashing against my side. The layered robes concealed him once more as he took up his post by the door.

Arro tossed off Yemailrys and snapped his fingers. His tattooed chest heaved, and the bottom half of his face gleamed. He pointed to the spot in front of him.

"Birdie, present yourself," he demanded.

Merrias. Grandmother, I may rid the world of men in their entirety.

"Yes, Arro," I acquiesced, lying down on my back and spreading my legs.

"This belongs to me." He entered me swiftly, fucking me so hard the bed inched away from the wall.

Ambrose! You better thank this fucking Baldorvan for holding me down, because I'm going to KILL YOU!

CHAPTER FORTY-THREE

BECAUSE I'M HUNGRY

CATO

"Apprehend him!" I hissed. "Useless fucking..."

The faceless guard moved like a wraith, a silent storm of smoke. My hands felt clumsy against his fluid fighting style. He seemed to weave in and out of my hold, disappearing the moment I thought him bound. I wished him the same frustration as I deflected and stopped each slash.

He evaded my companions with the same grace.

"No blood." I signaled in our wordless language as Ambrose flipped the piece of stock iron I had procured for him. He nodded and returned to guard the exit as I'd instructed, never allowing the faceless servant close enough to raise the alarm.

I gave chase, closing in on the guard, corralling him back toward the entrance to the Emberkin's rooms. He ran and, at the last instant, twisted, feinting left and exploding right. His momentum carried him past me, his back exposed for but a second. You can't dodge a blow you don't see coming. I struck, tangling my fingers into his voluminous sleeve and bringing his dagger hand down as my knee came up to meet his knuckles. With a cluster of staccato popping sounds, I broke his hold on the thin-bladed dagger and likely several of his knuckles. I caught the tumbling blade on an outstretched foot before it clattered to the floor, then slid it to Ambrose.

Caught in a grapple, the guard's tactics of exploiting openings and precisely timed retreats became useless. I dragged his trapped arm across my chest, pushed my hip into his, and sent him violently to the floor. I dropped, moving my center of mass, and drove my shin into his hyoid bone.

"Thank fuck," Ambrose said as the guard's twitching legs began to settle. "I see your grip strength has increased twofold. The upside to being alone so long."

"Shut up!" I whispered-yelled for the fourth time in a matter of minutes. It was dumb luck that the Baldorvans had removed the guard's tongues, and I was currently seeing the benefits of the practice myself.

Ambrose pursed his lips.

Satisfied the man was dead, I signaled to Evandr.

In his frost giant form, he took up a third of the entryway. His neck pressed against the ceiling, his marbled knees bent to keep his foot from popping through the door. For all the use a giant would have afforded us, he was effectively imprisoned.

He licked his lips and then squeezed his arm from its confinement, snatching the corpse in his massive paw.

"Evan, nip off his head and nurse the neck stump like a tit this time."

I wanted to tell Ambrose to shut the fuck up again, but, honestly, his advice was sound. The consumption of the first guard had nearly gone awry when Evandr sampled the man's leg *before* we had divested the corpse of his clothing.

The Frostborn had attempted to lick the blood-splattered pants clean, but in the end, I determined that the long overdress would cover Septimus's leathers. Besides which, blood was the least of our concerns. Already, the wooden platforms tucked into my and my uncle's shoes caused me significant discomfort. Goddess willing, they would grant us enough height to sell the ruse.

I rechecked my weapons before shucking my shirt and slipping the gown and head covering over my body.

Evandr bent his head at an unnatural angle and severed the guard's head with his sharp incisors. Blood flowed freely down the giant's gullet as he held the man by his legs, dangling the lifeless form above his mouth.

"Dear gods." Ambrose clutched his head and dropped to the floor in a dead faint.

I stared in confusion at the heap of priest's silks now sprawled on the floor. Ambrose had been outright giddy during the consumption of the first guard. The Baldorvan had sported a tattoo of a massive red dragon feeding on the unmentionables of a curvy elfin woman with flowing black hair—he'd proclaimed it the finest work of art of the age.

The door flew open.

Everyone froze.

No, no, no.

"I'll be right back, Arro. I'm dying of thirst, and that aggravating Father Regulus is taking too long." My wife stomped into the room, a grayish haze gleaming in her eyes, fists clenched at her sides. She was awash in rage, right up until the color drained from her face.

I lunged forward, cupping my hand over her mouth a split second before the muffled sounds of her cries spilled forth.

"Hush, my love," I whispered over and over again, turning her and shielding her eyes from the grisly sight. Thankfully, her shock rendered her incapable of tears. "You are okay. Breathe in slowly. I have you, love."

The crunch of bones and squelch of teeth through fat and viscera brought her to her knees. I lowered her to the floor.

For fuck's sake. Was no one capable of reading a situation?

I slashed my fingers across my throat, signaling for Evandr to stop. The grinding noise was too loud to go unnoticed with the door cracked.

"Sweetheart. Can you hear me?" Eira stared forward, her body trembling. "It will be over soon, but my love, you must return. Head back into the chamber, curse Ambrose's good name, sing your loudest Nortian ditty. Do what you must. I will be with you in"—I glanced up and made note of the remains—a shoulder and the hips, which had taken the most effort on the last man—"five minutes' time. Can you do this?"

I would find another way if not.

She nodded once, her bloodless lips quivering.

"Take my arms, here we go." I helped her to rise, not releasing her until she stopped swaying. "No, love. Don't look back." I guided her chin forward, forcing her gaze to lock on mine. "Are you well enough?"

Her lashes fanned over her cheekbones.

"Yes," she lied.

I leaned in to kiss her, to give her reassurance, but the confounded face covering blocked me. I settled for skimming my knuckles down her cheek before I opened the door and ushered her through.

A guileless smile curved her lips as she reentered. My chest swelled. Gods, but I owed her a better life. My eyes followed the sway of her hips, pride and jealousy colliding in an all-too-familiar feeling.

"Father got called out to bless a newborn. Are you ready for round two? I've always wanted to try taking a cock while a woman rode my face. Do you want to hear a song? I know a good one!"

I tucked in on myself, forehead to the floor, hands pressed to my ears. My mind told me to enter the rooms, cut out the Emberkin's heart, and toss it to the frost giant. Yemailrys could follow in kind.

Rhythmic clapping and loud whoops came from the bedchamber.

I signaled for Evandr to resume his meal.

"Do you like wits or nether bits?

With a purse like mine, everything fits.

'Cause it's emptyyyyy! I'm as poor as they come!"

My woman was a fucking warrior. Horrific musical taste and singing voice aside, she was an outstanding showwoman, unlike my fainting lov—friend? Brother? Gods, I didn't know how to refer to Ambrose anymore—whatever the title, he needed lessons in fortitude, and our wife could certainly give them.

I stormed to his lifeless form and tapped my boot to his cheek. His eyes fluttered open.

"Sh-she felled me with her mental lung capacity. He took my proffered hand, and I tugged him to his feet. "Threatened to kill me, though I am still unsure why. My gods, are her courses upon us? As you know, she is *your* wife when she bleeds."

"Can't buy you a mess of fish,

Or a whalebone comb or a new meat spit.

But in my purse you shall fit,

Sing it with me now!" Inside the chamber, Yemailrys clapped along to Eira's off-key warbling.

"'Cause it's empty! I'm as poor as they come!"

Ambrose rubbed his temples.

Loud moans and feminine shrieks were a godsdamn pickaxe through my skull. I fought the pull, the Bond—the feeling that right now had my stomach churning and my mind considering begging Evandr to rip me in two—but if she could endure it, so could I.

"Catommandus?"

"What?" I spat out.

A cool hand settled on my shoulder.

"What she must do bears no reflection on who she is... or whom she loves."

I allowed my tumultuous feelings to wash over me, accepted them for what they were, and moved on.

"Ambrose, collect the shredded clothing and prepare the acolyte's robes for when Evandr shifts back. Leave the exterior door cracked to rid the air of this stench and pen a letter to Emberkin Arro asking him to enjoy Eira's company for the night, as duty has called you elsewhere."

"Yes, sir." Like the soldier he was raised to be, Ambrose jumped to follow my directives.

With a final, morbid grunt of satisfaction, Evandr polished off the second guard.

"Disgusting." I grimaced as the giant rubbed his stomach and then scratched his saddle-bag-sized scrotum.

Evandr hoisted a middle finger, and his face split into an unsettling, fang-toothed approximation of a smile.

"We are a crew of disturbed individuals, are we not?" I whispered.

"Cato, go; her song has ended."

I opened the door wide enough to slide in and took up my post opposite Septimus, arms to my sides.

This was to be my nether—the most difficult mission I would ever endure.

He took my giggling wife again and again. Fucking her and kissing her. Running his hands over her curves, fisting her hair as she sucked him off, until finally he succumbed to exhaustion.

The room was pitch when Eira quietly backed out of the bed and tiptoed toward the bathing chamber. She beckoned with a soft cough, and I followed, my foot hitting the ground with the same cadence as Yemailrys's soft snores.

Her hands sought me, desperate and clinging, and I pressed her head to my chest and stood as the rock she needed—no words and no judgments.

"My vagina is chafed as raw as a priestess's knees after holy week."

I stifled a sudden burst of laughter, pressing my face into the crook of her neck. I smelled him... but beneath that, there was her scent, clean and uncorrupted, and that filled me with peace.

"And, he has two fully functional twats to choose from, but he insists on mangling mine." Her shoulders shook as we shared in a grim chuckle.

"You are like no other, my Eira."

"Cato, Yemailrys says the waterfall's flow begins in the Primus-King's study, two floors up. I have an idea but need your help."

"Name it." I rubbed circles on the small of her back, unwilling to break our embrace.

"I'll float up the falls. Instead of taking a chance on ingesting the poison, I'll lower something—a string, a rope, I don't know, whatever I can find that will catch in the current. Down here, you attach the vial, and I will reel it up like—"

"Like a fat fish on a Nortian dinghy?"

Eira smacked a hand over her mouth, but flatulence-like honks puffed from between her fingers. I dragged her into the back corner and caged her in, doing my best to muffle the sounds with my body.

In the mirror's reflection, I saw the flash of her teeth as she wiped her eyes. I draped my arms over her shoulders and pulled her against my chest. I would never get enough of her.

"Eira, if he is present—"

"I will end him."

"If he is not—"

"Then this fate will await him." Eira selected a vial from the cabinet. She pressed it to my palm. "This one."

I closed my hand around the warm glass, praying it was our freedom.

"Are you ready?" she asked.

"Unquestionably so. Let us close the book on this chapter." Stepping back, I gave her room to shift.

In the dark, the shimmer working across her irises looked anything but natural. There was no mistaking it for a trick of the light.

She paced the floor, wringing her hands.

"It's still not second nature," she whispered. "When I'm mad, no problem. When I'm nervous, welp, poof, I can't focus enough to become the shade."

"It is alright, love. I will be standing in this spot upon your return. And you *will* return. Come here."

Resting my palms on her chest, where her æther tended to collect, she tried again.

I blinked, and she was gone.

Chapter Forty-Four

How Easily Love Is Shared

Eira

Traversing the path of the waterfall was the simplest task I'd completed in the last year. Which meant I was sure to stumble upon a room guarded by a battalion of elite warriors, surrounded by a legion of horsemen, ringed by a circle of archers.

Instead, as I exited the watery cavern, it was into something a little girl had to have dreamed up. Bookcases were the majority of the furniture, filled to bursting with tomes. A mural covered both ceiling and wall, painted to look like an enchanted forest, complete with pixies riding on the backs of squirrels and sprites turning somersaults, their glittering, multi-hued wings mosaics of chipped gemstone. Copper pipes dropped from the ceiling, looping in concentric circles until they ended in glass domes of lavender and gold.

Snap! *Oof, that was jarring. I've got to improve my landing.*

My feet appeared beneath me, and my toes gripped the deep pile of a luxurious carpet. Overused vagina soothed and my knees less bruised, I squatted behind a tall-backed chair, thanking the Goddess for my unique gifts and the good fortune that not a soul appeared to be in residence.

There was no time to waste, however, because my "good fortune" had a habit of changing as fast as the flap of a bird's wing.

I peered around for something to send back through the waterfall—something that wouldn't visibly change the room. My eyes fixed on a swag of opulent teal blue curtains studded with silver rounds. I could pull fibers from their weft and—no, the stripes of missing threads would be a glaring indicator of tampering. The ties that held them open, though, they could—no. The rope lengths I'd have to destroy to make them long enough.

Crawling around a simple yet masterfully built desk, I peeked to the left and then right.

Children's toys lay scattered around an open chest, and it seemed that a little one had left behind a single knitted sock as well.

Something shiny caught my eye. On all fours, I inched forward until my mind put together what it was I saw. I brought the jewel-encrusted robe to my face and sniffed, my morbid curiosity getting the better of me. He'd worn this the day I encountered him in the brazier room.

I inhaled again.

The Primus-King smelled of fresh berries and liniment—the oil my gran used to rub into her joints.

"Why are you crying, Eira?" I hissed into the room. "Why sorrow instead of rage?"

I glanced down at the overgown. A trail of dried spit-up ran from collar to mid-chest, and a small, grubby pink handprint stood out against the smooth fabric.

He loved them. I'd seen it time and again.

He adored his family—and from the interactions and the stories I'd seen and heard, it was clear they loved him in return. Not only his family but his subjects as well. They trusted him. They were happy, healthy, and cared for.

I let the garment fall from my hands.

How could one character play two distinct roles in the same story? And how was it possible to shed tears over a life that I never lived? I loved my childhood, my father, the simplicity of our life back home, but how would things have been different with supportive siblings and a passel of nieces and nephews?

My long blonde strands fell into my eyes, and rather anticlimactically, it dawned on me how to retrieve the vial of poison. No one beats a Nortian at knotting and netting.

Plucking the strong fibers from my scalp, I gathered small bunches until there was a length long enough to drop two stories when tied together. Praise the Goddess, I didn't have to attempt it with the slick sticks that I naturally grew; they'd never hold a knot, even with my skills. As I looped the strands in square knots, I pondered an additional benefit. Who would bat an eye if globs of hair were found in the drain below or sticking to the side of the wall? Tub hair art was a favored pastime of many with lengthy manes.

I ducked back behind the desk as I continued to weave.

The rush of the waterfall soothed my nerves. The installation delighted each of my senses, from the smell of mist to the occasional refreshing droplet hitting my arms. The Primus-King was sure to cut a grand figure meeting with dignitaries and entertaining foreigners with this as his backdrop.

I laced the last of the fibers together.

Stepping over the slick rocks and potted plants that hid the floor grate, I fed the length through. The force of the falls took the handmade string so fast, I feared it might snap, but after less than a minute, I felt three distinct tugs through the line.

I reeled it in, and the vial appeared. I should have felt a rush of relief but instead was overwhelmed by feelings of trepidation.

Too fucking easy. I squeezed my eyes shut and waited for an explosion... for lightning to crash through the window... for wraiths to start chewing on my head...

I caught the vial, plucking it with two fingers and wiping it on my hair, lest it drip on the carpet. The Primus-King was sharp; no matter how insignificant, evidence of my trespass would alert him.

"Alright, let's off somebody's grandpaw."

Cato, I need your conscience... or should I say, lack of conscience? For a fleeting moment, I wished that our Bond allowed us to speak through a connection, but then quickly dismissed the thought. He'd order me around as often as he'd compliment me.

I scanned the room again, plotting my next move. I didn't want the poison falling into the wrong hands—a child's, or even Zephyr's. He didn't seem evil, but, did evil have a look?

As I padded closer to the desk, my eyes were drawn to a cracked wax seal. Its blood-red imprint, an oval surrounded by stars, brought anxiety and excitement—the seal of Verus Temple. I procured a discarded stylus, noting the angle at which it lay, and the location of its end and tip so that I might return it exactly. I lifted the missive's top half, careful not to disturb its placement.

"Majesty, We look forward to your visit and pray for a peaceful conclusion. The Baldorvan may not step foot into Verus's territory, nor may his soldiers accompany you. Though you have opened the doors of your kingdom, in the name of protection, one who condones the enslavement of humankind is not permitted on these grounds—now or in the future. Signed, Their High Holiness, the Goddess's Earthly Representative, They Who Are Exalted, Keeper of the Faith, Defender of Ærta, the Mantle."

My head bobbed saucily upon my neck as I read. *Good!*

Opening the vial as carefully as I could, I dipped his stylus into the blue liquid and skimmed the underside of a ledger and leather notebook. Carefully, I removed the folded linen that lay across a blown glass goblet and drizzled a few drops into the vessel. Like alcohol, it dried quickly and left no streaks. Unlike alcohol, I could only detect the faintest nutty odor.

A decanter of fermented tea sat next to his glass. I raised my arm and positioned the poison over its mouth.

Do it, Eira.

My hand quivered.

"Fucking do it," I whispered.

Eira of a year ago wouldn't have made it this far. She would have wrapped the confounding vial in layers of material, sealed it in a box, and buried it far from town... and then fretted over whether an animal might dig it up. Eira today knew the cost of peace.

"I could just turn myself over to him. Make a deal to let him bleed me once a week. Draw up an iron-clad contract." How had I never thought of this option? "He gets what he wants, and, and—"

My eyes caught on the words *offspring* and *recipient*.

I pushed off the chunk of malachite that held the notebook open. It was a chart. I traced my finger along its lines and columns. Dozens of names graced just this single page.

"Cindella and Marsh, Offspring Recipient: Guild leader Brooksdale. Zenith and Bryony, Offspring Recipient: Lord Hollowsford. Dæne and Wren, Offspring Recipient: Councilman Grinstead and Lifemate. Junnie and River, Offspring Recipient—"

Not Junnie and River, but Cato and River. It would be Cato's child if she conceives.

"Recipient: Lord of the Assembly, Julian Haycroft and Lifemate." The æther in my chest jolted to my arms. Electric snaps arched between the tips of my fingers. "The asshole who hit me?"

No. Absolutely not. Poison temporarily forgotten, I searched the drawers for a blade. Any Troth worth their status knew how to remove ink from parchment. I bent low and went to work, scraping the animal skin gently, lifting the fibers until the name was nothing but a memory. Next, I procured a smooth malachite stone and burnished the area, smoothing back the loosened material. I placed both items back in their spots, then took up the poison-rubbed stylus and dipped the tip into an inkwell.

"Magistrate Badyr and Lifemate Sparrow." I dotted the *i* and crossed the *t*, the final flourish mimicking the slash of pain that seared across my heart.

I scrubbed my hands in the waterfall, cleaned and secured everything I had touched, and before I could convince myself otherwise, dumped the poison into the decanter of tea—life was a game of chance.

Bitter, I let the æther flow and let the shade consume me until I stepped back into Cato's arms. Moonlight filtered through the diaphanous curtains that covered the chamber's large window.

"I am no longer the person I once thought I was," I whispered into the hood that obscured his face. I felt his nod. More than anyone, he would understand.

"Get some sleep. I will not leave you."

We parted, Cato taking up his post, while I slipped back under Yemailrys's arm. I closed my eyes but startled awake when gentle fingers caressed my cheek.

"Birdie, come back with me."

Hard fucking pass.

I smoothed my mouth over Arro's wrist, his pulse thumping steadily under my lips.

"My family would—no, I can't even consider it; my mother—"

"Think on it, and in the meantime..." He slipped the black opal ring from his finger and slid it over the knuckle of my thumb.

"Arro, I can't accept this. I'm not worthy to wear such a treasure." And I certainly didn't want to wear it with the ring that represented the love shared between my husbands and me.

"I have a dozen more back home."

My eyes widened.

"How haven't you been snatched up?" I joked.

He brushed my hair back over my shoulder, chuckling softly.

"Whenever the stolen daughter is found, I will set sail. There is time yet for you to change your mind. I cannot offer you a Hearthing, Birdie, as you are not Baldorvan, but I would see you in great comfort."

In chains, most like.

I sighed, letting go of a long-held breath.

"Arro, do you really believe that she exists? I think, perhaps, just as you are falling for this fantasy," I pointed to him and then myself, "her existence is but another romantic tale meant to evoke emotion and nationalistic fervor."

Arro shifted, scooting closer. He lifted my thigh and draped my leg over his lean hips. Yemailrys snuffled and rolled away, dragging the sheet with her.

"What a mind you have, my nearly illiterate farm girl. The warlord believes his betrothed is alive." I caught the faintest fracture of doubt in his voice, and though the design was to play the long game, I reckoned that such cracks might best be widened early on.

"And you?"

He shrugged an indifferent shoulder, but his mouth contradicted the nonchalance, tugging down almost sarcastically.

"It does not matter what I think. I receive an order. I follow that order."

I gasped and hugged my arms around his neck, pulling him close while I fought to bring tears to my eyes, hoping he'd see the glint of sadness in the low light.

"Birdie, what has caused you distress?" He tightened his embrace.

"I'm just—oh, Arro," I faked a piteous cry. "I hadn't realized you were his slave. I didn't know how your hierarchy worked until now."

The muscles in his stomach tensed.

"I am no man's property."

Thankful for the dark, I rolled my eyes to the sky. I sniffled and tucked my head into the crook of his neck.

"Truly?" I asked in a small voice. He nodded. "Thank the Goddess, I couldn't stand the thought of you bound in shackles."

I could stand the thought of you on the other side of the bed, though.

"Consider my offer, Birdie." He nudged my nose with the tip of his. "I am well aware that ours is a union of transaction and not emotion, but I am discovering that this liaison may be precisely what I seek."

"Like you seek the figment fantasy daughter?"

As he rolled on top of me, Arro laughed out loud. He spread my thighs with his knee and worked his erection into my body. I hooked my ankles around his back.

"No. A wife is *my* fantasy. A position you could readily fill without the emotional cost that comes from caring for a true Hearthmate."

Chapter Forty-Five

THE GODDESS'S WILL, MY FAT ASS.

Eira

"If I could make pillows as plush as your breasts, I would be the queen of the merchant class." I said, groggily opening my eyes to the satisfied smirk of Troth Yemailrys, who I could now say, with the full authority of my word as a professional liar, was a mistress of deception. She'd played her part impeccably. "If I can persuade the misters, would you be interested in the position of our fourth? I miss lady cuddles."

From the other side of the room, a throat cleared and another growled, in the mean way, not the sexy way.

"Right!" I hopped out of bed and headed toward the table, naked and uncaring.

Emberkin Arro had received a message from one of his captains and set out with the man, leaving his personal guards behind—because he didn't trust the whores but wished to allow them sleep. *What a kindness, slaver scum.* At least the interruption had kept me from having to endure a quiet breakfast and a stroll through the grounds with him. Poor man had fallen for the lure, and we reeled him in faster than a tuna in a chum cloud.

"Hmmm." I pondered a few implements scattered on the table's surface. "Butter knife, feather quill... what is this?" I held up the chunk in question so that both my Bonded creepers could see it.

"The antler of a buck. The slaver carves them while he thinks," Cato said from his post near the door.

I weighed the rock-like horn and tossed it back to the table. I picked up the quill and studied its sharp tip.

"This will work, I think."

Yemailrys yawned and fumbled into her cast-off garments. Her eyes tracked me as I walked to the door. "Will work for what?"

Cato moved closer, also curious.

"This." Æther arced from my fingertips in a violent burst. Septimus's hood lifted from his head, flying off and hitting the door behind him. "If you ever!"—I drove the metal-tipped feather into his shoulder—"Ever tamper with my conception control again... if you ever put your penis near my body again..."

Feminine shrieks pierced my ears. A nimbus of auburn curls streaked through my periphery. I jerked the quill back.

Oh, right.

"Holy fuck! Gods above!" Yemailrys screamed. "What's happening? Eira, what are you?"

Septimus's hand lashed out, speeding toward my neck. Cato intercepted and deflected it with a fast strike. Septimus pivoted, clawing for Cato's neck. The scuffle ended quickly, with the elder Monwyn pressed into the wall, Cato's blade to his throat.

"A conjurer, but not a mean one, despite what this looks like," I tossed over my shoulder.

"Holy fu—" She passed clear out.

"You made the offer, Enchantress," Septimus said with none of his usual malice. I looked into his sky-blue eyes, so coldly beautiful. My body reacted, the Bond drawing me to him.

"Do not touch her," Cato seethed. "Divine link or no, I could end you like any other man."

I gripped Cato's arm and pushed him back.

"Enchantress, I did the gods' will." Blood collected around the embedded shaft of the quill. "It was you, deceitful bitch, who called *me* to your whores' bed." Septimus pointed at Yemailrys. "What? Did you think I would have sullied myself in another's cunt?"

Cato's sharp inhale was a warning, the sudden coil of his muscles a signal of an impending onslaught.

Septimus knew he'd erred, and with a warrior's instinct, he twisted and ran, bolting for the far side of the room. Cato pursued.

"Rise, noble butter knife!" I raised my arm, quill clutched tightly.

The utensil hovered.

"Attack!" I shouted. It shot off, whistling as it cut through the air.

Septimus's eyes widened as he turned and saw the projectile hurtling toward him. I clenched my hand, a ripple of æther seeming to harden my fist. The knife warped and stretched, trapping his wrist as its point sank deep, embedding into the wall.

I rode the storm of my anger, berating him as I stalked forward.

"I made the choice not to bring children into this world, and you maliciously worked to thwart me. I don't care *whose* will you were doing. A single will matters when it comes to my body, and it is mine," I snarled.

Septimus jerked at the knife, entirely unmoved by words.

"His other arm, Cato, hold it."

"Do your worst, Enchantress. I regret nothing."

"Yes, yes," I said, rising on my toes to kiss Cato's cheek through his face covering. He leaned into me. "As long as it's the god's will, Septimus, you don't have to reflect upon your sins. Right?"

"I owe you nothing. You are nothing more than a bitch in heat—"

I slammed the quill back into his shoulder wound, working its tip in deep rounds, enjoying the give of his flesh. He gritted his teeth but made no sound, simply glared down his gorgeous nose.

"No, Uncle. My wife is a vision of beauty that blinds me anew each day," Cato murmured. He wrapped one arm around my waist while keeping Septimus pinned with the other.

"I am a thing of beauty only because you are a man who sees with his heart," I replied. The æther summersaulted and skipped, running along the side pressed against Cato's body.

Septimus spat in my face.

I went stock-still... and then a demented laugh escaped me.

Cato went in for the kill.

I flung my husband back and imprisoned him in a cage of black flame.

"Cato, my heart, though I understand your knee-jerk reaction to employ violence, that will never goad this tyrant. Humiliation on the other hand..." I snatched Septimus's handsome jaw with my left hand and with the right studied the bloodied nib of my quill. "Allow me to guide you in the true art of getting under his skin."

I dipped the quill into the bloody well of his wound and watched the dark ink travel up into its hollow. I squeezed his cheeks hard and forced his head back.

His proud forehead was a flawless parchment.

"M-i-s-o-g-y-n-i-s-t... hang on, I've run out." I stabbed the quill back into the wound, tunnelling deep. Across his cheeks and fine straight nose, I continued penning, "P-I-G."

"Eira, love, do not devalue the world's swine population."

Even through my flame and beneath his veil, I knew that Cato's lips twitched as he tried to suppress a smile.

"You've had your moment, willful cunt. Release me."

I tapped the feathered end of the pen against my chin.

"You're right, husband." I jabbed the quill back into the pool of clotting crimson; Septimus's arm spasmed like I'd hit a nerve. "Add a loop to the *P*, and a little line to the *I*... ha!"

I released the flames from my control, and they noiselessly dissipated.

Cato leaned in to inspect my handiwork.

"'Misogynist bag?'" He clutched his uncle's jaw and forced his head from side to side before shaking his own. "Is that supposed to be clever? I do not suppose I understand the joke."

"Well, it was that or pug, but I've seen a painting of one. Their little squished pupper faces are too darling to insult."

Cato barked a laugh and swallowed me in a hug of ochre fabric.

Yemailrys, unsteady on her feet, came up behind us, and, with no ceremony at all, shoved Septimus's hood back over his face. The covering fell into place, hiding the message and wound, just as I had intended.

Cato yanked the butter knife from the wall and stuffed it into a pocket beneath his gown. He took Yemailrys by the elbow as she swayed.

"Eira," she pointed at Septimus. "Next time I want that one, dick and all." Her eyes sharpened as she licked her lips. "He seems my type."

I gaped at my Troth sister, my jaw slack with shock.

"Warped by trauma and mentally ill?"

She nodded while rubbing her palms together.

"He's all yours, friend."

As her eyes seemed to disengage from reality, I took her other elbow.

"Eira, you have freaked me the fuck out. I need a meal and some wine, but then I'll get my hands on that betrothal contract." She combed her fingers through her tangled mass of hair. "It's going to take a pound of sugar or a pound of flesh..."

I nodded, loathing the need for more violence.

"Let me know what you require."

"A stealthy man with a strong blade," she stated, looking at Septimus with a hungry expression.

"He's indisposed," Cato growled.

"He looks fine to—"

"Back away, nephew, before—oof!"

Septimus collapsed, hands cradling his crotch.

Cato, like the most dutiful of men, offered an elbow to Yemailrys and escorted her to the door.

Our Mother Who Art In Cradle, Pillow Talk Be My Game.

Eira

I settled into the bath while my two Bonded creepers read each and every correspondence scattered about the table and floor. They worked as an efficient unit, almost as if *they* shared a mind Bond. Without asking, Cato retrieved the items Septimus looked for and vice versa, and when replacing the parchments, they measured out the precise distances using their fingertips and knuckles as guides. As I washed, I wondered, not for the first time, how Cato would have turned out if Septimus had *raised* him instead of *trained* him. How far would a hug have gone?

I let my legs float and in my solitude, become enamored with a school of red and blue fish swimming around under the glass floor. I had sown doubt about Emryss's existence into the mind of the Baldorvan, and I would continue to bury tiny seeds of misinformation, starting with the odds of her survival in the recent battles in Solnna. Then, in a few days' time, I would have Arro take me to the library—playing the farm girl wanting to be told stories—and pick out a tome about the Kingdom of Taleer. If Emryss had escaped Solnna on foot, her only option would have been to travel through the former kingdom's desert to seek asylum. A man as discerning as Arro should conclude on his own that a girl born to palatial comfort would lack the skills and fortitude to endure the rough terrain and live.

A crash sounded, shattering my musings.

An uproarious bellow came from the atrium. In unison, Cato and Septimus opened the chamber doors, admitting a furious Ambrose and seething Emberkin.

"Absolutely not! She is a prostitute, a strumpet—"

"Sex worker is the term I prefer," I said, loud enough that the two men disengaged momentarily and glanced my way before sizing each other up again. "If either of you were of the mind to ask, you would have known."

I paddled to the bath's edge and lay my chin on crossed forearms.

"Birdie, out." Arro snapped, a gesture I was coming to loathe. "Cover yourself at once."

I'm going to break his fingers, one by one.

Eira, out of the bath! I need your assistance in bringing him to heel.

I floated my way to the steps.

I will also be snapping off your digits, husband.

Emberkin Arro stormed to the table and began stacking his parchments, loudly thumping them on the table to bring them into order.

Ambrose pursued.

"I will speak slowly so you can get it through your head, Father Regulus. I do not dance. I do not make merry. What I do is get bored." Arro flung his chair back and dropped into the seat. "It is when I get bored that my true nature is revealed."

Ambrose scoffed and tossed back the lightweight silk veil that concealed his face. The soft gold enhanced the moss green of his eyes as it fell in loose frills around his neck.

"Baldorva sent their best general, I am told. Where is he?" Ambrose swung his head around, his palm over his eyes as if he were shielding them from the sun. "Surely, they sent a man who understands the necessity of basic self-control?"

Ambrose! Pull back. He's going to boil over, and he's armed.

Ambrose smacked his lips while studying his nails.

"Emberkin, what I think is that you are a man used to getting what he wants and acts like a bratty child when he's told no."

Towel-dried and wrapped in a robe of combed wool, I quickly padded over to Emberkin Arro and wrapped my arms around his neck from behind, pressing a kiss to his temple.

"How can you be bored after a three-hour threesome? And what is it the two of you are debating?"

Arro caught my arm and pressed a kiss to my wrist.

"The Naming ceremony. Father Regulus forbids your attendance on account of your employment."

"Then you must heed his counsel. He knows the laws and the customs of the land better than any." My long hair swept over my shoulder as I brought my lips to his ear. "I'd hate to be discovered and kicked out of the palace. I've grown fond of our nocturnal entertainments."

"No. I am not beholden to the laws of this continent, and your fucking Primus-King is well aware of it. I can and *will* muster my units and take them back to Baldorva. Where will the idiot be then? The warlord will rain fire upon him for wasting his time and resources."

"If you leave, then we never see each other ag..." I let my words dwindle away.

Arro wrapped my hair around his fist and drew my face to his. Our lips met.

Eira, you have my permission to go all puff demon and evaporate his pretty painted face. You could also, I don't know, cease your lip-lock before your husband takes leave of his sanity.

"Emberkin Arro, I must insist that Birdie stays confined to my apartments when not on an assignment."

"An assignment? Am I not the only man with whom she plies her trade?" Arro's hand inched toward his side. Though Ambrose could not see it behind the shield of my tresses, the glint of Baldorvan steel caught my eye.

"Arro." I touched his cheek, encouraging him to look into my eyes. "In these parts, Father Regulus is my owner, not you."

The slaver sat motionless, outwardly calm, yet a tempest churned behind his storm cloud-colored eyes.

Too much, wiflet. You've struck a nerve.

The air around Arro seemed to thrum, and when, finally, he broke his silence, his expression was bitter and measured.

"In this room, it is I you will call master." Striking fast as a falcon snatching its prey, he clutched a fistful of my hair and jerked me to the floor. The force of my fall sent pain through my knees, a sharp jolt of agony radiating up into my hips.

"Gods!" I cried, clutching my scalp. "Arro, please, you're hurting me."

Eira, debrief. Ambrose delivered the concern-tinged demand as sharply as Cato would have.

Stand down, my solace. The faux fibers make it bearable.

Behind me, I heard the subtle creak of Ambrose's chair as he sat back down.

"Obedience," Arro gritted out, "is the only assurance you have against punishment."

My contempt swelled, the foreigner's words feeding my indignation instead of cowing me as was his aim.

Eira, use caution. I will not maintain neutrality much longer.

The æther bubbled within my chest, eager to spill forth, though fully under my command. The realization that as fast as he could snap his disgusting fingers, I could rend shrieks of agony from his lungs tempered my burgeoning ire.

"Do you think you frighten me?" The words slid past my lips like a blade drawn from its sheath—quiet, deliberate, meant to pierce. Arro tightened his hold of my hair, but I held his gaze, unflinching. "You may command a person's body, may call them yours on account of writing their names upon your register—but their minds will always remain beyond your reach. You don't control those you think to possess, not a single one of them, and most certainly not your Ærtan whore."

Arro tensed; the tendons in his neck stood out, quivering beneath his ink.

"You know nothing of the power I wield," he seethed.

Eira, stop. Show contrition.

From the floor, I secured a parchment, crumpling it in my hand.

"Do you see this, Arro, how easy it is to control something with no mind? It doesn't respond when crushed."

He cocked an unamused brow, fingers still clenching in the tangled mass of my hair.

"What I see is a woman who needs—"

Crack!

I struck the slaver's cheek. The sharp sound resonated as his head whipped to the side. I ignored the sting of my palm and countered his stunned expression with one of submission. I lowered my gaze.

Tread carefully, Eira. Cato is near breaking. Septimus has a noticeable hard-on.

"Do you see what happens when you finally force the hand of someone who lives—who thinks and feels? They fight back, Arro, because they have nothing to lose." His fingers dug into my biceps; bruises would soon bloom. He shot to his feet and slammed my lower back against the table's edge. "I won't go to Baldorva in shackles."

"Who are you to—" he paused. "You've decided then? You will come with me?"

Not on your sick slaver life, motherfucker.

I reached up and straightened the collar of his gray undershirt, letting my fingers stray to the exposed skin of his neck.

"Arro, if I am going to travel to your lands, you must prove to me that I'll not be treated like an object. If you want *real*, if you want *soft*, then—"

His mouth sealed against mine in a bruising act of possession.

My fingers brushed the edge of his jaw, deliberately lingering as if I were savoring him. His breath came fast against my lips, and I urged him to take more. Every stroke of my tongue, every deliberate scrape of my teeth, was a calculated move disguised as my surrender. I kissed him as though he were the only man in existence, knowing lust would aid in obscuring my motives. His grip tightened on my hips, pulling me flush against the proof of his unraveling. I whined softly as if begging and pressed closer, letting the curve of my body meld into his.

Ambrose drummed his fingers on his armrest.

Well, I am just about done with this voyeurism business. It is cute with Cato, but I find my taste has soured on this one.

Arro pulled back.

"Birdie will not attend the state dinner, Father Regulus, but she will join me at the Naming ceremony. I have no place of honor there, so she will not be recognized for what she is, but I require her company."

I walked my fingers up his chest.

"So that you will have a dance partner?"

"I do not dance."

A man who does not dance? Eira, he is as uncouth as an ill-tempered bovine! I want you nowhere near such a—

"Then why do you so adamantly seek my company, Arro? Do you plan to flaunt my beauty?"

The Baldorvan brushed his thumb across my clavicle.

"I like talking to you."

The fuck did he say, wife? Talk to you? He takes pleasure in intimate conversation with my harpy? Wishes to speak of the mundane with my woman? Fucking you is one thing, Eira, but he will rue the day he moves in on my pillow talk, rue it, I say!

Arro and I shared a look in Ambrose's direction, and the slaver's oddly gentle laughter enveloped us.

Ambrose, calm down. Release your hold on the table and quit grinding your teeth. I can hear their scraping from where I stand.

Arro palmed my ass and ground his hips against mine.

"Leave, priest, so I can discover what delights my deviant little farm girl has planned for me this night."

I caught Arro's bottom lip between my teeth and tugged. He growled as he thrust his erection into my lower stomach.

"You wanna fuck a man of the cloth?" I let my eyes drift to my husband.

Chapter Forty-Seven

TRUTHS ARE SHARPER THAN LIES

Eira

"The slaver will never penetrate me, nor will I perform the dance of love upon his filth. It goes against all that I am. How you even suggested such a dubious act, I can't begin to comprehend." I stretched my legs out, kicking off the cover Ambrose insisted on pulling up to my chin.

I tipped back a glass of water and watched him rub lotion into the soles of his feet—not pointing out the hypocrisy of his argument. I was too shattered to argue with him. He still didn't have his full range of motion back, and I noticed that if he bent over too far, stress lines bracketed his lips. *Goddess, give me his pain.*

"Here, let me." Setting my glass aside, I took the jar of jasmine-and-chamomile-scented cream and sat cross-legged on the bed. "I'm tired of spending time with the Baldorvan. I miss my men."

As if conjured, the door opened, and Cato, in the guise of a palace servant, entered the chamber. His curls were parted at the center of his forehead, and each side lay smashed to his head, the consequence of the creeper's hood.

"Evandr is veiled and in my place. Before the ceremony, Septimus and I will resolve the issue of a certain Gaean with Yemailrys. In return, the original betrothal contract and the copy stored in the temple will pass into our hands. From digging around, it seems a pocket of despondent nobles feels the Primus-King owes them a hefty sum. Tonight, they send a message."

"That you and Septimus will deliver?" Ambrose said as flippantly as if it were a bit of low-stakes court gossip.

Cato kept quiet as he shed his pants and shirt, folded them into perfect rectangles, and then placed the stack on a chair. He kneeled next to me, yawned, and then attacked, wrestling me to the mattress.

"Cato!" I screeched. The lotion tumbled from my hands and splattered across the fine sheets. My mate, paying no mind to my laments or the mess, crawled across the bed, dragging me with him. He launched a full-scale cuddle assault, all hugs and love and tickling fingers.

"This"—*kiss*—"is where"—*kiss*—"I belong." He lay alongside me, molding his chest to mine. "I love you. Have I told you enough, Eira?" I fluffed his curls back to life, and while I scratched his scalp, he shook his foot like some silly pup with an itch.

"No. Not nearly." I said in the most sober voice I could muster. I blinked my innocent eyes and stuck out my bottom lip.

"No?" He blanched, hand to his heart, and mouth agape. "Were the fifteen declarations in the wee hours not enough?"

I shook my head, for in truth, I needed to hear it now more than ever.

"I shall directly make amends, greedy beast of a wife."

"Black Bear? You too?" I reached out and made grabby hands at Ambrose, who lay facing away, tucked in on himself. "Hugs, please?"

Ambrose glanced over his shoulder and, without saying a word, scooted behind me and took up his place at my back. He slipped an arm around my middle, and I couldn't help but notice that he avoided Cato entirely. Normally, he'd squish his fingers between me and Cato or allow his forearm to rest against Cato's elbow.

We had once been like a sheet of ice—strong, clear, shining, the way the lakes back home froze in winter. Now, though, cracks webbed through us like veins beneath the surface, thin at first but deepening.

"My heart, my soul." I simultaneously stroked Ambrose's knuckles and Cato's stubbly cheek. "Emotions are tense between us, yes?"

Gods, how stubborn my men could be. Behind me, I felt the shrug of Ambrose's shoulders, and Cato regarded Ambrose like he might a passing cloud—there, then gone, and not worth remembering. I felt like shouting, but knew it would accomplish nothing more than ratcheting up the tension. This was a delicate situation.

I cleared my throat.

"Cato, how are you feeling about us? All of us?" I asked, doing my best not to sound like a healer during an exam—he'd endured too many invasive procedures as of late.

His jaw tightened, but the thoughtful glint in his dark eyes told me he was weighing his words. I prayed their tone would heal instead of hurt.

He opened his mouth, closed it, and then tried again.

"I am cautious, but I am open."

Over my head, Cato rested his palm on Ambrose's shoulder.

I could have cried, could have broken down and sobbed.

"Ambrose, it is true that I entered this union with dubious intent. I used you as a means to claim what I sought." Cato paused to collect his thoughts again. I kissed his chest, right on his stupid harpy tattoo's face.

"Some truths are sharper, cut more deeply, than even the most expertly wielded lie," I said, curling my arm around Ambrose's forearm and weaving our fingers together.

I let my lips linger on Ambrose's knuckles, and he squeezed my hand.

"Ambrose? Where are you right now?"

My big, sensitive, and profoundly wounded husband swept his head back and forth, drawing lines on my shoulder with his nose. A cold tear dropped onto my shoulder and snaked a cool path to the mattress.

"I am... I am skeptical." His loud exhale ruffled my hair. He twisted away, and I rolled over, tucking myself into his side. Cato scootched forward, chasing the lost heat of my body. His hips cupped mine. "Though optimistically so."

My contract husband tucked his chin into the space between my neck and shoulder, and my divine one's heartbeat aligned with mine, as steady as our vows spoken before the stars. This was how we were meant to exist—three souls braided into a single Bond.

Cato, ever so gently, guided our palms to rest in the middle of Ambrose's chest.

We lay this way, not a one of us willing to break the spell until Ambrose found his voice.

"Catommandus. To grow this family, we cannot repeat the sins of our parents. There must be no secrets between the three of us."

Cato sat up, his frustration evident.

"Ambrose, I have informed you of my actions. Yes, this began as a farce, but I am willing to—"

"You misunderstand, Cat." Ambrose forced himself upright, every movement strained, as though the truth dragged him down. He gripped my arm and pulled me with him, his eyes never leaving Cato's. "It is my sin that must be atoned." His voice faltered. "There was an incident at the Cult."

I saw the explosion in my mind's eye... felt the shift in the atmosphere... wondered if I could contain the brothers to this room when all nether broke loose.

"I did everything in my power to stop your semen from being delivered into the womb of—"

Cato jolted off the bed and fell to his knees. He doubled over, clutching his head in his hands.

"Please, gods, please. Please, gods, don't tell me." He lashed out and sent the bedside table toppling. A stack of books thudded to the floor as he held his stomach with both arms. "Please do not. No. Gods."

I ran, emptied a bowl of fruit, and then placed the vessel at Cato's knees.

"Cato, it wasn't Wren. It was given to River. And, according to the healer, she was not in her fertile phase, and she's not conceived Junnie's child in two months of the experiment," I explained. "Ambrose tried. He did, my love."

Ambrose sat on the edge of the bed, head hung. He reached for Cato but hesitated.

"That is… is supposed to make this better…" Cato said as beads of sweat poured down his temples. "Eira, *we* decided no children. I do not want a child of mine walking this earth if they are not half of you."

Cato flung the bowl, and the vessel exploded against the wall in a spray of splinters. Heat radiated from his skin as he gulped the air. Ambrose lowered himself to the floor and placed his cool palm to Cato's nape, his touch gentle yet deliberate—support when the ground threatened to give way.

"Cat, we will steal the child away. Or, or send River to Monwyn. The baby is—"

"A violation," Cato breathed.

A choked sob tore from Ambrose's throat. No doubt Cato's words had reopened the old wounds of abandonment. He dashed the wetness from his cheeks and in the next beat of my heart, had Cato drawn into his embrace.

Cato reached for me. I fell into him and enfolded them both.

This was my world. No weight was too heavy, no path too treacherous, if it meant they were mine.

"We will bear the burden together," Ambrose whispered. "I love you."

Chapter Forty-Eight

BLIND DEVOTION IS THE TRUE CAUSE OF EARLY ONSET HAIR LOSS

Ambrose

G uilt is an emotion meant to dampen the spirit.

With renewed focus and my conscience clear, I threw myself into the task at hand… by sitting and thinking.

Cato, like the man he was created to be, set aside his emotions, and left with our uncle to carry out the slayings of five Gaean elites who had sided with the Primus-King in accepting not only the Baldorvans' presence in their kingdom, but also in demanding extra taxes that would be sent directly to the country and used to support their inhumane practices.

Septimus had been gleeful, claiming the targets were men "worthy of an unhurried and thoughtful death" while Eira had dressed a wound—an unfortunate incident with a quill, of all things—and fed him a drop of her blood. I plotted *his* unhurried demise as I watched the man's body writhe beneath her healing touch and, what was worse, hear her breathing turn heavy as she rubbed her thighs together.

I huffed, and the silk covering my face shuddered, drawing the attention of the priest at my side.

"Look away, Father Shawnai, I commune with She Who Judges You in my own way."

Though I couldn't make out his expression under his fluttering veil, I knew it was one of repentance. The cretin lowered his head.

If given the choice, I'd rather playact the guard. I was built for the role of grizzled warrior, handsome but hardened hero from the tough side of the river, not the constant aggravations of priestly life. All manner of people asked for intercessions as they hacked and coughed on my garments. And the kneeling, for the gods' sake, these religious types knelt for hours on end with nary a tasty puss or cock to keep them occupied. And the supposed charity foisted upon me by the nobles: "Here, Father, it's for the starving, distribute it as you see fit." Ugh! Nobody wants your day-old beans, Lucinda.

Across the hall, Eira entered the room, a vision of feminine beauty. I contemplated my wife through the delicate latticework embroidery of my semi-sheer, pearl-dotted veil. She was the image of perfection, which I'd ensured myself, despite the shouting match that ensued when she demanded to wear a gown of hideous green.

With her in her blonde era, I'd created a palette of pale gold and brown for her eyes and swathed her flawless lips with a mauve pigment mixed into oil. She'd not be mistaken for a servant with her multi-tonal braids woven around the top of her crown, their tails curled into fat ringlets that cascaded to her waist, nor would she risk recognition. I daresay her own Momma would have trouble identifying her in a crowd.

The Baldorvan stepped forward to meet her, looking for all the world like the cruel but undeniably sexy evil prince from a bard's tale. She lifted her chin and met his gaze, and my heart palpitated at the raw emotion I saw pass between them. *Eww.* She outlined the beasty inked on his forearm, and though the veil hampered my vision, I knew her pink peaks went to points. *Hmmm.* Perhaps I would reconsider my aversion to bodily modification and join Catommandus in an adornment after all—a petite violet satyress inked upon my bicep, a mountainscape in the distance, a rainbow arcing through the sky.

"Fucking filth," I muttered under my breath.

"What was that, Father Regulus?"

I whipped my head to the side and caught the priest tracking my wife as she moved through the crowd. He coveted her. There was no doubt in my mind that he was a lecherous ne'er-do-well, despite his years of humanitarian effort, and his dedication to the poor, and that time he threw himself into the path of a charging cow to save some blind child from a near-death trampling.

"Pluck the disgusting bouquet of hairs sprouting from your ear hole, you deaf bat. Meddling ninny."

The priest bristled. No, that was his cover. He shivered in delight, ogling Eira's curvaceous form. *Pervert.* If he wanted a set of succulent thighs, he should cease all the fasting and focus on a tried-and-true regimen. I knee-walked and sat my bulk in front of him. Gawk at my wife? I think not!

"Praise Her!" I bless-bopped the forehead of some odious Gaean toddler in desperate need of a nappy change. It laughed, smiling up at me with milk-crusted lips.

"May the Goddess shine Her light upon you, Father." The urchin's mother bowed.

"Sure, sure, thank you, move now, you block my divine line of sight."

The mother took her child's sticky hand and moved on.

There they were. *Oooo, but I hate him.* My vision sharpened on the spot where Eira clutched the foreigner's elbow.

On any other occasion, seeing Eira on the arm of another instilled within me an intense sense of pride, or at least got my dick hard from imagining potential couplings. The Baldorvan beast made my chilly blood boil. Why, currently, he blocked her from the assembly, purposefully shifting that exceptional ass with the intent of isolation. Cato had a habit of doing the same, but at least *he* was driven by some suntastic goddess's essence. The Baldorvan had no excuse other than weak mental fortitude.

Beauty was meant to be shared, not hidden. For instance, were I built like the slender, taut-muscled canvas that Arro was, a scenario would not exist where I would clothe myself in bagging layers of puff—I'd not clothe myself at all. His voluminous pants were a crime to seamstresses everywhere and no doubt broke the backs of many a weaver.

I'd not accomplish a single task if you walked the palace halls in the nude, Black Bear. Nor would any maid, guard, or noble.

I couldn't hide my wiggle of delight and basked in her praise like a cat in a sunbeam. I sent a quick prayer to the Nether Lord, acknowledging him for the blessing of our connection, and for the fact that not once had Eira mentioned my scars, not once had her gaze wavered to my disfigurement when we spoke.

That's because your ass is all I can think about.

"Care to share in the source of your chuckle?" A voice asked from behind. "What has you amused, Father?"

"Certainly not you, Shawnai, you prayer-interrupting piglet."

I bent and tapped my forehead to the floor, the knowledge that my wife still found me attractive close to my heart. My side ached from the motion, but keeping up appearances meant falling in line with the four other priests, three priestesses, and nine acolytes that shared the prayer carpet with me.

Wifey, do you think blind devotion is the true cause of early-onset hair loss, or do you think my sibling was trying to tell me something by sending me with this group of elders?

Eira smiled shyly at the Baldorvan and tucked herself further behind him, like he alone shielded her from the atrocities of the world. I grit my teeth. That was Cato's job.

Arms crossed and stiff-spined, Emberkin Arro smiled back at her false demureness.

No, I don't, my sexy Scion, but the Lead Healer sits four feet to your left. Share your hypothesis with him and see what research has been done on the subject. Maybe you could head a new branch of medicine.

Oh, hush, I can hear your sarcasm through the—

The bright glow cast by the bronze lanterns faded away, leaving only the hall's massive dais illuminated.

"It begins! Shawnai, breathe less loudly." I clapped, gleeful for the pomp to come. I relished a grand ceremony. "A deviated septum, from taking a falling beam to the face while rescuing geese from a barn fire is no excuse for nose gargles of that magnitude."

I turned my attention back to the reason for the occasion. The nobles took to their seats, and the lesser ones stood at their backs.

The throne room of Mynder Palace was *okay* in its grandeur, but honestly, I preferred the stone walls and marble columns of Cordillaria. I mean, yes, the carved wooden portrayal of the Ærtan pantheon was fine, and the twinkling of thousands of hand-hammered copper stars hanging from the ceiling created a charming visual effect. And I suppose the floor-to-ceiling oil paintings depicting Ærta's history should be noted as a fine addition but I simply could not ignore the overabundance of green—it just screamed commoner's hovel.

I disagree, Ambrose. The room reminds me of you and Cato. The mahogany dais is the same hue as his irises, and the heavy drapes surrounding the throne are the exact shade of yours. I would paint our chambers the same color and cherish it for all eternity.

"Phhftb." The derisive sound tooted from my lips. *You've no eye for fashion. The dress you chose hammers my point home.*

The heads of the surrounding priests swiveled in my direction.

"Pardon, it's the excess of curd they serve here."

A chorus began to sing from the loft above, the deep basses and baritones mingling with the highest sopranos in a soft but cheerful tune.

"The Royal Family comes!" A herald bellowed. Trumpets blared from the four corners of the room.

The sound of laughter greeted my ears as children of all ages walked or toddled into the hall. All dressed in the same uniform of—who would have guessed it—shades of leaf. They giggled and waved, happily calling greetings to their friends as they processed down the middle aisle.

Ambrose, you do realize that everything you wear in Monwyn is blue?

Begging your pardon, I own a wide-ranging selection of lightest sea spray to cobalt.

Pimply-faced youths arrived and—*Eira, look how many share in your eye color. Not all of them, but a vast majority.*

Mmhmm, I've noticed. Which is why I'm keeping my head down.

Good girl.

Next came a slew of adults and then a line of grinning wives, dressed in the height of fashion and all bearing thin gold circlets upon their brows.

Goodness, he does keep a menagerie of beauties...

Eira cleared her throat through the connection. My jealous little woman—I fucking loved it. My other partners had never given a damn about my comings and goings. My wife's envy was obsidian—sharp and born of heat.

They are pretty enough, but I bet none of them have fairy cunts. I know you're ogling the tall one's ass, Ambrose. Cut it out, do you hear me?

I cannot hear you over the snarling from your side of the room, my sweet bun-bun. Do you hear snarling where you are?

The chorus sang out, their voices brimming with an effervescent energy.

The Primus-King appeared in the doorway, a little girl in his arms. Beaded bracelets decorated her wrists and ankles, and the tubby folds of her belly protruded over her skirt of sunflower yellow. Chestnut hair stood straight from her head, and bright teal eyes cried fat tears. Her father consoled her, kissing her brown cheeks and whispering into her ear. She turned her small face into his chest, and he patted her bitty bum as he continued down the aisle.

The chorus quieted, and the Primus-King ascended the short flight of stairs to his throne. His wives' thrones flanked the Gaean high seat, and his children took their places standing behind their mothers.

He sat.

"She's a little shy," he said, scrunching his nose at his daughter. A ripple of hushed laughter rolled through the audience at his gently delivered proclamation.

"Do you want to tell them your new name or should Dada?" he asked his daughter.

"Dada," said the tiny voice.

The Primus-King kissed her plump cheek and settled the child on his lap. She immediately turned back into his robe, hiding her face in her dumpling-shaped hands.

"Most beloved citizens of Gaea, I would formally introduce you to my littlest lady, the newest princess of our realm, delivered by her mother Giavann a year ago today. We bestow upon her the name Aviana Blossom."

The crowd erupted into a thunderous applause but quickly quieted as the Primus-King held a finger to his lips.

After a few speeches and other such political nonsense, the girl came out of hiding and grabbed the stunning malachite medallion that hung from a thick golden chain around her father's neck. She gnawed on the centermost stone as the Primus-King bounced her on his knee.

Finally, the speeches ended with the child being promised to a Nortian lord, taking with her a herd of reindeer, three hundred fur pelts, and a sizable sum of gold.

The Primus-King stood.

"As per tradition, Aviana's mother should have the first dance with our daughter, but my gentle wife and Aviana's sister came down with an illness shortly after breaking our fast. I will rejoin them where they convalesce as soon as the prayers have been said in Aviana's honor."

"Clear the floor!" the herald boomed.

Oh, gods. Ambrose, the poison.

I felt her panic through the connection.

Eira, I know what you are thinking, but what are the odds they broke their fast in the man's study? Had they ingested the poison, it would follow that the Primus would have taken ill as well. He looks as fit as they come. I'm sure of it. Now, quit biting your lip and—ugh, I do not like him holding your hand.

Luckily, Emberkin fucking Arro would not see the grimace beneath my veil.

Neither do I. His palms sweat.

The Baldorvan ran his thumb along the edge of her jaw. He'd sensed her concern, and frankly, it made me murderous. Fuck her? Fine. Anyone with a functional ass could thrust a hip. Shower her with gifts? Yes, I'd seen the stunning ring she tried to hide from my gaze, but who cared? I could give her many. But attempting to become her emotional anchor without understanding the specific nuances of her needs? He had stepped much too far into *my* territory.

Ambrose, love. The room is cooling a little too quickly. Is that you?

Yes!

Slow your breathing. Think peaceful thoughts.

Peaceful? Peaceful is the opposite of what would calm me at this juncture. Pounding his chin onto a wedge and watching his head bisect like a glittering red geode would bring me utter relief, though.

The Primus-King took to the middle of the floor with his precious bundle.

A song played. Strings, flutes, and drums combined into a jaunty beat. The babe clapped her chubby hands, much to the delight of the assembled crowd, as her father moved in the steps of some bizarre dance ritual. How strange, the customs of these tree people.

Ambrose?

What?

I distinctly remember a scantily clad Minotaur slinking in my direction the night of our Joining. Was that not such a ritual?

Mouth closed, madam; I must concentrate on my piety.

Gaeans of all ages joined in the spinning and twirling, hopping to the left and bowing to the person at their right. On gold trays, servants passed around liquid libations and a honey-sweetened cookie—a special sugary treat for the extra-special day.

As the revelers continued their sweeping movements, the Primus-King meandered through the throng and came to kneel on the thick carpets lying before the assembled Verus escort.

I kept perfectly calm, focused on controlling the speed of my heart. He was sitting close enough that I could smell the scent of his freshly laundered tunic and see the single missing pearl in the exquisite embroidery of his fur-lined half-cloak.

"Esteemed guests from Verus Temple, Aviana Blossom and I are honored to receive your blessings. By the smell of her britches, you may wish to bestow them quickly, though."

I laughed with my counterparts and watched as the child moved from one set of hands to another. She was sort of cute. Not baby satyress cute, but I'd nibble those chunky knuckles.

"Aviana, may the Goddess bless you and keep you. Grow into a person of extraordinary talent," Father Shawnai said. "Little sign of love, bring peace to your family and grow wealthy in your spirit."

Across the way, between the arched arms of the dancers, I saw not one but two noblemen bow, asking for Eira's hand.

Emberkin Arro leered at each in turn, too uncouth to deflect them with polite rejection.

He'll not allow me to dance, and this song is one of my favorites.

How boorish. Only feeble men set such parameters. And perhaps Cato.

The tot passed into my arms—gods above. Was it possible to fall in love with a human you didn't know? My stomach bloomed with butterflies. Were Eira warmer of skin tone and wider of lip, she and Aviana could pass for—oh well, of course—sisters.

Altering my voice, pitching it a little higher than normal, I blessed the child who would soon find herself without a father. Her path would be a little less bright.

"Goddess of light and love, we pray that Aviana Blossom be a beacon of joy to her family, a verdant branch bearing fruit for all who know her, and a devoted servant tending to the garden of the Goddess's kingdom." The Primus-King looked upon his child with benevolence. You could see the pride in his azure eyes. "May she find a love for trees and a multitude of greens: celery, lime, and their more complex but superior cousin, mint." The acolytes and priests nodded at the solemnity of my words. I kissed the child's fat cheek through my veil, the warmth of her skin reminding me of my bitty satyress back home. Surely Cinden was seeing to little Verra's needs. I hugged Aviana close, inhaling her baby smell and rocking her in my arms. The Primus-King cleared his throat. "In the Goddess's name. Praise Her!"

A bobbing set of shoulder-length curls caught my attention, and I chucked the baby into the arms of the priestess next to me. Merritt, the fourth son of the Primus-King, spun Eira onto the floor, her smile as wide as it was beauteous.

I chuckled maniacally through the connection.

The Baldorvan couldn't deny a crown prince?

No, indeed!

Tension coiled in my stomach as Eira passed within feet of the Primus-King, who'd just accepted his daughter back into his arms.

I held my breath.

Thank the Cradle, her booger-green dress was so uninspired that it blended in with the surroundings, and he moved right on. No godly connection sparked between them; no fatherly recognition lit his face.

Godsdamn, husband, shut off the connection if you plan to disparage my gown.

Sugar buns, you are still the loveliest thing on the floor, with the exception of perhaps—

Don't. Finish. That. Sentence.

A throng of nobles pressed against the doors leading back into the palace proper, their polished boots scraping the floor as they jostled and spoke over one another, each vying for their place in the receiving line. The

Primus-King, ever patient, stepped forward, holding the child aloft. He presented her first to the highest-ranking lords, then moved carefully down the chain to the lesser nobles. One by one, they offered gifts—gleaming gold, glittering gems, bolts of rich fabric—each hoping to curry his favor. Servants darted forward to gather the offerings.

Amid the splendor, the little girl was utterly indifferent as she gnawed contentedly on her father's heavy medallion.

I rose, stretching my weaker side while scanning the crowd for the Baldorvan. Even then, my eyes flicked between the Primus-King and my wife as she twirled around the floor with an effortless grace.

Flanked by his twin guards, Arro cut an imposing figure. An abundance of metal jutted from his face, glinting in the lamplight like tiny, malevolent suns. I hated to admit it, the ink upon his skin—evidence of his ability to walk through the flames—gave him undeniable gravitas. Only those who wielded true power would attempt to cross his path.

I nodded a greeting to Cato, concealed under his ochre robe, and ignored his matching counterpart, opting instead to pray for my uncle's untimely death. The dual guards stepped back as I planted myself next to the Emberkin.

His gaze was unblinking as he followed Eira's every step.

"Territorial after only a matter of days, Arro? There was a reason Birdie was my first choice."

The Baldorvan leaned against a pillar whose complicated, woven knots looked to be carved into the entire trunk of a tree. I assessed his formal wear and experienced a brief stab of self-consciousness, daunted by his elegant upper half. The corseted back of his vest enhanced the taper of his torso, adding even more definition to the natural *V* shape. The darkest-gray brocade created a mesmerizing contrast with the goldenrod silk shirt he wore beneath. Swaths of black diamond and opal graced his neck, and a scarlet cloth belt, woven with fibers of gold and silver, tied about his hips and draped to his knees.

"In Baldorva, a woman chooses a man after a contract negotiation. Here, the father makes the choice for the woman, yes?" Arro asked. "As the Primus-King did for his daughter?"

"If you are referring to Birdie, no." I inched closer to him, my hands clasped behind my back. "She is in *my* service, contractually obliged for a year. I stand in her 'pa's' absence." Emberkin Arro crossed his arms. "If you are making inquiries, I will tell you upfront that I am loath to let her go. The last time we dallied, she choked me so hard I nearly called *her* father."

Was it possible to feel a man's eyes roll? Because from his position behind me, I felt Cato's do somersaults.

"Your *dalliance* has ended, Father. My men will move her belongings into my rooms this evening." Emberkin Arro waved a dismissive hand in my direction. "The Primus-King fears me like a child does a lion. He will transfer her contract to me."

Ambrose! My half-brother is delightful.

Eira twirled past us. Hair in disarray, cheeks bright.

He keeps falcons, Black Bear, and has a wife named Starling—bird name—and she lived in Nortia, right over the border! They met when he went on a trading mission, and he said it was love at first bite... because she was fishing! Is that not the cutest?

Eira danced out of earshot.

"Emberkin, if I may. Do not set your sights on the first woman to enthusiastically butter your cob. It would behoove you to remember she is receiving recompense for the service."

Ambrose? Can you hear me? He's never had cake. My relation has never tasted cake!

"This is different, priest."

Emberkin Arro motioned for his guard. Septimus leaned in while his employer issued a command and then shifted away when dismissed.

"There is a connection between Birdie and I."

"Oh, gentle-hearted slave monger... every man goes through this." In Monwyn's own Den of depravity, professions of love and proposals were common within hours of a tryst. It happened so often that in their dressing room, the dancers and workers placed bets on which patrons would be first to give up their inheritance for a betrothal. I myself once promised a man the jewel from my father's own crown. "Arro, Birdie has questionable hygiene practices and the table manners of a troll at high tea. Play with her for as long as you remain in Gaea, but... oh wait..." I bumped his hip with mine, much to his annoyance. "Does this mean you plan to take to the seas soon?"

The Baldorvan did not acknowledge me, just glowered at a happy prince and a laundress as they hopped around and tossed their hands in the air.

I shifted my eyes to the exit. The Primus-King's personal guard surrounded him as they ushered him away.

One less man to worry about.

"I believe, Father Regulus, it is time to consider that this Emryss is as mythical as the centaurs your people claim to have seen. I have made the decision to negotiate with the religious head of Ærta for what I seek."

I dipped my head in acknowledgment.

"You are a man of great wisdom. The Primus-King will be apprehended the moment he steps onto Verus's soil, and he will be turned over to you and your units off the coast of the former Kingdom of Hain. Your warlord and your God will be satisfied."

"I believe it will suffice, but the warlord wishes to procure a Hearthmate, and plurality is forbidden in my lands. The betrothal contract between Emryss and he—"

"It is taken care of... when you but say the word."

Emberkin Arro's head turned slowly upon his neck. His cool eyes regarded me with an expression of wary approval.

"Do it, priest."

I bowed deeply at the waist, recognizing the turning of the tides. Verus would deal with the Primus-King. My focus now? Eira's extraction.

Incoming! She sang through the connection.

Eira and His Highness Merritt bounded into view, sweat-soaked and laughing. With a final flourishing of her hand, my wife came to stand in the space between Arro and myself.

"Birdie, you are a lovely dancer, and I promise I will personally look into ensuring the purity recruits are given adequate time to recover between shifts. I hadn't realized the emotional toll they suffered," Prince Merritt panted out as he dabbed his forehead with a kerchief.

Eira performed a curtsy in his direction.

"And time to speak with a priestess when they need it? I'm telling you, some of the things I saw left me sleepless."

"Yes, yes." Merritt nodded and patted Eira's hand, which rested on his forearm. Her smile would have felled a lesser man. Merritt returned it in kind. "But, Birdie, sleep will soon fly the way of the south-seeking swallows when the blessing in your belly enters the world. My guess is a girl, and these hands of mine have never been wrong."

Chapter Forty-Nine

I'VE CHANGED MY MIND. MAYBE LIES ARE SHARPER.

Eira

A chilly wind blew through the hall, tossing my skirts around my ankles.

"Well, isn't that peculiar?" Merritt said, looking around for the source of the draft.

I could only grip the prince's elbow, too cowardly to face Ambrose. A haughty smirk of triumph was sure to be smeared across Septimus's face. And Cato...

"My dear? Are you well? Too much activity? Allow me to fetch the royal healer," the prince said.

My knees buckled as my breath caught in my chest. Prince Merritt's brows knit tight.

How long, Eira?

I couldn't answer.

How long?! His shout doubled me over.

Prince Merritt waved his hand in a summons.

S-Solnna, Ambrose. Maybe before. I don't know. Momma says—

Emberkin Arro grabbed my bicep and yanked me to his side.

My world tilted. The thousand copper stars on the ceiling spun. The joyous chorus of voices twisted into a grotesque cacophony as the eggshell I'd carefully crafted around my secret fractured, its yolk bleeding through the fissures.

Black Bear. This wasn't... I was going to—oh gods. I was going to birth the child and send them off with Momma. Ambrose, we cannot even protect ourselves!

The æther shot toward my back as a hand came to rest on my hip.

Cato.

I gulped the air, my breath coming too shallow.

Ambrose. Stop Cato. He will lose control. They'll kill him.

"You are sure, Your Highness? This woman grows my child?" Arro asked. He shifted in front of me and ran his palm over my stomach.

Over Arro's shoulder, Merritt's eye held mine. Understanding passed between us.

Ambrose, please, say something. I don't know what to do.

"My apologies, Birdie," Merritt said. "I have overstepped. The announcement should have been yours to make. Let us seek out my father for his blessing." Merritt angled his head toward the exit and proffered his elbow; his eyes brimming with apology.

Say nothing, Eira. Nothing!

Ambrose shook his head in shame as he placed a hand on the prince's shoulder.

"Highness, recruit Birdie is my laundress." He circled the fingers of his other hand around my elbow. "I should have kept closer tabs on her whereabouts, it seems."

I hung my head in disgrace.

"Was it that scoundrel Dæne from the Cult? Was your insatiable lust for choreplay your downfall, young lady? The aphrodisiac qualities of ammonia should be carefully studied." Ambrose wagged a finger in my face, slowly positioning his body nearer me. As he moved, I caught the exchange of something between his and Cato's hands, using me to shield the action. "Vigorous scrubbing mimics humping, Your Highness, but it is no excuse for the loss of one's purity. I take full responsibility and will escort her sullied self to Verus to atone." Ambrose pointed to the door. "Your reckoning awaits." His words struck with a quiet steel, cutting in their calm.

Ambrose, Black Bear, I will explain. I—

"Back the fuck away, Father," Arro's voice matched my husband's chilling tone. "Or one less priest will spout the Goddess's drivel."

In my peripheral vision, Cato stretched his head from side to side. *No, please, Merrias, no.* He would die trying to free me, and what atrocities would he commit for the child?

"A-Arro, calm down," I begged.

My men wouldn't bend, would not yield—they would bring this hall to ruins and drown in the blood of innocents before surrendering me. And Goddess help me, I would snatch the sun from the sky and cast the world into darkness before I'd see them fall.

I drank deep.

Like the moon to the tides, the undertow to an unobservant swimmer, I pulled, leaching the æther from the unsuspecting crowd: from Prince Merritt, the servant walking by, three children quietly playing with their dolls.

The æther coiled at the base of my spine and webbed a path through my limbs. My chest thrummed with energy, its discordant hum roaring in my ears.

Eira, remain calm. I am here. Cato and Septimus are behind you. Reach backward, ground yourself. Eira, this is not the end.

"Birdie, return to my rooms." Emberkin Arro snapped at his guards, but they made no move to obey. "We will make arrangements for our departure."

Ambrose moved into Emberkin Arro's path.

"You will do no such thing, slaver." Stripped of their warmth, Ambrose's eyes glinted with only ice-cold resolve. "Back away."

"You threaten me, priest? Would you pit your paltry temple guards against the units at my command?"

Without warning, Emberkin Arro lunged sideways, sweeping around Ambrose. He caught my wrist in his grip. My breath caught as he hoisted our arms aloft.

"In Baldorva, a Hearthing is an oath made!" Arro thundered, his voice cracking through the cavernous hall, drowning out the murmurs and setting every eye upon us. I could feel the weight of their stares.

Control, sweetheart. We will fix this. Cato and I will fix this. No demon puff's, not yet. Steady.

Arro snapped his fingers, and I felt the heat of bodies on my back as Septimus and Cato flanked us.

Okay, Black Bear. Okay. Please don't leave me. Please don't let Cato leave me. Please don't...

Merritt opened his arms as if inviting me into his embrace. "A beautiful sentiment, Emberkin."

The crowd, drawn to the dramatics, pressed in on us. Arro yanked me back, wrenching my elbow as I reached out to accept the prince's kind gesture.

Do you feel Cato? Eira, your eyes are shimmering. He is directly behind you, Eira. Reach back.

Pinned against the Baldorvan's side, I stretched my fingers and searched for my mate. Cato's thumb pressed into the center of my palm, grounding me in the moment.

I feel him.

Septimus's palm flattened on the small of my back. Their combined touch caused the loudly drumming æther to settle back into my control.

"This woman grows my future, and she has agreed to become my wife. There is but one creed intoned for a Hearthing in my land."

I didn't. Ambrose, I agreed to nothing.

I know. Remain placid, wifling.

"Let us gather and take refreshment, Emberkin. Such a union should be celebrated. Drinks for all." Prince Merritt turned around and hailed a servant with a fresh blue hanky from his short coat's breast pocket. As he did so, a woman some four feet to his right tilted her head nearly imperceptibly before she shifted her weight to the balls of her feet.

The Gaean soldiers stationed around the perimeter—twenty or more uniformed men—moved forward as several servants headed in our direction with their trays held high.

Arro saw them as well. His fingers dug into my wrist.

"As embers glow long in the heart of the flame, so does blood bind, unbroken, enduring."

Faster than my mind could comprehend, Arro pulled his dagger.

"No, Arro!"

Steel split the space between our linked hands.

Our mingled blood ran freely down our forearms, a gross parody of a Bond.

Fuck! Fuck, fuck, fuck. He has my blood. Ambrose?

Emberkin Arro dragged me behind his back, our blood spotting my dress and the floor.

"By the laws of Baldorva, we are man and wi—"

He quieted, brows knit taut in confusion. His lips moved, mouthing words that seemed to hang, impotent, in the odd silence. His silvery eyes found mine as he collapsed to his knees.

"Make no moves, my love. Wait it out," Cato whispered into my ear before rushing to his "master's" side.

Arro clawed at his chest, head thrashing from side to side. His body twisted in ways that made my skin crawl, back arching unnaturally, limbs jerking as if some invisible force suspended him from his navel.

Nobles backed away from the writhing man, but healers rushed forward to lend aid.

I barely registered Ambrose's arms until he pressed me forward at Merritt's urging.

"Goddess child, turn away. The Nether Lord has taken command of his soul!" Ambrose said loudly enough for the crowd to catch. He propelled us toward the veiled clergy of the Verus envoy.

The hall, once filled with laughter and song, burst into a tumult of shrieks and screams.

Children ran to their mothers. Baldorvan and Verus soldiers streamed through the doors, drawn to the commotion.

The glint of a mace drew my attention to the side split in Ambrose's robes.

"Keep moving, my child. You are surrounded by the Goddess's chosen. Here we are, right through the—"

"What in Mossius's divine wisdom... my gods. Em-Emryss. My child, is it truly you?"

The Primus-King's blue eyes fluttered in disbelief.

CHAPTER FIFTY

TWO PATHS

CATO

Soldiers: ninety-eight. Breakdown: Verus, twenty and four. Baldorva, thirty and one. Gaean, forty and three. More incoming. Exits: two. The southern blocked by fleeing nobles. Plan: Eira's safety. Nothing else matters. Weapons on my person: four. Mace passed to Ambrose. Weapons on Arro: three. Septimus: twelve. Frostborn: approximately twenty minutes to the west. Their delivery should be completed soon, and their return is anticipated.

The masses, once drawn to the spectacle of Emberkin Arro's "possession," shifted their attention.

"Emryss! Is it truly her?" a deep voice boomed.

"Our daughter returns to us!"

"She is delivered from evil! The Baldorvan brought her home!"

A throng of healers passed their hands over the Baldorvan's body as Septimus and I stood before them, keeping the onlookers at bay.

"Uncle, can you get to the Primus-King?"

"Yes," Septimus growled. "I will honor my Enchantress with his head."

"Go then. Do your worst."

My uncle dropped to his knees, knocking a healer from where he squatted over his seizing patient. Septimus trailed a gloved hand through the still-wet blood that had dripped onto the floor and pushed his fingers under his hood and into his mouth. He rose and faced me.

"There is a child." His voice was as I had never heard it, light and full of wonder.

I dipped my chin, the only action I could muster without sending my blade through the nearest body: his.

Yes, I'd heard. Eira's words had swept across me like the brush of a divine hand over my shoulders—rare and sanctified—the final threads woven into a holy tapestry.

But then I beheld my wife... *my* human. She'd flinched as if Merritt's statement were the strike of a mortal blow. And then her arms had crossed, not in defiance, but in defense. An emotion I had no right to question.

"Septimus, go."

He charged off, his bloodlust palpable in the swell of his chest, the aggression in his step.

A rasping cry echoed off the chamber's tall ceilings.

Emberkin Arro surged from the floor, eyes wild and teeth bared. The healers fought to keep him prone, but fortified with Eira's blood, he freed himself in an explosion of strength that knocked two healers down.

"We retrieve Birdie and make for the garrison." Spittle flew from his mouth as he snatched me by the hood and delivered the directive. "She bears my child."

My vision hazed. I reached for my dagger with the intent to drive it through the flesh under his chin, but a sudden clarity of mind overpowered my impulse. Another warrior netherbent on providing Eira protection would be worth swallowing my possessive impulses in the short term.

Let Septimus slaughter the Primus-King—fuck, let him get caught doing it. Let Arro flee to his homeland with Eira in tow—only for his contingent to be set upon by frost giants, all, including Emryss, crushed to unrecognizable paste. The warlord's calculations would change. He could negotiate for a new Hearthmate, and with Leyometh's essence returned to the god through the monarch's death, Ærta would look much less appealing.

Emberkin Arro ran, a blur combing through the masses, his feet and legs obscured by the smoke-like churn of his clothing. I followed in his wake, hand gripping the hilt at my side, not drawing, but prepared if necessity mandated its use. A ripple of space opened around the Baldorvan. They feared him, scrambling to part as he drove through.

"Do not touch her! Do not lay your fingers upon my wife, priest!" Emberkin Arro roared. He produced a blade and aimed it at Ambrose's back.

Two futures unfolded in my mind's eye... no... I heard them rather than saw them.

Let him die, Lykksun's Chosen, a feminine presence, with a voice like warm honey, said. *Your future is as bright as the rays of my crown.*

Would your lover love you still if you let my Chosen perish? This voice was deep, his tone biting as ice. *I will steal back your Frostborn if he falls.*

I wavered on my feet, caught in a damming spiral.

"What in Mossius's divine wisdom... my gods. Em-Emryss. My child, is it truly you?" The Primus-King dropped to his knees, his arms outstretched.

Chapter Fifty-One

SOMETIMES CHOICE IS ALL YOU HAVE LEFT

Eira

"You seek to deceive the warlord?" Arro Emberkin seethed, speaking through his teeth as he closed in on the Primus-King.

Liveried guards surrounded us, ready to protect their monarch.

The Primus-King knelt at my feet, blue eyes welling and hands shaking as they reached toward me. Cato stood at Arro's right, close enough that I could reach him in two steps, and Ambrose was at my back, not relinquishing his hold on my shoulder.

"Speak, old man! Before I take my horde and your head to my homeland."

The Primus-King flinched, taken aback by the vehemence flung his way. His eyes drifted to the blade in Arro's fist and then back to me.

"My daughter has returned to her fam—"

"This woman and I are bound. My seed swells within her womb, as told to me by your own touch-blessed son."

"This is *my* child, my daughter Emryss, born of my Lifemate's precious body." A pronounced tremor shook the Primus-King's hand as he raised his eyes to mine, his confusion evident. Without looking at the slaver, the Primus-King jabbed a finger at Arro's chest. "You've hidden her from me. In my own house!"

"Lies! She is nothing more than a servant who has sold herself for coin. The warlord will not take kindly to your attempt at gilding over the tarnish of your mythical daughter's non-existence."

The Primus-King caught Arro's hand as he rose to his feet. The Baldorvan wrenched away, but the Primus-King held firm.

"Emberkin Arro. Look closely and bear witness to my honesty. My boys, by the Goddess's grace, were blessed with a knowing touch... but *my* Emryss was gifted a healer's ability without parallel."

It was time—hidden within the folds of my skirts, the æther sparked hot between my fingertips.

Do not, Eira. If you strike him down and they make to imprison you, Cato and I cannot take on these numbers.

Then I will kill them all.

I jerked away to make my move, but Ambrose held me tight.

I love you with the weight of the mountains and the strength of a stone. Do not risk your life and that of... of the love within you.

"You are healed, Emberkin Arro. Not just bandaged. No trickery at play," the Primus-King murmured.

Arro glanced at his palm, turning it this way and that, seeking the open wound that had nearly knit shut.

The æther buzzed in my ears as I struggled in Ambrose's arms.

Let me go, Ambrose. This is my fate.

Cato would say something more poetic, like, "with a love carved in granite, impossible to erase." He will bludgeon me in the afterlife because he didn't get to say it himself.

Ambrose, stop talking like that and let me go!

I released a spark of black shade, with the intent of shaking off his hold, but he captured my arm and threaded his fingers through mine. A freezing snake coiled around my wrist and slithered upward. The æther died as the sensation traveled, the energy ceasing its churn. His touch tempered my black shade's heat, extinguishing its spark.

What the? Black Bear, what have you done?

"Im-impossible." Emberkin Arro dropped his hand, his face a mask of shock. "If the warlord finds out that I..." He hung his head, a man reeling from an unexpected blow. "In Leyometh's name, I swear I didn't know." He inspected his healed palm again, running his fingers along the fresh pink line that would eventually disappear. "The warlord can never know that I bedded his betrothed—the woman of Leyometh's bloodline."

The Primus-King signaled to his guards, his expression shifting from one of astonishment to shrewdness. The soldiers closed in, blocking the views of the interested crowd. He stepped closer to the Baldorvan and dropped his voice.

Over the Primus-King's shoulder and between two guards' helms, I caught sight of Septimus. In the regulation uniform of a Gaean soldier, he slipped through the crowd as stealthily as a cat through tall grass, looking for a way in.

"When the child comes, I will bear the burden of seeing it reared. You will take Emryss to her rightful husband in Baldorva."

Emberkin Arro gazed at his hand while pondering the Primus-King's words.

On Cato's signal, unleash yourself, my brutal harpy. Burn it all and then get to Aberus.

No! Not until you both get to safety! I still don't have the control to—

Leave no one standing—not the Primus-King or the Emberkin. Not a child or guard. Not Cato, not me. Rid the earth of all who might bear witness and then run. Find your mother and father and leave. Take Larm and Evandr and... and our child... and live a life worth living.

"No!" I screamed, the single word tearing from my throat. "No! None of you decides my fate! Do you not see the person that I am? The human that stands before you? How dare your desires trump my existence?"

The Primus-King's jaw tightened, his robes shifting as he stepped forward, hand darting out to seize mine. Cato lunged, propelling himself between us, his arm sweeping up to knock the Primus-King's hand aside.

"Call off your dog, Emberkin; my daughter will not be kept from her family by you or any other."

"Move away," Arro commanded.

Cato didn't budge, but I knew beneath his flowing garments and face-obscuring hood, his muscles coiled, just as I knew Ambrose's hand would be hovering above his weapon. I also knew, without a doubt in my mind, that if either of them made to raise arms against the Primus-King or Baldorvan, the guards would cut them down before they could take a second breath.

"Guards! Strike him down!" The Primus-King yelled.

I moved without thinking, ripping free of Ambrose's control, freeing a dagger from Cato's boot—he always kept one there—and planting myself squarely before him, protecting what was mine. I felt the heat of his body at my back, the hand that squeezed my hip in warning.

I found myself face-to-face with the Primus-King, my knifepoint steady, its tip resting above the shimmering medallion that hung from his neck.

"Daughter, what has the Solnnan queen done to you?"

The lies dripped as poison from his mouth, all to maintain the narrative he'd painted to save face.

Blades hissed free as the surrounding guards drew their weapons and charged. They closed in, the metal of their armor clanking with their footfalls, the steps ushering me closer to our end.

"Halt!" The Primus-King commanded, throwing his arms wide, his eyes frantic. The soldiers stopped as if the word itself staked their feet to the floor.

"Emryss, I have searched endlessly, praying for your safety."

Behind me, Cato made to move, the skirts of his robe brushing my calves. Dropping a single hand from my blade, I let the æther flow, suspending him in time, just as my father would do with a water drop or I a black flame. My mate would not fall this day, whether or not he'd hate me for my choice.

"A father's prayers are answered, and we will guide your mind back to well-being, daughter."

Did he think I'd not notice the reflection in his eye, the silent movement of some soldier over my shoulder? I dropped my knife hand, needing it to secure Ambrose and the approaching man. Both stilled.

How my husbands fought against me, struggled against my hold. I could feel it in the energy that flowed through them both.

"Merrias knows your heart, Primus-King, and the Goddess your deceptions."

Eira, transform! I am begging you. Get yourself far from here.
I have no life if you are not in it, Black Bear.

"Daughter Emryss, your mother has poisoned you against me."

"My mother," I breathed, my voice trembling but clear, "sacrificed everything so I might know love without fear. And I have. I have loved until I burned from the beauty of it. I choose to follow Momma's path, *Father*, her courage. Remember that... when you stand upon the blade."

"Take her." The Primus-King lunged backward as he gave his troops his orders. "Move her to the Cult for observation."

Movement exploded at the edges of my vision as the soldiers moved in from all sides. Septimus sprang forward, disarming a guard before twisting from the range of another.

"Assassin!"

"We've been breached!"

The air sang with the arc of Septimus's blade.

"*This* is my choice," my words rang loud with conviction.

He didn't see Septimus, or even me for that matter, but for once I saw myself in his face... for we shared in a stark and sudden end.

The guards reacted, redirecting their attention, and in that single heartbeat, just as Septimus buried his blade into the Primus-King's chest, I slid the dagger across my throat.

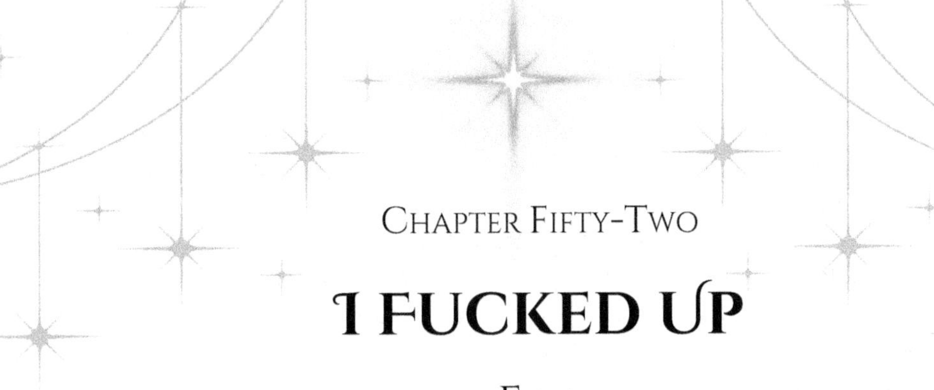

CHAPTER FIFTY-TWO

I FUCKED UP

EIRA

"A bold plan of action, granddaughter."

Merrias and I stood in the choir loft above, watching the chaos unfold. Singers clambered about, some hanging over the banisters, their expressions full of alarm—others hiding their heads in the chests of their counterparts, openly weeping, turning from what they had witnessed below.

Ambrose cast his veil aside, yelling for a healer. Cato held my body. His hands pressed against my throat in an attempt to staunch the sanguine flow. I wished to see his face one last time, but the concealing hood kept him from my view.

I lay my head on folded arms.

"My husbands will live. Leyometh's essence is returned, and the child I tried to prevent won't know a life in shackles."

The goddess leaned over the banister, stretching her neck out as another wave of soldiers rushed into the hall.

"Death is not the worst fate when greedy men rule the world."

Merrias sighed. "Granddaughter, why is it that human women seem to be the first to sacrifice themselves when their menfolk cause the issues?"

"I don't know. Ask your mother. She made them, after all."

Merrias laughed and then cupped her chin in her hands, watching the scene as I did.

"Though she created you with somewhat smaller frames, she gave you bigger hearts, I think—bigger brains, for certain."

"No. I disagree." I looked to where a group of healers now surrounded my body. Ambrose held Cato back as the husband of my heart struggled, clawing and twisting, doing his damndest to get back to my side. "Were my heart larger, I would have stayed. I would have fought to live, and despite my fears, I would have borne their newest obsession into the world."

"Eira, woman of my blood?"

"What?" I asked flatly, not caring about the turning of the world, not giving a single shit about the gods' essence or their master plans.

"Do you think I'll allow my line to end because you suffer human weakness?"

I faced my grandmother.

"I made my choice, and because of it, the *last* of your line won't be bled dry, or married off to a slaver, or forced to bend to the will of puppet masters. That may have been the plight of my mother and I, but no more."

Merrias chuckled, the mocking tone digging under my skin.

"Daughter of my daughter, when you make a decision of such import, wield the blade with more precision... or at least slash your throat in a city of imbeciles, not people of medicine."

"What do you mean?" I looked again, leaning over the half-wall. Below, blood pooled around my body, soaking the front of my gown.

"I mean, you aren't dead." Merrias theatrically cast her head from side to side as if she had lost something precious. "Do you see the Arbiter blade in my hand? No. Because this isn't your judgment, and hardly any of that is *your* blood."

Even on this divine plane, rage welled within me. It must have been Arro's or the Primus-King's.

The anger and æther pulsed through my limbs.

"Do you never get tired of meddling?" I seethed. "Of forcing your will upon others?"

Merrias pinned me with a look that should have sent me to my knees, but I fought the urge to prostrate myself at her feet.

"No. It is *I* who carve the paths that you humans only *think* you choose to traverse. You will live, Eira, my great-granddaughter will be born, and *she* will be the conduit that ensures my mother—the Goddess, in her rightful glory—remains upon her celestial throne. The Nether Lord will not usurp her."

I exploded—the æther surging, pouring from my hands, seeping from my chest in tendrils of black shade. The air cracked around us like the thrust of an oar through brittle ocean ice.

"You speak of thrones and legacies!" I spat. "Those are meaningless when built on broken bodies and stolen lives. The Goddess is love, and love is the only legacy worth bleeding for."

The world drowned in darkness, unbeknownst to those still bustling around the loft. Only the faint, pulsing glow of Merrias's veins remained visible. One breath, and her face, her fury-laden eyes, appeared scant inches from the tip of my nose.

"Do not think that you know an inkling of Her worth. She is the thread that ties humanity. Her unraveling would be the beginning of the end. Her worth is beyond that of a handful of lives—a dozen, a million."

Merrias's presence bore down on me, a weight unlike any I had endured, not a physical burden, but one of extreme awareness. I tried to look away but could not cower.

"If the Nether Lord ascends, the sun will bleed into the horizon and never once rise again. Rivers will choke off at their sources and cease to flow. Time itself will decay, and the living will become as still as the stone of his fortress."

At her temples, the soft webbing of pinkish veins illuminated her brown eyes. In them, flecks of green and deep bronze seemed to move as leaves upon the wind. They put me in the mind of the plants and flowers Cato had once gifted me, those that I had killed in a matter of days. Those eyes were deeper than I could fathom—they held the secrets of creation and the wisdom of ages—but there was something else there as well, an intensity that I recognized as surely as my own, a vulnerability so very familiar.

I settled my palm on her cheek.

"Even a goddess needs her momma."

The goddess lifted her arm, and her palm came to rest on the edge of my jaw, mimicking my touch, connecting us fully. At once, the swirling shadows of black fire burned out.

"Finally, granddaughter, you understand."

CHAPTER FIFTY-THREE

TCK, TCK, TCK

EIRA

Oh, fuck. Fucking kill me now.

Nan once told me that cleanly delivered cuts didn't hurt nearly as badly as rips or tears. She was either a godsdamned liar or... or maybe I was remembering wrong, and she'd said that the clean ones healed faster than the others.

"Her eyes," Cato rasped. "They open. Release me!"

Through the foggy haze of double vision, I beheld my world. Cato lurched from Ambrose's arms, that fucking hood still obscuring the face I loved. I just wanted to see him.

"She lives," Emberkin Arro cried out. He muscled past Ambrose. "Leyometh has seen to her return."

"Let them work! Do not impede their progress." Ambrose yanked both men back by the scruff of their garments.

Standing directly by my husband's side, judging from the way my body tingled, Septimus, the cunning wolf, had managed to slip back into his creeper uniform and loomed, arms crossed over his chest. I couldn't wait to hear how he'd managed such a feat. And I wanted to thank him for his willingness to kill a beloved leader in a crowd of his adoring subjects and family. *Morally charcoal.* Regicide was no small crime. Maybe I'd reward him with sex.

I tried to laugh, but nothing came out.

The heads of a half-dozen people, including healers Kristen and M'Xosha blotted out the view of my family. I tried telling them to move, but a sharp jolt of pain, followed by a rush of fear, kept me silent.

"Hold her down. Highness Emryss, don't thrash. We are here to help you. Hold her." Healer Kristen used the same comforting tone as she had with the boy, Gavin. Her calm was an anchor point. I knew she'd never hurt me, but a dozen hands rested upon me, working, pressing, holding, and I couldn't quell the terror. I tried to shout, to cry out for my mother, for Ambrose, but all I could manage was the click of my tongue.

"Tck, tck, tck!" I wanted Cato. His were the hands that restored me. "Tck, tck, tck!"

Metal implements and linen bandages passed above me.

"They've arrived. Place her on the board, gently now—do not add stress to the internal sutures," said Healer Kristen. "She clots remarkably well, but let us not chance it."

A rigid board slid under my back, and I found myself levitating. Four burly recruits, one of whom I thought I'd recognized, went running, the healers on their heels.

"Where are you taking her? We are bound by blood," Arro asked from somewhere behind.

"Speak the location," Ambrose said from the same direction. I could see his head towering above all the others as he attempted to force his way to my side. "Verus would demand my presence as Her Highness's spiritual advocate."

"Cult Mossius."

"Tck... tck."

Everything went black.

Visitation Hours

Eira

"She's been like this for days, but look at her neck, healed with hardly a scar. Our healers theorize that she remains unconscious from shock and not mortal injury."

"Fascinating."

I couldn't open my eyes or move my limbs, but I could smell the scent of ammonia wafting up from the hands that swabbed my neck.

"And, Archhealer, what of the Primus-King?"

I heard the scrape of metal against metal, followed by the hiss of shears through fabric.

"We are lucky our leader remains among the living. The sword pierced him through, right below his clavicle. The blade missed the major blood network. The Goddess was surely watching over him."

"Indeed. And the offender? Who would have dared?"

"You mustn't breathe a word."

"I swear it."

"Emberkin Arro's guards, the ones who do not speak, rooted out the assassin. The man had taken his own life already, but he left a letter. It insinuated that our illustrious Primus-King had taken part in nefarious dealings and that nobles would continue dying until the aggrieved party received their recompense."

"Good Goddess, and that would explain the horrific end of—"

"—the nobles who were found slain that same night. Yes indeed, it looks like they were breaking into the chroniclers' society."

"The chroniclers? Who would break into the old records room? Nothing but old paper and out-of-date annals."

I faded out once more.

"I failed you, Enchantress. It will not happen again."

"... and then I told them: Look, young people should learn to love their bodies and not focus their entire lives on maintaining their purity. Why do we deny what is nature? I'm not sure the Goddess would have given us natural urges if she didn't mean for us to explore them... or maybe she's a nasty bitch like Yemailrys. Wifling, we should teach our little one self-love, I think. That way, they will take care of their bodies, even if they aren't built like me, but instead take after their mama. Does that make sense? If someone were told over and over that their body was this way or that—too thick, too scrawny, too pale, too deeply complected, skin too coarse, head the wrong shape—well, I think for some it may inspire them to make changes, stick to a regime, or embark upon the daunting task of committing to an exfoliant. But for most, I am of the mind that it would have the opposite effect and make them loathe themselves to the point of harmful practice. You know, Mama loved her body, and she taught me to love mine. One of the things I find most attractive about you is that you love *you* and... and I would pass that on to our child—"

My Black Bear pulled a comb through my hair, his touch tender. Though I could feel the tines, I could not respond.

"Look, Ma, I'll be real. I'm kind of mad at you. Larm told me you were all love and hugs when you met him in the tavern. Me? One look and you almost barfed on the rug. In my defense, I was hungry, and we needed the guards gone. But anyways, me and Larm need you to wake up. I, specifically, need you to do better when you see me this time and give me a cuddly nickname, and maybe sit for a portrait with me and the old man. I'm pretty sure with looks like mine, I'll be your favorite. Oh, and are you actually knocked up? Cause we don't want another brother, especially if he's gonna be born all normal. How the nether are we supposed to teach some human kid how to hunt elk or swallow skulls?"

Minutes, perhaps hours, passed.

"Who's the daddy? Huh? Is it gonna come out perfectly pale like me and Septimus? Or will he have Cato's penchant for a butter-bellied boyhood? Oh, damn, or is it Ambrose's kid? Derros's dong, Nortia, Ærta can't handle another ego that size."

Tender hands brushed the hair from my face, and then a familiar weight settled next to mine, and a gentle warmth spread through me, reaching from the top of my head to my toes.

"As soon as you wake, my love, take to shade. Get to the meeting point."

I knew his scent—had already memorized the light hissing sound of the air traveling through his recently rebroken nose.

My skin tingled, just the pads of my toes. Perhaps the first physical indicator that reminded me I was still here.

"I cannot bear the silence, my love, for in the solitude I doubt my own existence."

"We ride to Verus tomorrow, Archhealer. Keep her under surveillance until the child can live beyond the womb. Use the elixir to bring about birth the moment life is viable. If it bears the gift of its mother and grandmother, it shall remain with us, to be raised in love, while Emryss is sent to fulfill her betrothal in Baldorva. No scar remains upon her hand. There is no proof of a Hearthing with Emberkin Arro. If, however, the child does not inherit her healing properties, send *it* to the slaver nation instead, for it will still bear the essence of Leyometh and should suffice in Emryss's stead."

"It will be as you say."

I tracked the sounds of light footfalls as someone paced the room.

A door clicked shut, and on my right side, the pillow beneath my head was reshaped and fluffed. The muscles of my back and shoulders sighed in relief.

"I've many regrets in my life, my daughter. More than I am able to count, and surely more than I am able to remember."

Wake, Eira, wake! I screamed. But my body would not, could not, heed my call to action. I called to the æther, I called for Ambrose, and then to my Pa.

The silence stretched on for so long that I thought perhaps hallucinations were setting in.

"I loved your mother. I loved her mind and her compassion, how she gave of herself to care for the downtrodden. Vonnie is my one true Lifemate, and she gave you to me. I would welcome her back without question."

I tried to spit, but my tongue remained as still as my arms and legs.

Fingers wove through mine. His skin was unnaturally warm, just like my own.

"I've yet to piece together how you came to be here, Emryss. My sister Hester blames herself and says she brought you here to rid my mind of its poison. She maintains that my judgment is clouded, but daughter, already you have kept a grandmother from leaving her children too early and, if you can believe it, healed the wounds of a boy who suffered burns over half his small body. My wound, which should have bound me to bed despite its lucky placement, healed within days of receiving your gift. And my wife and daughter, who took ill after ingesting a tainted beverage, have been restored to full health."

He squeezed my hand, and I felt the press of his lips to my knuckles.

"Why could you not have come of your own accord? I would have preferred you have a true life, not simply exist under the power of sedatives. Had I your gift, I would give of myself until the day I met Merrias—the pain I see in the world sometimes overwhelms me."

"Birdie... Emryss." Arro's voice pitched lower as he used the new-to-him name. "I am a man of decisive action. It has served me well in combat and in life. By the laws of Baldorva, the moment you set foot into Baldorvan territory, on sea or land, I am permitted to... take you into my household."

Enslave me.

"By Leyometh's divine plan, he has made *me* and *not* the warlord your seed provider. I have concluded that it is my calling to usurp the man who currently sits upon the Baldorvan throne. Our child, born of Leyometh's essence, is the future of our world. I do not pretend to think this is a match of love... but it is one of destiny."

Chapter Fifty-Five

SAFE HOUSE ENVY

Cato

To my front: bentwood trees arched in a tunnel, climbable, no issue. Flowerpots with human faces and statuettes of mythical creatures lining the pathway. A fanciful owner, then—likely no combat training. Copper light networks throughout the landscape. To the right: vineyard. To the left: pasture. Goats and horses located near the farthest barn. Ducks and chickens in the closest field. House beyond the archway... noble-owned, given the... no, scratch that. Merchant owned. Six visible wagons stored along the home's eastern wing, and those servants are not servants—prod of crossbow identified beneath half-cloak. Western wing—stone—fortified. Archers between rooftop crenellations: four. Rounded glass cupola atop the highest turret, three people moving within. Weapons on my person: four. Weapons on Ambrose: two. Woman running toward us.

My knees nearly gave way.

Eira's momma—she can be no other.

"This way, Highness Catommandus, Scion Ambrose." Gotwig led us through the tree tunnel, speaking as formally as if we were among the Devotees back at Verus. He wore three tunics, one linen and two wool, layered beneath a thick-knit sweater, and even then, he'd tucked a plaid scarf around his neck.

Eira's mother yelled and waved her arms above her head, but the high winds carried away her words. She pulled a thin leather coat around her shoulders as she steadily approached.

"Her status, at once!" the woman, Vonnie, demanded, still a few yards away. Her face was set in stern lines, her fair skin red from the burn of the endless gusts. "Describe the whites of her eyes. Temperature? Has she lost or gained weight?"

I have led men into battle, have negotiated prisoner exchanges between the continents, and have taken on the creatures of nightmares, and yet, here, in the path of this gray-haired matron, I stood as a mindless pillar of stone.

Peering into the eyes of the woman whose face mirrored my wife's left me without the ability to form words. And though there were differences—the bow of her top lip less pronounced than Eira's, her brows not as arched, her eyes the greenest aventurine instead of the color of an angry ocean—it pained me to look at her.

Ambrose opened his arms to intercept her; she dodged him smartly and barreled toward me, coming to a stop a foot away.

She looked at Ambrose and then back at me.

"You, pragmatic husband." She stabbed a finger into my chest. "Adorable like the neighborhood stray, two heads shorter than her Pa. Her words, not mine. Loosen your lips, son, and answer my questions."

"I…"

I could hardly muster the strength to leave Eira's side today. Arro left either me or Septimus to guard her room at all times. For days on end, I'd refused to allow my uncle to relieve me until Ambrose forcibly wrestled me to the ground and made me catch a few hours' sleep. His ability to defeat me told me he'd had the right of it.

Vonnie eyed me. She took my wrist and placed two fingers at its pulse point, tapping her foot in time with its beat.

"Did you travel here with information, or have you come to take in the fine Gaean air?"

Ambrose circled Gotwig, leaving in the midst of their conversation. He came jogging to my side and then slapped me so fucking hard, I stumbled forward, sidestepping Vonnie at the last possible second.

It was the jolt I needed, and instead of striking back, I accepted the assault as another bit of his odd wisdom, just the same as how he'd lured me from the Cult in the first place. 'You know which husband gets fairy cunted, Catommandus? The one who takes the time to give of himself and checks in on dear old Momma and Pa. Mark my words, brother-former-lover, it is my ballocks she'll be tickling as you perch upon the cuck's chair.'

With a curt nod and straight spine, I launched in.

"She remains unconscious. Pale, no bluish tint nor green, no indications that she struggles to breathe. Respirations are even. Temperature is cooler than her usual warmth. She has lost weight, but they deliver nutrition through means of a device placed in her stomach. It is not pleasant to watch, but her pallor brightens soon after."

Vonnie chewed on the information, fists on her hips, toe still tapping. Over her head, I spied Ulltan tugging Ambrose into a much-needed embrace—I'd been dead to affection the moment Eira laid blade to neck.

"Gather around," Vonnie said. "Everyone."

Gotwig was the first to her side, checking his timepiece as he moved. Ambrose and Ulltan swayed in their hug as if it were the twentieth and not the first time they'd met. They parted and came our way, not stopping to swipe the tears from their eyes.

Ulltan appeared to have aged a decade in a matter of weeks. He wore his grief for the world to see, and for a moment, I wished I were capable of the same.

I caught a noise, and my hand went to the blade at my hip as I spun.

"Stand down, Highness Monwyn," Gotwig cautioned.

A hidden door tucked beneath a trio of artfully arranged head-shaped pots opened at the archway's entrance. I had imagined the containers to spill over with leaves and fronds, forming hair-like foliage, but was taken aback when an actual human's head popped out instead.

"I am Rizellen." Half of the woman emerged as she climbed the rungs of an underground ladder. "I own these lands. You are welcome to my bounty, sons of Monwyn."

"Well met, merchant." Ambrose performed a short bow. I did not. "My wife mentioned your name to me in one of her lengthy reminiscences of her peasantry. You are the mercantile who visited her in Nortia as she grew from a Chosen child to Troth, are you not?"

Ambrose sidled up to Ulltan, who had not ceased his tears, and looped his arm through the man's elbow. He drew him to my side and leaned over, mouthing, "*sheath your weapon, imbecile*," while batting at my hilt with his other hand.

"Shall I not draw steel when the next goblin appears and begins teething on your leg, Ambrose? Mind your training. Complacency will see you dead."

I let my hand fall from my weapon, though my fingers itched to draw again. Trust was earned, and even then, it was a tenuous prospect.

"I am she. I sailed between Nortia and Gaea for nigh on forty years." The old woman replied, keeping her perceptive gaze locked with mine. With some effort, she climbed from the cellar and shut the panel, making sure to knock leaves and dirt over the low-profile hinges. "This one leads to the wine cellar, which then leads to the house, which then leads to the barn.

Take it further, and you will emerge near the tree line." She pointed to her right, indicating a field beyond. "Tell anyone outside of this circle and I'll see you silenced."

With a pronounced limp and unusual gait, she made her way to the ever-growing gathering. I inclined my chin and then looked beyond the archway to the house.

"When I had imagined a checkpoint, it was a dilapidated shack in the woods or a heavily concealed cave along a cliffside, not a thriving manor in Gaea's wine country. Pardon my wariness; it is my natural state of being."

Rizellen tipped her head in understanding, causing the glass beads on her tasseled headwrap to dance atop her shoulders.

"You will find me good company then." She sized me up, her rheumy and clouded eyes taking in every detail. "Tonight, when you return here with Eira, enter through the tunnel closest to the barn; it lies to the right of the round bale feeder. That location will draw the least amount of attention. The neighbors, though distant, are a curious sort and pledged to the Primus-King."

"Return here? With Eira? She cannot open her eyes, much less stand. She must remain under the healer's care. To move her would reopen her wound and spell disaster for her and the... the child." The last word caught in my throat. Did they not understand? A shaky exhale left my lungs. How could they think to risk Eira's life?

Vonnie gripped my forearm.

"No. Listen to me," she said. "Eiry should have woken by now. They are purposefully sedating her. I watched it happen for years at Cult Mossius—it happened to me more often than I can account for. Do not be deceived by what the Archhealer is feeding you. He sees to her personally, yes? Of course he does. The Primus-King would trust no other."

"He does," I breathed, my mind suddenly spiraling. Had my emotions clouded my vision? With my own eyes, I watched them change her bandage. Read the labels of each medication administered, and tasted each of the macerated foods forced into her. Had I missed something?

Vonnie's face hardened further.

"You will not have detected the means of sedation; his network carries out his orders independent of the Cult's healers. It will all have appeared above board. Hear me, my sons. Get her out this night. Bring her here, take her to Monwyn, find a ship and sail to another world. I do not care, but keep her from becoming the fountain from which humanity thinks it is saved. I will offer myself to the Primus-King if you cannot extract her. My child will not be bled into martyrdom."

Her words landed like blows. I pictured Eira's body upon the altar, not the throne that she deserved—needles and blades, bleeding bowls beneath her limbs. Feedings to keep her alive as her muscles atrophied from disuse. And... and the child. What cruelty would they rain upon the tiny, perfect connection between me and the woman I loved?

Strategies and scenarios, a flood of plans and contingencies poured through my thoughts, each rapidly assessed and then discarded.

"If your silence means you will not do it, I will go." Vonnie began walking in the direction of Mynder, tugging her jacket close to her neck. In my periphery, I saw her hair catch in the wind, a strand blowing free of her long graying braid. From the finality of her tone, I had no doubt she would.

"I should not have waited this long. Sid, Ulltan. If you make to stop me this time, I will have Rizellen lock you in the tower."

"And I'll do it." The merchant replied.

Ambrose stepped into the circle, holding his arms aloft.

"No, no, that's just his thinky face. Return, Momma-in-law." He ran to intercept her and offered her his hand. She took it and in the most Ambrose of moves, he slid forward and kneeled, hugging her about the waist. He laid his cheek on her stomach, and as if by instinct, she lowered her chin to the top of his head.

And then her tears came.

Gotwig edged to my side as Ambrose and Rizellen escorted a weeping Vonnie to her husband.

"Catommandus. Your thoughts." Gotwig tucked his gloved hands into his pockets.

"Plan A: The Frostborn creates a distraction, allowing us to remove her with the minimal presence of soldiers. Terror would reign in the barracks and town. Blood may be shed, but I care not as long as it is not hers. Plan B: a deceased patient transfer. At night, bodies are taken to the mortuary to be studied unless they are deemed useful for research, those go straight to the pyres. The dead are shrouded, and the lift is used to transport them. Plan C: dispatch the person administering the sedative. Allow Eira to wake and hold off any who might disturb her until she can take to the skies. This has the added benefit of allowing her to heal the injuries she may yet have."

Ulltan procured a linen from his pocket and passed it to Vonnie, whom he kept close.

"I'll go with ye boys, Sidnatious will stay with Vonnie. My baby needs her pa." Ulltan looked to Rizellen and then Gotwig. "Ye've got a room what can be made into a place for healin'?"

"Of course," Rizellen replied. "Under or above ground?"

"Above." Gotwig struck a match and held it to his pipe. "If we are found out or intercepted, she can flee from a window or the rooftop access."

"And the rest of us?" asked the merchant.

"Won't live long enough to worry, unless Gaean troops pursue us." He mouthed his pipe, chewing on its end. "They, we may stand a chance of outrunning. Not the Baldorvans, however. When my former master allowed me to see the sun, I watched them train and encountered their tactics on more than one occasion. Their efficiency at retrieval is unrivaled."

"I will take care of the Baldorvan," Ambrose asserted, his hand caressing the mace worn beneath his peasant's frock.

Gotwig puffed thoughtfully.

"I do not think that wise. His death would bring about certain war."

"You think to let him live? Claim my child as his own? My wife, his *property*," Ambrose whispered the last word. "I think the fuck not."

Gotwig raised his red-rimmed eyes, the wheels of his mind turning.

"My informants tell me he speaks of usurping the warlord. Several of the men under his command have pledged him their support. If he were to successfully remove their current leader, it would alleviate two issues—first, a war that Ærta will not win." Gotwig tapped his pipe to his lower lip. "Second. Through Eira, this spawn bears the essence of Leyometh. A man of Emberkin Arro's confidence, I am sure, is in a tizzy thinking that his god has *chosen* him to do his will and all that nonsense."

Ambrose recoiled, mouth agape.

"I am a god's *Chosen*; do not besmirch the gift of divine hands, you depressing little mite. What sacrilege."

Gotwig sneered.

"Thank you, Scion Ambrose, for modeling my argument in a way I never could have described through the use of simpler words."

"You are most welcome," Ambrose replied, not picking up on the slight.

"Come." Ulltan led Vonnie toward the manor house, where he urged her to sit upon a stone bench. We followed them in a morose line. The wind was harsher here, but Vonnie seemed not to notice. "I'll make ready. Sid, sit with her?"

Gotwig did as asked, and Vonnie turned to him, removed his scarf, and then tied it in a way that covered more of his face.

I mulled over my plans, viewing them from differing angles.

"Gotwig, do your spies have the ability to reach Troth Kairus? Can she be brought up to speed on what occurs here?" I asked.

"Of course they can reach Troth Kairus." Gotwig scoffed, holding off Ambrose, who had tried not once, but twice to lure him into a group hug with Vonnie.

"She may be of aid to Emberkin Arro in staging a coup. If she keeps him on that side of the world, they will bleed their strength as we work to build our forces," I said.

"Buying ourselves time buys Eira time," Vonnie stated with conviction.

I squatted, resting my arms on my knees. It was time for the conversation I'd been dreading.

"Mother Vonnie, are you privy to how long my wife has been baking our bun?"

Or... Ambrose could start the discussion.

In all honesty, it was probably better. I could not, in my current frame of mind, voice my thoughts without the Bond turning them toward violence—until I had control, as I did over the "warrior-king," it was safer to say nothing at all.

"She kept it hidden until this past month when she could no longer deceive us." Vonnie turned to her husband, drawing on his strength. "Living in such proximity, we would have been aware of the occurrence of her courses. When finally, her Pa and I sat her down to broach the subject, she was unable to recall the last date of a cycle. From what we could surmise, I would venture to say anywhere between three and five months. She wasn't yet showing when last I saw her, but that's not uncommon for women who are softer of stomach."

"Ah, it is no matter," Ambrose said, waving away the ambiguity. "Our focus is Eira, and her focus has never been children... even if contractually she'll need to provide me with a few."

Vonnie's brows went to points, but her retort was cut off by the return of her husband.

"Ulltan," Ambrose began, "stay with your wife and look after her. We have enough manpower to—"

"Ye'll not change my mind, husband number two." Ulltan bent and pecked Vonnie on her lips. "I reckon one of ye'll soon know what it is to shift the whole of yer world to ensure your little'un grows up good. I'll hitch up a wagon. If she's out cold, we'll need it. You ever moved a body?"

I cocked a brow as Ulltan turned to face me.

"A time or two."

Chapter Fifty-Six

Until the Soldier Softens

Ambrose

"Avast ye, Catommandus. Look alive, little princeling. We ride!"

I punched him in his sullen back, hoping to inspire his fervor. He snapped from his rumination and set upon me with a scowl that would have withered the tits off a turkey—not me, however. I was no lesser, fattened fowl. And nothing as minor as eye daggers would keep me from the task of freeing him from himself.

He struck, and I dodged, side-stepping the move that hadn't caught me unawares since before I'd turned twenty.

"We do not have time for your foolery, Ambrose," he bit out, even as he crouched and slid into a fighting stance.

I stared at the top of his short head.

I was in total agreement, and I knew my sullen, former-lover-brother would never have *actually* heeded my command to haul ass, but I had to interrupt the obsessive list checking and plot hole picking he was currently embroiled in. It would drive him mad, and that would lead to mistakes, and mistakes were—even more so than Septimus's ill-treatment—what had sent Cat into depressions so intense that our mother would sleep outside of his bedroom door.

"Smile, for fuck's sake," I hissed while saluting and bowing from the end of the manor's long pathway. "Reassure Vonnie, or she will set out after us and take matters into her own hands. Eira will *actually* kill us if that happens. Our marriage would not survive my death, and I have no wish to be resurrected as a Frostgiant."

Typical Cat. All he afforded the broken-hearted mother was a moment of eye contact before turning on his heel.

I felt Vonnie's pain to my very soul and wished to leave her with a glimmer of hope.

Gotwig, bless his perpetually ice-coated heart, just puffed on his pipe, taking it all in.

I fell into step beside Cat, letting Vonnie share her tears with her husband as she bid Ulltan farewell. I'd like Eira and me to be like that when her vagina ceased to make moisture and my soldier softened in his retirement.

"We were fools to believe it would take her this long to heal," Cato said. "She heals in a matter of days, not weeks."

"When a healer speaks, it is often wise to listen. You know this, and despite what they managed to hide from us, they have treated her well. Healer Ginnat bathed her and smoothed cream into her legs. The recruit that helps the Lead Healer stretched and moved her muscles, which was all above board, I should think."

We were far enough from the manor that the copper networks no longer cast light. The sun was dipping low on the horizon, painting the sky in hues that should have brought me a measure of joy: brightest tangerine and sea glass teal. The goats and horses in the pasture were mere silhouettes, fading into the dusk. Oh, no, my lenses were just covered with road filth. I brushed them on my loose linen pants and returned them to my face.

"Have you determined our course of action?" I asked, needing to bring my own wandering mind to heel. Though a brilliant tapestry of insight and intelligence, I, too, was consumed with a singular thought: bringing Eira home.

"Plan B," Catommandus stated, never turning to face me. "It is the cleanest operation by which to move her. I have the parchment, the signature. It carries the risk of recognition but presents the simplest path to freedom."

We walked in silence for a few moments, the rhythmic crunch of our boots a steady counterpoint to the drumming in my chest.

"The child," I began, my voice softer than intended, the vulnerability pouring from my lips. "Vonnie said she was three to five months along. And... she kept it hidden."

Cato's jaw tightened.

"She *did*, and she had her reasons," he lashed out. "And we will not question them."

"Reasons, yes, but more likely fears. One of those fears, perhaps, revolving around paternity."

Cat stopped in his tracks. The last rays of sunlight caught on the gold ring that he wore on his finger as he clenched his fist. I patted the silver counterpart where it lay hidden behind the Goddess's symbol, which hung from a chain around my neck. The bauble was a little much for the peasant frock I'd donned, but many of the lowlings I'd seen around the city wore similar.

"Speak plainly, Ambrose."

I raised my hands in a placating gesture. Though it would do him a whole mountain's worth of good, there was no time for a brawl.

Hearing the slow ramblings of a wagon on our heels, I turned. Ulltan, showing the same aptitude for fashion as his daughter, trailed behind us in a set of shabby, grime-green robes, sitting atop a wagon pulled by a team of long-eared, height-stunted ponies.

"The saddest steeds in existence. Rizellen is kind to give them a home," I lamented.

Cato rubbed his temples.

"You do not recognize your kin, jackass? It would behoove you to leave the palace more often, Ambrose."

I ignored the slight and refocused.

"You were with Eira. I was with her. And... there is Septimus."

Like the stench of a fart freshly passed, the name hung between us.

"It's not him," Cato said, his voice flat, devoid of the conviction I needed so badly to hear. "It cannot be."

I placed a hand on his shoulder.

"Hug me, Cato."

"Fuck off, Ambrose."

He shook off my hand, but I caught him with the other and slammed his chest to mine. He fought me, but I held fast. In all of his life, his greatest battles had been with himself.

His breath came fast; his spine stiffened. No matter. I swayed, forcing him into the rhythm.

"Regardless of who the father is, the child is Eira's, and that means ours."

CHAPTER FIFTY-SEVEN

I AM ONE OF THEM

EIRA

A stabbing jolt sent a ripple of pain through my head, sharp enough to pull a breath from my lungs.

"Steady now," came a warm voice. "You're safe, Highness Emryss. Just a sharp turn. A few more minutes, and we will see you comfortable again." Hands pressed gently to my forehead and then pulse points at my neck. Not rough hands. Not cruel. Soft.

I knew the voice, and yet... I couldn't reach the memory to discern to whom it belonged.

My lashes flickered.

The smell of home. Whale oil lamps. Not the vaporous scent of the copper systems of Gaea. Was I home? Where had I—

I moistened my dry lips, struggling to make words.

"Wh-where am?" It was all I could manage. I swallowed, and the bit of saliva traversing my throat felt like I'd gulped piping hot tea. I sputtered out a rasping cough. "Hurt." Single words were much simpler to manage.

The stiff board beneath me shifted again, and this time I caught a glimpse of the person walking beside me—a middle-aged woman with striking bronze hair pulled back in a ribbon. She wore the uniform of a recruit.

I wanted to speak, to ask again where I was, but voice already overworked, no sound came forth. Only a whistling breath.

"Don't try too hard, Highness. Though your skin bears no scar, the Archhealer says the nutrition device makes the throat burn something fierce. As soon as we reach the new accommodations, the healer will give you something to help you rest."

Rest? I didn't want to rest. I wanted to wake. I wanted my husbands. I'd swear to it that they were with me; I'd heard their voices. But now... had they been found out?

Ambrose? Husband, are you near? I need you! I screamed through the connection, but quickly ceased as it too felt heavy and disorienting to use.

Panic bombarded me, fear compounding as I realized I couldn't lift my arms. Fuck, I couldn't lift a finger and—I called out—where was the æther? Why couldn't I feel its hum? My heart pounded against my chest wall. It wasn't there. What had Merrias done to me? Had she taken my gift and left me to rot in a body that I could no longer defend?

Closing my eyes, like a conjurer fresh in the knowledge of their power, I followed the light like Papa Burchard had taught me. I squeezed them tight until, behind my lids, the lights and shifting colors appeared. *Breathe, Eira, you cannot conjure when deep in your feelings.* I focused on the brilliant flecks but sought what lay between. *One... two... three...* I fought to stay calm. I pursued the shadows—I was a creature born of night, born to hunt in the dark. The moonlight illuminated my path.

There was a slight stirring in my chest, eerily faint, like someone pressed the wings of a butterfly above my heart... but nothing more.

In that moment, as if I tapped into an underground spring, everything came rushing back. Emberkin Arro, the Primus-King, the knife.

The weight in my abdomen shifted slightly as we rounded another turn.

The child.

Merrias's sole focus.

My grandmother would see her line continue even if it meant I'd languish away, unconscious and immobile, under the sharp eyes of the Primus-King.

Why had the Goddess not answered my prayers?

The moment I realized my courses were not coming, I'd hit my knees, begging for it to end in miscarriage, then prayed instead that it would bear Cato's face, or Ambrose's darkly lashed eyes of green. Perhaps Cato's warm complexion and his curls? I'd fought the images of ice-blue eyes on its small face, too terrified by the prospect of looking at the child and seeing the loathsome man that was responsible for my condition in the first place.

Gods' will? Fuck their will.

We came to a stop, and the recruits used the sheet wrapped about me to transfer me to a bed. I stared at the ceiling.

I cleared my mind and allowed myself a moment of respite. I'd already spent two months crying and one vomiting, and the entire time after that was devoted to wondering if anything was actually happening or if it had all been a symptom of my menstrual irregularity.

And where were the momma feelings? Even before Ethens and she had Joined, Cinden was all doe eyes and tummy rubs. Where were those? And why was I so different from other women? These feelings, I knew, went beyond the twisted nature of this child's conception.

"Almost settled," the recruit said in a singsong manner. "She's waking faster than they said she would, and how exciting is that?" Someone pressed a cool cloth to my temple, but I couldn't see who.

I tried lifting my arms again. No luck, but I debated whether or not I'd felt the linen sheet slipping against the tip of my finger.

"Good, the Archhealer wants to assess her and ensure her cognition is sound. Says she needs to move and talk to the babe so that it's born unafraid of the world."

They don't know. They have no idea that I command the æther; they'd never allow me to wake if they did. I concentrated on the pitter-pat of that butterfly's wing above my heart, hope rekindling. A tiny spark prickled beneath my ribs. *Come to me, my darling flames. Dance upon my fingertips.*

My bitter laugh came out in a choke.

"Bushels and branches, it sounds like a toad resides on your tongue. Here now." The recruit turned away and then returned with a mug.

I shook my head. No fucking way I'd willingly ingest their poisonous concoctions.

The recruit frowned. "It's just water, Highness. I'd not trick you as we do the kiddos. Getting *them* to take their meds takes all of my cunning and most of my patience... Get it? Patients? Patience?" She winked and... Fuck it, I'd trusted others for less. Just hearing the water slosh from her pitcher blinded me with thirst.

I inclined my chin, and as she pressed the rim to my lips, the chilled liquid unlocked within me a need so powerful my gulps became audible.

"Slow as it goes, Highness. I've not cleaned royal vomit, but I'm sure it smells just as bad as the peasant stuff." She chuckled again as I slowed to sips. "And I did lie, you know, but just a teensy weensy one."

Panic surged, spiking through my immobile body, somehow making it all the more terrifying. I couldn't risk sedation. I was alone, and I'd require all my faculties to get out.

"Just a pinch of salt and a smidge of honey. It will soothe what ails you."
Oh, for fucks sake.
"Sit up," I managed to grit out through sudden exhaustion.
"I'll grab some pillows."

True to her words, the recruit left and then returned with a stack of shiny, silk-covered pillows.

"I'll support your head. Don't try and move on your own; you risk hurting yourself further. Ready and up you go."

Like that harrowing moment in the middle of a fall, my world spun, and my stomach flipped. Though my muscles didn't react to my internal plummet, a blessed rush of feeling returned to my toes—stabbing pins and poking needles.

I bit back a cry of pain.

"It's normal to feel disoriented, Highness." The recruit, still holding me steady, smoothed my hair back and ensured none of it was trapped under my back. "Shew, but you need a bath."

That I didn't doubt.

"H-how long?" The words were coming easier now, thank the Goddess.

"Three weeks since the assassin tried to take the Primus-King's life."

My big toe flexed. *He lived.*

"No, no. You're not going anywhere, you don't have the strength and though we praise Her name for the gift of our bodies, you are as naked as you came into the world. That's not how you want to greet the Others. Lie back, there we go."

"Oth-others?"

She stepped aside and swept an arm around the room.

And then I saw them.

"Your roommates."

It was a trick of tired eyes. It had to be.

Rows of beds lined each side of the long chamber. Some were curtained off, others wide open, revealing the patient within.

In the nearest bed was a gnome—just like Jilly—no taller than a child, mouth agape and breath wheezing from betwixt their lips. Their thin chest fell and rose, but they were not with us in their mind anyhow.

Two beds down, a satyress turned her head toward me, the whites of her eyes glassy and, like Verra, her irises pale lavender. She didn't speak, just watched. Behind her, curled on her side and bound at the wrists, was a young woman with pointed ears and brown skin—white freckles spread out over her shoulders, and she held her rounded stomach like some precious treasure.

Another, whose hands were concealed in quilted bags and whose arms were strapped to her sides, blinked hazel eyes through the tumble of sandy curls that reached her nose.

I had found the Others... I *was* one of the Others.

Merrias!
Grandmother!
Ambrose, hear me. Nether Lord, I call upon you! Leyometh? If you want me, hear me now!

CHAPTER FIFTY-EIGHT

IT. IS. ME.

CATO

*C*ult Mossius, fifth floor. A third of the way to Eira's room. Lamps lowered for evening hours. I cannot fucking see. I loathe this hood. Ambrose
at my left, footsteps timed to my own. Weapons on my person, enough to shear
the souls from a hundred men if they think to stand in my way. Greatest
threat: It is me.

"Do you think I fear you, Lead Healer? Do you think that I give a shit
about your status—that pretty fucking robe you wear?" A masculine voice
carried down the corridor.

The drawn-out, rending sound of silk tearing in two welcomed us to the
patient level of Cult Mossius, Birch Hall.

I tugged on the hood's hem to better assess the situation, but the godsdamned veil shadowed my already dim perception.

"If you do not comply with my demand, I will pull the nails from your
nailbeds. It is I the Primus-King left in charge of his kingdom!"

"It's Arro," Ambrose whispered, the wide sleeve of his vestments momentarily falling into my line of sight.

"Yes. I believe the whole of the Cult is now aware of his presence."

The door to Eira's room stood ajar, revealing nothing of those who
quarreled just beyond—shadows shifted on the opposite wall, voices rose
and fell.

As a purity recruit rushed out and closed the door, four men stood ill
at ease as they bickered. Emberkin Arro, the Archhealer of Gaea, the Lead
Healer, and Scion Amias were plainly at odds. The Lead Healer held his
torn robes together; his face contorted in fury.

Emberkin Arro caught sight of us and snapped me to his side.

I couldn't wait to gut the slaving shit stain. Even if I had to set sail and
track him across the oceans, I would have my satisfaction.

Scion Amias, ruddy cheeks flushed and in a fit, smashed his stylus against a writing board.

"*I* was tasked with looking after Her Highness. As the both of you know, she is in a precarious condition and cannot have just *any* remedies foisted upon her person. Who oversees her care now?"

I fought a stab of fear and took my place at Arro's side. If Scion Amias had been replaced, it meant the Primus-King was moving his people into position.

"I do, by command of the Primus-King himself." The Archhealer, a man whose title was more fearsome than his small stature, faced Amias. "And you will stand down, Scion Healer. The Lady Emryss is to have the best care the Cult can provide. I am the highest-ranking healer within these walls, and for good reason. Do you challenge my ability or just my authority?"

Amias shook his head.

"Neither, Archhealer."

"Then why in God's name are you not healing her, and where the fuck is my Hearthmate?" the Emberkin seethed.

Where is...

I struck.

Blade in hand, I drove it beneath the Archhealer's ribs and forced it up, jamming it into his chest cavity. Blood so dark it seemed black coated my hands in a series of hot glugs. I would play no more games.

A soft rush of air swept past me as the door to Eira's room clicked open—my uncle and I were of one mind.

"What have you done?" the Emberkin yelled. "I command you to—"

I jerked free a second dagger and slammed the steel into the juncture of the Archhealer's neck—his gurgling grated on my nerves.

Before the Archhealer's lifeless form could slump to the floor, Septimus tackled the body and propelled it into the vacant room.

"Guar—" Ambrose strongarmed the Lead Healer into the chamber before the man's shout could carry to the ears of others.

Arro grabbed my shoulders, peering intently into the mask that concealed my face.

"I'll see you flogged and executed. That man was the second-highest authority in these lands."

"You can try."

I ripped the hood away, and Arro pulled steel. The whisper of metal leaving the leather sheath was orgasmic to my ears. I rushed him, driving him into Eira's empty room. Less room to run.

The Baldorvan fell into a bent-knee stance, knife held aloft, the lines of his form a testament to his skill—not a brawler's posture but a warrior's stance.

Assuming his training had been similar to his guards, I became the aggressor—the role I was born to play. In a series of low, sweeping attacks, I deliberately worked to break his elegant foundation, to force him from equilibrium.

"Do you enjoy the cage, Emberkin?"

By now, he knew he was alone in this fight. He'd concealed the faces of his men, denied them their basic humanity, their individual existence, and turned them into tools. I turned his cruelty against him.

Arro's blade shimmered in the flame of the copper lights, a precise and intricate ballet of parries and deflections. He met my aggression with composed strength, not merely blocking but subtly redirecting my momentum, seeking to overbalance me, to create and then expand upon my vulnerabilities.

He could *think* he had the upper hand.

My next lunge, a half step too shallow, a few degrees from true, landed me in front of his viper's strike. I torqued my hips, just as the slash landed, and a familiar sting told me the blade had opened the flesh below my ribs. Sting was good; it meant a laceration and not a puncture. Punctures were very, very bad. The linen stuck to my side as blood trickled down my leg. Ah, yes... He was not enough of a warrior to keep the triumph from his eyes.

Through the tunnel vision of bloodlust, Septimus chuckled.

"You could help him, Uncle!" Ambrose bellowed while struggling to maintain his hold on the wildly thrashing Lead Healer.

"No need, false prince." He laughed again. In my periphery, I made out Septimus lounging against the chamber's threshold. I did not miss that he held the door's handle, ensuring none would enter. "Besides, if Catommandus should die, the path to my enchantress's arms would be free of the detritus that currently blocks my way. Just to be clear, I do not mean you. You pose no threat."

"Who are you? Do you work against the warlord or Primus-King?" Arro growled.

"Yes," I answered plainly.

I feigned a stumbling retreat, drawing Arro forward, allowing him to believe he had gained a decisive advantage. As he pressed, I gave ground, reeling him in by the line of his own anticipation. He grasped at my knife hand in the same instant that my heel bumped a heavy cabinet—his first, fatal, mistake. I pivoted sharply, letting him capture my wrist but simultaneously throwing my body into a punch that drove into his solar plexus. To his credit, he continued his hold on my wrist, but by then the fight was already won. He doubled over, and I dropped low, leveraging my foot into the cabinet's edge. I shot up, ramming my elbow into the same soft spot. He staggered and I capitalized, catching him around the neck and shoving his face into the feathered mattress where my wife should have lain.

"More pressure, Catommandus, end him quickly," Septimus counseled. "I am afraid your lover grows jealous of the attention you lavish on the Baldorvan."

Emberkin Arro thrashed and bucked, his eyes bulging. His struggles weakened as he clawed futilely at my arm. I squeezed until he stood upon the precipice of unconsciousness.

"Listen to me, you bag of filth. You have a single chance to preserve your wretched life."

He did not, could not, answer, but I knew he heard my words.

"You forced a Hearthing with *my* wife."

"And who else's?" Ambrose snapped as he continued struggling with the Lead Healer. "Ugh, hold still!" He smartened up and kicked out the man's knees.

"I am Prince Catommandus of Monwyn and—"

"And I a-am Prince Ambrose Burchard Berra Odel Ricard, second heir to the throne. *He* is but the third."

I closed my eyes, suppressing the impulse to incapacitate my relation.

"You have impregnated *my* woman, the Consort, the highest-ranking female in my kingdom. The disease in her womb—a womb for which I paid a hefty sum—will be deity-born. Are you listening, Emberkin?" I jerked his head back and allowed him a breath before crushing his windpipe again. "Adultery carries the punishment of death, and though she has made a cuck of me, my people will *never* know the blight she has placed upon my fine name. You have two choices. I shove my blade into her belly and carve out the sin you have created, and you return to Baldorva an empty-handed failure." Emberkin Arro made to growl, but I shifted my weight and cut off the sound. "Or you overthrow your warlord, free the enslaved class of Baldorva, and your child receives the honor of bearing my name. Your claim to my wife is void. The Mantle, the contracts, and the ring she wears upon her finger is proof that she is taken."

Emberkin Arro struggled again, fighting my hold.

"That is no bargain," he gritted out.

"The bargain is this—an alliance between Baldorva and Monwyn. We send our soldiers to aid you in your rise to power, and when the child is of age, you will select a Baldorvan for their Hearthing. A single attempt to thwart my will, and I will send you your child's head."

"Why the fuck should I believe you? Why is Emryss even here?"

"Because Scion Greggen, formerly of Baldorva, sold you out." Recognition flittered across the Emberkin's face. "I was aware of your movements before you set sail. And Emryss? She thought her father would save her from the likes of me. She chose wrong. She will *never* escape me."

Though he continued to lurch and twist, it lacked the conviction of his previous attempts.

"Septimus, remove his weapons."

My uncle casually stepped forward, patted the foreigner down, and tossed three blades to the far side of the room.

"Do we have an accord, Emberkin? Swear your oath to me, because I know the *exact* whereabouts of Highness Emryss and I require your skill at arms to retrieve her."

Chapter Fifty-Nine

WHAT KIND OF FUCKERY IS THIS?

Eira

"The Archhealer is held up, no doubt; it happens often to such an important man." The recruit patted the hand of the heavily pregnant person in the bed directly across from mine. The woman smiled tightly and applied pressure to the bottom of her rounded belly. "I know it's scary to start the birthing process early, but because your last two arrived still, we don't want to put you through it again. We grieve with you, Mizandra, the Primus-King most of all."

A host of concoctions, yellow, brown, and blue, sat in straight rows on the bedside table next to her. For the last hour, maybe two, I'd fixated on the largest of the jars, keeping my eyes narrowed, as I pretended to sleep.

Come to me, crisp water, sustainer of life. I looked inward, begging that flutter of æther to bloom within my chest. There was nothing more than that gentle pulse. *Please.* I struggled but only managed to lift the tip of my index finger, imagining the path the æther would take before it shot whatever liquid the jar contained straight through the Archhealer's temple. With him down and unable to sound the alarm, my hope was to cause a rukus so chaotic that no one would dare intercept me as I fled. I didn't want to scorch the victims in this room. I didn't particularly want the Archhealer to die—passed out would suit me fine, but above all and beyond anything, I didn't want to stay here.

I turned back to finger raises, as the liquid didn't feel the need to rise despite my desperate internal pleas. The exertion left me tired. I had determined I would need to buy myself a single minute, maybe a tiny bit more, as, though I couldn't see it, I did hear the faint and occasional slide of the lift door. Timing the seconds between the last slide and the moment a purity recruit came bounding in with their bucket and mop, it amounted to approximately a minute and fourteen seconds.

"You are awake! Ladies, elves and Others, allow me to formally introduce you to Her Highness Emryss, first daughter of the Primus-King." All in the room looked over to me, barring, of course, those unconscious few who made no movements save the rise and fall of their chests. "The lost daughter has returned to us, *and* she bears fruit!" The recruit fluttered around with the energy of Troth Richelle after drinking a coffee bean drink. She adjusted pillows, rubbed the legs of a lethargic gnome, and held a pan under the chin of the satyress who'd become sick. "I saw the Primus-King's face from afar when I received the debrief upstairs. He positively glowed while looking down on his daughter. A true miracle after the attempt on his life. Can you just imagine?"

"The Goddess's blessing." The woman across from me steepled her fingers and bowed her head. "May your time here allow the life within to flourish."

I tried to smile, to play the part of blessed daughter, but only a single side of my mouth pulled into place.

"The Archhealer will be here in a jiff, I've been informed. Let's get you all looking your best." The recruit produced a comb and a container of some sort.

I had to get out.

I narrowed my gaze again, tilting my index finger. *Come to me, water. I've need of you. We've need of you.*

The tiniest bubble floated from the bottom of the glass to the top. It was something, but needed it to become a much *bigger* something.

The recruit came to my side and held a mug to my lips. I sipped the honeyed water, hoping it would inspire some energy.

I heard the sound of the lift as it opened and closed.

Water. Hear me. Listen to your friend!

The Archhealer entered the room... and the liquid did nothing more than sputter up two tiny bubbles.

Calm, remain calm.

The man, outfitted in healer's robes, bore a tray laden with herbs and tinctures. From the back, the Archhealer looked different from what I had presumed he might, going off his daughter, Troth Chentel. She must have taken after her mother, for her skin tone was a glowing taupe brown, and this man was as pale as Septimus.

He walked to the back of the long room, and I tried summoning the water once and then again, failing both times. *Dammit!*

"Aunties, we prayed for your health and wellness at Temple," the Archhealer said while laying his hands on prone person's abdomen. The recruit followed with a parchment and stylus. "The baby's heartbeat remains steady." His brow creased as he tapped a finger to the recruit's forearm. "You will need to manipulate their limbs more to encourage blood flow, but be careful. The conjurer became combative when last she woke. Continue mild sedation."

He adjusted the brooch that held back his voluminous sleeves and then moved to the gnome. She shrank back into her pillows, fear plain on her face. The healer gestured to the recruit to move forward. The gnome relaxed as the woman went about combing and then braiding back the patient's hair. She had deep-maroon roots, just like Jilly.

"May I?" The Archhealer asked. The gnome nodded, and his hands went to her stomach. He cocked his head as if hearing something nobody else could. "Dani," he patted the gnome's hand, "the babe lives, but I am increasingly concerned about its health. In the next day or two, we should discuss the need to bring forth the pregnancy. We do not want the child to grow so large that it may not easily pass. You are much smaller than a human."

The recruit, knowingly, pushed a linen into the gnome's hand, just as tears cascaded over the tiny woman's ruddy cheeks.

"But healer, if the baby arrives healthy, I-I get to go home. The Primus said he'd take me home."

The healer nodded and took Dani's hands, placing them on her stomach.

"Pray to the divine. Every day miracles happen within these walls."

The recruit leaned in and hugged the gnome's shoulders. Dani clung to her, closing her eyes and slowly drawing breath through slightly parted lips.

"Thank you, Recruit Lymmia, you give the best hugs."

The Archhealer moved to his next patient, another comatose human; my guess was another conjurer. With his back to me, I turned once more to the jar across the room.

Please water, please!

Two bubbles and a third gurgled close to its rim, but more importantly, the fingers of my right hand twitched—all of them. *Yes!*

Come to me. Hear me.

"And here," the healer waved as he moved my way, "we have my sister."

"What?" I hacked out, followed by a short bout of coughs, sputtering on my own spittle.

The healer faced me, tears gathering in his eyes, the same teal color as was passed on to me. Lymmia patted me on the back and then fed me slow sips of water.

"I never"— the healer choked up —"we always clung to hope." He lowered his voice. "May I?"

My brother. Another one, and seemingly just as kind and caring as the last two had been.

A swell of emotion burst through my chest, one that continually confounded me. I had a family, Ma and Pa and Nan. Why was I so Goddess-damned overwhelmed each time I met somebody who shared the same tainted blood?

"Yes." I nodded. Holy Goddess above, but I nodded. Like dancing in Merritt's embrace, I wanted to know him better, to find out what kind of person he was.

He took my hand, resting his fingers on my wrist.

"Father mentioned to me that your purity belongs to the Prince of Monwyn and that he is your Lifemate. Plural marriage in Gaea is less common for women, but seeing as you are royal, Father will make an exception for the Emberkin." His eyes softened, lids lowering as if to shield them. "But... I must tell you, I do not think, given the timeline, that Emberkin Arro has fathered this child, which may complicate our dealings with Baldorva. That, however, is a conversation for another day." The healer waved over Lymmia, who turned down the sheets, exposing me to the hips. She then hurried to the other side of the room when the satyress became sick.

When his hands rested on my stomach, I could feel their softness. *I can feel.* His lashes feathered shut, and I fixed my sights on the mug next to my bed. An angry swirl of bubbles frothed at its top.

"Emryss, the babe within cannot live—"

"What?" A fist clenched around my heart.

"—beyond the womb, but you are very close to that point, and my niece or nephew has the heartbeat of a hummingbird. Can you feel them yet?"

"No." I shook my head. "Maybe? I thought the flutters were anxiety, but I just..."

"Pregnancy can be scary, yes?"

I glanced up, caught in the gentleness of his regard.

"I'm terrified." *For a hundred reasons. A thousand. A million.*

"Right now, Emryss, you're safe. The Emberkin won't find you here. Your sole job is to get stronger and grow this little life. Tomorrow, I'd like for you to speak to a priestess about the attempt you made on your person. That is not something we can dismiss."

How could such warmth live in those who served something so vile? And how could my heart hold both the desperate wish to be free of this child and the terror of losing it?

"What's your name?" I asked, needing to free my mind from its current direction.

"I am called Hollis."

"Are they…" I stalled, summoning the courage to hear the confirmation of what I already knew to be true. "Are they all bearing our, our father's children?" Slowly, I looked around, taking them in as a means to remember how to move my neck. I was stiff all over, but I managed an inch to the left and a little more to the right.

"They do, but with you home, this ends." He rotated his wrist in circles and stretched his fingers. "Years of trials, some wonderful, others ending in sorrow, and we could never create another like you."

"Like me?" I knew precisely what he meant, but I wanted to know more, wanted to continue building a body of evidence, so that, should I need to take more lives beyond that of the Primus-King, I could reconcile my actions.

Kind fingers rested on the back of my forearm.

"Emryss, you have within you the means to free the world of its human pains." He dabbed at the corners of his eyes. "Why couldn't all of us brothers and sisters have been born the same? I have prayed and prayed for the Goddess to bestow upon me the same blessing. Children will no longer suffer because of you."

My child will suffer. The thought made me ill. A baby with Cato's curls, purged and bled. Their tiny heels pricked until they grew old enough to have the vein in their elbow nicked open.

Grandmother Merrias, take this child from my body and whisk them away—leave me in this room. If this is to be their future, let me bear the burden in their stead.

"And the Others? Will they be sent home? What about their babies?" I asked, while steadily contracting the muscles in my calves and then thighs.

"The ones who survive are adopted into Gaean society and raised in the most loving of homes. We have placed three in the last decade, a gnome, and if you can believe it, two half-fae. You have never seen more beautiful offspring in your life."

Across from me, I heard sniffles.

"What if they want to raise their children?" I shouldn't have asked the question. Hollis's lips parted briefly and then settled into a grim smile. He patted my hand again.

"I am looking forward to getting to know you." His eyes were filled with genuine curiosity. "I cannot wait to hear of your Joining with the Monwyn. I'm a sap for binding ceremonies. Now, I must move on, but we have plenty of time to catch up. I'll bring breakfast in the morning, and if I can sneak him past Lymmia, my new kitten."

Hollis smiled broadly and then rechecked the closures at his sleeves.

"Mizandra, it's time to meet your little one." He walked across the room and tinkered with a few tools. He picked up the glass of pink liquid.

"Forgive me," I whispered.

"Pardon?" He looked back.

"To me!" I screamed as the æther burst free from my chest, traveled the length of my arm, and pierced my brother's temple. I threw my legs over the bed's edge and vomited as he fell to the ground, blood spilling from both sides of his head.

Chapter Sixty

THERE ARE THINGS NOT MEANT FOR A GROWN HUSBAND'S EYES

AMBROSE

"If you wish to remain alive, Lead Healer, you will convince the lift worker to lower us to the floor above the mortuary. Do not deny its existence," I warned the man who stood between Septimus and myself. "Or I will not deny myself the pleasure of slitting your stomach from hip to hip."

We marched the length of the corridor, Emberkin Arro and a cloaked Cato at our backs.

"Repeat the story, Lead Healer," I said, as much to reassure myself of our plan as I was to catch him in some fallacy. I was not teasing the man. My fingers itched to give him the same treatment I'd given the last troll I'd battled—blunt force injuries to the head.

The Lead Healer yanked free of my hold on his bicep.

"The false Father would trespass to pray over her body; the Baldorvan wants to shatter protocol to play husband."

Without slowing, I sank my fingers into his windpipe, walking him backward until, with a sickening thud, his head met the wall.

"Ambrose! Hold," Cato hissed.

"Shut up, you needlessly draw attention," Septimus said while attempting to pry my arm back.

"Given the taut skin stretching across your flawless old man's face, the haze of age that lingers in your youthful eyes, I presume you to be a recipient of my mother-in-law's blood or, Goddess save you if I find out, my wife's." Red crescents outlined my nails where they punctured his skin. "Unlike his Highness Catommandus, I do not endlessly ponder the future. I simply act. If you so much as flare your poreless nostril or give any outward indication that we are not on sanctioned business, I will waste every drop of your precious blood in the Gaean sewers."

And I would.

His wide-set amber eyes showed the proper amount of fear. Satisfied, I straightened his once-torn robe. I had only moments ago rolled and ironed the ripped edges with the heated tip of some flat healer's tool.

We approached the lift, and I mentally prepared for the eventuality of taking the worker's life if he gave any indication of being ill at ease.

"Level?"

"Root ward," the Lead Healer said quite casually.

The liftman hesitated, and I dropped my hand to my weapon.

"Signature."

"I do not require a signature," the Lead Healer sneered.

The lift attendant eyeballed our contingent.

"You don't, but they do. Signature?" the man repeated.

Cato stepped forward, producing a parchment from the bag at his hip. He flashed it above the Lead Healer's shoulder.

"Load up." The door slid open, and I breathed a loud sigh of relief as the contraption sealed us in.

The lift lurched and began its descent.

"How many workers should we expect on this level?" I asked. "Septimus, you dull-witted turnip, quit petting the man." My uncle stood barely an inch away, caging the Lead Healer into the corner, touching him on various parts of his body. "The fuck are you about?"

"Determining the plumpness of his veins. When we bleed him, you and I, we will slit the smallest to prevent a quick passing; they can linger for hours that way."

"Hmmm, interesting." I nodded. "Oh. My. Gods. Are we bonding?"

Cato shot his hand up and snapped his fist closed. *Silence.*

"Lead Healer, answer the question. How many workers?" Cato asked.

"Depending on the shift, between four and seven."

"Guards?"

"Seventeen.

The lift bobbed and then came to a halt.

"Goodness!" I grasped my temples to keep from pitching forward. "The sound is—*Wifey?*"

Ambrose! "Ambrose!" Eira screamed my name, her voice picking up through both connection and air.

We spilled from the lift and ran toward her cry. The corridor stretched ahead as it had the other levels, this one unnervingly empty.

We're coming, Eira. How many guards?

Fifteen!

"There are fifteen guards ahead."

"How the fuck do you know?" Arro shouted above our footfalls.

"He knows," Cato growled, daggers already in hand. "Maintain focus."

At the corridor's end, the panicked shrieks of a dozen or more voices amplified my already heightened fears. Drawn by the discord, we dashed to the left but came up short.

The Cult Mossius soldiers stood with their backs to us, their polished weapons gleaming as brightly as their bronze plate armor.

And there was my wife behind them, naked, crumpled in a heap on the floor, a stream of fuchsia liquid circling her fingers.

They surrounded her, a unit of grown fucking men standing against a single, obviously terrified woman.

"Drop it, conjurer!"

"Corral her into the confinement room. Hawthorne, get a message to the Archhealer and prince. She's killed three already."

My vision blurred, their voices muffled by the rush of blood screaming in my ears. A thin netting of frost crept across the floor.

Are you hurt? Report.

Just weak. Ambrose, head right. Get to the adjoining chamber. Her words were a blow to my still brittle pride.

I am not weak. I'm coming for you. The moment there is an opening, prepare for me to—

It's not that, Ambrose. Listen, we have to free them, please!

Emberkin Arro surged into the room, dagger drawn and biting. A guard turned at the surprise intrusion, barely registering the Emberkin before a strike sent him sprawling. A streak of crimson splattered across the immaculate flagstone floors.

Septimus charged, heading straight into the mass of men.

Who?

To the right! The urgency in her voice pushed me to obey.

I sprinted to the far wall and pressed my spine to its glaringly white surface. Slow, measured steps carried me toward the rightmost corner until only my forehead and the bare edge of my nose breached the wall's protective barrier—just enough to monitor for movement in the adjoining chamber. When nothing came hurling my way, I leaned out, sweeping my gaze over—*gods above.*

I stared into a room of bedbound creatures. Two tiny humans with tear-stained faces huddled and shook in a corner. Several lay prone, feet bound, hands entombed and strapped. And then—*No*—my gaze snagged on sharp horns, just like the ones my little Verra's would grow one day. The satyress's belly stood out, heavily distended on her thin frame.

We have to get them out. All the babies are his.

My eyes fell on the body of a dead healer, blood drying around the exit wound on his temple.

Ambrose, help them.

I warred with myself—weighing the reality of freeing them—eyes flitting to a grimacing mother-to-be who held her stomach protectively.

Eira, the seconds are already slipping away. I am sorry.

"Spread out! Keep their numbers fragmented!" Septimus barked, drawing my attention back to the fray.

Cato charged, a vision of calculated brutality. Wood cracked as he drove a heel into the shield of a guard who'd dipped his spear too low. The man tipped backward, colliding with another. Cato grasped the spear behind its point and ripped the shaft from his opponent's hands, using the man's momentum to his advantage. Cato spun the spear, and the instant the point was in line he rammed it into the strip of flesh between breastplate and belt, driving it so deeply he caught the man next in line too.

Already, the air stank of blood and piss.

Ambrose! Behind you!

I swung, my mace thudding, crushing bone in a back-handed sweep. I parried the swing of the next guard as he moved in. The point of his blade caught my shoulder, but the mace's haft took the brunt of the blade's bite. The guard shifted his footing, and a barrage of his strikes began.

Get away. Crawl, Eira, go!

A spaulder clattered to the floor, my mace taking it clean off its harness. My next blow glanced, and I prepared for his riposte.

They have done nothing to deserve this.

The tip of a spear shot over the guard's shoulder, and for a moment I feared I was outmatched. Then the tip raked the side of his neck, and he dropped to the floor.

"Catommandus, there are more. They are all with child, Others and humans alike. I am not sure our wife will leave without freeing them."

"She doesn't have a choice—Ambrose, duck!"

I dropped as Cato thrust his spear above my head—just as an axeman hammered his weapon down into what would have been my skull. A crack and a sickening snap drew my eyes up. The spear was shattered, and Cato's forearm hung at an unnatural angle.

My lover did not slow.

He lunged, driving a jagged shard of wood into the eye slit of the soldier's helm before plunging it into the soft, unarmored flesh of his underarm. I saw Septimus dodge a wild swing before stabbing and dispatching his assailant, and Emberkin Arro was holding his own against the remaining foes.

"Ambrose," Cato clutched my collar with one fist, while his other arm hung limp. "Get Eira, wrap her in a bedsheet. Fix your hair. It's standing straight on end, and we mustn't rouse the liftman's suspicions. Septimus and I will change into the costumes of the recruits, and we will—"

A piercing scream tore through the unnerving quiet. It was Eira. The sound jolted through my veins.

"Wife?" I looked around, shoving Cato aside, looking to the spot where she had lain. "How the fuck? Where are you?" *Speak to me! Report!* "Report!" I bellowed.

"Eira!" Cato flung around and saw for himself that she was gone. "Our inattention has been used against us." He looped a finger in the air and sliced two fingers across his brow, signaling for me to search the perimeters while he took the interior.

I ran, dipping my head in and out of the chambers that lined the hall.

Where are you, my heart? Speak to me.

On the other side of the connection, the sounds of choking and bitten-off words raised the fine hairs on my neck. The flames of both lamp and copper light flickered as I passed, sputtering out in the chill wind that seemed to propel me forward.

"AMBROSE!"

My heart stopped mid-beat. Cato—never had a sound so desperate ripped from his chest.

I pivoted, wheeling about, following the dying echoes of my name until...

Eira lay on the floor, hands bloodied, wrists bruised and torn as if her skin had been clawed away. Her eyes swelled, one already beginning to blacken. Protruding from the crease of her arm, a glass tube leaked a yellow substance. A funnel stuck out from her throat, and a handful of empty vials scattered about, rolling across the floor.

Cato straddled the Lead Healer, one-armed-hacking the man's head from his body. Blood splattered his ochre veil as he drove his blade over and over, until—

Black-black Bear.

I rushed to Eira's side and fell apart.

"I'm here, wife—We are here."

I sobbed, not knowing how to touch her, terrified to further hurt the one person who loved me most in this world. I willed my hands to move, to pull the tube from her throat, but all I managed was to tremble.

"Ambrose. I have you." Cato kneeled at my side. "Tip her chin and hold her neck steady." He took my hands in his, placing them on either side of our wife's throat. I nodded. "When I take this out, turn her. Ready? And go."

The stiff canvas tubing slid out, making an abrading sound as it issued forth; I gagged. It was much longer than I could have imagined, coated in mucous and tinged with bile.

"What did he give her? What did he do?"

Cato did not answer.

"I cannot carry her to the wagon." He gestured to his arm. "We must wrap her."

I swept my thumb across Eira's palm and brought her blood to Cato's lips; he accepted it without issue. His pain must have been unbearable.

"Come," Cato said.

I hauled my wife's perfection into my arms, and I followed him into the room where the Others were housed. Septimus and Emberkin Arro soon joined.

"What experiment is this?" Arro asked.

I lay Eira on an empty bed. She did her best to smile, but her eyes, I could tell, drifted in and out of focus.

"He stifled her ability. She cannot conjure, nor can she fight when unconscious," a gnome informed us.

I pulled the sheets around my wife's body, trembling as I neared the point where I knew I must cover her face.

Arro stepped to the opposite side of the bed and attempted to wrap the rest of her, but with a firm look, I cautioned him back.

I tugged the sheet across her head and tucked it securely around her neck and shoulders.

"We can take three of you." Cato stood in the center of the room, addressing the Others as he slipped from his robes and into the recruit's uniform. Septimus did the same. "We cannot treat your bodies gently, however. You will be shrouded in linen and at the end of our journey, loaded into a wagon bound for the pyres. We cannot draw attention by treating you as if you were alive."

"Me. Please." A small woman dropped her feet to the side of her bed and hopped to the floor.

Cato jerked his head over his shoulder. "Emberkin, take this woman."

A lovely creature, with delicate white freckles, drew our attention.

"I am too large to carry, but cut my bindings. I am a fae conjurer and can evanesce through the walls if my limbs are free. Take Amberline. They're unconscious and will look the part, but please be gentle if you can. Elves do not often carry children, and they are beyond excited to have made it this far."

"Septimus, they are your burden. You, do you seek freedom?" Cato asked, looking at another, no larger than my thigh. She nodded but did not look him in the eyes. "Can you cling to my arm if we wrap you about the limb?"

"Yes." The woman bowed her head. "If I cannot, slit my throat and leave me behind."

Cato, stronger of will than I could ever be, lowered his chin and his injured arm in acceptance.

"I am sorry we-we cannot manage you all," Cato stammered as the gnome or brownie or imp wrapped herself around his mangled arm. He hailed me over, and I fashioned a sheet around her body, making it appear as if he just held her across his chest.

"Go with the Goddess," the tallest woman, who looked like she'd give birth any moment, said, her voice steady.

And then we were in the lift and walking through the hall to Cult Mossius's entrance. Eira seemed to become more lifeless, more limp, the closer we got to freedom.

Seeing Eira wrapped in white made me ill—the Monwyn color of mourning carried with it profound grief. I wanted to smell her, see her, hear her. Instead, I prayed to the Goddess that I would meet Merrias before my wife. I could not stand this sight ever again.

We are almost free, Eira. Your momma is simply beside herself, and I cannot wait to see her face when we bring you through the tunnel. It's an underground chamber that leads to the house of Merchant Rizellen. She is thrilled to speak with you after so many years. She said—

I-I love you.

I breathed in, relief washing over me, just as we walked into the cloak of night.

And I you.

The ever-present rows of soldiers lined both sides of the pathway that led to the gates.

Eira, try not to make noise; prepare for a jarring toss. Remain slack. Breathe on impact, and do not stiffen.

Okay. The voice in my head was so soft, so faint.

"These all for the pyres?" Ulltan said from his perch on his wagon. "What's going on in that Cult, eh?"

Pa?

Yes, wifling. He is here. Be at ease.

"They are," Emberkin Arro replied, swaggering forward with all the confidence and authority of the man in charge of the entire kingdom. "The Archhealer suspects plague—the Lead Healer concurs."

Inwardly, I applauded the piece of filth for his quick wit.

A handful of soldiers shrank back. Several dropped their square-shouldered stances. Had they been men of Monwyn, Cato would have dressed them down so severely that they would have begged for contagion to take them.

The whispers began.

"Plague? Are you sure?"

"Did he say plague?"

"The last plague took nearly two thousand."

After tossing in his charge, Septimus climbed into the back of the wagon and held his arms out. Cato and Arro heaved their loads, and Septimus dropped them without a flicker of remorse.

"Father Regulus, I approve your request to go along and perform your rituals. I am off to the garrison to alert my units to the possibility of a fast-spreading," he looked to the wagon, "and decidedly fatal illness."

I heaved Eira's body, and by the Goddess, when Septimus caught her and tossed her atop the other bodies, I nearly lost my sanity.

I am so proud of you, Eira. It's almost over.

Ambrose?

Arro came to my side and took my arm. Though it would look to anyone like the man was aiding me into the seat by Ulltan, his fingers bit into my skin. I dipped my head while bending to pick up the layers of my priest's raiment.

Am-Ambrose?

"Tomorrow, find us at the estates of Merchant Rizellen, an hour due west of here."

He shook his head.

"Tonight. The wee hours at the latest." The Emberkin's tone held a note of finality that I knew would not be challenged.

I bowed my chin in acquiescence. Larm and Evandr patrolled the roads from Rizellen's property to the palace—they would sound the alarm if he thought to bring his units. And, if he did, we would carry out Cato's "the giants done ate all them foreigners" plan.

"Fine."

The Emberkin held my gaze, his threat silent.

Ambr—

Just a moment.

"Praise Her!" I walloped the Emberkin so hard he staggered back, releasing me.

Yes, my heart-snatching harpy?

I'm... I'm contracting.

BECAUSE A PERSON YOU DON'T KNOW IS STILL AN IMPORTANT ONE

Eira

The pain in my lower back intensified, but I dared not move a muscle. Beneath me, three bodies lay as dead, though I could hear the slight wheeze of one of the women as she attempted to pull in slow, shallow breaths.

"Let us be off, driver. If plague has its sights on Mynder, the Goddess's work must proceed expeditiously. The bodies must be burned and their souls sent to the Cradle," I heard Ambrose say to my father.

Hold tight. I am sure this is just a matter of physiology. Just your body responding t-to our son's growth.

"Tck, tck," Pa clicked his tongue, and the donkeys brayed as the wagon lurched and started to roll.

I couldn't muster tears. Not yet. They'd give us away.

The Lead. Drugged me. Said one of us would remain. Couldn't fight him. Too weak. I hurt.

The æther sat heavy in my chest. It was present; I could detect it, but whatever he'd forced into me had rendered my limbs near useless, though my mind felt somewhat clear.

"Ulltan, can you increase our pace?" Ambrose whispered from above. Our wheel hit a rock, and the jarring motion sent pain searing through my hip. "She requires her mother's skills."

Like a hand constricting around my womb, a distinct pressure tightened above my pubic bone. It was sharp, then dull, then sharp again, coming at faster and faster intervals. It had begun while lying on the floor and had increased in intensity as we rode the lift.

"Hold tight, minnow. Yer Pa is here, as are yer menfolk. We won't let nuthin' happen to our girl."

All will be well. Early pains are normal. Your momma can assess you when we arrive, and then I will run you a bath and pamper that beautiful body. All will be like it should have been all along.

I counted the clip-clop of the donkey's hooves on the cobblestones, focusing on the noise.

"Open the gates, plague abounds!" my pa yelled. "I smell the fester."

"Open the gates!" A guard yelled back. "Open 'em fast, Trevvon!"

Metal hinges engaged, the creaking sounds obliterating my focus on the hoof falls.

"Which way are you headed, Father, eastern or westerly? The captain can send men ahead to clear a path."

"Nay, my good son, cover your faces and hold back, lest the Primus-King's armies be brought low when they are needed most. Go with the Goddess."

"To you the same, Father." Minutes of silence passed as the gates continued their slow creak. "Soldiers, fall back! Wrest the towels from your packs and tie them about your noses."

My pains amplified.

Each peak was a mountain to climb, each valley a brief, deceptive reprieve before the next ascent. It was deeper than a menstrual cramp, and I felt it reaching into my back and beyond. I bit my tongue, stifling the moan that would betray us. The taste of copper mingled with the scent of iron as a wet warmth bloomed between my thighs. Weak though I was, I forced my knees together. Dead bodies don't bleed.

"Cat," Ambrose said softly, "the moment we clear the city, unwrap her; she's experiencing discom—"

"CONJURER! DRAW WEAPONS! WE ARE UNDER SIEGE!"

My pulse skipped.

We'd been found out.

"Yah! Yah, beasties!" Pa roared.

I drew from the bodies beneath me, pulling upon their energy and making it my own as I forced my crossed arms apart and battled the linen covering my face.

"No, Eira! Stop," Cato pleaded, dropping to his knees from his seat on the cart's edge. He lowered my body off the mound of Others. "We have not been exposed."

Shroud slightly parting, I saw who had.

Naked, clutching her rounded belly, and her eyes held wide, the fae conjurer from below had evanesced through the cult's wall. Her silver hair caught the glow of the moon, and her freckles sparkled like diamonds against her shadow-hued skin.

"Run it through the heart! You have to stab them through the heart!" a guard shouted.

I called to the æther, breathing through the pain in my abdomen and—a hand pressed to the middle of my chest, hindering its swell.

"Enchantress, her end cannot be prevented." Septimus's eyes were as fearful as the conjurer's as he struggled to bring the shroud back over my face. "Do not tax yourself. Blood pools at your thighs." He ever so gently rested his hand on my stomach.

My abdomen tensed hard, entirely out of my control.

"Save... save her," I slurred as my pains increased.

"Archers! Take aim!"

"Cato," I pleaded. "Don't let her die. She's—oh, gods." I silenced as the deepest pressure yet stole my words. Grabbing fistfuls of the shroud, I bared down as a wave of burning tension pulsed through my thighs. This was too fast. There was no natural way that the urge to push should be upon me. I needed to squat, or to get on my knees, but the shroud bound my legs. A low stretch and then burning fire caused my stomach to clench and vomit to burn a path up my throat and out my mouth and nose. The refuse smelled of herbs and pungent medicinals.

"My love?" Cato smoothed the hair back from my face, his fingers cool where they slicked through the film of sweat on my skin. He looked me over, his hands quickly assessing me for injury.

"P-please, Cato. Save her."

"Eira." He placed his hand on my stomach, opposite Septimus's. Though his expression remained one of utter calm, his eyes spoke of great concern. He set his jaw and then looked away. "Ulltan, increase your speed."

"Pa!" I summoned all the energy within me and cried out. "Save, save her. Please!" I pushed myself up to sitting, Septimus and Cato at my sides. "She's innocent."

Pa glanced over his shoulder. His face faltered—shock flickering over his features—before his eyes sharpened.

The telling sound of sabatons on stone alerted us to the presence of additional soldiers.

I called to the æther.

"Archers, fire!"

I screamed as the arrows loosed. A powerful contraction wracked my body, cutting off the æthers' flow.

"TO ME!" My father leapt to his feet and threw back the cape he wore.

I'd never heard him call the æther out loud, had never witnessed him at the zenith of his ability. From where the water came, I had no idea, but beads of moisture appeared, suspended in the air around him, swelling and then constricting, breathing in time with their wielder's lungs. Ambrose lunged for the reins still wrapped in Pa's hand. Upon contact, the floating water froze, turning white as it iced over.

Acting as if by nature, I summoned my æther, drew it from the bottoms of my feet, from the little life within me, from Septimus, and from the individual blades of grass on the ground. I poured the energy into my father, the connection between us a visible haze of gold. Like flames upon an oil slick, black fire danced across his palms, arcs bolting between his splayed fingertips.

"Gooooo!" Pa unleashed himself with a physical shove to the air. A blinding flash of light erupted, searing my eyelids.

The wagon shuddered violently, not from a divot in the road, but from a concussive blast that rattled my teeth and sent a fresh wave of agony through my lower back.

Pa stepped over me and the other bodies and stood at the wagon's rear, his face contorted as he wielded the sleet and sent it soaring, shredding through the ranks of men. Shouts followed—screams of fear, the clang of weapons, and the panicked whinny of horses. The guards, who moments before had been calling for a conjurer's death, now cried out in confusion. The æther pulsed around them in a chaotic blizzard that froze their bodies to ice before they crumbled into a pile of shimmering dust.

My skin prickled, but still I—this endless vessel of æther—infused my pa with all that I was.

Cato's face appeared before mine; he held my cheek. "You gave me a home. Make sure our child has one just as warm."

His lips brushed mine, and then he dove from the cart, running toward the conjurer.

"Cato!" I wailed.

An arrow buried itself in his shoulder, and another in his back.

But still he ran.

"No!" My screams tore at my throat. "Please, gods!"

The wagon lurched again, but this time it came to a trembling halt. I heard the distinct *thump-thump-thump* of bodies hitting the ground, then the sickening *crack* of wood splintering.

Flowing robes, like the twisting body of a wraith, sailed over my head. Ambrose leapt from the wagon, mace in hand.

"Don't take them!" I sobbed.

Below me, the bodies of the others stirred, no longer able to maintain the ruse.

"Septimus, the reins. Put the wagon into motion," Pa yelled above the cutting sound of the swirls of ice slicing through the air.

Scores of Gaean soldiers poured into the courtyard. Snow fell around us and covered the ground. My father took down the charging men three at a time, cleaving them with his blades of shade and ice.

Cato reached the conjurer and lifted her from her knees. He shielded her body as they ran toward the wagon.

"No!" Another arrow hit him, striking him through the forearm and embedding itself in the conjurer's bicep.

Ambrose ran to her other side and shoved his shoulder beneath her underarm, supporting her when she would have fallen. Together, my husbands bore her weight, and together they dodged and ducked.

I slid my hand between my thighs as the pressure in my pelvis offered no reprieve. I could feel the child's head, so low now, so close to entering this disaster of a world. And I knew that they were too small.

The wagon pitched and sprung to life.

"Please, please," I chanted in time to the frantic thud of Ambrose and Cato's feet as they hit the ground. Despite their efforts, soldiers closed in on them.

"Pa... Pa. They're dead. They are going to die."

Pa looked over his shoulder. "No, minnow, they shan't."

He closed his eyes, bent at the knees, and then lifted his arms in the air as if he alone could lift the burdens from the world. His arms shook, and his face mottled red, but snow, ash, and ice rose at his will. Pa rotated his arm—slow at first, then faster, until like a living thing, a cold vortex howled around my husbands, picking up speed as it spun—a shield of snow.

Soldiers screamed as their bodies split in two. Others ran in the opposite direction, only to be sucked back into the frozen wind.

From where they stood encompassed in the funnel, Cato, Ambrose, and the conjurer looked about in awe.

"Run!" I shouted.

Cato struck out first, pulling the other two along, and with Pa's protection, Ambrose jumped onto the back of the slow-moving wagon and pulled the conjurer up behind him. Cato struggled with his mangled arm.

On my side, I pulled myself forward, clawing at the wood until I could reach him. Ambrose got there first, yanking him into the wagon by the seat of his pants. My men fell around me.

"Oh, gods." My pain intensified. "We're safe, safe," I panted. "All safe. Safe."

"Ye are, tiny fish, hold on to yer men now. Septimus, go, man, and I will hold them—"

The bolt punched through his browbone, throwing his head back.

Pa!

My mind screamed his name, but no sound escaped my lips. My head spun—a sudden, catastrophic shift in my reality.

"Noooooo! Noooooooooo!"

As his body fell, a dead weight in the wagon, the final, relentless push of my own body brought forth a life.

A hot, slick weight rested at the juncture of my legs, unmoving. Born into a world of violence, an arrival amidst the screams of battle, this frail human lay still. I could not move, could not cry out, could not truly register its presence beyond the abrupt, profound emptiness in my heart.

"Cato, roll the body out. Lessen the wagon's load." Septimus shouted from the seat.

Ambrose blocked my view and then scooped the baby into his arms.

It was a girl, and she fit perfectly in the curve of his hand.

Flipping her onto her stomach, he patted and rubbed her tiny purple body, just as I heard the sound of my father hitting the hard ground.

The team picked up speed, the cart shaking on its axles.

Somewhere through the blur of shock, I saw Emberkin Arro, mounted on horseback, wave off the flow of soldiers, issuing orders to bolster the palace's units to prevent the next conjurer's attack.

The wagon thundered ahead as Cato sat behind me and pulled me into his arms. I leaned against him, my gaze drifting skyward. How pretty the constellations were—there was Cynder, the multi-headed dog, and the warrior bear Thoramika.

"Close your eyes, love. Take my strength. Take my breath if you need it."

In the dark, a thin but shrill cry sounded.

CHAPTER SIXTY-TWO

LITERALLY NOT AS BAD AS A SHOVEL TO THE TOOTSIE

CATO

Four lights flickering in the distance—a half mile, if not more. Winds: rough, blowing from the west. Rain comes. Safe house, another ten minutes. Weapons: No idea. Greatest threat in the vicinity: I don't care.

The wagon slowed, rambling its way to a standstill.

Vonnie and Rizellen came charging from the manor's front door. We'd had no time to bring Eira through the tunnels. The copper light network burned bright, and I gave not a single fuck as to what neighbor might see us. They could shout our arrival to the Primus-King himself, and I'd drive my blade through their face and his. Eira had been through too much, and I was beside myself at her silence.

"Daughter mine!" Vonnie cried as a shawl flew from her shoulders and landed in the dirt, entirely disregarded. Gotwig trailed the women. In the flicker of lamplight, I made out the steel in Vonnie's expression. She did not cry when she assessed the wagon's passengers; she simply marched into action. "Rizellen. Hot water, linens, a chair, sutures, and shears. Sid," she held my arm at the wrist, "Catommandus's arm is bad off. Eira's blood heals the skin, but the bone and tendons are a mess. Son? Son, do you hear me?"

It took me a moment to realize she spoke to me. I cradled Eira's head against my chest, my only thought her well-being.

"Do what you must. I'll not leave her side."

Sturdy fingers gripped my chin and tugged. Green eyes glared into mine.

"Absolutely not. You'll not add to her trauma. Has the afterbirth come away?"

My lips parted as she jostled me. I stared at her, unknowing.

Ambrose stooped and then knelt beside me.

"It has. I've wrapped it so you could check it for completeness. Will our daughter live?"

Ambrose thrust his arms forward and held the tiny priest-robe-wrapped body of… of… our daughter… into the stunned face of her grandmother.

"The babe lives?" Vonnie breathed, her hands coming to settle over her mouth. Ambrose flipped the shiny red fabric, exposing the child, and I caught my breath. How could something so small be so perfectly formed? How could her fingers be so tiny? Their full length that of my thumbnail.

Eira's mother clutched the baby and held her to the light. My hand shot out, fearful she would drop the girl, but Ambrose caught my arm and laced his fingers through mine, settling our hands between us.

"It's alright, Cat. She's got her. You, on the other hand, require attention. Brother, you are bleeding so profusely that it is likely Eira's blood is all that sustains you. Vonnie, the little one struggles to take air." Ambrose swallowed, his eyes glancing between Eira and our daughter.

Vonnie pressed a finger into the baby's mouth and swept her throat, then held the little one's sunken chest up to her ear. "She's come too soon, Ambrose. Much too soon."

"Prince Catommandus, you'll not be long for this world if you refuse treatment." Gotwig waved, and a massive shadow stepped from the side of the manor.

"Larm," I exhaled, relieved at the sight of my Frostborn.

"Pa-Cat," he replied, squatting and resting his enormous elbows on his knees.

Eira stirred in my arms. She said nothing, but caressed Larm's knee.

"Cato, you must receive treatment. I will stay with Eira." Ambrose squeezed my hand. "I will notify you of any change in-in either of their conditions."

I bent to my wife and kissed the top of her head before scooting toward Larm. Her arm snaked out and caught in my tunic. Her breathing accelerated as she began to shake.

"I will not leave you. I will stay. Eira, I will never—"

"Catommandus. You will go this instant," Ambrose clucked. He hopped down from the wagon and gathered Eira. She clung to him, burying her face in the crook of his arm. She was safe.

My Frostborn's arm cradled my back.

"I can walk Larm, but the others need to be moved as gently as possible. See them all located in a single room so that they may support each other this night."

Larm nodded and held his palms flat. Without any detectable fear, the elf and gnome sat on his forearms, and the others followed their example. It was a miracle that any of them survived.

"I will locate Evandr and keep an eye on the roads," Septimus said as he passed. He disappeared into the dark.

Our somber party crossed Rizellen's threshold and walked into a house boasting trinkets and decor from a multitude of distant lands—a lacquered music box inlaid with pearl, its lid carved with curling beasts; crystalline bowls that shifted color as we passed; a tapestry portraying acrobats woven from sun-bleached grasses. Not a single wall was clear, nor flat surfaces for that matter. The house was stuffed with mismatched furniture and smelled of an array of clashing scents.

After depositing the Others into a large living space, I was led, or rather, half-carried from Eira and the delicate life that had only hours ago entered the world. My arm was a mess, that I knew, but it was the ache in my chest that truly crippled me.

The manor's halls blurred by in a wash of color and texture. With uncharacteristic urgency, Gotwig, rushing ahead of us, ushered me into a second-floor chamber. A man and woman came forward as Larm, in his human form, entered the room.

"Healers?" I asked. "Cult Mossius?"

"Yes. Friends of Vonnie's. We anticipated the possibility of injury. Not to this level, mind you," Gotwig's eyes rested on the lifelessness at my side, he pursed his lips in disdain. "But here we are. We should have anticipated the need of a surgeon, given your penchant for, let us just say, getting into scrapes."

"I am Healer Glendall." The man lifted my arm and checked for pulse points. He searched and palpated, squeezed above and below the three most prominent wounds, and then repeated the actions.

"And do you—"

"I feel nothing below the shoulder," I said, having already anticipated his question.

"Sit." Glendall gestured to a sturdy wooden chair. I trudged across the floor, sat, and planted my feet on the ground, while staring into the merry fire of a small hearth. I had witnessed more battlefield examinations than most and knew they'd want to manipulate the arm to assess the joint. I pressed my back against the chair for stabilization. The healer procured a set of shears and cut the tunic from my body, pulling the blood-soaked linen off in ribbons.

"Your injuries are too significant to be healed by means of powders and poultices. Stitches can hold you together," the healer looked at me and then at Larm, "but blood no longer flows below your elbow. Amputation is required."

Amputation.

I forced my shoulders square, feet pressed harder into the floor as if I could anchor myself against what was to come. My fingers curled into a fist on my thigh. *Breathe in. Breathe out. Steady.* How many of my own soldiers had I held down when facing the same?

I would not cower.

The other healer, a woman of advanced years, dragged a table beside me and went about arranging her tools: A set of curved and straight blades, a saw, a basin of hot water, and a cautery iron. All were clean and placed in order of usage.

"Larm, to his left," Gotwig commanded, his voice devoid of any softness. "I shall take the right."

I bobbed a single curt nod. I was aware that the level of pain I was to experience would result in jerking or thrashing and that remaining as still as possible would yield cleaner results.

Larm's hand clamped over my shoulder, a steady and sure presence.

"Pa-Cat, Eira's blood will keep infection at bay, but the bone..."

Warm tears leaked from the corners of my eyes and streamed down my neck.

"Do it. My wife needs me and I her."

Gotwig braced my other side, unbothered as his hands slipped through the torn flesh and gore.

"We will work as swiftly as we are able. Do not fight the urge to pass out if it should come."

"Begin," I ordered.

The healers converged.

"The leather strap will slow the bleed—we must twist it as tight as possible." A belt cinched high on my arm, biting deep until the blood only trickled from my wound, and the crush of muscle to bone caused my fingers to go cold.

"Fuck," I groaned out loud in protest. A dull ache escalated to a pulsing swell that throbbed with each beat of my heart. My arm felt full to bursting.

The second healer raised their knife.

I sucked the air through my teeth as the sickening slice of a blade cut through flesh and then slid through tendon. The burn of open air on raw muscles warped my vision. My head tipped forward and then swayed upon

my shoulders, but I fought to remain aware. I had a family now. I was…
holy fuck, I was a father.

"Did you just smile?" Gotwig scoffed. "Monwyn men are a breed all
their own."

A guttural sound tore from my throat, raw and involuntary.

"Fuck! Gods almighty." My body arched against Larm's grip, sweat
dripping down my forehead and onto my chest. Short, ragged breaths
escaped my lungs. I shook and shivered like the earth trembling in a quarry
blast.

"Steady. Hold him steady."

Wheels of skin flopped wetly onto a tray, one atop another. The sound
was obscene, like meat slapped on a butcher's block. Each slice dug deeper
until the last shreds of fibrous tissue parted, revealing a chalk-white hint of
bone. Healer Glendall selected a saw from the table.

The door opened.

"Cat. Fuck, man. That's nasty." Evandr strolled into the room. "The
wife sent you something. Do I just pour it on or do you, like, dip your junk
into it?" He held up a dainty teacup and sniffed. "Oh, she said if you didn't
use it, she would file for a divine divorce."

I huffed out a bitter laugh and opened my mouth.

Evandr brought the cup to my lips, cradling my jaw like a mother would
her child. I drank deeply, quaffing the offering and licking the cup clean.

"Sir, kindly hold onto his feet," the healer instructed.

Evandr, the best of my soldiers, followed the directive and looped his
arms around my knees.

The healer positioned the saw at my arm, and I closed my eyes.

A grinding, tearing vibration echoed up my arm, through my shoulder,
and into my teeth.

"Aaaargh!" I could feel the grit, the separation of bone. "Stop!" I wailed.
"Gods, fucking gods!" My muscles spasmed uncontrollably in a futile
attempt to pull away. Larm's grip was unyielding. Evandr and Gotwig held
tight. "Mama!" I screamed.

The thunk of my limb falling into the basin brought up the contents
of my stomach. I retched onto the carpeted floor, passing in and out of
consciousness.

"Cauterizing the wound—"

"—your chance for bleeding—"

My breath came harder.

"—are lucky to be alive."

"Cat, it's no biggie. Remember when you lost your toe? This won't be nearly that bad." Only Evandr would think to say something so asinine.

I lifted my head, gagging on the bile pouring from the corners of my mouth.

"Promise you will see me to Eira immediately following the procedure. Swear it, Evan."

My friend bowed his head. "I will. I promise."

I gulped the air in a pointless attempt to cease struggling against my captors.

Healer Glendall heated the cautery tool over the hearth's open flame. It glowed a menacing shade of orange.

"Gentlemen," he addressed the men that surrounded me. "You too may feel faint. There is an inclination to hold one's breath due to smell, but for the sake and safety of the patient, attempt to breathe normally."

I jerked as the healer approached, my body screaming it was time to flee, even as my head knew I could not.

Heat seared.

Skin crackled.

My hearing dulled and—

Chapter Sixty-Three

SERPENTINE BLADEHOOF

Eira

A soft knock came from the chamber's door.

"Enter," Momma said from her spot by the window.

"Hey, hot Mama." Evandr poked his head around the door. "We've brought someone to see you."

Larm's hand appeared above Evandr's head, pushing the door wide. Between them, they carried Cato into the chamber, heavy wrappings binding his arm to his torso.

"Why is he unconscious?" I scrambled, tossing off the sheet that covered my legs. "Is he medicated? I saw him walk into the manor on his own two feet."

I didn't make it out of the bed before, with excruciating gentleness, my Frostchildren laid my husband on the bed next to a snoring Ambrose, whom I'd just convinced to rest.

"E, the injury was extensive," Larm said. "The arm couldn't be saved."

"You jest!" I rushed to Cato's side, my bleeding and the cumbersome padding stuffed into my underclothes all but forgotten.

I pressed my palm to his chest, feeling the rapid drum of his heartbeat beneath the bandages. My stomach twisted. He was alive—thank the Goddess he was alive—but the sight of him, so diminished…

"His sword arm." I sobbed into my hands, attempting to muffle the sounds of my anguish.

Larm led me around the bed. He ducked and lifted me, tucking me next to Ambrose just as gently as he had Cato. He pulled a handkerchief from his pocket and placed it in my palm.

"Your blood is already fixing him up." Larm sat on the edge of the bed and drew the blankets up to my waist. I took his hand between both of mine; his cool skin tempered the heat of my mounting fears but could not absolve me of my guilt.

Rusty-brown spots stained the bandaging below Cato's elbow, where the rest of his arm should have been. It would have been, had I not begged them to run in.

"Because... because of me. It's always because of me. I should have cut deeper when I pulled the knife across my—"

The baby squawked at my raised voice.

"She'll be the next victim of living within my proximity, Larm. How soon before she meets Merrias? Days? Hours, by the looks of it."

Tiny gasps punctuated each of the baby's exhalations. Mama placed wet rags on her chest, and the coolness seemed to still her struggles.

"You can't predict your time adrift when a ship loses her sails." Larm shifted and hugged me close. I winced as my bruised eye bumped into his shoulder. "Some catch the wind sooner, some never do... but while they float, they're still alive."

He would know better than anyone, having lost his family.

"How did you keep breathing, knowing that every breath carried you further from them?"

Larm didn't answer; he just squeezed me tighter.

"Eiry," Momma said. "Turn cloud and heal. Your menfolk are safe. Now you must be their strength."

She sat in front of the open window, rocking the little girl whose tiny body took up not even a quarter of the throw pillow she lay upon—the rise and fall of her chest uneven and too fast.

I shook my head.

"I don't deserve to be free of pain." I tugged from Larm's embrace and leaned back, gritting my teeth against the sting of the raw flesh at my wrists. "I will suffer as my people suffer."

"Eira Verras Chulainn, your pa would not have—"

"My pa would be alive, Momma. Your husband would be here to meet his granddaughter, whose life hangs in the balance. I cannot even feed the child; I've no milk. And I am not so blind that I think she might pull through. And the Primus-King... he still walks the soil. And what's more concerning is that I'm not convinced he should die. Have you met the people of Gaea? They are good. They care for themselves and each other. How is it even—"

"Hush," my mother scolded. "There will be time to mourn, but today we focus on what is happening in this room. The immediate."

The immediate.

"They need your strength, Eiry, and so does she." Momma dipped the tip of her finger into the well of a saucer and smeared another drop of my blood on the baby's tongue.

She was right, but wasn't she always?

Let it work this time. Let it work this time. I'd repeated the litany in my head the first, second, and third times she introduced it to the child. *Let it work this time.*

"My daughter, your pa knew the consequences of loving us from the very day he accepted us into his heart." Tears glistened in my momma's eyes; they slid silently into the dirt-smeared shawl gathered about her neck.

My pa. My big, cuddly, and kind pa. The father that all children should be blessed to know.

"The immediate," I spoke softly. "Larm, help me up, please."

I called to the shadows the moment my feet sank into the thickly carpeted floor.

"Eiry?" Momma's voice was soft.

"I'll see to Pa."

Shadows detached themselves from the corners of the room, swirling, coalescing around me, not in a sinister way, but like veils gracefully unfurling with an otherworldly serenity. I joined them in their soft gyres.

We took to the skies, a cloud of sorrow and shade. I was formless, vast, not driven by my anger or fear, only a deep and mournful pull toward the city.

The moon was my guide, shining bright on the rolling fields, the mud, and the animals in the pastures. I rode the high winds as I viewed Gaea from above. It was beautiful—even if I tried to convince myself it wasn't possible because of who ruled it. How childish of me. How had it taken me nearly thirty years to understand that the light and the shadows had *always* shared the same sky? That cruelty did not erase happiness, only made it rarer and more precious when found.

I passed over the Timber Tavern. Its windows were dark; no patrons staggered out the door. Naturally, soldiers combed the streets and ducked in and out of the residences, ensuring their terror-stricken citizens that all was well, and that they would keep them safe.

And they *would* remain safe, from me at least.

Cult Mossius loomed in the distance, and though it had been the epicenter of so much pain, I had to remind myself that it was also the salvation of many more.

Guards and servants were out in droves. Extra lamps had been lit to guide them in cleaning the heaps of glittering ash that littered the lawn and pathway.

A ring of healers surrounded Pa's body.

I descended and then released my shade, opting to appear as myself. I padded forward on bare feet.

"If you would be so kind, I'd like to see my father home."

"Emryss!" My brother Merritt jumped back, startled by my appearance. His mouth dropped open. "You are alive and, and my Goddess, you are a..."

"A conjurer *and* Goddess-born."

My half-brother rushed forward and placed his hands on my stomach.

"The babe?" He shook his head, a crestfallen expression marring his otherwise handsome face.

"Is not well. She is not..."

"She is too small." He placed a hand on my shoulder. "Emryss, I..." He looked around, patting his pockets like he was looking for something. "I will fetch my bag at once. Does she show signs of weak muscle tone?"

"She does, but is with healers and... and my Momma. You are needed here."

"Oh, my dear—Emberkin Arro, you will want your Hearthmate," Merritt chattered, turning circles as if his medical bag was close at hand. "His units are scouring the countryside, but I am sure I can locate him and have him return. How do I begin to find a man on a horseback..."

"*My* Lifemates are safe. But... but I am here for the man who raised me." I gestured to my Pa's fallen body.

The other healers shook their heads, and a priest took up an aggressive posture.

"But Highness, we are to examine any known conjurers for—"

"Not this time, no," Merritt silenced the man with a raise of his hand. He dipped his chin and shooed them back, clearing my path.

I called to the flames.

Come to me, friends.

The winds shifted around us as the black fire ignited, snapping and jumping between the tips of my fingers.

"Mossius alive."

"How is this possible?"

"The ones we have studied had no such ability."

I kneeled at my father's side. He stared lifelessly into the unknown.

"Defend His Highness!" Soldiers and guards ran onto the lawn, shouting and encircling us. "To arms!"

"Stay back! Do not draw weapons!" Merritt commanded, holding his arms wide.

The guards broke stride and held firm, still uneasy, their hands on hilts.

Merritt produced a hanky and laid it over the gruesome sight of the bolt lodged into my father's forehead, and then tenderly closed his open lids. He straightened the cloak that fell haphazardly around my father's wide shoulders.

"How can I help you, sister?"

"By bearing witness to the man he was."

His Intercession had begun. It was time to send Pa home.

"Ulltan of N-Nortia," the voice that I'd hoped would ring clear cracked. I drew in a deep, cleansing breath. "Husband of Vonnie, father of Eira." Tears fell, sizzling and steaming as they dotted my hands. "A minnow's first love."

I closed my eyes and thought back, my hand drifting to his beard. I used to stroke my fingers through its wiry frizz when he held me through my nightmares. It was probably my earliest memory.

"You made my first fishing pole, whittling the wood just so, even though I caught more twigs than fish. You bought me my first dress, the one with the little embroidered snowflakes. You told me that even though looks weren't important, I was still the prettiest girl in Silverstep. You—you took me to each festival, every single boring Troth dinner... and you'd stand there, beaming, drying the tears you never tried to hide."

I moved my hands, placing one on his shoulder, the other on his stomach, and asked the shadows to see him home. From my hands, tendrils of shade covered his flesh, bone, and fabric. Though the prince crawled backward and then stood, there was no chaos, no screams for aid, no destruction... only a quiet unmaking.

His cloak caught quickly, and black flames licked around my knees.

"You showed me what a partnership should look like, Pa: how spouses should love each other. How love doesn't hurt. Your strength was not in how hard you could hit, but in how softly you could hold. And you always held me, didn't you? Every scraped knee, every childish fear, every heartbreak."

I bent low and cradled him in my arms.

"And now I hold you."

I let go of my grief and the æther within me, the shadowy flames growing high.

The winds swirled into the courtyard, lifting bits of glowing ash into the air, taking them toward the night sky, where they danced gold in the darkness.

"Thank you for your kindness, brother. Perhaps one day we will meet again as family."

Merritt bowed low, and once more I took to the shade.

As quickly as I could, I circled what remained of my Pa, building speed until the ashes seemed to integrate into my form. I ascended, rising until the world below was distant, until the clouds lay beneath me. And then, with a final thought of love, I released my hold, the remnants that were my father, scattering like stardust.

Dawn was upon us, but I lingered for a moment before landing at the foot of Rizellen's property.

My feet appeared, solid and human. The pain in my face, arms, and abdomen was no more, but something was.

"Ouch!" I ran my hand over my scalp, where a sharp pain stabbed at my head. The blonde plant fibers had burned away, but in the nest of my shorter, tangled hair, something hard had embedded itself into my skin. "Oww, fuck, fuck." I dug out the fragment.

"Oh, Pa."

Unpolished and rough, a translucent stone, speckled with black and white inclusions, like it was sprinkled with a liberal dose of salt and pepper, sat in my palm—a raw and imperfect diamond.

I walked the road to Rizellen's as the dawning sun set its rays upon her property, needing time to be alone. The tunnel of trees came into view, and I turned down the path lest my nudity offend the neighbors. In the distance, the manor's door opened. Cato and Ambrose emerged. They didn't see me.

Ambrose supported Cato, arm wrapped below his waist. Cato cradled the baby.

He held her with the natural ease of a longtime nanny.

Standing at the edge of the archway, I followed them with my eyes. Ambrose lowered Cato to a bench beneath a budding tree and helped Cato sit before joining him. He produced a blanket from under his arm and wrapped it around Cato's back.

Ambrose pecked the top of his head.

Cato lifted his chin and placed a kiss on Ambrose's lips.

I muffled the cry that nearly spilled out.

How could a heart feel so empty and yet so immeasurably full? And how unearthly beautiful was my world?

Cato lowered his head and whispered something into the baby's little ear. Ambrose smiled, and then Cato's voice carried on the wind.

"Over time, baby mine, you will find
Some hills become mountains, but some remain small.
Hard to climb, by design, you will find
Some hills become mountains, but some remain small."

I went to them, not wanting to disturb, but needing them close. They were my people, my comfort... my home.

Cato saw me first.

His tearful smile stopped me short.

Had it ever been so brilliant? His face was pure light; the gold rings around his pupils glowed with an emotion so intense I thought I might falter.

Ambrose leapt to his feet, ran to me, and before I could stop him, was twirling me around.

"Come see her. She's perfect—a little wrinkly perhaps—but built like her father. Two legs, two arms, many fingers, many toes."

"Let me down. I can walk."

"No."

He carried me to the bench, placed me next to Cato, and then squished himself beside me.

"Hello, love," Cato whispered as he looked me over. "I am at a loss."

I nodded, similarly overwhelmed, swallowing back an abundance of tears, unable to form words.

Ambrose patted my back.

"Not his arm, Eira, his *emotions*. That is what he means."

Fucking Ambrose.

"How is she?" I asked.

Cato shook his head.

Slowly, he repositioned the pillow on which he carried her and sat it on my lap.

I held my child for the first, and perhaps last, time.

No heavier than a bundle of cloth, her limbs were thin and curled tight against herself as if the world were too loud and too bright. Her skin... gods, it reminded me of newly pressed parchment—soft and nearly transparent.

Her chest rose and fell in shallow, fluttering motions, each breath a fragile bargain struck between her and the Goddess. I traced the shape of her with my eyes—her tiny fists, the bend of her knees—memorizing her because I feared she might vanish if I looked away.

My mother and Gotwig emerged from the manor. He carried a bundle of cloth, she a wash basin.

"Daughter mine, put something on so your Frosties can come out."

Ambrose took the baby while Gotwig helped me shrug on a big black shirt that fit loose and hit me below the knees—it was Pa's. Ever thoughtful, Ambrose produced my ring. Cato plucked it from his fingers and slid it over my knuckles.

Larm and Evandr were already walking across the lawn, headed in our direction.

"What should we call her?" Evandr asked. "She needs a fine name, something like Iceblood or Bladehoof."

Ambrose snorted.

"She shall be called Ambrosia, of course," Ambrose said in all seriousness while kissing my temple. "She is my firstborn."

Cato grimaced.

"I think the fuck not. I do not care what she is called, but it will not be Ambrosia."

"Serpentine or Agate. Those are strong names," Larm piped up.

"Those I like," Cato agreed.

"My granddaughter, named after a rock?" Momma barked out a laugh. "Do you suppose to call her Serpent for short? I'll not have it."

I shook my head.

Momma stepped close and kneeled, placing her basin on the ground.

"Here Momma." I rolled the diamond around my fingers before tucking the flawed stone into my mother's palm. "It's from Pa."

Tears glistened in my Momma's eyes.

"Eira," Cato's voice dropped. "What would you call our daughter?" He dipped a finger into the baby's palm and stroked her purplish skin. She wrapped her tiny fingers around the digit and held tight.

"Nanetta. She will be called Na—"

"The Primus-King!" Septimus broke through the distant tree line. "He marches with three hundred men!"

Chapter Sixty-Four

ENCROACHMENT

Ambrose

"Emberkin Arro sold us out!" Septimus bellowed as he ripped across the grounds.

"My sword!" Cato surged to his feet.

"Cat, you cannot!" I shouted, attempting to grab but missing the sleeve of his uninjured side. "Get Eira and Nanetta underground."

He shoved me aside with a strength that in his current state, he should not have been capable of.

"Larm, my weapons!" Cato demanded again. His Frostborn did not hesitate and made straight for the manor. Cato clasped our uncle's shoulder as Septimus slowed to a stop. "Take Eira and Nanetta; protect them with your life. I am diminished, and the most skilled among us must defend them."

Septimus's head ticked to the side, his eyes sharp and focused.

"Enchantress, come." He took Eira's elbow, but my good girl flung him off.

"No, I will not."

"See, she understands." I cocked a brow while peering down my nose. "Now, Cato, take our family and—madam, what in the actual fuck are you doing?"

Eira pressed our daughter into the arms of my lifelong enemy. She slid her twisted metal ring from her finger and then held her hand out to me and then Cato.

"Septimus, keep her safe until... until she... promise me you'll stay with her until her time comes. Do *not* bury her in the ground."

I placed my silver band into Eira's hand, and then, as tenderly as she could, she worked the two larger rings over Nanetta's fingers where they encircled her tiny wrist. The third ring she snugged into our infant's swaddle.

"Now... now we are... are with her," Eira leaned into Septimus's side, and for a moment I thought she might falter.

"Eira, this cannot be the best method of handling—"

Cato cut me off with a glare and then pointedly looked to where Septimus cradled our child.

The same pale eyes that had instilled fear in me as a young one—and bitterness as a man—did not hold the familiar venom. He looked at Nanetta like, for the first time in his overly long and disgusting life, he understood love.

Jealousy cleaved me in two. The knowledge that he may have fathered my precious diamond grated on my heart.

"I will not fail you, Enchantress." Septimus fisted Eira's hair and brought his mouth to hers. She kissed him back—a pact sealed in saliva.

"I'll accompany the child to the tunnels. Sid?" Vonnie turned to Gotwig, and he, expressionless, bowed his head.

"Momma," Eira said, panic rising in her voice. "You can't! You must run. Take a horse from the barn and get as far away as you can. Go now!"

Steam rose from my wife's bare feet.

"I'm done running from the Primus-King, daughter mine. I love you, little minnow."

Septimus shot off. Gotwig and Momma trailed behind, carrying with them a newly formed piece of my heart.

Eira simply stood in her oversized shirt, and for once, I lacked the words to bring her peace.

Larm burst from the house, my mace in one hand, Cato's sword in the other, a jumble of mismatched armor clutched awkwardly under his arms.

A trumpet blared across the field.

The Gaean and Baldorvan contingents were upon us. Even from this distance, I felt the subtle shake of their army's perfectly timed footsteps.

"Larm, Evandr, circle around and take them from the side; do not hold back. Ambrose and I will stay at the manor; they will assume Eira to be inside, and we will work to convince them that it is so." Cato attempted to strap a too-large chest plate around his torso but failed. The armor clattered to the ground.

"Allow me." I procured the plate and snugged its leather closures behind his back. "The plan is a simple one, then: draw their attention, hold our ground, and buy time for Nanetta to get away. If they find her body, I am afraid of what they will do."

Eira shoved her way between us.

"The plan, husbands, is that the two of you stay alive and your wife will do the rest."

Cato's mouth opened, closed, then opened again, the words hovering in his mind but refusing to take shape.

"Eira," Cato began. "You must know something." I took up my place at my wife's back, prepared to shove her toward Cato when she puff-sploded, for I already knew the words he'd speak. "The Emberkin. If Nanetta... I promised her hand in exchange for the freedom of the people of Baldorva."

Shadows leaked from Eira's fingers, and her eyes glimmered in a shadowy gray haze. I draped an arm around her, settling its weight upon her chest, cooling the tempest within.

"Cato, my idiot spouse," I said, feeling the push of her flame against my skin. "You have willfully demoted yourself to second husband."

Cato frowned.

"He's. Not. Wrong, Catommandus," our wife hissed. "Stay alive so that I can remove your other fucking arm when this is over."

Eira snapped and took to the sky. I tumbled to the ground, arms empty, and watched her from my knees. Up she went, a streak against the morning sky. No matter how many times I witnessed it, I was always unfailingly awestruck.

"When you fuck up, Cat, you do so with aggressive aplomb."

"Shut up and run, Ambrose."

I rose, and we dispersed.

We rounded the manor house, and from a distance, I could just make out the fog-shrouded form of the man at the heart of this fiasco. I popped off my frames and gave them a quick clean. Cato paused his steps to determine our course of action.

"There are hundreds," Cato murmured. "I do not think three hundred, but certainly close to that number."

I bent the metal arms of my spectacles around my ears to secure them, and then looked from right to left.

Through the thinning mist, I spotted rows upon rows of forest-green tabards, a spear tips glinting in the morning light. Atop their mounts, the unit's standards stirred and snapped in the wind.

"Emryss! Show yourself!" The Primus-King rode forward on his armored warhorse as his cavalry took up their place behind him—armored riders atop destriers, heavy and finely muscled. "Vonnie, you have taken my child once again!" he shouted from a distance. "May the Nether Lord rise up and take you to your grave! Ride!"

His fist hit the air, and the mounted units spurred their horses to action, heading in our direction.

I swallowed down the lump in my throat.

"Hold, Ambrose. Stand firm."

"Catommandus. I love you."

"I love you, too."

"No, Cat. I love you as I love Eira. Though maybe not quite as intensely." I twisted my toe into the ground, finding peace in having vocalized my truth.

"And I you, husband."

I allowed myself a single second to close my eyes, to blink and imagine my arms wrapped around my loves, our little girl on her mama's hip... but not Cato-dog-mus. He was filthy and would never be allowed near our child.

The scent of damp earth mingled with the smell of burn and char.

Our wife had found her foes.

The thundering of hooves intensified.

I opened my eyes and—

"Get back!" Cato yelled.

I flinched, tossing my arms over my face.

Eira dove, erecting a crackling wall of black flame between us and the charging forces.

From above the black fire, I watched the Frostborn attack.

The cavalry on the right flank, that bronze wave that had seemed unstoppable moments ago, was in full disarray. Larm snatched a man from his horse, ripped him in two, and then sent both halves hurtling into the riders. Some attempted to re-form, their destriers snorting and shying away from the giants. Others, quite sensibly, tried to peel off.

"Bowmen at the ready! Spears to the front!" The Primus-King drew his sword and pointed toward the manor.

He was no fool. Even from this distance, I could see the calculation on his face.

A flood of shouted commands, followed by the rapid blowing of trumpets from deep within his lines, cut through the sounds of battle as the Primus-King changed tactics.

His heavy infantry raced around the giants, shielding his spearmen. Protected now, the long spears struck in a flurry, piercing the behemoths' skin. Streaks of blue ran from Larm's thighs down his legs.

Evandr bellowed, head thrown back as he took two spears and a sword to his hip.

"I will kill them," Cato hissed, holding himself back with every ounce of his control. "If they bring Larm down, I will—"

Behind us, a hair-raising scream shattered my calm. My stomach leapt to my throat.

I snatched Cato by his shoulder and shoved him with my body, forcing him to the side of the manor house, before venturing a look at the evil that could produce such a sound.

"Fucking Mother of All That Is Holy," I gasped.

In answer to the tyrant who led them, the demon army's roar washed over the field.

Cato jerked and tried to free himself, but I held firm. If he saw what was coming our way...

"Septimus! He's returned."

Hair flying, sweat pouring from his brow, Septimus tore past the barn in the far pasture, Emberkin Arro's soldiers in pursuit.

Above me, Eira circled, taking stock of the situation.

The Emberkin, bare-chested, riding atop a muscular black mule, was a thing of nightmares. A blackened helm covered his head, its visor hammered into the face of a dragon. Its long snout held two rows of razor-sharp teeth that glinted silver in the striking sun. Twin spears strapped to his back formed an undefined *X* behind him, and he brandished a long, curved sword in each hand. He didn't hold the reins of his animal but instead rode standing on the mount's back.

I pulled my brother to my side, finally allowing him to see what was coming.

"My dick is hard. Cato, my fucking dick is hard."

"Wait to fuck him until you determine whose side he is on."

Cato struck out running to intercept Septimus. Our uncle caught sight of us and sped toward the manor. We shielded him and our daughter, who was tucked tightly into the side of his leather jerkin, and the four of us took cover amidst a group of merchant wagons.

"Vonnie? Gotwig?" Cato asked.

"Underground," Septimus panted. He checked on Nanetta. She nestled against his bare chest, the slits of her eyes open, revealing that weird black-blue color that all babies seemed to share. "She is not long for the world."

"Did Arro give chase?"

Septimus nodded.

"When he saw I didn't have Eira."

The scenarios played out in Cato's mind, his eyes jumping back and forth between us.

"Retreat!" came a voice I recognized as the Primus-King. "Fall back!"

"But why?" I peeked from my hiding place.

"Cato, for fuck's sake, the Emberkin rides against the Primus-King."

The monarch bellowed to his remaining men, not to hold the line but to take to the woods.

Eira zipped through the sky and then plummeted, igniting a line of black fire between the shelter of the forests, cutting off their path to safety.

Cato and Septimus peeked their heads above the wagons a second before the armies clashed.

Arro's light cavalry, swift and relentless, tore a gash in the Primus-King's formation—a whirlwind of steel and hooves on a churned up, muddy pasture.

"Septimus, the baby. Take her and run. Get her body to the Mantle. He will see that she does not fall into the hands of those who would use her even after death."

"If you have ever borne me love, Septimus, you will do as Ambrose says," Cato rasped, his tone echoing the agony in my heart.

Septimus nodded and took off under the wagons, just as the air began to chill.

CHAPTER SIXTY-FIVE

FULL CIRCLE

EIRA

I ripped the very life from the pasture as I flew toward the forest, drawing the energy from all that lived. Blades of grass blackened and fell. I erected a wall behind me, keeping my family from the fight.

It was time for the story to end.

His troops turned... but I would not allow them to retreat.

I landed and took my human form, brushing my fingertips along the bark of an ancient elm. *Thank you for your sacrifice, old soul.* My flames raced up its trunk and swam out along its long branches. The trees nearest exploded into roaring columns of black shade, casting their morbid light across the battlefield. Pixies flew from the forest canopy and gave chase, rightfully, as I'd destroyed their homes. Though they dove and bit and stabbed me with their sharp little feet, I ran.

I had him in my sight.

My father.

Armored in bronze plate etched with the curling limbs of a mighty oak, he sat unmoving on his steed of white, relaxed and comfortable with a blade in his hand. A crown of twining branches rose from his helm in tangled arcs, and its nasal guard split and twisted like roots, framing the blue of his eyes in narrow slits. From his shoulders hung a cape—the left side a deep, Verus-red, the right a deep green—shifting like the wind-stirred leaves that fell from the trees behind him.

I felt a presence at my back.

"Larm?"

He grunted a reply.

My beautiful Frostborn, of course, my black fire had not stopped him; his cold skin was impervious to its burn. The air around me sang with sizzling pops and hisses, and then the earth below me lurched, sending me to my knees.

"He rises," I whispered.

Snow fell from a cloudless sky, melting into fat drops of rain as it encountered my fire. The temperature dropped.

He was coming. The Nether Lord.

A tremor began beneath the earth—a fissure slowly ripping open in the pasture's heart. A creeping freeze began at the mouth of the rift, clawing its way outward, coating the grass in a glaze of frost.

Men hit their knees and fell from their mounts as he rose, a mountain of marble-like stone. Soldiers ran for their lives... if their armor had not already frozen and entombed them.

The Primus-King's horse failed him, but he, like me, a bearer of Leyometh's essence—God of the hearth, protector of the flame—did not succumb like the others.

"Why have you come, Nether Lord?" I shouted. "Work your dealings with your own kind! Leave humanity alone!"

The God regarded me with a blink and then turned his sharply planed face until his eyes fell on the Primus-King.

The monarch ignored the god, his eyes tracking something far off. Immediately, I took to shade. What could be more important than a literal fucking god standing before you?

Septimus ran to the west, his arms wrapped protectively around himself. Around Nanetta.

The Primus-King sprinted, and I soared, speeding forward with all that I was. I'd not let him have her.

The sky splintered, parting like silk cut with sharp shears. A white-hot light beamed from the Cradle and drove back the encroaching chill. I was blinded and disoriented. The blaze burned away my shapeless form, and I spiraled to the ground.

"Merrias." I forced the breath from my lungs.

In her godly form, she descended, a shimmering beacon, both terrifying and beautiful. She was a massive orb of pure radiance.

"Eira!"

I turned my head, gasping for air.

My husbands charged toward me, Ambrose in the lead, able to withstand the cold, Cato dropping to his knees, the freeze making its way up his legs. He clawed the ground with his single hand, sinking his fingers into the ice-covered mud in an effort to keep moving.

Larm, my precious Frostborn, writhed in pain, caught in the beam of Merrias's light.

"Stop!" I screamed. "Take your fight elsewhere! Grandfather! Grandmother!"

"You have served your purpose." Merrias's voice felled trees and shook the earth. Stones tumbled from the roof of the manor house. "And I have come to collect her."

A shriek tore from my throat. I had to reach her. They all fucking wanted her, the Primus-King for her tiny drops of lifeblood. Merrias for her master plan.

The goddess took to her human form and ran toward Septimus, Arbiter blade in her grasp.

Still breathless, I rolled and stumbled to my knees.

I slipped in the mud but found my feet, barreling toward Septimus.

And Nanetta.

"Septimus!" I screamed, knowing I couldn't reach them in time, watching Merrias gaining ground and the Primus-King nearly at their side. "Septimus!"

His eyes met mine, icy-blue and focused.

For a fraction of a second, the universe paused. He pressed his hand over the mound that lay over his heart.

Nanetta.

A knowing passed between us, a flicker of understanding.

"I will not fail you, Enchantress," Septimus whispered, the words somehow carrying to my ears.

He pivoted, changing course, and took off in a mad sprint, heading toward the deep rift.

"Goodbye," I whispered. Better no life than one lived in a cage.

He launched himself, taking flight with Nanetta, eyes unafraid and wide open as he faced his end. And then they were gone, swallowed by the darkness.

"No!" Merrias screamed, "No!"

The Nether Lord canted and struck out, reaching into the rift with unfathomable speed.

"Noooooo!" Merrias screamed, bursting my eardrums and those of the soldiers lucky enough to remain alive. They held their heads and, like me, writhed in the mud until the sound ceased.

I rolled to my side and saw Ambrose collapse to his knees, screaming at the sky.

Cato ran to his side, blood trickling from both ears. He attempted to lift Ambrose to his feet, but Ambrose pulled him down, sobbing into his shoulder.

I staggered, walking and weeping, making my way toward them.

"Love."

I turned at the deep voice.

Evandr. He looked at the gaping fissure and then back to me.

"Love." I nodded in understanding.

My giant roared as he ran and launched his body toward the Nether Lord's retreating form. The god's hand opened as Evandr leapt.

"He has them—my gods, he has them," I said to no one as I glimpsed an unmoving Septimus curled protectively around Nanetta. Evandr landed on the god's fingers, just as the Nether Lord's head descended.

"It cannot be!" Merrias launched her blade, hurtling it toward the god.

The earth shook, and rocks and dirt tumbled into the fissure.

Point first, the Arbiter blade sank into the newly formed ground. Only seconds behind, Merrias snatched up her blade before turning her head to the sky.

The Primus-King stepped into my path, eyes wild and unseeing.

Finish this, granddaughter, Merrias commanded as she disappeared into the light. *I must protect the Goddess from him.*

"Daughter. Emryss. You are all that remains." He blinked at me while collecting his thoughts. "It should have been different between us." He looked down at his upturned palms, gazing at what, I didn't know.

Cato caught sight of me and jolted to his feet, setting out at a run—a bull protecting his herd.

"You and I, daughter..." The Primus-King raised a gentle hand, and I found that, looking at his shaking fingers, his worried azure eyes, that I didn't hate him. I... I pitied him and the path *he* chose. He looked around, taking in the carnage. "Together we could save them all, if you but trust me." His expression was sincere, his sadness genuine.

The mud beneath my feet put off clouds of steam, and I noticed that white clouds drifted from the joints of his armor as well.

"I have only witnessed the wreckage of your choices, Father." The word felt foreign on my tongue.

"Child, daughter, there is time to—"

Hot blood spurted onto my chest.

The Primus-King stilled, the tip of a spear jutting from under his gorget.

"Momma?"

"This is where it ends. It ends with me, daughter, as it always should have." She stood over him, wisps of gray hair flying, her chest heaving, the spear still clutched tightly in her hands.

His body hit the ground with a sickening thud.

CHAPTER SIXTY-SIX

WHAT LOVE DEMANDS

CATO

I reached Eira's side, my wounded arm searing in pain—the gods could take the other for the relief I felt.

I thought he would kill her—I imagined him falling upon her body and lapping her blood, stealing and consuming what was not his to take.

Vonnie reached for her daughter, and Eira went into her embrace, the man on the ground forgotten.

"It's over, daughter mine."

"But, Momma, at what cost?" Eira choked. Vonnie pulled back and held Eira's face in her palms. Green eyes peered into teal.

"What love demands, it returns. The cost is never wasted."

Gods knew I did not wish to interrupt a poignant moment shared between mother and daughter, but I needed to feel her, to ensure she was solid and alive.

I started and raised my sword as Gotwig popped from a tunnel a few feet behind Vonnie. As silent as ever, he climbed out and stood at her side. I nodded my respects, understanding now how Eira's mother had appeared like an apparition amidst the steam and erratic light.

"Wife, I have need of you." Ambrose breezed past me, wedged his way between the two women, and collected Eira in his arms. "Will we see her again? Will she live? Can you read her mind?"

How Eira did not tell him to fuck off was beyond me. No, not my wife. She just gestured for him to bend down, which he did on command, and then she held his head to her breast while he cried and babbled another string of incoherent questions. It is why they worked together and why *I* loved her.

Encroaching hoof falls turned my attention.

Emberkin Arro rode toward us, his people circling our contingent. Larm, in his human form, followed close behind.

"We have sworn an oath, Prince of Monwyn." He looked longingly at Eira and sneered at Ambrose. "In a month's time, I will march to your capital and collect your promised troops. Today, upon this field, your gods blessed the mingling of mine and Emryss's spirits. They too, believe I will usurp the warlord and free Baldorva's enslaved." He paused, letting his eyes linger on my wife. "Emryss of Gaea, when our child reaches maturity, a match with my people will be secured. I will select wisely from the best of my—"

"Like f—"

I lurched forward before Eira could spout off. I caught her by the bicep and then snaked my arm around her waist, squeezing. He had not seen the child; he assumed Eira still pregnant.

She leveled her gaze at me, and, Josa's taint... I near pissed myself at the flare of her rage.

"Emberkin Arro," Eira said through her teeth. "You, I am sure, have met Troth Kairus of Verus Temple? Assigned to Baldorva to secure trade negotiations?"

He spat on the ground.

Hmmm. He knew her well then.

"She and *only* she will preside over any and all contracts concerning *our* child. And before any bargaining is to commence, proof of abolition must be in my and the Mantle's hands. If I hear of a single instance where a person's life is not their own, *I* will mete out justice."

"As you wish." He saluted my wife in some odd palm-to-forehead gesture. "I will inform the citizens of Gaea that their monarch met a tragic end fighting an aggrieved mob of nobles—collect the body, Sergeant."

With that, the Emberkin rode hard to the east.

There comes a moment after battle when all is quiet. Where one's mind attempts to comprehend what it has seen but fails to form a coherent logic. I had not succumbed to such feelings in well over a decade, but I could see the disconnect in the others.

Larm and Vonnie sat at the front of the wagon, and though they kept their voices low, they chatted as if they'd been lifelong friends, discussing recipes and uses for whalebone. Leaning into the mundane; a common way to avoid the mental storm.

Eira rested against my chest, her head bobbing with the motion of the wheels rolling over the road's deep divots. Ambrose's cheek lay on my shoulder, his prickly mustache stabbing through the fabric of my linen shirt. His hand rested on Eira's stomach.

"Gotwig will see the expectant Others safely to Verus, and They will keep them safe, yes?" Eira asked for the third time.

"Of course, my sibling is the kindest and most understanding individual to live amongst humanity... and Others," Ambrose added quickly.

"They will give them a home, my love, or return them to theirs if They can," I assured.

Eira craned her neck to look at me.

She captured my hand in hers and placed them both atop Ambrose's splayed fingers.

"Home."

Chapter Sixty-Seven

THE PORTRAIT OF LOVE

Eira

"**I**'m fine, Black Bear! Well, I mean physically. Mentally, yes, I'm a little bit of a mess, but we've convalesced for two months now."

In actuality, it had only been five weeks since Gaea, and by convalescing, I meant engaging in nonstop preparations for Cordillaria to greet Emberkin Arro and his fucking terrifying band of soldiers.

We already had a plan in the works for me to feign morning sickness upon his arrival—the rest we would think up if Arro's campaign was successful. Until then, I'd relentlessly chastise Cato for selling off our child, and he would deal with my ire by taking out his anger on the royal guard, as he relearned to fight. He hadn't yet spoken to me of the loss of his limb, or loss of his child, but I knew in time he would.

"The healers can say you are fine all they want, Eira, but I know my wife better than any other." Ambrose sat at the table surrounded by bits of chalk and charcoal. "You require two hours of naptime per day, and you've been getting maybe one."

"And you?" I walked to the table, careful not to bump my pale-blue skirts into the mess he'd been making for days. "When I've been resting, you've been here, scribbling and scratching. Are you ready to show me what—"

I froze midstep.

"It is not perfect, but it is how I remember them looking."

Pa and Nanetta.

He'd captured the tiny, upturned nose, her almond-shaped eyes, the little wrinkles on her forehead. My father's busy beard and the detailed glint of his eyes as he smiled down in love.

I gulped back the tears, for fear that Ambrose would see and keep me confined. Momma said my emotions would be up and down for months to come, and so far, she'd been correct. I found myself crying at the most mundane of tasks—sitting on the edge of the tub, reviewing lodging plans, helping Bem pick nits from Richelle's hair. I took a fortifying breath and batted Ambrose's hand from my forehead.

"I'm okay. I'll be okay." *At some point.*

It still seemed surreal. All of it.

I could normally keep the sobbing at bay if I imagined her cradled in Septimus's arms—the sacrifice he made still astounded me. Maybe they all lived, Evandr's massive body looming over them in a giant-sized hug.

I pretended that she lived and thought that maybe one day I'd meet her again in a huge Frostborn body. I imagined Evandr telling her stories while Septimus scowled away all that frightened her.

"Now, sweetling." Ambrose produced a linen from the pocket of his leathers. He dabbed at my cheeks. "Let's get you back to bed."

"Nope, not doing it." I shook my head and reached up to tug his down for a kiss. "Shall we place it by the hearth in our room?"

"Yes, that or in the bathing chamber, so it is the first thing we see in the morning. Though her face was all squishy and red, I think her lips are shaped just like yours."

I couldn't make up the words to respond. I just ran my fingers over the short spikes of his freshly shaved head, loving the feel of them on my palms, even if he hated the style and once cried over the unshapely bump near his crown. Cato pointed out that his sibling had the same, and it seemed to placate the angry bear within. Soft lips brushed against mine, gentle as a leaf floating on the wind.

"Now come on." I grabbed his hand and dragged him through our apartment and into the common room. "I know that we are in mourning and that you hate the color white, but Ambrose, you are the most handsome man these eyes have ever beheld."

He managed the saddest little shimmy of his shoulders.

"Vonnie, is all well?" Ambrose asked my mother, who stood yanking on the balcony doors.

"It is, yes, but I cannot seem to dislodge the door. This room is stuffy and needs to air out."

Cinden told me that, after I'd flown away, Ambrose had sealed it off. The reminder of his mother's, Nan's, and Lilium's deaths had been too intense.

"I'll get it, Momma." I hurried over to the door and leaned in with my hip. I did my best not to wrinkle the heavy velvet curtains obscuring the windows. "Ambrose, help, please. I don't want Momma to feel stifled." I shared a covert smile with my mother.

He pressed his lips but, ever the gallant courtier, bowed at the hip and complied.

"Move aside, there is a trick to—" the door popped open with a simple push. "What is this?"

I nudged Ambrose forward and then turned to crack the door behind us.

"Deceitful harpy, what are you up to?"

Aberus, Richelle, Allaine, Greggen, Hughes, Bem, Cinden, Ethens, and their two little ones stood in a half-circle, all wearing various shades of blue.

"Yap, yap! Bark, yap!" I heard the best boy barking all the way from the hall.

"Here he comes!" I shooed everyone to the back of the balcony, my hands clammy with nervous sweat.

The apartment door opened and closed.

"Eira? The servant said you needed me. Where are you, love?"

My goodest pupper shoved the balcony door with his muzzle and came charging across the threshold.

Cato followed soon after.

"What is this?" He demanded, looking up at Ambrose, while shoving an errant curl back into his braid.

"I do not know!" Ambrose tossed his hands. "Stop assuming I am privy to the answers, Catommandus. You know the haphazard nature of the creature I have Joined better than I!"

"Gentlemen, I will explain if—"

"Bark, bark! Yap!"

"Ugh! Call off Dog-a-man-dus, nasty mutt." Ambrose shook his leg, trying to rid himself of his *new* mortal enemy.

"His name is Steelclaw Valedicto Barker's Vengeance." Cato narrowed his eyes. "Come, boy," He called out while proffering the flat of his palm. The one-eyed love, whom I personally called Steevo, released Ambrose's ankle, executed a flawless little spin, and bounced into Cato's arm.

Steevo bared tiny fangs at Ambrose—well, the one he still had.

"Eira, what is amiss? I was pulled from the sparring yard and—" He looked around at the crowd, confused.

"It's our Joining." I held my arms wide, not overly thrilled with how my carefully crafted plans were currently playing out.

"If-if you'll have me, that is."

"Eeeeeee!" Ambrose squealed and clapped his hands together. He shook me by the shoulders and kissed my cheeks more times than I could count.

Cato lifted questioning eyes to Aberus.

"I am the king." His brother tossed back his wild head of black curls. "I will allow this woman to Join with two men, but for the Goddess's sake, never ask it of me again. The Council has called for my abdication twice."

Richelle's fist shot out, punching Aberus on his backside. He glanced at her and shrugged, mouthing, *well, they have.*

"Oh! May I Join with Cat, too?" Ambrose questioned. His smile stretched from ear to ear.

Aberus began to sweat, the underarms of his embroidered tunic going dark. Richelle fanned him with both hands.

"No. I have managed to appease the citizens this once, by expending a tremendous amount of political capital," Aberus waved a hand between Cato and me, "on the basis that Eira is of noble Gaean birth and they permit plurality. I do not feel that I could convince them that brothers should Join." He grimaced. "And I am firmly against it as well."

"Uh! But we share not a speck of—"

"Ambrose, please," Aberus said, holding his palms out placatingly. "Already I seek a way to heft my bulk over this railing to run."

My Black Bear rolled his eyes.

"Fine." Ambrose crossed his arms and cocked a hip. "But everyone here, look me in the eye and say, 'Ambrose is husband number one.' Do it, or I shall throw a fit that will put tiny Verra to shame."

I rolled *my* eyes but waved my hands like I was conducting a choir.

"Ambrose is husband number one," the dull voices chanted in unison.

"Alright, now, Cat, you stand there, and Eira, you here." Ambrose fluttered around and positioned us just so. He straightened the pinned sleeve of Cato's shirt and reshaped the braid that ran down the middle of his head. "Oho! I am glad I forced you to shave up your sides and trim that gnarly beard you sported. You look positively scrumptious."

Ambrose kissed the tip of Cato's nose.

"Ahem, if we may, I have a state meeting to attend." Aberus ushered forward a priest.

The representative of the Goddess stepped between us and drew their veil back.

And Ambrose lost his composure.

Tears practically shot from his eyes.

I knew he'd have trouble not being the center of attention... so I'd planned accordingly.

"Ræyel... Sibling!" Ambrose embraced the Mantle, much to the horror of the two priestesses at Their side. "Oh, my Goddess, I thought it would be a full year before we would meet again." The siblings hugged. My heart was happy.

"I am to stay for a fortnight and will leave after the Emberkin disembarks. Troth Eira negotiated the arrangements."

Ambrose's bottom lip quivered, and there was no stopping my tears. He caught me and pulled me into a shared hug with his sibling.

"Am I romantic, husband?"

Ambrose tilted my chin.

"No, beautiful harpy, but you are thoughtful beyond measure, and I think that may be much more worthwhile. Now, let us begin. Cato, will you Join with this woman?"

Ambrose pushed me back into position and arranged my gown.

"Yes. For all to see and hear, yes." Cato's hand found mine, warm and steady, and I closed my fingers around his as if I could hold time in place. As his tears slipped free, the golden auras in his cinnamon brown eyes shone bright. I caught each drop with my thumb, as the æther spun in slow-moving gyres at the sight of his smile—wide, unguarded, and so full of abundant love. "This Bond was always meant to be."

Chapter Sixty-Eight

A Bonded Bundle Bedding

Eira

"Will you both hush?"

I sat between Ambrose and Cato, resting my chin in my hands.

Tell him to quit acting like it doesn't bother him.

"No." Cato balled his fist and struck the table. "Do not speak in the brain bond as if I do not exist."

I flicked my gaze between my husbands, wondering what kind of insanity I suffered to legally bind myself to both. Ambrose tugged the seat of my chair toward him. The legs shrieked as they scraped across the floor.

Cato jerked, dipping to pull the chair back over, only... he couldn't.

He closed his eyes when he realized what he'd done.

"You're a fucking asshole, Ambrose," I chastised him with a wagging finger to the nose.

"Well, it was an effective conversation starter; perhaps now, he wishes to speak openly with his spouses."

"May I?" I pointed to Cato's lap. He nodded and sat back in his seat, bracing one foot on the chair leg. I stood and then lowered myself to his thigh, breathing in the scent of the soap that clung to him: cedar and clove. I smoothed my finger over his short, cropped beard. "Cato, we're both worried about you. Ambrose just shows it in a louder and more antagonistically irritating way."

"Uh, how dare you insinuate that—"

"Hush!" I snapped at my more-than-a-contract husband. He crossed his arms and glared.

Cato patted my thigh.

"I thank you both for your concern, but I am not yet prepared to discuss my feelings."

"Okay. In time, though, please let us in?"

Ambrose grumbled.

"Of course." Cato kissed my neck.

"Well, while we're all here, would either of you mind if I brought up a concern? One that we *all* need to deal with."

"Of course, my love." Cato pressed his lips to my chin and then awkwardly tried to stroke my back while keeping me balanced on his lap.

Ambrose scooted closer and lifted my hand to his lips, holding it like some piece of precious blown glass. He turned it and placed a soft, reverent kiss on my wrist. "You are our priority, wifey."

"Okay, good. That's good. Because sex is a priority of mine, and currently we aren't having it."

Ambrose's eyes turned to saucers, and Cato looked away.

"Now, husbands, I'm not... I don't want to pressure either of you, but I think we should make an attempt. I feel that physical closeness is important for us all."

"An attempt should be made?" Ambrose repeated rather flatly.

"Yes. To fuck. I want to fuck. Is that clear enough for either of you? Ah, I feel that it was clear enough for Cato."

Beneath my thighs, he hardened, and I just barely stopped myself from sighing in relief, worried that if I did, he might take it as poorly as he took everything these days.

Ambrose cleared his throat. "I know there to be a, ahem, waiting time after delivery."

I blinked at him like he'd taken leave of his senses. Never did I want another person who'd experienced birth to know that with a puff, I'd healed back to my norm, or that, because she was so small, in the back of my mind, I felt like I should have endured much more. The medication had made me dilate so quickly and—

Cato squeezed my hand, pulling me from the dungeon of my thoughts.

"Are you sure you are ready?" he asked.

"No," I admitted, "but I'd like to try."

"Then we shall try," he stated softly.

Ambrose nodded in agreement, though his eyes held a trace of wariness.

"Then, gentlemen, husbands, I will lead the way."

I stood and walked to the door... alone.

I glanced over my shoulder. "I will be highly offended if the two of you continue looking as though you are walking to the executioner's block."

Ambrose rose, straightening his tailored coat before squaring his shoulders.

"Goddess save me," I muttered. "Cato, bring the cake."

He glanced at the absolute frilliest of confections, which Cinden and Ethens had commissioned for the day of our Joining, and frowned at the blue-on-sapphire-on-aquamarine layers of swirls, flowers, and flourishes.

"Who am I to deny you?" Cato clutched the platter, balancing the weight in his hand. "After you, Ambrose, *first* husband."

I threw my hands up in near defeat, but opened the door to our bedchamber.

New sheets filled the room with the scent of freshly laundered linens. As requested, the chamberman had turned the lamps down low, creating a soft and sensual ambiance.

I felt the presence of two bodies at my back.

"You all sit at the end of the bed. Set the cake on the floor." I pointed to the far right, and Cato, with less than his normal amount of grace, lowered the sweet where I bid.

I bit back a smile as they both perched on the bed's end, stiff-backed and looking as though they were presiding over one of the kingdom's state functions.

"Are you ready to begin?"

Cato nodded curtly, a soldier going into battle. Ambrose rolled that fucking wrist of his, acting all nonchalant when I could clearly see the outline of the bulge at his crotch.

"Alright. Well. Here. Let's start with something easy."

I bent over, grabbed the hem of my gown, and wrestled myself free of its volume.

There was an appreciative murmur from my audience as I stood in my fancy brocaded silk chest support and matching underwear. Embroidered harpies made up its complex pattern. The blood-red of their background complemented my skin better than any color ever had, and I felt amazing in the newly commissioned set.

Ambrose's tongue darted out, moistening his bottom lip, and the erection in Cato's pants continued to thicken. Heat pooled between my thighs, pressure and pulse building.

I untied the side lacings from my support and let the garment fall.

"Gods damn!" Without unbuttoning them Ambrose pulled his coat and undershirt over his head, casting them to the floor.

"Help me, Ambrose, dislodge these confounded clasps." Ambrose's hands went to Cato's crotch.

I squeezed my thighs together at the sight, imagining the possibilities.

Cato's cock arose from its confines, thick and heavy, and that rhythmic throb in my passage intensified—already I was slick.

"I thought you'd like them. One for you, Black Bear... this one"—I pointed to my left nipple and fingered the just-healed piercing—"is called a moss agate. It reminded me of your eyes." Eyes that were currently riveted to my chest. "And this one." I pinched my right nipple and dangled the bead. "Is called—"

"Cat's eye."

"Cat's eyes, that's right." I preened at how *my* Cat's eyes roved over my body. Gods, how I'd missed this—the closeness and the connection. The power that came from surrendering yourself to the ones you trusted most in life.

I pulled the ties of my underwear and then tossed them aside.

"What's next?" Ambrose asked, a fully immersed, ready, and willing participant. "Did Cato fuck you first on the night of our Bedding? Or was that me?" He tapped his chin thoughtfully. I pointed to his pants.

"Off."

"Yes, wife."

Ambrose followed my order, unbuckling his belt and plucking his laces The sides of his pants hung wide, and the waistband slipped low, revealing the *V* that pointed to my current desire. I groaned. He was so long, and I craved the feel of his tip rubbing my cervix.

I let out a long exhale, reminding myself that this was to be a slow seduction and not a fast fuck in some shadowy corner.

The tickle of my wetness escaping my vulva made my eyes roll back. Oh, what these men did to me. *Goddess, you have smiled upon your Chosen One.*

"There's something I've wanted to try..." I said, sauntering forward, too overcome by the delicious weight between my legs to feel bashful. "For quite a while."

"Proceed," Cato barked, ever the commander.

"Hands back, both of you," I ordered, and then just as quickly winced, hoping my careless directive didn't hurt Cato's feelings. I squinted sheepishly, but he'd not even registered my misspeak. He just rested his weight on one arm, instead of two, which made his bicep swell beneath his shirt.

"You have on too much clothing. Allow me, your meek and sub-servient wife, to serve you."

"Meek, my ass," Cato quipped.

I worked his buttons open, one by one, instead of ripping the garment from his body like I wanted. His inked harpy stared back at me until Cato flexed his pec and made her head bob.

"Be glad she has my face, sir."

Mmm, his body is simply delicious, is it not, wifey?

It surely is, husband. I can't wait to see you sliding up against it.

Ambrose's breath caught as I pushed Cato's shirt over his shoulders.

"Now, husbands, watch as I combine my two favorite things." I dipped down and scooped up a fingerful of frosting. "Who's first?"

"Me!" Ambrose's hand hit the air faster than Cato could balance himself and try. "Another game I will win each time, one-armed Cat."

Cato laughed before I could wallop Ambrose. The unguarded sound caught me by surprise. It slipped into my heart like a forgotten but beloved melody.

I stood between my men and slowly slathered the sugary goodness from Ambrose's base to his crown. His hips lifted, seeking my touch.

"And now some for you." I repeated the action but twisted my finger around Cato's broad head until a clear bead welled from his tip. "There we go."

"Hurry. Put your mouth to good use, wife," Cato gritted out.

The æther spread along my arms and legs, sparkling and dancing as it traveled to my fingertips and toes.

"Here's the fun part!"

The frosting's rich vanilla scent made my mouth water as I lowered myself to the floor. I didn't wait. I swept my tongue over Cato's head to collect the pearl from his arousal. The whipped butter and sugar combined with his salty flavor, and I couldn't stop myself from licking him clean. He didn't seem to mind, just closed his eyes and groaned his pleasure into the room.

Ambrose needed attention; he shifted his hips, trying to keep himself calm.

"Mmm, sweet cream and..." I lifted, and a string of pre-cum stuck to my lips and cheek.

Ambrose struck, capturing my chin. He guided my face to his mouth and lapped Cato's semen from my chin.

I licked my lips, more than happy to share.

"Take your cream, love." Cato fisted his hand into my hair, tugging on the dark length I'd asked Allaine to add on a few days after our return. He guided my head over his cock and tilted his hips while I bounced my head up and down his length. I relaxed my throat and took him as far as I could while rubbing my tongue over the flare of his head.

"That's a good wife. So fucking talented. Now, stop."

"No. Not done." I took him in, slowly, until he bottomed out and my eyes began to water.

Cato pulled my head back, my neck arching, not allowing me to suck him down like I wanted.

"But Cato," I whined. "It's been so long."

He brought my head forward and crushed his lips to mine. Our tongues tangled and rubbed, sought each other and danced until we were both panting. He forced my head back again.

"This is why she needs two cocks. Ambrose, might I interest you in some of the finest lips Monwyn has to offer?" Cato tugged my hair once and then again, watching my breasts sway with each yank.

"Why, sir, I would be honored to partake. Follow my rhythm, if you will."

Ambrose wrapped his hand around his erection and slid his palm up and down.

"Open, wife."

I parted my lips at Cato's command, and still holding my hair, he steered my mouth over Ambrose's frosted cock. On Ambrose's downstroke, Cato pushed my head to meet my husband's ringed fingers. I licked his digits as I descended, not willing to lose any vanilla deliciousness.

"So wonderfully hot," Ambrose purred. "Fuck me, but your mouth is scalding. So fucking brilliant. To think I once thought this god-given coolness a curse."

Ambrose scooped his hips as he jerked himself into my mouth.

I moaned and gasped, needing more, wanting to give more, until it dawned on me—

Black Bear?

Hmmm.

Give me your other hand. He can't do it himself anymore.

Ambrose understood immediately. He sat up, and our fingers met around Cato's erection.

"Right. Fuck. There are two of you." Cato's laugh turned into a drawn-out purr of satisfaction. Goosebumps broke out over my arms and breasts.

I switched over to Cato's cock and slurped the remnants of icing while Ambrose and I handled him together, slick, sticky hands moving over the man we loved.

I was burning for friction of my own.

"I'm ready." My lips popped off Cato's tip, and I hopped to my feet. "Can you all be ready? I'd really like you to be ready."

What happened to slow seduction, wifey?

Stay out of my head.

Ambrose lashed out, and as he shot to his feet, he tossed me face-first onto the bed. He sank his fingers into my hips and pulled me backward.

"Are you ready, Eira? Truly?" He slipped two fingers inside me, and I nearly saw the stars. "Mmmm, I think you could use a little encouragement first."

He flicked his fingers in a come-hither gesture and tapped on that glorious spot deep within.

I rocked back, riding his fingers, while Cato parted my cheeks for a better view.

"Cat, find a hole to fuck; I'm getting lonely." Ambrose positioned his head at my entrance, and I shoved back, taking him halfway before pressing forward and pulsing back again. "And she's getting feisty."

Ambrose wrapped his arm around my hips, his length slowly parting me and filling me fully, as Cato knee-walked across the bed.

Ambrose stilled his hips.

"Fuck me, Ambrose, why did you stop?" I cried out. "Should it be this difficult to coordinate—" Cato filled my mouth, just as Ambrose bucked.

I sucked him hard, hollowing my cheeks, using the force of Ambrose's thrusts to plunge me forward.

"Cato, may I bestow upon you a kiss, you know, for good luck on the occasion of your Joining?"

Ambrose leaned over me, fucking me harder. Cato's cock hit the back of my throat as I peered up and saw his tongue push between Ambrose's lips.

And then, I was coming.

"Oh, gods." Waves of pleasure crashed over me as Ambrose gripped my ass and sank his fingers into my flesh, fucking me with fervor, finally not holding himself back. My eyes no longer saw, and my ears no longer heard.

"Fuck, yes, wife, you feel incredible." Ambrose stiffened behind me, and I felt him pulsing as he released himself into my body. "Fuck, Eira, gods, no one compares."

He pulled free and fell onto the bed, panting.

"You alright, old man?" Cato teased. "I recollect a much more vigorous lover some months past."

Ambrose's eyes popped open.

"Are you up for testing his vigor, Cato?" I asked, angling for a second go-round.

Cato's brows furrowed.

"What is it you have in mind, Eira love?"

I smiled coyly.

"Ambrose, on your knees, please. Sit against the headboard, facing me."

Consider my interest piqued, wiflet.

Ambrose crawled by, and I delivered a sound slap to his ass. His penis began to fill again.

"Black Bear, I am still in awe of your swift refractory time."

He giggled his most manly of giggles, and I forced myself not to cry at the joyful sound.

I looked around Cato to find Ambrose exactly where I wanted him, on his knees, hands clasped behind his back.

You are such a good boy.

Thank you, wifey.

"Cato, if you don't want to, I understand, but if you would like to try… I have dreamed of riding you… while you… rode him."

Ambrose squealed through the connection.

Cato looked over his shoulder and worried his bottom lip.

Ambrose gnashed his teeth.

He's vulnerable, you ass. Tone it down.

In his ass?

I ignored him and focused on Cato.

"I will try it once, but I do not know if it will become a habitual practice."

"Ambrose, are you willing to—"

"Yes! Of course. I took your maidenhead, and now I will take his. This is much more poignant than a formal Joining."

"It absolutely is not," Cato informed him.

"Um, yes, it is," Ambrose countered.

"Let us get on with it, for the Goddess's sake."

I helped Cato to his feet, and he stomped across the bed, turning pillows over in his wake.

Ambrose reached into the bedside table and withdrew his Solnnan oil. He smeared it on his length, and my mouth went dry. Focus was becoming more difficult by the second.

"I have not an inkling of how to make this work," Cato said.

"You squat and relax; I shall do the work." Ambrose flashed me a smile that I quickly returned.

"Right." Cato bent his knees, and I appreciated the swell and expansion of his muscular thighs. Beneath Cato's widespread knees, Ambrose took his own erection in hand while he caressed Cato's hip with his other. Both husbands were beyond beautiful in my eyes.

"We will go slow," Ambrose said, his voice pitching lower. "Do you feel me at your entrance?"

Cato bobbed a single curt nod.

"Lower and—Eira suck his dick; it makes it all the more enchanting."

"No. I want you here." Cato caught my hand and drew me closer. His eyes bore into mine. Behind him, Ambrose shifted, tilted his hips, and lifted. Cato's face slackened as he experienced a pleasure all anew.

"Eira, you have mended the parts of me I thought irrevocably broken. This is not just love we share but an unyielding foundation..."

Gods alive, he's going to make it about rocks.

Ambrose, shut up!

"The very bedrock beneath us, strong enough to build a lasting future."

I fucking told you.

"Ambrose!" I sputtered out a laugh. "Why do you ruin the most beautiful things!"

"Are you all? Fucking brain bond. The two of you deserve each other. I am never to have—"

Fuck him, Eira, do it quick, silence the tirade before it turns into a full lecture!

I pounced and pressed my lips to Cato's, consuming his words while straddling his hips, letting his thickness fill me like no other could. He moaned into my mouth as I nipped him gently and ground my clitoris into his pubic bone.

The æther knew its Fated Bond. It spiraled and then knotted in my womb, and as I contracted my thighs, seeking my own pleasure, riding him faster, it traveled lower.

"Holy fuck. So good. So, fucking good. The two of you..." The rest of his words never came.

Ambrose's fingers slid into my hair; where he touched me, steam rose, encapsulating us in a cloud.

Cato pressed his fingers into my clit, and my mind went to that place where nothing and everything existed at once.

"Love you," I panted. "We love you."

Over Cato's shoulder, Ambrose offered me his mouth. I took it greedily as I bounced harder, fucking Cato to the wild rhythm that I adored.

Ambrose shouted, tearing his lips away and guiding my mouth to Cato's as he poured himself into our man.

Our man.

Ours.

I spread my legs wider, and Cato's arm snaked around me. In a frenzy, he fucked into me, yanking my hips in time with my thrusts.

His triumphant shout sent me over the edge, and we came together in a tangle of limbs and muttered professions of love.

Cato lay me on the bed, while Ambrose tucked a pillow under my head.

"Where are you going? Don't leave us," I cried out, not ready to be separated by any measure of distance.

Ambrose rolled his eyes and strolled out the door.

Do you think you can survive alone for the duration it takes me to shit?

I laughed out loud, much to Cato's confusion.

"Thank you, Eira."

"For what, Cato?" I asked while twirling one of his curls around my finger. He said nothing, just ran his fingers over my body, tracing the dips and hills.

Ambrose strolled back in with a basin of steaming water and a stack of linens. He laid the bowl on the bedside table and submerged the cloths before offering one to Cato. Together they skimmed the soft linens over my body, erasing the sweat and remnants of our lovemaking. When done, I fished a warm rag from the water and returned the favor twofold.

"Look at the scars I've given you." I blotted the welts on Ambrose's abdomen and then turned to Cato and gently ran the cloth over the knitted but still angry flesh of his amputation. My never-ending supply of tears pricked the backs of my eyes.

Cato caught my hand.

"Not scars, my love." He traced my fingers over his elbow and down Ambrose's side. "These are a map of our journey. The twists and turns, the valleys and the mountains. The path that led us home."

EPILOGUE: THE NETHER

SEPTIMUS

"Well, little Nanetta... you have your father's eyes."

A MESSAGE FROM E.A.

Thank you for making this journey through Ærta with me. When I set out to write this story, I never could have imagined the positive response to something I feared might make many uncomfortable. Romantasy does not often combine the traumatic and real aspects of the human condition, but I felt they deserved a place. We all have dealt with loss, and many of us—though perhaps still wading through rough waters—have gone on to live lives full of love.

That is my hope for you, dear reader: that you may know abundant love in your life, even if the one who gives it to you is yourself.

What now? Perhaps a dark Baldorvan romance, or maybe a soft, cinnamon-roll love story set back in Monwyn. Of course, a tale from the Nether may not be too far off. Or maybe I'll try something entirely new!

IF YOU HAVE ENJOYED THE OBLIGATES OF ÆRTA, PLEASE CONSIDER LEAVING A REVIEW OR SIGNING UP FOR MY NEWSLETTER AT FORTNEAUX.COM.

CONTENT WARNINGS:

ABORTION (MENTION OF), ABUSIVE RELATIONSHIP, ALCOHOL CONSUMPTION, AMPUTATION, ANXIETY, ASSAULT, ATTEMPTED MURDER, BLOOD, BONES, BULLYING, CHEATING (KINDA/KINDA NOT), CHILDBIRTH IN VARIOUS FORMS DISCUSSED AND ON PAGE. CHILD LOSS IS A THEME AS WELL, CULTS, DEATH, DEMONS (MENTION OF), DEPRESSION, DIVORCE (MENTION OF), DUBIOUS CONSENT SCENARIO, EMESIS (BARF), EMOTIONAL ABUSE, FIRE, GORE, MISCARRIAGE (MENTION OF), MISOGYNY, MURDER, NEEDLES, POISONING, PREGNANCY, PROFANITY, PROSTITUTION, RELIGION, SCARS/BRANDS, SELF HARM/ATTEMPTED SUICIDE, SEXUAL HARASSMENT, SEXUALLY EXPLICIT SCENES, SLAVERY/ENSLAVEMENT: MENTION OF AND ON PAGE. I WANT TO BE VERY UPFRONT. IT IS NEVER GLORIFIED IN THIS BOOK, NOR WILL CHARACTERS MIRACULOUSLY FALL IN LOVE WITH THOSE WHO PRACTICE ENSLAVEMENT, BECAUSE, BARF. SNAKES, TORTURE (POORLY EXECUTED), VIOLENCE, WAR (MENTION OF)

www.ingramcontent.com/pod-product-compliance
Lightning Source LLC
Chambersburg PA
CBHW070925100726
47908CB00001B/108